By the Same Author

Novels

in chronological order

THE GILT CAGE
DUEL IN THE DARK
THE RELUCTANT MADONNA
THEY THAT GO DOWN
WHERE THE WIND BLOWS
UNICORN
THE WISE AND THE FOOLISH VIRGINS
STALLION
SPIDER
MATADOR
THE TAVERN
THE ONE-EYED MOON } (*Spanish Trilogy*)
RETURN OF A HEROINE
THE MARRIAGE WILL NOT TAKE PLACE
WHO WOULD HAVE DAUGHTERS?
FAMILY TIES
THE SUN IS MY UNDOING
ROSE TIMSON

A KIND OF INSOLENCE (*short stories*)

Plays

MATADOR (*with Matheson Lang*)
FRENCH FOR LOVE (*with Derek Patmore*)
OAKFIELD PLAYS (*for children*)

Biography

THE LOST ONE: *a biography of Mrs. Perdita Robinson*
HUGH WALPOLE: *a critical and biographical study*
WILLIAM NICHOLSON

Belles Lettres

GRANADA WINDOW

PEEPSHOW: *a book of amateur stage production*

In Preparation

PHOENIX RISING: *the third book of the House of Flood*
LOOKING GLASS: *autobiography*

To. Pat with my very Best Wishes on your Birth day. 1949.

Willie

TWILIGHT ON THE FLOODS

TWILIGHT ON THE FLOODS

BY

MARGUERITE STEEN

COLLINS

ST. JAMES'S PLACE LONDON

1949

PRINTED IN GREAT BRITAIN
COLLINS CLEAR-TYPE PRESS: LONDON AND GLASGOW
1949

FOREWORD

TO many people 1900 seems almost like the immediate present, and it is true that the impact of two great wars on British West Africa has been light in comparison with their effects on other parts of the Empire. It is easier to get a historical perspective on 1800 than on 1900, and, in writing of the latter, far easier, unfortunately, to draw upon oneself a volume of correction from those whose memories provide them with matter for which the writer has had to rely on research and hearsay.

To avoid some measure of reproach, I have therefore set the Gold Coast episodes in two imaginary places: Charlestown (in *The Sun Is My Undoing*, *Fort Charles*) is " somewhere along the coast " between Cape Coast Castle and the mouth of the Volta, and Omo is a state on the Ashanti-Akim border. In Book IV, which deals with the Ashanti war of 1900, while keeping as closely as possible to the chronological order of events, I have mixed fact with fantasy in the names of people and places; my main object being to create a picture of this campaign, hitherto ignored in fiction, of its peculiar brand of horror and heroism, due to the conditions under which it was conducted.

It is in the hope of sparing my readers, as well as myself, some troublesome correspondence that I would draw attention to one small technical detail; that, while narrative may reasonably be assumed to embody the writer's personal views, dialogue belongs to the character. The persistence of some of my readers in identifying me with my characters has, from time to time, involved us in arguments from which neither has derived satisfaction, through failure to convince the other.

I therefore beg to disclaim, in person, the opinions voiced by several of my characters on mission work in West Africa. These are based—in some cases, reproduced practically verbatim—on conversations and discussions to which I listened when little more than a child, and on the explicit statement of the late Miss Mary Kingsley, in her *West African Studies*, that the missionary movement is the cause of our wars in West Africa. Whether or not this happens to be fact, it was a view generally held by trading circles, at the time of which I write. For the incident of " ringing out " the mission boy, Somilu, I have the authority of a contributor to Miss Nancy Cunard's anthology, *Negro*.

CONTENTS

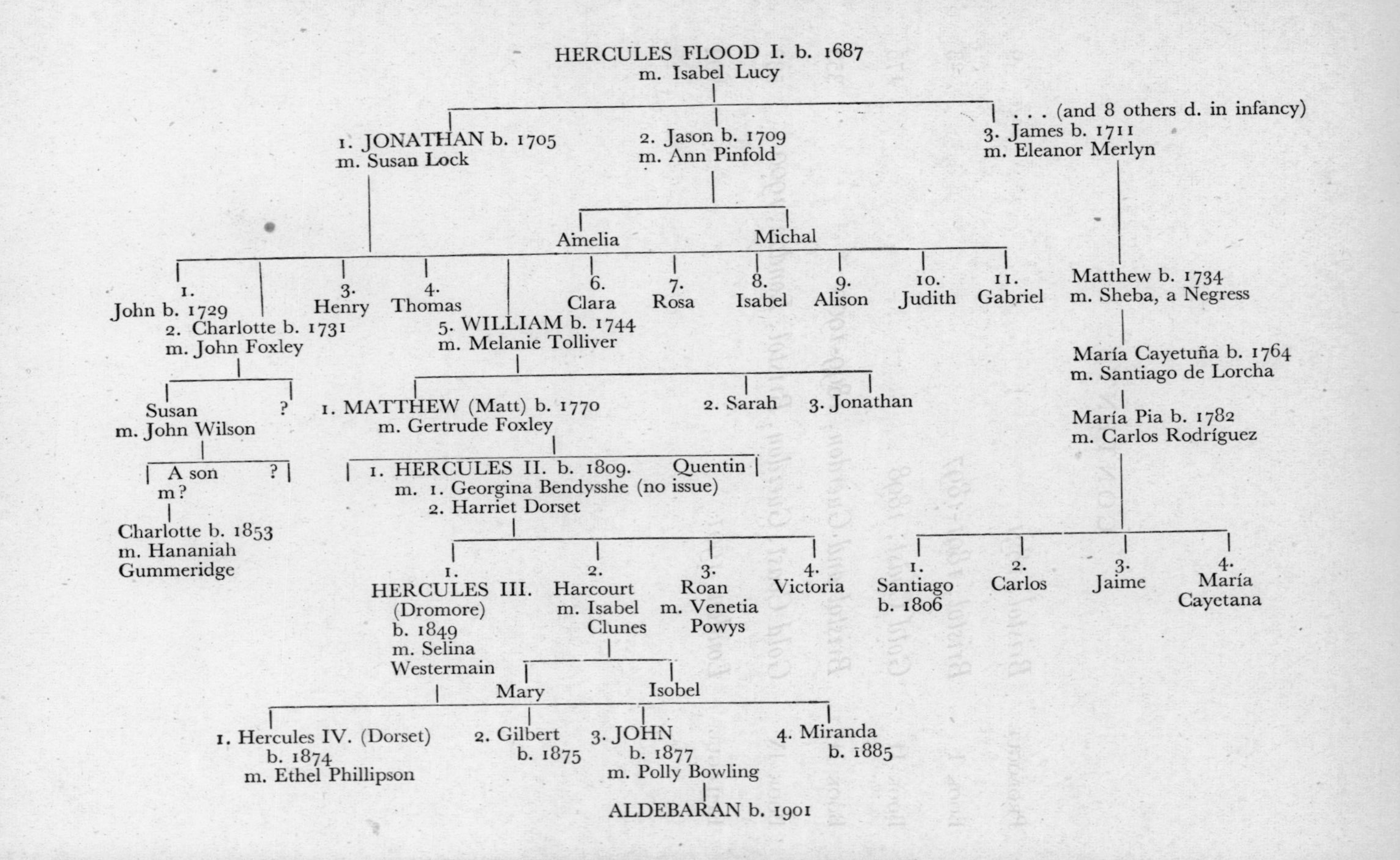
HERCULES FLOOD I. b. 1687
m. Isabel Lucy
1. JONATHAN b. 1705
m. Susan Lock
2. Jason b. 1709
m. Ann Pinfold
3. James b. 1711
m. Eleanor Merlyn
. . . (and 8 others d. in infancy)
Amelia
Michal
1. John b. 1729
2. Charlotte b. 1731
m. John Foxley
3. Henry
4. Thomas
5. WILLIAM b. 1744
m. Melanie Tolliver
6. Clara
7. Rosa
8. Isabel
9. Alison
10. Judith
11. Gabriel
Matthew b. 1734
m. Sheba, a Negress
María Cayetuña b. 1764
m. Santiago de Lorcha
María Pia b. 1782
m. Carlos Rodríguez
Susan
m. John Wilson
?
A son
m?
?
Charlotte b. 1853
m. Hananiah
Gummeridge
1. MATTHEW (Matt) b. 1770
m. Gertrude Foxley
2. Sarah
3. Jonathan
1. HERCULES II. b. 1809.
m. 1. Georgina Bendysshe (no issue)
2. Harriet Dorset
Quentin
1. HERCULES III.
(Dromore)
b. 1849
m. Selina
Westermain
2. Harcourt
m. Isabel
Clunes
3. Roan
m. Venetia
Powys
4. Victoria
1. Santiago
b. 1806
2. Carlos
3. Jaime
4. María
Cayetana
Mary
Isobel
1. Hercules IV. (Dorset)
b. 1874
m. Ethel Phillipson
2. Gilbert
b. 1875
3. JOHN
b. 1877
m. Polly Bowling
4. Miranda
b. 1885
ALDEBARAN b. 1901

PROLOGUE

Bristol

1831

I

ON Monday, October 31st, 1831, a vast cocoon of smoke hung over Bristol: was tweaked, shredded and carried downriver by the breeze. A ship was coming in slowly; her passengers, clustered on the decks, sniffed, wrinkled their noses and cried aloud their comments on the prospect ahead. It was the hour of dawn, and the eastern sky should have been silvery; instead, it was as though they were bearing down into the heart of a thunder-cloud.

As they continued on their way with the slow Avon tide, canvas sagging in a reluctant air, they got the facts—or some garbled version of them—from the small craft of the river; the tale was trumpeted from scow to wherry, up the tall sides of East Indiamen and through the ports of West African traders—of Bristol's retort to the opponents of the Reform Bill; of the burning Mansion House, House of Correction and Customs; of fires that raged from the Floating Dock to the Bishop's palace; of oil and spirits running in sheets of flame between the warehouses of King and Prince's Street, and the whole of Queen Square a vast bonfire that was expected to consume the entire city. Hell was let loose, Bristol in the hands of a mob of incendiarists, of criminal gangs which, escaped from the prisons and drunk on loot and the plunder of the taverns, would assuredly not abate their activities while tar, tow and tallow remained to feed the flames.

So much was shrieked by panic-stricken refugees from the barges and rowing boats which, charged by sanctuary-seeking victims, were sunk almost to the waterline by their unaccustomed loads, and increased the apprehension of those whose voyage seemed likely to have so grim an ending. Even on the river the heat could be felt; there was a rumour (which later proved false) that the shipping was ablaze off the south side of Queen Square; above the human hubbub the crash of falling masonry sent sparks swirling through the pall of smoke that tangled itself in the spars.

Where was the military? The inquiry, bawled from an upper deck, brought a howl of rage from water level. Mackworth's Dragoons were charging about the streets, sabring those who tried to escape and driving them to their death in the burning houses. "They" had sent to Keynsham, to Bath, Frome and Cardiff for reinforcements—"If we ain't to burn they'll massacre us!" a woman shrieked, with a horribly mutilated boy of ten or twelve clasped to her bosom. Others, more sober, allowed the military had been late in coming—some muddle, it was said (by the charitable) between the civic authorities and the representatives of His Majesty's Government; the fires were dying down—were a mere glimmer to the scenes of the night, when one could see to read the newspaper as far as Dundry tower; but the town was in the hands of low Irish and the ruffians of miles around, and there was no telling what would be the damage before another dawn.

The ship—*Bafangh*, out of Bristol, on the West African trade route—lay off-shore for twenty-four hours ; none but a few daring sparks regretting the captain's decision not to land his passengers until he could do so with some assurance of their safety. Most of them spent the night on deck ; there was little to see, but plenty to freshen conjecture in the sounds that came out of the dark—a sudden clatter of hooves, a brief crackle of musketry, a woman's wail or a ragged outburst of shouting, which told that Bristol, although in darkness, was far from sleeping. Now and again a glow of red marked the fanning of embers by a freshening breeze ; in the parish churches, which had been taken over as headquarters by the military, lights burned steadily. It was an eery night, out there on the black water, within earshot of terrors too vague for definition, to which the lapping of the tide and the creak of cordage and timber contributed.

The dawn came, icy with rain. The ship docked during the late afternoon ; from the light, it could have been nightfall.

Flanked by a mountain of baggage, three passengers, separating themselves from the rabble, stood on the dockside, blowing the smuts off immaculate broadcloth, coughing into fine cotton handkerchiefs, spitting the taste and smell of burning out of their lungs, and cursing volubly, in outlandish accents, at the absence of porterage for the conveyance of themselves and their belongings to whatever hostelry might remain in the reputedly burnt-out city.

It was discovered that Reeves' Hotel, in College Place, the headquarters of the Dragoons, had escaped damage, beyond the loss of a few windows, and, a coach having been procured, and ordered to drive by the scenes of the worst destruction, the travellers looked with curiosity upon a spectacle which, however far their imaginations had taken them, could hardly have corresponded to any description of the great West Country port with which they were familiar.

Through the raw dank of the November afternoon, steam still rose from the blackened shells of one-time mansions ; smoke wreathed itself about lead festooned like black icing from the ruins of classic porticos. Stuck in the lead of the Customs House porch, like flies in treacle, were shapes that called a sharp exclamation from at least one of the party : shapes whose human origin was partly lost in the charring action of the flames. The rain beat down on others, trampled in the gutters, on fallen timbers and on the muddy shards of glass that heaped the sidewalks, to which it had already been swept by order of the officers commanding the troops which, on horseback, still patrolled the streets. The sightseeing party drew some sour attention from these ; there was still enough to do in rounding up the rabble that, rat-like, scampered through the ruins, without the added responsibility of protecting folk who invited undesirable attentions by the evident opulence of their attire.

Death carts collected unrecognisable remains from the débris ; passers-by, slipping and falling, rose streaming with blood, and, from the wreckage of their one-time property, figures so smirched and scarred as to seem hardly human, bewailed with half-crazed gestures their inability to find records which alone stood to them for a life-time's labour.

Young Quentin Flood, pale above the flashy collar of a new travelling coat, said, in a voice whose unsteadiness drew a quizzical look from his elder brother, Hercules:

"It would seem, Papa, that the family has chosen an unfortunate moment for its return to Bristol!"

There was a curious eagerness in the hunched shoulders of the eldest member of the party, as he pressed his face closer to the window of the coach, to peer through the rain swilling down the ill-fitting panel of glass and dripping down a muscular calf into the top of his shoe. His retort was absent, a little contemptuous, and characteristic of the speaker.

"God damme—if you'd the wit to see it, we could not have chosen better!"

II

Through the devastated streets passed, on the following morning, the funeral of an old lady—all but unnoticed. A few pale faces turned towards the modest cortège, a few antick shapes mopped and mowed, in ancient Bristol fashion, beside the hearse; but, for the majority, the horrors of the week-end had subdued Bristol's enjoyment of a funeral—an important funeral. Moreover, the commonalty was absorbed in its own little buryings; the numbers of victims had not yet been computed, and the task of identification still occupied scores who sought their dead among the ruins. At least one unseemly incident disturbed the propriety of the short procession: the breaking through between the coaches of one of the ringleaders of the night's disasters, who seems naïvely to have assumed that respect for the panoply of mourning would restrain his pursuers. But the law, in such cases, knows neither respect nor sentiment. Eye-witnesses have left an account of the sudden rearing of terrified horses, the crackling of the carriage-pole, horse and driver down, splathering in the mud, while the alarmed occupants of the coach leapt out on the cobbles: of the hearse, separated from its escort, setting off at an indecent gallop, while fourteen of the Bedminster Yeomanry charged in the wake of their quarry.

If any old Bristolians remembered old Miss Burmester, it was to curse her, for she had been foremost among those who, by opposing the Slave Trade, had robbed the city of its richest source of revenue. Yet, under normal conditions, curiosity, if nothing better, would have drawn the general public to her funeral.

Instead of the tremendous crowds which would have followed her remains if she had elected to die twenty years earlier, a poor half-dozen coaches—one having been abandoned—passed over the bridge to St. Mary Redcliff. The Mildenhall coach was one of them; his lordship of Paragon, too frail to support his rôle of chief mourner, being represented by his eldest son,

Leander, a handsome, cold, young man, a little bored by his obligation, but sober, dutiful, and very much on the alert for any want of proper deference to the memory of his great-aunt. Already thunderous at the previous débacle—among the onlookers of whom Lord Leander did not approve was a flashily-dressed, foreign-looking individual who, in the very porch of the Redcliff, suspended the interesting operation of picking a set of lavishly gold-filled teeth to gape at the mourners, as they followed the bier into the shadowy interior.

Toothpick in hand, he stared with a curiosity as simple as it was bare-faced at the late Miss Burmester's great-nephew.

He was wearing a truly astonishing costume. Even the eye educated by Prinny to the rococo in tailoring might well have flinched from a vast and obviously bran-new surcoat in the brightest sapphire blue, tremendously frogged and collared with an upstanding pelt that threatened to nudge the white beaver hat off its wearer's head : the whole thrown back to display a sumptuous lining of quilted crimson satin. Across a waistcoat of florid embroideries, clashing with breeches of mustard yellow, a veritable chain-mail of gold supported at least a dozen seals on the ample curve of his stomach. Some devilish costumier had been having a jest at the expense of an obviously moneyed patron, whose yellowed complexion suggested the tropics, as the blackness of his eyes and brows laid him open to the suspicion (an unjust one) of coloured blood. A disgusting-looking fellow, in the estimation of Lord Leander Sax, and nothing short of an outrage at the funeral of an English gentlewoman.

Lord Leander shot a glance at his sable-suited supporters, and took a step out of the procession.

" Your hat, sir ! Your hat ! "

The furious whisper took the stranger unaware ; more used to giving orders than to taking them, his countenance, as he snatched the offending object from his head, showed such a mixture of affront and apology that it was almost ludicrous. His face empurpled, his eyes starting from his head with choler, he stood uncovered, glowering after the party which, on its way to the chancel, passed the foot of a tablet which, a few minutes before, had been engaging his attention.

Snapping his fingers to summon an aged nondescript, hovering in hope of alms, he learned the name of the dead : a Miss Pally Burmester—" that done a power o' good to poor folk like we, in this city ! "

The stranger's mouth dropped open ; first incredulous, then delighted, a smile broke in wrinkles on his face—like rings made by a stone dropped into a muddy pool. With an oath that must have resounded in the church itself, he slapped his thigh ; then, having tossed a coin into an expectant palm, he turned and tiptoed rapidly back into the building from which he had just emerged. Remembering, this time, to remove his hat, he took his stand in the rear of the mourning party : with no assumption of modesty, but with an assurance intended to show that he was as much entitled to his place there as any member of the congregation. More so than some ! He smothered a smile in the cavern of a doeskin-covered hand, as he reflected that, of all the company, none had more cause for gratitude to the late Miss Burmester than he—if they but knew it !

" O death, where is thy sting ? O grave, where is thy victory ? "

Where indeed. Matt Flood bowed his head with an admirable simulation of reverence, but laughter rumbled in his belly. To arrive in Bristol in time to attend the funeral of his old benefactress was surely one of those signs (like most irreligious men, Matt had his superstitions) that spell luck to an enterprise. Did her quiet dust stir, at the presence of one who had reaped the harvest she—with what different intention !—had sown ? There was no foretelling the workings of Providence ; so God rest the old woman who, by meddling with the Slave Trade, had diverted a golden stream into the pockets of all men of foresight, boldness and enterprise—such as Matt Flood.

Moved by the reflection, he even took a step towards the bier, as it passed, on its return journey, down the aisle. The bearers, disconcerted, faltered a little ; but it was again Lord Leander who stepped apart, his voice shaken with passion, his face like a bleached bone with rage which the solemnity of the occasion obliged him to repress.

" What is the meaning of your intrusion, sir ? "

Matt bowed slightly, as one who recognised the trappings of grief, and, in the circumstances, could afford magnanimity ; but his heavy lids did not quite conceal a glint of mockery, nor an appropriately lowered tone control the rolling unctuousness of a lip more used to the expression of scorn than of sympathy.

" I am paying my respects, sir, to one to whom I owe a debt of gratitude, and for whose memory I cherish an esteem."

There was no possible retort to such a speech. Lord Leander smothered an exclamation with the desire to hit the speaker between the eyes (after all, his great-aunt had had the most unlikely connections) and swung on his heel ; while Matt turned, chuckling, to the tablet which, for him, placed the coping stone on a most unexpected and diverting situation.

MATTHEW
grandson of Hercules
son of James Flood & hys wyf
of this city
lost in the Cassiopœa
off the coast of High Barbary
in the year 1764
Also his wife
Sheba
and his daughter
MARIA CAYETUNA
who died in Cuba
1794

MATTHEW FLOOD
who by ye Mercy of God
was restored to this City in ye year 1799
Died 1807
the year in which the Task to Which
he dedicated his Life was
accomplished,
viz, the Abolition of Slavery
for which the Lord's Name Be Praised.

Praise it indeed, piously murmured Matthew Flood's kinsman and namesake, as, jerking up the fur collar about his chin and driving his hands into the flapped pockets of the preposterous overcoat, he stepped briskly forth into the town whose misfortunes represented so rich a field of opportunity.

Not for the first time, Matt Flood proved his luck, and also the soundness of his judgment. He might, in ordinary circumstances, have lived ten years in Bristol without impressing himself on its inner life and politics, as the disastrous events of that winter week enabled him to do.

Having made his survey, he marched boldly to the Council House and sent in his name—as a more modest individual, in the circumstances, would surely have hesitated to do. But he was right in his calculation. On the tired, red-eyed men, sick with their responsibilities, who sat about the table, the announcement of royalty itself would barely have made an impression ; but there were those among them to whom the name of Flood, even after a lapse of twenty years, was a word of magic. Startled eyes queried the identity of this Flood—this ghost of a glorious past—that rose from the ashes of Bristol's grandeur.

As a ghost, Matt Flood can hardly have been orthodox, but he was convincing. He was not actually among the twelve commissioners appointed to enforce the Compensation Act passed to deal with the claims (computed at nearly £150,000) proffered against the city by those who had suffered, it was said, by the negligence of the authorities. But all " in the know " admitted him as a power in the background. It was he who advised the raising of a Government loan, to avoid the necessity of the ruinous tax of ten shillings in the pound on rateable values, which was threatened when the immediate liquidation of the claims was finally assessed at £68,208 ; and it was his scheme that eventually procured a reduction of the one-and-sixpenny levy suggested by the Corporation for the clearance of the debt to the Government.

In wards and committee rooms the name of Matt Flood, Esquire (he deliberately encouraged the diminutive, with an eye on posterity ; having no mind to be confused, by future generations, with a cousin whose claims to local eminence were based on other, and, in Matt's own opinion, inferior, grounds to his own), was speedily synonymous with wisdom and authority. He was called in on secret sessions, consulted confidentially by public bodies and private individuals, deferred to by Mr. Alderman Daniel on an important public occasion, and invited to houses which would not, even for the name of Flood, have opened their doors to an obscure newcomer from the little-known British property of Barbados. As a grandson to the Mr. Jonathan Flood who was one of the principal claimants to the fabulous Flood estate (which, owing to circumstances no one remembered clearly, save that it concerned a Negress and the Jesuits, was set adrift sometime in the latter part of the previous century), he commanded some little respect with the elders ; but it was on his personal qualities that Matt ingratiated himself with influential circles in the city politics.

He contributed generously to various funds which were opened for the relief of suffering among the poor, caused by the disaster, and even (it was whispered) lent money—on sufficient security—to those temporarily embarrassed through the destruction of their business or trading stock.

It appears to have occurred to few, at the time, to question the sources of affluence of a gentleman self-rated as a planter (retired), with some small interest in shipping. Regarding the latter, Matt seems to have been almost simperingly modest ; he had had, for a while, a few shipping shares ; he had interested himself in the American trade and picked up a bit of lucky money, here and there. It was generally accepted that Matt Flood was one of those who, by some means or other, having made his pile, had, very properly, come back to spend it in the home of his forefathers : an idea admirably calculated to advance his popularity with Bristolians.

As a widower, with two grown-up, unmarried sons, he was socially in demand, and would have liked, for the sake of prestige (of sentiment he had none) to establish himself in the old home of his family—used for several years as an annex to St. Peter's Hospital, but evacuated some ten years previous to his arrival, when a fund started by the late Miss Pallas Burmester had enabled the trustees to build and endow an institution which finally replaced the " Old Mint " for the housing of pauper lunatics. Triton Lodge, however, was in such a state of disrepair (and, moreover, threatened with the encroachment of other properties which, during this epoch, had started to invade Brandon Hill), that Matt, whose mind ran towards park lands and eminence in the county, began to look around him for more suitable domicile.

It was at the beginning of 1833 that he heard of the old Misses Centlivre, and of a mansion, said to be of striking beauty, somewhere between Westbury and Henbury ; and without ceremony, drove out to inspect it.

He met with an icy reception. The house, he was informed, by Miss Corinthia Centlivre, was *not* for sale. Was it not ? inquired Matt, with an ironic eye on rusted tapestries, rat-ridden floorboards and the threadbare liveries of servants. He knew the smell of poverty, had too often exploited it to his own advantage, to be impressed by pride or pathos, when either happened to stand in his way.

It is not known what means Matt Flood employed to bully and browbeat the old ladies Centlivre out of the home which had belonged to their family since the early part of the reign of Elizabeth. The scandalous small price he paid for it is among the blacker records of the house of Flood. Within a month of his first visit, a wretched little wagon, a coach with drawn blinds, passed out of the lower lodge gates. Matt had bought the place, lock, stock and barrel. Of that which was beyond repair, he made bonfires ; a legion of workmen was turned in, to deal with the rest.

Matt concluded the purchase of Guerdon, with its adjoining lands, farms, holdings, glebes and messuages—which included the church, of which the living was in Guerdon's gift ; he thought it might come in for Quentin, who, when he was told, declined the offer with roars of laughter. Even the pleasures of a sporting parson's life would not, he declared, compensate for the sheer grind of taking Holy Orders !

He bought himself a coat-of-arms—a monstrously showy affair : for which he supplied much detail of tropical fauna and flora to the draughtsman of the College of Heralds, and which he had blazoned, at vast expenditure of gold leaf, vermilion and sapphire, on the panels of his coaches. (He toyed with the notion of Negro supporters, but was advised that Negroes went down ill with the Abolition gentry. The somewhat ambiguous classic figures that flank the escutcheon are still a puzzle to the present generation.)

And, among other purchases, he bought a wife for his eldest son, Hercules.

III

" But I don't understand !—after all Papa has said——"

" I have always told you, Georgina, that one of the marks of breeding is to forget what people say. It is usually—particularly in the case of your dear Papa—quite at variance with their actual opinions."

" But he said he would rather resign his Hunt membership than have to be civil to a nigg——"

" Georgina ! You forget yourself."

" And you too, Mamma ! You yourself told me to look the other way when he—when the odious creature ogled me at the races. Not that I'd have allowed him to speak ! I loathe the very sight of his swaggering demeanour, and the insufferable air he has of expecting women to fall down and worship him——"

" You are making my head ache," says Mamma exhaustedly.

" Shall I look for your salts ? But really ! That smirk of self-satisfaction——!" Even the search for the smelling salts does not make Georgina relinquish her subject.

" He is probably used to admiration. I suppose one could call him handsome—if one cared for the type."

" As if anyone would ! "

" A little unrefined, perhaps ; but one must make allowance for foreign blood."

" And for coloured blood ? Ugh ! "

" Pray don't repeat that vulgar scandal. It is well known the Floods are a very respectable old Bristol family."

"Well, it was Papa who said——"

"Georgina! I must positively forbid you to repeat any more of your father's remarks. It was most unbecoming of you to listen to them."

"One would need to be deaf, Mamma——"

"Like most Englishmen, your Papa is a little prejudiced. I remember he was just the same about Italians, when we went on the Grand Tour; and I'm sure some of them were most elegant and agreeable, when one came to know them."

"You will hardly suggest that the Floods are either elegant or agreeable! 'Purse-proud, ignorant vulgarians!' I've heard you say so a dozen times; and I must say I'm astonished, Mamma——"

"That is enough, Georgina. . . . And you will wear the white India gauze to-night."

"Oh—*no*, Mamma!" Aghast, incredulous, the girl's indignation is halted. The India gauze—so carefully cherished; destined for another's eye——? "But I—I'm keeping it for the Hunt Ball! It's much too fine for a dinner at home."

"Don't argue, I beg of you, Georgina; and do remember it is your Papa's wish that you should be very agreeable to Mr. Flood, and—and to his son."

"Oh! This is really outrageous of Papa," she fumes, and is checked again by a tremulous gesture.

"It is my painful duty to tell you that your poor Papa is in great—in very great difficulties."

"*Papa?*"

"It appears he has lost a great deal of money—I don't quite understand how——"

"I could make a good guess——" Georgina is pert because she is frightened; her eyes avoid her mother's quivering face.

"My child, you must help us, if you can. You wouldn't betray your parents, who have done everything in their power to make you happy——?"

"Of course I wouldn't, Mamma. What does Papa wish me to do? Sell my jewels?" Her voice is shrill with rising apprehension.

"Mr. Hercules Flood has expressed. . . . His father has approached. . . . Oh, my child: I implore you not to oblige me to say the rest!"

"I don't know what you mean, Mamma. I don't. . . . You can't. . . . Oh, God, have mercy on me! It's not true! Tell me it's not true!"

. . . It was a conversation to be repeated, with variations, as, succeeding generations of girls of gentle birth and breeding paid the price of parental indiscretion, which was also the price of their husbands' social advancement. Of all those pale brides who went veiled to the altar, did none love the man she married? It is hard to say. Floods did not make bad husbands—to their own kind. Here and there a marriage, of coarser texture, was acclaimed a success; here and there a child was born, not of pride and sacrifice, but of mutual love.

As may be seen from the tree, Georgina Bendysshe was the first of the delicate daughters of impoverished families to bring the strain of a higher race into the earthy stock transplanted by the second Matthew from Barbados into English soil ; she was the beginning of the legend of shadowy women who served the Floods in the transmission of their seed, and lapsed into invalidism or nonentity when their duty of supplying the heir was accomplished. Their family names form the grace-notes in the elaborate genealogical table which was drawn to the order of the third Hercules, grandson of Matt, himself great-grandson of the Hercules who founded the House of Flood.

Matt spent long enough at Guerdon to make sure his plans were working out properly, then betook himself to an establishment of his own, and a counting house, in Queen Square—one of the few that had escaped serious damage in the riots, and next door, as it happened, to that which, in the last century, had been occupied by the Jason Floods, and of which only a shell remained. He could not be content, at fifty-nine, to follow the easy life of a country gentleman. Of his numerous activities in the city of Bristol, as well as the interests he contrived to maintain on the other side of the Atlantic, no more need be written. He became, as his great grandfather had been before him, a pillar of the church ; he built and endowed a charity school at the economical cost of £680—buying salvation, as his descendant, Miranda Flood, was later to write, at bargain price ; he figured on the City Council and graced in due course the Bench of magistrates.

His son, Hercules, carried on the greater functions of the estate, and, by astute manipulation of his wife's connections, got himself accepted in a society sufficiently amenable to the advantages of wealth not to be vulgarly inquisitive about the sources from which wealth derived. His secret and inordinate pride was when he was elected Master of the local hunt ; his secret and no less inordinate mortification, the obstinate refusal of the greatest of the local families, the Mildenhalls of Paragon, to acknowledge his existence, save by the frostiest of nods. What must have been his satisfaction, when he made Lady Orabella Sax, the youngest sister of the reigning marquess, his mistress may well be left to the imagination.

Still, Hercules had had his set-back. In the third year of their marriage, Georgina had died at the birth of her first child—still-born. After a riotous interval of restored bachelorhood, egged on by old Matt, he had married again—a Miss Harriet Dorset, a daughter of one of the great West Country families—penniless, but of very different mettle from the pale Georgina. With a certain dry philosophy, if little enthusiasm, she bore him three sons and a daughter, and superbly ignored his extra-marital diversions.

Victoria came to the throne, and the fashion for piety set in. By that time the Floods were landed gentry—which amused the sticklers for breeding, and would surely have made the first Hercules, had he known of it, chuckle in his grave.

Sixty years after that night of burning indirectly responsible for the restoration of Floods to their native soil, Matt's eldest grandson, the third Hercules (he was also christened Dromore, after a side branch of his mother's family), was lord of the manor of Guerdon : a lord viewed sceptically by his tenantry. This was hard on Dromore; hard on a Christian gentleman (none but the socially captious denied him the title) to come into the backwash of a legend established in the rip-snorting days of his father and uncle around the manor. To be a sober squire, to educate his sons in accordance with what he seriously regarded as their high estate and to consolidate the family's standing in the records of his county and country were Dromore's blameless ambitions.

It seems strange that an intelligent man should have overlooked that freakish corpuscle in the blood which, in a previous century, had blazoned the name of Flood across two continents: or that he should have discounted its possible revival in the rising generation.

BOOK ONE

Bristol

1891-1897

CHAPTER ONE

I

ALL the town was frail, empty and echoing, like a hollow shell: the buildings powder-like, the gas lamps, not yet extinguished, pale tulips isolated in their globes of glass. It was like something dreamed, not something familiar, with associations going right back into childhood. It was like being invisible, like the wind moving along the streets, where soft, new-fallen snow muffled the footsteps of the few who were abroad. With faces buried in collars or shawls, they hurried past; emphasising by their own evasion his invisibility, his complete, breathless aloneness.

The sky was the colour of smoked glass, with a hardly perceptible tinge of pink behind it. Under the arch, and up the slope of Broad Street—where shutters concealed the coloured jars, the noble castellations of Brown Windsor, the leeches swimming in their dark bottles, at Hodder's, the chemist's; and, on the corner of Tailor's Court, Mr. Searle's waxen dummies, crowned and befloured with specimens of their owner's hirsute art. Inside, slung from its great hook in the ceiling, was the dead bear, presently to be boiled down and applied in the form of Mr. Searle's famous pomade, to the customers' heads.

The façade of the *Western Daily Press* offices, with lights still burning behind the windows and snow along the ledges, looked like the frosted cut-outs which, at Christmas, replaced the Valentines and birthday greetings in the Miss Ollivers' shop. Below, along the curb, the horses waited between the shafts of the delivery vans, their patient heads enhaloed with silvery breath, the snow beneath them golden with their steaming dung.

On, still invisible, still possessed with the same sense of dreamlike unreality—past the chequered cliff of the Dutch House, and down the slope of High Street to the Bridge, where the wind gullied by Baldwin Street meets the cold stream from the Welsh Backs and sweeps one across the Floating Harbour; and so—by Redcliff Street and the Redcliff Parade, with the ship's weathervane swinging above Merchant King's offices—at last, to the Basin.

He felt his heart leap to his mouth. She lay there, calm and still, as though carven in fishbone: the square-sterned barque, with her three masts and the cobweb of her shrouds sketched upon a smoky sky. Against a background of dark, rust-coloured buildings she was spectral—a Flying Dutchman of a ship: liable at any moment to dissolve and vanish in thin air. But she was *there*!—frail but permanent. He stood still, gulping his breath; not realising that, all the way from the Bridge, he had been galloping, driven by a fear that far out-paced his original dread of interception. She was there, like the Word of God, like the calm asseveration of a sacred promise : "*Sailing Day February 22nd. Join your ship at Bathurst Basin 6 a.m.*" With his heart pounding against his ribs, he prayed forgiveness for his doubt.

The wind drove from Canon's Marsh, straight across the Basin, puffing a flurry of snow, thin and dry, like salt, into his face. He stepped aside quickly, into the partial shelter of a doorway, to compose himself : putting up his hand, as though to draw a mask across a young, thin face, frozen into greyness, with a ragged thatch of nondescript hair that the wind whipped forward across high cheekbones. The eyes were blank, the mouth and jaw grim ; he was exaggerating the blankness and grimness, for reasons of his own. He waited, half-concealed, getting his breath, his hands pushed down into the pockets of a short freize coat of which the sleeves were a little too short, as were the legs of a pair of well-worn trousers.

A growler was disgorging someone's baggage. A spattering of figures crawled, like black-beetles, across the snow : men in oilskins, with mufflers round their heads and ears ; a few women, clutching shawls tightly about faces nipped into patches of white and blue by the cold. The eyes of some were red-rimmed and glassy ; the face of an elderly woman was drawn into a hideous grimace of grief, from which he looked hastily away ; a pregnant girl started to whimper, and was hushed by her companions.

His eyes were glassy too—but not with tears. An artery, throbbing in his throat, forced him to swallow quickly, and shivers ran down his body, accompanied by a shocking paralysis of self-consciousness. Two men lurched by, propping a third, who could barely make the passage ; a pungent trail of liquor hung on the air. They were all carrying bundles—and he realised for the first time that he had no bundle ; nothing whatever but the clothes he stood up in !—a shameful state of affairs for a man joining his ship. He tried to imagine the sort of things he ought to have : oilskins, he supposed, and perhaps a sou'wester. Certainly a change of underclothing. These were what he was expected to buy with his advance—of which he had been green enough to let some water-front crook relieve him. There must be some junk shop, some ship's chandler close at hand, where, if there were time, and he could persuade the owner to take a jack-knife, or a watch, in exchange, he could remedy these deficiencies. Otherwise—he had a sweater, and a shirt, and a woollen vest under his overcoat ; he would have to make shift with these. . . .

He pulled himself together. It was too late for misgivings. Cold, broad daylight, increasing every moment, stripped the scene of its Breughel-like picaresque. Stony-faced, with hands driven into his pockets, he tramped across the squalid snow to the landing plank.

II

" How old are you ? "

" Sixteen, sir."

Something like a flat-iron caught him on the side of the head and slammed him against the lockers. As he picked himself up, he muttered indignantly :

" What's that for ? "

" That's what you get each time you lie, my lad," said the captain pleasantly. " Come to think of it, you're due for some more. Whaddya think you're doing on my ship ? "

" You know. . . . You know the ship's boy broke his leg—and I saw it happen—and I came aboard and asked you for the job." He scowled resentment of this injustice.

" Very pretty. Very simple and pretty ; just the sort o' thing you read about in story books, ain't it ? By thunder, you want keel-hauling ! I was a sick man—*very* sick," repeated the captain, on a note of serious self-pity, " and you took sneaking advantage of me not being myself to pitch me your confounded cock-and-bull yarns that made me take you on—undersized little runt that you are ! "

" You wanted a ship's boy—and I've done my job, haven't I ? " he muttered.

" Try them tricks on again "—the captain's voice had sunk to a whisper more menacing than any bellow—" and you'll get a work-up you won't forget if you're fifty years at sea. In my young days you'd have holystoned the jib-guys for it. And now : what's your age ? "

" Fourteen "—defiantly.

" Is your name Jake Waters ?

His lips tightened. When the answer came, it was,

" No."

" Ah-h-h. And it would be too much, I suppose, to ask you the truth about that ? "

The eyes of the man and the boy met, each recognising the unbending quality in the other. After a pause :

" So you signed the articles in a false name. I suppose you know that's illegal."

The boy calling himself Jake Waters maintained a stubborn silence.

" Police matter that is." The captain chewed, scowling, a hangnail on his thumb. " I've a good mind to hand you over to the dock coppers." A sly look, to observe the effect of the threat, brought no confirmation of suspicion. The boy's eyelids were lowered ; his jaw tightened a little, but there was nothing to betray the fugitive from justice. A weedy-looking youth, shooting out of his clothes—but no scallawag. He stood up straight and, if he was scared, knew better than show it.

" You made a bad start, Jake." The mildness was unexpected.

" What made you do it that way ? "

" I want to go to the Coast."

" Well——? "

" I was afraid somebody 'd—stop me."

It had taken him several seconds to grasp that the stocky individual in front of him was the one with whom he had had his previous interview. The captain of the barque *Aldebaran*, afloat, was, it appeared, a different being from the unsteady and all but unintelligible person who, first swearing at him for impudence, trespass and a variety of crimes he was not aware of having committed, and which he afterwards discovered were attributable to his predecessor, with whom (under stress, no doubt, of illness) the captain continued at intervals to identify him—eventually despatched him in lurid terms to " get on with it." The *Aldebaran* had already missed two tides, and Bristol dock dues were heavy. He had known enough to bank on this for his gamble.

Freshly shaven, dapper, with a peaked cap aslant on a big, square head furnished with a sandy-grey, spade-shaped beard and a pair of crimson ears so large and so outstanding that they appeared to act as floats, wafting their owner from place to place with a curious, swift, sweeping motion at variance with his clumsy build—Elias Wildblood had held his master's ticket for fifteen years, and, for twelve of them, followed the West Africa trade on behalf of his employers, the shipping firm of Runstable. Wildblood had had better offers, but was loyal to his owners ; it was said he got more pleasure out of bringing off small triumphs over rival skippers than he would have had from the bigger money offered by Floods and Kings. A light way with sea law and an absence of aversion to certain small but tricky practices had made him valuable to Runstables, who showed their appreciation, if not in cash, in kind. Captain Wildblood enjoyed a cosy little house at Pill, as a result of the foreclosure of one of the Runstable mortgages, and an interest in one of the numerous public houses that catered for the illimitable thirst of Pill inhabitants.

" Now listen, young fella." He addressed the boy after a pause for reflection. " If any trouble comes of this, it's your look-out, not mine. I won't lift a finger to get you out of it."

" No, sir."

" I've a darn good mind to send you back when we take the powder on at Kingroad." An obviously empty threat, since the chances of picking up an extra hand in the roadstead were sufficiently remote to call for no comment.

" Well, you done it, my lad ; and I'll take my oath you'll wish you hadn't, before we're half-way to the Coast. Bear this in mind : there's no favours asked and none granted in this ship. You signed on as Jake Waters, age sixteen, and Jake Waters, age sixteen, you are, from now on, whatever it costs you. So don't come snivelling you'd like to go back with the pilot when we're off Lundy. Fetch me a pot of tea and look sharp about it." Captain Wildblood faced about, and, propelled by his ears, floated out of the cabin.

In the foc's'le tempers were short, as they usually are on sailing day. A rich, ripe hangover lay on the ship's company. No one gave him any succinct instructions in his duties—which, up to now, appeared to consist in hanging about within earshot of the captain's cabin and keeping from under people's feet.

Every part of his body ached, and there were special little areas of pain, in his shoulders and loins, which kept him from falling into complete lethargy. In a sense, he was glad of the pain—proof positive that the events of the last twelve hours had existence, apart from his imagination ; it would be there next day—that gnawing discomfort of wrenched muscles, together with a little stab in the lower part of his belly, which had started with a click, while toiling between store-rooms, lockers and lazarettos, on the previous afternoon. And, above all, he craved for sleep : the sleep he had not dared to snatch, for fear of missing the morning summons.

Very slowly the banks of the Avon went by. At one moment the suspension bridge swung its great metal cradle over their heads ; then there was Nightingale Valley and the winter-coloured woods of Clifton and Leigh on either hand. Patched with snow, the familiar gentle landscape assumed a strange indifference to the fate of its children, being borne slowly away from it on Avon tide.

When he had delivered the captain's tea, and made a clumsy, amateurish job of filling a pipe, in the art of which he received a lesson, and the admonition, on pain of some violent-sounding punishment, not to need telling again—they were down at Pill : with a handful of watchers waving from the jetty, and something that looked like a scarlet petticoat flapping from a window—in compliment, perhaps, to Captain Wildblood, who made a stately appearance on deck as the *Aldebaran* swung round on the race of the tide and caught up with the fleet of bumboats making for Kingroad. A sudden brilliant whiteness from the east struck the boats, silvering the wings of gulls and carving out the reflections of boats and banks in jagged black, far into the steely water.

A curious, numb emptiness, starting when the ship nosed her way from the Basin into the Floating Harbour, had so far dulled his perception of all but the external. But when they reached that loop of the river which is overlooked from the heights near Henbury—those heights and hollows that cup the fair estates, the noble manors whose names make Gloucestershire history—he went quickly into a cabin and sat down on a locker. Setting his elbows on his knees and his knuckles against his temples, he closed his eyes. He found he had to swallow hard, to get rid of a succession of lumps in his throat.

III

". . . I assure you, the police are doing all that is possible."

"The police—oh, heaven !"

"I understand from the Chief Constable that they have already communicated with Scotland Yard."

"Do they—do they think he has been kidnapped ?"

"An unlikely hypothesis." The speaker arched his eyebrows, then drew them into a frown which deprecated melodrama, as conveyed by the suggestion. "Although short, the boy is extremely sturdy."

"Sturdy ! As though a child like that would have the least hope of defending himself against those dreadful, dockside ruffians !"

"His appearance is hardly such as to offer temptation to such people. Pray, Selina, calm yourself; you are allowing imagination to run away with you."

"Oh, Drummy, take care!"—a feminine plea. "I think Selina is going to faint——"

"No, I'm *not* going to faint. Go on!"

Women, thought Dromore Flood, are excessively tiresome. They may be counted upon to complicate every situation which calls for presence of mind by the intrusion of emotional outbursts. He sent a cold glance of warning towards his wife.

"We have at least one consolation. In the opinion of the Superintendent, there has not been an accident."

"How can he possibly know?" cried the mother, scornfully.

"Without distressing you, my dear," said Dromore, striving for patience, "I can only ask you to accept my assurance that every possible line of investigation has been pursued."

"I suppose you mean they have dragged the river?" The startling interruption came from the farther end of the room.

"That, Mamma, was what I was trying to infer, without emphasising a painful possibility," her son reproached her.

Mrs. Harriet Flood was not, however, the kind that accepts reproaches, particularly from her own offspring. Dromore should have known better. She rose, her neat figure, its elegance emphasised by the tight bodice and arum lily-shaped skirt, assuming the character of a small crystal pillar, lapped by the billowing liquefescence of Selina and Vicky, both prostrated by her candour.

"Selina, you had better have my smelling salts. It is not a matter of emphasising painful possibilities"—her intonation set a delicate edge of derision on the words—"but of bringing intelligence to bear on all possibilities, whether painful or not. It would be a relief to dismiss that particular one from our calculations."

"You may do so," her son told her frostily.

"On whose authority?" Her raised brows put Dromore in his place. "How far is it from the town to Avonmouth? You can hardly pretend they have had time——"

"I assure you a thorough examination has been made—of the usual places." Dromore was flustered, and, for once, betrayed it. Really—Mamma! And with Selina in her present—one might almost say, her usual—condition . . .

"The 'usual' places!" She snorted. "And what may those be? The Basins, I suppose—and under the suspension bridge. For pity's sake, Selina!" She turned to snap at her daughter-in-law. "Stop snivelling! You know as well as I do that nobody *falls* over the suspension bridge; and even you are hardly fool enough to credit your son with suicidal tendencies!"

"Oh, Mamma—— !"

"We are all fully aware that the boy swims like a fish. I suppose you've informed the police of that? Or are you allowing your friend the Chief Constable to save his face by wasting time and public money on dredging up all the insanitary contents of the Avon, on the chance——"

"Lamentable as it may be to contemplate." Dromore had had enough; he raised his voice. "The police have come to the conclusion that the foolish boy has run away."

"Run away! Run away from his beautiful home, from his devoted parents! Oh, God, spare this blow to a mother's heart!" moaned Selina collapsing in her chair.

"Hold the salts to her nose, Vicky, and push her head down. And what, pray, was your answer to that?"

"I said, naturally, that I found the suggestion preposterous."

"Not preposterous at all. You, Selina, are his mother, and you, Dromore, odd as it may seem, his father——"

"You will permit me to observe, Mamma," said Dromore huffily, "that your qualification is in the worst of taste."

"There is no need to be pompous. My remark was not intended to reflect on Selina's virtue, about which there is, happily, no question. It had quite another implication——"

"I should think so indeed!"

"The fact remains that, as parents, you have always exhibited a singular stupidity about your children. I don't suppose, for instance, that it has ever occurred to either of you that the boy hates school."

"Ridiculous! All boys hate school. It is natural and—and healthy for a boy to hate school."

"Really, Drummy, I think there is something in what Mamma says." The elder Mrs. Flood snorted. "I mean, there is *everything* in what she says," amended her daughter hastily. "And in what you say, too, of course." Victoria became confused under her brother's cold stare. "I dare say it's quite usual for boys not to enjoy school—though the others seem quite happy at Harrow and Winchester. But—but Curbham's different, isn't it?" she stumbled on. "Perhaps you could see your way to making a little change——?"

"I should be obliged, Victoria"—Dromore's look was awful—"if you would reserve your comments. No spinster knows anything about bringing up a youth."

"Vicky's the boy's aunt, and she knows as much about bringing him up as you or Selina." Vicky turned purple at this unwonted commendation from her mother. "More, I should say," pursued the elder Mrs. Flood. "Who found out about the abcess in his tooth? And the time when he complained of an ache in his side, which you all said was 'growing pains,' and turned out to be a cracked rib? And perhaps you remember when he came back from school with his hair in that disgusting condition——?"

"That is really sufficient, Mamma! We have never denied that Victoria has looked after the boy's physical health in an admirable fashion. Discipline, however, is another matter——"

"Discipline—pah! Why don't you discipline your eldest son? Why don't you make Gilbert into something better than an idle, destructive, young wastrel ? "

Surprisingly enough, it was Vicky who, encouraged, perhaps, by previous approval, struck in :

" But what are we to do now, about Johnny ? "

Selina broke into a wail.

" Oh, to think of a child of ours running away from home—not thinking of the pain he would cause—the terrible, terrible disgrace to the family ! "

" Oh, goodness ! " Her frail hold on commonsense broken, apparently, by this reminder, Vicky's jaw dropped. " Oh, mercy—what will Lady Gannet think ? "

" I am glad "—Dromore spoke with satisfaction—" that this aspect of the situation has at last dawned on you both ! You will perhaps understand my anxiety to keep this unhappy event out of the newspapers. We cannot hope, alas, to check the gossip."

" Gossip ! " A small, silver gamecock, the elder Mrs. Flood returned to the attack. " I'm the boy's grandmother, and I happen to care more about that than about local tattle. You appear to have forgotten, all of you, that I've lived down worse than the disappearance of a grandson in my time. Gossip ! There would have been no occasion for any, if you had ever shown the least sense of parental responsibility. Kindly do not interrupt me ! You, Dromore, have had no eyes but for that bumptious young cub, my grandson Dorset ; Selina has left no stone unturned to make Gilbert an even greater fool than nature intended. So far as the pair of you were concerned, Johnny might have had no existence. He has been snubbed, pushed in the background for the sake of the others, on every possible occasion. You didn't even think it worth while to send him to a decent public school ! He was ' only Johnny '—the youngest—of no importance where your precious family was concerned ! And I, for one, am in perfect sympathy with his effort to prove that he is not the nonentity you have tried to make him."

" Then you don't think he's dead ? " gasped Selina, when she had grasped the import of her mother-in-law's utterance.

" Don't be a fool ! " snapped old Mrs. Flood. " He's no more dead than I am." She turned back on her son. " Unless you and your famous police find a better way of handling this, I shall deal with it myself."

" Perhaps you will be so good as to explain yourself, Mamma," he answered her coldly.

" A boy—your son," she emphasised, " has been lost for forty-eight hours, and all you think about is ' discretion ' and ' losing face ! ' Unless we get news to-day I am going to the printers. I'll have bills printed and get them circulated all over the country. I'll put advertisements in *The Times* and all the local papers, and I'll offer a reward for information. A hundred pounds ; does that shock you ? A hundred pounds for foreign missions : to put natives into cotton shirts and give them tuberculosis—that's quite in order, isn't it ? " she jibed at him. " Well, you'll spend a

ds on finding Johnny ; and a few unfortunate Negroes can
:aths, for once."
only presume that you are unwell, Mamma." Dromore was
ave never heard you speak in such a manner before. I may add
that I am deeply wounded by your suggestion that I should be unwilling to
pay a sum—any sum "—he gulped—" to discover my unhappy boy again."

" Then you needn't look at me like that. I am *not* unwell, and I mean to find my grandson. I'm perfectly indifferent to the family credit—if there is such a thing by now !—or to anything you and your friend the Chief Constable may have to say about it——"

" Oh, Mamma . . . you're so impetuous ! Let us at least reflect—let us be sure that whatever we decide is for the best. . . . Oh, dear ! " moaned Selina, and fell back with her handkerchief to her eyes, as one who founders beneath the final straw ; " here's Uncle Quentin ! "

". . . Well. Has he turned up yet ? "

" No."

" Of course he ain't." The Flood lip curled, the Flood nostril sneered at the folly of a younger generation. " I lay you a pony to a banana he's half-way to the Coast by now ! "

IV

Scuttering most of his time in the bowels of the ship, he felt like a rat, or like one of the big, lethargic cockroaches with which not only the holds but the cabins were infested. The berth he shared with the second mate—a cupboard, carved off by the shifting of a bulkhead in one of the passenger cabins aft—was alive with them ; awake in darkness, he would hear the beasts rustling like shells on a beach, over and under each other's horny bodies ; or one would drop on his face, and he would hurl it from him with loathing. Once, getting into his bunk when the light was out, he found a handful of them in his bedding, and guessed that this was one of the pleasantries in the invention of which his shipmates excelled.

His days, to begin with, consisted of a squalid jumble of tasks that brought on him the continual mockery of his companions and the animosity of the mate, whose knife had been into the ship's boy from the day he came aboard. It was he who circulated the rumour that the new boy was an " owner's pet : " a rumour the victim had no means of contradicting, as even the well-disposed among the crew, not choosing to set themselves up against general opinion, were chary of advances.

" Where d'ya think y' are—in a young gents' academee ? " was a frequent taunt. " Whatcha hangin' about for ? Waitin' for somebody to fetchya afternoon tea on a tray ? " a jibe that brought sycophantic grins from all within earshot. To such he returned no answer but a sidelong glare, but his fingers curled into the palms of his hands. Yes ; every day his fists were getting harder ; the time was approaching when one of his tormentors would get a reply he was not expecting.

The duties of a ship's boy, he had discovered, consisted of everyth. too menial, too trivial or too filthy to be foisted on other members of the ship's company ; from swilling the heads he was yelled at to attend the mate in serving out rations, and not given time to wash his hands before he was handling the food he had to rush to the galley. " Don't shake the measure when you're dipping up peas or rice, you silly young beggar ! Put it in quick and skim off the top to the rim of the pan." " But that means we don't give proper weight." " I'll knock your bleedin' block off if you start arguing with me ! " Or the task of filling the lamps would keep him busy up to the moment he was to serve dinner in the cabin, and a plate would shoot from his fingers, slippery with paraffin, and earn him a crack on the head from whoever happened to be nearest.

Now and again would come a " good " day, when he helped the cooper whittle pegs or cut tin patches for the oil casks ; or cleaned the ship's firearms—a task to which he was promoted after he had succeeded in convincing Wildblood that he had had the handling of guns since childhood. But from this he would be called a dozen times to dance attendance on the cabin passengers—a couple of clerks, going out to their Company's hulk on Bonny river, who gave themselves airs and were universally unpopular ; two ambiguous individuals whose sole motive in making the trip was apparently to get through, at record speed, the cases of spirits they had brought aboard and stowed in their cabin, which was always in disgusting condition ; and a missionary with a coloured youth in his charge, who was being returned from school in England to his family on the Coast. These were the duties which he loathed the most, and in the avoidance of which he grew gradually more cunning as the voyage went on.

It was long before he became conscious of the miracle of the sea : of the mobile green wilderness, ruffled with white, that changed at nightfall to liquid jet, blurred with the magic of phosphorescence ; of the night and day rhythm of ocean, and of that unearthly singing note that follows a ship across deep waters—thin, sweet and continuous as the music of a horn, celestial accompaniment to the sounds made by the ship herself, as she thrusts her timbers, her sheets and her canvas against the pressure of wind and water. " The music of the spheres : " the phrase rushed into his mind the first time he heard it, and he thrilled as one of the early venturers may have thrilled, coming on the tracks of Columbus. Perhaps this was what old Pythagoras meant, and Shakespeare quoted, and had turned up suddenly in a memory not addicted to literary tags. . . .

Then there was the slow sinking of the North Star and the rising of the Southern Cross, as they dropped towards the Equator ; and the south-east wind, bringing its shoals of albacore and benito, of the flying fish and of butterfly-like Portuguese men-of-war.

It was long before he knew the dizzying delight of looking up, into the profound, blue vault of the sky, then down, to the billowing spread of the main royal, which, according to the list of the ship, revealed or concealed the hive-like activity of the decks. That first time he got his arm over the truck, and clung fast, the breath whistled through his teeth ; he almost ceased to breathe as the wind freshened, and the whole ship, and the mast, and himself, like a beetle clinging to a blade of grass, bowed down towards the racing waves, for seconds that were like eternity. During those seconds it seemed as though the *Aldebaran* must turn right over, and lay her beautiful sails flat on the waters, to drift like a drowned bird . . . then she righted herself, and the laughter puffed out of him with relief.

He learned in time to take his share in stowing a sail : standing on the foot-rope, his feet pointed aft, to throw his weight forward and wait for the chanty man at the bunt to strike up :

> " O now you Johnnie Boker
> Come now and turn me over
> Do my Johnnie Boker do——"

—and on the last " *do* " to heave with all his might, while the sail went rolling up to the top of the yard. Standing at Wildblood's table, holding down the charts, he learned the compass—though doubtful of the lubber's point—and enough of latitude and longitude to follow the captain when the latter was plotting the course ; and he worked at his knots until there was no danger of a reef turning out a grannie—as had happened, to his shame, after his first lesson from the cooper. " If you go and make a grannie on a topsail, it'll jam, and somebody'll get killed. Get it right, you young juggins, or you'll get no breakfast this morning ! "

As they were approaching the Doldrums, the weather changed. The water boiled under a blackness of cloud which, suddenly prolonging itself seaward in a gigantic nipple, drew up the waves and joined them to itself in a column like a sea-serpent suckling on an immense black breast. Then there was the metamorphosis of the serpent into a hydra-headed monster, spreading and writhing over its dark host—and the humans' fearful struggle for breath inside a green glass case, as the waterspout dropped on the decks, smashing the *Aldebaran* deep into the sea-trough from which she rose trembling, gushing from all her hatches. Scrambling, half-drowned, through the swimming cabins, helping to rescue their débris from the flood, he had for the first time a deep sense of unity with those who fought to relieve her of her burden.

Then came the storms : lightning that danced in the shrouds, fused a sheet and filled limbs with cramps and lungs with the choking fumes of sulphur. Packed so full of terror that he wondered if his skin would crack with it, he fought to conceal it. At one moment a yelp went up, as lightning struck dead within inches of the powder magazine. The man who shouted looked sheepishly across his shoulder, then, seeing only Johnny, with a stolid expression on his small, sallow face which had turned to the colour of lead, he grinned.

" S'welp me, that wos pretty near Kingdom Come for you and me, mate ! "

He stuck his hands through his belt and winked, to conceal his immense satisfaction at being addressed, for the first time, as " mate." The other guffawed, and caught him a clap on the shoulder.

" Wot price a life on the ocean wave now, cully ? "

V

" You'll be back—when ? " demanded Harcourt Flood.

His captain, a man of few words, planted a thumb on the calendar lying flat by the Chairman's elbow.

" Then-abouts—the Lorrd permitting." A dogged Presbyterian, it pleased him now and again to launch these small testimonies in the teeth of a godless employer.

" Then, if the Lord can spare you from His service long enough to attend to mine," said Harcourt, with immense irony, " you'd better pick up a nephew of mine you'll find somewhere between Accra and Grand Bassam. Do him good to stop there—but his mother's whimpering."

A slow satisfaction spread over the skipper's face.

" That wad be the yin as shipped wi' Runstables ? Och, weel, I jalouse he'll ha'e lost his taste for the sea forbye."

" Then he can work his passage home," was the grim rejoinder.

CHAPTER TWO

I

SELINA FLOOD would have swooned if she had beheld her fourteen-year-old son reared in luxury—or such approach to it as wealthy Victorian parents permitted the sons whom most of them considered it their moral duty to " harden "—washing out a trading skipper's singlets, pipe-claying the deck shoes of a vulgarian from Peckham, or making unskilled attempts to patch a pair of trousers which might fitly have graced one of the Guerdon scarecrows. The idea, to a Victorian, of a schoolboy's bathing in warm water, sleeping on a sprung mattress—or that equivalent, dear to the Victorian sybarite, a feather bed—or lolling on a cushioned couch, was incongruous, if not actually degenerate. Rich and copious meals, hand-and-foot service, the rigorous enforcement of the rule that one did nothing for oneself that could be accomplished by the ringing of a bell were, however, part of the essential upbringing of a youth of good family.

One horror, at least, Selina would have been spared : Johnny flatly refused to perform any of these services for Master Kaboha Komuntale.

" Boy ! Oh, you boy ! "

He turned ; and something—some garment still warm from its owner's body—wrapped itself round his face and slid down on his shoulders. The Negro youth stood grinning.

" You ship's boy ? Berra well. You wash dem shirt one-time. I wear him to-night—savvy ? "

"Wash your own dam' shirt!" Furiously he tore it away and kicked it to the speaker's feet. "And if I've any more cheek from you, I'll beat the guts out of you—you—you black pot-walloper!"

The youth—he was little more than Johnny's age—stood with the smile still a bright ivory gash across his face.

"You too much palaver for ship's boy. My name Amankwa Kaboha: Amankwa—all same prince, savvy? My father king out where we go. I done English school—got book. I not take palaver from ship's boy—white trash—come on board for chop."

"You—perishing nigger!" gasped Johnny, as his right fist drove straight for Master Komuntale's jaw. It was with some surprise that he found the other fully prepared to fight. An unexpected blow in the ribs cooled and made him more scientific in his attack; a second jab—this time at his face—advised him of that diabolical trick of the fighting Negro, of pushing the thumb up between first and second finger, so as to use the nail as a knife-blade, gouging out flesh at every hit. He felt the blood start down his cheekbone, and went in hammer and tongs, raising blows on whatever part of his adversary's anatomy presented itself within his short range. The Negro boy took it stolidly; he had at least four inches advantage in height of Johnny, and each blow he landed was like a sledge-hammer. It would have gone badly for the ship's boy, had not a hand plucked him back by the shoulder, while the other dealt an open-handed slap on the Negro's face. Panting, they fell apart.

"The dirty nigger! The foul, cheating, dirty-fighting bastard!" Johnny was screaming, beside himself with wrath.

"Shove your face in the bucket—you're making a muck of the deck." It was Wildblood speaking coldly; the sun shone through his ears, so that they stood out like two crimson danger signals on either side his head.

"Did you see what he did? He stuck his thumb out—like this!" spluttered Johnny. "God dammit, look at my face!"

"Lucky for you he hadn't got his bracelets on." Wildblood seemed unmoved.

"Bracelets?" Johnny shook his head; a spatter of scarlet flew across the deck. The Negro boy had vanished.

"Wait till you see a real nigger mix up. They use them ivory bracelets like choppers—so, slantwise"—Wildblood illustrated—"with a pull-down behind it. I seen a couple o' blacks carve chunks out of each other with the squared-off edges. Go and find the cook and tell him to patch your face up. You'll get a work-up, you know, for this."

"A work-up—for a damned nigger?" Johnny's jaw fell with indignation.

Wildblood was plucking his lower lip, a trick he had when angry, or perplexed.

"Black or white, he's paid his passage, like the rest of 'em. Your job's to wait on passengers. Black or white, if they're passengers, one's as good as t'other. That's owners' orders." There was that, however, in Wildblood's voice, which showed he was not, for once, in agreement with his owners; from it, Johnny took courage to mutter:

" All right ; I'll take the work-up. But I'm washing no bloody nigger's shirt for him."

" You'll do what you're told. By *me*. That Komuntale," mumbled Wildblood, who, for a while, had skippered Runstable ships up the French canals, " is what they call a movay soojay." Johnny's jaw stiffened, in grave acceptance of Captain Wildblood's French. " They vary—as you'll find, when we get out there. I hold no brief for niggers ; good or bad, I got no use for them—out of their proper place : which ain't among whites. There's one thing you can bear in mind, young fella : you can't do nothing with a nigger, after the missionaries have got at him."

Watching the captain tacking for'ard, with the wind in his ears, he wondered what Guerdon would find to say to *that*. He also wondered whether Captain Wildblood had forgotten the work-up, or whether . . . " *When we get out there.*" His heart quickened. Always, when he thought of it, impatience sent the blood pumping through his veins. *The Gold Coast*. Words of magic ; magnetic words—echoing down imponderable channels of heredity to young Johnny Flood. Even as a child they had come to him with a roll of drums, through long, moral disquisitions on Christian endeavour among the denizens of Darkest Africa ; they were like bars of black and gold, emblazoning dreary narratives of native contrition and conversion. He could smell them, taste them on his tongue ; they set themselves to a tune to be marched to. They were fetish words, to be guarded cunningly, as symbols of a forbidden cult ; used by the initiate, there was no telling what powers they could release. Terrible and wonderful words : whose secret meaning had lured Johnny Flood, as the report of some fabulous beast may lure the hunter, on an adventure which, for him, was less of an adventure in itself than means to an end.

. . . Squatted on the fo'c'sle hatch, Eddy the Painter drew two wavy lines with a brushful of Reckitt's-blue paint across the lid of a packing case ; sucked the brush, spat out the residue, loaded the brush carefully with Chinese white, drew four more lines, and achieved an effect which, half a century later, would probably fetch forty guineas at a Bond Street dealer's. Its value to Eddy was, with luck, a pipe-full of Mabel's Mixture. Somebody would now and again give a bob, or a tanner, for a painting of " foreign parts ; " if they didn't, the painting was there, to hang up between the daguerreotypes of Eddy's parents and his grandparents, each over-shadowed by its shell-encrusted frame. Eddy, a wizened creature, bald as a coot, gave the impression that the sea had ground him down, like a piece of foreshore, to bedrock : eyebrowless, toothless, with the sharp nasal promontory jutting from an ageless, bony face, it was a mystery to most of his companions, how he had come to the fo'c'sle. Eddy had " got book "—a term which, translated from trade English, meant that his education was superior to that of his shipmates for'ard.

" Why don't you paint the sunset ? " Johnny loitered at his shoulder, on his way to turning in ; it was his turn for the middle watch.

" What sunset ? "

Johnny, gaping, pointed to the monstrous aniline flame mounting from the horizon to the zenith itself, where it lingered for those few ecstatic seconds before the swift onrush of tropical night beat it down below the distant band of the sea.

" Can't see it."

" Can't *see* it ? But——"

" Can't ever see anythink I'm looking at." The Painter stuck to his point stubbornly. " Not in the way of setting it down in drawin'. I never draw nuffink I sees—not till afterwards. Then ev'rythink comes up clear—ay, down to the Old Man's Sund'y-go-to-meetin' pants hangin' out to air in the ratlines, an' a loaf o' bread some seagull's forgotten, a-bobbin' about in the wash ! " He chuckled, stopped abruptly, and his tongue followed the direction of his brush, as it laid a thin streak of lamp black, symbolising the smoke from a distant steamer, from west to east of his work of art. Having achieved this to his satisfaction, he directed an elfin twinkle upwards at Johnny. " That's how it's done, mate ! T'ain't what you see at the time, but what sticks in your mind, as counts. Face stinging yet, ain't it ? "

" Like billy-o." Johnny dropped his hand from the cross of plaster on his cheek, to which it had gone involuntarily, as his wound flared under the sun and the spray. It had been getting steadily sorer as the day wore on, and he had been stoical about it up to now. " My face feels like a boil," he muttered, under Eddy's kindly regard. " I'd not be surprised if he's given me blood-poisoning—the black swine ! "

" How much diff'rence 'ud it make, if he was white ? "

" How do you mean ? " Startled, Johnny turned on his interlocutor. He found himself looking down on the top of the Painter's head, polished and coloured like a chestnut.

" ' Black swine '—' Damn' black nigger : ' you got it all off pat, haven't you ? You'll be all right, when you get out yonder." A note of irony in the speaker's voice checked Johnny and made him vaguely uneasy.

" I don't know what you're getting at. You can't say a white man, even the worst sort of cad, would fight with his thumb-nails ! " His tone was aggrieved.

" I ain't saying so. All I say is, a dirty trick's a dirty trick, whether it's a white or a black as uses it," was the calm answer.

" Well—yes, of course. But what about it ? " Puzzled, he crouched on his haunches, staring, with folded arms, at Eddy and at the canvas.

" This about it," Eddy spoke slowly, after a pause. " The colour of a fella's skin didn't ought to be used against him, no matter what crime he's committed. That's supposed to be a law in our courts—but I seen more cases when it did than when it didn't."

" Well, I suppose one can see how that comes about," said Johnny. The Painter, intent on his foreground, had given him time to think it over. " I don't suppose our judges mean to be prejudiced ; but you've got to allow that there's a lot of beastly customs and crimes that go on among the blacks which simply don't belong to the white races."

" It depends what you call beastly. I've heard tell of white folk doing things that 'ud make a savage's gorge rise. See here, Jake." The Painter had thrust the handle of his brush, crosswise, between his toothless gums while he sought among his paints for a fresh tube ; his words came mumbling past the obstacle. " There's one thing strikes me as not fair, however you look at it ; and that's the way a nigger's marked down, wherever he goes, by the colour of his skin. Kids in the streets, runnin' after them : ' Black man ! Nigger ! ' Folks turning round and starin' ; sometimes they laugh, sometimes they frown. Whichever way, they don't bother to hide it—like's if the nigger's some sort of dummy, that doesn't know when it's being talked about. It's a joke, with a lot o' folks, just to be black. You give kids black dolls to play with ; folks black their faces and twang banjoes on the beach ; there's nigger minstrels. Laugh ! Laugh ! Anybody that gets himself up like a nigger's sure of a laugh. Stop laughing, and you hate. That's how it is among the white people."

" Missionaries don't hate—and they don't laugh." Johnny answered out of profound experience. " They've got a whale of a pluck, you know—going out and getting themselves caught by the Ashanti, like those Ramseyer people ; did you ever read *Four Years in Ashantee* ? It's as good as a ' blood,' any day ! And I've got a sort of cousin——" He broke off, biting his lip, but the Painter did not appear to have noticed.

" The Lord made white and black. I'm not religious, and I don't swallow half what the parsons tell us. But He'd got the doing of it. If He'd wanted, He could have made the whole boiling white, and saved a lot of trouble. What beats me is, if He wanted the two sorts, to keep 'em from getting mixed, like, what's the notion of settin' the whites on to make the blacks as much like themselves as possible ? It oughta work both ways," said the Painter solemnly. " Why don't we get blacks telling us how to run our lives and our societies, and making it damned uncomfortable for us, if we don't do as we're told ? "

" What ? Teach us to take it out on each other with witchcraft, and give us a taste for human chop, as a change from beef and mutton ? " jeered Johnny, assuming his companion was jesting.

" Pah ! I tell you one thing," said the Painter, and set his board aside to find his plug and knife. His toothless jaws champed for a few seconds before he continued, fixing, as he spoke, a bright, sandy eye fiercely on Johnny. " A thing you'll not find in any nigger colony till it's had the whites there to show it the way : and that's a knocking-shop. You know what I mean, Jake, though you're not old enough to have sampled 'em. There's more moral decency among the pure nigger races, away off our trade routes, than ever you'll find in so-called ' civilised countries.' "

II

He had barely had time to glance at the magic coast, as they approached it on a sea so steady that it was as though the land moved nearer, while the ship stood still, clamped in her malachite cradle, with the long grey pencil of the shark that had followed them from Formosa nosing at her stern.

If not lugging goods into the " trade room " on the after deck, helping the cooper to knock the hoops on to the oil casks, or lending a hand at dragging the big canvas hose from the starting tub amidships to either end of the deck, Johnny was manufacturing dash-heads of tobacco for the trading small fry that swarm in the tracks of the coastal capitalists, and having his first lesson in preparing the dash-rum cask from which every purchaser, however insignificant, expects the free drink that lubricates trade. Blinded with sweat, he toiled between the main deck and the trade-room, filling the two hundred and fifty gallon tub with its quotas of rum, salt and fresh water, bilge and damaged tobacco leaves, which were ambrosia (so he was informed) to the native palate. Curiosity prompting him to sample the brew, he retched, vomited and acquired a horrified respect for native digestive processes, together with the resolution never to subject his own to the test again.

He had no time to think. And there was no hope of sleep, when he crawled into the bunk over the second mate's, for the ache in his loins and the twitching of muscles that felt as though they had turned to red-hot wires inside a thin casing of burnt-up flesh.

At first he lay naked, in a pool of sweat, heedless of the warning passed on by all old Coasters, to " keep wool next the skin " from the time of arrival in the fever belt. At the end of an hour's twisting and turning, raucous snores from the bunk below adding to his torment, he lowered himself painfully over the mate's comatose body, and, having dragged on his trousers, crawled out on the deck.

A greyness which was neither light nor darkness lay over everything, reducing all colour, all solidity, to cobweb. Silence. Then a soft soughing of tide. Then silence—in layers under the thick African mist that blotted out the moon. A faint, unreal silver-point, the hummock of a headland, crested with palms, drew itself across the *Aldebaran's* stern, land and water merging imperceptibly in a band of white vapour at sea level.

Half-surprised that his feet did not sink through the faintly shining surface of the deck, he laid his hand for reassurance on a rail, saturated with moisture. Under the rail dew was collected in heavy drops ; aloft in the shrouds rustled the rats, drinking the dew caught in the furled sails.

" Well. Here's your Gold Coast, Jake." Eddy the Painter—or some ghostly version of him—had loomed out of the silver mist.

" Yes." A shiver ran between his shoulder-blades. This spectral land, this waste land, this limbo ! How far, how far from all he had pictured.

" Peaceful, ain't it ? "

He nodded.

" You're a rum kid. You ain't seen nothing yet."

" No."

. . . Like being dead. Suspension in some no-man's land—some inter-planary space. Yet not empty. Something watching. Something crouching. Something that pullulated endlessly—some threadlike octopus—through layers of silence and mist. Again the shiver slipped down his naked spine.

" Gives you the willies, don't it ? "

He hesitated. The Painter's hand fell on his bare shoulder.

" This ain't your watch, mate. Go on, turn in. Don't you know that's Yeller Jack, waiting for ye, out yonder ? "

He turned and padded back, his feet making no sound on the dew-soaked deck. It was only when he lay in his bunk again that it occurred to him that he and the Painter had never raised their voices above a whisper. . . .

III

It was a shock, next morning, when the captain came out in full splendour of ducks and pipe-clay, in place of the ragged singlet, old serge slacks and carpet slippers of recent weeks. Johnny, entering with the teapot, nearly dropped it at the spectacle of Wildblood, solicitously trimming the beard which, since leaving Bristol, had grown half-way down to his midriff. The captain pointed to a steward's white jacket, mysteriously produced from one of his lockers.

" You got to smarten yourself, young fella. You ain't going to wait on His Majesty King William of Half Jack in that rig, are you ? "

" Do you mean we're faking ourselves up like this for the benefit of a bunch of niggers ? " Johnny, his hair pomaded, his lower half clothed in a pair of sea-stained but clean bell-bottoms he had been ordered to borrow from Alf the cooper—his own amounting by now to little more than a piece of cobbled patchwork—snorted disgustedly as he buttoned the steward's coat round his naked ribs. The cooper, a short, spare man, not much longer in the limb than Johnny, but with the chest and shoulders of a gorilla, sniggered.

" Don't you make no mistake. 'E's a great man for comp'ny, is our Elias, when we gets into port. You wait an' see ! "

By noon, there was no peace aboard the *Aldebaran*. Wildblood and his cronies, captains and mates of other vessels lying off the headland—Johnny assured himself, after a moment of panic, that there were no Flood ships among them—one or two white traders, a missionary and, by courtesy, the passengers, celebrated his arrival in a style that kept the ship's boy on the gallop from the arrival of the first canoes to the departure of the last.

Among the earliest arrivals was a state canoe, escorted by a fleet of smaller ones, which encircled the ship three times with great parade of chanting and swinging paddles, before it disembarked two immense chiefs who, on account of their corpulence and the volume of their ceremonial robes, had difficulty in negotiating the ladder which had been run down on the port side. Escorted aft with great ceremony, a wave of singular majesty passed in their wake along the observant decks. Standing aside to give them way-room, briefly conscious of two pairs of eyes, almost eclipsed by the heavy lids half-closing over toffee-coloured eyeballs, of the intolerable lips of absolute despotism, Johnny was startled by a brief reminder of his

Uncle Harcourt. The same kind of brutal grandeur! The chiefs passed on, their enormous bellies supported by hands that spread themselves there, as much for that purpose as to display their load of ivory and gold.

While these magnates were received with every mark of the respect that accrued to their exalted rank, the decks swarmed with eager Kroos, bargaining through their headmen for terms that would enable each, on the conclusion of his twelve months' engagement, to purchase a new wife, and send him back to his village with some show of prosperity. Johnny, rushing between state-room and galley, ran a perpetual gauntlet of flashing teeth, snapping fingers and innocent familiarities which, not knowing how otherwise to respond, he ignored. What sort of an attitude was one supposed to take up with these cheeky niggers? There was no time to reflect on this.

He did not at first recognise the slim, proud figure in a long white loin-cloth, its neck hung with many-stranded necklaces of gold and shell, its arms loaded to the elbows with ivory, that passed him on the middle deck. One of the sailors grinned and jerked his thumb.

"What price our Ponto this morning?"

Wiping the sweat out of his incredulous eyes:

"Good gosh, he hasn't got his trousers on!" gasped Johnny.

"Trowsis? 'E's all togged up to meet 'is Da. The old geezer 'ud say 'e'd got witch if 'e turned up in pants. 'Ere, you, get a move on; yer wanted in the trade-room."

"How the hell can I be in the trade-room and keep on filling that lot up in the cabin?" muttered Johnny, as he hurried back to his duties of handing round cigars—it was noticeable that the chiefs, now richly amiable, picked out the best of the Havanas—and replenishing beakers with liquor that bore no relation to the contents of the dash-cask. There was a lot of good feeling going round; the chiefs roaring at Wildblood's stories, of which it is doubtful whether they understood more than a fraction, and Wildblood roaring with them; but there was a glint in the corner of his eye which told that for all this show of geniality, chiefs Kufi and Quah would not be "jumping ship" with a few unreckoned but valuable pieces of dash concealed beneath those flowing robes.

In between summonses to the cabin, he was toiling in the trade-room, one of three told off to check on the Krooboys' assembling of Chief Kufi's order; and was presently sent to superintend the loading of the hogheads of rum, cases of guns and powder, cloth and tobacco, which were going off in the canoes. It was thus that he came, for the last time, face to face with Kaboha Komuntale.

He looked with curiosity at the Negro youth, as he followed in the stately procession of his father and uncle to the head of the ladder. Since the fight, which had left its permanent scar on Johnny's cheek, the two boys had ignored each other. Master Komuntale, warned, doubtless, by his guardian, had let the ship's boy alone, Johnny behaving with scornful aloofness when duty obliged him to enter the Negro youth's cabin. He was aware, however, of a vague disturbance, as he looked at the transformed being who gazed across his shoulder towards a land in which his own race was master.

The sniggering arrogance of the Europeanised Negro had slipped from Komuntale with his European clothes. It was as though the sun, striking across the water and burning his naked torso, restored to him something which his year among the white people had taken from him : some pride, some decency, some assurance of his own dignity. He stood there quietly, with suitable decorum, during the leave-takings between his relatives and the ship's officers. Although barefooted, he seemed to have grown taller ; the poise of his head on his shoulders was that of a young forest animal, innocent and proud.

A phrase came into Johnny's mind from an old Hausa grammar Eddy had produced one night from his locker. Possibly Komuntale did not know Hausa ; still—he took a step forward, and held out his hand.

" *Sai wata rana*, Kaboha. Good luck."

The ivory gash appeared in the Negro youth's face ; he shot out his hand and gripped Johnny's, without speaking.

" Goodbye, my boy—goodbye—and God go with you ! "

The missionary who had brought him out leaned over the rail to call to his departing charge, who grinned upwards as he waved farewell. It was no doubt by chance that a gob of Captain Wildblood's saliva dropped into the water just short of the state canoe. The missionary, a simple-hearted creature (" Wait till he gets up against some of them black sprucers at Winnebah ; he's a natural for 'em ! " Wildblood had said, more in sorrow than in anger, after a more than usually glaring sample of the Reverend Pilbeam's naïveté), turned with moist eyes towards the farewell party. " Poor lad ! I fear he takes the Lamp of the Lord into dark places."

" Lamp of the Lord ! " Wildblood snorted. " There ain't much Lamp of the Lord about that one."

" We must pray for him," said the missionary, simply.

" If you want to do any praying, padre "—Wildblood had had as much as he could take of Master Komuntale and his relatives that morning—" you can pray he'll forget the white vices he's learned before starting to mix 'em up with his black ones."

The canoe boys began their chant, into whose rhythm there came now a note of joy and triumph for the return of a chief's son. The weight of the potentates in the stern sank the canoe almost to its gunwale under the state umbrella. As the paddles struck the water, Johnny saw Kaboha rise ; saw him turn his back on the ship and, with a movement as grave as a religious rite, loose the loin-cloth and let it fall from limbs smooth and perfect as ebony ; saw him stretch out his arms in the gesture which is that of the Cross, but which seemed like an offering—the offering of the returned exile, who brings all of himself, all he is and will be, back to the land of his people. In the midday blaze of the sun, the palms, the land itself, quickened with welcome, as the canoe shot like an arrow towards them.

Moved, without knowing why, Johnny started as Wildblood cuffed his shoulder.

" Get aft, you, and clean up the cabin ; it's like a piggery, after that black scum."

IV

On the following morning, trade began in earnest. Long before midday, the palaver in the cabin had risen to pandemonium. Chairs, table, every available inch of locker-room was crowded. Palm oil, gold dust, ivory, ebony, logwood, coconuts were offered in token against liquor, guns, powder, neptunes, cloth and the welter of shoddy and pawnbrokers' trash that made up the trading cargo ; orders and counter-orders, the breaking of manillas in token of contracts accepted, came to a crescendo in the handing out of trust. The air was solid with nigger-smell, rum-smell, the smell and smoke of tobacco.

His jacket no longer white, but grey, and plastered to his body, his eyes streaming, Johnny pushed his way round with the cans of " chain-lightning " liquor, and marvelled at Wildblood's coolness, the quickness of his calculations, amid chaos created, often, expressly to confuse his reckonings. Runstable's captain was one of the smartest traders on the Guinea voyage : knew to a nicety those who were worth seventy-five per cent, those who were good for fifty, the doubtfuls to whom it was rash to allow more than twenty-five in trust ; those who would sell slaves to honour their commitments, and those who would try to get out of them on a hard-luck story, or pretended misunderstanding of the bargain.

At sundown, to the relief of all, the last of the visitors, at the end of a long chaffering which Johnny, by then, was too stupefied to follow, was bawled off the ship ; Johnny was ordered to fetch bass, and, rocking on his feet with fatigue, was offered a mug, in acknowledgment of his industry. The captain's mood was gracious.

" You ain't done so bad, for a beginning. Well, Jake ; you seen your first day's trade. How d'you like it, eh ? "

Johnny grinned. He felt, actually, a little drunk. Steadily, since the opening of the palaver, the excitement of the scene had been mounting to his head, and he had followed each chaffering bout with eager interest, or, when an order or a summons elsewhere robbed him of his climax, with a sense of keen frustration.

" It's grand fun, sir. They're a slippy lot, aren't they—some of those nigger traders ! "

Wildblood chuckled.

" ' Softly, softly catchee monkey.' I reckon we can match their slippiness, when we got to. That reminds me—I got a nice job for you to-morrow." He flung himself back in the chair and roared with laughter ; stopping as suddenly as he began to scowl impressively at Johnny. " Twenty-two passengers, my lad. You got to be ready for twenty-two passengers to-morrow."

" Twenty-two ? " Johnny gaped : for a moment wondering whether alcohol and sunlight had, for once, gone to Wildblood's well-seasoned head. " But—we've only got four passenger cabins, and—and nobody's left the ship, so far but Kaboha—— ! "

" Twenty-two," repeated the captain solemnly, " and we're putting 'em down below. So you got to make it all shipshape and Bristol-fashion in the morning, bearing in mind that ladies is particular——"

" You're pulling my leg ! "

" Be damned if I am ! Twenty-two black females we're carrying—a little token of good feeling from my pal Quah to old Billy at Half Jack. It'll be your business to look after 'em, and you mind what you're about. We got to deliver them twenty-two Venuses right side up with care ; William's got a rare eye for the ladies. They're coming aboard . . . When are they coming aboard, mister ? " he shouted at the mate, whose lean body appeared, blocking the door.

The mate spat, with his usual look of malevolence at Johnny.

" We going to wait and pick up them niggers for Half Jack ? "

Wildblood swung round sharply in his revolving chair.

" Sure. I got it fixed with Quah's headman. . . "

The mate said nothing, laconically shifting the plug he was chewing from one cheek to the other. Lolling in the doorway, his eyes fixed on the horizon, he began to whistle a tune from *Floradora*. Then he turned his head slowly, and looked at Wildblood, who had not finished his sentence.

Wildblood said, " Grand Gobro—— ? " And the mate nodded.

Staring at the floor, the other began to swear, in a deep, continuous and profane rumble. Then, reminded by the shadow flung across his feet, of Johnny's presence, he turned to bellow, " Get out, you ! " and Johnny, appalled by the prospect before him, was thankful to obey.

CHAPTER THREE

I

" HE'S right, all the same. Them Grand Gobros have been laying for us, ever since we was off here last trip."

" We oughta've upped anchor an' 'opped while the goin's good —an' to 'ell with ole Billy's concubines."

" Tain't so convenient, to fall foul of Billy, or of Kwaw neether, for that matter ; 'tween the pair of 'em, they can make it pretty 'ot for us, down this bit o' the Coast."

" 'Lias is scared of getting a peppering, if we turn up at Half Jack without Billy's skirts !"

" We'll get wors'n a pepperin', if them Grand Gobros start in on us about that powder we sold Kunkumi, after promising it the Grand Gobros."

" What's 'e *done* it for ? " An aggrieved whine in the background. " Landin' us all in a pickle like this——"

A shrill laugh mocked the speaker's simplicity.

" 'Cos Kunkumi offered double the Grand Gobro price. You don't 'spect 'Lias to turn that down? That's 'ow a trading skipper lines 'is pockets."

" An' what about British credit? 'T'ain't ethical," gloomed the aggrieved one.

" Blow ethics; 't'ain't *safe*, with sprucers like these Grand Gobros around."

" 'E didn't oughta 've bothered with Billy's concubines."

" Wot—an' leave Floods or Kings to collect the passage money? That ain't 'Lias's way!"

" 'Ush. Listen. . . ."

The fog was thicker than ever, the second night they lay off the headland. It came over from the lagoons behind the cocoa palms, sticky with fever. Few feared the fever—an odds-on hazard of their occupation: but there was that in the white plasm, pressing upon them all, moulding itself into the human body, that lit up imagination in the least fanciful, and roused apprehensions which each knew he shared with his companions.

" Hark at them Kroos. They got the wind up—and no mistake."

" No wonder neether; 'alf of 'em 'ave 'ad their uncles an' cousins boiled an' roasted by the Grand Gobros; they know what's coming to 'em, if we get some o' them pickles aboard."

" Might as well be roasted as feed Old Faithful, that come down with us like Mary's little lamb——"

" 'E's 'ad a couple o' Kroos for supper. I guess the 'ole boiling of 'em coulda got away, if they'd 'ad the sense to go over all together. Even a shark don't ask for collywobbles by swallowin' more'n two Kroos at a sittin'."

Half-dead of exhaustion as the crew were, none save a couple of fo'c'sle hands who had gone down with a preliminary bout of fever had turned in. All were jumpy, worried by the fog, worried more by uncertainty of what the night might bring, by the difficulty of identifying each other in the thick white brume which, blurring the lights, played grisly tricks with human proportions. Somebody's mumble that it was like a blurry winding sheet brought jeers from those within earshot.

" 'Ark at 'Arry! 'E'll 'ave 'imself dead an' buried next! One thing—Old Faithful 'ull save us the trouble of breakin' up one o' them gun-cases for 'is coffin."

" Cockroaches bin at you yet, 'Arry?" came the pointed inquiry. " You ain't dead till you got them gentry atween yer toes!" cackled the speaker.

" Here's Alf." Eddy the Painter ducked his head and made an ineffectual attempt to rub fog out of his eyes. " Lumme, Alf, you don't 'alf look a fine figure of a chap, seen through a fog. It's a proper shame your girl can't see you. Alf . . . Alf?" he repeated uncertainly, as the figure made no answer.

Suddenly the man between Eddy and the form he was addressing leapt to his feet with a shrill scream.

" It ain't Alf! It's . . . *Jesus*! They're 'ere!"

. . . In a series of soft thuds, the Grand Gobros dropped from the rails on to the decks. For a while there was hubbub and somebody let off a firing piece ; but in the treacherous fog no one could shoot without risking the lives of his shipmates.

". . . What for you no trade with Grand Gobro man ? "

" That's my business. I can trade with who I choose, without asking the likes of you."

Backed up against the rail of his chair, sullen, implacable, Captain Wildblood glowered at a ring of towering figures that dripped water on the floor of his cabin. Each carried a knife in his loin-cloth. Captain Wildblood looked away from the knives. He was a brave man, but he had a delicate stomach. The notion of one of those knives, driven in just above the top button of his trousers, upset it.

" No, Cappy, no can do. You done trade with us, and Grand Gobro paid fit time. You blood brother with damn' black nigger Kunkumi, you let him have plenty guns proper."

" Get off my ship, you dam' black nigger."

" No, Cappy, we no fit for go till you give us plenty guns too, and powder to blow dam' black nigger Kunkumi to bad place ! "

" Unless you jump ship one-time, I give you fumfum," muttered Wildblood. A square, middle-aged man, knowing his own helplessness, he sat there, bluffing, for he knew the odds were against him.

The failure of crew or passengers to come to his support had told him the ship was in the hands of the raiders. All he could do was play for time. Through the crack of the door, where the fog was wreathing, came the shuffle of innumerable bare feet : the ship was alive with Grand Gobros. They must have surrounded her, creeping up in their canoes under cover of the fog, then stopping at a safe distance to take to the water—having, no doubt, their own way of taking care of Old Faithful, already gorged by his earlier meal. But for the howling of the Kroos below, they must have been heard. . . . Passing through his mind quickly, these things explained, without offering a solution to, his present situation and that of his passengers and ship's company.

" We want dem powder and guns, Cappy. If you no get we cut your throat proper like bosilla. You come for trade with Kunkumi. Tink you go away and gib no powder and no guns to Grand Gobro. No can do, Cappy. You do it one time, we no catch you. Next time we say we catch you, you gib us guns proper. Savvy ? "

" White man no take orders from you, you black gorilla ! You too much big mouth. You no start palaver when Governor Daddy send gun-boat down from Cape Coast, blow you to bits bang bang ! " Captain Wildblood held to his point stoutly, seeing that the mention of Cape Coast made an effect.

An uneasy look shot sideways from the eyes of the one who, so far, had acted as spokesman. Among those who pressed forward to confer with the leader was one whom Wildblood identified, as much by smell as by the eccentricity of his appearance, as the village fetish man. Reeking of rancid fat, with hair teased up into enormous horns on either side a face striped with ochre : his chest and arms smothered in the diamond-shaped cicatrises of palaver-marks, and a collection of unsavoury-looking objects round his neck which included human bones, and were recognised by Wildblood as juju—this one was evidently urging the headman to defiance. The cabin stank of tanyard offal, hummed with the insects the open door had let in, which whirled about the lamps, struck them with loud pings and fell sprawling on the furniture. The yellow of the lamplight and the black of the Grand Gobros' bodies ran together in a blur made by the invading fog.

The leader turned at last from his conference.

" White gunboat not frighten Grand Gobro man. Got witch for beat gunboat," he announced triumphantly.

Captain Wildblood sighed. It was what he had expected, after seeing the fetishman. Well, that finished it. He made a movement to rise from his chair.

In a flash, four knives were at, respectively, his eyes, his throat and the pit of his sensitive stomach. He managed to control a shiver, but closed his eyes, because the light quivering down the knife-blades made him squint ; and his voice was a tone higher than its usual bass note, as he muttered :

" Where's your order ? "

A hasty fumble in the woolly recesses of somebody's head produced the crumpled paper.

" We want plenty dash, Cappy," the ringleader had the impudence to remind him.

A sigh of relief went along the ship as the captain emerged from his cabin. Held frozen at the point of the knife, crew and passengers had reacted according to their kind. He smiled grimly at the sight of the Reverend Pilbeam on his knees, and at one of the Bristol drunks, trying to buy himself off with a bottle of gin. The Grand Gobro men took the gin, but did not relax their attention to their captive.

Called off by the headman, the Grand Gobros lolled, while the crew dispersed ; some to open up the trade-room, under Wildblood's orders, some to mount guard over any removable property to which their visitors might take a fancy. The imprisoned Kroos, silent as they had previously been noisy, lay quiet, doubtless in fear of their lives, under the hatches.

Johnny's hand, piloting the lamp between the kegs of powder in the magazine, shook, as much with excitement as with fear, now that the worst was over. The whole affair was too fantastic, too much like a *Boy's Own Paper* thriller, to carry conviction. Even with a Grand Gobro knife at his ribs, he had found himself unable to visualise the possibility of that knife driving home ; of blood—his blood !—dripping on the deck ; of pain and anguish before dying—Johnny Flood dying !—on a Bristol ship, in a fog, somewhere along the West African coast. Try as he might, during moments that prolonged themselves into hours, he failed to imagine it. In the stories there was always the rescuer ! . . .

Conquering a Lower School impulse to jeer as the knife was withdrawn, from its uncomfortable proximity to his vitals, he swaggered slightly, when, obeying the order to fetch an anchor light, he followed Alf and another hand down to the magazine.

" Here—hold that lamp steady ! "

" I am doing ; but it wants snuffing all the time." The foul air in the magazine beat down the flame. Impatient of wrestling with the metal latch of the lantern, Johnny took the candle out and wedged it carefully between two of the gun-powder kegs ; the ship was steady as a rock, she barely lifted to the oily suck of the tide.

" Have a care ! " yelled Alf. " If one o' them kegs catches, you an' me an' everyone else 'ull go sky-high ! "

" Rats," muttered Johnny. " There's plenty of water in the buckets "—and caught the words back on a sudden gust of memory : Guy Fawkes' Day—he, Dorset and Gilbert—wet gunpowder—and a match. He held his breath ; then—" Alf !—*Alf !* " he whispered more urgently, down the dark tunnel of the magazine. . . .

In the trade-room they were checking the guns. The Grand Gobro headman was taking nothing for granted. Each case had to be opened, the twelve six-foot Danes it contained verified and the lid nailed down again, under his eyes. Someone nudged his neighbour to draw attention to the figure of Wildblood, his feet apart, his head lowered like the head of a charging bull, his fists clenched behind his back as though he could not trust them not to fasten themselves upon the throats of his black tormentors. The passengers stood in the background, an indistinct group, silent before the unedifying spectacle of a British skipper, held up by a bunch of natives. " Serve 'im blurry well right. 'E got us in this mess : teach 'im to trade proper next time, instead o' trying to slip a fast one across the customers ! " was mumbled among the crew.

Apart from this brief interchange, and the incessant chattering of the Grand Gobros, there was dead silence in the trade-room, where men stumbled around with anchor lamps in their hands and murder in their hearts, intent only on getting through with an ignominious business. A crisis arose, however, when the headman, evidently intoxicated with his own triumph, indicated that he expected the loading to be done by the sailors, and not by his companions. It was at this moment that the cook, a big Galwayman, let out a howl of rage, drew a pistol from his belt and, by firing it, would have precipitated disaster—when a sudden yelp, followed by fizzing and a puff of black smoke, made those who stood near the open hatch of the powder magazine leap back. A piebald figure, bursting into the trade-room, screamed :

" We're done for—she's alight—she's blowing up ! "

A moment to make sure, a moment of petrification, while smoke billowed from the hatch : and the trade-room was empty, save of the crew. Yells and splashes told that Grand Gobro had taken to the water. There was a general leap for the fire buckets, while Wildblood stood still : wondering whether to order the ship's company overboard—into the jaws of Old Faithful—or to allow them to meet their doom on the doomed ship. Slowly he became aware of two grinning faces black as his departed visitors', in front of him—of a strong smell of singeing, and of a familiar voice.

"That's fixed 'em nicely," said Alf the cooper.

II

Beyond the flashing wall of the surf and the yellow strip of the foreshore ran the "town:" starting with the native huts, then the more formal, though no less decrepit, buildings housing white, or near-white, officialdom; the whole petering out in a welter of tin roofs that were saloons, factories, storage sheds and the offices that centralised trade on this stretch of the coast. Behind them, the coco palms brushed a sky heavy with heat.

A telescope purloined from Wildblood's cabin gave him the rainbow of the surf, the ant-like population fulminating along the waterfront, and the detail of the buildings behind them, among which he thought he could detect at least one store whose proprietor, according to the numbers pouring in and out of his door, was doing a lively trade. Johnny marked it with satisfaction. He had money in his pockets, and it was the first sizable town at which they had touched, in their leisurely nosing along the Coast. Wildblood had his contacts to make, and time was less valuable to him than the collection of a cargo that would bring the utmost profit to himself, as well as to his owners.

The two Bonny river clerks showed off their familiarity with the local layout to the drinking couple, who, much the worse for wear, had had their baggage brought up to quit the ship at Charlestown—formerly Fort Charles; Johnny's eyes glued to the telescope, his ears followed the high-pitched Cockney voice which identified, for the benefit of the strangers, features of the shoreward scene.

"Floods"(his heart gave a tick) "—that's only one of their sub-factories: they don't do much along here these days. McKittricks—they're newcomers, trying to nose in on the oil; they won't last long. Dalton's. Then there's the Old Fort, and back of it—you can't see properly from here—Rodríguez and Plant. Most of their stuff goes to the islands." The speaker broke off with a snigger, nudging his companion, who asked what the joke was.

"A funny set-up, that—ain't it, skipper?"

Captain Wildblood had floated up and Johnny hastily concealed the telescope. The master of the *Aldebaran* turned a look of sultry dislike on the speaker.

"Captain to you, Mr. Smith. What's a funny set up?"

"Rodríguez and Plant—that dago-Yankee combine." The clerk named Smith winked, in no way put out by the snub.

Wildblood shrugged his shoulders.

"Same as the rest—jockeying for position with the nigger chiefs and grumbling about local tariffs," he grunted.

"Ay, but there's more to it than that, isn't there?" The other clerk spoke up: a thin-faced youth with a ruddy complexion, whom Wildblood marked down inwardly as a " natural " for the mosquitoes. He was a pleasanter type than his jaunty colleague. " I've always wondered about the rights of that old Abolition yarn——"

" Abolition must have made a sore difference out here." One of the drunks fixed a gloomily retrospective eye on the shore line. " I reckon it was worth having a cut at the Coast trade in those days——"

" You bet that's what Plant thought, when he picked up Rodríguez for his partner." Smith sniggered. " Back them Yanks for having their eyes open—yes, siree ! "

" Let's have the yarn, captain," urged the younger (and less damaged) drunk.

Wildblood snorted, made as though to rest his arms on the rail, remembered, and saved himself a blistering.

" The trade had been running down, you know, for quite a bit before Abolition. Folks was getting queasy—there was a lot of Quaker interest among the shipping fam'lies. There was Rathbones, making a fuss in Liverpool, and a gang o' females, beaten up by an old witch called Burmester, that was driving the Bristol owners crazy."

" Ay, ay, we know all that."

Damn you, what do you want to cut in for ? Johnny's ears were pricked for the rumble of Wildblood's voice.

" Well, this Yank—Plant, he called himself—had been working on a design that 'ud beat the patrol ships on the old slaving routes. He kept it quiet, till Abolition was a cert. Then he got this fellow, from Cuba, to finance him, and they had the ships built up at Galveston—long, narrow, plenty o' sail ; greyhound type. There wasn't anything afloat that could beat 'em."

" I get you. Then—bing ! comes the Abolition bill, and——" The elder drunk was grinning.

" They cleaned up a packet, in the ten or twelve years after the Bill went through. You oughta get Rodríguez himself—the present one—to tell you about it. The Spaniards aren't sheepish about their slaving connections, the way we are, in Bristol," said Wildblood dryly.

" How about Plant ? Is there a Plant now, by the way ? "

" Oh, well, there's a ditty-bag o' yarns about him. Nobody ever saw him. According to some, there never was a Plant—and, I warn you, you'll get no satisfaction from Rodríguez on that score. If there was a Plant, he ran the other end of the racket—clearing the cargo up to Texas, that was doing big business in nigger flesh just then."

" Never got caught, eh ? " This, to judge by the inflection, gave the speaker satisfaction.

A smile dawned slowly on Wildblood's features.

" Not them. They ran the whole cahoot under the Portuguese flag, so's to avoid trouble with us, or getting crosswise of anti-slavery interests in the States. Here, you ! "

Johnny started ; absorbed in the yarn, he had not noticed Wildblood, edging round behind him.

"What're you doing with my glass?" The telescope was whipped out of his hand.

"You weren't using it," Johnny defended himself.

Wildblood's ears, always the index of his mood, were empurpled.

"I wasn't using it! And maybe I wasn't using my ruler the other day?—or my water-bottle the day before that? By heck, I'll teach you the meaning of property, my lad, if I tan the hide off you! I suppose you'll be helping yourself to the anchor next, if it happens to take your fancy?"

Johnny shrugged this aside as persiflage. Old gas-bag! . . . And there were things to see and things to buy, across the dancing water. . . .

"The boat's coming," he mentioned. The canoes which were to take the passengers ashore and the first batch of men on shore leave had negotiated the surf. The crew had drawn lots for the privilege of first leave, and Johnny had been among the lucky ones. Luck having gone to his head—"I'm in the first lot," he jubilated, not caring who overheard him.

The crimson passed from Wildblood's ears into the whites of his eyes. His voice dropped to a croon.

"You are, are you? Then—*get for'ard!* And if I have any more lip from you, you'll get a work-up in place of shore leave, young fella. Get your cloths and do up them brasses; they look as if a whale's been breathing on 'em."

The canoes had come alongside, and were lifting and falling at the foot of the ladder. The passengers and their baggage were established, Alf the cooper and half a dozen of the fo'c'sle hands had scrambled in, and varied flourishes on mouth organ and concertina with derisive whistles at their less fortunate shipmates. "'Ere: we're a man short. 'Oo's the eighth?" Alf was shouting.

He took a quick look up and down the deck; Wildblood was not in sight. A sheet of tarpaulin covered the baggage in the nearest canoe; under that was safety. Let there be a work-up when he got back. No one —not even the captain—had a right to interfere with the fair chances of the draw.

Acting on impulse, Johnny made a rush for the ladder. Within a couple of rungs of the bottom, as he was about to let go and drop into the canoe, a roar from above made him lose hold prematurely. The last thing he saw before shooting into the pellucid water was Wildblood's infuriated face, thrust over the rail.

"Bare-faced insubordination; so that's the latest, is it? Listen you; I got plenty to say to you."

He stood, with eyes fixed stubbornly on the planks on which his garments were streaming. The tar, bubbling in the seams, sizzled as the drops fell on it. For the first time since sunrise, he was cool—which was more than Wildblood could claim!—standing there with his fists swinging, his head down, as though about to rush at the dripping figure before him. The snigger Johnny was at pains to stifle was smitten from him by the first words.

"The hero! The chap that saved the ship when she was all but lost!"

The sarcasm biting into him like acid, Johnny flung back his head and glared Wildblood in the face ; his own had started to burn.

" The fella whose shipmates gave him a tarpaulin muster, to show their gratitude—— ! "

Furiously, he plunged his hands in his pockets, brought out the money and flung it on the deck. The coppers, the threepennies and sixpennies went rolling away into the scuppers, chipped off in bright flakes of bronze and silver that fell in parabolas to the water.

" Take it ! I suppose I get my pay ? I've earned that ! "

" I been watching you the last week or two, and it's pretty plain you got a fine idea of the fella that calls himself Jake Waters ! I don't know where you come from, and I care less. You come aboard, looking a reg'lar young tramp ; that was part of your game—to pull the wool over my eyes. But your folk wasn't tramps, and you wasn't brought up trampish fashion."

His eyes were lowered again. The mask of secrecy he had assumed on the day he came aboard slipped back over the pallor and humiliation of his face.

" You wasn't brought up to know what these "—he pointed to the few coins that had settled in the scupper—" meant to the men that gave 'em. Pick 'em up. *Pick 'em up, I tell ye !* " The voice, hardly more than a whisper, reached Johnny where he stood, dazed by the unexpectedness of Wildblood's line of attack. " By the living Jesus, who are you to despise the offerings of fellas, the worst o' whom's better than a cockahoop braggart that can't carry his corn ? "

As he knelt to recover the coins, shame crimsoned his face and drove disgraceful moisture to his eyes.

" They didn't think much of you when you came aboard, Jake Waters, and neither did I ; and I think less of you now. But sailors are a soft-hearted lot. They see you come aboard without a ditty-bag. Without so much as an odd pair o' pants to change into. And, like a lot o' mutton heads, they jump to the conclusion you're hard up. So just to show they appreciate not being made into a pot-roast for Grand Gobro, they take up a collection —give you a tarpaulin muster——"

" I—I didn't want to take the money—— ! "

"—and treat you from then on like one of themselves. And what comes of it ? You give yourself the airs of a lord of creation. Besides taking liberties you'd not have dared to do before we had that set-out down at Kunkumi. Your work's bad, you give anybody lip that tries to put you in your place, and, by heck, with this last trick of yours, you've put the crown on it. Instead of going ashore you'll take your work-up at the wheel, my lad. It's time you had your lesson."

III

He tried to pretend for the first hour that he was enjoying it. The soft aquamarine swell lifted the ship and lowered her ; sea-birds perched on the yards, cocked bright eyes down on him—he could just see them, through a gap in the palm matting which roofed in the main part of the deck, and had given the *Aldebaran* the outlandish air of a great, masted ark, since her arrival on the Coast. But for one unfortunate, doing a work-up on the main-mast, the men left aboard were having an easy time. The ship was strangely silent. Wildblood and the mate had gone ashore.

But, as the sun shifted, depriving him of his small patch of shade : as a burning iron bar of heat, seemingly driven through his body, nailed him to the deck, the illusion of pleasure was no longer tenable. Faint with the pain of the heat, sickening with it, thirst became agony.

He managed to claw the water and the biscuits, which a grinning Kroo had left beside him, into his fettered hands—no easy achievement—and drank most of the former : tepid, by then, like glue. No one came to refill the can. His tongue swelled up and became a wedge of rubber in his mouth, his lips also swelled, and stiffened into a thick bandage between his nose and his chin.

Half comatose, he was not aware of the clouding of the sky; of the freshening of the Harmattan. He staggered, and was thrown to his knees, as the *Aldebaran* rolled.

From then on it was torture. Each lunge of the ship made the anklets drag on the naked flesh, sweat-softened. Presently the blood began to run down between his toes ; made a dark pool on the planks on which he was crouching. Light-headed with pain, he heard himself sob. He had not known there was such pain in the world, or that it was possible for the human body to support it, and to survive. Consciousness began to ebb and flow ; deep sunk at one moment in a bottomless trough of agony, at the next he swung to some ecstatic peak from which his spirit, looking down on the tormented body, took pride in its capacity for endurance.

Sunset came, and the dank, shivering dew ; and Johnny Flood hung there in the chains, a boy who had taken a man's punishment : a frail human shell, lit by thin pride, like the small flame of a rushlight.

IV

" What have you got to sell ? "

" Plenty gold, Cappy ! "

For a morning and the greater part of an afternoon, Wildblood had been asking the same question, getting the stock answer—given always with an air of beaming confidence : receiving across his table the bags or calabashes of dust handed over by dealers, of whom every man-jack was positive that the sandy and highly adulterated rubble known as " Guinea gold," washed down from mountain pockets, traded from village to village, or taken by bloodshed, until it reached the coast, was worth a (Gold Coast) fortune.

Johnny had got the procedure by heart. Wildblood tipped the contents of the calabash out on the table—not troubling unduly about grains that went into the cracks, or lodged under nails grown deliberately long for the purpose : shuffled it through expert fingers : decided privately the amount of brass filings and sand its artless owner had blended into the mixture, and announced laconically its weight in ounces—a weight, needless to say, always much beneath that reckoned by the seller.

" 'Right. Now we'll try it with firewater."

The company pressed in eagerly, to watch the work of the acid, whose fumes rose overpoweringly into the already overcharged air. Wildblood had had a fan fixed up ; it was one of Johnny's duties, when the stench became unbearable, to pull on the string of the fan, wafting gusts of tobacco smoke, trade spirits and the pungent, ammoniac smell of the Negro body towards the open ports, allowing a faint current of exhausted air to enter from the door. Otherwise, his business was to keep an eye on the dust, to prevent too close encroachment on the table, to push Negroes who showed signs of being overcome by the combination of liquor and acid fumes into the open air, and to regulate the flow from the dash-cask—a process still novel enough, to him, to be interesting : as were the disconcerted faces of the vendors, as their " gold " packets emerged from the action of the acid, thirty, forty, or even sixty per cent lighter than the original load.

" Him firewater. Him eat gold. Him devil. Him witch." The ripple of misgiving ran through the ranks, swelled into the haggle for prices.

The second mate was at the door, making signs. Johnny pulled on the captain's singlet to attract attention. For such occasions Wildblood discarded the refinements of society ; he was back in the singlet and carpet slippers of the earlier part of the voyage, with the substitution of an ancient pair of jeans for the serge slacks of cooler latitudes.

The message which the mate bellowed across the roomful of frizzled heads and polished shoulders froze Johnny's blood.

" The *Rembwe's* in, cap'n ; hailing you now."

" Go on—be off, the lot of you." He indulged for a moment the wild hope that the captain was too deeply absorbed in his task to accept the hail, but it appeared that Wildblood welcomed the diversion. Lumbering from his seat behind the table, he waved them out, swept them, scuffling, protesting, out on the deck like black beetles. " Bring me the speaking trumpet, and padlock the hatch behind you," were his parting orders, that Johnny obeyed with a sinking heart.

Too well he knew the *Rembwe*—latest and fastest of the Flood barquentines : launched only a year ago from Hill's yard, and christened by his aunt Venetia (who, in accordance with custom, received a very handsome piece of jewellery for her pains). There lay the *Rembwe* now, anchored in the roadstead, dwarfing, with her towering masts, her air of proud patronage, the humbler shipping clustered off the mainland. How like Floods ! For a wild moment he meditated confession and appeal—and knew it was too late.

" Ahoy ! *Rembwe*, out of Bristol, calling. Captain Macphairrson wad be wishing a worrd wi' Captain Wildblood."

" Ahoy there, captain. How's things with you ? " Lifting the trumpet to his lips, Wildblood let his voice roar across the water. On the poop of the *Rembwe*, Macpherson's beard burnt like an oriflamme. Johnny took care to keep out of sight. " Will you be coming aboard ? "

" Nae fear," was the ungracious answer. " We're making for Accra. We've got mair to dew than daunderr aboot the Coast like some folk ! "

" Ay, that's how you come to miss so many bargains." The captain of the *Aldebaran* joyfully took up an ancient feud.

" I'll be sending the gig. I thocht ye might dae wi' a pack orr twa cockroaches."

The welkin rang with the unprintable—the implication of the offer being that a ship overrun with fleas and lice often sent for cockroaches, which regaled themselves on the smaller vermin.

"—an' when ye've stowed 'em "—the shrill, Gaelic accents rose like the screel of bagpipes above Wildblood's profanity—" ye can send back the gig wi' oor property in it."

" What the hell do you mean ? We got none of your lumber aboard, ye old rot-guts ! "

" Ye've got the Chairman's nevvy aboarrd. I wadna say ye'll no be sued for abduction of a minorr," piped Macpherson with unction. " Things get ca'd by fancy names, the higherr ye climb the social ladderr. Not that ye'd know ought aboot sichlike. Shanghai-ing it's ca'd, befoor the mast. Ye can pit Johnny Flood i' the gig——"

The hand holding the trumpet dropped slowly to Wildblood's side ; he blistered Johnny with a look before lifting it again.

" You can keep yer gig ! And I'll be dining with you to-night—that's to say, if there's anything fit for human consumption aboard a vessel run by a porridge-eating pound-and-pinter out of the Gorbals !

". . . So that's who you are." Ignoring a howl from the *Rembwe's* poop, he swung slowly on Johnny. " By thunder, my lad, you've played me a nice trick ! "

Assuming the conversation with the newcomer was over, the traders were eagerly closing in on him ; he waved them off.

" Get back, get back ! No more trade to-day. You—and you "—he singled out a couple of pock-marked faces—" go on, get aft, and I'll settle up with you. Here, mister ! " He bawled to the mate, hovering curiously in the background. " Clear the ship. We're shutting up shop for to-day."

An hour had passed ; the swift dusk was falling, bringing a cool breeze. The *Aldebaran* lifted herself, and sank back on her moorings with sighs of relief. A faint prickle of stars showed through the faint gauze of the sky.

" So you're Johnny Flood. What's that mean ? That you're the son of old Iron-Guts, in Queen Square ? "

" No, sir. My father's Hercules Flood—he's usually called Dromore—of Guerdon." A naïve surprise tinged Johnny's voice, at any Bristol man's ignorance of the Flood hierarchy.

" Never heard of him. I take it you're one of *the* Floods, the shipping family ? "

" Yes, sir. The Chairman's my uncle."

"Why didn't you come out in a Flood ship?"

"My—my father's got no interest in the Company," stammered Johnny. "At least, only an indirect one. I thought it might put the Chairman in an—an awkward position."

"Indeed? A very pretty bit o' fam'ly feeling!" Despite himself, a smile twitched at the corners of Wildblood's mouth. "Well, Johnny Flood, you've got me in a nice pickle. So a Runstable captain's to be robbed of his ship's boy by one o' Floods! By thunder, it's the sort o' thing a man don't live down—not if he gets to be a hundred!"

"Well—but I've signed my articles, haven't I?" asked Johnny anxiously.

The smile had disappeared from Wildblood's lips, and his brow was darkened with a scowl of serious perturbation. It would rock the Coast, for sure, if the tale got about that Floods—known always as the autocrats of the Guinea voyage—could help themselves to his ship's boy, as easily as pull a fish out of the water! For everyone who knew the truth, and exonerated him of the charge of pusillanimity, there would be a dozen at least who picked up only half the yarn, and not a few, probably, who, knowing the correct version, maliciously withheld information for the pleasure of getting a rise out of Runstables. As touchy of his firm's prestige as of his own, Wildblood's teeth gritted with mortification.

"Then I'm articled to you for the voyage," Johnny was insisting. "You can raise that as an objection, sir, can't you, if Macpherson—Mr. Macpherson—tries to take me off? Then he'd have to go down to Cape Coast to get it settled, and I should think they'd be bound to uphold you." His voice shook a little with anxiety. In anticipation of some such contingency, he had had it all thought out.

"Pish." It appeared that Wildblood was in no way soothed by the tribute to his authority. Although he would sooner have cut out his tongue than admitted it, he knew well enough that the authority of a Runstable skipper would not for a moment avail against that of the Chairman of Floods.

"If this business had turned up a month ago," he said slowly, "they could have had you—an' welcome. You ain't perfection as a ship's boy—not by a long chalk; but I'm not denying you've turned over a new leaf. So you don't want to go back with Macpherson?" As an attempt to keep satisfaction out of the speaker's voice, it was not successful.

"No, sir." Johnny's tone was equally committal.

"Then what the blazes are we going to do?"

"Can't you say you're standing by the articles?" he pleaded. "After all—you've got to say something, sir, if you're going to supper on the *Rembwe*."

The other stared at him blankly; then, as a thought took slow shape behind the square block of his forehead, Wildblood suddenly flung back his head and burst into a bellow of laughter.

"You mayn't be much of a hand at your job, Jake—Johnny, I should say; but, by thunder, you know how to scare the back teeth out of a bunch of niggers. It's a pity——" He stopped again, staring at Johnny as though seeing him for the first time. " By heck, I'll do it !" He brought his fist crashing down on the cabin table. " I'll teach that cross-eyed, carroty-jowled slob of a Glasgow skipper to give his orders to a Runstable captain !

" Going to Accra, is he ? " Wildblood's progress across the cabin was like that of a tea-clipper running before a quick gale. " We'll make for Apam, and oblige him to follow us ! That'll take him nicely off his course, and teach him manners to his betters. There's a nice capful o' wind coming up, and we got the tide with us. We'll show that Scottish bargee what Runstables can do—— ! " He was pushing Johnny out on the deck.

They stood for a moment in silence, the man and the boy, looking at the bare masts and shrouds of the *Rembwe*, enmeshing the stars ; and the thoughts in Wildblood's heart were similar to the thoughts of the boy of fourteen. She was a great ship, and so beautiful, at peace on the water, with her topmast almost touching the tip of Orion. . . .

" She'll overhaul us, of course," he was murmuring, " with all that sail. But it'll be a good laugh on Macpherson—and it'll give you a good last run for your money, my lad !"

The order " Up anchor ! " startled the ship. It had been taken for granted she was in for a long stay in her present waters ; tarring had started, and, as each member of the crew knew, the trade room was ready for a " big show " on the morrow. Charlestown was one of their best trading ports, although small as such ports ran along the Coast. But the palm awnings were furled and the windlass manned with a rollicking shanty, while still a few bedazed voices queried the captain's sobriety.

" Our Bo'sun's a goggle-eyed son of a gun,
Blow, my bully-boys, blow.
Lights red or green, they are not seen,
Blow, my bully-boys, blow.
Belaying pins are flying about. . ."

The cheery strain, carried by the breeze towards the *Rembwe*, roused curiosity on her decks ; there were shouts, and presently a blare from Macpherson's trumpet, demanding to be told what the *Aldebaran* thought she was about.

" Taking a bit of a cruise for the good of our health ! " bawled Wildblood: turning to Johnny, assiduous as a spaniel at his heels, to add with a grin not quite devoid of gravity, " If ever you think of quitting the sea, my lad, and going into steam—just you think of to-night. There'll be no chance of jaunts like this one, when you've got to account to the owners for every ton of coal in your bunkers ! " And a thrill went through Johnny, at the unspoken assumption that his future belonged to the sea. Unlikely as he knew that to be, he felt his heart swell at what he recognised as the best compliment it was within the speaker's power to bestow.

Pipes shrilled aboard the *Rembwe*, the screel of her windlass and the rattle of her cables started ; her shanty lifted itself like a battle cry. But the

Aldebaran had the advantage ; her anchor was up. She slid from her moorings like a cat, making the most of tide and following wind. The bo'sun's pipe sent the crew leaping to their stations on the gantlines. Presently she broke sail ; slowly her canvas shook itself out, blotting the stars, and for a moment she trembled, waiting for a wind. It came, and she swept forward—with the *Rembwe* in her wake : their departure followed by the horns and bells of every ship in the roadstead, wondering if Floods and Runstables had taken leave of their senses, and what profits might be made out of the absence of these two formidable competitors, for once, from the trading arena.

It was a short chase and a gay one—never to be forgotten by a fourteen-year-old boy—down the spaces of the night : with the water creaming away from their bows and racing backwards in great flutings of black glass, patched with phosphoresence, with the broken reflections of their port lights and with mysterious flashes of submarine silver. Embarrassed at last by the commotion he had caused—for, by now, all knew what was afoot, and the jest of having a Flood as ship's boy had spread from cabins to fo'c'sle—Johnny took refuge in a favourite hiding-place, a corner of the after-deck, where he could almost imagine the ship deserted and himself alone.

An overpowering sadness had come over him, that threatened to drown excitement in tears, as he crouched there, hearing the rush of the waves, watching the great white V carved on the indigo water by the *Aldebaran*, and the *Rembwe*, now hidden, now faintly visible, with the starlight on her sails—not so very far behind, alas, in pursuit. He knew, with a sudden rush of sad realism, that it was as hopeless to outpace her as to evade the future of which she was the symbol ; and there seemed something foolish, even childish, in prolonging the chase. It seemed to him that Wildblood, who had initiated it, was the boy, and he the man, tolerating a boy's mischief ; for Johnny Flood, like many another, had left his boyhood on the coast of Africa, and, although he might return, in search of that bright youth, it could never be the same again.

CHAPTER FOUR

I

THE Guerdon bays, with sunlight laid like varnish on their mottled quarters, stepped sedately down Park Street, aided by an adroit manipulation of the brakes which alone prevented the barouche from over-running them. In the barouche, which was open on account of the mild weather, Mrs. Harriet Flood—known as " old " Mrs. Flood to the vulgar—stiffened her back and braced her small feet against the footstool placed for that purpose against the panelling of the opposite seat. In common with many, she disliked driving down Park Street ; her daughter-in-law, Selina, a nervous creature, preferred to walk, and, leaving the carriage at the top of the hill, chose usually to teeter down on her own low heels and the arm of her maid. It took more, however, than an inclination of one in five to dethrone " old " Mrs. Flood. Straight as an arrow, she kept her eyes severely on the back of the coachman and footman, who, braced as stiffly as their mistress, preserved the classic attitudes of carriage servants, and showed the Bristol public how " the quality " should be attended on its jaunts abroad.

Restored to the horizontal on reaching St. Augustine's Parade, the horses, as though to show of what they were capable, broke into a stately trot, which swept them presently into Queen Square.

Like all people of cultured taste, Mrs. Flood admired Queen Square, and deplored its latter-day prostitution to commerce. What a fine place it must have been at the beginning of the century !—when its greensward served for the stately promenades of people of quality, and its sidewalks were not polluted by whistling errand boys, pert young clerks and the vulgar, although affluent, population that follows a flourishing trade; when powdered footmen and small Negro pages carried messages between the dignified houses, and torches slanting from their iron brackets proclaimed the entertainment of company behind the fine, square windows ! Unlike many in her position, Mrs. Flood did not despise that bygone race of Bristol " gentry ; " born and bred an aristocrat, she found nothing ridiculous in the pride of a society which had grown out of honest endeavour, rather than of privilege. Proud as she was, and assured, of her own privilege, she knew exactly what had drawn her son Harcourt back to this setting of his forefathers, and respected him for it ; as she despised her son Dromore for his tacit repudiation of the commercial origins of the family.

She sat for a moment, in contemplation of the pleasant scene, before allowing her footman to hand her to the steps before which the carriage had halted. Not choosing to ring a bell, she paused in the bare, handsome hall, with its mouldings by Grinling Gibbons and its red mahogany doors ; furnishing it, in her mind, according to her period and taste. Rarely as she visited it, her foot trod its stone flooring with the confidence of authority. She marked with asperity the absence of porter or doorkeeper, before mounting the broad, uncarpeted stair curving towards the first floor ; commerce or not, it was surely a matter of dignity to keep some attendant in waiting on callers such—for example—as Mrs. Harriet Flood !

Her small figure, strikingly slim and fashionable for a woman of her age, took the stairs a little more slowly than it might have done if she had had an audience. Tight-lacing, even when a matter of long habit, shortens the breath, and coolness and self-possession are essential attributes of a lady. She paused just long enough to be sure of both, before rapping with the handle of her parasol on the door which confronted her at the head of the stairs.

" Good God—Mamma ! " Harcourt Flood, gaping across the gallery of his vast desk at the farther end of the room, lumbered to his feet at her entrance.

" I hope you are not occupied ? "

His heavy mouth curved into a smile, as he set a chair for her. She viewed it with distaste, and chose to stand.

" May I ask if all your clients conform to these proportions ? " She indicated disdainfully the capacious seat, the suggestive breadth of the arms and the lofty back of the Chippendale—one of a dozen pieces which yet left the room half-empty, relying on its proportions for the dignity she appreciated while affecting to deride it.

" I'll lift you into it, if you like ! " He grinned at her.

" You will do nothing of the sort. And, as I dislike being made ridiculous, you had better sit down," she added sharply : an order which he obeyed, because he knew she preferred it so.

One of the private satisfactions of Harcourt Flood was that of being the only Flood of the century to measure up to the fabled proportions of his gigantic ancestor, that Matthew who, after a life of more or less discreditable exploits that included slaving, died in an atmosphere of Abolition and sanctity highly gratifying to the family, and to none more than to Harcourt's elder brother, the third Hercules, commonly known by his second Christian name, Dromore. Harcourt had worn a suit of Matthew's at a costume ball given in honour of the Diamond Jubilee—and worn it badly, for he had all the aversion to " fancy dress " of the average public school Englishman.

Yet, in his high-buttoned cheviot of daily wear, and the grey stove-pipe hats he affected for business, he had a distinction of his own. His port-wine colouring and prematurely snow-white hair, stiff as a clothes' brush, caused strangers to take him for considerably more than his age ; there were even those who spoke of him as " old " Mr. Flood—a description to which he took no exception, youth having no meaning for him since the death of his wife Isabel. The white moustache bunched out over the ugly Flood mouth ; the eyes, dark as prunes, had the black bar of his brows across them—the Flood trade mark. He walked stiffly, with an air of sultry authority, looking over the heads of most people, but touching the brim of his hat to those who showed him recognition ; and there was that about him that kept familiarity at bay.

He sat there, looking towards his mother, with a kind of grim deference based on no filial feeling, but on character : her own. There was no member of his family whom he admitted as his equal, save her in whom he recognised, with amusement, traits which, exaggerated in his own case, accounted, at least in part, for the position he held as controller of the family fortunes.

And she stood before him, a porcelain figure in a grey moiré gown : her lips pursed with the exasperation with which she invariably regarded this incredible fruit of her womb.

" Well, Mamma, it's a pleasant surprise, to see you."

" You'd better save your compliments, until you've heard my reason for coming," she rapped at him.

" I don't suppose that's pleasant, but you're welcome, all the same," he mumbled, on his guard.

" If it were pleasant, I'd have called on you in Berkeley Square, not visited your office." She grimaced.

" What's the matter? Are you overdrawn again?" He came bluntly to the point.

" How like you! to imagine that anything unpleasant must be connected with money."

He guffawed outright.

" Hardly that, Mamma! Money's a deuc'd agreeable commodity, providing one has enough of it."

" You can hardly complain on that score," she reminded him dryly.

" I don't," grunted Harcourt. " Except that that old fool Salisbury's landed us in a mess with the Assinee tariffs, and God knows what it's going to cost us before we get the damned French back to their senses. Not that that interests you."

" It does not."

" It will, when you find you've got less money to fritter on fal-lals than you've been used to."

" Nonsense." Her foot tapped the carpet impatiently. " I've come to talk to you about your nephew Johnny."

" What's he been doing? Running away again?"

" It's not improbable he will do. You've got to do something about Johnny."

" I've got enough to do with my own litter, thank ye, without taking on Drummy's."

" That's absurd. You never pay the least attention to Mary and Bell."

" I pay their bills."

" And Miss—what is her name?—Vertigen does the rest."

" What do you expect me to do? Button their petticoats? See they brush their teeth?"

" It is a sad pity Isabel never gave you a boy, Harcourt." She spoke gently, but it was his turn to glare.

" What's this about Johnny?"

" They're ruining him—as they ruined the other two."

He looked at her curiously.

" That's a change, isn't it?"

" Not in the sense you mean. He gets no spoiling; very much the contrary. Since he came back, Dromore's behaviour is outrageous; there are times when he's positively inhuman."

" That'll do Johnny no harm. The young beggar's been a dark horse, you know, Mamma. We all thought he'd not got enough in him to come out of the rain——"

" Speak for yourself!" was the spirited retort. " Johnny is far from a fool. The truth is—and you very well know it—he has never had the slightest chance, as the youngest, of getting his fair share of attention. His sickliness as a child, and Selina's long illness after he was born, all helped to keep him in the background. He has never had the privileges or the advantages of his brothers, and he has always been made to feel the odd man out in anything concerning the elder two."

" He should stand up for himself," growled Harcourt.

" Stand up for himself—against that great, hulking Dorset !—against Gilbert, who may be an imbecile, but is as cunning as a fox in getting his own way ! Don't talk nonsense," she answered scornfully. " And," she added, " he is more than capable of standing up for himself now—given the opportunity."

" Very well. So much the better for everybody."

" Yes, it would be gratifying to see Dorset put in his place ! " Some memory seemed to amuse her. " Well, it is about time they learned to respect Johnny, who has a finer character than either of them will ever have," said the grandmother fiercely. " Or would have—if Dromore, with his continual fault finding, and his absurd resentment of what amounts to very little more than a high-spirited prank, does not break his temper and make him as stubborn as a badly-schooled horse."

" Well, Mamma, you can't expect me to interfere with the way Drummy chooses to bring up his family," said Harcourt, after a pause.

" You can take Johnny away from Guerdon."

" What on earth do you mean ? " He gaped at her.

" Just what I say." Forgetting her previous objection, she seated herself in the chair, as in a side-saddle, one tiny foot swinging under the flounce of her gown. " Let me tell you what is going on. Johnny, as you know, was brought back by your Captain Macpherson——"

" As his parents wanted. I'd have left him with Runstables ; he'd have had a tougher time than ever he'd get in one of our ships."

" It's only natural he should be bitter and resentful : no one in his senses would take any notice of it, after the experiences the boy must have had. But Dromore is not in his senses, where Johnny is concerned. He carps at him until the boy is driven nearly crazy. Johnny is not to be allowed to hunt next season. He is forbidden to accept any invitations—even to the Gannets at Frenchay : although Penderel Gannet is his particular friend, and Lady Gannet has been most sympathetic—having sons of her own has taught her to be sensible, I imagine ! When the other boys go to the races, Johnny is left at home—if he were a leper," cried she, indignantly, " he could hardly be treated more disgracefully ! Even his mother thinks it is unjust——"

" Well, I suppose she could interfere, if she chose," he muttered, resenting, manlike, her attempt to involve him in matters that did not concern him.

" Selina ! She is too flaccid to bestir herself on her own behalf—let alone Johnny's," was the contemptuous answer. " All she does is weep over the boy, until he dreads the sight of her."

" It's no affair of mine." He brought his hand down heavily on the desk. " This is the way to look at it : Johnny has played the fool, and he's got to pay for it. I allow he has more spirit than we credited him with, but it was a devilish silly way of showing it. If he wants to go to sea, he must wait until he's older and have it out with Drummy. I've got something to do beside taming a young scapegrace his parents can't handle ; and I take it you're not thinking of putting him with Mary and Bell, to be spoon-fed by Miss Vertigen ! "

" You could take him into your office. Why not ? " she demanded, as he stared at her. " You have boys of his age—though what you do with them I can't imagine ; I expect they spend most of their time with pocket knives and catapults, destroying your property."

He could not restrain a smile, at this original conception of the duties of a junior clerk.

" And you think Johnny would be better employed doing the same ? "

" Well, will you have him ? "

" No ! " he shouted at her ; stuck his hands in his pockets and strode to the windows from which—the room was at the back of the building—he could look down on the decks and rigging of the small craft tied up along the wharves.

Harriet was unmoved—as she had learned over the period of her married life to be unmoved—by Flood ill temper and ill manners. Of her three sons, Harcourt—she admitted it without prejudice—was the best value ; Roan, the youngest, most to her taste. For the sanctimonious, pompous Dromore she had a mild, contemptuous dislike, while according him, on most occasions, and invariably in public, the deference due to the head of the family. Having dedicated a moment's silence to Harcourt's ill humour, she said, as though the matter had ceased to interest her :

" Well, I suppose you know your own business——" Ending on an upward inflection which queried, without stressing her scepticism, his own certainty.

His huge body turned towards her sullenly.

" You know my opinion of the Guerdon lot."

She shrugged her shoulders.

" They're your own flesh and blood."

" And yours—eh ? Your luck was out, Mamma, when you married a Flood."

" You can at least leave it to me to say so."

His hard eye softened ; he knew and respected courage when he met it. Yet he blamed her for the adulteration of the stock.

" I've got no use for Drummy's children—a soft, spoiled set of young parasites, that fancy their upbringing entitles them to patronise the world ! To patronise *me*, by God !—because I'm in trade : as we'd all be, but for Grandfather's damned folly. Guerdon ! It's a fraud ; and you know it, as well as I do. Here's the reality—here." He made a clumsy gesture. " Flood and company : a title that's held good for seven generations. Not a flimsy upstart of the last fifty years, like Hercules Flood, Esquire, of Guerdon Manor, Gloucestershire. Esquire: God save us ! Harcourt Flood, Merchant: that's good enough for me. That's worth more than all your esquires——"

" What a snob you are ! " She said it lightly. " One might think you were blaming me for giving you gentlefolk among your ancestors. You're entitled to the ' Esquire,' you know, from my side of the family."

" You can keep it, thank ye. I don't mean to be offensive, Mamma, but our standards are different. You probably understand the Guerdon tribe better than I do. All I say is, I'd sooner take the devil into my business than one of Drummy's idle, self-sufficient whelps. In any case—good God, who'd hear of it? Since we got into Burke, trade's poison to Drummy." He laughed harshly. "Let Drummy bring up his sons as he chooses. I'll have no finger in that pie!"

"You are very different from your brothers," she reflected, with her eyes on his heavy face.

"Ay; a throw-back. You find 'em in most families," he told her ironically.

"I suppose it has not occurred to you that Johnny might be a throw-back, too?"

"Eh? That undersized brat?" Instinctively he flung back his shoulders. "Pish. There's not much of a Flood about him."

"There is no need to blow yourself out like a peacock," she snapped, "because you happen to be physically abnormal! Character, allow me to remind you, my dear Harcourt, bears no relation to brawn and bones. In my opinion, Johnny has his full share of qualities on which you Floods pride yourselves; combined, happily, with a few more likely to recommend him to people of refined perception."

Again she had drawn from him his reluctant smile.

"You hate us, don't you, Mamma?"

Her eyes, the colour of moss agate, set in their curious, diamond-shaped lids, returned his look levelly.

"No, I pity you."

She had startled him.

"Very civil of you—'pon my soul!"

"Your sense of values entitles you to pity; it is so very impermanent." As often, she baffled him with her passionless impersonality; yet he was stung, and showed it in his reply.

"You don't know me, Mamma."

"I think that is possible," she agreed. "My knowledge of Johnny derives from his unlikeness, rather than his resemblance, to the family."

"Very likely, very likely." He spoke testily. "Now let me say this. Like all women, you've let sentiment run away with you. Johnny, because he's the youngest, is, in your opinion, the neglected one of the family——"

"He is not the youngest; you've forgotten Miranda."

He waived the interpolation. It was foolish of her not to remember that girls never entered into his reckoning.

"He's done a showy thing, so you make a hero of him."

"You flatter me! I doubt if anyone could make a hero at present out of your nephew. He's a sullen, bad-mannered youth, with a grudge against life in general and us—you see I include myself—in particular——"

"He wants a damn' good hiding," growled Harcourt.

"I agree it would be better for him than his father's method——"

He cocked an eyebrow.

"Prayer," she said succinctly.

"Damn' nonsense!"

"That's as it may be." Her air of open-mindedness amused him. Like all Victorian women, she made a duty of her church going, but he had a shrewd idea that her natural cynicism protected her from its consequences. " I have an impression, however, that he won't put up with it much longer."

" What do you mean? He'll run away again?"

" What would *you* have done," she countered, " if your father had opposed you in everything you wanted?"

Harcourt looked mulish.

" What's he want? To go back to sea?"

" My dear Harcourt, there is no means whatever of finding out what he wants. He refuses to speak to any of us."

" Let him alone," he counselled. " He'll get over it all the sooner, if no one pays any attention."

" No one does pay, or has paid, any attention. That is exactly the position," she persisted. " A slum child has hardly had less attention than Johnny, from the day he was born."

" Oh, come! Vicky was always coddling him."

" Johnny does not want ' coddling,' as you call it. He is a particularly manly boy, though he had an affectionate disposition—until this happened. Not that he showed it, excepting—I am not boasting—to me. He reminds me of an animal—very easily won by kindness—"

" No, Mamma, you can't make out that Drummy isn't ' kind ' to his brats! I've been sickened, often, by the way he fusses over those great lads——"

" My dear boy, I know Dromore! There is nothing about Johnny that appeals to his vanity; he is not handsome and impudent, like Dorset, or correct, like Gilbert. He is short, plain and—I suppose you would call it-insignificant. Add to this that his adventures have rather coarsened his speech and made him careless of his manners, and you will see that Dromore has—or considers he has—a grievance. One knows, of course, his attitude to your business"—she shrugged this aside—" but I don't think his opposition would be very serious, if there were an opportunity of getting Johnny away."

" It's no use, Mamma." He spoke after a silence. " I can't stand Drummy's children, and, in any case, I don't hold with taking relations into the business. If you take my advice, you'll leave Johnny to settle down."

" Settle down—to what?" She clung to her point.

Irritated by now, he answered:

" He's got a couple more years' schooling, hasn't he? What that youth wants is discipline and the company of men. There's too many women at Guerdon; he's likely to go on making a nuisance of himself, if he's got you and Selina and Vicky, all crying over him whenever he starts to sulk."

" Nonsense. However, if you insist, there's nothing more to be said. I should have thought it was a good opportunity to work a younger member of the family into the Company, as you have no one to take your place when you retire."

She did not see the angry suffusion of his features.

" Will you leave me to handle my affairs in my own way ? Get that lad back to school, and——"

" The headmaster won't have him back."

" That's not surprising," grunted Harcourt. " It doesn't take much imagination, to picture the effect on the school, when young Johnny starts to brag about his adventures ! Of course they won't have him back—at Curbham. What's Drummy thinking about ? Send him to Clifton—as a boarder, of course ; and let Glazebrook lick him into shape. I don't suppose they'll want him there, either, but I can fix that—or Drummy can do it with the Board of Governors," he corrected himself hastily. " Drummy can do it, of course ; tell him to make a donation to the college mission, and leave me out of it. I don't want to have anything to do with this—or with young fellows that go mountebanking off to the Guinea Coast to escape their Latin declensions ! "

" Unfortunately for your admirable suggestion," she interrupted him, " Johnny himself refuses to be sent back to school."

" I'd like to see him refuse if he was a boy of mine ! " blustered Harcourt. " Refuse ? I'd soon knock the refusal out of him——"

" And then, no doubt, you'd handcuff him and send him off in a prison van," said Mrs. Flood innocently. " I am not particularly well informed in the family history, but I can't help feeling that is quite in the tradition."

" Now, I ask you—— ! " Losing his temper at last, Harcourt pounded the desk with both fists. " Can you—even you—imagine anything more preposterous than a man of Dromore's age allowing himself to be defied by a boy of—how old's the fellow ?—thirteen ?—fourteen ? "

" Johnny was fifteen last birthday, and the question of age does not enter into it. Can't you use a little imagination, Harcourt ? " Her energy had flagged, in the sudden, disconcerting fashion of a person no longer young ; her voice betrayed her, it had lost its crisp incisiveness. " Think ; Johnny has been living, for nearly a year, as a man among men. His interests are no longer those of a schoolboy ; even beside Dorset, who is now quite the man of the world ! Johnny seems startlingly mature. The truth is "—she paused, as though seeking for words—" the boy is bewildered by the puerility of the life to which he is now expected to adapt himself. Backward as his education may be, and he was never a bright scholar, it would be sheer inhumanity to send him back to the school-room, where he would be shockingly out of place, and, very likely, a butt for younger boys, quicker at their lessons than he."

Damn women ! Harcourt Flood was thinking. They always find some way of justifying themselves when they've set their minds on the impossible. It was not from conviction, but from the desire to put a stop to an argument which had become intolerable, that he said, at the end of a scowling, nail-biting silence :

" Well, Mamma, you're certainly a determined advocate. I'll see if I can do anything. But only on one condition ! If you say any more about my taking Johnny into the firm, I'll wash my hands of the whole business. That's understood, is it ? "

She gave him the smile which had made her devastatingly beautiful in youth, and still had power to quicken the pulses of those on whom she bestowed it. Friends, servants, children knew that smile of Harriet Flood's : so rare, yet so exquisite that the remembrance of it would go all through a day, like a thread of spun gold.

"You will hardly accuse me of unintelligence ! "

"No, that I won't ! " He grinned as he helped her to her feet. "You're as sharp as a weasel and as stubborn as a mule, and, by God, I sometimes wish I'd got you on my Board ! It 'ud be a pretty sight to see you and Sam Killick come to grips. Don't forget yourself, and start trying to foist Drummy's lad on me again—that's all. And I'll tell you something," he added, to her twinkling eyes and smiling lips. "If I'd started to consider it—which I hadn't !—you knocked that neatly on the head just now, by reminding me the fellow's a dunce at his books. What were you thinking of, Mamma ? Your mind must have been on something else ! "

He was chuckling when he left her in the carriage ; he did not see the look she flashed at him—the vicious lift of her head, like a little adder, taken by surprise. She was a great woman, Mamma : he never quite got over the astonishment her "greatness" caused him—he who, in the main, could hardly have held a lower opinion of women. But she was a confounded nuisance, coming and pestering him about Drummy's lad ; what had come over her ?

It was this nonsense of living by herself at the Dower House, he decided, which had turned her peculiar—turned her maternal ! A lot any of her own children had had of her maternity ; yet they had been fond of her, in their way. She had not inspired tenderness ; but Floods were not naturally tender. And they had all given her her due for the way she kept her chin up, under the repeated blows of their father's misdemeanours. It was she who, after the death of the second Hercules, and the discovery that, due mainly to his extravagance, the estate was seriously encumbered, had supported Harcourt in his proposed revival of the commercial tradition of the name of Flood. It was she who—for all her blue blood !—had mocked at Dromore's anger and encouraged Harcourt who, a heavy, bored, young man, had had no taste for the monied idleness to which, under his father's rule he was dedicated. He hunted, shot, did a little clumsy whoring, and was a gross eater and drinker by the time he was in his twenties ; but once the idea of trade had got hold of him, it was like setting a match to gunpowder.

Dromore might sneer : Dromore, intent on his career as a county magnate and philanthropist, out on the farther side of Henbury.

"It's high time somebody made money, for it looks as if Drummy's heathen are going to cost us as much as the Pater's women," Harcourt had said gloomily, after his father's funeral and a disquieting interview with the solicitors.

"All right, old fellow ; you get on and make it," was Roan's easy answer. "You've got my moral backing, though I'm afraid my brains won't be of much use to you. You're the only one that's inherited the family flair for finance."

"I can do without yer morals, thank ye. But I'll have your money, and I promise you won't be the loser. I tell you a thing I'd like to do, Ro." He spoke almost shyly, biting a hang-nail on his thumb. "Fetch the West African trade back to Bristol. It don't seem natural, somehow, to have no Flood ships trading direct with the Coast."

"You can trade with the Antipodes, for all I care : so long as you make me enough to pay Venetia's bills and keep me on the right side of the bookies. Chin-chin ; who wouldn't sooner be a rich merchant than a poor squire ?" They lifted their glasses of champagne to each other, at the end of the first Board meeting in the long panelled room on the ground floor which had been Matt's office, and which, since his death, had been let, with its adjoining premises, to a firm of brokers who had taken over Matt's various interests, the "hobbies" of his latter years. The lease having ended opportunely, Harcourt was quick to reclaim a property valuable to his new enterprise ; but it was Roan who voiced the thought in the back of his mind. "I'm glad we're starting here ; it seems like a good omen."

So Guerdon was saved ; and, on the few occasions when he was forced face to face with reality, Dromore had to accept that it was Flood and Company that maintained Guerdon acres, that fattened Guerdon cattle, that covered Guerdon women with appropriate silks, filled Guerdon loose-boxes and subsidised his preposterous charities ! Dromore was a "gentleman." But Bristol had its aristocracy—of commerce ; to which Harcourt was proud to belong.

He dealt tersely with the business his head clerk brought him, and saw from the calendar that there was a Board meeting on the morrow : main item on the agenda, the opening of a Liverpool branch—supported by Samson Killick, who had an axe to grind, a son-in-law whom he hoped to put in as the Liverpool manager ; opposed by himself—for various reasons : of which the strongest was the stubborn aversion of a Bristol man to having any truck with a port offering so bitter a rivalry. God damn those skin-flints on the Dock Board !—who, by raising the dues once again, had just driven another nail into Bristol's coffin.

He signed his letters and looked at the clock. It was his custom, when his work was done, to go to the club, where he dined, played a game or two of whist with some of his cronies, and, having made sure the governess and the girls were in bed, went back to the big, empty house in Berkeley Square—his concession to a wife who declared that, although she appeared to have married a tradesman, nothing, nothing would ever induce her to live in that noisy, vulgar region down by the wharves ! He'd get rid of it, when the girls were married ; what did a single man want with a place of that kind, and no one to leave it to ? He would furnish a couple of rooms above the offices—or he would go and live with Kitty Prior ! That would serve them right, thought Harcourt, grinning evilly—his mother in particular. She had got him on the raw, with her championship of Drummy's lad ; her intolerable reminders of the fact that he, Harcourt, had no son to carry on his name ; her impudent offer of young Johnny—faugh ! the throw-out of the Guerdon litter—as a substitute for the boy Isabel should have given him.

So that was what they were banking on ? Guerdon for Dorset, the army for Gilbert, and for Johnny—unworthy of higher things—the business ! Harcourt swore, deeply and obscenely. Marry again he would not but it would serve them right if he were to produce Kitty's bastard—for Dromore's horror, Roan's cynical amusement, the ladies' distress and the scandalisation of the girls : done out of their expectations by a natural brother, arbitrary heir to his money, and, incidentally, to a controlling interest in the Company! It would be a pretty sight—Guerdon kow-towing to the bar sinister !

At the juncture of Broad Quay with Baldwin Street he was all but run down by a pair of spanking chestnuts, drawing a showy kind of brougham, whose occupant leaned forward, to express with the horrified gesture of a jewelled hand her relief at the avoidance of an accident. All Bristol knew that carriage—as all Bristol knew the house, number 30 Trenchard Street : with its visitors' book which (so it was said) could do more to wreck Bristol reputations, if it fell into improper hands, than any police court record.

For a second he hesitated. It was years since he had been to Trenchard Street—a resort of the dashing young blade, rather than of sober and respectable citizens. A bottle of " the widow ; " some sprightly company to drive away dull care. . . . No.

The flash-house was no longer the answer to the mental and spiritual vexation that possessed him. Harcourt thought, I must be growing old.

CHAPTER FIVE

I

" THAT," said Venetia Flood, " will be a menace in a couple of years. Did you ever see anything so irresistible ? "

" And fully aware of what you are thinking of it," said Mrs. Flood shortly ; she turned from the spectacle of her grandson Dorset, vaulting the five-barred gate which led from her lawn to the bridle-path across the paddocks : making a perfect landing, and turning to wave to the spectators on the veranda. And Venetia—foolish creature !—was clapping her hands and laughing in that way that even a schoolboy may interpret as a tribute to his own achievements.

It was her birthday, and there had been the usual ceremonies : a family luncheon at the Dower House—Dromore, with Selina ; Harcourt, and, of course, Victoria ; Roan and his wife Venetia—come specially from town. Why ? In heaven's name why ? Why six busy people—seven, including Uncle Quentin, who could not be said to qualify for the adjective—should set aside their own affairs to celebrate her birthday passed Harriet's powers of imagination.

It was Vicky, as usual, who had organised it ; Vicky, who, at her age, ought to know better : ought to know that after the age of thirty-five each anniversary of a woman's life should be kept in decent seclusion, since it marks the falling of another petal from the rose of youth.

Well, well. Vicky was a stupid woman, but well meaning. No doubt it gave them satisfaction to come with their presents—Dromore and Selina with a specially-bound, large-printed psalter, inscribed, " *To dearest Mamma, for her birthday, from her devoted son and daughter* "—surely a tactless reminder of the fact that she had recently found it necessary to use a magnifying-glass to follow the lessons ? Venetia had done better—presenting, on behalf of herself and Roan, a really handsome Staffordshire group. " Isn't the little lady adorable ? I told Roan we had to get it, because she reminded me of you ! " A pretty speech ; Venetia was good at them.

Vicky had worked one of her endless tea-cloths ; poor girl, there was never anything original about her presents. There was a bracelet from Harcourt, and old Quentin had dug up some bit of possibly valuable junk from one of his magpie collections—West African stuff : *cire perdue* technique, she had heard it was called—together with a compliment which was worth more than the rest of their offerings put together. Harriet smiled reminiscently ; she had a taste for compliment—a taste which had not often been gratified within the family circle to which her marriage had introduced her.

The lunch and service were excellent, and Roan and Venetia, those bright visitants from gayer spheres, had successfully kept the conversation away from domestic and local subjects. Quite a gala, in fact.

The young people arrived after the others had gone back to the house, and Harriet had had her rest : Dorset, Gilbert, Miranda (age seven, in her wheel chair ; the poor child was delicate—some spinal trouble which might, or might not, clear up when she was over the " difficult " age), and a gawky, spotty-faced girl, with her governess, from one of the neighbouring manors. Selina had confided to Harriet that Allice Montagu was earmarked for Dorset, and Harriet kindly forbore to point out to the poor, foolish woman that Dorset's tastes were already sufficiently marked to make it positive that no Norman lineage would induce him to look twice at a girl who took sixes in shoe leather, and whose pronounced buck teeth lent her an unfortunate resemblance to one of the less attractive carnivores. She was kind, however, to Allice Montagu, who had evidently been prepared for her fate, and whose submission to it took the form, from the moment of her arrival, of all but lying flat on the ground and inviting Dorset to walk over her—in which there was no harm, as that one gave no sign of recognising her existence. But Harriet, who knew her Dorset, wondered.

In his Harrow blazer, with superfine flannels and a rose in his buttonhole, the youth was almost indecently handsome : filled with sensuous awareness of his own good looks, good fortune and physical excellence ; except for blue-grey eyes and lightish colouring, a typical Flood. The boys had been bathing ; on Dorset's head the wet hair rose in thin metallic flakes ; he sauntered beside his sister's chair—the heir-apparent, crowned! Harriet would have liked to slap his face.

As Miranda held out a pin-cushion—evidently the produce of her own efforts—towards her grandmother, Harriet saw traces of tears on the small, wizened face, although the wide eyes, gipsy-dark, were dry.

" Why has Miranda been crying ? " She had a trick of disconcerting observation—particularly with her own sex—to which her family was hardened.

" She always grizzles when Johnny's not about. Many happy returns, Grandmamma." Dorset presented his bouquet of carnations with a bow, and stood back for Gilbert, weaving and waving above her like an amiable caterpillar, to produce his offering : a box of chocolates tied with a monster bow of satin, for which Selina must have been responsible, since it was inconceivable that the pin-brained Gilbert could have thought of it for himself.

She expressed her thanks in suitable terms, turning on Gilbert, whose shadow, swinging between her and the sun, she found distracting.

" Good heavens, boy, how tall are you ? "

" Only sus-six feet and half—half an inch, Grandmamma," stammered Gilbert, always reduced to the dregs of his infinitesimal intelligence, in the presence of his grandmother. His pale face, blank as an egg, with one brow lifted, the other lowered, as though in rehearsal for the monocle he was later to adopt, stared down at her with a ludicrous effect of apology.

" Six feet ? And you're how old ? Sixteen ? We shall soon have to climb a beanstalk to talk to you."

" It's a gug-good idea, you know, if you're an off-officer. I'm going to my crammer's next year," Gilbert brought out, in exculpation of his offensive height.

" Well, I expect you would all like a game of croquet. No, I won't play ; at my age mental exercise is quite enough," said Harriet, thinking of her luncheon party. " I dare say you would like to join them, Miss—— ? " She turned to the governess, who looked embarrassed.

Dorset's pimple-faced intended gave a giggle.

" I don't think she would. She's been bilious all day. She might be sick ! "

" Really, Allice—— ! There is no need to be indelicate—— ! "

" I bet Polly will play. You're not bilious, are you, Polly ? " It was Dorset who covered the lady's confusion.

" Polly—— ? " Harriet looked round. Having the habit of not noticing servants, she now saw, for the first time, that the figure at the back of the little group was not Mytton, Selina's maid, who usually attended the wheel-chair.

A girl in her early teens stood, with hands primly folded, but eyes dancing with merriment, just behind Gilbert. At the moment, a bright tide of crimson had all but effaced the small golden spangles on a cheek freckled like a cowslip. Plump and glossy as a young calf, there was something in her that vibrated, even in repose : some abounding energy, expressed in a springing head of well-brushed hair and in the brilliant scarlet of lips she was biting to suppress, perhaps, an ill-timed smile.

"Ah—Polly Bowling." What a contrast between this daughter of the soil and the poor, attenuated product of Norman chivalry! Harriet was thinking, as she nodded kindly at the blushing girl. "Well, Polly, have you forgotten your curtsey?" Curtseys were going out, but Mrs. Flood believed in keeping the younger generation up to its observances. "And what are you doing here?" she added, as Polly, by now crimson in the face as a dahlia, hurriedly repaired the omission. She did not tell "old" Mrs. Flood that she had been told not to curtsey since she left the village school: that the curtsey, symbol of servitude, was not for girls in her position; that a polite "Good day, ma'am," was quite enough from a farmer's daughter —even a tenant farmer, renting his land from the manor of Guerdon.

"Polly came up with some eggs, Grandmamma—and we met her, and I asked Mamma if she might come down here with me, instead of Mytton," Miranda was explaining.

A reasonable preference. Polly, by reason of her connections, was, after all, almost a member of the household. Harriet looked with approval at a clean, sprigged gown, modestly high at the throat, and at the sun-bonnet with which the girl had covered her exuberant hair.

"I suppose we'll be having you in service, one of these days?"

"No—please, ma'am." Polly shook her head. "I'm going to boarding school."

"To—*what*?"

"Yes, ma'am. I'm going to Miss Kempster's, in Bristol." Her blushes died down, as she smiled with the confidence of simplicity at her inquisitor.

"So they are going to make a 'young lady' of you." Harriet spoke dryly. It occurred to her that Selina would have said something cutting; but, after all, what did it amount to? Times were changing, and she—Harriet—would be dead, please God, before all the girls of Polly Bowling's class had started, as shop assistants did already, to consider themselves "young ladies." "You boys had better get the mallets, and have your game before the dew begins to fall."

Allice Montagu claimed Dorset, and Polly cheerfully enough accepted the lanky Gilbert as her partner. The governess, at Harriet's suggestion, went to "sit down quietly" in the drawing-room.

Harriet watched the pretty scene for a while: the smooth green turf, the young figures flinging their long shadows across the hoops—all very well behaved, very innocent; the boys, following the stalwart British tradition, all but ignoring their partners, and concentrating their attention on flogging the balls; Polly playing sedately—it appeared she knew all about croquet; where had she learned it? And Allice Montague, who chose to ignore her existence, uttering small squeals and plaintive requests for her partner's advice or assistance every time she struck a ball. Even from a distance, Dorset's response was plainly perfunctory.

"He'll soon have enough of *that*," soliloquised Harriet, "and then, my girl, the trouble will begin! Don't you know a boy of that age only cares about winning the game? If you were very pretty and very entertaining, he *might* forgive you for making him lose it. As things are——" She gathered her shoulders in a delicate shrug, turning to Miranda to help her out of her chair.

Drawing the child to sit on her lap, she rested her cheek for a moment against the dark, silken head. The tobacco plants along the border below them had begun to give out their evening scent, and a cloud of mayflies executed their dazzling dance against the setting sun.

"And now"—instinctively she lowered her voice—"where's Johnny?"

"I don't know. He didn't have dinner with us." Midday luncheon was still "dinner" to Miranda, who had her supper in the school-room at seven.

"Do you mean, he did not come in?"

"Papa was angry with him again. It was something about"—Miranda's brow crumpled—"about money, I think. You see, he hasn't got any."

"Hasn't got any——?"

Outrageous. While the others had the run of their father's pockets for whatever extravagant project occurred to them. Harriet's lips tightened as she resolved to repair this state of affairs—if necessary, out of her own pocket. But not before she had had a good try, for the benefit of his soul, to bring Dromore to his senses!

"So Johnny said—he said," stumbled on Miranda, "that unless Papa gave him some money, like he gives Doss and Gilbert, he'd go away and earn his own living. I expect he's gone to Bristol, to look at the ships. Or perhaps he's met some of his friends—the ones he met last time he went away. But he promised me—he promised me he wouldn't—without telling me first——!"

The child had been struggling for self-control, but suddenly, with what Harriet felt to be a shocking inevitability, the dark eyes filled and a stream of crystal poured down her cheeks. Instinctively the grandmother caught her to her bosom.

"Listen. You must never cry. At least, you must never allow anyone to see you cry." Quickly finding her handkerchief, she dried the small, woeful face.

"Once upon a time, it was thought that tears became a woman. All that is changed. From the moment a woman weeps, she loses her power over the person she wishes to influence." Without thinking, she spoke to the child as though Miranda were the same age as herself. It was a habit of hers which unconsciously had endeared her to her grandchildren. Yet, in the present instance, some fear of failing to make herself clear, checked her. She paused, and holding the child away from her, so that the two pairs of eyes—the topaz-coloured eye of her own family and the dark, dolorous, Flood eye—met; shook her slightly; and Miranda stopped crying, out of astonishment.

"Do you understand what I'm saying? I am talking about men. About boys. Even about Johnny.

" You say he promised not to go away again, without letting you know. He would mean to keep his word. But suppose you made it so hard for him that he could not? Boys—men——" She corrected herself, and wondered why she had done so; for what was Johnny but a boy? A boy of fifteen, who, in the normal course of events, would have been at school. " Hate to see a woman weep. They will do anything—they will even break their word—tell an untruth—run away—anything—to avoid it. You must promise me you will never let him see you cry again."

II

The game of croquet, as Harriet had foreseen, was not going smoothly. Twice Gilbert and Polly had beaten Dorset and his partner, and Dorset was a bad loser. Allice Montague, her lips pinched with mortification, was missing the easiest strokes and Dorset punching the bells viciously, with complete disregard for the safety of his companions. Gilbert took a crack on the shin at short range, and hopped about on one leg, saying, " Hang you, Doss! Hang you!" which made Polly laugh inordinately. Her laughter acting as fuel to Dorset's rage, he let fly with his ball at hers neatly placed six inches in front of the hoop. The impact which, unchecked, would have sent both balls careering into the depths of the herbaceous border, separated from the lawn by a broad flagged path and a dozen yards of turf, made Polly's ball climb the hoop, hurtle into the air and drop on its owner's toe. Polly gave a sharp squeal, set her teeth, walked up to Dorset and did what Harriet had been longing to do for years: slapped Dorset's face.

Harriet watched with curiosity to see what would follow.

Dorset dropped the mallet and seized both of Polly's wrists. A tussle developed, which went on so long that Harriet, having twice called, and been ignored, or unheard, by the combatants, put Miranda off her knee and rose to interrupt it; when she perceived that it was a half-hearted affair on both sides.

Polly, although pretending to fight, was smiling at Dorset, who, still in possession of her wrists, was laughing excitedly, making a feint of letting her go, then drawing her back, close to his young, sturdy body.

" Stop it, you two—we want to go on playing!" Gilbert was stuttering, and Allice Montague, beside herself with jealous resentment of Dorset's attention to her rival:

" You—what's your name—you *Polly* girl! Let him go this minute! I never saw such vulgar behaviour!"

Polly, inarticulate with laughter, was gasping.

" I'm not holding him—he's holding me!" And, as was obvious to the onlookers, not making the least attempt to escape.

" Dorset!" Harriet spoke sharply, immediately behind the combatants. She could hear their quick, excited breath, Dorset's muffled chuckle; see the swing of the ardent young bodies—Polly's much overdeveloped for a girl of her age! Trust Dorset to notice that—and she sensed instinctively the profound sexual undercurrent in the struggle, of which the participants might be unconscious—although she doubted it. Dorset was seventeen; Polly a year or two younger.

"Dorset!" Her voice at last penetrated their absorption in each other. They dropped apart, shame-faced.

"You should be ashamed of yourself!" she told her grandson freezingly. "As for you, Polly Bowling, you had better go home at once. It is to be hoped your boarding school will teach you better manners than you appear to have learned in the village."

". . . You mustn't be angry with Polly, Grandmamma." Gilbert had shambled off to put the mallets away, Allice gone offendedly in search of the governess, and Dorset, leaving, as usual, the tedious jobs to others, leaned gracefully on the back of his grandmother's chair. "I was the one to blame—I was, really. I lost my temper——"

"I'm fully aware of that." She gave him no quarter.

"The truth is, I'm a confoundedly ill-tempered fellow," said Dorset, with that air of rueful self-deprecation which seems rather to confer an added virtue on the speaker, than to detract from his charms.

"And, by admitting, you excuse it, I suppose?"

He laughed outright. Yes, laugh, thought Harriet. That's how you will get out of everything, all your life. You will laugh, and people will tell each other what a delightful good fellow you are, really! To herself she was obliged to admit it was an irresistible laugh: rich, easy, full-hearted. Strangers had stopped, even when he was a little boy, to listen to it. It was as though, by his laughter, he could draw to himself everything pleasant, satisfying and luxurious that he had ever known, and drape himself in it, as in a mantle of gold, whose warmth he was pleased to share with his companions. It was, of course, beside the point that he could, at his pleasure, twitch the mantle away, keeping himself snug, and leaving them to shiver in the cold.

"That's too bad! But you're quite right." His frankness was engaging. "Only—what matters is not getting Polly into trouble, Grandmamma. Her mother is a regular dragon, you know; I believe she even beats Polly sometimes."

"To judge from this afternoon, she probably deserves it. And how, may one ask, do you come to know so much about Polly Bowling's mother?"

"She chased me off their garden wall one day!" The youth was in no way embarrassed. "We were just chatting about the hound puppy she's walking for us—and I believe Polly had given me a bit of their honeysuckle. My stars! We might have been planning an elopement, from the way the old vixen went for me!" A reminiscence which appeared to afford him amusement.

Harriet looked at him. Really, he was preposterously good looking. In view of past history, it was no wonder cottage mothers discouraged the young Floods from hanging about their daughters—especially if they were as plump and pretty as the Bowling girl.

" Take care, Dorset. Polly Bowling is only a silly, ignorant village girl, and you have had much more experience, as well as a better upbringing, than she."

His look of astonishment was genuine enough to be reassuring.

" Why, Grandmamma, you don't think I'd be such an ass as to—fool about with the tenants' daughters, do you ; like—— ? " He broke off ; his face flamed.

She looked round. Allice and the governess had volunteered to accompany the wheel-chair back to " The House." The three figures moved slowly towards the gate in the ring fence. Calmly, she finished his sentence for him.

" Like your grandfather, you were about to say. Like your Uncle Quentin—and others of your family." God in heaven ! did Dromore never talk intimately to his sons ? Did the boys' moral education stop at the sermon on Sunday, the family prayers which were instituted on the day Dromore became master of Guerdon, and Dromore's dreary homilies on abstract virtue, which he had a way of producing—in his mother's opinion —on the most unwarrantable occasions ?

" I see I have shocked you," she continued ; Dorset, in fact, was shocked into silence. No more averse from indelicate conversation between members of his own sex than the majority of his contemporaries—that his grandmother should open her lips on such a subject petrified him. A lady—and his grandmother ! Outwardly cool, save for heightened colour, Dorset suffered, inwardly, an exquisite embarrassment.

" You know the countryside as well as I do," she was saying calmly. " You have listened to its gossip. And, presumably, you have used your eyes. It is difficult to overlook the family traits ! In previous centuries, and, in fact, up to my own time, the lord of the manor was supposed to enjoy a kind of *droit de seigneur*." She allowed her voice to trail away on a note of distaste. " May I be allowed to remind you that times have changed ? That departures from—shall we call it convention ?—are no longer considered, at least in the society to which we belong, good form ? And that their indulgence is hardly admissible to a person who calls himself a gentleman ? "

" Of course I know that, Grandmamma." She saw she had been right in appealing to his dignity ; but how long, she wondered, would social consciousness hold out against that restless blood ? " Why, here come Uncle Roan and Aunt Venetia ! " said Dorset, on a note of relief. " I thought they were dining at The House ; did you invite them ? I say "—he dropped his voice to a man-of-the-world inflection that brought a smile to Harriet's lips—" what an awful fine woman Aunt Venetia is ! Quite a beauty, isn't she ? Do you think people climb on chairs in the park to look at her," he inquired ingenuously, " as they do for Mrs. Langtry ? "

Harriet said gravely that she had not heard of such a demonstration in the case of Mrs. Roan Flood, perfectly grasping the implication. Dorset had been invited to stay with his uncle and aunt in London ; the obvious climax of such a visit would be to squire a woman to whom such tribute was shown.

" I must say I agree with the fellows who say a girl can't hold a candle to a woman of that age, if she happens to be a real stunner, like Aunt Venetia ! "

My dear boy, thought Harriet, as she moved forward to greet her visitors, there's really no need to underline it so heavily. I fully understand that village beauties have nothing to say to a person of sophisticated taste !

They were indeed a striking couple, she reflected, as she looked from Venetia to Roan—the only one of her children who favoured her side of the family. Tall, with the angular elegance of the Dorsets, Roan looked as young for his age as Harcourt was old for his. The pair of them might have been in their thirties, instead of . . . What is age ? she interrupted herself to reflect. Age is pain, disillusionment, endurance and, finally, wisdom ; and what of all these had come in the way of Roan and Venetia ?

Roan was the only one who appeared to have found happiness in his marriage. Saved by an early and brief engagement from making a fool of himself, he and Venetia were admirably suited to each other : modern and frivolous in their outlook, frequenting cosmopolitan society, extravagant, and united in their determination to have a good time. Roan did not mind Venetia's smoking a cigarette in her own or her friends' drawing-rooms, and Venetia only laughed when Roan came in, a little less than sober, confessing that he had lost at Crockford's the price of her promised furs. She knew she would get them, sooner or later.

Childless, they were frank enough to admit they were glad of it. Roan's income—he was on Harcourt's Board, held a few other small directorships, and had done fairly well out of the Ebuassi mines—was not equal to his tastes ; and if there had been nurses, tutors, governesses and schools to pay for, they would have had seriously to curtail their pleasures.

" Harcourt insists on carrying Roan off to dine with him in town ! " cried Venetia gaily, as she came within her mother-in-law's hearing. " We came to say goodbye, for our train leaves early in the morning, and I'm quite sure I shan't see Roan until he meets me at Temple Mead ! "

" How you young people rush about." This seemed to be the tolerant comment. " Arriving yesterday, leaving to-morrow morning ! I'm afraid my birthday has put you to a great deal of inconvenience."

" Oh, no. It's a rushing age," Venetia assured her with charming seriousness, " and it will be more rushing still, if we all take to these horseless carriages everyone is ordering. I've made Roan promise to give me one, as soon as we may be sure of not having to get out and push, whenever they stop on a hill. I'm sure there'll be a great demand for them in Bristol, if they ever become really dependable. Think of coming up Park Street by machinery, instead of behind two panting horses ! "

" I suppose there must be progress; but horses will do me for the rest of my time. It is time you were going, Dorset ; you will be late for dinner." She paused a moment before adding, " And if you see Johnny, remind him he has not yet been to wish me many happy returns of the day."

Having made his adieux, Dorset departed, hallooing for Gilbert, who came loping, with stained mouth and hands, from the strawberry beds, where he had prudently retired on gathering, from a word or two, that Doss was in for a jawbation from Grandmamma ; and the two set forth for the bridle path.

It was then that Venetia made her indiscreet remark—her pretty eyes following the retreating figure of her nephew Dorset with an interest which, in Harriet's opinion, was less that of tolerant relationship than of feminine response to something which, a short while before, had quickened the breath of Polly Bowling, and earned Dorset a slap and a smile.

III

". . . I've made Roan take that house I wanted—you remember ? I wrote to you about it. The one in Halkin Street."

" I thought he didn't like it ? "

" *I* like it." Venetia pushed the bright hair back from her small, jewelled ears and smiled at her mother-in-law. She was an entrancing creature, with her small, brilliant face and dark-crimson, pouting lips.

" You are a very clever woman," said Harriet after a pause. " You have married the third most selfish man in England and you get precisely what you want out of him."

" The third most selfish—— ? " Amused, Venetia's brows queried the description.

" My son Dromore and my son Harcourt," said Harriet calmly, " are, each in his way, more self-indulgent than Roan. Dromore shows it in his personal relationships, and Harcourt in his indifference to all but the interests of his business. My husband," she added on reflection, " was the worst of them all."

" Roan and I are each quite selfish, in our separate ways," admitted Venetia, " but I'm the one who wins in the end ! Isn't that true, by the way, of all of us ? I wonder how many women really allow themselves to be dominated. I know very few—from the Queen downward !—who believe in the theory of an inferior sex. It's so funny—how furious the Queen is about these people who want votes for women !—although I actually find myself quite in sympathy with her, for once. I'm sure we shall have much fewer privileges, when we insist on being treated as equals by all the men who, for the present enjoy patronising and humouring us. They'll be much less accommodating when they're obliged to be, by Act of Parliament ! Of course the Queen knows that ; for all her stupidity, she's as cunning as a weasel about getting her own way."

" The Queen is a very great woman." Harriet solemnly voiced the creed of her generation.

" And a shocking killjoy ! Well, Mamma, you at least cannot complain of not getting your own way. Everyone does exactly as you tell them—even Dromore."

" It is one of the penalties of my age." She spoke with a strange sadness.

" You call it a penalty ? " Again Venetia arched her flexible brows.

They were indoors. Harriet moved abruptly to avoid the too-strong beam of the setting sun, streaming across the flowers back in the *jardinière* that filled the bow of the window. She stopped to rub a leaf of lemon verbena between her fingers before answering ; its crushed sweetness in some way comforted her.

" You are a frivolous and sometimes a light-minded woman, Venetia, but you are no fool. You know as well as I do that a society which ceases to be dominated by its men is a doomed society. You can see it around us to-day."

". . . Is anything the matter ? " Venetia looked at her mother-in-law curiously. It was unusual to find Harriet in this tenebrous mood.

" Nothing that affects you. It affects me because, in the many years I have been married, I have learned a good many lessons. I have learned, for example, to respect the Floods. I recognise in them a kind of warped—I had almost said a pitiful—greatness, that comes from one thing only : from the worship, generation after generation, of one god——"

" Their money ? " ventured Venetia. " I tease Roan sometimes, about being purse-proud."

" The less is included in the greater." Harriet's dim smile glimmered. " Shall we say, of their money they make a continual burnt-offering to their god, which is themselves. I am a foolish old woman, and you do right to pay no attention to me "—Venetia flushed, caught in the act of strangling a small yawn—" but I have my moments of guilt. You should have them as well ; for we are both blasphemers in the temple ! " She had settled quietly into the wing chair which was her favourite, looking out across the blue-green evening landscape. " You and I, Selina, Isabel and Georgina Bendysshe, who was my husband's first wife, have each done our share in breaking the chain of worship, by withholding our contributions to it. We have not loved our husbands, Venetia, and, without love, there can be no domination."

Venetia's eyelashes flickered. She gave a little laugh.

" And Vicky ? She is a Flood as well ; sometimes I think she is the most *deeply* ' Flood ' of them all. How does she fare, Mamma, in your summary ? " Fascinated, as she always was, by her mother-in-law, she leaned a little forward ; the perfume of her gown met that of the verbena Harriet still held in her fingers, struggled with it, surrendered, at last, its *fade* exoticism to the verbena's clear, triumphant scent.

" Victoria," said Harriet, " is in a peculiarly strong position. Although she is not good looking, she could certainly have married, if she had chosen. Her dowry was arranged as soon as she was presented, and I should have been very glad to see her established in a home of her own. As it is, she stops with Dromore—the sole surviving believer in the family godhead ! Her faith has never wavered ; she does, most truly and sincerely, believe in the divine right of Floods, and this, I am sure, is why she never married. Yes, I know it argues an almost celestial stupidity on Vicky's part ; but as it is the mainspring of her life, why disturb it ? "

" Well, Mamma, if the ' godhead '—I like your name for it !—has got mislaid in the present generation, surely it has some hope of revival in the next? Let's admit, for the sake of argument, that we've damaged it, between us, by our wicked refusal to accept our husbands as supermen—for which, personally, I feel they're as much to blame as we are ourselves. And, anyhow, my taste doesn't run to supermen.

" Let's admit, if you like, that we've let them down by failing to love them. But suppose the wind is changing? ' By the pricking of my thumbs—— ! ' Dorset, Mamma; have you forgotten Dorset? Prince Charming—with all the girls in the county crazy about him already, and, I'd take a safe wager, most of the elder women as well. You weren't at the Hunt ball, where that one was calmly taking his pick of all the prettiest and most elegant partners; when they were practically fighting and scratching to get their hands on him, and one girl was taken home in hysterics, because she failed to have Dorset's name on her programme! Dorset won't lack for love, Mamma; he's more likely to have a surfeit, and sicken, and so die. Why, he has ' Lothario ' written across his brows——"

" Does Lothario ever know love?" queried Harriet Flood. " Passion, no doubt; but love—— ? Dorset will rouse passion; may even be capable of it himself; though I am inclined to think he is more likely to mistake a perfectly commonplace biological disturbance for the authentic fire!

" Is it not strange, Venetia," she pursued, " that this powerful, this—*monstrously* endowed family has been denied the one thing that might have made it invincible? It can command almost all the kingdoms of the earth; but it cannot command its women."

Venetia nodded slowly.

" I had not thought of that before. It explains—much."

" It explains why Dorset, who has yet to come face to face with his family's bane, has the air of a young immortal, wreathed in his immortality! When he discovers the truth, he will be merely another blustering Flood, snatching everywhere at power for the concealment of his shame, and believing that the secret of strength lies in inhumanity."

" How ruthless you are. Then—it's *kaput* for them all; is that what you mean?"

" There is Johnny."

" Oh—Johnny. You've always been—tender "—she had nearly said " foolish "—" about him!"

" Johnny is simple, and humble, and doubtful of himself. So far. He sees people as human beings—not as pawns in a diplomatic game, to be played for his own advantage. And how long will that continue?" Harriet shook her head. " Unless God looks after him, they will make Johnny like themselves. But perhaps," she added simply, " something will happen, to save him."

" Poor Johnny. He's certainly having a bad time," Venetia conceded.

" Don't be sorry for Johnny," said Harriet tersely. " Save your sorrow for the others, as I do. Deeply as they have wronged me, much as I have been made to suffer through them, I pity them so deeply, Venetia, that if I could spare them by any personal sacrifice, I would make it. An old woman's life," she said, smiling, " is not worth so very much, I agree! Nevertheless, I'd give it—just because I can't bear to watch human beings in torment. In seeking to escape from their own suffering—which they are not even intelligent enough to recognise—they have destroyed us ; but we, in our turn, will destroy them. There is no help for it. It was natural law that made man the leader, and gave him woman for his complement and counsellor. We are stronger than our men, Venetia ; and God help us if we ever oblige them to admit it."

" Where have you been ? They will be sounding the gong in less than five minutes. You'd better let me come and help you to dress, or Drummy will be in a towering temper ! "

" I've been at the Dower House, talking to your mamma," gasped Venetia, as she and Vicky ran upstairs.

" Talking to Mamma ? What on earth was she talking about, to keep you so late ? "

" Red ruin and havoc on the House of Flood ! " She could not resist shocking Vicky ; who stood for a moment, taken aback, until a smile dawned on her plain, wholesome face.

" Oh—Mamma ! She thinks we're terrible people. But it's just her way of paying a compliment ! " A nod settled that. " Do put on the dark plum-coloured gown again ; it's Worth, isn't it ? I wish I had the figure to wear such things," said Vicky wistfully.

CHAPTER SIX

I

HE set three small objects down carefully on the edge of her card-table and straightened himself, watching for her reaction. She laid down her patience pack and bent to inspect them: three little—hens, were they supposed to be ?—in graduated sizes : of brass, or lead perhaps. She weighed one curiously in her hand, noting the fine yet primitive carving.

" Very pretty. What are they ? "

" I thought they'd do to hold down your papers. I brought them back from the Coast. The natives use them for weighing gold."

She looked up at him ; at the smiling lips and smileless eyes. Her heart, which had leapt at his entrance, sank again. Where was the grandson she had known ? A thin barrier, to be felt though not seen, had descended between her and the stranger standing there with Johnny Flood's features and Johnny Flood's untidy, dust-coloured hair. Change, change ; the word rang in her mind like a small, melancholy bell. The change went deeper than the pigment which, rich brown on his return, had now faded to a leaden hue that added to his strange, derelict look of a boy out of tune with his circumstances. A boy ? No boy of fifteen should have on his face that expression of dogged resistance : resistance to—what ? It was as though he held the world at arm's length, with some profound mistrust of its motives towards him.

" I thought you had forgotten my birthday." She spoke crisply, dismissing sentiment.

" No, I hadn't. But I couldn't—find "—there was a slight pause before the word—" those things."

" Well—I appreciate your remembrance. They will do admirably, as paper weights." She moved the little hens neatly aside. Her hands, exquisitely pretty for a woman of her age, and hardly larger than Miranda's, started to shuffle the patience cards. " I take it you have had—a meal."

" Yes, thanks. Let me do them for you." He stretched out his hand for the cards. As he took them, she looked at it quickly ; it was clean, pink from a recent scrubbing, but the nails were terrible, the edges split, with dirt ground into them and round the cuticle. That was how they were when he came back ; but he had seemed to be getting his hands in order. He saw her look, and hid them quickly.

" Sorry. I'd have tidied up, but I was afraid if I took too long you'd have gone to bed," he muttered. She saw him glance round the mellow room with the air, almost, of seeing it for the first time.

" Where have you been, Johnny ? " Despite her vow, never to question him, the words slipped past her control.

" In Bristol." His eyebrows lifted slightly, as though the answer were to be taken for granted, while he shuffled the cards with the expertness of the gambler. She remembered how, in the old days, Dorset and Gilbert had jeered at young Johnny's clumsy manipulation of the pack. " There you are, Grandmamma." He set them in front of her quickly and hid his hands again.

" I suppose you went down to the docks." Carefully casual, she began to lay out the cards.

" I did, as a matter of fact." His voice had broken ; deep and slow, it reminded her a little of Harcourt's, but less implacable. " How did you know ? " The naïveté of his surprise brought a laugh from her.

" My dear boy——! "

" Grandmamma . . ."

She did not look up ; her hand, holding the ace of clubs, poised itself over the green baize, the lamplight striking sparks of rainbow out of her diamonds and throwing a subtle ivory into the lace dripping from her wrist.

" Well——? "

She heard him scuffing his chair across the carpet towards her ; his fist —he had remembered to tuck the fingers inside—appeared on the table at her elbow.

" I hadn't mislaid those weights. I pawned them."

Raising her face, with its beautiful smile, she lifted her hand and pushed the hair back lightly from his puckered brow.

" You did—what, my boy ? "

" I'd got no money when I came back to Bristol. You see "—he took it for granted she would want an explanation—" if I'd come back on the *Aldebaran*, I'd have drawn my pay when we docked ; but though they made me work my passage back—that was Uncle Hacky's idea—I hadn't signed the articles. It was pretty cute of old Macpherson! He's a real pound-and-pinter"—a description that eluded Harriet's comprehension—" and I bet he slipped the surplus in his own pocket. So I was on the passenger list, but I was sweated like a fo'c'sle hand and Floods got an extra hand, for nothing! Pretty bl—pretty funny, when you come to think of it." He laughed, and for the first time she heard cheer in the sound; the short, dry, obligatory honk with which he had received some of her previous attempts to divert him gave way to the gusto she remembered. It was funny, when you came to think of it: Floods economising at the expense of one of the family. Her laughter rippled out in echo of his.

"Go on; tell me more about it," she encouraged him.

"Well, when we docked—I'd got matey by then with some of the chaps for'ard, and we went round to one or two pubs." He paused, aghast.

"I may be ignorant, but I am quite aware of the habits of sailors when they come ashore at the end of a voyage," said Harriet. Johnny grinned cautiously.

"Well, they treated me, and of course I wanted to treat them when my turn came round; but I hadn't got a red cent——"

"Surely the purser, in one of our own ships——!"

"The *Rembwe's* not a slap-up Atlantic liner!" he reminded her. "The captain did our banking, and it's easier to get a red-hot sixpence out of hell than a copper out of a Glasgow skipper's breeches——"

"*John!*"

"Sorry." He blinked contritely. "I'm afraid I've not had much parlour talk lately," he mumbled.

Her look pardoned him.

"There's certainly something a little—bracing, about the fo'c'sle vocabulary."

"Phew! Too bracing for you, Grandmamma. But I'll be careful from now. Well, I was in a real splice, because, of course, they all knew who I was, and it looked pretty poor cheese for the owner's nephew not to have the price of a pint on him. So I went and got my ditty-bag——"

"And what might that be?"

"Oh, a sort of canvas sack the men keep their things in. One of our chaps died when we were in Grand Bassam, and they auctioned his traps—that's the usual thing," explained Johnny. "So I got this bag, and of course I'd picked up a few bits of curios—sharks' teeth and native carvings and things of that sort; so I popped them with old Solomon in Guinea Street. I didn't want to give him your weights, but he'd hardly allow me anything on the rest—the old muckworm! Sorry——"

"A very pithy old English term," Harriet contented herself with observing.

"So I had to throw them in with the lot——"

"And how, pray, did you recover them again?"

The light went from his face.

"When I'd been home a few days, I naturally asked the guv'nor—father—for some money."

" You used to call your father ' Papa,' " she reminded him. " A childish term, I admit. Dorset's name, ' the pater,' is probably more suitable, although I can't think why children of to-day can't call their parents simply ' Father ' and ' Mother,' as we did in my young days."

" I call him ' sir ' when I speak *to* him. When I speak *of* him—it won't be often," promised Johnny grimly, " I'll call him Mr. Flood."

" You must please yourself. And what did he say, when you asked him for money ? "

" I'm not to have any, ' until I can be trusted to use it in an honourable fashion,' " She bit her lip, to hold back an exclamation.

An honourable fashion ! Who were they to prate in that style ? Was Dromore ' honourable,' when he spent vast sums on the charities that bolstered up his pride while neglecting the obscure needs of his own tenantry ? Harcourt with his furtive affairs with women, and Roan with his gambling, his trips abroad and his pandering to his wife's entravagance ? Young Dorset, betting on the sly, and Gilbert apparently maintaining a tapeworm—to judge from the quantities of plum cake and sweetmeats he stuffed into his pipe-stem of a body—were they being ' honourable ' too ? —Her angry partisanship rose in Johnny's defence, although she would not let him see it too plainly.

" You should have come to me——"

" To you, Grandmamma ? No fear ; thank you. I don't sponge on women."

She bent her head to conceal a smile. At what moment, she wondered had the sovereigns she slipped into his hand, the tips she gave him at the end of the holidays and the money orders she would sometimes enclose in a letter to him at school passed into the category of ' sponging on women ' ?

" The others could have let you have some ; they both have far more pocket money than is good for them."

" Oh, yes, they'd have forked out, if I'd asked them ; but I wasn't going to. After all, it comes out of *his* pocket, doesn't it ? " She winced at the bitter adjective.

" You have not told me yet how you got it," she said tartly.

" I found a job at the City Docks." He said it brusquely, as one forestalling expostulation.

" What sort of a job ? "

" Actually "—he had the grace to look sheepish—" she was a coast steamer, in for bunkering. Coal, you know. It was rather a mucky job, but it was all I could get ; and I didn't find that until late in the afternoon."

" You've been heaving coal ? " asked his scandalised grandmother.

" It's not so easy picking up a job as it ought to be. There's not nearly enough shipping in—and there'll be less still," he said gloomily, " if the Dock Board doesn't get rid of some of those old muffin-heads that keep on chucking rocks into the dockisation schemes. All sorts of things got done, when Portishead and Avonmouth were under their own Boards ; but ever since the Corporation took them over——"

" Those are matters you can discuss with your uncle. So that is how you earned the money to get my birthday present out of pawn ! " Her eyes glittered, and she could not keep the note of triumph out of her voice. " One of Drummy's idle, parasitic brats ! " All the same, even Harcourt could hardly be expected to bring enthusiasm to bear on an exploit which, if it got about the town, would shed a peculiar light on the way Floods treated their sons ; and Dromore, of course, would be out of his mind, if he heard of it.

" That wasn't the best part of it ! " He twinkled at her. " When I got to old Solomon's, it was pretty late, and the place was locked up. I nearly hammered the door in, but I couldn't make anyone hear. I was in an awful steam, because I wanted you to have those things on your birthday. Then just by luck, I happened to notice a sort of attic window, half-open, on the roof."

" Don't tell me you've added housebreaking to your other accomplishments ! "

" It didn't take long to nip up there, and after that—well, it was nearly dark, and I had to keep on striking matches. Looking for a needle in a haystack wasn't in it, and I made sure the old bast—Shylock had sold them : which he'd got no business to do, because the time wasn't up, and I'd got the tickets."

" So you stole them."

" Stole be—— Of course I didn't steal them. I left the ticket and the money on top of it——"

She could not help it ; she leaned towards him and brushed his brow lightly with her lips.

" Thank you, my dear. You've taken a lot of trouble."

An hour passed ; they had been talking easily—like old friends—on no very serious matters, and on nothing that concerned the adventure which, so far as Johnny was concerned, appeared to have been dropped to the bottom of a deep well.

" Ought I to go, now ? "

" Go—where ? "

" Why—home, of course. They'll all be in bed—and I'm sure you should be, Grandmamma ! It must be after midnight."

She glanced negligently at the clock on the mantlepiece, flanked by its two elegant Capo di Monti figurines.

" So it is. I had not noticed the time."

" Shall I wind it up for you ? " He did it very carefully, replacing it exactly in the spot from which he had taken it. No one but herself had ever touched the little French clock ; Harcourt had once been caned for playing with it.

They stood on the verandah, her hand lightly on his shoulder. A sky thick-sown with stars arched itself over the profound hush of the English countryside. She felt him shiver slightly, and, as though ashamed of it, draw away from her too-intimate hand.

" There's the Plough ; it's upside down after you cross the Equator," she heard him murmur. " Good night, Grandmamma ; I hope you've had a happy birthday."

She hesitated, and gave him deliberate answer.

" You have made it quite perfect."

" Me ? " He sounded startled. " I've done nothing——"

" But you might so easily have spoiled it ! "

The moonlight, shining full on his face, showed her the boy with manhood struggling inside him. She stood silent, still fighting her desire to question him, to attack the barrier which remained—although no longer inimical—between them. She heard him draw a long breath.

" It's all—queer——"

She held her peace.

" Queer—and so different——"

" Different—from what ? "

" From what I thought it was before I went away."

She looked at him mildly.

" Kind of—imitation," he blundered.

" You have seen many strange sights." It was like encouraging a timid animal. " Tell me about some of them."

" I'm no good at describing." She felt his retreat, like a mouse into the wainscot. I know, I know, her heart was saying ; we're all fine and critical, and prepared to be shocked ; and you're afraid of saying something —or saying it in some way—that offends our pampered gentility ! Was not Dromore perpetually hammering at him for roughness of speech or of pronunciation ? Instead of leaving all that alone, and allowing time to uncover the original grain, and polish away the shallow damage of a brief experience.

" Sometimes—sometimes—I see a picture . . . I could draw it—if I could draw ! " he mocked himself. Suddenly he turned to her. " It's what sticks in the mind that counts, isn't it ? "

" I should say, as a rule, yes."

" You do something, or see something, and it's all mixed up with a thousand other things, and you get a sort of idea it's important. . . . Then, when you've forgotten all about it, something else bobs up, like a jack-in-the-box—which you never even noticed at the time, and the whole picture's altered ; and the thing you thought important isn't, and the other thing is . . ."

Oh, my dear. How easy to imagine Selina's yawn, Dromore's expression of disgusted impatience—Dromore, so fluent and so studied in his periods ! " My dear John, until you have acquired some command of the English language, you can hardly presume to inflict your maunderings on civilised listeners ! "

" Have you something in mind ? Something in particular ? " If he would but let her help to withdraw his thoughts from the tangle of the past.

" There was a fellow—a nigger ; he gave me this." He touched the scar on his cheek, about which she remembered them all questioning him, and he had evaded their curiosity. " And one day I saw him standing up in a boat, facing the sun, with nothing on, like this——"

He had turned his back to her and stretched out his arms. Crude as the gesture was, she saw it : the naked boy, dedicating himself—to what ? She found she was holding her breath.

He had dropped his arms. Clumsily, almost furtively, he snatched her hand, and, after a moment's hesitation, pushed his lips against it. Then, all but flinging it from him, he was running away from her, his shadow trailing him across the grass.

No more the rough hug, the soft cheek rubbed endearingly against her own. He had shown her how it was to be for the future, and, proudly, she accepted it.

II

Early morning sun sucked up mist from the stream. Out towards the river mouth, the heat haze, merging water into sky, held the shipping impaled like butterflies on a background of translucent grey. The pastures shone like satin with their load of dew and buttercups.

A lively rattle of locks, the flinging open of doors and windows, proclaimed that Guerdon, like a complicated piece of machinery, was cranking itself up for another day's activities. Lights rose in green-houses, slid down from frames over which an anxious gardener pored to see what nocturnal damage the slugs had done to his cherished seedlings. The sweet heads of horses hung gracefully over the half-doors, awaiting the men with the morning feed. Milk arrived from the home farm with a clinking of churns. The cows streamed slowly into the meadows, to be greeted by Miranda's donkey from the linhey.

In a saucer on the commode were the remains of a half-smoked cigarette. A paper-backed novel, tumbled on the floor, displayed its frivolous cover and its title, *A Fair Parisienne*. Only Dorset would have dared to leave such incriminatory evidence to catch the eye, perhaps, of a housemaid ; but no female servant ever betrayed Dorset. Gilbert, on the other hand, had been " given away " for the small crime of leaving fruit-drops stuck to his pillow-slip. He—Gilbert—had recently been promoted to a room of his own : mainly because the beds in what, for two generations, had been known as " the boys' room " no longer accommodated his abnormal length of limb. The notion of Gilbert wallowing in the four-poster of the Regent's chamber (the future George the Fourth being reputed, on the thinnest possible evidence, to have passed a night at Guerdon on his visit to the West Country in 1808) was offensive to both his brothers, but, for once, even Dorset's protests made no impression on parental decision. Dorset, the Brummel in embryo, must continue to share a room with his younger brother—for reasons with which neither was favoured.

The noise of water being poured into the shallow tin tub that stood in a patch of sunlight wakened neither of the sleepers. The groom who poured it stooped, soaked a sponge, and, with the mechanical indifference of one performing a familiar rite, pressed it down on Dorset's face. The latter's yell roused Johnny, who had time to yawn himself into consciousness, while Dorset stumbled from bed, had the nightshirt twitched over his head and blundered, still half-asleep, into the icy water of the tub.

" How the devil did you get in last night ? " Rosy, now, and sumptuous, he stood up to towel himself, smiling on Johnny, as though surprised to find him there.

" Through the window."

" Liar. You couldn't come in through the window, unless you climbed over the roof."

" What's a roof, when you've been over the main royal ? " The taunt was irresistible.

" I'll kick your backside, you know, if you put on airs about your sea-going ! I bet you didn't come over the roof."

" I'll do it again, if you like," yawned Johnny, " and you can hang out and watch me."

A reluctant admiration kindled slowly in Dorset's eye. He chuckled. " You *are* a fellow. Lord, what a thundering morning. For the love of snakes, look at Aunt Vicky ! I lay five to one she's off at the bend. Hi-i-i ! "

Snatching the towel modestly about his torso, Dorset thrusting up the window, emitted a piercing yell. Miss Victoria Flood, on her new " safety " model, let out a short, sharp bark, and was salvaged by a young gardener, who staggered as he received Miss Flood's not inconsiderable weight on his shoulder. Despite Dromore's embargo on public appearances, Vicky was determined, for her own pleasure, to ride a bicycle. She had even sent for one of the " rational " costumes which went with the newly popular sport : bodice and bloomers, the latter modestly concealed by a full skirt—prevented by an elaborate contrivance of netted string from tangling itself into the spokes of the back wheel. Secretly, she thought she looked well in it ; fussy, femmine attire had never become her. Such, however, was not the opinion of her grinning nephew, who dodged out of sight, as, once more on the good earth, and straightening her hat, Vicky glared up at the window.

" About twenty geraniums this morning "—Dorset summarised the damage of his aunt's exercise—" and two of the new standard roses. Won't Braddock be mad ! " He glanced at Johnny, stepping gingerly into the tub, and glanced away again quickly from the small, sallow body marked with weals which, long as it was since his own had been similarly decorated, made Dorset's flesh creep in sympathy. That last tanning from the pater must have been a brute ! What an ass young Johnny was, again to put him in a rage.

" Here, you—what's your name—George." Superbly nude, he lounged elegantly on the window-sill. " Hand me the cigarettes. What's up with you this morning ? " he asked, with the good-humoured scorn of perfect physical well-being, of the groom who brought them. " What a misery you are, George ! You look as if you've been drinking vinegar." Guffawing at his jest, Dorset held out his hand for the matches.

"I were only thinking what the master would say, if he smelled your cigarette."

"Oh—mind your own business. One needs to smoke, when you're in the room! You positively stink of the stables. Here, what's that you've put out? Didn't I say I'd wear the new breeches this morning, you forgetful scoundrel?"

"They haven't come yet, Mr. Dorset." The man stood awkwardly, the condemned garment dangling from his hands.

"Confound it." The glory departed, Dorset became merely an angry young man, puffing viciously on his cigarette. "Then you can go and get them after luncheon."

"I can't do that."

"Why not?"

"I've been given the afternoon off," he muttered.

"Well, you'll go and fetch my breeches, all the same." Dorset's voice was quiet, his eyes shining. "And you'd better remember in future—your afternoons off depend on our convenience, not on yours."

"I've been given my afternoon, and I'm going to take it." The man's face was like grey clay; fear and defiance glistened in the roots of his hair. "It's the first I've had since Christmas——"

"Listen," said Dorset, and leaned forward gently. "You'll do as you're told, or you'll get the sack."

The man's fingers twitched into the palms of his hands.

"I don't get my wages from you. And we aren't black slaves these days, Mr. Dorset."

"You impudent dog!"

As Dorset moved, Johnny, as if by accident, stepped from the tub, into which he was nearly flung back by the impact of Dorset's body. In his rage Dorset hit out blindly, and his fist thudded into Johnny's ribs. Johnny, struggling for his balance, flicked Dorset's face, and stepped neatly aside, as the latter struck back. The door closed behind the vanishing groom. Johnny's fingers had closed like strips of steel round his brother's wrist.

"Wait a minute."

Taken aback by the unexpected strength of the grip, Dorset stood still, his ribs heaving under their sheath of ivory flesh.

"What's the sense of losing your temper? You're bigger than I am, but that makes no odds. I learned a few tricks while I was away, and—well, I might forget and use them: that's all," concluded Johnny, as he allowed his hand to fall to his side.

"You—little—*rat*!" There was as much incredulity as fury in the tone.

"You see, men don't fight for fun where I've been," said Johnny calmly.

"For two pins I'd break every bone in your body!"

Johnny shook his head.

"Of course you could smash me, if I fought by the book. You've given me many a lamming, but I just don't happen to feel like taking one now. Why should I, when I know I could beat you in my own way?"

"I bet it's some sort of a rotten way!"

"It is," Johnny agreed cheerfully. "They don't hold with Queensberry rules, you see, out on the Coast."

"You make me sick."

Turning aside, Dorset began to pull on his shirt, fighting irascibly against the drag of the material.

"If—if I ever lay a finger on you again," he spluttered, as he drove his head through the neck of the garment, "I'll damn' nearly kill you! God knows what you've sunk to—among your filthy niggers! I've done my best, so far, to take your side with the pater, but you can go to hell in future, for all I care."

Too well accustomed to such outbursts to be moved, Johnny stood still, looking at his own reflection in the glass over the chest of drawers.

"All the same . . . he was right. And he only said what others think."

"What others?" Dorset spun on his heel to face him.

"If George thinks we're slavers—well, I bet he's not the only one."

"Let him wait; he'll pay for it," muttered Dorset.

"What's the good of that?" He said it wearily, not as he would once have said it, dodging a clout for impudence from an outraged senior; and a stab of quick longing for those years of childish awe went through him. "You can't make people 'pay' for being human beings. Perhaps he'd got a girl waiting for him."

"What business is that of mine?" blustered Dorset.

"Oh, hell, I don't know." Shrugging his shoulders, Johnny picked up the brushes and attacked his straggling hair.

Dorset glowered and chewed his lower lip. As quick in recovering as in losing his temper, he was already simmering down. Stupefied by the tug of a variety of emotions, of which by far the strongest was an overwhelming curiosity, he could not maintain wrath with Johnny. Having consistently bullied and persecuted a defenceless youngster, his resistance to Johnny's new-found independence was oddly mixed up with an uneasy feeling that Johnny was unhappy. Having, in common with his kind, no objection to making people miserable for what he was pleased to call their own good, Dorset objected to an extraneous misery which trespassed on his own peace of mind. Moreover, while his acute sense of social propriety deplored Johnny's escapade, he had a secret respect for the spirit it had proved.

"You've really been a deuce of a fellow, you know, since you came home. What's the matter with you? You're setting everyone against you," he complained. "One might think you hated the whole lot of us!" After a pause: "Do you hate me?"

Johnny turned slowly. He had a momentary impulse to strike that face —that handsome, serious face, on which was written its owner's conviction, that no person in his right mind could hate Dorset Flood! He wanted to shout, "Yes, I do!"—and knew, with despair, it would be a lie. For what he really hated was what Dorset stood for; and this was beyond his power to explain.

"Don't be an ass. Of course I don't hate you."

" I just thought you might feel sore," blundered Dorset ; " because of my being the eldest, and coming into—all this—when the pater's gone."

Johnny opened his lips—then closed them again. He answered presently, with a faint smile :

" It's all right. I bear you no grudge for being two years older than me."

Dorset straightened himself, with a laugh of relief.

" That's good. I didn't suppose it was that—but I'm glad you told me. It would be a wretched sort of thing to have between us." As Johnny stood mute, envying Dorset's power to recover aplomb—" Come on, old fellow ! " It was Roan's voice, rich, warm, irresistible—" why don't you say what's gripping you ? I'm getting the blues, you know—watching you moping around every day ! "

" Nothing. I just want to get away—that's all."

" Away—from Guerdon ? " Dorset's brows gathered in bewilderment. " I can't make you out ; upon my soul, I can't. I know we led you a dance, as a youngster—confound it, you'd got to be put in your place ! But it's all different now—and when Gilbert's at Sandhurst and I leave Harrow, there's no end to the good times we can have—— ! " As Johnny was stubbornly silent, Dorset persisted, " Don't you *like* Guerdon ? "

Johnny was silent, then shook his head.

" You must be crackers ! Good lord, it's the greatest place on earth ! Every time I come home I think what a lucky devil I am, to have a place like this to come to. Gilbert's the same. We'd no idea you weren't—you didn't——" Dorset, it seemed, was shocked briefly into silence. " But, good lord, don't you see it's your *home* ? " he ended weakly.

" I can't help it, Doss—and I can't explain. And if I did," he said hopelessly, " you wouldn't understand. But, if you want the truth—I *hate* Guerdon. So now you've had it."

" But you must have a reason ! "

" I haven't. At least, nothing you can pin down, and say, That's it. It's more a feeling—a feeling that we've none of us—got any business here."

" Speak for yourself ! " The other was offended. " I have plenty of business, as you call it, here—and so could you have, if you had any sort of sense of your responsibilities." He turned towards the window, overlooking all that spread of rolling and wooded country that was Guerdon to the horizon ; it was as though he swelled with possession.

" Responsibilities—to whom ? "

" To the property, of course. You wait till I'm the squire," muttered Dorset. " I'll make Guerdon as much of a place as Paragon, before I've finished."

" What will you do ? Take in more of the farms, to make the park bigger ? And make some more of the tenants go off to the next county, because there's nowhere for them to live ? "

" Suppose you mind your own bloody business ? " An ugly gleam had come into Dorset's eye.

" Well—I wish you a good run for your money, Doss. And I hope it will be a long one," said Johnny sincerely.

The haughty stare flickered, relaxed, and the smile of goodfellowship—his greatest stock in trade—broke once more on Dorset's face.

"Damned if I can quarrel with you, you exasperating fellow! For God's sake get dressed; we're going to be late for breakfast."

A light tap on the door and a feminine voice interrupted their colloquy.

"Are you both presentable?"

"Come in, Aunt Vicky." Dorset draped a towel negligently round his waist, to spare his aunt the spectacle of two muscular legs emerging from the shirt hem, and flung open the door with a flourish. Vicky, in her "rational" suit, flushed with exercise, entered. "You look wonderful! Quite the modern girl. Won't you——?" He offered her the cigarettes, with solemn impudence.

"Don't include me in your misbehaviour. Pah—you're a savage!" Affecting to cough, Vicky waved smoke away from her face. "Don't you go near your mother, smelling of that disgusting tobacco. I don't know what the world's coming to, with this horrible cigarette habit."

"To which, my dear aunt, your sex will soon be addicted, as much as ours! Now, Vicky, don't tell me you haven't longed sometimes to puff your cheroot, wearing a dream of a plush smoking jacket, with a dear little Turkish cap on your head. I'm sure you'd be ravishing——"

Johnny let out a honk of laughter, which drew his aunt's attention on him.

"Johnny! Oh, my dear boy, will you never learn to tie a bow properly?" She tweaked at the knotted string under his collar, holding up her skirt out of the pools of water on the floor. "You're dreadful, the pair of you! Don't you know the water soaks through the ceiling of the Dutch room?"

"That's all right, Aunt Vicky; they're used to it in Holland."

"Hold your tongue, Johnny—and be quick; your father wants to see you before breakfast."

Dorset pursed his lips and began to whistle the Dead March. Outwardly indifferent, Johnny had sudden sickness at the pit of his stomach. There had been many such interviews, all ending in the same way: mutual bitterness, mutual defeat.

"In his dressing-room." Vicky was pushing him through the door. On the broad landing, barred with morning sunlight, she laid her big practical hand on his arm. "My dear"—her plain, kindly face was lifted to his, her eyes swimming with tenderness and anxiety—"do try to be reasonable with him this morning. I know how hard it is for the young to realise—but we're all so troubled about you, Johnny, and your father most of all."

He drew himself away from the restraining hand.

"I don't know what you've got to be troubled about, Aunt Vicky," he muttered. "I'm all right."

And he went sullenly towards one more scene with his father.

CHAPTER SEVEN

I

HE had never seen so exquisite a child.

It was odd that he thought of her as a child, for she could hardly have been more than a year younger than himself. He had never noticed a girl's clothes before ; he did not notice them now, save as a general effect of soft darkness, but all his life he was to remember Emily, as he first met her on the terrace, smiling at him from beneath the brim of her wide black hat.

" Johnny—it's Johnny ! "

Miranda was lurching towards them, with that perilous walk of hers, that became so much worse when she tried to control the painful twist of the hip, the lag of the right leg, which made sensitive grown-up people look away. Johnny never looked away ; nor, unless she let him see she wanted it, did he help her ; with the result that in Johnny's company she very often forgot she was not like other children, and seldom if ever tumbled.

" Johnny ! This is my brother Johnny," she told the other child proudly. " This is Emily Temple, Johnny ; she's come to live near us. Isn't it fun ? Now we can play together." She took Emily's hand with the protective air of the hostess. " What sort of games do you like best ? Do you play you are climbing up a precipice, and down below there are lions and bears, and One False Step means Destruction ? " gabbled Miranda.

Emily stood smiling, a little doubtfully ; not at all the kind of child to play such games as Miranda was describing. Her small, luminous face, into which the black straw flung a darkness of grey pearl, had the delicate drawing of childhood, but there was something more than childish in the lilac-coloured eyes and the pale, soft mouth, a little large for the rest of the features. From the way she held out her hand and said, " How do you do ? " it was plain she was well trained ; if shy, she had been taught not to show it.

" She's got no parents, and she's come to stay with Lady Cullen." Miranda's black eyes caressed her new companion as though she found in Emily some new and entrancing form of plaything off which she could hardly keep her hands. " I want to show her the stream, and the kingfisher's rock, and Falada's baby. Johnny, Johnny, do fetch Falada and come with us ! Then we needn't take ' The Grim,' " petitioned Miranda. " The Grim "—officially Miss Seagrim, the governess, was a recent infliction : a bright, self-confident young woman much disliked by Selina and Vicky for an unbecoming independence of manner which did not fit into their design for governesses. However, she was inexpensive, and fulfilled her requirements.

Selina—already ballooning out with another of her pregnancies, which, after a lull between Johnny and Miranda, had annoyingly started again-observed the group from the window of the Little Drawing-room, and agitatedly beckoned Vicky.

" I suppose it's all right—— ? " She lowered her voice to avoid being overheard by Dromore and their visitor.

" All right ? Whatever do you mean ? "

" I suppose Johnny can be trusted with the girls ? Lady Cullen would be terribly upset, if——"

" Really, Selina ! Your own son ! " A little guilty, because she knew she would not have ventured to say it to Dromore, Vicky flushed with indignation. " What do you accuse him of, now ? "

" I don't accuse," pouted Selina. " But considering all those dreadful people he has been mixing with——"

" I don't know much about sailors' society," said her sister-in-law stoutly, " but, from the little I know, I should say it's very unlikely to teach Johnny disrespect for his sister." They were going too far—much too far—with Johnny. Mamma was right ; this continual attitude of suspicion was enough to break the boy's temper.

Selina's mind would have been set at ease, if she had accompanied the three to the stream, where, knee-deep in grass, and relieved of the light basket saddle that carried Miranda, Falada peacefully suckled her foal—the grey velvet miniature of herself, that Emily overwhelmed with kisses and caresses as soon as it appeared, pressed shyly against its mother's quarters. Johnny proceeded to entertain the girls by wading into the stream and bringing out clumps of the big, wet king-cups, whose stalks he dried on his handkerchief before giving them to Miranda, who declared her intention of making a crown for Emily. The stalks were tough, and resisted her small, soft finger-nails.

" I could split them, if you lent me a knife," Emily offered.

" You might cut yourself," he said. " I'll do it."

" . . It's a bore ; it takes too long." Miranda stopped, smiling her apology at Emily. Recognising the formula for announcing that her hip was hurting, Johnny said :

" Why don't you lie down and have a nap, Winkle ? "

" Winkle ? Is that what they call you ? " Emily was gently amused.

" It's what Johnny calls me ; the others aren't allowed. We don't use it in front of people, generally," said Miranda, while Johnny went to get the thin Afghan rug which was folded in the saddle.

Emily helped him to spread it over the tussocks ; in doing so, their hands touched, and her eyes met Johnny's. They both smiled. It was as though the use of the little secret name, the act of tucking the child up and making her comfortable, had narrowed the gulf of shy politeness between them and banished their self-consciousness.

" *You* may call me Winkle, if you like," murmured Miranda, as she sank into the strong, resilient grass.

The heat was oppressive, and the sky had clouded over ; the dandelions and buttercups had become a shoal of yellow wafers, sown on dead green baize, as the meadow lost its satin gleam. The sky seemed darker, more solid than the earth, that gave off a rich, acrid scent, faintly anæsthetic.

"It's nice for Miranda, that you've come." He brought it out with an effort, for the sake of saying something.

"And for me too," she replied, in her polite, grown-up manner.

"Haven't you really got any parents?"

She shook her head.

"Are you the only one?"

"Mamma died when I was born"—she nodded—"and I lived with Papa until he died, some time last year."

He plucked at the grass, uncomfortably tender for her.

"It sounds—lonely."

Emily appeared to consider, before replying.

"So it does," she said, as though this had not struck her before. "I suppose one doesn't notice being alone very much, when one is used to it. I didn't really know Papa very well. He was almost always abroad, and I was left in London with my grandmother. She is very ill now," explained Emily. "I think she'll probably die too. That's why I'm staying with Lady Cullen. I like it very much," she concluded, as one who has at last made up her mind on an uncertain matter.

"Do you ride?" asked Johnny, searching for subjects away from the funerary theme.

"Only a little. Papa has taken me, once or twice, in the Row."

"It's a great hunting country——" he began, before remembering that he was not to hunt that season. He crimsoned, but she, apparently, had not noticed, when she replied:

"Oh, I don't ride well enough for that! Besides, I don't suppose we'll be here then. Lady Cullen is always in town, after the beginning of October."

"You'll have to meet my grandmother; she's a great person," he tried again.

"I think I have had enough of very old people, just for a while," said Emily reflectively. "I think young people are more interesting. Especially boys. I have never known any boys at all." Her delicate pronunciation gave the word an exotic flavour; as though "boys" were something rare and mysterious, yet to be added to her collection of human specimens.

"Well, there are three of us——" began Johnny: and made the odd discovery that he did not want Doss and Gilbert to know Emily Temple.

"Tell me about yourself." Instinctively she employed the all-time feminine gambit. "Miranda told me you had just come back from West Africa. Tell me about that," she commanded. Her lilac eyes embarrassed by flattering him with attention.

"There's not much to tell. One just went in a ship—and came back in a ship," he ended lamely; immediately afterwards regretting his inarticulacy. There were many things he might have told her—would tell her, when the chance came again: things that would have interested no one else, but which—he began dimly to perceive it—belonged to no one but

Emily. Strange light on coloured waters; the grey, pointed sail which was the fin of a shark; the iris of surf along a yellow beach—these needed a vocabulary, which he must discover before trying to describe them to her. "Tell me about yourself instead," he was inspired to ask her.

"Oh—it would take too long." All the same, she began. Her voice was very soft, and she shaped her words in a fastidious manner, as though they were sweet on her tongue.

"We lived in Paris when I was very small, and Papa was at the Embassy. We had a house on the avenue Gabrielle—do you know it?—just by the Champs Elysées."

He shook his head, feeling very rough and ignorant. All he knew of Paris was that "the Roans" went there often, and Aunt Venetia was always talking about the dress shops.

"My *tutu* used to take me in the gardens, and there was Punch and Judy, and little horses of wood that went round to a tune. There was a smell"—she paused to identify it—"a smell of coffee and lilacs. Sometimes we drove in the Bois. There was a Madame de Séguin, who was a friend of Papa's. . . . Once she came and visited us in London. I think she tried to persuade Papa to let us go back and live in Paris. I don't know why we didn't, because he was always saying London was so dull, and London people were not beautiful and witty, as Parisians are. He always made me speak French to him; he said it was the only civilised language, and Roman Catholicism the only civilised religion——"

"Are you a Roman Catholic?" To a Flood, this was startling. Roman Catholics—he had some indistinct recollection of a family legend—were supposed to have swindled them out of a fortune, some time in the last century. And, in evangelical circles, the Church of Rome was always the Scarlet Woman.

"No. But I might be, when I am older. We went once or twice to the Madeleine—that's the great church at the top of the rue Royale, you know. It was funny"—she laughed a little—"going to church and then coming out and sitting at little tables in the street, to eat *babas* and drink wine! I liked the robes the priests wore, and the smell of the incense. I was never allowed to go to church in England——"

"Haven't you been to church—the Protestant, I mean—at all?" This, to Dromore's son, was astounding.

"Once. My English nurse took me. She got into great trouble with Papa. I expect I shall go, though, now I'm living with Lady Cullen—shan't I? I suppose she keeps Sunday very strictly," said Emily with gravity.

"Oh—I expect so. Most people do."

She sighed.

"When Papa was at home, we were very gay on Sundays. People came and played cards, and sometimes there was music." All this was hardly less foreign than West Africa to one reared on Guerdon strictures in regard to Sabbath-keeping.

"You'll find our Sundays pretty dull," he warned her.

"Well, there's always reading, isn't there?" she consoled herself. "I will lend you some of my books, if you like. Most of them came out of Papa's library, so you won't find them too—womanish ! I am reading one now, called *Travels in the Himalayan Provinces of Hindustan and the Punjab* ; it's old, but it's very interesting. You will have to write about your travels some day," she told him graciously.

"Me ? Good lord, I couldn't write a line."

"*I'm* going to write books." Miranda, it appeared, was not asleep.

"What sort of books, Winkle ? " he teased her.

"Will you write novels ? " asked Emily seriously.

"I expect I shall do historical romances, like Sir Walter Scott. The Grim says my history is good—but I can't spell," admitted Miranda. She lifted her hand, palm upwards. "It's going to rain. I felt a spot. Do you like being out in the rain ? "

"You're the only one who's got an umbrella ! " Pointing smilingly at her hat, he felt suddenly very bold—daring to make fun of Emily Temple. "Come on, we'd better go before we're drowned. You're right, Winkle ; it's going to pour."

In confirmation of the statement, Falada lifted her head, stiffened her legs, and, showing teeth the greenish-gold of old ivory, went into the prolonged bray of a rain-apprehensive ass. They laughed, while Johnny lifted the basket into its place and strapped the girths. As he did so, the rain began to fall in large, heavy drops that dimpled the smooth stream and made a noise like pebbles on the broad flag-leaves.

Miranda set her teeth as he lifted her on to the donkey ; she never showed, if she could help it, how much it hurt to be lifted. If lifting had to be done, it had best be by Johnny, but she hoped they would not have to hurry ; it hurt badly, when Falada broke into her jerky trot.

"Let's make for the grotto ; the house is too far."

They stood in the rustic arbour, watching the rain advance in clouds across the meadows—" as though," said Emily, " someone was blowing smoke along the ground." They had taken the foal into shelter with them ; Falada stood with her head inside the grotto, shivering the water off the mossy stubble of her coat, as it dripped from the eaves.

"Are you very wet ? " Johnny asked Emily.

She did not seem to mind that the brim of her hat was dipping round her ears ; she had folded the front part back from her brow. She looked lovelier than ever, the strange shape adding quaintness to her small face. Miranda began to laugh.

"You look like somebody in a picture book : one of those French fisherwomen—or, perhaps, a nun——"

"There was a nun," began Emily, " a Prioress, named Madame Eglantine, who ever shyly smiled——" She stopped and blushed, as though conscious this was too personal.

"Go on," encouraged Miranda.

"Don't you know the *Canterbury Tales* ? "

"No." Supporting each other's ignorance, the young Floods stood sheepish before superior knowledge.

" Neither do," I said Emily disappointingly. " Only the children's version. The real one has queer words in it ; words no one uses any longer."

" I know some poetry," asserted Miranda. " I know :

> " ' Paddles none had Hiawatha,
> Paddles none he had or needed,
> For his thoughts as paddles served him
> And his wishes served to guide him. . . .' "

" I like that ! " Emily's eyes shone. " ' For his thoughts as paddles served him. . . .' " She turned to Johnny. " You say some poetry now."

He shook his head. He would not for the world have repeated the only words that came into his mind—a jingle Roan sang sometimes, in his pleasant tenor voice :

> " It's no matter what you do
> If your heart be only true,
> And his heart *was* true to Poll."

" The rain's stopped ! " cried Miranda. She leaned over to tap Falada's ears. " You big silly !—making so much fuss for only a shower."

The sun burned a sudden hole in the clouds over the elms which Emily had called oaks. The strange, dead pasture land broke into its customary glitter of green and gold, and began to give off steam from the heated soil.

" You'll get your feet awfully wet before we're on the drive." Johnny was lifting Miranda back into her saddle. " Why don't you get up behind Winkle ? Falada can easily carry the pair of you, if I shift this contraption a bit forward——"

" Oh—*bother*," he heard Miranda say. " It's Doss."

Dorset—of course. Arriving from the pools, upstream, with net and basket over his shoulder ; soaked garments adding, in some inexplicable fashion, to his splendour.

" Hallo. You do look a lot of drowned rats ! " His smile, lingering on Emily, exempted her from the unflattering description, and showed plainly his surprise and interest.

" It's Emily Temple—a friend of Miranda's," Johnny heard himself mumbling. It was like Doss—suddenly to appear, and steal to himself everybody's sunlight.

Dorset and Emily were looking at each other : his face brilliant with the charm that descended on it always when meeting a stranger ; hers bleached, set in its lines of childish beauty as though she looked upon the medusa. Only her eyes, which had widened excessively, were alive—with a life of which she seemed neither to be aware nor able to control : a clear, blank aliveness, like swiftly running water.

Suddenly aware that he was staring at her, Johnny dragged his eyes away. His brows gathered in a frown, he jerked at the straps on the donkey's harness.

She was putting out her hand and saying, " How do you do ? " as she had done to Johnny : but as if she would rather not, and had barely touched Dorset's brown fingers before she drew her own away.

" Confound the rain ! They were lying like the dead. I tickled an enormous fellow just now, up in the White Pool ! " His smile confidently claimed her admiration of his prowess.

" Pooh ! " Miranda, leaning from the saddle, poked up the lid of the basket. " They're not so *very* big ! "

" You'd have done better in my place, eh, Winkle ? " he teased her.

" And don't call me Winkle ! " she shouted.

For the rest of the journey to the house, Emily hardly spoke, except to answer " Yes " or " No " to direct questions, and Miranda allowed it to be scowlingly apparent to whom she ascribed the change in their gay companion. Dorset, it is needless to say, was unaffected by Emily's silence ; he liked shy girls—so long as they were pretty, well-mannered and impressed by his charms. With easy grace, as befitted the heir-apparent, he constituted himself cicerone to the party.

" We must show you round next time you come," he was saying, when they came face to face with an agitated group on the terrace. Miranda was snatched by the Grim and hurried into the house, Emily swept by Lady Cullen towards the waiting carriage. Dorset took himself indoors, and Johnny, left to unsaddle Falada and turn her loose in the paddock, whistled softly as he attacked the buckles.

" So that is how you look after your sister ! "

" What ? " Wrestling with Falada's girth—she had the playful trick of blowing herself out while she was being unsaddled—Johnny did not look up to observe the blackness in his father's face.

" No gentleman," stormed Dromore, " would have allowed those girls to get wet to the skin. Emily Temple—a visitor ! You act like a complete savage."

" What was I supposed to do ? Act like God : hold the rain off ?" A wiser man than Dromore would have sensed danger behind the flippancy.

Johnny straightened himself. He stood upright, his hands on his hips —like a groom, thought Dromore disgustedly : though any groom would have received a sharp reprimand for addressing him in so disrespectful a posture.

" Do you know who you are speaking to ? "

Johnny shrugged his shoulders. A sudden indifference to consequences combined with a sense of bitter injustice to make him insolent in his reply.

" Yes. But I was wondering if you did."

Dromore's lips trembled as he fought inwardly for self-control. His heavy, handsome profile presented a slight but distinct resemblance to that of the Prince Consort—which, in deference, to an already almost legendary hero, he chose to emphasise by the cultivation of short side whiskers. He sincerely aspired to be worthy of that " white flower of a blameless life " which the Laureate had conferred upon Albert, and he found it hard to forgive those who made the struggle difficult.

" Go to the library," he said, almost in a whisper.

Johnny shook his head.

" No."

" Do you defy me ? "

" Yes."

Dromore stood silent. His right fist clenched itself, as though to strike—and he saw Johnny sneer at him. The sneer undermined all the foundations of his personal dignity : there was something so adult, so distantly removed from the boy he thought he knew, in it. He knew he could easily overpower Johnny by brute force ; but to do so would add to his humiliation. The puniness of the boy's stature added—as it frequently did—to his resentment of Johnny's insubordination : that any Flood should be so physically unimpressive, so small, sparse and lacking in the qualities that command respect from less nobly endowed mortals, appeared an outrage. He stood aghast before the unchristian prejudice evoked in him by his youngest son.

" Have you gone out of your mind ? " he whispered—almost hoping it was true : that Johnny's experiences, or some mysterious devil entering into him, had turned his brain.

" No," said Johnny coolly. " But I'm not going to the library, and I'm not going to take any more thrashings from you. Not that they hurt much ! " He could not resist the taunt, which was not exactly truthful. Dromore was a muscular man, and had been an athlete in his youth. He thought of his work-up at the wheel. " I just don't hold with them ; that's all. You're beating me, not for my good, but for your own satisfaction. And I don't see any reason for giving you the fun of it any longer. Ever since I came home, you've treated me as if I was a criminal. I've done nothing —have I ?—except go away, for a few months, without your permission. I wasn't idling my time away ; I was slaving, most of it, like a navvy——"

" That is enough, John." His father's uplifted hand checked the outburst. Johnny lapsed into sullen silence, while Dromore struggled with the torment in his soul. At last—" It is evident you have gone beyond our discipline," he said heavily. " A bitter reflection for a father ! Well, you have made your bed, and you shall now lie on it. Since you have this craze for going to sea——"

Johnny's head came up with a jerk.

" Who says I want to go to sea ? "

Dromore gaped.

" Your Uncle Roan suggests we should send you into the navy ! "

Johnny's mouth twisted.

" That's very classical, isn't it, sir ? The eldest son for the estate, the second gets a commission in the Guards and the youngest serves Her Majesty's Navy ! By God, we Floods have come up in the world, haven't we ? " His sneer was a thin reflection of Dromore's.

Dromore stood speechless, as well he might. Johnny's tirade hit him in two spots : first by its irony, and second in its reminder of an evolutionary stage which Dromore, quite sincerely, had forgotten. For him, as for the rest of his generation, the tree started with the establishment of the family at Guerdon.

" Your manner," he said at last, " is singularly unbecoming. Your use of God's name, though common, I fear, to the kind of people with whom you have been mingling, shocks me deeply."

" I'm sorry." Johnny rubbed a hand confusedly over his forehead. " I didn't mean to swear. I don't want to be a sailor. I went to sea because it was the only way of getting to the Gold Coast——"

" Why? Why should you wish to visit West Africa ? '

" People want to see foreign places. . . . It's not unnatural, is it ? " he stammered.

" I fail to understand you."

" Considering our tie-up with the Coast, it seems plain enough to me." Suddenly calm, he faced his father.

" You seem to be under a curious misapprehension," said Dromore, after a pause. " Your great-grandfather, as you must know, came from the island of Barbados. There is no known record of his ever visiting the Coast."

" He got his plantation slaves from there, didn't he ? And *his* great-grandfather, the first Hercules, was a Bristol slaver. His uncle, Matthew——"

" I had no idea you had made so close a study of the family tree," sneered Dromore. " Your ancestor, Matthew Flood——"

" I know ; he was an Abolitionist. But the Abolitionists didn't bring it off, did they ? There was plenty of slaving after 1807—there's plenty now, if you want the truth of it—and, what's more, we lend ourselves to it. Blackbirding, it's called ; and it's not confined to the native kings——"

" You are not suggesting that you want to take your share in such abominations ? "

" I don't want to trade niggers, if that's what you mean, sir. But since the English took over the forts, there a lot to do out there, and it seems to be pretty hard to find people—the right people—to do it."

" And you think you qualify for the post ? I am afraid, my boy, that your nature is more deceitful than I had realised. I must admit that there have been moments, in the past, when your diffidence caused me some anxiety ; when it amounted almost to an unmanly shrinking from the assumption of your proper dues. This, it appears, was no more than a cloak for a conception of your own importance that far outsoars anything I had imagined ! "

" Well, there's nothing like experience for taking conceit out of a fellow." He came out with it bluntly : " Can I go to West Africa ? "

" The White Man's Grave ? Certainly not. Your mother would not hear of it." He straightened his shoulders ; the mantle of his own omnipotence, of which Johnny, for a brief while, had rudely bereft him, descended on them again. " Now understand me, John. There is to be no more of this romantic vapouring—the outcome, no doubt, of the tuppence coloured trash you read and of your careless interpretations of a record you would do well thoroughly to study, before basing your conduct on it. If you must emulate the exploits of your ancestors, let it be the worthier ones : not those which brought the blush of shame to the cheek of those who indulged them ! And if, for some inexplicable reason, you continue to interest yourself in the affairs of our West African colony, there is always the Foreign Office——"

" Civil Service ? I'd never pass the exams ! "

" That rests with yourself. We should have to find a tutor for you. You have already idled away the best part of a year——"

" A lot of idling we did in the *Aldebaran* ! " he was driven to retort.

"—and, unless you agree to enter the navy, you must make up for lost time at home." Turning on his heel, Dromore left Johnny to follow him, with the laggard step of the unwanted, into the house. In each was a sense of dull relief—not in the outcome of the conversation, which was far from satisfying—but in having brought the tension of the past weeks to some kind of a climax, although not without shame to both : for Johnny a barren triumph—he knew his father would never beat him again—for he had destroyed, with his desperate insolence, the habit of filial respect in which he had grown up, and the shards pricked him ; and for Dromore the pale consolation, at least, of knowing what was in his son's mind—though that indeed was baffling enough to murder sleep for nights to come ! On the act of defiance itself, Dromore did not choose to dwell ; there are sores it is wiser not to aggravate.

At dinner, the master of the house was sunk in a morose silence. The chatter of Selina and Vicky sounded thinly down the long board ; even Dorset was quiet, after a glance, with lifted eyebrows, to right and left ; he was an adept at taking the family temperature. A nasty, low fever, he diagnosed, having observed his father's lowering brow and the food he left on his plate, at the conclusion of each of the courses.

Gilbert, as usual, was too busy stuffing himself to be affected ; Johnny's appetite seemed normal. And Uncle Quentin—by God's grace, even Uncle Quentin, intent on sampling the last consignment of claret that had come up from the docks, spared them his usual reminiscent ramblings. Dorset sighed and settled down comfortably to duck and green peas. That little Temple girl was very pretty ; very shy, but very much of a lady. A presentable sample to produce on ceremonial occasions. Mamma must be persuaded to keep in close touch with the Cullens. . . .

John must be sent away as soon as possible, was the thought in Dromore's mind.

And, in Johnny's : I wonder if she caught cold, with being out in the rain. I wonder what made her behave so queerly, after Doss joined us. I wonder what sort of a girl she really is—not to fall, as all of them do, for Doss.

CHAPTER EIGHT

I

OF all the crosses Dromore Flood had to bear, Uncle Quentin was, without question, the heaviest.

After a lifetime spent in gadding about the globe, he had returned, a bachelor, some six months before the death of his brother Hercules, settled into Guerdon like a fledgling into its nest, and, unlike the fledgling, refused steadily to be dislodged. Harcourt and Roan in turn, prompted by Dromore, offered him temporary domicile, which he declined. For his own mysterious reasons, he liked Guerdon; it suited (he said) his old age. It also suited him to be occupying two of the principal chambers on the main gallery, to everyone's inconvenience (considering its size, Guerdon was singularly short of bedrooms) and Dromore's indignation. So indignant, in fact, was Dromore, that he went so far as to call a committee of his brothers, to discuss the raising of a family fund to set Uncle Quentin up in an establishment of his own.

"What for?" Harcourt was blunt about it. "The old boy isn't hard up, and you can't force him to live in a place he doesn't fancy."

"What do you want to get rid of him for, anyway?" asked Roan, with the indifference of the unaffected. "You can't pretend there's not plenty of room for him, since Mamma went to the Dower House."

"You know perfectly well why I wish to get rid of him." Dromore viewed his youngest brother with disfavour. "He is already beginning to have an undesirable effect on the young people." Dorset and Gilbert: at that moment about to commence their schooling at the hands of the local vicar—incumbent of the living turned down by Quentin in the past.

"I don't suppose he'll start them on the bottle yet awhile," said Roan, with gravity; and Harcourt:

"If you wanted him out, Drummy, you should have acted before now. Ten years' domicile gives right of way, you know."

So Uncle Quentin—blissfully unconscious of attempts to dislodge him—stayed on at Guerdon. He had lived past his rioting in foreign cities, and was content (so he said) to die at peace among his own people—who, with the exception of Harriet, for whom he showed marked affection, as well as respect, he appeared cordially to detest. He got so much fun out of baiting Dromore, however, that he was practically fond of him. He terrified Selina, though treating her, invariably, with an elaborate politeness. As a matter of fact, his manner to all women was perfection: a fine blend of old-fashioned gallantry with a dash of the gay dog which made Dromore's insistence on treating him as an *âme damnée*, and his assumption (in Uncle Quentin's presence) of the rôle of protector of feminine virtue more than a little ludicrous. Uncle Quentin loved it. His acceptance of Dromore as a licensed droll prettily rounded off the picture.

If Uncle Quentin flustered a few housemaids, or allowed himself too free a manner with some of the more elderly village matrons, it was as far as he went in these, his days of discretion. He liked best to spend his time in his own apartments, among his collections of books, documents, drawings and West African incunabulæ gleaned from other parts of the house.

Guerdon was rich in West African trophies; Matt had plastered the mansion from floor to ceiling with objects—a few valuable, the majority merely curious—whose proper place was in native huts, fetish houses and palaces of Negro justice. The effect, against Guerdon panelling, and under its diapered ceilings, was bizarre in the extreme. His son Hercules had been content to leave them there; Dromore, on succession, had made a clean sweep—from no æsthetic motives. A family which had found its way into Burke had no occasion for flaunting its mercantile origins. Besides, what had these oddities to do with Barbados? Matt's collection, actually, was an atavistic eccentricity; and, as an earnest Christian, Dromore felt the impropriety of living surrounded by the symbols—in some instances highly embarrassing—of heathen cults.

Uncle Quentin, swooping with glee upon the gems of the collection, bore them in triumph to his own quarters. A purist in his way, he rejected anything south-east of Benin; some remarkable stuff from the Cameroons, the Belgian Congo and the islands he left to his nephew, who had it conveyed to the attics—periodically raided by Vicky for her charitable raree-shows. Uncle Quentin sneered finely at the innocuous junk she selected as suitable to her rustic audience.

"Why don't you show 'em the masks? The necklaces made out of 'uman teeth? Old What's-his-name's household dummies?"

Vicky, who had her own ideas of what constituted amusement without vulgarity for the villagers, refused his offer of his finest piece—a ram's head pendant, *cire perdue* technique, and a Dahomey Protector of the House, which, in deference to his niece's modesty, he had thoughtfully put into a petunia silk overall of his own fashioning. Fully aware of what lay under the overall, she sucked in her cheeks to repress a giggle.

Alas, Uncle Quentin, in his eighties, was passing into the stage when conversation consists mainly of reminiscence of a repetitive character. Dorset and Gilbert, who could recite the history of the Fires of Bristol word for word before they were out of their petticoats, had the Slave Risings on Triton, Halifax and Foxley by heart, and could quote fluently from speeches made by the Barbados planters when arguing the proposals made by the British Government in reparation of damages sustained by the stoppage of their main labour supply—found him an old bore. Only Johnny perceived in Uncle Quentin the fascination of some rare and exotic plant, which continues ceaselessly to reward observation.

At a loss for other employment, he had got into the habit, since his return, of dropping in on the old gentleman in the big, stuffy room overlooking the side lawns, which had once been an important guest chamber and would now, according to Selina, take a quarter of a century of purification, before it was again fit for human occupancy. Neither welcoming nor the reverse, Uncle Quentin might, or might not, look up from his researches, leaving Johnny free to pursue such investigations as might be prompted by his surroundings.

"What d'you want to go to the Gold Coast for?" he mumbled, on one such occasion. "Nasty, unwholesome place. Fever, bugs an' mission'ries. No place for a gentleman."

"You've not been there yourself, have you, Uncle Quentin?" He said it wistfully.

"Good God, no." He appeared to be shocked by the suggestion. "No use for slummin'. Awful place; no s'ci'ty, no women, no *cuisine*! Y' know"—he swung his handsome old head heavily towards Johnny—"if you must go gaddin' abroad, you should go to Cuba and look up your culluh'd relatives."

"My—*what*?"

Uncle Quentin chuckled.

"Mean to say you don't know that What's-His-name—Matthew—married a nigger? I don't mean your grandfather." In talking of the past, Uncle Quentin was apt to slip a generation. Dorset, a specialist in genealogies, would have corrected him, Johnny was content to let it go. "I mean the Abolitionist fella—died eighteen-o-seven," brought out Uncle Quentin triumphantly; lost in the last three decades, he was clear as daylight on the first half of the century.

"Do you mean he really *married* a nigger?" This was incredible; leaning across the back of the chair beside Uncle Quentin's, Johnny held his breath.

"Bell, book an' candle—accordin' to the scriveners: though it took a fortune to prove it. Not a pop'lar subject with Drummy." He gave Drummy's son a conspiratorial wink. "Descendants out in Cuba now. Rich as Crœsus. Ought to go out there and get yerself a wife. I nearly did——" He heaved a sigh of regretful reminiscence; it was evident his mind was adrift down the alleys of the past.

"Strappin' fine gel. Touch of the tar-brush—funny, how it comes up, after all these gen'rations. Gives 'em something . . ."

His eye strayed vaguely towards the picture gallery which the young Floods accepted as "views" of the plantations. A faint wash, by an amateur hand, of a factory building, with a stream of negroes bearing the bundles of cane on their shoulders, was signed "Gabriel Flood"—Quentin's great-uncle, who had got himself killed in a plantation rising in Cuba, some time near the end of the last century. There were two or three handsome houses, of Palladian design, and some drawings, probably of coloured servants. These artless works were varied by photographs, mostly of the size known as *carte-de-visite*, of a galaxy of female charmers, languishing (by precept of Monsieur Daguerre, or of his disciples) against their backgrounds of plush and potted palms.

Johnny, who had never before gone closely into Uncle Quentin's beauty chorus, drifted over to look at them, conscious, as he met those pictured eyes, of a world beyond the small orbit of his own experience.

"Is she among these——?"

"That's her." Uncle Quentin, pointing, ignored the rules of grammar; adding, on an emotional note, "Had it done specially for me—Havana, 1855." He pronounced it Habanna.

"She's like us. She's got our eyebrows." There was something fascinating in identifying, in the faded portrait of a tall, full-bosomed girl, across the pale spread of whose crinoline poured a torrent of black hair, the features of one's own family.

"Got more than that. You wait till you've met those creoles, my boy. Not that they've all got Tana's advantages. Nigger, present tense, is a stink. Nigger, in the past—it's honey: sheer honey, like you get out of the heart of a bunch of calla lilies!"

"What did you say she was called?"

"Cayetana. Tana I called her, for short. Cayetana Rodríguez—a big sugar-growing fam'ly at San Juan de Remedios; they're all tied up with the Bonadventura de Lorchas—living like lords, like kings of the island!" He chuckled. "Makes you smile, when you see Drummy puttin' on airs about Guerdon! Guerdon! It's like a gatekeeper's lodge, beside the Rodríguez place at San Juan."

Rodríguez——?" Something stirred in Johnny's memory; he knitted his brows, trying to remember.

"One of 'em was in partnership, at one time, with my Da."

"What—in the plantations?"

The question had a curious effect on Uncle Quentin. An expression of caution, almost of cunning, came into his dark eyes, which stared irascibly at his great-nephew.

"Ain't you got anything better to do than hang 'round all day?" he demanded querulously. "Good God, at your age I'd have been across a horse, or I'd have had a fishin' rod in my hand, or I'd have been fishin'—in a diff'rent sort of water altogether!" he added, on his graceless chuckle.

"It's not much fun for me, having nothing to do," Johnny defended himself. "But, apart from the fact that I'm not allowed to do most things—I don't seem to be interested in the things I used to like before—before I went away."

Uncle Quentin snorted, but not unkindly. His attitude of toleration to the younger children, although strictly regulated by the amount of trouble they gave him, expanded into something like warmth for Johnny.

"You're growin' up—that's all. And damme if I see why there should be such a precious fuss about it." He rustled the papers before him impatiently. "Now then, be off. I've got more to do than sit gossipin' with you like a couple of old maids at a christ'nin'."

II

Moonlight lay across the landings. Through the open windows came the drip of trees and the indescribable scent of vegetation respiring after rain. There was no light under Uncle Quentin's door.

After a while, he ventured quietly to open it. The room, barred with moonlight, sealed against outer air, reeked of tobacco, of snuff, of spirits and of the curiously spiced contents of Uncle Quentin's treasure chests ; it was like going into a foreign country. And yet not foreign to Johnny Flood. It was as though he had known, from the beginning of time, that rich, organic aroma, with its vivid intimations of a life but briefly glimpsed, which was yet the background to all his imaginings.

He waited for a moment, getting his bearings in this strange room : this room which, even unoccupied, vibrated with the presence of its owner. Presently he sought for matches, found them, and, in some dread of disturbing Uncle Quentin, presumably asleep in his adjoining chamber, lit a lamp.

Holding it in his hand, he began cautiously to tiptoe round the room not sure of what he was seeking, but determined to find it. Covered by the soft, mocking eyes of Uncle Quentin's charmers, he passed slowly, attentively, by sheaves of native weapons and sunbursts of carven paddles ; by the longitudinal half-section of a Guineaman, glass-encased and realistically mounted on its foundation of sea-blue wax, with a foam of white cotton-wool round the hull ; by two or three cabinets, containing ivories and surmounted by a formidable array of teeth, polished and curved like scimitars. There was a horn through which, as children, they had delighted to blow, although no one could produce the long, hollow note that was drawn from it by Uncle Harcourt, on occasions when he condescended to demonstrate.

In a corner of the room stood the most grisly of the exhibits : a deep show-case, containing all the implements of the slave trade—chains, manacles, branding irons, speculum oris and so forth, which, to Dromore's disgust, Quentin had bid for, as it stood, in a local sale, and of which he avowed his intention of leaving it to Bristol museum. This, naturally, had been the boys' favourite ; Johnny himself had been as thrilled by it as by any specimen in the Chamber of Horrors at Madame Tussaud's. To-night, in the strange mixture of lamp and moonlight, he felt a recoil : as though the rusted iron gave up in the silence some of its burden of human anguish.

On the wall, above the show-case, were a number of framed diagrams which he had never troubled to examine closely, recognising them vaguely as " something to do with the slave trade."

He set the lamp down on a table, and lifted one of the frames cautiously from its hook, realising, as he did so, that the drawing under the glass was a cross-section of a trading vessel. Having carried it, and its companion prints, over to the light, he drew up a chair, and sat down to examine them in detail.

It was easy to see why they had not particularly interested him ; to the casual glance they might have been sarcophagi, covered with a close design similar to those found on Egyptian papyrus. The " sarcophagus " proved, however, appropriately enough, to be a slave ship, and the " design " a series of rows of diminutive human figures, reduced to a formula, placed transversely in close alignment within the periphery of the hull. Slaves, naturally. Diagram of stowage of cargo—phew. Each man, flat on his back, touched his neighbour on either side. A narrow, central passage, corresponding to the keelson, was filled with figures placed longitudinally, touched on either side by the feet of the transverse bodies. In order that no space should be wasted, the rounded end of this monstrous, mass coffin was utilised for the irregular disposal of a group which, no doubt, had to find its own arrangements for limbs forced out of their natural positions by the conformation of the timbers. Two decks and two quarter-decks were occupied with this cargo, as was plainly shown in the long section accompanying the cross one.

Twelve months ago, the diagram would have been a diagram and little more, to Johnny Flood: holding some documentary interest, but "historical," and therefore impersonal. Since then, he had sweated under tropical sun; had known the innumerable discomforts of life afloat, although free to enjoy its pleasures. Reared in conventional horror of the slave trade, he had never felt *in himself*, like the turn of a screw, the agony and degradation of the human body condemned to its tortures.

Now, however, it all came back; the intolerable stench of the bilge, simmering under tropical heat, the loathsome effluvia of human flesh, even in the case of men at liberty to avail themselves of such cleanliness as their quarters afforded, and the obscene smell of the vermin swarming between decks. He too had known—for a few hours only—the galling of irons, worn by slaves, sometimes, throughout a voyage; and the rats would smell that blood, and crawl over bodies to get at it. In the oven of the holds, human creatures would die of suffocation, their last agonies augmented by the cockroaches fastening on their feet and hands. He found himself sweating, as, with his face twisted in an unconscious grimace, he bent over the next diagram, which, but for the outline being longer, and fully a sixth narrower, was identical with its companion.

Inspection showed, however, that the arrangement of the "design" was different. In profile, instead of flat, the figures lay in a double row, transversely down the hull. Round the hull itself ran a thin, continuous chain, head to foot, touched by the transverse ones. Four decks there seemed to be, not two, in this precious vessel, and a faint pencil note in the corner of the sheet stated: "Arrow, R. & P. Accommodation, with false deck or grid—447." At the foot, in another handwriting: "1837-38 Texas—15,000:" obviously a later addition.

He tiptoed from the room and stood for a moment on the gallery, his heart thudding. The old house whispered about him and he felt the sweat gathering in the palms of his hands. There was something, slipping down the generations—slipping towards him, Johnny Flood: panic-stricken, he turned and fled from it. His bare feet padded along the carpet, carried him into the labyrinth of little staircases and passages of the upper storey: past closed doors, whose sunken thresholds let out on him the creak of wire mattresses, snores from the servants' bedrooms: rushed him to the low door on to the leads. Still in flight from the inapprehensible, he scaled the tiles and gained, at last, the roof-ridge, where he sat astride, gasping, and looking down on the strange, moonlit design of Guerdon: the terrace and lawns, the formal gardens to right and left of the house, the great sweep of the avenue crossing the park and ending at the high roads, drawn like white ribbons north and south of the wide demesne.

Slowly his panic passed, his breaths grew even, and his brain resumed control of the wild, unreasoning emotion which a few moments before had governed him. Slowly, like a plant that shoots forth its buds, grew in Johnny that motive, half-romantic, half-practical, but wholly serious, that was to shape his future. Hazily, with no distinct perception of the form it was to take, the idea of atonement was born in him : not that he had yet found the name for it. Somebody, some day, had got to pay for that outrage on human flesh and blood for which his forefathers had been responsible. Somebody . . . perhaps himself.

III

To his friend Penderel Gannet, who came galloping from Frenchay as soon as he heard Johnny was at home, and was loud in condemnation of " this awful bally rot of your guv'nor's—not letting you come and stop with us ! " he had been at first communicative, and then shut up like a clam.

A sudden gulf had yawned between him and people of his own age with whom, previously, he had been friendly. They were still friendly—something more than that. Whatever might be the attitude of parents, terrified of such example to their offspring, the young folk were prepared (outside his own family) to accept Johnny Flood as a hero. But he would have none of it. The rôle of demi-god, freely offered, embarrassed him ; he felt a fool in it.

Perhaps he had been a fool, to reject Dromore's offer of the navy? Perhaps a few sharp years of sea discipline would have helped to bridge the gap of which, without analysing it, he was constantly aware, between himself and his contemporaries. He had come back—a misfit : faced at every turn by his inability to adapt himself to the interests and the ways of thinking common to the society in which he had been raised.

Separate and lonely, he saw little of the family, save of Harriet and Miranda. Sometimes Emily Temple was there. Shy as he was of visiting the schoolroom, as the rather sordid parlour where Miranda did her lessons was called, or of intruding on the girls' society, they made him welcome. A little scornful, he would sometimes share in their occupations. Although six years the elder, Emily was charming with Miranda, and was adored by her ; she had brought into the crude matter-of-factness of the schoolroom routine something delicate and fantastical, the product of her own nature, and the very different character of her own education. And she, on her part, had begun to shed something of her own over-serious air, to join in Miranda's games, to capture the spirit of a childhood she had never known.

It was Emily who drew from him, gradually, tales that delighted them both—tales of his adventure : innocent enough, yet thrilling to the girls.

Innocent as they were, these tales were responsible, one day, for a scene in the schoolroom.

Thinking, from the silence within, that the room was empty, and in search of a jacknife he had mislaid, Johnny walked straight in : to find his sister sitting alone on a stool which, from time immemorial, had been associated with nursery punishments. He could not withhold laughter from her glowering little face and her air of black resentment. Enraged by the laughter, Miranda dragged her lips back from her teeth in a villainous grimace, stuck out her tongue and ended by spitting at him.

" You little—vixen ! I'll box your ears if you do that again ! "

" Stop grinning then ! " snarled Miranda. Hunched like a witch, she bent sideways, to relieve her hip. " Pig—swine—camel ! " she added, with the evident intent of making her attitude clear.

" What the dickens is up with you ? "

" If you want to know, I'm being punished," she mumbled, through the tangle of her unplaited hair.

" What for ? And where's Emily ? "

" I told her to go to—Jericho ! "

" Did you, then. And, for the love of snakes, how've you got yourself in such a filthy mess ? "

The front of Miranda's checked pinafore was streaked with black from chest to hem ; she appeared to be wearing a black breast-plate. Her hands were black, and so were her sleeves ; there were smears of black on the side of her face.

Without answering, her sullen eyes went to the schoolroom sofa, whereon sat a row of objects that again brought laughter whooping out of Johnny : Miranda's nine dolls, their faces painted with a streaky jet, and more than a trace of the altered pigmentation on the frills and flounces of their petticoats.

" Oh, life ! oh, lord ! What a set of freaks ! "

Miranda burst into a loud roar, which Johnny interrupted by snatching her up and setting her on his knee.

" *Shut up*, for pity's sake ; they'll hear you in the yard ! What on earth have you got on you ? You're all sticky, you little beast ! "

" Boot-blacking. I got sick of their silly pink faces. So I made them into niggers. I can do as I like with them, can't I ? They're *my* dolls ! " howled the descendant of slavers.

" You've made a filthy mess, and they're not a bit like niggers, if you want to know."

" Aren't they ? " Startled into self-control, Miranda gaped, crestfallen. " But look : I rubbed the blacking all over them, even in their hair ! It's a bit sticky now, but it won't be, when it's dry. Won't they be like niggers then ? "

" No, not much." He suppressed another gurgle, out of kindness to the artist.

" Damn," said Miranda calmly : an expression she had learned from Uncle Quentin, but was wise enough to suppress in adult company.

" Is that what you and Emily quarrelled about ? "

" Oh—pooh. *Emily*—— ! " There was evidently more in the matter than the dolls.

" Now, chuck it, Winkle. What's Emily done ? I suppose she guffawed, like I did, at those nine sights ? "

" No, she didn't, then ! I did them after she went."

" Went where ? "

She wriggled off his knee, limped over to the window, and, planting her elbows on the sill, glared over the roofs of the stables.

" I wish Doss would keep away. He never comes when I'm by myself. He spoils everything."

" What's Doss got to do with it ? " His voice tightened.

" Everything. Emily hates him."

" Does she say so ? " he asked quickly.

" No. But she goes all different when he's here. She hardly speaks, and there's no fun in her any longer. She might as well be deaf and dumb as go on in that silly way ! " was the scornful reply.

" I'll tell you what." Johnny had an inspiration. " Next time she comes, we'll take her to see Grandmamma. She'll like the Dower House ; and we can show her the pigeons, and Grandmamma's little temple on the lawn."

Miranda snorted.

" Pooh ! He's taken her."

" Who—when ? "

" Doss—just now. We'd settled down to play Native Villages, and in he comes. ' Oh, Emily, you've not seen the Dower House, have you ? Come along, I'll take you down in the dog-cart.' *Dog*-cart ! To go to the *Dower* House ! Just showing off—because Papa said he could take the new mare out——"

" But she went—did she ? " said Johnny bitterly.

" Oh, she pretended she didn't want to leave me by myself," sneered Miranda.

" How do you know it was pretending ? If she didn't want to go with Doss, she'd got to find some excuse."

As long as he could remember, the Dower House and Harriet herself had been his, in a way he had never attempted to define. Even at parties, when all the children were there, all, apparently on equal terms, he had that secret sense of security and privilege, as though the others were visitors and he the son of the house. Harriet contrived to give him this in a look, in a touch, in a dozen small ways that amounted to a secret code between herself and her grandson. And he felt he could not forgive Dorset his treachery.

Miranda was there, pushing herself against his side.

" Emily's awfully silly. She'd much sooner have gone with you. But when Doss is here she's just like a silly, hypnotised rabbit ; she does whatever he tells her."

" Who cares ? " He pushed her aside and slouched over to the row of staring dolls. " Do you really want these things black ? "

"Why, yes." She accepted, with apparent relief, the reversion to the original subject. "I mean to get Emily to help me. I want a native village, like you told us about, with huts and a—what do you call it?—a fetish house, and everything. And that fool Maud"—she indicated, contemptuously, the most imposing of the transmogrified beauties—"can be the lady witch doctor and the others are just wives. I'm the chief," she announced, with decision.

"Well—I dare say I can fix it. I saw a can of black paint they've been touching up your chair with, this morning, in the coach house. I don't know what you'll do about the hair—unless you knit some sort of a woollen wig——"

"Polly Bowling can do that!" cried Miranda, delightedly. "She's awfully good at knitting. I'll tell her, next time she comes up to the House. Oh, Johnny, thank you; it's a marvellous idea."

"And I should think you'd better wash yourself," he advised, as he scooped the viscous collection under his arm.

"Oh, I can't do that." She shrugged her shoulders. "I've got to learn 'Almighty God, thy piercing eye,' for Aunt Vicky, before I have my tea. . . . I wonder," she reflected, "what Almighty God's piercing eye makes of those dolls."

"I'd like to know what it makes of you," retorted Johnny as he shut the door behind him.

So that was it again. Just as, in their childhood, Dorset had managed, in the most casual way, to gather all the attention and all the interest of strangers to himself, so, now, he was preparing to conquer Emily. Struggling for loyalty, Johnny told himself it was not done deliberately; Doss could not help being handsome and gay, and having all the qualities that attracted people, and made them—even grown-up people, like Papa, and Sir Maxwell Gannet, and Uncle Quentin—want to please him. I am just the same as the rest, he reminded himself; I get so mad with Doss, sometimes, I could almost kill him; then he says something, or does something, or looks in some way, that makes me ashamed of myself, and I'd just turn myself inside out, to get a smile from him!

And yet . . . Emily. Why should she be expected to be immune: she, a member of that sex which, already, showed itself weak as water, where Doss was concerned? And yet, foolishly, one had expected, or at least, hoped for it. One did not ordinarily make friends with girls, unless they were the tomboy kind, like Penderel's sisters, who, but for their skirts and flapping hair, might be a couple of fellows! And, to have found such a friendship possible surely argued something above the common in the one who inspired it? It hurt, in a stinging, unaccustomed way, to find Emily just one of the foolish majority.

For the next hour, squatting in the coach house, he tried, like Miranda, to forget the bitterness of first betrayal in transforming the sticky complexions of nine erstwhile waxen beauties with the help of a tin of Aspinall's black enamel paint.

CHAPTER NINE

I

SHORTLY before the end of the summer holidays, when the elder boys were gloomily contemplating their return respectively, to Harrow and Winchester, and Johnny was wondering when his own fate was to be decided, Flood and Company held one of its monthly Board Meetings which, as Roan said, no civilised being would call at a time when all presentable society was in Scotland, at the seaside, or bracing itself in continental spas for the serious demands of the hunting season.

He did not, however, allow his grumbles to keep him from his duty. Venetia was quite happy catching salmon ; Roan, an essential Londoner, always a little *dépaysé* out of hearing of Piccadilly traffic, arranged to combine a couple of nights at his deserted club with popping over to Bristol to humour old Hacky—who, of course, would as soon think of setting fire to a pile of banknotes on College Green, as of allowing his pleasures to interfere with a Board Meeting !

Old Hacky, it appeared, was in need of humouring. Roan was not the only one tactfully to conceal surprise at the Chairman's tetchiness, the vicious way in which, on a couple of occasions, he over-rode his fellow directors. Roan marked, without comment, the unhealthiness of his brother's appearance. The leaden colour, the pouched eye and smouldering ill-temper were ascribed by the majority to a hang-over from the previous night. But with whom had Hacky been drinking ? He had left the club early : earlier than was his custom. He had been seen in none of his usual haunts, had accepted invitations from none of his cronies.

Roan was none too bland, for him, either. Dromore's invitation—amounting to a command—had been handed to him on his arrival in Queen Square. He showed it vexedly to Harcourt, before the meeting.

" What's all this about ? Confound the fella, I had arranged to dine in town."

" In *London*, I suppose you mean," snarled Harcourt, to whom, as all his acquaintances knew, the sobriquet for the capital was anathema. To Harcourt, Bristol was " town ; " he damned the impudence of those who conformed to snobbish custom.

" My dear fella ! To everyone I know, with the exception of yourself, ' town ' means London." Roan cocked a quizzical and slightly irritated eyebrow.

" Then you've got a poor ring of acquaintances," snapped his brother.

" Well, what's it mean ? Drummy and I saw each other on Mamma's birthday. What's he been churning up since then ? "

" Don't bother me," muttered Harcourt. " I've got more on my mind this morning than Drummy's fiddle-faddle." He broke off as someone came into the room, and lumbered away to wash his hands—actually as well as metaphorically—of Guerdon's intrusions upon the firm's business. "All the same," he turned at the door to add, "you'd better be there." And slammed the door on Roan's sudden look of surprise and annoyance.

Harcourt had had a blow. A blow in his self-esteem—which is the tenderest part in the make-up of a cold, proud Flood.

He would have had nothing further to do with her, but for the boy.

A coarse, hearty creature, who had caught him briefly in the net of animal desire—her own as much as his—she was as much taken aback as he was himself, when it appeared that the moment of self-indulgence had to be paid for. Concealing his annoyance, he told her shortly that she would be looked after, and set her mind at rest on a matter that was fretting it: she should not have to go crawling to the Samaritans, or ring the night bell of the "Temporary Home" in Southwell Street; after the child was born, she could either put it out to nurse or look after it herself—he would see to the payments. And he would see she got her job back again, as chambermaid at the Royal.

Kitty behaved well; he had no intention of denying it. Free and easy with all, she in no way altered her public manner to him. Meeting him, she would wag him a cheerful "Good day, sir," with nothing whatever in her demeanour to suggest former intimacies; no airs of privilege, and no hint of dissatisfaction or of attempt to claim more than was in their bargain. The few shillings she had named as adequate for her purpose reached her each week through an agency he knew he could depend on; he took it for granted she would let him know if they were insufficient. No, no one could call Kitty a grasper.

And it was at least four years before he knew that she had borne him a boy.

The shock of his first meeting with Kitty Prior's lad remained vividly in his memory: Kitty drooling along Wine Street, with a shopping net on her arm, and the boy rolling his hoop in the gutter. Mechanically tipping his hat-brim to Kitty, Harcourt did not notice the child, until she turned round and called out sharply, "Here, Joe: take off your cap to Mr. Flood."

The urchin caught his hoop, stopped astride the causeway and pavement, and, clutching his cap, brought it off with a jerk that left his red head—the colour of Kitty's—aflame with short, upstanding hair. He was big for his age, and sturdy as a little oak tree; he had a benevolent grin and a pair of light, intelligent eyes. Kitty caught Harcourt's eye, and she winked: her one and only gesture of complicity in all their years of acquaintance. Harcourt thought, "Great God: this is my son."

The girls were coming in from their walk with the governess on Brandon Hill: Mary, as usual, nervously dodging her father's eye, and Bell, the younger and bolder, sniffling with the beginning of one of her recurrent colds; both of them sallow and lanky, without that indefinable something which is in children who grow up in the glow of parental affection. He stared at them without pity. By the contrariety of fate, Kitty Prior had given him a son who had no claim on him in law: while these two dismal moppets were the lawful fruit of his loins. A bitter thing, for a man with ambition.

Little Joe Prior benefited, during the next few years, from his natural father's solicitude. He showed all the aptitude and quickness for which such children are frequently notable. Taken from the National school, where he squeaked and pullulated in an ant-heap of similar little maggots, and sent to the school endowed by his (unadmitted) great-grandfather, he proved a bright boy, at work and at play. Hearing, by chance, that his mother was going to cut short Joe's schooling, and make him into a page at the Royal, Harcourt, after some sour soul-searching, intervened. Twelve months later, he was an office boy in Queen Square, shaping to be a junior clerk. No one connected the bright youngster with the Chairman ; if they had done, Harcourt would not have cared. Joe Prior certainly had no preferential treatment ; and if he got into less scrapes than other office boys, it was probably because he managed to behave himself.

Then Harcourt met Kitty—at the opening of the Industrial Exhibition, down on that piece of ground between the Old Drawbridge and the Harbour which had been reclaimed and covered over, and was seized upon by the promoters of the Exhibition and utilised while the Council haggled over its ultimate purpose. There was Kitty, all dressed up, among the fine folks who, paying five shillings for the privilege of exclusivity, strolled to the strains of Sousa under the looped bunting of opening day. Amused to find her there, he wondered if Kitty had backed a winner ; she sometimes got tips from her customers at the Royal.

" I'd like to have a word with you." She had looked round cautiously, to see if anyone was noticing, before she caught his attention.

She had never asked such a thing of him before. Because of the boy, Harcourt asked :

" Where ? "

" You'd better come to my place. There's nobody in on Saturday afternoons."

He noted her choice of day and time—both, fortunately, convenient to him—and wondered if she had left the Royal. She gave him a little nod of confirmation and walked briskly away ; her gown fitting her broad back smartly, and springing into a lavish bell below her tightened waist. She held up the train with a quirk of her little finger—quite the woman of fashion ! He would tease her about it.

" The fact is," she told him, when they sat together in a small, dark room which he supposed was her parlour, " I'm going to get married."

" You are ? I'm glad to hear it." He was thinking that Kitty, for all her hard work, had worn well. Her coarse hair had greyed at the temples and her high, plump cheekbones were netted with little purple veins ; but there was still about her plenty of the vitality which had tempted him in the first place. But for a falling-in about the mouth, due to loss of teeth, she could have passed for less than her age—of which he had no idea. " I thought there must be something in the air, when I saw you the other day."

" What—me among the nobs ? " She laughed, taking no offence. " I thought you'd wonder where I'd got the five bob from! Waste, wasn't it, when I could've got in next day for a shilling. Well, it's nice, to be a bit wasteful, for once."

He had the grace to feel ashamed that he had done nothing, ever, to enable her to be wasteful.

"Who's the lucky fellow?"

"Well, now, that's what I was coming to." She bridled a little, coyness sitting oddly on her hard, middle-aged face. "He's from Chicago; now what do you think of that?"

"So Bristol men aren't good enough for you?" he quizzed her.

"Bristol men don't hold with the parson and ring," she retorted.

"Yankees are supposed to be rolling in money, but I see he hasn't given you a ring yet." He paid her back for her cut at him.

"Well, to tell you the truth, I've not said I'd marry him—not yet," confessed Kitty; her big face had coloured. "You see, there's Joe."

"Where does he come into it?" Despite himself, a note of possession, a note of self-interest, quickened in Harcourt's tone.

"He comes into it like this. If I marry this chap—this Eph—I've got to go and live in Chicago."

Don't be a fool, he warned himself. He waited, before saying cautiously: "Well? America's the country of opportunity: so they say. What's wrong with that?"

"Nothing for me. But I don't want Joe to grow up a Yankee. I'm Bristol born and bred, and to me there's no place in the world like Bristol," said Kitty softly. His heart warmed to her. "I don't want to take Joe out there, and have him forget—all that." She lifted her ugly, work-worn hand to point to the window: to the slender spire of the Redcliff, and the glimpse of the Harbour, with its shipping, which was visible from where they sat. Behind them was the jangle and clatter of the railway; several times, while they sat talking, the rumble of a passing train had made the squalid little room vibrate. "Besides—I don't think Eph understands Joe; it seems like he's not like American boys——"

God forbid. "What do you want me to do?" For all his resolution to do nothing beyond the narrow bounds he had set for his natural son, the words were torn from him.

For a moment, she evaded the question.

"It would be grand, marrying Eph." It was as though she spoke to herself, rather than to him. "His people are well off. They've got a house with a real fixed bath in it—like at the Royal: just think of that! They keep a carriage and two horses—I bet you can't fancy me in a carriage of my own!" There was a note of appeal in her laughter, as though she were hoping he could imagine her in it. Harcourt scowled: a braggart, of course, like all Yankees. She'd probably find herself living in a shack in the fifteenth precinct, with a saloon on one side and a bawdy-house on the other; he had visited Chicago.

"I tell him he's soft. Fancy choosing an old bag like me, when he could take his pick—with all that money!"

Her humility annoyed him ; it was out of place in the woman he had favoured, the mother of his son !

" He knows his own mind, I suppose. I take it he's not a youngster ? "

" Oh, no. Eph's been married before—if it comes to that. She died : poor thing. Eph says the sanitation out there's something shocking. That's another thing ; I wouldn't want to take Joe where he might get sick——"

" I'll keep my eye on Joe." The words were spoken before he had time to weigh their implication.

" That's what I was hoping you would say," she said simply. " It's not I want to part with him, but the work's getting too much for me. My legs are in a proper state." He forestalled, with a gesture of horror, a movement she made as though to raise her skirt for his benefit. " I reckon I've earned a bit of peace, over the last fourteen years ! " She looked him in the eye and he accepted her meaning. All the same :

" I hope you get it," he told her sardonically. " You're going to a queer place for it."

" So far as I'm concerned, peace means a place of your own and somebody to keep you," she took him up on a note of sharpness. " Now, see here —sir." The respectful address came oddly, as though against her will, on the top of her forthright manner. " It won't be long before Joe's old enough to look after himself. I tried to make Eph see that, but there was no making him. He's made up his mind he's not going to wait. He's set his mind on an English wife, and if it's not me, it'll be somebody else. I know who it'll be, too "—her lips tightened into a line of vicious resistance—" and she's not got a boy to bring up, or a pair of old crocks under her like these." She pushed a foot out from the hem of her skirt, and, although he looked quickly away, he had been obliged to see the swollen, misshapen extremity which pushed, with its carbuncles, against the new leather of her shoe.

" I'd have to give up working sooner or later, and who's going to keep me ? Joe ? Not if I know it ! " she asserted. " A boy's got enough to do to keep himself. And I don't want charity, either."

Harcourt, who had lifted his head quickly, mumbled :

" Wait till it's offered."

She tossed her head.

" I'm not one of them that holds with waiting. Go and get it, if you want it : that's my motto," was her tart rejoinder.

" Even when it means getting more than you wanted ! " Harcourt, who liked people to stand up to him, threw the dubious jest at her with a wink, and was rewarded by her roar of laughter.

" There's one thing they can always say about you "—she leaned over to slap his thigh with the palm of her hand—" You're never short for a bit of fun ! As good as ever you were, aren't you ? " Her fingers, which had lingered, kneaded his muscle inquisitively. " You old—— ! "

" That's enough ; behave yourself." Dealing in familiarities when it pleased him, he would brook them from no one—certainly no person in Kitty Prior's position. " Where'll he live ? " he interrupted her, as she began to stammer an apology.

"I'll fix him up a lodging. There's the wife of one of the waiters; she's got a boy of her own. Joe and him could share—it's not like a grown-up person, that wants a room to himself."

He wanted to say, "Send him to Berkeley Square," and knew the folly of it. I might as well advertise to the whole of Bristol that he's my son, thought Harcourt bitterly; and remembered the numerous bastard Floods who flourished round and about Guerdon, none the worse, apparently, for being ignored by their fathers. Where would Joe fit in Berkeley Square? In some closet in the basement. Mary and Bell in their spacious first-floor chamber, ringing a bell for all their needs, while their brother—their brother, by God!—ate his meals with servants and slept on a groom's pallet. That would not do.

"Fix where he's to live, and I'll see to the rest," he told her shortly.

The compact was vividly in his mind, on the afternoon when Harriet infuriated him by suggesting he should take Johnny into the office.

Much as he cared for her, he knew he could never forgive or forget her attempt to foist Johnny on him in place of the son he had never, so far as she knew, begotten. Each time he saw a red head bent diligently over a ledger, or passing cockily under his window, he remembered it.

Everyone in the office liked Joe Prior. For all his youth, and his inevitable, boyish love of mischief, he was a steady lad, a lad of goodwill and of decent respect to his betters. He never "gave lip," as some of the boys and younger clerks did, to their seniors, when reproved of misdoing. Was this Kitty's training? Harcourt preferred to put it down to his own share in the boy's breeding. Joe was bold, independent, well-mannered; he had looks, too, of an unassuming sort—his mother's healthy frame and high colouring translated into terms suitable to a boy fourteen years old.

Harcourt had to be careful; he had to take pains not in any way to betray a greater interest in Joe than in the rest of the young office staff. But he had eyes in the back of his head and his ear to the ground; no tremor of the office grape-vine ever escaped him. And he was sorely put to it, on an occasion when Dromore patronised Queen Square with one of his infrequent appearances, not to point to Joe Prior, and say—"How's that, beside your phenomenal Dorset?" Not that Dromore would have admitted the lad's superiority; but it would have been fun to shake Drummy's vanity, in being the only one of the three of them to enrich the family with sons.

On the evening Harriet left him, he had taken a vow never, in any circumstances, to take any of his brother's children into the firm. He had always resolved not to do so—although feeling that, owing to Dromore's objection to "trade," the question was unlikely to arise. He now took the vow formally, phrasing it to himself: There shall never be a legitimate Flood to jeopardise the chances of young Joe, if any offer, under his father's roof.

Supposing the boys, working together, were to run neck to neck for promotion: the coveted appointment was bound to go to Johnny. Public opinion would force it. To award it otherwise would be to start a tornado of whispering, and resentment among some of the older members of the staff, who would rather accept a young Flood as their equal (and perhaps, in time, their superior) than a popular but unaccounted-for newcomer. Floods had always run on tradition. Kitty Prior's bastard was accepted on his own merits, but when it came to putting him in authority, over a Flood—there would be another tale to tell. Whereas, without Johnny there, to crowd him, Joe might, with industry, rise in time to a position of importance on the staff.

II

It was Joe himself who, as usual, brought the morning's mail in, and laid it on the Chairman's desk. If Harcourt was busy, or was talking to one of the clerks, he might tell Joe to slit the envelope ; this gave Harcourt an opportunity of watching him. He got a bitter kind of pleasure out of the lad's look of cleanliness and health, the clearness of his skin, the impudent flame of his hair.

The narrow ivory blade slid between the fold and the gum, and Joe laid each envelope, as he slit it, on the Chairman's blotting-pad. When he had done the last one, he went out of the room.

Harcourt's eye lit on the top of the pile : a cheap, common envelope, an illiterate hand. He knew that kind of cover ; people in his position got plenty of them—anonymous abuse, whines for charity ; the first, in his case, predominating. There were few naïve enough to ask alms from the Chairman of Floods. A generous giver to organised charities, he let it be known he had no time to spare in investigating private claims. He would, however, advise the writer, if persuaded of the authenticity of the appeal, where to apply for the needed help.

He sneered as he picked it up. What this time ? A threat of personal violence for some obscure grudge cherished by the writer ? An attempt at blackmail, on account of some imaginary sharp practice in his business affairs ? A sheet—often illustrated—of obscene abuse ? He had been advised to pass such things on to the police ; despising, he dropped them in the waste-box, for the delectation of any who cared to read them. There was no better way of advertising his inviolability to his enemies.

He read it twice, before his mind took in fully the message it contained :

> " Fancy you being fool enough to let them clap the horns on you ! Joe Prior no more your son than the Pope of Romes. Ask his mother about the commercial chap that stopped at the Royal in Agricultural Show week, 1875.
>
> " A Well Wisher."

. . . Kitty was in Chicago—or on her way there—safe from questioning. Joe came in, with a parcel.

" Where will you have it, sir ? "

" When were you born ? "

" In—in eight—eighteen hundred and seventy-six, sir ! " Joe showed his astonishment in his stutter.

" I mean the date, boy ! " Harcourt hammered at him.

A sudden bright flame ran up the boy's cheek.

" I—I'm not sure, sir. Mother didn't remember." His voice was low with shame.

Not remember the date her son—*his* son—was born ! Yes, she'd fooled him prettily—*the bitch* ! It was common knowledge, among the Royal's patrons, that the red-haired chambermaid was an " easy " one. He sat there, dumb before his own simplicity in accepting her story. Yet——

" Surely you've got your birth certificate ? " he insisted. " Where were you christened ? "

" I don't know, sir." The boy was now miserably embarrassed.

" But you were born in Bristol ? "

" I don't think I was, sir," he stammered. " I've heard my mother speak about going to some relatives—out in the country——"

" I suppose you were baptized ? "

" Oh, yes, sir."

" Have you been confirmed ? "

" Yes, sir ; while I was at school."

Then surely at the school——?

Joe had been his nominee—one of three each adult member of the family had power to nominate annually. Under his ægis it would be a simple matter for Kitty to fill up the entrance form—which he remembered giving to her signed, but not completed—with any fiction she chose. The governors were not likely to question any statement that came to them with Harcourt Flood's signature at its foot. Sometime, out of curiosity, he would ask to see the record. For the present . . .

What had anyone to gain by planting a falsehood on him ? He had betrayed to no human soul his interest in Joe ; no one, to his knowledge, had suffered by Joe's appointment to his humble position in the office. It was an act of pure malice, on the part of someone who knew—*the truth.* Who, moreover, had been mocking him for the partiality he believed he had concealed.

" Do you want me, sir, or shall I go ? " He had no idea how long he had sat there, silent, until an unsteady voice recalled him to the present.

He looked up heavily. The boy stood there, holding himself stiffly, like a soldier on parade, but with the colour drained from his cheeks, and a look of tense perplexity in his eyes ; aware that something was gravely wrong, but transparently unable to imagine what it was. Harcourt looked at him for a long time, before holding the dingy page out to him, across the desk.

" Read that."

". . . Am I . . . your . . . son ? " Half-dazed, the boy raised his eyes, after a long silence, from the scrawled words.

" Did your mother never say anything to you ? "

"No, sir."

"Nobody else?"

"No, sir."

"Have you any idea of who might have written that?"

"No, sir."

"Nor of why they might have written it?"

"No, sir." Joe's face quivered; he scowled and bit his lip suddenly, to control it.

"You had no idea who your father was?"

"No, sir," he whispered.

Harcourt said, after a long pause:

"And it looks as if we'll never know. That will do, boy; you can go." He had risen from his chair; he dropped a hand on Joe's shoulder—did it shrink from his touch?—and pushed the boy gently from the room. Then he locked the door. Never, since he took possession of the room that had been Matt's, had the door been locked; but there must be no risk of some early arrival for the Board Meeting coming in to witness his hour of weakness.

Facing the window, but well back from it, so that he should not be seen from below, he allowed the tears to burn slowly down the empurpled folds of his face. He did not allow—he could not check them. Tears of wounded pride, of hope relinquished, of pity for himself—as dupe of a cunning woman's deception—and of humiliation, on account of that enemy who, somewhere, was laughing at him. Ignoble emotions, but none the less painful. He pulled the great banner of fine linen from his breast pocket, blew his nose, rubbed his eyes that were the colour of fire and went back to his desk—having unlocked the door. While he went through the remainder of his correspondence, the poison generated by his mental torment—that which the French call *mauvais sang*—escaped from him in a violent attack of belching; the raucous sounds tore themselves from his belly, until he rose, went to the corner cupboard, where he kept the liquor for the entertainment of his associates in business, poured himself out a glass of brandy, and drained it, neat.

I'll get married again, he told himself. By God, I'll do it. I'll have a son, by God, if I burn for it!

There had not been wanting, since the death of Isabel, those who had advised him to remarry; nor even those to offer themselves, delicately but unmistakably, in consolation, and in regard for the welfare—so they insinuated—of his two little daughters. But Harcourt had had his fill of domesticity. Mere lust should not drive him to the marriage bed! Nor—this secret he shared with none but his mother—would he marry another woman, to find, after he buried her, the sealed packet of her lover's letters in a hidden drawer of her escritoire. Isabel—the perfect wife! "How great a comfort it must be to you," some sentimental old cousin had written to him, when it was all over, "to have known those few years—alas, *how* few!—of perfect trust and perfect confidence in one who rewarded you with the same. Oh, my dear Harcourt"—and so forth and so on. It was

Harriet's coming upon him when he was bent double with derision at this admirable effusion that obliged him to take her into his confidence ; he had to share the jest with someone.

As time went on, he had toyed occasionally with the idea of finding a hostess for his hospitalities in Berkeley Square ; but he had abandoned these from the hour he tacitly accepted little Joe Prior as his son. He might never acknowledge him publicly as such ; but the mere fact of the boy's existence furnished him with some obscure satisfaction, inexplicable save to those who knew Harcourt Flood. Of this satisfaction the writer of the unsigned letter had reft him ; and the man who turned to greet Roan, on the latter's debonair entrance, was as dangerous as a tiger with the smell of blood in its nostrils.

III

Dromore, Harcourt, Roan, Uncle Quentin, Dorset, Gilbert, Johnny, Selina, Vicky : Harriet had been invited, but had declined on the pretext that she had begun to find evening engagements rather an effort ; a palpable excuse. It would really be a relief when Miranda was old enough to join the company. Surrounded by an overwhelming male majority, Vicky sometimes felt like saluting Selina, at the farther end of the table, as "Mrs. Livingstone, I believe ?"

She had thought of asking Mary and Bell, but Harcourt was always sulky when he had to escort the girls. He would really have soon to recognise his duty to his daughters—Mary nearly eighteen, and Bell well past her sixteenth birthday. Mary should be engaged by now, and Bell, at any rate, have admirers. Poor girls ! Much chance they had, with Hacky positively growling every promising young man away from the door ; although, from his conduct to his daughters, one might imagine he would be only too glad to get them off his hands. Such a pity Hacky, who was eminently unfit to deal with the female species, had had daughters ; he would have been an excellent father to sons. Ah, well ; perhaps, one day . . . although indeed he must shrink—poor Hacky !—from the thought of replacing Isabel : so right, so conscious of her duty as wife to a Flood.

He looked terribly sulky this evening : as though something had badly upset him. That wretched Dock Board probably—as usual ; one hoped nothing more serious. Especially as Drummy was uncommonly gay ! It was long since he had been so genial—so willing to contribute to the pleasantries about the family board. That was probably because he was placed out of sight of Johnny—well away, at the farther end of the table, next to his mother.

Vicky heaved a sigh of contentment ; she had really managed the arrangement of the table rather well, considering the difficulties it presented, on these occasions of family reunion—placing herself next to Uncle Quentin, so as to be able, at a moment's notice, to draw his attention off Dromore, with Gilbert and, beyond him, Johnny, on her right ; then Selina, and

Drummy, at the head, Dorset, Roan and Harcourt, conveniently placed so that Dromore, if he had any statement of importance to make, could, without the trouble of turning from side to side, address what he was pleased to consider the less unintelligent members of his audience and not be put out by the vacuous majority.

Dessert was over, and the port had made its first solemn circle of the table. Vicky saw that Selina's glass, as well as her own, was empty. The servants had left the room. Vicky wondered whether her sister-in-law had forgotten to " catch her eye."

CHAPTER TEN

I

" WELL; I suppose all this fuss is about the memorial."

" Don't foul Drummy at the gate." Roan lit a cigar, with a bow of thanks for permission to Selina.

" About *what*, Uncle Hacky ? " Dorset's ears were pricked ; he leaned forward, to sparkle at his uncle, who glared past him.

Dromore raised his hand, with a glance of thanks to Roan, for his considerate observation of the priorities. " We're off," murmured Roan, under his breath.

" Although we elders are aware of it, you young people have not heard that it is proposed to erect a memorial to your great-grandfather, Matt Flood."

" Good egg," said Dorset comfortably. Scornful as he might be of Bristol as a centre of society, he was by no means averse to the glorification of an ancestor in its streets.

" First I've heard of it," mumbled Uncle Quentin ; accepting, across Vicky, a light from Gilbert, who, only able to think of one thing at a time, was letting the match burn down to his fingers, in gaping his interest at his father's announcement, until Vicky snatched it neatly from him and dropped it in the ash tray.

" I hadn't heard about it either," she consoled Uncle Quentin. " That's very nice indeed ; isn't it, Selina ? "

" Very," agreed Selina, on a note that suggested she couldn't care less.

" What sort of a memorial ? " Roan was non-committal. He vaguely remembered getting some kind of a memorandum, which he had scanned quickly and tossed over to Venetia, who had been very much amused, before using it to light her cigarette.

" A full-length effigy in bronze is projected, to be erected on St. Augustine's Parade——"

" Golly, the town's going to be bristling with statues ! " Dorset—as none but he would dare—interrupted his father. " Wasn't there something at the last Council meeting about Mr. Wills presenting one——? "

"With the trifling difference," murmured Roan, as Selina hushed her eldest son, "that it's not to glorify the family of Wills, but in honour of Edmund Burke. Sorry, Drummy; pray continue."

"I'm surprised I've not had any say in the matter, considering Matt was my father." Uncle Quentin was peevish.

"An oversight, sir, into which inquiry must certainly be made." Dromore raised his eyebrows, in deprecation of the oversight; so bland that he could be courtly, even with Uncle Quentin. "I assure you I will have it looked into immediately."

"Never mind about looking into it; I want to know whose notion it is." Quentin tapped the table. He had straightened his shoulders and looked every inch the fine, well-preserved old Flood he was, finer and more distinguished in appearance than any of his descendants, with the exception of Roan. "Who's presentin' it?"

"It is being erected by private subscription: the subscribers being a few people of exalted standing in Bristol, who wish to commemorate what our family has done for the town."

"I don't know who your exalted subscribers are, but I heard about it six months ago," grunted Harcourt. "And I told 'em I'd have nothing to do with it."

"What's your objection, Uncle Hacky?" It was, naturally, the irrepressible Dorset who spoke into the silence of the rest of the company.

"Never mind. I've got one."

"I am bound to say I had not anticipated your attitude, Harcourt." Dromore had recovered his composure, momentarily disturbed by the note of dissension. He, as well as Vicky, had noticed their brother's uncertain mood, and, like Roan, he was prepared to humour it. "We will return to it presently. Have you anything to say?" He turned to Roan.

"Nothing—except it's a pity they can't make a family group of it. We'd all look rather pretty, in bronze, noddin' and bobbin' at Burke, down there on the Parade"—a ribaldry that drew a guffaw from Gilbert, always responsive to very simple jokes.

"Uncle Quentin?"

"My dear boy, you are the head of the family; it is not my place to question any decision of yours. I hope the sculptor will do justice to his subject—that's all," concluded Uncle Quentin huffily.

"In this case, we may pray for mercy, rather than justice!" Roan's eyes were on the portrait of Matt, which hung, the work of a local artist, immediately behind Vicky's head. She managed to kick him under the table, but Gilbert, unfortunately, had gone off into another explosion, which drew her attention from her brother to her nephew.

"It would seem"—majestically ignoring all three of them, Dromore turned to Harcourt—"that your objection is unsupported."

"No. I object."

Everyone started.

"Johnny, be quiet!" gasped Selina.

" Your opinion has not been asked." Dromore crushed him with a glance, from beneath which Johnny struggled out with :

" I thought we were all being asked—and that's why we're all here." He threw a glance, half-sullen, half-apologetic, at his uncles, across the table.

" And what might your objection be ? " Harcourt peered curiously at his youngest nephew, down the length of the board.

" I'd sooner not say—unless I've got to," muttered Johnny. The scar on his cheek stood out like a crimson circumflex against its sallow background.

" Well, of all the brassbound nerve ! " Gilbert was gasping, while Dorset burst into the attractive laugh with which, so often, he bridged conversational dilemmas.

" That will do." Dromore rapped the table.

" I'd like to hear Hacky's objections, all the same," put in Vicky. According to her calculations, Harcourt, unless given an outlet, was likely to burst. It was, however, several moments before, having, apparently settled something in his mind, Harcourt spoke.

" You've asked for 'em ; you can have 'em. Look at the docks ! "

" Oh, those docks ! " An irrepressible wail broke from Selina ; she had acted too often as hostess to Harcourt, not to know what they were in for.

Dromore settled dutifully to attention. Uncle Quentin was making smoke-rings, as if the whole matter had ceased to concern him. Roan's face was blank, Dorset's so politely interested that it amounted to an impertinence. Gilbert had tilted his chair back and was staring at the ceiling with his lips pursed for a whistle that Vicky was only just in time to check by jerking him forward in his seat. Selina's eyes were streaming with her strangled yawns.

" Ay ! You can smile, you can sneer, you can patronise ! " Harcourt's voice thundered down the table, and only the small grey face of Johnny, his arms crossed on the table, gave him the attention he spoke for. " You set up effigies to the past ; you build churches for the heathen ; you head the subscription lists of missionary societies and hold garden parties to put decent savages into cotton drawers ! "

Uncle Quentin ceased to blow smoke-rings, and nodded appreciatively, while Dromore winced.

" We've got eleven and a half thousand paupers in Bristol—three hundred and twenty-six to each ten thousand of our population. Ain't you ashamed of it ? "

Selina, whom he seemed to be addressing, started violently.

" Oh, dear, I'm so sorry, Hacky——"

" Eleven and a half thousand paupers ; eleven and a half thousand parasites, sucking the life out of the city. Three times the return from Birmingham ; more than Liverpool, Manchester or any other big town in England. More than any town can carry."

" It's not carrying it," pointed out Roan, as Harcourt paused. " Charity's been the fashion here for at least a couple of centuries. You must admit we've done our share——"

"And a damn' bad fashion!" retorted his brother. "Pauperisation breeds trouble—in the long run. May not be in our time; but I wager . . . Nay; you can't wager with the unborn. Let it go." His voice had softened, was almost regretful. "Yes, I'm as sure as I am that we older ones 'ull all be in our graves that, fifty years from now, Bristol 'ull rue its charities. Charity ain't healthy, Ro—for the human soul. It's poison. And it works slowly."

"Then what's the answer, Uncle Hacky?" Even Dorset was impressed.

"The answer, boy, is the Docks. The mile of quays, the eight-hundred-and-fifty-foot entrance lock, the graving docks and low water piers we ought to have, if Bristol's to be saved from starvation." Harcourt spoke absently; it was hardly worth while talking to Dorset, but he had become aware of Johnny's attention. That was an odd young shaver, down there. He looked as if he thought things out on his own, instead of accepting what he was told, to save himself trouble.

Dromore, as well versed in the perennial squabbles of the Dock Board as any layman in the county of Gloucestershire, intervened.

"No doubt you are right in what you say, Harcourt. But I fear you are too late. Thanks to the Board's unfortunate policy, other ports have seen their advantages and taken them, by now."

"What advantages?" he challenged the speaker. "Mileage! That's what counts, in these days of steam. We can give Liverpool a hundred and sixteen and London a hundred and fifty-five nautical miles on the Port Said passage. We can beat Liverpool by thirty-two out to Montreal. We've got 'em all beat for distribution, and we've got the coal on our doorstep——"

"In fact, we have everything but the ships!" Roan smiled at his brother. "And we can't get the ships because Avonmouth won't take the big, new stuff, and, if it would, nobody in his right mind would pay Bristol dues when he can get in at Liverpool at cut price. The Port of Bristol isn't going to fetch down its charges after it's spent another couple of million on the dockisation scheme, Hacky. Your mile of quays, your giant entrance lock and your low water piers are going to look pretty foolish, sitting empty, while economical skippers take their ships up the Mersey! You won't have—what was it?—eleven and a half thousand paupers then. You'll have every ratepayer in Bristol scraping the dust out of his pockets to meet the Council's levy for your new toy!"

"You fool!" muttered Harcourt. "What do you know about it?"

"Not so much as you, I grant you, old fella—but——"

"He's right," piped Uncle Quentin unexpectedly. "The life of Bristol's always been in the shippin'. It was so in my father's time, and it was so when his great-grandfather ran the nigger trade——"

"You see what I'm driving at." Harcourt turned on Uncle Quentin, while Selina, her eyes on Dromore, shuddered. "It's like watching the blood run out of a body, with no one having the sense to apply a tourniquet. Put that tourniquet on our shipping, and, in five years' time, you'll have no able-bodied fellows whining for coppers on our pavements ; you can close half the alms houses——"

" I'm sure I'm very stupid," said Vicky at this point, " but I can't quite see the connection between all this dock business and the statue to Grandpapa. I suppose you mean we oughtn't to spend money on statues, when——"

" May I add something, sir ? " Dorset appealed to Dromore, who nodded gracious assent. Dorset turned to Harcourt with a becoming air of diffidence which only managed to cast a thin veil over his self-assurance.

" I don't pretend to know anything about the shipping, sir, but, as I see it, the people who want to contribute to the effigy scheme aren't the sort who will give vast sums for your dockisation. As a matter of fact," he added, as Dromore again signalled his approval of his firstborn, " they've proved they aren't already. You haven't, you can't, and I'm afraid you never will raise the enormous amount—whatever it may be ! " he threw in, with his charming smile—" that would be needed to carry out these plans of yours."

" Then Bristol's finished, and there's no need to put up statues—to Matt Flood or anybody else," said Harcourt flippantly. It was not worth while losing one's temper with Dorset, or even to point out to him that the plans were not " his " plans, but the outcome of a long struggle against the self-interest and prejudice of a large body of obstructionists on the Dock Board ; or to assert his own inextinguishable belief in Bristol's future, although he thought it very doubtful he would live to see her deliverance from the shackles which had come near to being her ruin.

" I suppose people like to remember their benefactors." Vicky sounded thoughtful. " Bristol was very grateful to Matt Flood, after the Reform riots."

" A man's best monument is in his works," said Harcourt. " Bristol's got plenty to remember Matt Flood by, and shows it, in ways that are plain enough to Bristolians—although maybe a stranger would not recognise them. But what have strangers got to do with Bristol ? "

" That's the stuff, Hacky ; that's the way to talk, my boy ! " Uncle Quentin had evidently forgotten that he was, virtually a stranger ; that, even in the days when he used to potter about Bristol, peering into the antique shops and pestering second-hand book dealers for his favourite subjects, he was always getting lost, mistaking one bend of the Floating Harbour for another—or even for the river itself—and generally behaving in a manner highly unbecoming to a Bristol Flood.

" Thinking it over "—after a pause : Roan was examining his beautifully-shaped nails—" I'm not sure that I don't agree with you. With all the poverty you describe, there's something a little—cold-blooded in raising a public subscription——"

" A *private* subscription," snapped Dromore, whose conclusions were foregone.

" My dear Drummy ! " Roan smiled. " I'd like to see anything kept private in Bristol. Before the list's closed, they'll have done everything but publish the names of the subscribers in the *Times and Mirror* ! They'll get a sly bit into the *Evening News*, and tie it up with a piece in the *Observer* at the week-end ! On the whole, I think we'd better sink the memorial——"

" I can see no reason why there should be any more objection to this than about the Wills' presentation ! " Dromore spoke heatedly, the flesh at the base of his fine nose flushing slightly, as it always did when he was seriously annoyed.

" Except that Willy Wills is giving it out of his own pocket ; he's done plenty for the town, and if he wants to throw in a bronze statue nobody's likely to make a fuss about it. Whereas, in Grandfather's case—unless I'm much mistaken "—he caught Harcourt's eye, which flickered slightly—" the people who are likely to subscribe—we know who *they* are without my mentioning them, I think, Hacky ?—have in the majority of cases not given a brass farthing or taken the least interest in anything that concerns the town."

" On a point of fact, I'm with you," said Uncle Quentin handsomely. " Matt was my father, and a great old English gentleman, on a pattern you don't often meet to-day "—others beside Matt himself would have been startled by the description—" and I am the last to slight his memory. Nor, by heaven, would I let anybody else slight it ! If anyone thinks that, in supporting Roan on this point, I'm wanting in respect to my dear old father, they can think again ! "

There was a confused babble, out of which came Harcourt's voice. Shrewd and silent while the others chattered, he had seen which way the tide was running.

" We'd better have a show of hands on it."

" Nonsense ! This—this is a family affair——! "

" Even in a family so united as ours, my dear Drummy," said Roan, on the lightly cynical note that never failed to irritate those of his own flesh and blood on whom he employed it, " it is possible to have two opinions ! Come then : let's vote——"

" And let the boys vote as well," Harcourt surprised the table by proposing. " Matt's their ancestor as well as ours, and they'll have to suffer this precious effigy, if it materialises, longer than we shall ! "

Dromore, who had been about indignantly to scout the proposal, gave a quick glance round his board. He was sure of his two elder sons, and he was sure of the women ; that made five, not counting the possible support of Uncle Quentin, whose last-moment decisions were notable for their freakishness. Had Harcourt not realised he was beaten ? He gave in with a show of graciousness. " As you will." And leaned back in his chair, concealing a slight smile by raising his glass to his lips.

" Well ? " Harcourt spoke gruffly. It may have been unintentionally that his heavy glance, travelling down the table, lingered for a moment on Johnny. For a mere flash of time, the two pairs of eyes, dark prune-colour and indefinite blue-grey, met and exchanged something. " Are we ready to vote ? Those in favour——"

Dromore's hand was raised solemnly ; Dorset's and Gilbert's shot up at the same time. Vicky, after a short pause, lifted her own. She was not quite easy about it ; Hacky was very shrewd ; he knew the trend of public opinion. But it was her duty to support Dromore. She lifted her hand a little higher, firmly, in token of asseveration. Dromore smiled his approval at her ; his glance, passing over Johnny as though the boy were not there, rested on Selina, who, in her usual absent-minded fashion, was playing with the fringe of her shawl, drawing it across the back of her left hand, watching the threads catch in the settings of her rings—for all the world as though a matter of vital importance were not under discussion !

"Selina, my dear." Her husband admonished her. "We are waiting for you. Those in favour——?"

"Oh . . . yes. No, I mean," she corrected herself. She raised her large, fair head and looked steadily down the table at Dromore. "I'm not in favour. That's why I didn't have my hand up."

"Those against——" Harcourt spoke evenly, before Dromore's expression had time to register with the others.

Harcourt, Roan, Uncle Quentin and, this time, Selina, raised their hands. Johnny still sat with crossed arms, his fingernails biting into the sleeves of his dinner jacket. His Uncle Roan looked at him quizzically.

"Well, Johnny?"

"I'd rather not vote." He did not look at Harcourt.

"Changed your opinion?" It was Gilbert, nudging him.

"I prefer not to vote."

Harcourt said in an expressionless voice :

"Four to four. The casting vote lies with——" He was so used to having the casting vote that it did not immediately occur to him that he was not entitled to it on the present occasion.

Dromore leaned forward, with blackness on his brow. There was no question his side was the poorer, the lightweight one. Harcourt, Roan, Uncle Quentin, all ranged against him. Not that that altered his views.

"As head of the family, the casting vote is mine." The harsh ring in his voice was at variance with its usual mellowness. "I give it to——"

"Is this in order, Hacky?" Roan did not care a rap ; he merely shared, with Uncle Quentin, a taste for baiting Drummy. "Johnny's already expressed his sympathy with our side ; morally, it's five to four, isn't it?" He winked at his brother to return the ball. But Harcourt was not playing.

"He has not voted." What was the boy up to, landing them in this *impasse*, which he must have known would be the result of his withdrawal? Dorset and Gilbert were grinning at their father ; Vicky, with a vexed expression on her face, had her eyes on her folded hands ; Uncle Quentin, once more withdrawn from the argument, was making a business of lighting a fresh cigar. Only Selina's eyes rested, with a mild, reflective curiosity, on her youngest son.

"I give my vote in favour of the proposal," said Dromore clearly ; and Harcourt, on a dry note :

"The Ayes have it."

" And I think there is no more to be said." Dromore glanced triumphantly at Roan. Selina's gown rustled, as though she were about to rise, and Vicky began to feel hastily for her slipper, which she had kicked off under the table.

" Hard luck, old man ! " Dorset leaned across the table to say to Johnny.

" I hope "—Dromore addressed his brothers with the magnanimity of the victor—" you will at least let us have the benefit of your opinions, when it comes to the approval of the model."

" Vicky can do my approving for me." Harcourt shot a vicious look at his sister, who gave it back to him, not vicious, but reproachful. There was no use losing one's temper, when one's side had lost ! It was a pity they had not talked it over together ; she still had an uncomfortable feeling Hacky might be right. If he had explained his views to her more fully, it might have been possible to persuade Dromore . . .

" Is the statue going up ? " Johnny's voice, high-pitched, reached her from the farther side of Gilbert.

" Naturally," said his father coldly.

" Well—it can't ! " A note of panic drew the eyes of the adults towards him quickly. Harcourt took a long breath.

" The discussion is now closed. Selina ? " Dromore bowed coldly to his wife, with whom he was displeased. If she had voted in support of him, as duty should have bidden her, all this annoyance would have been avoided.

" You can't put up a statue to Matt Flood," said Johnny, in a small voice. Dromore clicked his tongue impatiently ; what was the boy's mother thinking about, sitting there, paying attention to him, instead of bidding him hold his tongue ?

" That is sufficient, John——"

" *You can't do it*," repeated Johnny, on a stronger, more emphatic note. Harcourt leaned forward. " Because Matt Flood was a slave trader. Ask Uncle Quentin if it isn't true ! "

II

" It's true enough." The diamond in Uncle Quentin's ring was shooting off little sparks with the slight vibration of his hand. He kept them all waiting while he puffed vigorously on his cigar ; through the smoke he peered mischievously at their faces ; Roan, of course, ready to burst out laughing ; Hacky's like a wall ; Selina all bright and interested, for the first time in the evening—handsome woman, if only she'd show a little more animation ; and Drummy—Uncle Quentin let out an irrepressible little puff of laughter at the sight of Drummy's face. " Cheer up, my boy ; there's no need to look as if you'd seen a ghost ! What did you expect ? Do you think a sugar plantation, from 1802 onwards, could make enough to run a place like this ? I'm surprised none of you thought of it before ! "

" I had thought of it." Harcourt's eyes smouldered upon his uncle.

" I hadn't," confessed Roan. " We must all have been pretty simple when you come to think of it ! " Suddenly he let his laughter go. It was very infectious laughter ; even Dorset and Gilbert joined in it, though their eyes were bolting out of their heads. A dazed smile appeared at the corners of Vicky's mouth, although she was too sorry for Dromore to join in this unseemly outburst of ribaldry. Really, they might have some consideration for Drummy. Even Selina was laughing, in a soft, silly, malicious way, as though not quite sure what she was laughing at. The exceptions to the general mirth were Dromore, who sat as though turned to stone ; Harcourt, who was scowling, and Johnny himself, who, white-faced and with glittering eyes, had half-risen from his chair, to lean across Gilbert and his aunt, and address Uncle Quentin.

" Rodríguez and Plant. Plant was great-grandfather, wasn't he ? "

" 'Pon my soul, this is funny ! It's a pity my Da isn't here to listen to it ! " Quentin gave an unregenerate chuckle.

" Selina." It was less a voice than a croak that came from Dromore's lips. " It is time you were in bed. Dorset, ring the bell for your mother's maid."

" Oh, no, thank you," said Selina brightly. " I have just begun to enjoy myself. This is all very interesting."

" To *enjoy* yourself ! " The croak trembled into reproach. Even Vicky, with her eyes, begged for pity—pity on her tormented brother.

" I did not mean to be unfeeling. Of course, I realise that this must be rather distressing for everybody." I have never, thought Vicky, known Selina so completely to disassociate herself from us before. After all, she has no right to do so ; she has been a Flood by marriage for a great many years.

" Go on, tell us about it, please, Uncle Quentin ! " Gilbert's jaw was hanging open with his excitement, but Dorset, she noticed, was a little flushed.

Uncle Quentin, the cynosure of all attention, settled comfortably back in his chair, which he had swung a little away from the side of the table.

" Well, when the plantations began losing, my father sold out—retaining a certain interest, of course—to a Foxley. Some connection of the family ; one of Jonathan's girls married a Foxley—mixed-up sort of business ; we bought a plantation from 'em in '92—1792, I mean," said Uncle Quentin meticulously ; " just a hundred years ago. Then we sold it back again, with Triton and Halifax, the old fam'ly holdings, as well. That's when we went to live in America."

There was a pause, before Dromore said hollowly :

" I did not know you had ever lived in America, although I knew you had visited it."

" Even you, my dear fella, don't know everything," said Uncle Quentin blandly. " Well, we did. We lived in Galveston, while Papa's ships were building. Your father and I, as boys, had our schooling in Galveston—and a pretty tough schooling it was ! It ended up by shockin' Mamma into her grave, so they sent us up to our grandmother's in South Carolina——"

" Just a minute, Uncle Quentin : was your grandmother an American ? " Even Dorset had begun to be confused.

" A Virginian," Uncle Quentin corrected him. " Mayflower family. Married my grandfather William after the wars—damnation, why can I remember these things, and not be able to sort you all out one from another ? Do you mean to say you know no more than that about the fam'ly tree ? "

" It's a little muddling, after Jonathan," Dorset apologised. " Your grandfather was the third son, wasn't he—the one who went and fought in the wars and lost an arm—— ? "

Quentin waved William aside.

" Grandmother took us in hand and civilised us. Then we went back to Barbados, were joined by Papa, settled up the estates and—arrived in Bristol in time for the fires."

" But did—did you actually *know* your father was trading—conducting the slave traffic ? " Vicky stammered ; it sounded terrible, but anything—anything to head Uncle Quentin off 1831 !

" My dear lady." He turned on her a vague look which struggled for a moment to place her as one of his kinsfolk, relinquished the effort as unrewarding, and changed to the expression of slightly reverential politeness with which he approached the rest of her sex. " Neither my brother Hercules nor I knew the least thing about it until long after my father's death—when I visited Cuba and met our Rodríguez relatives. Young Santiago Rodríguez let it all out to me—under the natural impression that I was *au fait* with the whole affair," concluded Uncle Quentin.

" That great-grandfather had taken the name of Plant, and that he'd designed the new-pattern slave-ships, with the false deck and the narrow hull, that would take the same number of slaves, packing them closer ? " persisted Johnny. He seemed determined to get this hammered in. Harcourt looked at him ; the boy had guts, driving his point home under the inimical gaze of his father.

" Good business man, my Da." Quentin wagged his head, tapping the first knob of ash off his cigar.

" He must have felt a bit sheepish about it," Roan offered ; " otherwise, why call himself Plant ? I suppose he was trying to save his British bacon."

" You seem to forget there was another Matthew Flood operating, on very different lines, this side of the pond," Harcourt reminded him dryly.

" He died in '07. There wasn't much danger of confusion, was there ? " frowned Dorset.

Suddenly Gilbert broke into a guffaw.

" I've got it—jolly good, by jove ! It was a 'plant' on the other Matthew, wasn't it ? I say, that's a joke—old Matthew, preaching anti-slavery over here, and young Matt in the States getting ready to rush in and make hay out of Abolition, the minute it went through ! "

" Be silent, boy ! " thundered Dromore.

There was a pregnant silence, broken, uncertainly, by Vicky.

" Well—this is quite a private matter, I suppose. It can hardly affect——" Her glance appealed to Dromore.

" You are right, Victoria." His eyes, haggard and pitiful, rewarded her. " I suggest "—he returned to the company at large—" that the subject is closed. It should never have been raised."

" What difference does it make, to close it ? " Johnny's face was hardly less haggard than his father's. " Uncle Quentin's given us the facts. We're sitting round this table on the proceeds of slave trade. Everything we've got "—he pointed to the rich panoply of the table : the painted Champion plates, the crystal bubbles of the wine glasses, mounted on their fragile spiral stalks, the Queen Anne silver, Selina's gold and white jade *bonbonnières*—which he might have excepted—the vast gold and ivory casket, one of Matt's presentation pieces, which Quentin had adopted for his cigars—" the food we eat, the wine we drink, the cigars we smoke—they've all come to us through slave trade, which we were brought up to be ashamed of ! The thing all decent people in Bristol want to forget ! And when it comes to shoving the statue of a slave-trader under their noses——! "

" Steady, boy." But Harcourt's look, under his black brows, was kindly.

" You have said enough," Dromore was beginning.

Johnny ignored them both. He rushed on :

" There in the Redcliff : ' Matthew Flood, who by the mercy of God—died in eighteen hundred and seven, the year in which the task to which he dedicated his life was accomplished—the Abolition of Slavery, for which the Lord's Name be praised.' What about that ? A nice idea, isn't it, to shove up a slave-trader's statue in the face of that ? A member of the same family—with the same name ! Standing out there on the Parade, to mock everything the other lived and—and died for——"

Harcourt sat very still. He had never held a lower opinion of himself. Knowing all he knew, he had left Johnny to pull the chestnuts out of the fire for him—and, by God ! the youngster had done it, royally. All very well to say he had had, until to-night, no confirmation of his suspicions. He should have found means of confirming them. Instead of trying to baulk the issue by his (perfectly sincere) raising of the question of Bristol's poverty, which he had hoped would divert Drummy's attention from the matter at stake.

The boy had integrity : which, for all their parade of schoolboy " honour," was missing in the others. Even in the righteous Dromore ! He—even he, the angel of the flock !—was preparing, if Harcourt knew the signs, to compromise, to conceal, to lay unction to the pride which Johnny had so deeply wounded. Where had the lad got his information ? How long had he had it ? Harcourt would have given much to know.

Roan was saying, on a note of curious satisfaction :

" Well, I take it that's knocked the effigy on the head."

And Selina, drawling :

" It will be rather a difficult thing to explain, won't it, to the people who proposed the memorial ? " with a glitter in her usually lifeless eyes.

" Not difficult at all ! " Vicky challenged her—no devoted sister-in-law, for the moment, but a Flood, indignantly defending Floods. " There is no need whatever for explanations ; I'm sure Drummy agrees with me. I really don't feel we require to justify ourselves, at this time of day." Squaring her shoulders, she looked round at her brothers, as though daring them not to support her. " The Matt Flood that Bristol wants to commemorate is the one who, by his wisdom and foresight, helped Bristol to recover after the terrible affair of the Reform riots ; the one to whom Bristol, as a town, is normally and financially indebted. How he came to be in a position to help so many people is beside the question ; it's certainly nobody's business to-day," she ended stoutly.

" Especially if nobody knows about it—eh, my dear ? " Uncle Quentin chortled in her ear. She turned on him a resentful shoulder. Really—Uncle Quentin ! She felt she could not forgive him for allowing himself to be drawn into so unseemly a state of communicativeness, by Johnny—with whom, despite all her past partisanship, she was seriously offended.

" If nobody knows about it ? " Roan had caught the old gentleman's mutter. " Exactly. I wonder how many do ? I don't feel particularly easy, myself, at the idea of being a public laughing-stock, each time I happen to pass old Matt on my way to a meeting of Hacky's Board."

" That is absurd." Dromore's face was heavily congested. " Who should know about it ? We did not even know about it ourselves——"

" If you've got any sort of worldly experience, Drummy, you'll know that the last person to hear of a shady piece of business is the person most concerned." Harcourt had just had an unpleasant sample of it himself. " So far as I'm concerned, the subject's closed." He pushed himself up from his chair and went to the end of the table, to bid Selina good night. " Good night, Selina. Your cook knows her business ; you'd better send her in to teach mine how to do a bisque ! " He raised his finger across her to Johnny, who, looking half-stunned now it was over, slumped in his chair. " Go and tell them to get my horse, boy."

As Johnny vanished from the room, he faced his host.

" Take my advice and get this quashed as soon as possible. And, if you've got any sense in your head, be thankful to Johnny for saving us all from a damned awkward predicament."

Glowering at his neglected wine, Dromore made no reply. Vicky offered her second brother a cold good night. Discarding Dorset's invitation to a game of billiards, Roan yawned that he supposed he might as well go to bed, and following Harcourt from the room, while Uncle Quentin observed, to no one in particular.

" Dammit ! Why wasn't Harriet here ? She'd have enjoyed herself." Ending with a graceless chuckle. The boys made themselves scarce, and Selina, suddenly exhausted, now that the entertainment was over, asking Vicky to see her to her room—the master of Guerdon was left to chew the cud of bitterness in solitary state at the head of his table.

" What do you make of that young Johnny ? "

Harcourt and Roan stood on the steps, waiting for the former's horse to be brought round ; Harcourt, like a giant, his white head all but brushing the lintel, as he preceded his brother into the cool, night air. Roan, well above the average height for his sex, seemed fragile, beside that immense figure.

" Make of him ? 'T'aint my business to make anything of him—thank God."

" Rats ! I saw you watching him all the time he was speaking, you old ferret," was the easy answer. " He's really an extr'ordin'ry fella. All these years we've been taking him for granted as something of a milk-sop, then suddenly he goes off, like a time-bomb. Extremely disconcerting for Drummy ! I'm willing to wager there are a lot of headaches coming in the near future to our Hercules." He smiled his light, maliciously reflective smile.

" Storm in a teacup," mumbled Harcourt. " Time-bomb !" he snorted. " Damn' silly way of exploding it. That's the worst of the young—they're either lollin' about like cattle, or actin' as if they thought they were on the Lyceum stage, with a blob of limelight on the end of their noses and somebody banging a sheet of tin off. Pah ! "

" I like you, Hacky, when you're metaphorical. I wish you'd do it more often," murmured Roan, and yawned again. The horse was coming round from the stables, with Johnny on its back ; perched up there on the huge chestnut, he looked hardly bigger than a child. " Well, I'm away to my bed. I'll leave you to deal with your Lyceum villain—or hero ; which is it ? Perhaps you'll let me know some time."

Johnny slipped from the saddle, gave the reins into his uncle's hand and obligingly held the stirrup for the latter to mount.

" Sorry you were kept waiting, sir. I think the groom was tight. But the girths are all right—I saw to them myself."

The towering man on the towering horse sat still, and looked down on this—this *sliver* of a Flood !—who, with the light from the hall lamps behind him, shrank to even less than his just proportions against the massive shoulder of the animal.

" The others go back to school next week, don't they ? "

" Yes, sir."

" And what are they going to do with you ? "

" Goodness knows," shrugged Johnny. He muttered, as Harcourt continued to stare down at him, " There's some talk of a tutor. If I don't get quodded for to-night ! " He meant it as a jest ; the pale wedge of his face, upturned towards Harcourt, dragged itself into a smile.

" Don't be bombastic."

Harcourt, still scowling into the whispering trees. A disillusioned, in many ways a corrupt man, he was uneasily aware of young honour standing there beside him in the darkness. For himself, he did not give a damn that the Barbados Floods, as well as their forebears in Bristol, had been tarred with the slave trade ; had he lived in those days, he would doubtless have taken a cut at it himself. Nor did he care if the facts were published to the whole of Bristol ; there were few eminent Bristolians who had not had their thumbs in that unsavoury pie ! But he would have cared at least as much as Drummy if the family had been held up to public ridicule for an act of arrogance for which, after all, they were not directly responsible : and his own suspicions, unfounded as they were on any sound data, had brought him to Guerdon prepared to fight to the last fence this nonsensical proposal. And, if Drummy had proved obdurate—the matter must, eventually, lie in his hands—he would have taken him quietly aside and given him something to think about, before crossing his Rubicon : not blurted the whole thing out over the dinner table, to make gossip between the women and provide the boys with a sensation—as Johnny had done. In Harcourt's opinion, it you wanted to keep a matter private, you let as few people into it as possible.

However, that was the way of the young. Johnny had certainly popped the cat among the pigeons !—and, reluctantly, Harcourt was obliged to honour him for it. There were no signs of the broken spirit Harriet—like a woman !—was bewailing, in this young sprig, sailing straight into the wind of his father's wrath. But Roan had been right ; the sprig must be a devilishly uncomfortable companion for Drummy, who disliked an independence unclothed in the graces with which Dorset so well knew how to adorn it.

" Would you care for a drink, sir, before you go ? I'll bring you one out, if you like ; I don't suppose they'll have locked up the decanters yet."

Harcourt. As he sat there, with the chestnut now and again tossing its head, blowing the moths away from its nostrils, striking an impatient hoof on the gravel, he was profoundly conscious of his loneliness, his mental unsettlement. Unused to the sensation of tiredness, it troubled him. He was tired, tired. Too tired to care about much, too tired, even, to hate Kitty Prior.

Joe. Joe. Joe. For the last several hours Harcourt had forgotten his existence ; with the stab of reminder came the slow realisation that now, in actual fact, he owed nothing to Joe ; no more than he owed to any promising youth to whom he paid his wages.

Johnny came out with the brandy—neat, as Harcourt always took it. He did not trouble to be surprised that the boy remembered ; he took the glass and drained it at a draught, then handed it back to his nephew.

" You'd better come and see me to-morrow."

" Yes, sir." The reply was noncommittal. " At the office ? "

" At Berkeley Squ——" he was beginning, and checked himself angrily. None of that, you fool ! " At the office—ten sharp ! See you're not late—and good night to you." He touched the chestnut's neck with his crop, and it strode away into the shadows of the Avenue.

There was no harm in finding out if the youth was such a fool as he'd been painted, he justified himself—and was irritated to find he had the need for self-justification. It was perfectly clear Drummy was not the one to handle him ; there was alien fibre there—alien, at least, to Drummy's technique in dealing with the young ; a toughness, a lack of smooth adaptability that grated, of course, on Drummy's sensitive surface. A duffer at his books, so they said ; well, there was no place for duffers in Flood and Company. But it might be possible to find a pointer or two, that would prevent the boy's riding off in a bad direction. A Flood, *détraqué*, was an uncommonly tricky proposition—bad for himself, bad for those who had to do with him, bad for the family. And the family came first. For the sake of the family, Dromore had better revise his ideas about young Johnny; better listen to the advice of people more favourably placed than himself for judging what was good for a youth who had spent the best part of a year in doing and seeing things which did not ordinarily come in the way of boys of his age—not, at least, the kind of boys to whom Dromore and Selina were accustomed.

As he passed the Dower House, there was a light in Harriet's bedroom window. Mechanically he tipped his hat to it, smiling to himself. Uncle Quentin was right; it was a pity Mamma had missed the scene. She would have appreciated it.

CHAPTER ELEVEN

I

THE day after what was ever after referred to as 'Johnny's scene" dawned in one of those soft, grey, incalculable downpours that, sweeping in from the sea, enfolds the West Country in a silver trance. From the windows nothing was visible beyond the low yew balcony of the terrace; through the whisper of the rain came the whisper of fecund earth, of grass blade and flower stalks, thrusting upwards in the warm moisture, of swelling fruit and ovule gorged with sap.

In the ugly schoolroom, the two little girls bent their heads over their needlework: Miranda's a much-crumpled, much blood-spotted strip of flannel, which she reluctantly covered with rows of feather-stitching and faggoting. Emily, aware that it was Miranda's sewing hour, had brought with her the handkerchief on which, much to her companion's awe, she was embroidering a monogram.

"It's for Lady Cullen's birthday," she explained, when questioned as to the destiny of this work of art.

"Huh! I shouldn't think she'd ever dare to blow her nose on *that*! All those teeny-weeny little stitches; it must take millions of hours—oh, *Polly*!" Her black eyes behind the steel-rimmed glasses sparkled, as the door opened and a beaming face appeared. "Oh, Polly, are you going to sit with us? Now we can have fun!" rejoiced Miranda.

"Looks like fun, doesn't it?" But she laughed as she lifted the basket, piled high with darning. The laugh came rippling out of her, as though to show it would take more than a basketful of stockings to daunt Polly Bowling's spirits.

"What a pity we don't still wear woad!" Emily made room for her at the side of the table. "Oh—oh, what terrible holes! You'll never fill those in, will you?"

"Just you wait and see," promised Polly, as she plucked the threaded needle out of the bosom of her print frock, thrust her fist into one of Dorset's socks, the knuckles through the hole, and made them into a funny face, which made the girls laugh. " I bet that's Mr. Gilbert's. He ought to have tin caps on his toes and his heels." She set to work light-heartedly to cobble, while Miranda lifted her head and frowned at the window.

" Isn't the light bad ? Oh, there's a magpie." As a flash of black and white crossed the pane.

" '*Une pour tristesse,*' " said Emily.

" What ? " Miranda stared.

" *Une pour tristesse,*
Deux, seras gai ;
Trois disent mariage,
Quatre, quelqu'un de né ;
Cinq pour un violon,
Six pour une danse,
Sept, vieille Angleterre,
Huit, la belle France,"

recited Emily, smiling.

" I know ! It's 'One for sorrow, two for joy,' isn't it, in French ? "

Emily nodded.

" One for sorrow——"

" Oh, there's always another round somewhere," said Polly, as she thrust back the curtains. Her eyes, returning, dwelt respectfully on Emily. " Say it again, miss, will you ? It sounds pretty."

Emily, it appeared, had learned all her English nursery rhymes in French ; presently she had them all gabbling " *Voici la Maison que Jean a bâtie,*" to the delight of Miranda, who had the memory of a parrot and a tolerable ear, and to Polly's confusion, as she stumbled through the phrases to bursts of laughter.

" Oh, Polly, don't ; you're giving me a pain ! " Tears rolled down Miranda's cheeks as Polly wrestled with " *Voici l'Homme tout déguenillé et déchiré* "—she having none of Emily's polite inhibitions about laughing at someone doing her best. She took off her spectacles to wipe them, as she said apologetically to Emily : " When you say French it doesn't sound a bit like the Grim and her French irregular Verbs."

" What are French irregular verbs ? " Emily asked, in all innocence.

" Don't you know ? You are lucky," sighed Miranda.

" I only learned to talk French. I don't know any grammar," said Emily, with humility.

" I expect they'll teach me French when I go to boarding school." Polly spoke up for herself in the face of all this erudition.

" Are you really going to boarding school ? It's going to be a nice thing, I must say, when you've gone away and Emily's gone back to London," pouted Miranda.

" Oh, my, wouldn't I love to go to London ! " Polly allowed her hands to drop in her lap, for a moment of wistful contemplation.

" But we'll be coming back soon, Winkle," Emily comforted her. " It's only for the funeral. You see, now Grandmamma's dead, Lady Cullen is going to be my guardian."

" What is a guardian ? It sounds like a kind of warder ! " scowled Miranda. Resentful, protective, her skinny little hand shot out and gripped her beloved Emily's. " Why should you have a warder ? "

" Because——" She flushed, remembering a conversation of the morning. An heiress ; what did it mean exactly ? Something about money, which would be hers when she came of age ; and well-brought-up people did not talk about money. " It's not like prison, Winkle," she explained carefully. " It's only having someone to look after one until one's old enough to look after oneself. And I'm to call her Mamma," said Emily thoughtfully. " That will seem very odd ; I've never had anybody to call Mamma."

" Oh, dear ; does that mean you've got to live with her, for ever ? "

" Why ? " The words " for ever " seemed to startle her.

" I prayed last night that you came to live with us, and we all grew up together, and "—Miranda dropped her voice, as she screwed her eyes over her stitching—" you'd marry Johnny."

Bent over the work, she did not see the sudden flame leap up Emily's cheek.

" Who are you going to marry, Polly ? " demanded Miranda, after a pause.

" Me ? Oh, mercy, give me time ! " cried Polly. " I'm but a year older than Miss Emily ! "

" Isn't it funny ? I always think of you as quite grown up—only in a *nice* way," amended Miranda. " Not the sort of grown-up that grown-ups are, if you get my meaning ! It does seem as if people lose a lot of sense as they get older," she sighed. " And, anyhow, I expect you'll be engaged in another couple of years ; all the girls here get engaged as soon as they're sixteen."

" I shan't be in a hurry ! " Polly tossed her head. " Why, goodness me, I'll only just have left boarding school ! I want to have plenty of fun, before——" Strangely enough, she too was blushing, like Emily.

" Well, I'm sorry for both of you, having to get married ; I haven't got *that* to bother about," said Miranda off-handedly.

The needles of both the elder girls halted in air ; neither lifted her head ; it was as though each had felt a touch which, momentarily, paralysed her. A cloud of painful embarrassment, overwhelming them both, avoided Miranda and left her free to look up, in surprise at the silence.

" Sing for us, Polly ! "

With a gesture of relief, Polly flung back her head, her face like a damask rose, and started to sing. Polly's voice was pure delight ; it bubbled out of her young throat like the notes of a thrush and charmed, inevitably, those who listened.

Emily swept back the wave of dusky hair from her brow and smiled as she pointed to the window.

" You've sung the rain away ! Look, it's fine, again."

" The sun will be out next ! " Miranda clapped her hands. " Go on—sing some more. Now ' Grandfather's clock,' " she prompted, having, like most of the young, a taste for the doleful. She joined in triumphantly when it came to :

" And it stopped—short—never to go again
When the old—man—died ! "

" Who is that singing ? " Harriet, below, in the yard, stopped to inquire. Loving horses, " the old lady," as she was respectfully known, seldom paid a visit to the house without going round the stables. Her hand lingered on the soft nose of Selina's mare as she lifted her head to listen.

One of the young grooms squirmed.

" It's my—my cousin, ma'am ! "

" Your cousin—— ? "

" Polly—Polly Bowling," stammered the youth, hoping he was not getting Polly into a scrape, but trusting to " the old lady " not to make trouble.

" And what is Polly Bowling doing up here ? " she asked Vicky, whom she met at the entrance to the Dutch garden.

" Polly—— ? Oh, Polly ! " Vicky's mind had been full of other matter when, hearing that her mother had arrived, she hurried round to meet her. " We asked her mother to send her up to help with the mending. The boys going back to school makes so much extra work, they can't manage it in the sewing room. And the governess—tiresome creature—had to have the afternoon off ; something about a tooth," muttered Vicky. " So Polly was sent to the schoolroom, to look after the girls. I hope there's nothing wrong ? "

" Come round here and listen," smiled Harriet. Leisurely, her skirts brushing the wet box edges, she led the way, now and again using the point of her umbrella to lift some battered spray, or drawing a rose towards her, to inhale its sweet, wet scent.

" And it stopped—short—never to go again
When the old—man—died ! "

floated in a triumphant chant from the schoolroom window.

" What a voice," murmured Harriet. " A pity it should not be trained."

" Yes——" said Vicky vaguely. " Oh, Mamma, I was coming down to see you—I've got so much to tell you——"

Harriet stood still, her hands clasped on the handle of her umbrella, and turned a quizzical smile on her daughter—the smile Roan had inherited from her. She should, of course, have remembered that Vicky was practically tone-deaf, that she could not be trusted to keep in tune on *God Save the Queen*.

" I noticed you were agog with something. Well ? You had better get it off your mind."

. . . The schoolroom door burst open.

"Oh, lord—a make-and-mend !—I heard your caterwauling half-way down the avenue."

"Oh—are you back ?" beamed Miranda.

"No, fathead, I'm still in Bristol!"

Johnny rumpled her hair, picked a ball of stockings out of Polly's basket, kicked it neatly up to the ceiling, let out a whistle and, with his hands in his pockets, cut a few steps of the hornpipe. Emily sat wide-eyed, smiling, her hands in her lap ; it was the first time she had ever seen a boy behave—like a boy. She found it fascinating, as she would have found fascinating the antics of a young animal in a zoo. Was this, perhaps, the way boys always behaved—when they were excited about something ? Looking at Johnny, she found herself looking at a stranger ; having taken the short cut through the shrubbery from the lodge, his head and shoulders were splashed with the wet from the trees ; on his brow and cheekbones the drops glittered like little diamonds there was a kind of diamond-like glitter about him altogether, making him different from the sober person she had always known. It was interesting—like the transformation scene in a pantomime.

"It's you does the darning, is it ?" He had turned on Polly now. "Well, the last pair of socks I put on had rocks in them. My hat ! If I'd done the captain's socks like that, I'd have had a work-up that would have laid me out for a week. Why don't you learn to sew ?"

"Why don't you darn 'em yourself ?" squealed Polly. The next moment the air was alive with stockings, Johnny and Polly pelting each other with all the force of their muscles, Miranda screaming and dodging each time a missile came her way.

"*Pax !*" shrieked Miranda suddenly, and, to Emily's surprise, all three stood still. "Oh, goodness, I'd forgotten ! We've got to have tea with Mamma, Emily. Come on—we must wash our hands." She scrambled down from her chair and limped hurriedly to the door. "Come on, Polly, you've got to brush our hair."

When Emily returned—alone—Johnny was sitting on the window sill. They looked at each other shyly. To-day she was wearing a grey silk frock, falling straight past her knees from its smocked yoke ; her hair was drawn back from her broad, tranquil brow into a soft bow of black satin. Johnny, who had never seen a "Liberty" dress before, thought she looked odd, but very sweet.

"Hallo," said Johnny.

Emily said : "Hallo," then, helpless before a shyness which she had managed to conceal at their first meeting, but which suddenly overwhelmed her, she knelt down and began hurriedly to collect the stockings which were scattered all over the floor.

"I say—don't do that !" He leapt across the room to take them from her. As he snatched them from her hands, she sank back, momentarily speechless, on her heels ; then, before he could give her his hand to help her, jumped up, and stood blushing, smoothing the creases out of her grey dress. Johnny rammed the stockings back in the basket, trying to think of something to say. She was acting almost as if she were frightened, and he felt ashamed of himself, for being the cause of her fear. Presently he muttered :

" You're not used to that, are you ? "

" To—— ? " Emily cleared her throat.

" To people yelling and—and chucking things about."

Her lips parted suddenly in a smile.

" It was—fun." She found her voice had come back, and with it her self-control. " Where have you been ? " she asked him.

" In Bristol, seeing my Uncle Harcourt." The flamboyance of his entrance had dropped from him ; he was almost as shy as she. " I'm going to work in his office."

She looked at him sweetly.

" You're very pleased about it, aren't you ? "

" Well—yes. Though I expect it will be tough, to begin with." He had meant to tell no one, until he had told Harriet. Why, now, was he telling Emily Temple ? He frowned as he ran his finger along the moulded edge of the table, wondering what had possessed him to blab to her. To ask her to keep it a secret seemed childish, and, in some way, rude to Emily : like saying that she could not keep things to herself.

Emily was saying :

" It is very nice to be a man, and lead one's own kind of life."

" I don't think I know what you mean."

" Neither do I," admitted Emily. " But it is rather dull, for a girl, to have to—to have to——" Wait until someone marries her, was in her mind ; she would have said it in all innocence, half an hour ago.

" Of course, I'd sooner be a man than a girl," said Johnny seriously. He looked at Emily ; there was something so soft, so delicate, so smooth about her ; she made one afraid of ruffling her. He was glad Dorset and Gilbert had gone to play fives with the Gannet boys. " It's man's business to look after girls," he stammered.

Emily said, with her darling smile :

" Would you look after me, if I ever wanted you to ? "

". . . Why . . . yes," stuttered Johnny. " I expect I could manage you—as well as Miranda." And could have kicked himself, afterwards, for mentioning Miranda.

Emily came first. Of course, always, Emily would come first.

II

" Joe."

The boy, who was slipping out of the room without speaking, turned, keeping his eyes on the ground. Harcourt gave him a quick look. There was something in the young, humiliated face that touched an organ he was seldom aware of possessing.

" Joe. Come here. That which I showed you yesterday makes no difference."

Joe looked up, and lowered his eyes again ; they were red-rimmed. The clear, white skin of his face had lost its gleaming quality ; it had the lifeless look of a blossom that the frost has blighted.

" So long as you behave yourself," said Harcourt deliberately, " you're here, in the firm. You'll get the same dealing and the same opportunities as anybody else who works for Flood and Company. Is that clear ? "

" Yes, sir," was the mechanical reply. But the boy seemed to shiver. Harcourt's brows drew together.

" Have you had your breakfast ? "

He shook his head.

Harcourt pushed his hand in his pocket and brought out a handful of coins. Carefully selecting a shilling from the silver, he held it out.

" Go and get some." Something prompted him to add : " Come, lad ; look up. There's no disgrace "—in not being the son of a Flood ? He muttered, with an impatient gesture : " Go on ; be sharp. You may be wanted."

A watery smile dawned on Joe's face. He touched his forelock as he took the coin.

" Thank you very much, sir. I shan't be long." The smile suddenly broadened. " Thank you very much, sir ! " he repeated, as he hurried from the room.

Ignoring, for once, the pile of mail on his desk, Harcourt thrust his hands in his pockets and paced between window and door. Ought I to have shown it to him ? Whatever might be the answer, the damage, if damage there was, was done. Ashamed of the weakness, Harcourt had no shame, or at least no regrets, for that which was irrevocable. If he had made an error of judgment, he was prepared to stand by it. A tap on the door swung him towards it.

" Come in."

" Good morning, Uncle Hacky."

It was Johnny, very grave, very sedate, in a suit Harcourt guessed to be his best : clean collar, neatly-tied bow (he had, for once, allowed it to be tied for him), hair plastered to the high crown of his head. He had left his soaked raincoat downstairs, and, while waiting, had borrowed a cloth and removed the mud from his shoes. Insignificant ; yet, in some way Harcourt was at a loss to define, well conditioned : the small offspring of a good stable.

" You're late." He scowled at the clock.

" I've been waiting downstairs. They told me you were engaged."

Harcourt grunted. He sat down—and did not invite Johnny to do the same. The boy stood there : his feet slightly apart, his hands clasped behind his back, his shoulders straightened—sturdily. No air of dependency ! —rather as one who had as little time to waste as his interlocutor. Making the most of himself. Harcourt repressed a smile. This cock robin !—that he could crush by merely reaching out his hand.

" Well ; what's to be done about you ? They tell me you're a dunce at your books."

"I've missed ten months. I wasn't very bright before," Johnny conceded, "except at figures. They came easily to me, on the whole."

"What do you want to do?"

"I told Mr. Flood——" began Johnny.

"You told *who*?"

"I told my father," he corrected himself, with a bright flush, "that I want to go out to the Coast."

"What for? What's there about the Coast, that appeals to your fancy?"

"I'd like to work there." An edge of stubbornness met the note of mockery in the other's voice.

"Be specific, boy," snapped Harcourt. "What sort of work?"

"I can't be specific," rapped out Johnny, "without knowing what kind of things are open to a fellow like me. There are plenty of Britishers out there; I'm ready to do anything—be a clerk, or something of that kind, while I get the hang of things. I mean, a clerk to one of the factories—not Civil Service."

"We've got our factories out there," scowled Harcourt. "Why didn't you come to me?"

Johnny looked him in the eye.

"To be candid, sir, because I didn't think you'd take me seriously."

"Hrrumph. I don't know that I do now."

"Then there's nothing more to be said." Johnny turned abruptly on his heel.

"Don't be bumptious!" bawled Harcourt. "Now, what's at the back of this? What are you pleased to imagine you'll find on the Coast?"

"It's no use my pretending to know," said Johnny, after a pause. "I've always had a 'pull' towards it; that's all I can say. I feel it more strongly, of course, since I was out there."

"Blowing niggers up with gunpowder, eh?"

Johnny's face crimsoned.

"Who told you about that?"

"Never mind. By the way, have you ever had your pay from Runstables?"

Johnny's jaw dropped.

"By George! I'd forgotten all about it."

"That's a business man for you!" jeered Harcourt. "A fine sort of clerk you'd make."

"I'd like to be a trader, eventually," stuttered Johnny—on the principle of in for a penny, in for a pound.

"And what do you know about that?"

"I've watched them trading gold. I know how the nigger's mind jumps. After all, one's got to get one's experience——"

"You won't get your experience at my expense, thank ye. What do you know about cocoa?" Harcourt shot at him.

Johnny paused again to consider.

"Nothing much. Only that Columbus discovered it in 1519. And it was introduced to the Gold Coast in 1879 by a chap called Tette Kwesi, who brought the pods from Fernando Po. They say it's doing well—but the beans take five years to mature."

"What about concessions?"

"They'd have to come through the native chiefs," said Johnny, after consideration. "The Government doesn't encourage industrialisation, does it?"

The lad's no fool, thought Harcourt.

"Go on," he grunted.

"I can't go on. I don't know any more. But from the talk I've heard, they seem to think cocoa growing's an economic proposition—if there were better means of transport. Of course, that applies to everything on the Coast," answered Johnny.

He hasn't wasted his time, thought Harcourt. He keeps his ears open, and remembers what he hears. It's more than you'd get from the average schoolboy, filibustering round the Coast, playing penny-shocker antics on a bunch of niggers. He muttered:

"To begin with, you're not old enough to go out to the Coast. You can't use it, and it can't use you—except to send you home with a dose of Yellow Jack and give your mother fits. You'd better come into the office and get some of the flim-flam out of your head."

"With a view to going out there later?" He stood his ground, hammering his point home.

"With a view to nothing!" roared Harcourt. "Why, you impudent young shaver! Do you know there are fifty boys of your age in Bristol, who'd give their eye-teeth to get into Flood's, without having the sauce to make conditions about it?"

"I'm not making conditions," said Johnny coolly. "But I guess I've got a right, haven't I, sir, to know where I'm going? I don't want to waste time, or, for a matter of that, to disappoint you, by taking what you offer me, and then turning it down, because something turns up that seems to promise a quicker way to what I've got in mind."

Harcourt was quiet, recovering his control. One could not but admire the boy's obstinacy, his independence and his self-assurance.

"Look here, Johnny—siddown," he muttered. The lad might be only fifteen, but he spoke, and acted, like an adult, and was worthy, at least, of the courtesy due to his elders. "Look here, my boy. It's no good your thinking there's a royal road to West Africa—because there isn't. It'll be surprising"—he broke off to soliloquise—"if there's any road at all, for the British, in ten or fifteen years' time, if the Government goes on the way it's going at present. Never mind. You know, as we all know, that you've made a mull of things up to now. Wanting to fly before you can walk is just as silly as never wanting to fly at all. Look at yourself! Here you are, fifteen years old, and there's not a decent school in the country that'll take you in."

"I've done nothing disgraceful," he muttered.

"Don't be a dolt! Do you suppose parents all over England want their boys to follow your bright example of running away to sea? Young lads are as imitative as a pack of monkeys, and half the skippers round the country would be driven mad by youths in their teens trying to trick their ways on to the ships!

"I'll tell you straight: I don't want you in my office. I've made you an offer—which you can take or leave, as you please—because you're one of my own family, and I'm giving you a chance of showing yourself ready to make good, instead of stravaging round like a madcap, driving your parents crazy and ending up as a ticket-of-leaver—which is just about what will happen to you, young fellow, unless you mend your ways. Come in the office, and see what trade really means—instead of imagining yourself king of the castle because you can bamboozle a bunch of ignorant blacks into parting with their goods at a few farthings under the honest price! Oh, yes, I know Runstables' methods," quoth Harcourt, "and I don't care for them. A bargain's a bargain, whether you make it with the President of the United States or with a pock-marked up-river nigger that doesn't know B from a bull's foot!"

Anæsthetised by the slow rumble of his uncle's voice, Johnny, so far, had not attempted to speak. As Harcourt stopped, he asked:

"Do I decide now?"

"Now, by God!" Harcourt brought his hand down heavily on the desk. "You've given us enough trouble, without shilly-shallying when somebody tries to get you out of it."

"All right." He lifted his chin and looked Harcourt in the eyes. "I'll come."

Triumphant, Harcourt returned the look slyly.

"And supposin' Drummy makes a fuss?"

"I'll still come," said Johnny without hesitation.

Harcourt chuckled.

"Ring that bell, boy." He drew his pen and a sheet of paper towards him. He had written the date when Joe came in.

"Yes, sir?"

"Send Mr. Derbin. This, by the way, is Johnny Flood. You can take him downstairs until I ring for you again."

The two boys stood grinning at one another: Joe taller by a couple of inches than Johnny, heavier, although no less lively in movement. By far the better looking of the two, thought Harcourt, with a tick in his heart. If there had but been some sign—some unmistakable mark of paternity! He turned impatiently back to his desk, swearing as Johnny, in the grip of excitement, slammed the door behind him.

"Golly!" Joe was grinning on the stairs. "If you're going to be with us, you'll soon learn not to slam the Chairman's door!"

Bending over the desk, Harcourt wrote:

"My Dear Drummy,—

"I have seen Johnny, and he is coming to work in the office. If you listen to my advice, you won't make a fuss about this. It is more than obvious he'll do no good in the career you are planning for him. . . ."

III

Lady Cullen also had picked up her pen. An indefatigable correspondent, her letters inflicted (as a rule) boredom on the wide circle of her acquaintance which had learned to flinch from " poor Edith's " writing on an envelope.

"I am deeply touched, my dear Constance, by the kind letter in which you express your sympathy in my enterprise. For such it appears, no doubt, to many of my friends ! For a quiet, middle-aged couple to adopt a child is a grave step, and one which we have taken—I will be frank with you—more from a *sense of duty* than because we are either of us, in the general application of the term, *child-lovers*. I pray it may turn out to the good of all. A *heavy responsibility* indeed !—especially when one considers the heredity involved. Still—there was *no one else*. The Vanbrughs—poor dear Amicia's family—made no advances ; and the Temples—that particular branch—became extinct, as you know, with Everard's death. One had to do *something*——

" I must tell you, the little girl is very good, gentle and (seemingly) well disposed—though it is early days to speak of *character* and there is *much in the past* to make us *anxious* and *watchful*. It is hardly necessary to add that she has been beautifully trained in the social observances. I receive many compliments—even from comparative strangers—on my ' daughter's ' manners.

" These, however, are shallow considerations. It is my earnest prayer that we shall succeed in implanting in our little ward that *true regard* for Christian principle which has, alas, been neglected by those responsible, so far, for her upbringing.

" I should be most grateful if you, from your wider experience, could recommend me a young *Protestant* gentlewoman, who may be trusted to continue, and *to correct*, an education which appears to have been conducted on *somewhat peculiar* lines. At present Emily is having some lessons with the Floods' governess, but as Miranda is very backward, in addition to being much younger, the arrangement is far from satisfactory.

" There are *three boys* at the manor ; the eldest, a handsome fellow, is at Harrow and already regarded—according to gossip, to which, as you know, I pay little attention—as quite a parti in the neighbourhood. It is a mercantile family, which had made *great strides*, and although not very well viewed by a few of the county, I must admit we find them agreeable neighbours, and shall doubtless see more of them now that our young people have made friends. *She* was a *Westermain*. Some of the people we have met are inclined to make a joke of the fact that the

Floods marry for social advancement, but one naturally ignores this kind of ill-natured comment.

" If it were not for Sir Vaughn's addiction to his clubs and to his circle of scientific friends, I should be quite content to settle down in our quiet country home and assume the responsibilities of our station in the direction of our humbler neighbours. It may, however, be better for Emily that she shall learn, when young, to contrast the more worldly life of London with the simple pleasures of the countryside, to the advantage of the latter. I sometimes feel that I could wish for her nothing better than the calm dignity of one of these great country houses which, despite the *disruptive* spirit of the times, one is thankful still to see exerting their great power and influence for the general good of the community. One is bound to admit that Mr. Flood takes his duties as a squire *most seriously*, insisting on the punctual attendance at church, not only of the indoor and outdoor servants and the tenantry, but of each member of his family : a *rare* and *beautiful* example—in these days ! They should indeed do well—with such a tradition behind them——"

" My poor Con ! That's your tenth yawn ! What earthly excuse can any correspondent find for inflicting such boredom on her reader ? " The speaker mocked gently, through the smoke of his cigarette, at his companion's occupation.

She flicked the closely written pages across the table.

" Edith—preparing us for the fact that she means to marry Mishy Temple's girl off to one of the young Floods. Who cares ? . . . All the same, it's rather hard on the girl." A pair of pretty eyes pondered reflectively on their *vis-à-vis* : relaxed, tolerant, genial, after the devilled bone, kidneys and bacon of English breakfast. " Of course, she's Everard's daughter, as well as Mishy's."

" Meaning—— ? "

" That she may have a will of her own. As I had. Why—didn't you know they wanted me to marry Harcourt, before you came along ? "

" The devil they did ! " This was startling information. " By Gad, *did* they ? Damned impudence—— ! "

She patted his hand soothingly.

" Why worry, old boy ? ' The best-laid schemes ' are no use against a woman's will, when she chooses to exert it ! And, you know——" She paused.

" Well ? Out with it ! You're looking dev'lish knowing," her spouse was pleased to encourage her.

" Oh, nothing in particular. Only—it would be funny if she did. The girl, I mean. Marry one of those boys."

" Funny—for who ? "

" *Not* so funny for the young Flood, I fancy. That Vanbrugh blood ; you know—— ! "

" Pretty washy, isn't it ? " with a raised eyebrow. " I seem to remember the mother—rather a colourless specimen, wasn't she ? "

" Mishy ? " She gave him the irritatingly superior smile of her sex. " Stick to horses, darling ! " she advised him. " You're so much cleverer about them than you are about—us ! "

And, in the West Country, Miranda Flood was saying to her brother Johnny :

" Isn't Emily *nice* ? You like her too, don't you ? "

" It hasn't taken you two long to ' chum up ! ' " He evaded the issue. Hugging herself with her thin arms, Miranda appeared to consider.

" I think it's because she's so unlike any of us," she offered. " She's like —well, it's as if she was made of silk, and we——"

" Well, what are we made of ? " he teased her.

" Oh—any old thing." She shrugged her shoulders. " *Bitty* stuff—with knots in it—and loose threads here and there—what they call shoddy ! Except you——"

He burst out laughing.

" You are a cuckoo ! Look : I want a pencil. Find me one, will you— like a good Winkle."

She limped before him into the library—the long, narrow room, dark with the darkness of a rainy morning, and of a room which has not yet come to life ; for it was yet half an hour to breakfast. An anxious immaculacy lay on the furniture, on the chairs and hassocks placed in readiness for prayers, on regimented writing materials and on journals arranged in mathematical precision. Glass fronts of bookshelves gave back their ghostly reflections, as Johnny and Miranda tiptoed uneasily towards the desk which spread its vast barricade across the bow of the window.

While he rattled the papier maché tray, in search of the special kind of pencil that would look well in the breast pocket of a smart young man of business, he heard her say " Look ! " " *Look*," she repeated, with a note of urgency in her voice that finally drew his attention. He glanced at the volume she was pushing towards him across the shining leather of the desk.

" Burke ? " He turned away impatiently. " I want a copying pencil— be sharp, Winkle : look in the drawer. I'll be late—if I don't look out——"

" Look," she insisted. " It's *marked*."

He bent reluctantly over the small print that her finger indicated, noticing, as he did so, the slip of paper which had marked the page.

> " Temple, Everard Lygon Chichester, b. 1848, y. s. of the late Lord Percy Temple (*see* Chieveley), m. 1872 Amicia, dau. of the late Lionel Vanbrugh, Esquire, of Boltings, Norfolk, d. 1879. Had issue one dau., Emily, b. 1879——"

He heard himself saying :

" It's an old edition, because it hasn't got her father's death." And found Miranda clutching his arm, her dark, short-sighted eyes staring wildly at him.

" *They've put a cross against it.*"

A lightly pencilled cross, marking Temple—as it had marked Montague ;

as it had marked Cholmondeley ; and Pelham ; and half a dozen more. They—the children—were not supposed to know the meaning of the cross ; it was Dorset who had found out—and been very funny about his parents' ingenuous plots for his future. Funny—with a glitter in his eyes : the glitter which came there at any reminder that he was the heir to Guerdon.

" Johnny—be quick ! You—must—be—*quick*." She was panting. " You've got to make lots of money—and marry Emily ! "

" Shut up—you little ass."

He flung the book away from him and rushed out of the room, and out of the house. He had left Dorset's bicycle—the bicycle Dorset was too grand to use—carefully propped in readiness under the open barn where they washed the carriages—and some officious underling had put it away. A groom came running at Johnny's furious roar. The coach house was unlocked, the bicycle wheeled out—with a flat tyre.

" Give me that thing ! " Snatching the pump, Johnny disposed of the youth's clumsy fumbling with the valve. Swept with sudden panic of being late, his heart pounding, he drove the air into the tyre and felt it slowly hardening : only a slow puncture, mercifully. But he had six miles to go and it might let him down again.

Tearing down the muddy avenue, he felt a sick emptiness, and ascribed it to having had no breakfast. That was because he had forgotten to remind anyone of his early start. He had meant to call in on Harriet, when passing the Dower House, grab a cup of tea and a hunk of bread from the kitchen and gnaw the latter as he went along ; but a glance at the stable clock had shown him he could not risk the delay. Harriet, waiting behind her curtains to wave him godspeed on his new adventure, caught only a glimpse of the small figure on the bicycle, as it flashed between the lodges, and wondered if the boy had eaten ? Vicky's business, of course, to look after such things, but she was perfectly capable of assuming, unless he had reminded her, that Johnny would sit down to breakfast with the family at the usual time. Her lips tightened with annoyance, " old " Mrs. Flood descended for her own breakfast, irritated to find she had no appetite for a meal she normally enjoyed.

He was sweating by the time he reached the common, the discomforture of his speed increased by the drag of the overcoat on his shoulders and armpits. He must ask for a new one ; this was ridiculously short and tight—he had only put it on because it was his best, and he did not want to cut a poor figure, on his first (official) appearance in Queen Square. Why not—the thought flashed into his mind—go and order one for himself ? They knew him at Cole and Pottow's, and would doubtless be pleased to open an account for an independent young gentleman with an income of his own ! That the " income " was not likely for some time to provide for the purchase of overcoats was beside the point.

Johnny drew in a deep breath and looked round him. A heavy sea mist lay across the common, swathing the tree trunks and lending a soft, drowned aspect to the grass. Only a farm cart or two, a few labourers, clomping in their hob-nailed boots, had passed him since he set out ; the men wagged their heads at the young fellow on the bicycle, one nudged his companion and the pair of them put their fingers to their forelocks sheepishly. Pedalling on, he could imagine their comments : One of the young Floods—ay, the young 'un ; him as ran away to sea. A reg'lar character, that one. Looks like he's up to something else—eh ? The penetrative curiosity of the countryside followed him ; he smothered a laugh.

It was almost like that other morning—ages ago, now, it seemed : only not so early, and dew instead of snow on the ground. But there was the same sense of breathless adventure, not to be destroyed by the cold interview with Dromore, or the incredulous mockery of Dorset and Gilbert. Let them scoff—they—still in their public schools, subject to the authority of ushers, the discipline of the cane, while he, the youngest, was already a man of business, a man of means, earning the pocket money for which they had, virtually, to beg ! He coasted, with a whistle, down to Redland Green, with its fringe of villas at which the milkmen were just concluding their morning rounds, and paused, to examine his wheel again ; it would not do to arrive in Queen Square on a flat tyre.

Not quite like the first time, of course ; there was not the sea at the end of it, the heart-stopping moment of sighting the *Aldebaran* at her berth, the stumble up the landing plank ; and yet . . . the end : was it not the same ? Far away, beyond the green trees, the grey Georgian façades of the square, surf beat on a waiting shore ; drums sent forth their summons, to be carried in the cordage of a homing ship and tremble finally in the ear of a boy on Redland Green. . . .

Whiteladies Road was lively with opening shops, with scurrying assistants, with men who looked at their watches as they hurried towards the tram terminus or made for their offices down near St. Stephens. He had a thrilling sense of being part of this active life of Bristol ; impatience to take his share in it had banished the cold moment when, looking at a pencilled cross, he had seen in it memorial to Emily.

IV

A smart young clerk took his place briskly at the desk indicated to him on his arrival ; hung up his hat with a flourish, took in with pride the stretch of mahogany of which he was master. A ledger, a box of envelopes appeared at his elbow ; his immediate duty—he was given to understand—was to address envelopes. He dipped his pen in the ink ; in his best handwriting he began to transcribe the addresses he had been given.

At the end of a couple of hours, with an aching hand (it was an effort to keep up the standard of penmanship he had set himself for this, his first official duty), he took a look round the office. All his colleagues appeared to be fully occupied. At intervals, wire baskets were carried in by office boys and their contents distributed among the desks—but none delivered at the newcomer's. Now and again, a senior clerk received an entire basketful.

The smart young clerk looked at it with envy. He was getting a sense of inferiority. He bent earnestly to his task again, determined, at all events, not to incur the charge of idling which had already been levelled at his neighbour by a censorious superior.

A basket arrived on his left—it was for the idle one. A basket on his right; and an elderly, bearded person claimed it intact and dealt with it nonchalantly.

He found Joe Prior at his elbow: a basket in Joe's hand, a single manila envelope in it, addressed in a clerkly script to "Mr. John Flood." He snatched it with relief; recollected, and dropped it like a hot cake in front of him, assuming the air of bored preoccupation that goes with custom. He forced himself to address six more envelopes before opening it.

He found himself goggling at the contents.

"Dear Sir,—

"We are advised by your Chairman, Mr. Harcourt Flood, that our account with you remains unsettled. Apologising for the oversight, we therefore enclose you a money order for the sum of Three Pounds Seventeen Shillings in discharge of our indebtedness for services rendered. Kindly receipt and oblige.

"Your humble servants,

"J. J. Runstable.

"p.p. (illegible) cashier."

At noon, a smart young clerk put on his hat, stepped out briskly, and, with a fine sense of direction, made for the Llandoger Trow in King Street; ordered a beer, drank it with appreciation, ordered another, and was tapped on the shoulder by a smiling stranger.

"You're Johnny Flood, aren't you?"

"That—that's my name," he stammered. A bony hand, ink-stained to the knuckles, shot out to grasp his own.

"Well, Johnny Flood! You've seen we don't lose time in discharging our liabilities—when they're brought to our attention."

"I don't know who I'm speaking to."

The stranger apparently found this a great joke.

"Got to find your feet in shipping circles yet—eh? I reckon you heard from Runstable's this morning."

The colour ran up the smart young clerk's cheek.

"Yes. I'm obliged to you." (A formula of Harcourt's, in dealing with inferiors.) The Flood eyes dealt summarily with the stranger—a middle-aged, slightly seedy individual, in need of a shave, whose meaningful eye on Johnny's tankard indicated his preparedness to accept hospitality. Johnny leaned over and tapped him smartly on the shoulder. "And harkee: if occasion rises again—there's no need to address me through the Chairman. I deal with my own affairs."

With a finger to the brim of his bowler—a gesture which with its dismissal of familiaries, might have been Harcourt's—the new representative of the shipping firm of Flood opened the door and stepped out on the cobbles of King Street, leaving his unsavoury acquaintance agape.

A smothered titter brought an oath from the Runstable clerk's lips.

"Didn't land your herring that time, did yer, Sam? Who's your dandy pal?"

The burst of profanity with which the other satisfied their curiosity drew interest but no sympathy from his audience.

"Must have gone soft—trying it on with one o' that lot!"

But the word went round, and it was with respect, that time alone was to change to liking, that Johnny was received on his next visit to the Llandoger Trow.

CHAPTER TWELVE

I

"I THINK Harcourt, with that great house at his disposal, might have offered Johnny accommodation!"

Selina was outraged at the idea of a son of hers going into common lodgings. Vicky took a saner view of her brother's conduct.

"I'm sure Hacky has his reasons. He probably feels it would not do, to single Johnny out in so conspicuous a fashion, among the other clerks."

"His own flesh and blood——!" fumed Selina.

A suggestion that he should be apprenticed to the firm had been turned down, by Johnny himself. "I'd rather begin as an ordinary clerk, and earn my wages," he gave as his reason; and out of these unmunificent wages he insisted on paying for his lodgings. Even Harriet lost her temper with him.

"As though there were any virtue in living in a style totally different from anything to which you have been accustomed! Play-actor!" she stormed at him.

"I'm not pretending to any virtue." His jaw set stubbornly. "But as nobody approves of what I'm doing, I'm not going to take money for it."

"You are just doing this to annoy me!" She pointed a disdainful finger at the little heap of gold which lay between them on the table. "Take it! And owe it to me, if you like. You can give me an I O U—if you're so much of a shopkeeper as to insist on it!"

He could not help smiling at her disgust, but he stood by his refusal. After he had gone, she flung the sovereigns into a drawer; her eyes were bright with mortification, as she locked it. For the first time in her life, Johnny had hurt her; but she would have died rather than admit it to the family, to whom she boasted of his independence.

Snow had lain for ten days deep across the commons, when it became inevitable that Johnny should lodge in Bristol. Joe Prior's landlady in Ship Lane had, it appeared, a "false loft" off one of her rooms that would accommodate a truckle bed, and could be made into a chamber for Joe's friend. This, at least, was the solution Johnny found for himself, and which scandalised the family. Appealed to hysterically by Selina, Dromore shrugged his shoulders. John—it was useless to blind oneself—had the instincts of a vulgarian ; so far as he—Dromore—was concerned, he might find his own level.

During the seven years that followed, Johnny Flood learned to be what his forefathers had been : a man of Bristol. In the long, light summer evenings, when other youths swaggered over their pints in the alehouses, trailed the giggling trollops of Cock and Bottle lane along the pavements, or applauded from the gallery the star turns in Broadmead's music hall, he and Joe Prior explored the antique beauties of the town—to which he found Joe no less receptive than he was himself. Every alley and corner became familiar, from Pie Poudre Court to Christmas Steps, down to King Street and on to the Redcliff Hill. Rooting in curiosity shops, where they were both welcome as soon as it appeared their interest was genuine, and not confined to the facetiæ that usually drew such customers to the premises, they would sometimes find a few pence to spend on one of the family-engraved old bill-heads or tradesmen's cards of the last century ; or a broadsheet, or a play-bill of Jacob's Well ; and once—a rare treasure—a bill of sale for a small consignment of slaves, to be disposed of at the Llandoger Trow, which, since it cost half a crown, Johnny had to ask the shopkeeper to put aside for him, until he could spare so large a sum from his weekly pittance.

And when the days grew shorter and nights were cold, the two boys would pore by candlelight (the landlady was parsimonious of her oil) over books borrowed from Uncle Quentin or picked up in the twopenny trays of booksellers : books always on the same subject—West Africa, that Johnny read word for word, storing up their information as a squirrel stores nuts, filling his head with a jumble of miscellaneous knowledge that only time would resolve : with, now and then, a flash of triumph in the detection of some mis-statement made by the author, which even his small experience enabled him to correct.

"See here : this juggins says"—he would read the passage out to the respectful Joe—"whereas, of course, the truth is——"

"It's a pity the fellow that wrote that rigmarole didn't come to you, before making an ass of himself." Joe's simple belief in his friend's infallibility had the effect, occasionally, of making Johnny ashamed of himself.

"Rats. It's easy to make a slip."

"I wish," he said on an evening when they were lying under the hawthorns on Brandon Hill, looking down on the tumbled roofs across which the chimneys drew their thin web of smoke, "I wish I could get hold of a book on native dialects. It would be jolly useful, when I get out there. . . ."

Joe looked up quickly ; he had not missed the "when" in place of the "if" Johnny might have used.

"You're going back—really?"

"As soon as I get the chance. Why don't you come too?" It was no more than a bit of friendly rhetoric ; Joe for all his goodness and loyalty did not fit into that world which was a background to all his thoughts.

The other shook his head slowly.

" No ; I guess not. It doesn't call me, the way it does you."

A curious look passed between them.

" Shall I tell you something ? *I hate the Coast.* I'm scared stiff at the notion of going back. But I've got to ; d'you see ? "

" No, I don't," said Joe bluntly. " If I was scared of a thing, I'd lay off it—you bet ! But I'm not made the way you are," he added, with humility.

" No, but—listen : don't you know that thing that makes people who are frightened of heights feel as if they've got to throw themselves over ? "

" But they don't," said the literal-minded Joe.

" How do you know they don't ? And there's another thing. I know a fellow who's scared to death of bulls. But he can no more pass a field with a bull in it than fly ! He just has to get over the stile and go towards it, as if he was magnetised."

" I bet he'd get back over the stile pretty quick if the bull was to start out for him ! "

" Yes, but he's *got* to do it ; that's the point. And that's more or less how I am about the Coast," he muttered, half-ashamed of the admission.

" What are you scared of ? " Joe knitted his brows, trying, in his simple fashion, to find a reason for so eccentric an attitude.

" Oh—cut it out. It's just a lot of rot ! " He flung himself over on his face and plucked at a head of clover, to crush the honey-laden bases of the blossoms between his teeth. Joe said softly :

" Do you think there's anywhere—any place in the world—as beautiful as Bristol ? "

They lay for a moment, silent, looking down from their green eyrie on that russet-and-purple dimness where already, in small houses darkened by their eaves, pale buds of light bloomed here and there ; and a ghost rose, laying its hand softly on the shoulder of Johnny Flood. He said in a hushed voice :

" It must have been a fine sight—the old ships—lying right up here at the city wharves. We'd got a house, once, somewhere near where you and I are lying now." So strong was the past, he almost expected to see it as he looked round. " Triton, it was called——"

" What happened to it ? "

" Pulled down, I suppose." He shrugged his shoulders. " I've heard Uncle Hacky say some of the stone was used to build Berkeley Square."

The boy with no background stared at the boy with so rich a tapestry behind him.

" I bet you're proud, sometimes, to think of all your folks have had to do with Bristol."

While Johnny sought an answer to this, two feminine figures, to whom Joe instantly transferred his attention, appeared on the lower slopes. More mature in sexual matters than his companion, he was accustomed in deference to Johnny's youth, to conceal his bashful concern with a sex which held no particular fascination for one immunised by his home circle.

The two slim creatures, bending against the slope of the grass, were unconscious of their voices mounting upwards, as they started what was evidently a race to the top of the hill. There was little to be seen but the crowns of two flower-bedecked hats and the umbrella-spread of " epaulettes " recently launched from the great fashion houses of London, and already imitated with ardour by young provincial ladies who founded their wardrobes on *Weldon's* and the *Lady's Journal* ; but Joe's face was burning. All womanhood, for him, was filled with exquisite possibilities ; his misery was the bashfulness that limited his advances.

" Oh, stop, for mercy's sake ! "

The leader of the two paused to look down with laughter on her breathless companion.

" Why, we're not half-way yet—— ! "

" It's all very well for you, but I've got on my new diagonals ! "

" What are you ? I was eighteen and a half, last time I measured myself." Johnny nudged his companion, at this cryptic saying.

" I've set my heart on getting down to seventeen," panted the other, blissfully unaware of the still air that broadcast the recondite information to the interested listeners.

" You'll be green-sick, if you don't look out. I read in the paper, only last week——"

" Good lord, it can't be—it is Polly Bowling ! " Johnny scrambled to his knees to wave wildly. " Hi, Polly ! Polly ! Where on earth do you think you're going at this time of day ? "

Her lifted face lit with pleasure.

"Why, Mr. Johnny ! Well—of all things—to think of meeting you——! " Taking the remainder of the slope at a run, she stood before them, her hands on her hips, her bosom, above the eighteen-and-a-half-inch waist, rising and falling under its swelling plastron of imitation lace : a different Polly from the one in a sun-bonnet, who had curtseyed to " old " Mrs. Flood and slapped Dorset's face. Johnny grinned appreciation of the change.

" My word, you are a swell ! Is that how you dress up to run races on Brandon Hill ? "

" Silly ! " She dimpled at him. " We've been to the review ! Connie's brother's in the Volunteers—oh, this is my friend, Miss Ives—Mr. Flood," she ended, with demure recollection of the proprieties.

An anæmic brunette gave them each her hand, in the fashionable " swan's neck " style which was supposed to be current in " smart " society —so deprived of breath by her climb that she was incapable of more than an agonised smile.

" If this isn't a joke ! " beamed Polly. " And me only here for the night—stopping with Connie ; we were both at Miss Kempster's, you know." With a friendly nod to Joe, as though to prevent his feeling he was left out of the greeting.

" This is Joe Prior. So now you're back at Guerdon? Sit down and tell us about it." Johnny patted the turf invitingly.

" Goodness, no ; we mustn't stop—must we, Connie ? " Still speechless, Miss Ives shook her head. " Oh, yes, I'm back ! " gurgled Polly. " And Ma's doing her very best to make a dairymaid of me ! You should see me at the churn. Next time you're home you'll have to taste one of my cheeses ; they're good, aren't they, Con ? " she appealed to her companion.

Finding her voice at last, Miss Ives agreed they were " quite de-*Licious* ! " with an accent whose gentility was increased by her breathlessness.

" I'll keep you up to that ; I'm at home every Sunday."

" Are you ? We don't see much of them now : only Miss Miranda. She comes with Miss Emily, when it's fine."

Emily ; it gave him a pang to remember that he had only seen her across the aisle, in the big Cullen pew, for months. She never came to Guerdon on Sundays : was it because she was not allowed, or because she did not care to see him ? Miranda said it was because the Cullens would not have out the carriage, except for church-going, on Sundays : a poor reason, it seemed, with Champion Court, the Cullens' place, less than a mile away across the park.

" Well—you'd better let us walk you home, hadn't you ? " To change the subject, Johnny drew out his watch. " It will be getting dark soon, and there's a lot of roughs about—after the review."

" Oh, we don't live at all in a *rough* part." Miss Ives was evidently pained by the suggestion. " But we don't mind an escort, all the same ! " Her smile was for Joe, whose silence she openly preferred to Johnny's nonchalance, interpreting it as a tribute to her charms.

" Connie's people live on Richmond Hill—all among the nobs ! " Polly winked cheerfully. " Her father keeps a tobacco shop. That's nice of you, Master Johnny. Well, this *is* a surprise," she observed, as, taking precedence of the others, they crossed the crown of the hill, to see the lights of Clifton twinkling before them. Her skirts swished on the short grass ; she tilted her head to catch the liquid note of a thrush, that poured its final ecstasy from a bough in Berkeley Square. Suddenly she burst into laughter. " Wouldn't Ma be in a steam if she could see me ! "

" What about ? "

" Why—*us* ! Walking by ourselves, at this time of the evening. I'd have a lecture an hour long. You won't say you've seen me, will you, Mr. Johnny ? " she pleaded.

" No, I shan't say anything. All the same, I don't see why she should mind. We've known each other—as long as we can both remember ! " He frowned at the foolishness.

She gave him a quick look, not telling him that that would add to the offence. Ma was ridiculous about the Floods—she really was ; it was sheer folly, considering Bowlings were Guerdon tenants, whom it paid to be on good terms with the Manor. As though she—and the Flood boys as well, if it came to that—did not know how to behave themselves !

" Have you ever been to the Redcliff ? " he was asking her unexpectedly.

A little confused by the change of subject, Polly shook her head.

" We used to go to St. Nicholas, from Miss Kempster's."

" There's something you ought to see there—that might interest you."

" Is there? I'm not awfully keen about old tombs and monuments and things," confessed Polly frankly. " Still—what is it? I might go and have a look, sometime—if I've got the nerve!" She gave him her friendly smile. " Why don't you take me? I don't have to go home until to-morrow night."

Privately considering the suggestion rather a pert one, Johnny agreed, after some hesitation, that he might manage it.

" We get about an hour off at half-past twelve," he told her, with a lack of enthusiasm that might have abashed a more self-conscious young woman than Polly Bowling. She appeared, however, to be delighted with the concession.

" That's fixed then! And listen: I'll fetch Connie, and you'd better bring your friend Joe along. Then, if anybody happens to tell Ma, there won't be trouble."

He felt the precaution to be a stupid one, but promised to observe her wishes.

" I'd give plenty to have your way with girls!" burst from Joe, as the pair of them were returning across the bridge.

" My way with girls!" Johnny gaped with astonishment. " What the dickens are you talking about?"

" There you were, gabbling away with the one you call Polly, and blowed if I could think of a word to say to the other, that walked with me!"

" Why, you ass! Polly and I have known each other since we were children. She's a daughter of one of our tenant farmers." He stopped, his face reddening; it was one of the few impediments to his intercourse with Joe that he felt constrained, always, to suppress anything that might remind the other of the difference in their respective status. " By the way, we've got to take them to the Redcliff to-morrow; it's an awful nuisance, but I didn't quite know how to get out of it, when she asked me. As a matter of fact, I thought it was rather a piece of cheek——!"

The darkness concealed the difference of Joe's opinion from that of his companion, but no more was said on the subject until they had had their supper and were going to bed.

" I say—I've got something to ask you."

" What's up?" yawned Johnny, glancing with surprise at the scarlet face of his friend.

" You might take that dark-haired girl, and let me have the other—for a change. You know—to-morrow—when we go to the Redcliff!"

Johnny burst out laughing.

" All right, you can have Polly! She'll do all the talking, if that's what you want. But I've got something to show her, which wouldn't interest either of you, particularly."

" That's very decent of you, old chap!" Joe was now purple with embarrassment and gratitude. " I suppose—I suppose"—he blurted—

" you wouldn't lend me that tie I borrowed last week ? The kind of speckled one—— ? "

" Good lord, take it. I'm not going to doll up."

" You don't need to," said Joe humbly. " But," he added, with a simplicity the more touching because it was genuine, " I've got something to do to cut you out with a girl like—Miss Polly ! "

II

The midday sun lay in long shafts on the aisles of St. Mary Redcliff—" the fairest, the goodliest and most famous parish church in England ; " the dark effigy of the one who so described it looking down on the four young people, as they entered by the porch in which, some six decades before, the ancestor of one of them had paid ironic tribute to the memory of a great lady of Bristol. The little statue of Chatterton in his school gown attracted the frivolous attention of Polly before they passed into the church with which both Johnny and Joe were familiar.

To Johnny it was particularly dear ; less for its architectural beauties, of which he had no more appreciation than the average youth of his age, than for its association with the history of his people. Why were they not still buried here ? Matt was the last Flood to be commemorated in this place ; his huge, ornate tablet flanking the long marble slab which almost amounted to a genealogical table of three generations. Matt's son Hercules was interred at Guerdon, where, doubtless, the rest of them would lie. Johnny never looked at that earlier record without a wistful hope that he, when his time came, might rest near these Bristol ancestors to whom, more truly than to Guerdon, he felt he belonged.

He had no desire, however, to share these emotions with present company, with whom, regretting he had brought them there, he had begun to feel impatient. It would mean nothing to Connie Ives and Joe ; and Polly, although on her best behaviour, was obviously on the alert for anything that might relieve the over-sobriety of their surroundings.

He shot out his arm to point brusquely to a narrow brass plaque, placed humbly at the foot of the great Flood marble—" There it is ! "—and saw her stoop to read it.

Joe, whether from tact or by means of coercion—Miss Ives had shown herself patently dissatisfied with the change of partner, which Johnny, on Joe's behalf, had skilfully organised immediately on their encounter—had taken Connie into the side chapel, to show her the great rib of the mythological cow, and save for a few sightseers drifting between the pillars Johnny and Polly were alone.

As she straightened herself and looked at him, he saw, to his surprise, like a light cloud across the incorrigible levity of her plump features, an expression of awe and wonder.

" Who was it ? "

" *J. R. Bowling, faithful servant, good friend*," he read aloud, from the

Gothic lettering on the brass plate. "I only know he was a sailor on one of our ships, and he died in one of our almshouses." It seemed a meagre record. "I just thought you'd like to see it; he might be a relative of yours."

"I'll ask Ma; she knows more than Pa about the family." She reached out her hand with a shy gesture, to touch the simple inscription. "I wonder who put it there."

"I asked the Vicar that"—he was glad to be able to produce some more substantial information—"and he said he believed it was a Miss Burmester, who had a lot to do with Abolition and was probably a friend of the family. She must have known J. R. Bowling—whoever he was."

"I like it," said Polly. "It's plain, but it's kind of—noble: isn't it?" she added unexpectedly.

His heart warmed to her, to the sudden gravity of the face under the flowery hat, to the way her gloved hands had folded themselves, as though she had suddenly remembered she was in church and had put off folly for a while.

Alarmed, himself, at the possibility of showing emotion, he spoke in an offhand manner.

"Anyhow, it seems like a pretty good reason why Floods and Bowlings should still be friendly, the same as they were in the past, doesn't it?"

She flushed, then nodded, rubbing the back of a finger across her eyelashes as though finding moisture there, and went back quickly to the others, advancing up the aisle. She evidently did not tell them about it, or ask them to come and look, for the three of them turned and went towards the door; and Johnny, following them, liked her for treating this as a private matter, concerning only himself and her.

III

The century was gathering itself for its last lap. As Venetia Flood had said, the age of speed had set in, with the arrival of that yet incalculable monster, the motor car. As though in protest against the headlong tendency of the times, the Queen, it was said, had taken to a bath-chair, while her son, heading the Marlborough House set, charged about the country in his De Dion Bouton; and the expenses of young men-about-town were increased by the insistance of their charmers upon the provision of the electric brougham for the display of their graces in the park.

Harcourt Flood was among the first of the local magnates to invest in the new means of travel; but it was remarked that he kept to his horses when it was a matter of urgent punctuality. Speed invaded Bristol, with the electric tramway from Old Market Street to Kingswood; speed even affected the Docks Committee, which, with a sensational *volte face* of policy, suddenly voted enormous sums in the effort to reclaim that which was already lost. Labour, which had demonstrated its restiveness with torchlight and broken heads at the beginning of the decade, settled down into a rumbling more ominous because it made no spectacular claim on public consciousness, and a gulf hardly less marked than that which existed in the previous century yawned between the prosperous and the indigent sections of the community —a gulf into which philanthropists flung their charitable mites, in the hope of postponing that which clear-sighted people were beginning to recognise as a social menace.

Wine Street was broadened, and the prices of building plots kicked the beam. The Suspension Bridge acquired an unsavoury reputation for suicides. Following on some calamitous incidents caused by storm and high tides, a scheme was instituted for the disposal of flood water. A little crop of baronetcies was collected by city worthies—and the Floods refused one. In a gush of patriotic sentiment, Bristol turned itself into an electrical bonfire for the Diamond Jubilee. The University College launched an appeal for ten thousand pounds, to satisfy pressing needs for its development, and the Cabot tower rose majestically on the site of the first Hercules' pleasure grounds. Someone got fidgety over the defenceless condition of the Bristol Channel, and a gunboat and the re-arming of the fort at Portishead contributed to an increase of civic dignity.

Progress was the catch-word of the age, and some curious misdemeanours were committed in its name—as when some bright spirit had the inspiration of driving four ventilation holes through the Jacobean ceiling of the Old Mint : a project mercifully thwarted at the eleventh hour by the intervention of local antiquarians, who, however, failed to preserve some relics of old Bristol being rapidly swept away to make room for commercial expansion.

Thus the town, keeping itself abreast of modern issues. At Guerdon there were few changes. Dorset came of age, with pomp and circumstance, presentations from the tenants, and a grand fête, culminating in a ball at which was rumoured—without confirmation—his engagement to Emily Temple. She, grown very beautiful, had had several proposals, but was understood to be reserving herself for Dorset. And Gilbert, passing out of Sandhurst with a commission in the Foot, was posted as subaltern to the West African Frontier Force : a bit of bad luck for one who had seen himself in more choice surroundings. Still, he had made it only by the skin of his teeth, failing three times before he passed into the Royal Military College as a gentleman cadet ; and big game potting was at least a fair recompense for the polo on which he had been counting.

Selina, after her third miscarriage, sank blissfully into a life of invalidism, leaving Vicky established as virtual mistress of Guerdon ; while Dromore directed the ardour which the family doctor had privately advised him to bestow elsewhere into that orgy of Christian endeavour which, according to skippers up and down the Guinea Coast, was doing more to prejudice our commercial interests in foreign parts than any measure so far instituted by the Colonial Office.

In his uncle's office, Johnny plodded on through the years which it would have been false to call years of advancement ; promotion, in the Flood Company, was slower than the wheels of time. Such small credit as was one's due was reaped, as a matter of course, by the head clerk, through whom all approach to the higher powers had to be made. For the small fry there was little but the sheer, mechanical grind of copying, dictation, order sheets and bills of lading—tedious because it made small demand on anything but one's powers of application and accuracy.

For Johnny it was less tedious than for some ; names of places and commodities, coming up in the course of his labours, evoked scenes of a past now so remote that it had lost reality—as a dream, vivid on wakening, loses reality in the course of a day. Visits to the ships, to the Customs sheds, to the offices of the Dock Board, where, dancing attendance on a superior, he suspected that his presence was more by way of lending prestige to the other than of value to the business he represented, were all too rare interludes in long hours spent over ledgers ; the most they brought to him was a deepening perception of the death-clutch maintained by the Committee on Bristol's trade. He came gradually to marvel that a firm like Floods could keep its position against competitors operating from ports whose authorities were more alert to modern developments in ocean commerce.

Ignored by the senior clerks, reverend elders, several of whom had been with Matt, and had emerged from the interim hibernation to put their services at Harcourt's disposal, but much discussed in camera among the younger faction, was the Liverpool branch, which took the Chairman up to the Merseyside port on two days of the week. Occasionally a clerk was transferred from Bristol to Liverpool, and this, by the majority, was regarded as promotion, and inspired envy of the favoured one, who usually made his departure an occasion for jubilation and modest " treating " his colleagues left behind.

" None of your pen-pushing, up there in Water Street ! They do everything by typing machines," gleefully reported one returned from a preliminary survey of his new place of employment.

" They're saying Liverpool's going to be Head Office, and we're only going to do coastal work from here," was another rumour that ran round the desks on an autumn morning. Johnny and Joe exchanged looks of dismay, until the former shook his head and shaped the word " Tommyrot ! " with his lips.

" I hope to goodness they won't send me to Liverpool," mumbled Joe in the dinner hour : thinking less, at the moment, of Queen Square than of Polly Bowling. There were few Sundays, now, when he did not accompany Johnny to Henbury, where, while the latter went on to " The House," Joe might with confidence seek welcome at the farm.

Johnny shrugged his shoulders ; he was mortally sick of Queen Square, and sick of the evidence, patent on every side, that Bristol was no longer a first-class port.

" Do *you* think they're going to make Water Street Head Office ? " Joe persisted. He found it difficult, sometimes, to believe that the Chairman's nephew knew no more than he knew himself of the secret workings of the House of Flood.

" Not while Uncle Hacky's alive ! "

His eyes were fixed enviously on two men at an adjoining table, one of whom was having difficulty in negotiating the soup between his plate and his chattering teeth. The skin of both was of a malarial yellow that Johnny recognised ; their suits, good in quality and little worn, were crumpled, and diffused an odour of moth balls that told of long bestowal in store. They were Flood clerks, on furlough from the Coast, and he was determined to make their acquaintance before the dinner hour was over.

He muttered an excuse to Joe, and for the next half-hour the air chimed with the names of Coast towns : Half Jack, Jack-a-Jack, Grand Bassam, Assinee, Ancobra, Axim, Takoradi, 'Mina, Anamaboe, Apam, Winnebah, Charlestown, Whidah—and so on, from the Ivory, to the Gold, to the Slave Coast, and so up to Lagos. The two men, amused by the youth's eagerness, were ironic towards his envy of their occupation.

" What's wrong with the Coast ? " he asked defensively, when mockery began to gall him.

The men exchanged glances.

" It's not what's wrong with the Coast," one muttered. " It's what's wrong with the folks that run it."

As Johnny was about to demand elucidation of the statement, Joe's hand fell heavily on his shoulder.

" Have you retired from business ? It's going half-past," he reminded him. Johnny snatched up his bowler and the pair of them set off at the run for Queen Square. To be late was a penal offence at Flood's, and Johnny, as he ran, reflected on the many times Joe might have saved himself being reported to the head clerk, had it not been for his loyal determination to share any trouble in which Johnny involved himself.

" Look out ! " he gasped, just in time to save the pair of them an embarrassing encounter by pulling Joe into a doorway, as Harcourt and a companion paced gravely on their way to Baldwin Street, for luncheon at the Constitutional Club. Johnny looked curiously after his uncle. " Did you see who he's got with him ? Now I wonder what these two are cooking up between them."

" Young Mr. Arnold, wasn't it ? " Joe was not as familiar with the figures of Bristol magnates as Johnny, but he knew enough to recognise the dapper figure accompanying the immense one of Harcourt Flood through the midday crowds on Queen Charlotte Street. The Arnolds were brothers who, it was said, held extensive West Indian interests in the cultivation of cocoa, and were seeking affiliations with the great Bristol firm of Fry. Knowing Harcourt, it was not likely, thought Johnny, that he would waste his luncheon-time in making himself agreeable to a newcomer, unless the latter's brains offered pickings to a vulture of Uncle Hacky's proportions.

" I'd give a shrewd bet they're hatching something." He loitered for a moment, staring after the couple, as they vanished round the corner into the big main thoroughfare. " Why do all the beans go into Liverpool, and have to be brought down here by rail ? And why doesn't our company do any direct trade with the West Indies ? " He shook his head ; the solution of such problems was not within the scope of a junior clerk—although he had recently, owing to the sickness of a senior, had the handling of some more confidential papers than usually came in his way. It was these, whose contents he was in honour bound not to divulge, even to Joe, that caused him to add, with a chuckle :

" Make Liverpool Head Office, were you saying ? Not on your life, my boy ! Old Iron-guts "—he had cheerfully adopted the office name for the Chairman—" has got too many eggs in the Bristol basket, to go where he can't keep an eye on them ! "

" You're late, Flood."

" Six—no, seven minutes," he corrected himself by Matt's big round clock over the office mantelpiece, as he slid up on his stool.

" Well, you'll make up for it with extra time this evening," the head lading clerk retorted, slapping, with malicious satisfaction, a thick sheaf of papers on Johnny's desk. " It's Board meeting to-morrow, and we're behind-hand with our statements. You've got those to copy out in quintuplicate before you go home, young man ! "

" Oh, hell," muttered Johnny, as he surveyed the formidable task before him. Smitten by a sudden recollection, his jaw fell in dismay. " Look here, I can come early to-morrow ; but I can't do these to-night. We're parading at half-past six and I've got to get back for my belt——"

In common with the majority of able-bodied Bristol youths, rumours of unrest in South Africa had sent both Johnny and Joe rushing to join the Bristol Volunteers : a body formed at the time of the Peace of Amiens, whose ranks had since expanded to include Naval Artillery and Engineer Corps, as well as the Artillery and old Sea Fencibles of which it was originally composed. The Engineers, which the two young men had joined, held their drills, as a rule on Saturdays, in the large drill hall and armoury in Trinity Street ; but in view of the Queen's visit to Bristol, at which the Volunteers were to reinforce the regulars from the barracks, the Gloucester and Somerset yeomanry and a detachment of army veterans, extra parades were called which, for the honour of the corps, few would willingly miss. Shocked at the idea of doing so, Johnny stared aghast at the senior, who sneered at his inferior's perturbation.

" Even in defence of your country, Flood, I'm not at liberty to excuse your duties to the firm. It's your own affair, of course, if you choose to discuss the matter with the Chairman."

" Old bastard," snarled Johnny under his breath, as the other went away. " Just look at this damn' great whack of copying ! Why the hell we can't be like other firms and use a duplicator, God only knows. Pah ! Uncle Hacky capering about in his Panhard, and the office run as it was in great-grandfather's time ; it's a marvel we aren't expected to use quill pens—oh, *sod* it ! " he muttered viciously, as he dropped a great wad of copying paper on the floor with an inadvertent thrust of his elbow.

" Quietly, please, quietly ! " The reproof came rustling from one of the survivals of Matt's day, whose desk was opposite Johnny's. In Matt's day, young clerks did not drop paper and use bad language with impunity.

His task was not much more than half-finished, when he saw, with a desperate glance at the clock, that it was after six. Joe had been sent out with a message to one of the counting houses, and had to go on from there to Royal Insurance Chambers in Small Street, where the Post Office had just established its parcels department; that would make him late as well. Fuming with rage as he drove his pen along, Johnny at first did not hear when he was addressed across the long slopes of mahogany.

"Flood!" It was the head clerk's voice, old, quavering, and as excruciating as the squeak of a slate pencil. "Dear me, do you know I've spoken four times? We don't often have such an example of industry!"

"Sorry, Mr. Derbin; I didn't hear you." Johnny lifted his head to force a smile. Derbin wasn't such a bad old billy-goat! Better than that swine in the lading department. The mild, elderly face nodded; Johnny wondered what it was like to have spent sixty years in the service of Floods—first with Matt, then in some capacity or other on one of the Barbados plantations, and, after an interval of well-earned retirement, back on the treadmill at the bidding of Harcourt.

"You're to go to the Chairman," piped Age. "And be sharp, my boy; Mr. Harcourt is just ready to go home."

IV

The occasions on which, since his enrolment in the firm, Johnny had been called to his uncle's room might be counted on the fingers of one hand; there was no need, even, he reflected, as he took the stairs in a series of strides, to include the thumbs! Four times in all, and each occasion an unpleasant one; he grimaced, as he rapped on the panelled door. This, no doubt, meant that he and Joe had been seen skulking in the Coal Office doorway, when Harcourt and his companion turned down Queen Charlotte Street.

There was nothing, however, particularly ominous in the Chairman's aspect, as he peered up from the cigar he was lighting to nod at his nephew. The thought flashed through Johnny's mind that he would ask to be let off for the parade. Harcourt was hardly likely to oppose the natural desire of a member of the firm to cut a good figure in the forthcoming celebrations!

"Siddown," grunted Harcourt, surprisingly. Hastily controlling a start, Johnny sat, not quite easily, on the edge of one of the chairs. Harcourt, in gracious mood, inspired misgivings. His next remark was even less reassuring. "Well, how's your mother?" A query with which Selina would certainly not have been favoured before she earned his approval by her oddly unexpected support of him, on the night of the discussion of the Flood monument.

"I—I believe she's quite well, sir." Johnny failed to keep astonishment out of his tone. "I don't see very much of her at week-ends; she keeps a good deal to her room."

"H'rumph. She hasn't got your grandmother's stamina," snorted Harcourt, and was silent for a few moments, glaring at Johnny through the smoke of his cigar. "Well, haven't you got anything to say for yourself?" he demanded, as the latter maintained a nonplussed silence.

Johnny gaped, then laughed, despite himself.

" I didn't know I was expected to do the talking, sir——"

" You weren't," snapped Harcourt. " Well, thank God you're not a poll parrot, like your brother Dorset."

" I've not got as many things as Doss has to talk about."

" How old are you now ? " his uncle interrupted him to ask.

" I'm twenty, sir. I'll have my twenty-first birthday in a few week's time."

" Damme, you're no taller than a boy of twelve ! " scowled Harcourt—basing his statement on Flood proportions, rather than on the average.

" Five feet seven ? A pretty good height for a fellow of twelve," Johnny grinned at him. " Gilbert's monopolised the height in our generation. I don't show up so badly, apart from the family." He remembered Joe had three inches advantage of him, and closed his lips.

" You've now had seven years with the Company—nearly. Well ; how d'you like it ? "

Johnny hesitated ; it would be the worst policy, he knew, to tell his uncle that he was bored all but to the limit of his endurance ; that he felt himself to be, as he had dreaded, in a blind alley ; that, for months, he had been meditating a request to be sent to Liverpool, where the tide of commerce ran more swiftly than in the Bristol backwaters. But to do this, he felt, would be sorely to offend Harcourt. He answered, with caution.

" I think I've learned—a fair amount, sir."

" You'd have learned more if you'd been an apprentice."

He was silent, knowing it was true.

" We'll have to send you to Liverpool, to sharpen you up." The tone was bitter enough to warn Johnny not to show too plainly his satisfaction in a prospect he had not dared to consider.

" Thank you, sir," he said discreetly. " It will be a change."

" So that's what you want : ' a change,' is it ? " The query was ironic.

" Well, sir, I'd like to feel I was getting on a little—gaining some more experience."

" All you young people are the same," grumbled Harcourt. " You seem to think that the only way of getting experience is tearing about the world, filling your heads with a lot of twaddle you never give yourselves time to digest."

" You can't say I've done much ' tearing about ' in the last seven years," said Johnny, with justice.

" Well—you can have your ' change,' " mumbled Harcourt. His large, handsome hand reached out to tap the ash from his cigar into the great brass bowl supported on four tusks of rhino that stood on his desk. " We're giving you a holiday."

" A holiday ? " It was the last thing Johnny had expected. They did not have holidays, at Floods. Never, since the Company was formed, had its Chairman taken one ; never, following his example, were the old clerks absent from their desks. It took courage, on the part of a junior, to ask for his " week " in the summer, which, although it was granted, enveloped the recipient in a blight of disapproval it took hardihood to withstand.

" We're sending you to the Coast."

. . . The blood drained from Johnny's heart. He recovered, at last, sufficiently to moisten his lips. He whispered :

" Thank you, sir." And waited to hear more.

" You'll sail from Liverpool on the twenty-fourth," continued Harcourt. " Your passage is taken—and you'll get off at Sierra Leone. That's all—for the present."

" But don't I have any—any instructions ? " stammered Johnny.

" God damme, boy ! " roared Harcourt. " What sort of ' instructions ' do you want, to take a holiday ? Great God Almighty, at your age I didn't need tellin' how to go and enjoy myself ! "

All very pretty, thought Johnny ; but, if I know the old devil, there's a catch in it somewhere ! I wonder what he wants—what he expects—of me.

" It's very good of you, sir," he heard himself say ; the words sounded flat, colourless, empty of the joy he would like to have put into them : but how express joy, where joy was not ? In this moment of realisation of a dream, he felt emptied of everything ; as though the shock had atrophied all of his power to think, to feel, to rejoice. " How long have I got ? " he asked dully : the only question that occurred to his deadened perceptions.

" As long as you choose to take," Harcourt grunted. " That is, you can stop out there up to twelve months, if you please. I reckon that ought to kill or cure you of your fancy for the Coast. If you come back wiser for your trip, we'll see what use can be made of your wisdom. If you get ill, or homesick—well, that's your affair ; your mother'll have the vapours about you, anyhow ; no doubt she'd rather have you back in a damaged condition, than delivered in a wooden box ! " Over which grisly jest Harcourt shook a chuckle. " In plain words "—he was suddenly serious—" I'm giving you a chance to prove yourself. If your interest in the Coast is something more than hot air, and a sentimental sort of throw-back to what you're pleased to consider the land of your forefathers—you'll find it out. I've got a notion you'll find it a lot less picturesque than Matthew Flood found it when he went out in 1763. But you may find other things. . . .

" You may find, for instance "—he threw the dead cigar into the bowl—he never smoked a cigar more than half-way—and bit the end off another—" why West Africa, one of our richest potentials, only returns a third of the revenue it should contribute to the British crown."

" Don't you know why—yourself ? " Suddenly alert : as though Harcourt's words had injected some powerful stimulant into his blood-stream.

" Pah—know ? I've got every theory advanced to account for our failure in West Africa at my fingertips ; but there's a difference between theory and the evidence of one's own senses. If I were your age, I wouldn't be sending you off to act as eyes for me. I know the politicians', and the soldiers', the traders' and even the missionaries' end of it : and I discount the lot of 'em. Why ? Because they're all interested parties : each one grinding his own particular axe, with our colonial system for a whetstone.

you've got no stake in West African colonisation, and nothing to gain by distorting the facts, as you see 'em. Facts! Facts! Facts! That's all I want; no comments, and no half-baked conjectures on 'em. You can leave me to do the conjecturing. I'm quite capable of drawing my own conclusions, if I'm given the material to base 'em on.

"There's something damned queer going on on the Coast, and I don't expect you to tell me what it is; but there's a chance you might fetch something back that 'ud put me on the track of the trouble."

"I'll do my best. But—I'm terribly bucked, of course, sir, about all this—but I still don't understand why you've picked on me—I mean, there are other fellows, like Lynd and Farquarshon, whom I was talking to this morning"—Johnny stammered, in his anxiety to give credit where it was due—"who've got all the experience I haven't——"

"Pish," said Harcourt. "I can buy experience, of the sort you mean, by the bushel. You're observant, and, for some reason, you've got this Gold Coast bug in your head. I hear, by the way, that you spend every penny you earn on books; what d'you want to do that for? I've got the finest collection of Gold Coast stuff in the country. You could have borrowed it, if you'd chosen."

"I—I didn't know, sir," said Johnny, wondering who had been reporting on his extra-office activities to Harcourt.

"Some damn' queer stuff among it," chuckled Harcourt. "Things about fetish, and the leopard societies, that you won't find in the libraries: for fear it gets into some old maid's hand and she starts a brawl about it. I got 'em from Quentin. You'd better come up one night and take a look at them; you never know what comes in useful, if you happen to be in a tight spot."

"I'd like that!" His eyes sparkled at the prospect.

"Been learning up the languages, haven't you?"

"I'm blowed if I know who's told you!"

"You've got enthusiasm, and you've got youth. There's those who'd call the last a disadvantage. You ain't callow, like those brothers of yours." Johnny opened his eyes. Dorset—*callow*! "And you get on with people, because you don't throw your weight about," concluded Harcourt, astonishing Johnny more and more by this summary of virtues he had never connected with himself. "A fellow of your age can ask questions, without starting people wondering what he's driving at. And they tell me you've got a good memory. All right, then: ask questions, and remember the answers. Never mind if it's the truth or not; you can leave it to me to sort out the grain from the chaff. Don't discount what anybody says: whether he's a Customs House clerk, a nigger policeman or a ticket-of-leaver with a quart of Van Hoytima inside him. If you're chary of anybody, let it be of the Civil Service high-ups; the Foreign Office has got them, body and soul, and what they say will be pretty much what we hear from the newspapers—so you can save your time. Do you know where you are now?"

Johnny nodded. with tightened lips. The stupefaction of the first moments over, wave after wave of excitement was beating up in him; already, in imagination, the Atlantic rolled between him and Queen Square.

"Very well; be off." The chair creaked as it was relieved of Harcourt's immense weight. "Be off—and have your rumpus with the women! Or, if you're wise," he added, as an afterthought, "you'll say nothing, until you're off. You've got enough to see to, between now and when you sail, without adding their snivelling to your occupations!"

His heavy lips parted in the rare smile that held some of the sweetness of his mother's. Johnny thought, What a grand fellow he is, when one gets down to the bottom of him! They stood for a moment, facing each other, the huge man and the small one, with a wave of that rare affection which exists only between men travelling between them.

"Well—go on; what are you hanging about for?" Harcourt, grumbling, reached for his hat and gloves. "I want my dinner."

"I was only thinking," said Johnny, "it would make it easier—I could probably bring you something more useful—if I knew what you've got at the back of your mind. There's something—isn't there, sir?"

For a moment, Harcourt stared at him, wall-eyed. It was not his way to take people into his plans, before they were fully ripe. He stood silent, weighing the integrity of the youth before him. Having decided:

"There's some talk about cocoa concessions." He evaded the question. "Arnold wants to get in on them—the West Indian crops have done poorly, for a couple of seasons. We'd handle the cargoes direct; possibly have an interest in the planting. . . . I've got an idea it's a wild-cat notion. Anyhow, it depends on a lot more than getting the concessions out of a bunch of double-faced niggers; it depends—God damme!" exploded Harcourt. "D'you think I've got nothing better to do than stand here talking to you about my private business?"

He stumped out, leaving Johnny to follow at his leisure his white head, as it sunk into the darkening well of the stair.

V

When Johnny went to say goodbye to his uncle, he was a little damped to learn that Harcourt had gone to London. There was, however, sufficient hand-shaking, back-slapping and general well-wishing to make up for his want—not of ceremony, for the Chairman of Flood's owed no such thing to a junior clerk; but of avuncular feeling. Johnny was surprised to find himself a popular figure; he was, in fact, both touched and embarrassed by the amount of interest that attached, unexpectedly, to his departure. Even old Derbin took the trouble to come and shake hands and wish him Godspeed, while the valedictory spirit of the smaller fry broke out after office hours, and, starting at the Trow, took in all the taverns of King Street.

It was a moonless night, with gusts of rain that laid a thin, muddy film over the cobbles, but King Street was like a feast of lanterns, every orange-lit window sending its invitation, every doorway its warm, malt-laden breath of welcome to the revellers, as they rollicked from house to house : from the Trow to the Coopers', to the Royal Naval Volunteer, to the Bunch of Grapes and the Theatre Tavern ; to the Old Duke, the Cardigan Arms, the Britannia, the Oddfellows' Arms and the King William the Third ; floundering back to take in the Green Man, the Cornish Arms and the Waterloo House. Never was a short street more richly endowed with the ingredients of good cheer and good fellowship, and to " do its round " was an exploit reserved for those rare occasions when the convivial spirit was matched by the state of the sportsmen's pockets. Pay day, however, was luckily at hand, and there were few among the improvident who had not managed to raise a few shillings in anticipation of settlement when Saturday came.

It is to be feared that King Street recaptured, that night, some of its old reputation for carousal : that old boys and old girls in the Merchant Seamen's houses wagged their heads, winked at each other, and that a few of the abler and more sportive strutted out of their courtyard for a peek at the fun ; that in the Central Public Library mouths were pulled down, shoulders shrugged and deploratory murmurs expressed regret that, in the whole of Bristol, no place should have been found for the seat of civic culture save this one, in a quarter opposed to culture of any kind.

Every now and again, a thought of Guerdon, crossing his mind, brought a smile to Johnny's lips : Guerdon, dark, dignified, disapproving—expressing with lifted eyebrows and tightened lips its opinion of his announcement of his intention of spending the night in Bristol, on account of the early start in the morning. Only Uncle Quentin had winked, in bidding his nephew farewell ; Uncle Quentin had probably enjoyed enough send-offs in the course of his wanderings to appreciate the situation—though the old gentleman's fruity snobbery would not be likely to admit some of the elements that contributed to Johnny's farewell.

The parishes of Bedminster, St. Gabriel and St. Nicholas were all represented in King Street, and did not provide, in the strict sense of the word, a " high-class " clientèle ; the ships patronised King Street, and the theatre, and the wharves and warehouse regions all along the Welsh Backs and off the Redcliff Hill—men of good will, and good stomach, and good voice, whose geniality was prone to break out in song, in the skirling accompaniment of accordions to music hall choruses, and, as the night wore on, to old and simple ditties whose tearful sentiments have woven themselves down the centuries into the texture of British farewells.

As the atmosphere thickened, faces grew redder and the company more charged with the voluptuous melancholy of unlimited beer, Johnny found himself accepting what his companions appeared to believe : that he was leaving Bristol for ever, that he was looking for the last time on all the old familiar faces—most of which he could not remember ever having seen before—and that nothing could ever be the same again, once the refulgence of Johnny Flood's presence was withdrawn from the haunts of his youth. Midnight was striking when a small group of the faithful, still lugubriously carolling, managed by a series of miracles to circumvent the harbour, to get themselves across the bridge and to deposit Johnny and Joe safely on their doorstep in Ship Lane.

It was a very pale and shaky couple of young men who shivered their way to Temple Meads soon after dawn to await the arrival of the train that was to take Johnny to Liverpool. Chins sunk into upturned collars, they paced the platform in a salty drizzle ; it was Johnny who, at last, in desperation, led the way to the steamy refreshment room, where they sipped and shuddered a little over the Martell that had occurred to him as a final gesture of munificence. Under its influence he felt himself mellowing into the young man of the world, the experienced traveller, the genial recipient of Joe's respectful admiration.

The guard was waving his flag when Johnny recognised, in a man who came running alongside the train, one of the servants from Berkeley Square. He had just time to snatch an envelope before he was swept away—with Joe's serious, rather stunned face left behind : all the familiar squalor of the town rolling backwards beneath the windows. . . . Johnny yawned.

It was not until the train reached Crewe that he awoke, and began to read Harcourt's letter.

". . . I want you to get to know men." This was the first sentence that struck him.

"I know what you're thinking," it went on.

"There's no shortage of men in Bristol—thank God !—and you've had plenty of chances of mixing with them. But your mixing, so far, has been against a background of privilege."

He was suddenly wide awake. It would be interesting to hear Harcourt's views on privilege, as it applied to a minor servant of the firm of Flood !

"Since coming into the business you've gained, I hope, a more realistic outlook on things and people than they gave you at Guerdon. It's dawned on you, perhaps, that being born a Flood doesn't confer omnipotence on you. There are plenty of people in Bristol whose positions rest on foundations more secure—and a damn' sight more distinguished—than ours. All the same—it means something to be a Flood.

"You may fancy you've been accepted on terms of equality by the people you've been working among. Up to a point, that's true ; but I wager the thought at the back of the mind of nine out of ten of them is your name, and mine. *That*, whether they know it or not, colours their attitude—either in your favour or the opposite, according to whether they're friends or enemies of mine. It's taken me a long time to discover that, as a Flood, you can't live in Bristol on your own merits. They're going to ascribe to you virtues or vices you know nothing about. They're going to set you against some sort of an artificial standard they've built up for themselves, out of the old records.

"It comes down to this : what *are* you, besides being a Flood ?

" The atmosphere of Bristol is an atmosphere of security. Most of the people that come your way, and mine, live in circumstances, whether high or humble, defined for them by their parentage. They're *safe.* And, because they're safe, they do all in their power to secure safety for those who stand for safety to them and to their belongings. What they actually do is live on risks taken by other people. That's what I do myself.

" Sounds smug, doesn't it? Well, we are smug, because we can't help it. We take ourselves and each other solemnly. We are puffed up about our own importance. We sit in our offices and see the world through our office windows. Our outlook is bounded by the interests of our city, by our banking accounts and by our ledgers. We're the top layer.

" Remember the top layer's only a thin crust. What matters is what lies underneath. And there's a damn lot of trouble going on underneath. I don't believe—as a lot of people do—that it's a matter of politics. I've got a notion that men—the kind that matter—aren't fussing about political labels and creeds; they're too busy doing the things that need to be done. But that's not the question.

" Get out where living's hard, and get to know the people that are coping with it. People who've got no sort of influence behind them, that are doing their jobs—they don't know why—with no sort of prospect before them and nothing in particular to make them immediately worth while. Have it in your mind that those are the people who are paying for Guerdon, and for me, and for your relatives in London. The underdogs.

" You met a few of them in your first escapade. You were too young to profit by it. Now you're old enough to know that life is not a picturesque adventure. What is it? I'll expect you to answer that question when you get back.

" Use your eyes and your brains and keep your mouth shut. Enjoy yourself in Accra.

" Yours faithfully,

" HARCOURT FLOOD."

BOOK TWO

Gold Coast

1898

CHAPTER ONE

I

IT was a steamy, busy morning, with chunks of swamp mist that the sun had sucked from the crocodile beds lying like cotton-wool across the camwood trunks and knotted into the yam clusters. A rainbow shimmer trembled in the umbrella tops of the coco palms, and the heat had not yet degenerated into the sweaty anæsthetic of advanced day.

Akosua Ngomi, standing in the doorway of her hut, scratched herself through the robe of big-flowered cotton one of her sons had bought her from a Dutch trader. She had plenty on her mind, because, although her son, Kufi Kaboha, was nominal ruler of the village, she knew, he knew, and every member of the community, down to the smallest infant, knew that all forms of jurisdiction, every major decision, every matter affecting the personal and communal life of the village was referred back to her for ultimate settlement. She was a queen without a crown : a queen whose authority royalty itself, at the head of the province, respected.

Akosua, who occasionally went behind her son's back, had just concluded, privately, a deal with her friend and rival, the formidable Ya Ashantua, up at Ejesu, which, affording the greatest possible satisfaction to both ladies, might, one of these days, bring home to young Kufi, in a very surprising fashion, the extent of his mother's foresight and resourcefulness. The Ashanti were an unpredictable lot ; living on their borders, it was no bad notion to be on businesslike terms with them.

Akosua was feeling pleased with herself. She had this morning decided that one of her granddaughters was ripe to leave the fattening huts for marriage with a nephew whose first wife—a feckless creature—had foolishly succumbed to a suhman exercised (so the wife believed) by a rival. Akosua, who was tough and sceptical as the majority of her sex, and who, in her youth, had once got herself into serious trouble by poking her nose into one of the leopard societies, was pretty sure it was a straight case of kraw-kraw, mishandled by the local lady witch doctor. The nephew's wife had never been popular with Akosua, who despised any female with insufficient sex appeal to keep her man off the lhiamba. There was Quisi, at this present moment, when he should have been out with the rubber gang, hack-hacking his guts out, and trying to smother it for fear of his aunt. *Chi !* As if she did not know the noise made by lhiamba smokers—apart from the way it spoiled their tempers. It was a good thing Quisi was marrying again, if only to give him something better to think about than the poisonous little plant.

Her toothless jaws champed on the aromatic pulp of a malaguetta pod, and she spat the stinging seeds reflectively across the woolly head of a young relative, who, squatted in the dust, was submitting to the cicatrisation which was the brand, in the tribe, of newly acquired manhood. He grinned up at her proudly, as the thin knife slid under the oiled satin of his shoulder-blades : as the flesh was lifted, and the silk-cotton fluff tucked in, like narrow white worms, to make ridges of the wounds. Akosua nodded absently, approving the pattern. She appreciated fortitude.

Under her close-cropped skull lurked memories which, although faded by time, seemed vivid in comparison with the experiences of her latter years. The record of her youth was one of warfare and bloodshed. Flaming villages, the murder and rape of her kinsfolk formed the background of her adolescence and early married life. Life was now easier, but duller : the young men softer, more inclined to live on their wits than on physical prowess, than in her youth ; and there were influences which, for all her scepticism, made Akosua uneasy.

She stood still, to squint beneath the palm of her hand up the hill behind the village ; and what she saw she hated, with a deep, mistrustful hatred.

The white people. In the old days you knew where you had them. They wanted you for a single purpose. To them you represented gold, cowries, basins—or whatever was valuable to white people. So they had straightforward compacts with the kings : who, for the sake of guns, powder, liquor and finery, plundered your villages, burned your huts, captured your warriors and sent you downriver and overseas, to perish in far-off, unimaginable lands.

But the British Government put an end to this, and to the rich revenue enjoyed by the kings ; which might have been a good thing, but for what followed.

Akosua had never forgiven the white people for coming and setting up their fetish house here, in the village her husband had governed. Had he lived, she thought scornfully, no such outrage would have been permitted ; nor would the priests have tolerated the intrusion, on their sacred ground, of a foreign god.

The missionaries had arrived, many years ago, in the middle of a yam festival : taking advantage of everybody's distraction to establish themselves on the hill. By incessant nagging, and total disregard of the feminine principle of minding her own business, Akosua had goaded the men of the village, including the local fetish house hierarchy, into a palaver that continued for days ; went into chattering frenzies when it appeared no action was to be taken, and prophesied every sort of disaster if the white Wanga was allowed to take root in soil dedicated to darker spirits. Forgetting her open profession of scepticism, she haunted major and minor witch doctors, beat up a panic among the women, and started a sasabonsum scare that very nearly had the effect she was seeking.

But the conclusion of the palaver was that even sasabonsums were less to be dreaded than the action of the British Government if the village took the good, old-fashioned way with missionaries. There was a quick trade in expensive ju ju and the committee decided to spend a certain sum on magic which might or might not settle the hash of the intruders. As none of these took effect, it was conceded that the whites had got a powerful ju ju, and

Akosua sulked. An ounce of poison was, in her opinion, worth a pound of witchcraft, and the knife better than either; but her son Kufi was against these things, and she was obliged to accept his ruling.

As time went on, she was wise enough not to say, "I told you so." Among the older members of the community, the white Wanga appeared to do little harm; its effects on the younger element—even among members of her own strictly governed household—was disastrous.

Seldom a week went by but one of the young wives came howling because, her husband having taken up with the white Wanga, she was left to do all the work of the household and nursery—the white Wanga, forsooth, forbidding a man to have more than one wife; a preposterous state of affairs for any girl of decent upbringing to have to submit to.

The girls in the fattening huts were perpetually snivelling that there were not enough men to go round—with the result that there was always a lot of lawless scampering behind the huts, and young women losing their characters, to the annoyance of parents who were naturally no less anxious than their daughters to have the latter made honest women.

And the boys, instead of exercising their brains and their muscles in exploits becoming to their sex, spent their time lounging round the mission in white cotton shirts, giving themselves airs, jabbering trade English, and generally allowing it to be seen that they considered themselves superior to their elders and betters. Bumptious, cocksure and self-opinionated, they had no use for the village, no share in its interests—save of the most frivolous. They joined in the dancing at the Yam and Bantama festivals but looked sheepish when it came to the blood rites. Akosua, who, decked in the canary-green powder, her neck and arms laden with gold, had swung the fans for Bantama, was scornful. Her family had killed and eaten two native communicants of a foreign mission and paid up with dignity in teeth, rubber, pissava and cheeses. She had no use for the prissy boys of the mission, and let slip no opportunity of scoring a hit on them.

She looked up viciously at the mission, and wished that in her youth she had paid more attention to her grandmother, a skilled practitioner in ju ju, instead of larking about with the boys and fooling with her hair and her trinkets, to make the other girls jealous. Her grandmother would have made short work of the white Wanga and its priesthood. There was the Drum charm, or the Face charm, or even that simple business of driving a nail through a man's shadow, which would surely have put a stop to the activities up on the hill. Unfortunately she could not clearly remember any of them, and the local Fetish Man had, in her opinion, already shown how little he was worth, by failing to put up any effective opposition to the magic of the whites. Their magic was worse than their material power, and had beaten her country's gods. Her hatred lashed out and coiled itself like a burning snake round the white witch doctors, who, with their teaching, had let disorder into the tribe.

Still, her family was in fair order. Quabina Mukama, her third son, had done well, both in timber and rubber, and had acquired five wives.

The second boy, snatched in the nick of time from mission influence, had been successfully headed off in the direction of music, for which, as a mere infant, he had shown uncommon aptitude, and was already making quite a career with his song-net—although his grandmother would have preferred him to have taken up a more virile occupation. However, she was bound to admit it—there had always been music in her family; an uncle had been famous on the sirimba, and there were several harpists in her own generation.

And there were ways—small, negative ways, mainly—of getting one's own back. She prided herself on the best grape-vine in the locality, flinging its tendrils well into the neighbouring state of Akim, up through Denkera and Ashanti as far north as Kintampo and down to the Coast—where one of her young relatives had got himself employment with the Customs. There was little the whites were up to on which she was not informed in advance.

She had succeeded, for instance, in blocking the project of cocoa planting, to which Kufi had been disposed, at first, to lend a receptive ear. She had at last convinced him that cocoa would not pay as well as palm oil or rubber; that it was not only harder work, but did not carry those opportunities for adulteration on which emolument depended: all those cunning little tricks she, as past mistress, had imparted to her daughters-in-law, which could make a good agiratsche's worth out of a mere agiratschifa's worth of gum.

She had organised resistance to a recent call for native labour levies by the simple means of sending off all the young men into the bush, and representing the village to the recruiting agents as a colony of elderly dotards, women and children.

And now—she chuckled and scratched herself with added gusto at the thought of that very pleasant little compact with Ya Ashantua, to which the hourly expected visit of the white traders so opportunely lent itself.

II

" *To Mr. Joseph Prior, 8 Ship Lane, Bristol.*

"December 16th, 1898.

" DEAR JOE,—Just a line to let you know I have arrived safely, after a very good trip—seventeen days fourteen hours out of Liverpool, allowing for twelve hours at Grand Canary: not bad going for one of our old barrels! We had a grand time on board, as nearly all the passengers were old Coasters, and I need not tell you we kept the bar steward galloping after dinner. I had to put up with plenty of leg-pulling, and heard enough traders' yarns to fill a book (*n.b.* remind me to tell you the one about finding the trouser buttons and the Ingersoll watch inside the paw paw). I'm afraid I had one or two " thick nights," but thanks to the captain's medicine chest, which seems to be equal to anything from bubonic to mosquito bites, landed at Sierra Leone in fairly good shape. Am now at Accra, and will give you all the news in a few days' time. My regards to Polly when you see her.

"Yours,

"JOHNNY."

It was, however, more than "a few days" before that popular young gentleman, Mr. John Flood, got down to his neglected correspondence.

Mindful of Dromore's instructions, he wrote his name at Government House: a formality which, he was agreeably surprised to find, carried with it election to membership of the Club. Having thus made his debut in Accra society, an avalanche of invitations obliged him for the first time in his life to keep an engagement book: balls, amateur theatricals, dinners in the officers' mess, parties for the races and for shooting, tea-and-tennis, and, on Boxing Day, the Officers v. Gentlemen match, in which Johnny, much to his own satisfaction, carried his bat, followed one another in breathless profusion. Any suggestion on his part of more serious preoccupations than these was met by good-natured derision, and, apart from a few qualms of conscience that soon subsided, he was ready enough to follow the primrose path of his new acquaintances.

Reared in the shadow of Dorset and Gilbert, and under the hard rule of Harcourt, Johnny would have been less than human if his first taste of social success had not gone slightly to his head; less than himself if reaction had not come sharply, as time and the subconscious brought their intimations of depths over which he and his companions were light-heartedly skating.

He recognised—the first impact of its novelty having worn away—that Accra was as foreign to the Gold Coast as he was himself: a little chunk of Great Britain deposited on African soil, smugly superimposing its British habits, conventions and manners on its immediate surroundings: floating on them like oil on water, breaking here and there into globules, but needing but the faintest movement of the supporting element to draw them together again. There is something almost miraculous about the way in which the Britisher, wherever fate may transport him, will produce, from the most unpromising materials, a replica of home conditions; something sublime in his power, when ensconsed, to ignore as completely as though it were non-existent, the environment which conditions his life and his actions.

With some such reflections in his mind, albeit indistinctly, a somewhat subdued Johnny sat down on the eve of his departure from Accra, to fulfil his neglected duty to his family. Like the majority of young men, he disliked letter writing; like most people in his situation, he chose the easiest of his correspondents for the first of the pages he covered in his stiff, clerkly script.

"I wrote this down because I thought it would interest you," he told Miranda, "and also as an exercise in the language for myself: it is the song of the boys who take the surf boats between the ships and the shore—a pretty exciting trip, as you will imagine. First you are sucked up a glassy slope of water—something like the wind-up to the starting platform of a switchback railway; then there's a sort of dizzy moment at the top, when you see everything through a rainbow of spray ; then you go crashing and spinning down into the next hollow, and so on. This is the song :

"My boat my strong boat carves the water
because I am strong
my arms are of steel and my back is iron
and I shoot my boat out on the water
like an arrow—like a spear
cut the water with a knife
with the curved tooth of an elephant
to make way for my boat my strong boat
for my boat that is like a shark
rushing through the water.

"They make this into a sort of chant, keeping time with the strokes of the paddles."

Yes ; that was what it was like. He paused for a moment, to muse on an experience which already seemed so distant from the recent artificiality of his life ; glanced at his watch and concluded hurriedly :

"I expect Emily will be at the Court for Christmas ; don't forget to remember me to her."

Then there was a waste of time while he hunted for some notes he had made for his letter to Dromore, on whose behalf he had, in desperation, cut a day's shooting, to visit the Botanical Station and Sanatorium at Aburi, and the Technical School and Hospital, with its adjoining laboratory, where research was going on into the origin and possible prevention of tropical diseases ; these were at least fig-leaves on the disgraceful nakedness of his report on his own activities, since his arrival in Accra, and must serve for Harcourt, as well as for Dromore.

"Useful labour done by native prisoners—carpentering, weaving, tailoring, bootmaking," scribbled Johnny. ("Blast 'em to hell. Where've I put those perishing bits of paper?") And, memory refusing further assistance, concluded on a placatory note :

"I am glad to tell you the missions here are very active. Many denominations are represented, but the Basel Mission is generally considered to have covered the widest ground and, in conjunction with the Government, to have done most to make the Negro a self-respecting and useful member of society. I will remember to make a point of looking up the missionaries at the various ports of call we make, and have made a note of the names of Mr. and Mrs. Gummeridge. I will try to find out whether there is any truth in the report you have heard, that they are related to us."

It was the kind of letter, wholly impersonal and artificial, that Dromore would expect, but he was not ashamed of it, as he was, for some uncomfortable reason, of the letter to Harcourt, in which one paragraph might, he hoped, atone for the paucity of the remainder.

"I have heard of several chiefs who may be useful to us : one a fellow called Kufi Kaboha, at Omo. The soil there is said to be particularly promising for cocoa growing and the natives not so averse from hard work as some of their kind. This country lies inland, behind Charlestown, which I gather is rather a dead end since they started sending the rubber down to Anamabu, but it will be interesting to see a place so closely linked up with our family history."

I bet the old boy sees through it, he reflected ruefully, as he thumped the flap of the envelope down ; but it's no good giving him the impression I've turned into a blasted social butterfly since arriving on the Coast. The women—Harriet, Selina and Vicky—would, he knew, revel in his "Society journal," but might pass it on to Harcourt, and it was wiser not to risk it. One piece of reassurance, at least, he could afford them.

"I have had the luck to find a very good 'boy,'" he wrote to Harriet. "Or rather, he was found for me. 'Tich,' as he is called, is twenty-two, and has been in British service up and down the Coast ever since he left school. I can't describe the difference a decent boy makes to one's comfort, especially when, owing to the heat, you are changing four or five times a day. Tich's last boss must have been a bit of a dandy, judging from portions of his wardrobe which Tich has inherited, or acquired *we won't ask how* ! Anyhow, he knows all about putting links in, and gets a knife-edge on my nether garments which would startle you if you saw it."

The heat was smothering, and he stopped to plunge his head into the bowl of tepid water on his wash stand. The bungalow in which he was staying—one of the new, "long-legged" ones out in the Christiansburg district—commanded from the height of its ten-foot iron supporting posts a general panorama of the town. He looked down through the dimming screen upon the strange patchwork of his surroundings and felt, not for the first time, uneasiness in the dusk.

It was not hard to forget, on the club veranda, or with a shooting party in the hills, the festering dung-pit of native quarters, the poverty, disease and vice of the cabins, or the unspeakable things that went on within the toss of a ball from one's own cool, sanitary dwelling. It was not "done," in Accra, to discuss such subjects ; for the Negro, if he ever intruded into conversation, there was a special formula of reference. "What wonderful work dear So-and-so is doing among the blacks !" "Have you heard the latest about So-and-so's houseboy? These blacks are too comical, aren't they—when they're not being maddening !" *If you don't laugh, you hate* : who said that? Was it imagination that caught, now and again, the flash of hatred across the smooth, civilised, British face? Hatred—of what? Each time the thought cropped up he had jerked his mind away from it. Hatred—that has its roots in fear. It was absurd to attribute hatred to the great, secure, superior race of West Africa's conquerors.

He had received many warnings, direct and indirect, not to meddle in "the nigger question," and knew them to be reasonable—if only on the grounds that "what can't be cured must be endured ;" and it was perfectly plain that, for anyone who had a job of work to do on the Coast, the Accra way was the only way to approach the Negro, even if it led to occasional injustices. It *must* be right, because it was the outcome of a century of experience. It had evolved through the wisdom and the integrity of those whose duty it was to govern this imponderable stretch of British territory and it was, in the main, successful. So Johnny told himself: conscious, however, in his bones of that grey, impoverished, subfusc community, cringing and assertive, with no status of its own, that crawled like fungus, like a parasite through the fine social structure raised by its overlords. Now and again, in a face that was neither black nor white, he recognised, with a shock, something that challenged his loyalty to the prescribed attitude, and recoiled from the question it raised: a question which, if he had put it into words, would have ostracised him among his own kind.

It was only in rare moments of solitude that Johnny had had time to indulge in these reflections, of which he knew Harcourt, as well as his friends at the Club, would highly disapprove. Of what use were they? Save to divert him from the real object of his visit to the Coast.

The pen handle was wet when he picked it up again and scrawled to Joe a brief memorandum of his plans.

"I'm taking advantage of an offer from a skipper of one of the small coastal steamers to have a look at some of our smaller trading settlements. Tich and I are off to-morrow and, grand a time as I've had here, I'm not sorry to be going. So far it's been like looking at a picture in an artificial light, or in a fancy frame that makes the picture look better than it is—if you get my meaning! Anyhow, I've seen enough to realise that the Accra picture isn't the Gold Coast, and I hope to find the real thing when I get a little more off the beaten track."

Colourless as they were, the words sent a thrill through him as he re-read them: recognising in them his pledge to adventure

III

The steamer had let our four throaty whoops and the surf boat was bobbing at the foot of the ladder. Johnny's declared intention of going ashore was clearly looked on by both captain and mate as high-grade lunacy, but the former shrugged his shoulders.

"Mappin's a bit hard of hearing; may be he'll not have heard the horn. It's a good two miles to his place: follow the creek, if you want a walk. You can't miss it."

. . . The heat dithered over the huts, and over a woman with lopsided breasts, scraping up goat dung with her hands. Five or six children, with sore eyes and sore feet, churned up the dust, scuffling after a small, lame monkey, that screamed and gnashed its yellow teeth at them; then, suddenly giving up hope, squatted and covered its face with its hands, a picture of despair. Catching sight of the white man, the children vanished, and, within seconds, the empty space in front of the huts was covered with a mob that seemed to boil up out of the earth.

They pressed in on him with a purposeful curiosity; when he stood still, and pulled a match box out of his pocket to light a cheroot, they followed his every movement with their eyes ; one or two fingered him slyly. They were mainly old people and children ; the sounds they made were shapeless, like sounds made by the deaf and dumb, and their faces held a uniform lack of intelligence. It was a little eery : like coming upon a colony of man-fashioned apes, identical in all save mental equipment with their human prototypes. Perhaps this was the way it had been in the Garden of Eden ; perhaps this was the norm, and he himself the freak, the circus animal, the Talking Horse. . . . Johnny pulled himself hastily together, and from the mass Face in front of him, inquired the way.

After an ineffectual ten minutes, having failed to produce the noise, or series of noises, that made sense to his audience, he decided to continue on his way. It seemed to him that he must already have come more than the two miles described by the captain, but so far had found nothing recognisable as a white man's dwelling. He was followed between the towering citadels of the bush ants by the entire community ; they crowded on his heels, now and again coming round in front of him, as though to refresh their memories of his appearance, and dropping quietly back again. It did not add to Johnny's enjoyment of the walk to notice that one or two were marked with leprosy. Then the path took a twist, and there was a rough clearing, and the house, with thatch coming down low over a broad veranda.

Since leaving the beach, he had been looking forward to a rest out of the sun, and a drink—even if it was only the sweetish, flat palm wine : but something—whether it was the shut-in-ness, the loud buzzing of flies, or a curious impression of unhealthiness that hung about the place—took both desires out of him. If alone, he would have turned back—the house was so evidently unoccupied ; but to retreat meant cleaving one's way through the solid bodies behind him. It seemed better to go on, to go in, and wait a little—giving his escort time, perhaps, to exhaust its curiosity and retire. So he beat his way through the high, rank grass, a little faster than was prudent, and only when he reached the veranda remembered the danger of snakes, and considered himself lucky not to have been bitten. The escort came about half-way, then stopped, and took up an unblinking watchfulness on his procedure.

He was aware of his own heart-beats, as he stood there on the clay platform : wondering what had happened to Mappin, and how he had come to miss him, as there was no other discernible track to what was, evidently, the factory. A shout or two having produced no answer, it took an act of will to enter a room apparently used as a dining-room : there was a rough table, made from the cross-section of a vast tree trunk, and some stools and chairs, similarly fashioned, all scattered with carcasses dropped by the spiders from their webs overhead. The sound of his own footsteps and the endless, metallic humming of the flies were the only breaches in the silence, which lay on the house and on the clearing, pressed down, heavy with a stench that made him feel sick.

He went out again on the veranda, sheepishly conscious of a desire to bolt, but resolved, before so doing, to penetrate the mystery of this strange, empty house. The humming had risen to a trumpet-note, and he suddenly saw whence it proceeded. Across the clearing, between the trees and a shuttered window on his right, a continuous skein of flies formed a broad moving belt of blackish iridescence in the sun. He watched it, feeling his flesh creep, feeling under his skin some obscene purpose that drew the creatures to their objective, that crusted them upon the shutters, through whose slats they crawled. The noise behind the shutters was that of a gigantic hive about to swarm. He had forced himself to take a step or two in the direction of this closed room, when a noise within shot his heart into his throat and froze him to the spot. There was something inside, beside the flies—something that slithered, broke into an occasional patter, and then was silent.

" Hallo."

The act of turning was fraught with curious difficulty.

" Hallo," said Johnny.

The figure which had appeared below the veranda wore a sun-helmet; a towel, knotted chastely about the hips and a pair of light yellow riding boots alone supplemented the thick web of hair, bleached silvery by the sun, which covered an immensely long and muscular body. Over his head the stranger carried an egombie-gombie leaf, which cast its green reflection into the thin, tobacco-yellow of a face reminding Johnny of an amiable bull-terrier's. He felt his lips move stiffly into a smile at this unexpected apparition.

" Are you Mappin ? "

The stranger shook his head, moving the leaf casually to dispel the flies.

" Luckily—no." His eyes considered Johnny, before he added, " I guess it's just too bad—if you're a friend of Mappin's."

" I'm not. I was just—dropping in. Isn't this his factory ? " There was another pause, while the eyes continued to measure him ; something in their steady regard suggested to Johnny it would be better to explain himself. " The steamer's lying off there—waiting for him. I walked up, in case he hadn't heard the horn."

" Trader ? "

" No—passenger ; that's all."

" You wouldn't—by any chance—have the Book of Common Prayer on you ? "

" Why—no." Uncertain whether this was meant to be taken seriously or as a jest, Johnny went poker faced.

The other sighed.

" Didn't think you would. All right—we'll manage." He turned and spoke to the two Kroo boys behind him in a vernacular unknown to Johnny. They came up on the veranda ; both were carrying spades, and one a big calabash bowl of the kind used for displaying fruit in the markets. Johnny noticed that the rest of the company had, for some reason, withdrawn ; they were standing in respectful silence on the far side of the clearing, under the trees.

He remembered it all later, as part of a nightmare : the opening of the door, and a sudden rush of rats, the size of rabbits, that leapt from the veranda into the long grass ; and the Kroos going in, and coming out, presently, with something in the calabash, and the flies that made a cloud about them, singing resentment of their disturbance. Then the stumble through the grass to a freshly-dug hole, and the boys tipped the calabash into it and used the spades to slap at the flies, while Kershaw, under his green leaf, naked but for the towel and his yellow boots, stooped down to throw a handful of dust into the hole. "I heard a voice from heaven, saying . . ." And then the green had seemed to rush up and hit him between the eyes.

" It's one of the things you get to take for granted."

They were on the steamer, and it was evening; a strip of raw sunset ran along the horizon and the water in their wake had turned to a dark amethyst with pools of indigo in it. They were up in the bows, to escape the stink of the oil, and Kershaw had produced from somewhere a pair of ragged dungarees and a thin sweater that was tied by its sleeves about his neck. Leaning on the rail, with a pipe clamped between a set of teeth which owed more to the dentist's zeal than to its owner's vanity, he held forth with lazy acceptance of his companion's attention. Johnny had begun to recover from the humiliation of his own weakness—to which no reference had been made by its witness, since they came aboard.

" What killed Mappin? It could be snake-bite, or fever, or any of the odd things that catch you in the bush: who's to know? Who cares? One day he drops down—and rats and the heat do the rest. Then I come along —or may be you—and clean up what's left. ' Man that is born of woman hath but a short time to live. . . . He cometh up, and is cut down, like a flower.' Excuse the quotation, I'm not Biblically minded, but bits like that stick in one's memory. Hell of a fuss made about death—among the civilised peoples. Damn' ridiculous. All part of evolution—might as well raise a hullabaloo about cutting a tooth. What are you doing out here, anyway?" A glint of half-humorous curiosity narrowed the speaker's eyes.

" Just having a look round. Making for Charlestown, ultimately: that's where I'll be ending my trip."

" Charlestown!" The sleepiness had gone out of Kershaw's voice. " Why in thunder Charlestown?"

" Why not?" Johnny was at a loss to account for the look of incredulity which had come into the other's odd, long-nosed face.

" Charlestown—well," said Kershaw, shifting round so that the weight of his body was carried on his elbows, set back on the rail. He spoke lazily, with his eyes still on Johnny's. " I guess you picked out about the scabbiest hole on the Coast. Ever seen the Sargasso?"

" Sargasso Sea—where all the rubbish of the Atlantic drifts?" Johnny shook his head.

" Ay, there you've got it. Charlestown's the Sargasso for all the garbage in the Colony."

" Sounds a good sort of place to get out of." His lips stretched into a smile.

" 'Bout as simple as getting a ticket-of-leave out of hell," grunted Kershaw. " If you take my advice, you'll give Charlestown the go-by. If they'd got any sense, they'd let it run back to seed, to sand—to whatever it was before we started using it as an outlet for nigger flesh."

"What about trade? We've got several factories there, haven't we?"

"Had," Kershaw corrected. "Most of them's packed up, since the swamp's cut off road communication with the inland. Charlestown's one of our local Golgothas." He grimaced. "Well, you'll see, if you ever get there."

"What's the point of our hanging on to it, then? I suppose it costs the Government something in maintenance. I thought the Colonial Office was keen on economies."

Kershaw emitted a honk of laughter.

"You've said something. It's district headquarters—the D.C.'s got his staff there. If the railway to Kumassi ever gets going, it might take on another lease of life. Or death," he concluded, as an afterthought. "Or death—ha ha!"

The little steamer continued to chuff its way slowly through deepening darkness, the air freshened and the dew felt like small rain.

CHAPTER TWO

I

IT is the hour of the native: the hour when local society rouses itself from post-prandial coma and tunes up for the activities that keep decorous citizens in a state of anticipation, pleasurable or otherwise, according to their natures, of what nightfall may bring forth.

Odours of frangipanni and orange flower penetrate the thick human and vegetable and excremental effluvium which stretches like a tangible web between the more or less presentable, though ramshackle, façades of the main street, and the crumbling dwellings, housing most of the town's mixed population that form their background. An exquisite light—the brief, extramundane twilight of the tropics—moving under the pepper and eucalyptus trees that fringe the turfed broadwalk, lends to the figures parading there a theatrical unreality: an illusion of the theatre heightened by costumes as various and fully as fantastic as those of carnival.

High-grade bucks, in cotton of English tailoring, whose original owners, quiet under snake-infested grass, no longer have use for it, flaunt that touch of the rococo beloved of the Negro in some exotic form of headgear—a West Country policeman's helmet, or the cast-off millinery of a Liverpool belle. Here a military belt, there a strip of tarnished galloon suggests dandyism latent in a scarecrow whose lack of means, or of enterprise, limits his wardrobe to a flannel petticoat, or to the loin-cloth which, along the coast, brands its wearer with social inferiority.

As the green light drops into dark, spangled with the white flash of teeth and eyeballs and the glowing tips of cheroots, through the close ranks of the male weave the women : from the giggling tee-tees, pranked out in mission frocks and critical of the number of pigtails rampant on each other's woolly heads, to a few Europeanised local Aspasias, in Manchester-made frills and flounces of styles already historic. One, in a crinoline which, lacking its cage, hampers her progress, hitches it boldly about her beautiful bronze thighs, down which her companion's hand slides impatiently ; but the majority content themselves with showy lengths of traders' cotton, which, worn by the more modest with the mission blouse, or leaving their torsos naked, mould their narrow hips into the grace of Attic urns.

With the coming of the women the atmosphere thickens ; a vibration of simple, mindless pleasure is in the air, in the glutinous bubble of negro laughter, in the rhythmic shuffle of feet on a patch of bare earth, in the yip and yap and oh-ah-oh of the priapic votary already surrendered to his god, who rises smoke-like under the branches.

But darkness does not lend itself to negro revelry : it is not long before the lights of saloons and parlours draw the promenaders from the avenue of trees—leaving their innocence behind them. Only a few besotted lovers remain, clamped against tree trunks : hearing only each others' breathing and the booming of the surf. Neither the heavy dew-fall nor the sudden chill of night disturbs their dark, serious and implacable purpose.

Back in the town there are kissing and fighting, and kisses that turn to fighting and fighting that resolves itself in kisses ; and two Negresses tearing each other's hair out over a comatose Appolonian who, in a few hours, has made up for the liquor restrictions enforced by the Goldfields corporation, and drunk away the wages of a year's labour in the Ebuassi mines. And the empty bottles of Peter's gin crashing merrily behind the counter in Sam's Select and a wedding party driving its way through the crowds—the men in hired frock coats, white kid gloves and top hats into the bands of which are thrust the invitation cards—gilt-lettered on shiny pink pasteboard—commanding the bearers to the " hymeneals." The best man and his boon companions are out to make a night of it, to show off their fine feathers and dance the stars down the sky with cakewalk and juba, so long as horny thumbs thrum on the banjos and palm wine succeeds gin in the saloons.

Gambling halls and flesh shops are in full swing, stores packed with girls persuading tipsy sailors to buy them dress lengths, earrings, necklaces and iron basins from the heterogeneous display on the shelves. And a bunch of Kroo boys, iron-muscled from taking the boats through the surf, dances like mad, a sleazy mulatto tries to sell off a packet of dirt as gold dust to a suspicious Dutch skipper, who wants to toss him for it, double or quits.

Above the tin roofs that act as sounding boards rises the din—the infinite variety of noise with which the Negro expresses light-heartedness : ranging from human gabble, through the estoric jangle of the mechanical piano to the horns, the drums and the stringed instruments of the West African orchestra : beneath which, in an insistent obbligato, runs the orchestration of Nature herself—the shrill of cricket and cicada, the grinding rattle of frogs, the innumerable anonymous whines and grunts and squeals which, swelling through the hours of darkness, reach their climax in the piercing whistles of birds that announce the dawn.

Beyond them all, the crash of the surf and the endless, rainlike rustle of coco palms keep the exile under the Southern Cross in remembrance of the distance that stretches between him and the sweet, still, English night.

II

Dodging backwards and forwards along the coast, Dixcove, Sekondi, N'Banta, Anamabu, Apam, Shama, and a host of places too small to have names, left on Johnny's brain a kaleidoscopic impression, blurred with everlasting surf, framed everlastingly in yellow of sand and blue of sky. He reached the point of forgetting which place he was in, and indeed it made little difference in the universal pattern of wood buildings, tin roofs, stink, blacks, dirt. The redeeming feature was the company of Kershaw, who, mining engineer by profession, with seven years' experience of the Coast, revealed himself as a natural vagabond, the mystery of whose independence worried Johnny as little as it appeared to worry Kershaw himself.

"They'll run me out one day," he cheerfully informed Johnny; "but, so far, it don't pay them! Between ourselves, administration's in one hell of a muddle, and somebody who can turn his hand to anything that crops up's worth plenty to the departments. The thing to do's keep on moving around; you're all right, so long's you don't give them the chance to put a tab on you."

The following extracts, undated and taken at random from Johnny's letters home, cover in cursory fashion the stages of their pilgrimage. That they follow no set geographical progress may be due to the vagaries of transport—Johnny's addiction to ships and to the company of sailors leading him, whenever possible, to "take a lift" to whatever port of call the ship he favoured was making for.

"It will give you some idea of how small the Coast world is" (he wrote to Dromore) "when I tell you that, overhearing me mention the Gummeridges one day, my boy Tich told me with great glee that he is a convert of 'Mister Gummijo's,' and had attended the mission school in his village up-country, before his family moved down to live on the Coast. The Gummeridges are at Charlestown, towards which we are making, although it may be some weeks before we get there, as my travelling companion has various places to visit and we are dependent on casual transport.

"Tich is being of the greatest service to me in practising the native dialect, for I have forbidden him to talk to me in traders' English, which all the house-boys use, and we are beginning to get on quite well, with the help of a few words of Hausa, which I speak better than he."

Not without mischief, he wrote to Vicky, whose horror of insectivora had furnished ground for some of the brighter practical jokes of her nephews during their school holidays:

"You will gather I'm in very different surroundings from my fashionable setting in Accra ! Kershaw and I share a corrugated tin hut, called by courtesy a bungalow, with (don't shudder) about ten thousand mosquitoes, about a thousand billion sand-coloured ants (which means we have to keep all the food in bowls of water, or hung from the rafters on coir ropes) and as nice an assortment of scorpions, centipedes, spiders and variegated beetles as you can imagine. I must single out for special mention a small lizard with a head the colour of a red-hot cinder. When you meet a couple of these, after a convivial evening, you feel preciously near signing the pledge.

" The heat inside our tin dog kennel is like a bakehouse until just near dawn, when you suddenly feel as if you have been packed in cold, wet mud."

Heat is, naturally, a recurrent motive of the correspondence, although it is only to Joe that he admits :

" The heat's getting me down—though, so far, I've kept clear of fever : largely, I fancy, through smoking like a chimney and laying off spirits. That's not to say I've gone T.T. ! I generally have a few drinks at sundown, when the mists come up and everything sweats and drips and the air feels like the hot springs at Bath. One of the bitterest charges against the missionaries is their persistent preaching teetotalism in a climate where it practically amounts to suicide.

" These swamps along the coast are breeding ground for mosquitoes and for the dreaded tsetse fly. I'm about inoculated after all my bites, but the beggars keep one awake at night and rather get on one's nerves."

" Tich, my house-boy, confides to me that he's got a girl in Charlestown he's most anxious to marry, but it appears her parents are ' old-fashioned nigger,' and won't hear of the ceremony taking place according to mission customs. The mission people don't approve of Tich's marrying a heathen, so the poor chap is in a splice. Another complication is, the bride's parents want twenty pounds English, forty bags of salt and I forget how many goats before parting with their Ewe lamb (that's a pun, but I'll have to explain it when I get home). So it looks as if Tich's luck is out, especially as his mission teaching forbids him to ' buy ' a wife. Not that that would stand in his way, I fancy, if he had the needful. I expect I could raise the cash, but I want to have a look at the girl first. Tich is too good a sort to tie up with one of these coast hussies.

" I'm nearly as keen as he is to get to Charlestown. I was sick at not getting ashore last time I was there, but am looking forward to exploring the scenes of our ancient crimes, and trying to imagine what the Fort looked like when all that schemozzle took place between Matthew Flood and the Beautiful (? ?) Negress. Question mark, because I have never yet seen a female who wasn't more or less revolting, along these shores.

" Thank you for the message from Emily. Please tell her I am trying to find something nice for her. There are astonishingly lovely carvings and gold ornaments. Unfortunately, they are all very expensive."

Apart from Miranda, the only member of the family with a gift for letter-writing was Harriet : and it was probably her long and eagerly awaited letters that evoked from Johnny replies fuller and more interesting than those with which he favoured his other correspondents. In a ribbon-tied packet found in Harriet's bureau was one which, in the light of later events, carries a significance which warrants its reproduction in entirety.

" My Dear Grandmamma,

" Back again at N'Banta !—after a refreshing interlude at Cape Coast Castle, where we stayed with some friends of Kershaw's who have one of those really grand old stone-built mansions with high-walled courtyards and sculptured entrances that the eighteenth-century merchants built for their residences when they visited the Coast. Those old boys certainly did themselves well—and they hadn't the stink of the rubber to contend with ! However, it was worth the rubber smell to sleep a few nights in a high, cool—well, cool-ish—room, and eat at a clean table. I made the most shocking bloomer, by the way : picked up my wine-glass and started wiping it all round the rim with my handkerchief ! I could have sunk through the floor when I saw my hostess staring. Of course I apologised, and she burst out laughing and said she quite understood, which was really very handsome of her.

" The Maxteds (Kershaw's friends) seem very hospitable people. There was a lot of company, and I was interested to meet one of the officers from the barracks at Elmina, who was in the last dust with the Ashanti, and had some very interesting—and gruesome—tales to tell. This led to a discussion on whether the Ashanti were really beaten, and whether there was question of another rising. Captain Allen inclined to be noncommittal, but the general opinion was that it was out of the question. The Ashanti have lost their king and have yet to pay up the indemnity fixed by the British for the last campaign.

" Kershaw, however, when we were by ourselves, took another point of view. He says Prempeh (who, by the way, I saw down at Sierra Leone : having quite a cosy time is a political prisoner—old scoundrel !—and polishing off a joint that would have kept a family of six for a week) doesn't amount to anything, and they've still got the Stool—as they call their throne. Any time they feel like having another king, they've only got to dig up the Stool, and—bingo ! All set for another rising. I must say that would be a pretty look out for trade, with every nigger on our concessions scouting round with firearms, instead of looking after his oil and rubber. Let's hope it doesn't come off.

" From the papers it looks as if we've got our hands full in the Transvaal, doesn't it ? I hear some of the West African Frontier Force are being drafted down there, which looks like business. I've been wondering if Gilbert's battalion has gone—the lazy fellow never writes, but he won't be pleased if he has to leave his polo and hippo-potting, to chase Oom Paul's riff-raff round the kopjes !

" Guns, by the way, account for our return to this far from salubrious spot. The blacks are allowed to import a certain number—' for the maintenance of order and inter-tribal defence '—but they're supposed to buy them through us and the issue is limited in accordance with the district : i.e., if the buyers are known to be well disposed or otherwise to

British rule. It is needless to say this order is more honoured in the breach than the observance. It is absolutely impossible to keep tabs on the chiefs, who sell and exchange and buy all over the place, so no one actually knows where the firearms get to.

" But a tale's gone round that the Dutch, who, at the best of times, are slippery customers, and are of course all agog over the rows between the Volksraad and the Uitlanders, have been slipping them guns on the sly, snd that they have been coming in here, at N'Banta, which is a small place—hardly more than a native settlement—within ten miles of Cape Coast Castle, but awkward to get at, because of swamp and sand-bank. As usual, there's not enough police to go round and the authorities have their hands full with the penal settlement at Elmina.

" So Kershaw and I volunteered to come down and see if we can catch them. We've been here a week, and no luck, so far. I think the beggars are too sly, they'll have tipped off their Dutch partners, who no doubt have found another spot for the exercise of their ingenuity."

A postscript, dated ten days after the foregoing, adds :

" Still after those damned Dutch—now in a place called Shama. Not a sign or a sniff of them. Kershaw enjoying himself enormously. To be candid, I've had enough.

" I had a real ' go ' of home-sickness to-day. I believe it's the smell (or smells). An old boy I met at Cape Coast said : ' You'll meet plenty of bad smells along the Coast, but you won't find a chemical reason for all of them.' First there's the rubber—you get used to that—and the oil. Then coconuts—rotten. I absolutely cannot describe the stench of these, when left to decompose in thousands under the palms. Brackish water, fish offal by the ton and all the filth the natives leave piled up to accumulate round their huts or houses. There's also the nigger smell itself, for which I can find no description except a kind of hot fustiness, mixed with the rancid oil and grease they rub on their skins and into their hair. These make up ' Gold Coast Bouquet ' (Kershaw's name for it)—plus all the strong-scented plants and flowers which, to begin with, one finds rather agreeable, and which end up by sickening one. It gets into your nostrils and clothes and everything you eat or touch. Even the water (boiled) that you drink tastes of it. I find myself longing for the clean, fresh tang of a frosty morning, such as you must be having now.

" If Charlestown's any worse than this place I'll eat my hat. Time's getting on, and I am absolutely determined to get down there and up to Omo before the rainy season sets in. Kershaw for some reason keeps on putting it off : he says it's ' the dead end of everywhere,' and thinks I'm crazy to go there. If he won't come, I'll go on by myself : and if I can't look after myself, after all his ' tuition,' there's something the matter with me ! "

III

" Mistah Flood ! You come at last—oh, sah, I too much glad to see you ! "

Johnny stared up incredulously into a big ebony face, raised like an exotic bouquet on the holder formed by a wing collar, whose whiteness was matched by the grin that seemed, like lightning, to dance all over it's owner's personality.

" It's not—— ? Komuntale—by gad ! Where on earth have you sprung from ? "

The sally brought a guffaw of laughter which drew an audience, of which Komuntale took immediate advantage by bending his knees, leaping suddenly into the air and coming down in a position that brought his face more or less on a level with Johnny's.

" Dass good ! " He guffawed. " Oh, my, oh, me, dass mighty damn' good ! " He slapped the great thighs straining against the cotton of his trousers. " Oh, my, Mistah Flood ! I done spring plenty place dese lass few yeah ! "

" Well, you look as if exercise suits you." There were few traces left of the narrow youth of the *Aldebaran* in the vast figure before him. Komuntale slapped his chest with another whoop of delighted laughter, making it plain by the radiance of his welcome that he bore no grudge against an ancient enemy.

" You bet I plenty fit strong fella ! " He turned sharply on the grinning circle of his retainers, now jostling and pushing for the privilege of watching the scene. " Get out, all you dam' black niggers ! Don' you see you make you'selfs discomformable for gennelmun like us ? Mistah Flood come special for see me ; we know each other all our lifes—know each other from boy, like brothers. Mistah Flood : I tell all dese innorant wild people how much you love me——"

" Oh, do you. Well, you might leave them to find that out for themselves. I'll be seeing you—one of these days." He broke off, looking down at the black hand laid, with assurance, on his sleeve. " I'll be seeing you," said Johnny curtly, and stepped aside—unexpectedly enough for the hand to be dislodged though not to shake off its owner.

" You see me, sure ! " There was evidently to be no doubt of it. Komuntale drew himself up with hollowed back and chest so expanded that the coat he was wearing gaped between the spotted bow tie and the top button of his trousers ; it was as though the white stuff opened over fleshings of dark-brown satin. " I big fella in Charlestown, Johnny ! Big man in Gov'ment office——"

Before Johnny had recovered his breath at the impudent use of his Christian name, the other continued :

" You come see my house some day ! I got plenty big fine wife ! " A gesture defined the evidently generous contours of Mrs. Komuntale. " Got t'ree, fo' chillen in school. You have tea with my wife : she damn' smart

Gov'ment lady ! Friends with all de white ladies in Cha'lestown ; don' make no 'count of all de innorant black women in dis place. She make you tea like you' wife make yo' at home——"

The inscrutable looks of the one or two white men within earshot warned Johnny to cut it short.

" Very kind of her. I'm looking for someone called Prewett——"

" Mistah Prewett ? Sho', he'll be long presently. He busy with captain for minute or two—ho ho ! " A wink and a lifted elbow indicated the nature of the business. " Oh, my, oh, me—yo' sho' is jess the same as you used to was, in dem ole days on de ship——! "

" Well, I'm going to see to my baggage." The time had come, to curtail familiarities ; to make his début in Charlestown under the ægis of a cheeky Customs clerk would not, Johnny knew, advance his credit among the white community. Again, a large, prohibitive hand checked his departure, and, this time, he jerked it aside, with no pretence at accident.

" You don' have to bother 'bout no baggage, Johnny."

" My name's Flood ; Mister to you. I wouldn't forget that if I were you—Mister Komuntale."

" Yes, sah. Please, sah. I don' forget nutting, sah ! " The instant servility was typical of the coastal Negro. " Yo' leave me look after yo' baggage, sah. I big fella—dey shiftum one-time fo' me."

" Yes, but——" He checked himself ; there was no point in inviting more impudence by admitting that he had yet to find a place to lodge. Komuntale took advantage of silence to press his services.

" You don' have to t'ink of nutting. I know ship an I know skipper : he goddam bloody thief ! You tell me how many pieces, I watchum like dey crown of England ! "

Johnny was obliged to surrender.

" You'd better hold them at the sheds, till I send for them." What, he wondered, would be regarded as adequate remuneration for this service ?

" Please, Mistah Flood, it is notting. You are my bess friend," Komuntale was assuring him. " Anyt'ing yo' want, yo' only ask me. I t'ink yo' like to give me somet'ing " An engaging freedom from inhibition in the asking of favours shone in his smile. " I big fella. I t'ink yo' not dash me fi' bob, six bob, same yo' give small fella—ornery carrier boy ! Perhaps you dash me ten bob——"

" Here's five." Johnny handed it over, glad to know, on coastal arithmetic, where he stood.

" That is too much kind of you." Komuntale accepted it cheerfully. " Amankwa Kaboha "—as son of a chieftain, Johnny was forced to admit, he had no overblown idea of his cash value.

" And now, as you are my bess friend, you do me a little kindness. Please have you got some English newspaper ? Always I try to make improvement in my reading——"

" Well, I don't think I have——" The request was surprising. Johnny nodded and prepared to side-step his companion.

" Please, Mistah Flood—I t'ink you have got some newspaper ! "

" I haven't seen a paper since Cape Coast ! " Johnny was beginning to be irritated by the other's persistence : but remembered, and, not to seem churlish, added : " I got an old *Times* from a man off the mail boat. I believe my boy used it to wrap up the laundry. He's somewhere round about, if you want to look for him."

" That is too much kind of you." Komuntale repeated his formula beamingly, holding out his hand, which Johnny contrived not to see, and turned firmly away.

" Are you Flood ? "

" Yes. I suppose you're Prewett ? Kershaw told me to be on the look out for you." There was a short, antagonistic silence, while a pair of disillusioned eyes, tiger yellow in a tobacco-yellow face, allowed Johnny to see that his hobnobbing with a native had created no favourable impression.

" I'd heard you were on your way down. We've got no social amenities, you know, in Charlestown."

" Hell—I've been here since November ! "

" Quite an old Coaster." This time, the sneer was patent.

" Old enough to know what to expect, by now." If that was the tune, he could pipe to it.

" By God, if you do, you know more than the rest of us." He turned away to spit ; the spittle, as it hit the rail, sizzled. The ship stank of oil, and the chatter of the Kroos made coherent speech difficult. " Had a nice trip ? " he queried ironically.

Johnny stared, smiled and stuck his hands in his pockets. He was not going to feed this line in persiflage.

" Captain says they're going on to San Paul de Loanda. Not a bad place—San Paul. You might," said the other, " take a fancy to it."

" Who knows ? "

It was Prewett's turn to shrug his shoulders. He turned on his heel. Johnny, following the direction of his eyes, looked steadily towards the shore. He felt he knew it all : the sloping beach, thinly tufted with coco-palms, and the straggle of tin roofs behind them ; beyond them, wooded ranges whose infinite depth was lost in the steam that blotted out the horizon. A featureless mediocrity, exuding something that crawled out, across the beach, and the band of the surf, and the deep, translucent green of the roadstead.

He found Prewett looking at him oddly.

" Well—— ? "

" Well—what ? "

" Smell it ? " said Prewett curiously.

He did ; he had even, in unoccupied moments, gone so far as to try to analyse the strange, creeping fetor—sometimes faint, sometimes strong, but always there—which he had learned to accept as the smell of the Gold Coast. So much per cent malaria ; so much per cent mangrove ; so much per cent native ; and the rest—— ? The unknown quantity—X. X stands for Africa.

" Where's Kershaw ? " Prewett was saying.

" He's coming on the next boat—with luck. They're doing some repair on the telegraph lines, and the man in charge has gone down with stomach ulcers. Kershaw's holding the fort until the relief gets down." He felt disinclined to answer the curiosity in the other's eyes by a full explanation of his reason for coming in advance. It was Kershaw who had said, after the last thunderstorm, " You'd better go on and get the Omo trip fixed up, if you're set on it ; when the rain starts and the creek rises, there'll be no way of getting up there till the end of the wet season." He had recommended Prewett for advice about land and water route, the movements of traders which might be of service to them and any formalities that might arise under administration, which, he had been warned, was particularly lively in the district to which they were travelling. It was a piece of bad luck that Prewett had turned out so surly a customer ; certainly his reception had not turned out as Kershaw had led Johnny to expect and he felt at a loss to account for the former's confident recommendation.

Still, there was nothing to be gained, now, in boggling over the matter ; it must work itself out in its own way, and, for all one knew, Prewett might be suffering from some private disgruntlement that had nothing to do with his present company.

It was cooler on the water level. The wall of the surf cut off the shore line. There was nothing but water and sky, both of the same rattling blue, but the sky was hummocked with cloud along the horizon—a reminder that the dry season was coming to an end. At a shout from the headman, the rowers unshipped their paddles, and the boat leapt suddenly from its patch of shadow towards the hidden shore.

The surf was worse than usual, and they were soaked to the skin when they scuffed up the beach, the sand plastering itself into the wet stuff of their trousers.

Prewett turned when they reached the littered broadwalk, where a bunch of girls looked slyly across their shoulders, to look at the diamond-white wall that piled itself up, and crashed, and broke in thunder behind them.

" I doubt they'll get another boat off to-day. Come on, let's get a drink."

" I expect you've got jobs of your own. I can push round—get a line on the layout." At a glance, the layout would not take much mastering.

" I said, let's get a drink. I can't put you up," said Prewett abruptly, when they had found crates to sit on in the shack, half-store, half-saloon, which Johnny was to know later as Easy Emma's. " I've got a chap stopping with me. We don't reckon to cater for company and——" The realisation of his ungraciousness appeared to strike him ; he mumbled : " Batty might fix you up ; or Lewis. There ain't many of us, you know—outside the staff." Taking this to refer to the District Officer, Johnny nodded. " It's a nigger town mainly." He spat into the dust. Suddenly he gave a harsh laugh. " There's the Gummeridges ; I forget them."

" The missionaries, you mean ? Yes, I'll have to look them up one day," said Johnny cautiously. He shook his head, as he caught the meaning of

Prewett's cocked eyebrow. "No, thanks; I won't plant myself on them. It might turn out awkward—for all parties. Don't put yourself out; I'll find a shakedown for myself when I've had time to look round."

"There's Vicker's place," said Prewett. He said it doubtfully, after a long silence.

IV

"*To Mr. Joseph Prior*, 8 *Ship Lane*, *Bristol*.

"Dear Joe,

"As this may be the last letter you'll get for some time, I'll try to make it a long one. This letter writing is getting beyond me. As well as writing to you and the family, I am trying to keep a log for Uncle Hacky, though I doubt it will give him much satisfaction. I have to do most of my writing by night, and in spite of shutting doors and windows, every sort of pestilential bug seems to get it and start its antics round the light. A thing the size of a bat, but with hard wing-sheathes, has just hurtled past, nearly putting my eye out, and something that looks like a bit of rope, and is actually a small mamba, is dangling down from a roof beam, about a yard and a half from my head, and I'm damned if I've got the energy to get up and kill it.

"I can hardly believe it's only a few weeks since I was playing cricket at Accra; at the present moment I feel just about equal to patting a ping-pong ball across this table. "You will guess from the gloomy tone of the above I've got a slight touch of fever. I've just had fifteen grains of quinine, instead of the customary five, and a filthy decoction of hot lime juice that my houseboy, Tich, insisted on pouring into me. I'll also take an opium pill when I turn in, and hope to sweat it out before morning; I was given some by one of the Bristol skippers, together with the cheery reminder that eight-five per cent West Coasters die of fever, or return home total wrecks! Death, by the way, is the Big Laugh out here. Any joke that's got death in it is a huge success, and gets handed round till it's a chestnut. Whimsy, but you get in the way of it, in time.

"There's really not much point in writing, as I've told you most of the things already. To be quite candid, the sameness of life out here is a little depressing. Apart from Accra and Cape Coast, each place is the same as the last, and the people are the same, and it isn't sameness on a high level, if you know what I mean; it's a kind of sticky squalor, that spreads itself over everything, and infects people's actions, and even the way they think. I'm beginning to wonder if conditions need really be as bad as they are, but I'm d——ed if I know how to begin to alter them. The fact sticks out a mile, that everybody on the Coast—I'm speaking of the whites, of course—is doing his damnedest to make a go of his job; it only gives one a bit of a shock to see how little has been effected, at such a frightful expenditure of life and labour.

"There are many things I'd like to talk to you about, but they don't seem to fit into a letter. I've tried a number of times to put them down, and when I read it over, I find it's actually nothing like what I've written. The minute you try to put certain things on paper, they get all fogged over, like a glass that is breathed upon. The solemn thought that emerges from all this is, of course, that I'm not a writer, and never will be! Which is a pity, when you consider I'm seeing things that few people get a chance of seeing, and every now and then I get the same sort of thrill you would get (I imagine) by going behind the scenes in a theatre: only that would be enjoyable, and this . . . well, I guess this is the point where authors take refuge in asterisks.

"Another reason I think it's better to cut down on letter writing is that I'm pretty sure, in my present frame of mind, I'd exaggerate, and give impressions I'd be sorry for, and have to correct later on. On the other hand, there are a great many points I want to make sure of not forgetting, so I have decided to start a kind of diary; at least I can tear that up, and it will have done no damage.

"Joe, there's something awfully wrong somewhere. It's completely undefinable, but you can feel it on the back of your—and other fellows'—necks; it's there when you wake up, like a bang in the chest. If I feel it, what do you suppose it's like for people who haven't got a chance of escaping from it? Sometimes, when a bunch of us are together, and the phonograph's going, and everybody's a bit 'merry,' I tell myself it's imagination. Then it's there, all of a sudden, at the back of somebody's eyes. Do you remember that night we talked about ghosts? Well—(*the next three lines are erased*).

"Another positively god-damned thing is the way we scrap among ourselves. You'll hardly believe I had a regular up-and-downer with a fellow at Shama, over nothing more important than putting a dish on the table. He said to put it in one place, and I, thinking of something else, put it in another. Then he called me something, and I went one better. We were having chop, and he'd got a knife in his hand; he jabbed it into my knuckles and I slugged him one with my left and cut his lip open. It looks idiotic, written down, but it's how people get, when they're cooped up together, day after day, irrespective of tastes, and with no sort of outlet for their free time energies. (Not that those amount to much! Half of our people look more dead than alive, and few seem to have energies for sprees.) And of course there's this absolute dead-line between us and the black and half-caste population, which drives us in on each other and increases the tension between the whites.

"Now, it's easy enough to put all this down to climate, but that, between ourselves, is rot. Allowing climate to be fifty per cent responsible for our troubles—what makes up the other half? Well, Joe, it looks to me as if that fellow Sisyphus had got no worse a job than we have, trying to govern territory seven-eights of which hasn't even been prospected, and of which it is impossible to take a census. That's a kind of generalisation which I'm trying on Uncle Hacky's behalf, to reduce to plain facts. It all seems to be the same thing wherever you turn—a vast muddle of squandermania and niggardliness, of bureaucracy and *laisser-faire*: the kind of thing that drives people with any sort of conscience crackers and, of course, leaves every sort of loophole for abuse of power and neglect of duty. Not that I've seen much of either ; but that's just a matter of the British character. It all reminds me of a machine, running down for want of attention. You ought to hear the traders. . . .

" Well, here I am at Charlestown, which, as I told you, used to be one of our great trading posts in the eighteenth century. It is now pretty well derelict, with a white population (not counting the missionaries) of not more than a score, but every variety of half-caste and three-quarter-caste you can imagine, as well as the Negro. One can hardly picture it as a flourishing centre of the Slave, and, later, of the rubber and oil trade, which it remained up to about ten years ago ; all the factory and storage buildings are in a tumbledown condition, and it has the thoroughly squalid aspect of a settlement that has ' gone back to nigger.'

" Now I think this is enough—more than enough !—for the present. Tich, of course, is in a state of high feather about getting back to his home town. Did I tell you he's got a girl here ? I'll be in a pickle if they elect to get married, because finding a decent boy is a deuce of a gamble and it's a plague to break a new one in to one's ways. He gets more of a dandy every day—not, I am thankful to say, on my wardrobe ; it's just a piece of luck that nothing of mine will meet round his waist or across his chest. I notice, however, that he makes a point of making up to the washerwomen in each place we come to, and hate to think how many people, by now, are bemoaning the loss of their best shirts and hosiery !

" I shall only stop here long enough to make my arrangements for the trip up-country to Omo ; I was rather taken aback to find you're supposed to have a permit—I hadn't imagined there would be any let or hindrance to prowling about on one's own ! As the District Commissioner is away, I have to wait for his return, but I have small temptation to linger in my present quarters, which are eery in the extreme.

" Now, Joe, I will finish. Give my best regards to Polly, when you see her. I wish she would send me a line ; I expect she goes to the house sometimes, she and the girls used to be great chums. . . ."

V

On her mat, in a corner of her parents' compound, Akiki howled quietly. Akiki, doing as her parents bade her, had refused to go in church with her lover, Somilu, to make public declaration of repentance for letting him put a baby in her, to wait for the mission ju ju to work, and finally to be married —not according to the rites of her own people, but by white customs, to which Somilu was foolish enough to subscribe.

The coloured population hummed with the affair, one faction for Akiki's people, another for her lover—who, after putting a baby in her, had gone away, leaving Akiki to swell and swell until now, within a couple of moons of delivery, there was not the remotest doubt of her unseemly and foolish behaviour. The younger and more frivolous set decided unanimously that, in Akiki's place, they would have defied parental objection for the sake of the bridal gown, the veil, the bridesmaids and all the delightful paraphernalia accruing to marriage on the mission pattern. Akiki, who, despite her one disastrous lapse, was essentially a home girl, with a strong respect for the ties of family, stopped at home and howled : partly because she was sick with love for Somilu, partly because she too would have liked the veil and the bridesmaids, and a great deal more because her father had beaten her with his stick which had a powerful spirit in it. Ever since childhood she had watched him giving it its proper offerings of rum and calico ; now she snivelled, remembering how much rum and how many pieces of calico had gone to the sore places on her arms and her buttocks.

But she knew she had been a silly girl. She suspected, rightly, that her father's wrath was less due to the slight on his tribal gods than to his being out of pocket over the affair. Akiki's price had been fixed at twenty pounds English, forty bags of salt and ten goats : enough to give any girl a good opinion of herself, and to keep off light-minded philanderers. And now she was not worth a brass halfpenny, and all the girls who had previously been envious were laughing themselves paralytic over her downfall.

" O you Akiki ! " they sang, with the light-hearted cruelty of their kind :

" O you Akiki !
You are the girl that nobody cares about
Whose lover has gone through the high forest
and into the unknown dens of leopards
and out on the seas before the quick-running winds
and into towns where there are women
whose clothes smell of musk
and who hang little small moons in their ears—
Sooner than stop home and look after you and your baby !

He left his town and he left his father's house
and he left you on your mat
and he went down the dark forest path
where the snake lies waiting
and the elephant tramples
he walked across rivers on the heads of crocodile
and left his shadow in a pool of blood—
Sooner than stop home and look after you and your baby !

There were about twenty more verses, because the girls were good at this kind of thing and enjoyed themselves thoroughly when once they got going : Akiki spat at them and threw stones, which they promptly bowled back, but she knew the song was stupid. Somilu had done none of those things ; he had never seen an elephant, or a crocodile, in their living state, since his family came down to the coast from their village, when Somilu had reached the age of puberty. He had gone straight from mission school into domestic service, and he had left Charlestown because his employers, one after another, had all had business which took them up and down the coast. It was sheer bad luck that just before she found out she was going to have the baby, he had been swept away to Accra—a place of whose splendours Akiki had no idea, and in which she had not the remotest interest, when Somilu tried to describe them to her. The only thing she had against Somilu was that he talked too much, and expected her to listen ; to Akiki, a girl who did not care to talk, and who went to sleep when she had to listen, this was a trial. But, apart from it, Somilu was perfect.

And he *had* promised to come back to her. In bidding her farewell, he had assured her of his return, and of his having, by then, saved enough money to pay what her parents demanded. For once, Akiki had listened ; she even went so far as to remind him that her father would never, in any circumstances, consent to her marrying according to the customs of the Water-god men, and Somilu, after consideration, had promised to find a way of getting round his future father-in-law's objections. If necessary, they could have a secret wedding, in the bosom of the family, and the Water-god people would just have to make the best of it later on, when they found out.

But when the baby developed from a suspicion into a certainty, a slow terror took shape in Akiki's mind. It was not much of a mind, and what there was of it was now wholly taken up with her lover, and with the plight they would both be in, on his return. Realistic in her way, she fully realised that it would be unreasonable now to expect Somilu to pay the full price for a privilege he had already enjoyed : and this in itself would embitter the relationship between him and her parents. A stern view was taken, in her family, of girls who parted with their virginity on anything less than a sound cash basis, and there had been one or two grisly instances of reprisal on betrayers who failed eventually to come up to scratch by purchasing indemnity from the results of their impetuosity. A good deal was made, also, of the marriage rites themselves ; no Noncomformist community could have been stricter than the tribe to which Akiki and her father and mother belonged, in enforcing sexual propriety between its younger members. To begin with, therefore, Akiki was afraid for Somilu ; it was just possible that her father, or one of her elder brothers, particularly if he happened at the moment, to be under the influence of alcohol, would not wait to argue the matter of the money, the salt and the goats, but would proceed immediately to a form of reckoning which, while not rated technically as murder, usually, in the long run, worked out as such, unless the victim himself forestalled it by committing suicide.

The idea of fetish, also, troubled Akiki dimly : the fetish of the Water-god people, to whose customs Somilu subscribed. Her own father was a considerable fetishman, and the children had been brought up in respect, not only for the whole range of manu, abambo, miode and oginga—not one of which Akiki was capable of distinguishing from another : the ombuiri, sasabonsum, and sisa hierarchy : all Keepers of the House and domestic gods—but also for the fetishes of other people. They had been taught politeness to these, because, just as the powers of one's own fetish might be directed, in time of stress, against an enemy, so might the disciples of another school employ their fetish against anyone who offended its principles.

Supposing the Water-god men withdrew the protective virtue of their fetish from Somilu? Or, worse still, set it against him? He would be like a butterfly, crushed out between clappers of iron. The wrath of the Water-god meeting the occult forces invoked by Akiki's father could only mean annihilation for the victim who lay between.

Akiki lay on her mat, shivering and hoping Somilu would not return.

Only that afternoon she had met Mrs. Gummijo.

To any other of the white ladies in Charlestown (there were not more than six, counting the Commissioner's sister, who, married into the Civil Service and living at Accra, occasionally paid a visit to the Residency) Akiki would have been just "one of the nigger girls." To one who prided herself on having the best eye and memory for Negroes on the West Coast, she was definitely (and unfortunately, as she felt, in the circumstances) "that girl of the carpenter's—you know, the heathen family—in whom Thomas is interested." Thomas—as Somilu was known in the mission: he answered with equal readiness to Thomas, to the name bestowed on him by his parents and to Tich, the facetious invention of his first employer—was one of Mrs. Gummijo's pets, one of her husband's earliest converts. She looked with a sour eye on Akiki, after several years' efforts to make a convert of her. But Mrs. Gummijo—the native version of Gummeridge—was not the kind to be beaten by heathen resistance to the Word. Akiki, although she was never allowed by her parents to attend the mission school, in common with her friends partook of most of the mission junketings: at least, she had done so up to the time when instinct warned her that it might be better not to flaunt her swelling breasts, her beautiful, big, round stomach under Mrs. Gummijo's eye. Instinct, and not reasoning, told her that these additions to her charms, of which she was proud, although they got her into trouble at home, would not be approved by Mrs. Gummijo; in fact, she had it from one of the Water-god girls that, according to the Water-god, you had no business to be that shape at all, unless you had first worn a white dress, cocked a crown of white flowers over one eye and pushed a brass ring over the white cotton finger of a left hand glove. Akiki's private view was that this Water-god custom was silly, as who could help getting a baby inside her? She felt, however, that it would be wiser, for the present, to keep out of Mrs. Gummijo's way.

How right she had been came to her in a flash, when she came head on against Mrs. Gummijo, just outside the hospital. As the sun-bleached bow on the top of Mrs. Gummijo's bonnet—she seldom condescended to the sun helmet worn by the majority of her colleagues—stiffened: as a pair of lashless and somewhat protruberant eyes took stock of her appearance, Akiki smiled sweetly, hoping to put Mrs. Gummijo in a good temper.

"Have you been getting married?" One was obliged to use the term, even for those improper heathen ceremonies.

Aiki showed her teeth politely and wriggled, bringing the less presentable aspects of her anatomy even more pointedly to Mrs. Gummijo's notice.

" I thought you were going with Thomas." If Akiki had been used to the English inflection, she would have detected a note of relief in the comment. But the only word of which she was sure was Thomas, which she recognised as Somilu's mission name, and to which she nodded vigorous assent before replying, in the trade English which was her only means of communication with the white people, and to which her mild, obliging manner contributed a charm in which it is usually lacking.

" Thom-O good bwoy, Missy Gummijo. My Daddy mad too much, say him blow him headbone inside. I say, not blow him headbone. Dem bwoy lib fo' marry me." And she went serenely on, unconscious of the emotions she had kindled by her proud little speech.

It was only later that she remembered, and was frightened, and began ardently to hope that Somilu, after all, had found it impossible to keep his word to her ; that he had stayed safely in the big coast towns with his master—even that he had become temporarily enslaved to one of the town women, whose clothes were scented with musk and who wore little moons in her ears—rather than, by returning, place himself within the inimical power of the Water-god people, and the no less dangerous reach of her own family.

Mrs. Gummijo stood in the sun, looking after her with tightened lips. As one capable, in her time, of keeping a whole village of temperamental Akim in order, she was not to be defeated by one young Fan girl. And Thomas was her favourite convert. The implication of Akiki's words, that he was the one responsible for her indisputable condition, hurt Mrs. Gummijo deeply. Though practical in the main, she could not get over the fact of a young man practising the Christian religion behaving in so thoroughly un-Christian a manner—and with a heathen girl above all. And as she trudged home through the dust, she decided that if the rumour that Thomas had got back from his costal travels was true, he must be given a sharp lesson.

VI

In the town itself the people acted as if they were anæsthetised. The men stood along the sidewalks with their hands in their pockets as though each had had a knock on his head. The women squatting on the doorsteps had an air of waiting without hope or interest, for something which never came along.

Apart from the hospital and the mission, every building was in ruins. A dead indifference lay, like a fog, over everything. Even the passing of a stranger roused none of the interest it usuall did, in the small towns along the coast.

Out at Endor; where, on Kershaw's instructions, Johnny went, to pay his respects to the District Commissioner, and, as a matter of courtesy, mention his plans—it was the same. Nobody there but the janitor, and a clerk who informed him he must wait for a permit to go up-country to Omo. From whom did he get the permit? From the District Commissioner. Where was the District Commissioner to be found? No one knew. When was he expected to return? No one cared. It was the first obstruction Johnny had encountered, in his travels along the Coast; the first wet blanket which, so far, had been cast upon his projects. A little of the dimness which, apparently, enveloped Charlestown descended upon him; to combat it, he decided on physical energy—incompatible as that might be with the climate and with the hour.

For want of other occupation, he set himself to clamber over the ruins of the Fort, whose echoing emptiness seemed that of the town itself. The sand, deep-silted in the dungeons to which, at last, he penetrated, rose to the level of the rusty chains cemented by their rings into the walls. The sea air had perished the cement, and he pulled a ring out easily, and held it in his hand: until a sudden shaft of horror sent him scrambling away, up towards the light.

The arch of the gallery along which he was walking gave under his feet and shot him down in a cloud of dust and rubble. Only a hell of a climate, reflected Johnny, as he spat grit out of his mouth and rubbed gravel off the palms of his hands, could reduce a place originally so solidly built, in little more than a century, to a mere shell. It was his second narrow escape: once the tread of a staircase broke suddenly into air above a yawning pit of darkness. But he persisted, through patches of darkness and of light—where the roof had fallen in—past nests of snakes and scorpions, until he found the old powder magazine, and a gun-turret, filled with the droppings of birds.

Cautiously, having learned his lesson, he perched himself astride a block of masonry and looked down at the beach below. It was empty, and strangely colourless, as though the sun, in its sinking, had dragged down below the horizon all the blue and the gold. Kershaw was right; it was the god-damnedest place they had struck, so far, along the coast.

The first instalment of the baggage had arrived, by the time he slithered, scrambled and rolled down to the hut, and Tich was mounting guard over it, with a puzzled expression on his face.

"And there are the three long ones," he pointed out, when Johnny had finished checking over the collection of crates and bundles which, by some means, had attached themselves to his modest load, since leaving Accra, "each of a size to contain the body of a man—that came among the others on board the ship."

"What is this, of long ones?" Johnny scowled. "I know of none such."

"Yet, lord, they are here." Three long, narrow, coffin-like cases confirmed the claim: done up with wire and nails and labelled Machinery—which Johnny examined in vain for signs of ownership. Could they belong to Kershaw? It was unlikely he would have sent them on, as advance baggage, without mentioned the fact to his travelling companion. Much more likely that Komuntale's zeal on behalf of his "bess friend" had overleapt itself in claiming more than Johnny's share of the goods that came up from the hold.

It's probably for the mines. I bet some unlucky devil's cursing the non-arrival of some vital bit of his working parts, thought Johnny. I'd better report that in the morning. " My belly is thin ; make chop one-time," he told Tich laconically, and stepped out for a last sharp walk along the beach before night fell.

Yet, at the touch of the brine-laden air, the desire for movement went from him. It was as though the air were dead, and laid a sticky film over everything.

He turned to look at the hut—the first stone house he had occupied since coming to the Coast : built out of boulders which, at some time, had formed the outworks of the Fort, or, perhaps, of the old barracoons. Whoever built it had taken a rampart of the Fort for the fourth wall ; in the twilight it melted into the rampart, became part of the Fort itself. Its single virtue was its thatched roof—there had been enough rain at Shama to give Johnny a lasting distaste for tin roofing.

What kind of a hermit-like soul had been this Vickers, Johnny wondered, to inhabit a place so isolated from human sight and sound ? The noise of the surf cut off all of the echoes of the town ; the Fort itself formed a barrier between the hut and its nearest human habitation. A man might live and die—*and die*—and his nearest neighbours be none the wiser, unless chance, or curiosity, took them round that great mass of crumbling stone. . . .

After chop, he spent an hour on his Hausa grammar and wrote out a number of phrases he had memorised from Tich—by then retired to his mat. At liberty to go and visit his girl, he had postponed the reunion : Johnny suspected, because the boxes with his best garments had not yet come ashore.

He conducted his usual hunt for scorpion and other live stock which, however many precautions one took, seemed always to find their way into the bedding. For a moment, after blowing out the light, he opened the door.

The moon was at full and lent an easy look to the foreshore. The blocks of stone, tumbled from the Fort, took on odd shapes in the moonlight : he picked out a ship, a headless man, the forequarters of a horse, some sort of a prehistoric monster, with prognathic jaw and serrated spinal fin. The sand itself was alive with small black crabs, dazzling as an ant-heap. The wind had risen with the flow of the tide and, now and again, blew spray, or sand, against the windows.

He wondered what they were all doing at home. He wondered how long it would be before Kershaw arrived.

CHAPTER THREE

I

Johnny's Diary

"HAVEN'T been able to write for the last two days—hands being done up in bandages. They are better now, though fingers still raw at the ends, and there's a nasty gash between the thumb and the first, on my left, that will take some time to heal, as it keeps opening when I use the hand for anything. Must just jot down briefly how I got in this mess.

"I suppose I'd gone to sleep, but all of a sudden I found myself awake, with a feeling there was somebody round the hut. When I opened the door there did not seem to be anyone about, but it was cloudy, and there was plenty of cover among the rocks ; so, knowing what cowards the blacks are, I took a chance and pumped a couple of shots out of my Colt at the nearest chunk of rock, and, sure enough, there was a sort of yelp and a scuffle, and I think I caught sight of three or four figures making a bolt for it. Tich, of course, came, yelling with fright, out of his quarters, and it took me a good ten minutes to quiet him down.

"I don't know what put it into my mind, but after I got back into bed I got the idea that the visitors were after those cases of machinery. It struck me that it would take a pretty strong inducement to fetch them here at that hour of the night—the Fort not being a favourite resort after sunset. And a simple robbery seemed unlikely, as the natives don't go in much for petty thieving, outside their own circles—white men's equipment being too difficult to dispose of without starting inquiries.

"To cut it short, I decided to have another look at the cases while the coast was clear : Tich by now snoring on his mat, and a good three hours more to go until daybreak. So I lit one of the palm-oil lamps, which are all the illumination we have got, until Kershaw turns up with the kerosene one that belongs to him (and a miserable light they give : about two inches of wick, floating on oil in an old cigarette tin), and went into the dugout at the back of the hut, which someone presumably intended for stores and baggage.

"I had guessed by now what was in the cases, but I opened them carefully, in case I was making a blunder. It took a long time, as I hadn't got the proper tools, and had to make do with my knife and a bit of iron bar that, luckily, was lying about. I kept thinking how Kershaw would curse, when he knew he had missed the fun : and of all the hours we'd spent, hiding in swamps, dodging through screwpine and making raids on perfectly harmless huts, for the very things fate—in the shape of Mr. Komuntale—had dumped on my doorstep !

Three dozen Danes: a dozen in each case. No wonder Tich couldn't lift them.

"I sat there a bit—getting my breath and wondering what to do about them. I hadn't got the hang of things yet: I didn't want to go rushing up to the wrong person with my thirty-six Danes—wagging my tail, like a puppy with a bone. Also, I had an idea it would be better to lie quiet until Kershaw arrived. The question was, what to do with them, and what to do with the boxes: as it was all Africa to a chaney orange someone would have another go at collecting them—either openly, or in the same way as the party that had just bolted—and who I was quite sure would not come back that night, after the scare I had given them.

"After a lot of thought, I came to the conclusion the best thing to do, first, was to get the guns into a safe hiding place, inside the Fort itself. None of the natives ever go in there, and it is as safe as the Bank of England. And while I was carrying them into the old magazine, the second part of the scheme came to me, though I doubted whether I could carry it out by myself.

"It was broad daylight before I had finished filling the cases up with pieces of rock, packing them so they would not slip about, with all the old rags and blankets I could find: then getting the lids on again, with the nails in the right places and the wire twisted so as to look more or less the way it did before I started my excavations. It's lucky the black isn't observant. A white man would have spotted it at a glance, and known the cases had been tampered with. I had taken great pains not to tear the labels, which—again by a fortunate chance—were not stuck across the join between the lid and the box. I hoped, also, that no one would notice the bloodstains—my hands by this time were torn to pieces: but if they did, they would probably only think someone had been mauling the cases out of curiosity.

"I was more dead than alive by the time this was finished, and could hardly crawl back to my hut. Tich was still asleep like the dead, although it was going on for five, and the cocks were crowing their heads off.

"To-day I am pretty tired, but feel much livelier and better than I have been in every way since leaving Accra. Think it's the deadness of everything that gets one down—after the novelty has worn off. This gun business has made a pleasant diversion.

"Tich, on the other hand, looks, for some reason, like a wet rag. He has hardly been off his mat, except to cook chop, and I've never known him so gloomy. Don't know whether he has had a row with his girl. I asked him if he wanted the evening off again, but he said no, and, in fact, seemed terrified I would order him to take it. I've given him a dose of cascara, so hope he'll run it out of himself—whatever he's got. For once, I don't think he's malingering. He looks a very sick black, and wouldn't, or perhaps couldn't, rouse himself to give me my usual lesson in conversation, which, as a rule, he enjoys very much. It makes him feel superior, and then he gets cheeky, but in a harmless fashion that is really very amusing, although I have to kick him for it. He is an excellent specimen of his type, and one of the few I have come across who seems to be no worse for his mission training ; quite fairly honest and as devoted as a spaniel. Like the rest of these Coastal blacks, however, he has no stamina. They're all the same : the least little complaint, a bellyache or a bad tooth, and they wilt like faded violets !

" So I have been making lists of words, and feel quite encouraged by the extent of my vocabulary. I am now practically fluent in Hausa, and can make myself understood in two of the dialectic variations that complicate one's dealings with the countryfolk in this part of the world. All this in preparation for my trip to Omo—I shall look a fool if it doesn't come off ! Kershaw says the linguists are not really to be trusted, and it will certainly look better if I can palaver directly with the chief, instead of through an interpreter.

" I keep on thinking about those guns. I am as certain as one can be that Komuntale knows about them. I haven't reported the cases, am just letting nature take its course. Something will turn up, one of these days."

II

In all the other places he had visited, whether towns or small stations, there had been some mitigation of the general discomfort : some grotesque incident, or character, on which to pin the humour in which Coastal society is by no means deficient, some focussing point of interest, for the stranger, in local occupations or diversions.

The District Officer at N'Banta, the smallest station he had stayed on, was back from furlough with a selection of the latest phonograph records ; the fun of watching the reaction of the guileless inhabitants of the adjacent bush had not yet started to pall. It was worth while dropping in at Shama to have an evening of Duncan's yarns, highly apocryphal, mainly concerned with panjandrums of the Civil Service, and guaranteed to remove any unwholesome tendency among new arrivals, or reverence towards their betters.

At Duke's there was an orgy of energy round the construction of a new road, supposed to connect up with the main carrier route, and vastly to expedite the flow of supplies from inland to the seaboard. Nobody, yet, had started to worry about whether or not it would be completed ; the whites were content because they had plenty to do, and the blacks because there was money about, and gin parties, and congas every night. To celebrate the general feeling of prosperity, the mission children had given a concert, of which the high light was a translated and dramatised version of *Father, dear Father, come home with me now*, to which a small boy in a top hat, carrying a swagger cane, contributed a lifelike impression of the inebriated parent.

And Bfuma was still laughing itself sick over the story of Carter, who, electing to die in the rainy season, had to be ballasted top and toe with bottles of the respected Mynheer Van Hoytima, to prevent him floating to the top of his hole and bobbing off down the creek. Then came the dry season—in more senses than one. For some reason, Bfuma's liquor consignment did not turn up ; Spike, who kept the store, was driven frantic by customers who threatened to break up his premises unless their demands were met ; and was obliged to call on his old friend Carter for the relief of a very ticklish situation.

That story was a great success when Johnny recited it in Easy Emma's, and advanced his credit with those who were inclined to be stand-offish. To tell the truth, Charlestown did not know what to make of this thin, grave, little man who had dropped casually upon it, with no ostensible pretext for his presence : and Charlestown did not care for people who failed to produce pretexts. Who the hell was he ? What was he after ? No one in their right minds came to Charlestown " on holiday." Suspecting, to begin with, some departmental snooper, Charlestown lowered its eyelids, put its feet up defiantly on its office benches and refused steadfastly to pretend it had any work to do ; made rude noises at Accra, and, in general, turned thc cold shoulder on the visitor, who—by Jesus !—had popped himself down in Vickers' old place. Prewett was responsible for that—and may be Prewett knew what he was doing. Still—a certain amount of morbid interest must attach itself to anyone cracked enough to pop himself down in Vickers' shadow. Fishy, said Charlestown ; recalling the fact that the few misguided strangers who, in a moment of aberration, " dropped off " for a day or two's visit, invariably made hot-foot for the Commissioner's, or scrounged quarters at the mission, while waiting for the boat. One or two of the more nervous dusted the ants out of their files, scrabbled anxiously for mislaid forms, took a hasty glance at their accounts and, in the usual fashion, contributed small sums out of their own salaries to cover an awkward hiatus between debit and credit, due to the embranglement of Coastal arithmetic, where everyone was always borrowing and paying back, and by far the lengthiest item on the books was the page headed " Loans." But the sturdier majority were prepared to go to hell, sooner than fuss themselves.

So Charlestown laughed, albeit guardedly, at Johnny's anecdote, and a little sandy-haired, snipe-faced trader, known as " Foxy " Biddle, wagged his head across his rum and lime. Foxy was shrewd ; he was also, as a transient, immune from Charlestown's local idiosyncrasies. Some time, earlier on in the drink session, he had decided this young 'un was all right. Which did not restrain his curiosity about Johnny's activities.

" Have a drink." A voice inert with heat, or liquor, or both, broke the brief silence following the laughter.

It was the dinner hour. Most of Emma's customers took their midday meal from the bottle, but one or two were shovelling down platefuls of hash that the proprietress herself dipped out of a pot on the hearth. Emma's was used as a canteen by anyone who happened to find it convenient : whites mainly. There were few of the coloured community who had not, in one way or another, call on a communal pot somewhere in the rabbit-warren at the back of the town. All over the floor, and in the corners, swarmed the endless progeny of Emma's four daughters : scuffling, fighting, biting, in a soft, endless turmoil briefly checked by a kick or a smack from one of the parents. One of the girls slapped down a plate of hash at Johnny's elbow.

"What's the mee-nu ?" Foxy leaned over, to sniff amiably. "Pigs' innerds ar lar kerosene—m'm. Got no chop to-day, chum ?"

"Nobody to cook it. My boy's got the gripes."

"I'd give him gripes," said Foxy comfortably.

"You—Flood : I said, have a drink."

"It's Prewett." Foxy nudged him. "He's had a basinful. Pay no regard."

Prewett, however, peeled himself off the counter at the far end of the room and sat unsteadily on the table between Johnny and his companion.

"Blast your liver, don't you hear me ? Have a drink, and talk. I'm sick of talking to these bastards. Only two subjects—shop, and smut. I've got a nice line in smut, but the hell of it is, just when I'm off on a nice bit of smut, I get an idea. And that's the end of it !"

No one moved. No one seemed to listen. And yet the air was filled with a kind of resentful attention. One man had his head on his arms, pretending to be asleep.

"Ideas unpopular—very. For instance." The slight pedantry of the lecturer entered into the blurred accents of the speaker. "Take integrity. Maudie doesn't know what the word means—do you, Maudie ?" He turned to the girl who, too bored, too scornful, or possibly too ignorant to pay attention, hung her weight on the counter, smudging the wet rings left by the glasses into one another with an idle thumb fine and curved as a scimitar. "How should she ? They don't teach 'em words like that at the mission."

He lifted a long forefinger and wagged it impressively at the room.

"The integrity of the individual derives from the integrity of the tribe. If the tribe loses its unity, there's no focal point for individual virtue. Tha's pos'tive." He appeared to wait for a contradiction ; receiving none—"Now : effect of British rule in gen'ral—disintegration of tribal unities. Result—demoralisation. Perf'ly simple : all works itself out like a problem in al-algebra. Hell of a lot of long words," said Prewett gently. "Too much for Maudie. Or for that black son of a bitch behind the counter."

A flash of white at the level of the latter's mouth betokened his acceptance of the compliment.

"Yes, sah. Yes, Mistah Prewett. I got book, but dem word too big fo' me !" Laconically, without being asked, as one who knows what is expected of him, he filled another glass and put it at Prewett's elbow.

"Monograph on Results of British Administration on the Indigenous Population of the Coastal Districts of West Africa ; I must work it up one of these days. Give Maudie a drink. She's suffering—though she doesn't know it—from disintegration of her tribal unities. Why don't you forget about your unities, you silly bitch, and have a drink ?"

Maudie answered in one syllable—not current in polite society. Her thumb went on breaking up the patterns of the wet glasses. Her flesh showed golden through rents in her flounced gown, and her mouth, in the floury mask of her small, sullen face, was like an aneurism.

" Have a drink," Prewett was saying. Petulantly, rather than angrily, he pushed the fork Johnny was in the act of raising to his mouth aside. " And tell us what you're doing in Charlestown. Doing in our fash'nable spa—the brightest jewel in the Empire's crown ! Matter of public interest, y' know, when a person turns up in Charlestown, with no partic'lar excuse to show for it. Starts a lot of gossip." He wagged a reprobatory head. " Can't have that, y' know ! Can't have gossip in a nice, clean-minded place like Charlestown."

He stopped abruptly ; blinked, jerked his head sideways, like a horse jibbing at a hurdle ; looked round in a puzzled way, and, as though taken aback by the silence, lunged towards the door.

With his going, the clatter of spoons in plates, the boom of male voices and the shrill squeals of Emma's girls were resumed. Foxy Biddle lifted his mug, drained it, set it down with a clap and picked up his sun helmet.

" Well, so long, chum." A faint movement of his head appeared to invite Johnny, who, finding his appetite gone, left his plate unfinished, to follow him.

Outside Emma's a gang of labourers slumbered in the sun. The shadows of passers-by, patterning the foul mixture of dirt and dust underfoot, the hot, living air, trailing over them its burden of insects, of microbes, of the insanitary effluvia of the quarter, left them untouched. An elderly Negress emptied a slush bucket into the street drain, raising a swarm of flies and disturbing a sow that suckled her stringy offspring in the bottom of the gully. Away through the jewel-like light wavered the figure of Prewett ; a sudden dappling of shadow from the eucalyptus trees dissolved it into its background.

" Thank God," Foxy was saying, " I'm a simple, block-headed trader, with no brains to get addled in this garbage dump ! A month of it, all the same, 'ud send me barmy. 'S a mercy my job keeps me movin' around. Have you had a look at the swamp yet ? "

Johnny admitted he had not. " But it's no different from any other swamp, is it ? "

" Come to think of it," allowed Foxy, " I don't suppose it is. Still—there's one or two things you might find out, if you was to take a stroll round that way. You might find out, f'rinstance, how Prewett comes to be the way he is. You might find out what makes a chap spend five years of his life middle-deep in liquid malaria, and what accounts for everybody in Charlestown being three-parts cracked. Even the blacks are cracked : haven't you noticed it ? There's something god-damned about Charlestown," confided Foxy, " and, if you ask me, the answer's there—back o' those god-damned trees." He added, unexpectedly, " Prewett ain't a bad sort of chap, you know."

" I can't make him out—but I can't say I've taken a fancy to him ! It's a bit difficult to get a line on a fellow who's plastered all the time."

"Him and me's been stable companions, in a manner o' speaking, for quite a while. I been thinking—when I clear out you might do worse than dig in with him. T'aint so bad, up at his place. Prewett won't bother you; t'aint often he gets one of these talkative spells—and he gen'rally works 'em off at Emma's."

"I'm all right, where I am." Johnny could not help showing some surprise at the unexpected suggestion.

"What—at Vickers'?"

"Kershaw'll be here, any day, and we're planning to go up-country." What, he wondered, was the queer look in Foxy's eyes about? "I won't be sorry to get out," he blurted. "I guess you're right—it's the swamp that makes everybody here more dead than alive. It's certainly the damnedest climate I've struck since starting along the coast."

"Oh, climate—pish. I'm sick of hearin' everybody put things on the climate. It ain't done anything to me, has it? O' course you know the yarn——?" He gave a sly look at his companion.

"Yarn? What yarn?"

"Basinful o' trash," grunted Foxy. "You know the tales that get around when you've got a pack o' niggers all mixed up with mongrel whites, and they get crackin' in the cabins. All the same, they *do* say"—Foxy lowered his voice and looked sheepish—"Charlestown's got a curse on it. Some old wives' tale about a chap that lived here in the slaving days, and got his nigger woman pinched by one of the merchants: I can't recall the details, if I ever heard 'em——"

"That was my—one of my ancestors."

"Go on."

"I'm not kidding," grinned Johnny. "It's part of our family history. I've got relations, somewhere, who are descendants of the—ah—nigger woman." In politeness to Foxy he adopted the former's phraseology; but the word "nigger" had become distasteful to him, with its connotation of contempt. There were individuals—he thought of Kaboha Komuntale—whom it was a pleasure to call nigger, as a term of abuse; but he had come across others for whom it was a patent insult.

"Well, no offence meant." Foxy was obviously embarrassed. "Of course, that alters the picture. Anyhow, it's a lot of ballyhoo. What's wrong with Charlestown is that bloody swamp, washin' in behind us, every year a bit nearer, with a few more billion tsetse breedin' on it: while we wait for our lords an' masters in Whitehall to make up their minds to pack it up. If ever you got a sample o' nature beatin' 'umanity—here it is!—and it'll be int'restin' to see how many 'uman lives it takes to make the Gov'ment admit it's had the count."

"Well—but swamps have been beaten, haven't they? I was told they've got a terrific scheme on in one of the French districts: nearly thirty miles reclaimed already and no prospect of unemployment for the next five or ten years!"

"Don't talk to me about the French," said Foxy fretfully. "They can give their people landin' piers, can't they? And a proper patrol system up an' down the rivers, an' their *Chargeurs Réunis* steam line. The French take colonisation seriously : the British play at it. Beatin' the swamps ! That's where Prewett comes in—poor bastard."

" That's what I gathered from Kershaw. He said Prewett was one of the brightest chaps they'd ever had in Public Works."

Foxy snorted.

" Ay, that's how he comes to be in Charlestown. He got at loggerheads with somebody in Accra, and they sent him down here—may be to teach him not to be so bright. Told him to prepare his scheme, make out an estimate of costs, and, assurin' favourable consideration, make himself gen'rally useful, till the Big Job came along. One day," said Foxy, after a pause, " Prewett'll go mad. Not just cracked, the way he is—the way most of us are : but stark, starin' crazy. The sort o' crazy that goes round with a knife in its hand and sticks it into the first thing that happens to come handy. Pity some o' them Colonial Office big-wigs couldn't be around when Prewett gets hold of his knife. Well, I got to get over to the factory——"

" You don't know, by any chance, when the Commissioner's supposed to be back ? "

" Morris ? " Foxy swung on his heel. " I reckon it 'ud take second sight to cast Morris's movements. Is he a pal o' yours ? "

" No. I'm waiting for my permit to go up to Omo."

" Permit ? " The other spoke sharply. " What's the game ? You don't need no permits for this part o' the world."

Johnny shrugged his shoulders.

" That's what I was told, at Endor."

" Suthink new, so far's I'm concerned," grunted Foxy. " Well, you can always depend on Morris for a few surprises. You'll like Morris," he offered. " Plenty o' folks are scared of him and some think he's mad : but he's the finest Commissioner in any of the districts and he's got one hell of a job in this one ! Queer," he mused, " if they're expectin' him already ; he don't gen'rally publish his movements, and it's not more'n three weeks since he went up-country. Sounds as if you're in for a long wait . . ." he ended dubiously.

" I'll wait," said Johnny.

" Listen, chum." Foxy dropped his hand on the younger man's shoulder ; there was a serious look in his eyes. " Don't stop too long in Charlestown. Folks have been known to catch more than fever, down here."

III

All day long, Somilu, whom his master called Tich, and the mission Thomas, had felt terrible ; he had pains in his bowels and his belly, and a fluttering in his wrists and behind his knees, which drove him to his mat. Fludi had given him a dose of something which, if anything, had made matters worse. He had been obliged, repeatedly to get up, crawl round the corner and crouch on the rough branches of his latrine. As he crouched, his head swam, and he felt he might die at any moment, and tumble into the hole underneath.

He had felt like this ever since, strutting up the town to see Akiki, to show off his new clothes, and to impress her parents with his wisdom and importance, he had been waylaid by one who told him something that so frightened him that, instead of going to Akiki's, he took promptly to his heels and spent several hours shivering with terror in one of the disused sheds down by the Customs.

It at first seemed unbelievable : this terrible thing which had happened to him and Akiki—only because they loved each other, and would have been married long ago, if other people had allowed them to mind their own business.

Then it came over him, in waves of horror, that, if it was the truth, he had not only offended Akiki's family in a dangerous manner, but had sinned against his mission teaching, of which he had always been extremely proud, as it lent him superiority among uneducated people, and earned him respect from those who employed him. But now, he remembered, Jesus-God would be angry, as well as the gods of Akiki's people, and, in His anger, might withdraw the protection of His ju ju—leaving His servant open to the attacks of all the spirits which, dutifully, on becoming a Christian, he had forsworn. Panic romped about in Somilu's intestines, turned his sinews to water and his heart to a lump of cold wet jelly, slopping about in the noble cavity of his chest.

Perhaps Fludi would protect him. Perhaps they would be leaving Charlestown soon. Every now and then he clutched at a ray of hope, and it eluded him, like a butterfly.

Slowly, however, as the throes and agonies of his disturbed interior began to die down, stray passages of Mr. Gummijo's teaching, which had always laid great stress on the quality of mercy, revived in his mind. Slowlier still, the natural resilience of Somilu's temperament began to reassert itself round this idea of mercy, which took on brighter and brighter colours, the more he thought of it. So that when—several hours after Johnny's departure for Easy Emma's—one of the young catechumens appeared, with the news that Somilu's return was known to Mr. Gummijo, and that he was expected to make an appearance at evening service, Somilu felt almost cheerful.

He got up, and put on the suit of clothes he had inherited from his former employer, Mr. Holbein, delighted with an opportunity for showing them off. They were not improved by his night in the Customs shed, but a candy-striped bow tie and a red and yellow ribbon round the straw boater would surely draw attention from creased and blackened trousers : particularly if he stopped in at the laundrywoman's on the way, to have a sharp line pressed down each trouser leg, and a flourish to the lapels of the coat.

Everyone would look, and everyone would think what a fine, town-style boy he was ; and Mr. Gummijo would say, " Come along, Thomas, I respect to welcome you, for I know what a good boy you are and how well you work for your master. . . ." Like all Negroes, Somilu had an unbounded capacity for wishful thinking, and while one half of his mind pondered the idea of putting on his shoes, and rejected it, because his stomach was still too queasy to deal with the complications of eyelet holes and laces, the other half was occupied with the scene to come.

Although, according to his informant, Mr. and Mrs. Gummijo knew all about himself and Akiki, something would have happened, some miracle—as they called the God-men's witching—and the hearts of Mr. and Mrs. Gummijo would be filled with mercy and love at the sight of their returned disciple.

These and other pleasant thoughts were in Somilu's mind as he obeyed the summons of the mission bell ; its djang, djang, djang spoke to him of the mercy and love of Jesus-God, and even banished his tendency to dodge the purlieus where certain members of Akiki's family might be lurking. Jesus-God was speaking to him through the bell : Come along, Thomas, everything will be all right, there is no need to be frightened of anything. . . .

When he heard the summons to come up to the front seats, right ahead of all the congregation, he leapt to his feet with a proud, bright smile, glad of his candy-striped tie and pleased to have all heads turning towards him. His strut up the aisle was practically a cake walk : he could just not control the joyful prance of his legs in Mr. Holbein's trousers, which were held up by Mr. Flood's best Sunday silk handkerchief about his excited hips. There were Mr. and Mrs. Komuntale looking at him in admiration, and Mr. and Mrs. Judson of the Post and Telegraphs, and Mr. Artemidorus Come-all-ye-faithful Smith, who looked after the Commissioner's house at Endor, and all the cream of coloured society, collected to give him a big welcome. . . .

There was Mr. Gummijo, waiting for him : waiting to say, " Never fear, Thomas. You are a good boy, and you shall marry Akiki to-morrow, the way her people want you to marry her, and then you shall have a great, big wedding, here in the church, so everybody will be pleased, and there will be no trouble with her spirits or with yours." Then he would say : " Please, sir, please, Mr. Gummijo, I can't pay the money." Then a bright light of mercy and love would shine all round Mr. Gummijo's bald head, and he would say : " Don't let that bother you, Thomas, because I will go myself to Akiki's parents and tell them you are a good boy, and it is lucky for her she get husband like you. And then we will arrange something about the money. . . ."

Then Mr. Gummijo started to speak ; and the shining mist of Somilu's romancing shivered, thinned, and grew cold. For what Mr. Gummijo said was nothing like the speech Somilu had invented for him.

And, at the end of it, the bell began to ring.

IV

He felt the crust give under his feet, letting him down into putrescence. All around, like skeletons of extinct monsters were the mangroves. It was the patch immediately behind the richly wooded region bordering on the creek which ran down between Charlestown and Endor, and it was like passing from life into death. Silence, and death, and the bone-grey roots of the mangroves, risen above the mud from which they had sucked its vital essences.

He lost count of time—gripping the roots, using their tortuous network for foothold, working his way through this starvation belt into the swamp itself. He knew he was getting close to it when the silence gave way to a web of small noises : clucks and suckings and whirrs. The heat was that of a Turkish bath ; a light steam, skimming the black batter that was the swamp, was laden with flies, and held in on all sides by the green-black walls of the mangroves. It was almost impossible to realise that one was within little more than a mile of civilisation : that this was no " lost land " of the interior, but that, somewhere at hand, was the landing places for canoes and the beginning of the main waterway between coast and up-country.

It took little stretch of the imagination to recognise, in the bubbling, scum-laden surface, one of those vortices which generate superstitions governing the length and breadth of the bush. Shaking himself free of the clutch of fantasy, Johnny set himself conscientiously to examine his surroundings.

Almost at his feet, sticking up through the mud, were the remains of a pipe-line. Glistening with slime and crusted with larvæ, some kind of a primitive pump suggested past attempts to drain the water into a channel whose commencement was visible in half-submerged earthworks behind it. One more sample of the ineffectuality of which he had seen plenty. It was after he had taken in these things that he saw Prewett.

Prewett had a lump of lead on the end of a piece of string and was lowering it at intervals into the mud ; waiting for it to settle and the string to tauten in his hand ; then pulling it up and examining the mark made by the mud on the string. There was something childish and amateur about the performance that embarrassed the watcher. Then he went clambering among the mangroves, and Johnny saw that these, here and there, were marked on their stiltlike roots with patches of black. Now and again Prewett marked another, daubing it with his hand with the mud of the swamp. He himself was black to the waist, and the flies made a cloud of black about his head and body. His movements were slow, impeded by the mud and by his evident exhaustion. He went on with his task, which, to the watcher, had no end and no meaning. A human maggot, crawling through the cosmic intestine, towards eternity.

" It's gone down about two inches."

He spoke calmly, accepting the other's presence as though he had been aware of it all the while. As he waded heavily in Johnny's direction, the disturbed slime threw up a nauseating stench of decaying matter. Behind him, on the surface of the swamp, a log stirred. Johnny let out a shout.

" Look out ; there's a croc behind you."

" We know each other ; he's having his afternoon nap. This is where the old carrier road came down." He drew himself up casually out of range of the drowsy monster, which settled again ; he stood, holding by the roots, his light yellow eyes resting on Johnny, hardly more human in aspect than the mangroves around him.

" How far does it go ? "

" What ? The swamp ? " Prewett shrugged his shoulders. " About two miles north—the main stretch. It's pushing out west now, towards Endor. Greedy things, swamps." He laughed softly, shortly, without mirth. His tiger-yellow glance flickered from point to point, reading in slime, in floating branch, in the discoloration of an aerial root, a case-history illegible to his companion. Then he was off again, clambering over the roots until Johnny lost him in their meshes ; driven by his mysterious obligation. . . . There was nothing to do but get back ; nothing to be gained by lingering in this compost heap of disease germs.

" Tich. Tich, you lazy devil."

Oh—foxing, after all ; gone off in the town. Swearing, Johnny stripped, snatched a towel and took a dose of Warburg's.

V

The headman, grinning explained there had been a mistake. The three long cases that came up with the lord Fludi's baggage belonged elsewhere. The carriers had mixed it. He had orders to collect them. All of which, to his surprise, he was told to repeat, not in trade English, but in the dialect. This in itself was disconcerting : it was not the business of a newcomer to be fluent in the vernacular. Out of nervousness, the grin became impudent. The small white man to whom it was addressed remained impassive.

" How do they call you ? "

In his surprise, the headman gave his proper name, not that bestowed on him by a race notorious for its evasions of the native nomenclature with sportive inventions of its own.

" They call me Mfabo."

" Then, Mfabo." Johnny removed the pipe from his lips ; he addressed a polished chest indifferently, as though finding it as much to his purpose as the bullet head above it. " You will take the boxes, and you will carry them ten times round the Fort. This will teach you not to make mistakes again."

" Master," said Mfabo, with respect, " it is just punishment, for these boys are fools and should suffer for it. I myself will count the ten times, so there shall be no question about it."

" There will be no question ; for I will count and you yourself will carry. And there are three boxes, which means that ten times each will make thirty times, which I will mark here on the sand—"

" That will not be needed ! " Mfabo indicated with a flurried gesture the row of Kroo boys behind him. " The lord sees these men are here for the purpose—two to each box: for it is beyond one man's strength to lift them alone!"

Johnny allowed his eyes slowly to travel up the vast human column in front of him.

"O ko!" The degree of scorn with which the simple ejaculation was loaded made Mfabo wriggle. "So that is how it is? You are the rotted arm of a tree, that needs but a tap and it falls, showing the dead wood within? Truly," said Johnny, wagging a thoughtful head, "the sickness takes strange forms, of which I had heard, but in which I had not believed until this day. So, since it is not well the strong should be governed by the weak——"

"That is not so, lord!" Stung by the aspersion on his physique, Mfabo hastened to vindicate himself. "I can lift an elephant by its hind legs!" he boasted. "The weight of a full-grown palm is nothing to me! It is for this that I am chosen to put fear and restraint into this dung of camels." He spat with accuracy towards the nearest Kroo, whose mirth had become unseemly.

"Either you lie," came the calm rejoinder, "or the boxes to you are but as straw. Come. Lift."

In a cleft stick between pride and ignominy, Mfabo stooped sullenly. The box was not "as straw:" so much was shown by the swelling of his muscles as he lifted it to his shoulders. Staggering a little, he glowered at Johnny—conscious that the sniggers of the spectators had turned to respect. So far, at least, he had justified his boast; but the triumph was a brief one.

"It is true you are strong, Mfabo, and you are not sick—although you may be, when I have done with you. There is the path, and you will follow it; and as it goes but one way, I will remain here, and count the times as you pass. And this will make much laughter, for it will show you are a bad headman, who cannot keep those under you in proper order."

"That is bad talk," scowled Mfabo, "for it is not for the lord to put shame on one who is not in his service, and does only that which he is bidden."

"Bad talk it may be, but it will be worse for you and for those who employ you, if I send a book to Those Who Are Higher. The palaver is finished. Now—walk."

"Master," gasped Mfabo, at the end of the seventh round. Outside the patch of shadow in which, at Johnny's order, they had placed his chair, the midday sun burnt up the dust and rubble, the sandflies swarmed. The joke of seeing their headman trot round and round the walls palled on the Kroo-boys, most of whom, in boredom, sank to their haunches and nodded, with their heads between their knees; but the performance still drew a fluctuating gallery of coloured small fry, of humorously-minded idlers, whose witticisms Johnny took wall-eyed, though they added visibly to the discomfort of his victim. "Master, the load is heavy."

"Walk," said Johnny, and swished at the flies with the horse-tail set in ivory he had bought in Accra. There was something in his dispassionate stare that quickened Mfabo's reluctant feet.

At the end of the eleventh round Mfabo collapsed, face down in the sand. Although suspicious that the fall was histrionic, Johnny let it go at that. His purpose was achieved ; not only had the headsman lost face, but whoever was employing him ; the tale would be round the town by nightfall.

VI

" You've let your coffee go cold, Hananiah. Goodness me, you're more trouble than a child. Come right in and I'll make you some fresh."

The strong, positive voice, a voice that never seemed to doubt itself or its owner, and was therefore invaluable to one given, as the Reverend Hananiah Gummeridge, to self-question and self-criticism, jarred for once. Sensing the reaction, his wife added, more gently, " What's the matter ? "

" Listen," said Hananiah.

She listened. The mission house was a little removed from the town's centre, but, at this hour of the night, the usual waves of sound, beating on the air, set up a corresponding vibration in the ear-drums. Charlotte Gummeridge listened attentively, but heard nothing that was not familiar.

" Well, what is it ? "

His sudden, jerky movement knocked the chair from which he had risen against her knees ; she saved it expertly. How was it that Hananiah, so strong in the spirit, was so helpless and so clumsy in ordinary ways ? She felt his helplessness like the fluttering of a moth in the darkness of the porch.

" Listen," he said again, and she heard his teeth chatter. Had he taken his quinine ? Yes ; she herself had seen to it. She listened stolidly.

" It's only sailors ; I expect there's a ship in. Come in and drink your coffee."

" I ought to go and sit with Cator ; I fear the poor fellow hasn't got long——"

" You'll drink your coffee "—she gave him a quick frown of anxiety—" and then you'll go to bed. It's where you ought to have been the last two hours."

She pretended to be occupied, but was sharply aware of him sitting by the table, his back bowed in weariness, his long melancholy head bowed over the bowl of coffee he held in both hands ; apparently he had forgotten to drink it.

" You've heard our bad news, from Omo ? " She nodded, her lips pursed. " They've given up the mission." He spoke slowly, incredulously. " A sad set-back. A heavy cross for our brethren to bear."

" Now, Hananiah, you've got to be practical about these things," she rallied him briskly. " You know it's very largely a question of lack of funds. And it's better to break new ground than go on digging a plot that's ceased to be productive. We've got to face the fact that that Omo mission had worked itself to a standstill more than twelve months ago."

" Yes, but one wonders why. Don't you remember how we all gave thanks, some years back, for the chief's conversion? And Brother Hall himself gave me a promising account of the school—I was wondering——" began Hananiah, and stopped.

"I know what you were wondering." She took him up astutely. "You were wondering if it would be possible to work Omo from here; that was it, wasn't it?"

"I confess, Charlotte, that was in my mind."

"Then you can put it out of your mind," was the terse rejoinder. "You know I'm willing to carry your share of the burden as well as my own, but stop here while you wear the last of the flesh off your bones"—she looked at him with affectionate disparagement—"in canoes and hammocks, I will not."

"I was only thinking of it," he apologised mildly.

"What's the good of thinking? Brother Hall is a stalwart soldier of the Lord, but even he couldn't make headway against that two-faced Kufi and his bad old mother. I'm willing to wager he was attending the services and conducting all his heathen rites on the sly. Of course, if you insist," she was shrewd enough to add, "I'll go up with you, but I don't mind admitting I've had enough of the Ashanti, and I don't look forward to settling on their frontier again."

"You are a brave woman." He looked at her lovingly.

"Fiddlesticks. You're the brave one." She spoke gruffly, her heart quickening to the memory of his unfailing courage during their travels up-country, the calmness he had displayed in the face of mortal danger, his unshaken belief, when death—a peculiarly unpleasant form of death—stared them in the face, that they would be delivered from the hands of their enemies. "Let it be, Hananiah," she said quietly. "It can't be many years now, before the old woman's dead, and then we can try again. If you succeeded in converting old Akosua—well! They ought to put you among the great evangelists."

"It is hard, all the same, on Hall's converts: surrounded as they are by the troops of Midian, we can only pray for them."

"I'll do all the praying you like," promised Charlotte. Her slight acquaintance with Omo had always disposed her against belief in the authenticity of its conversions.

"I've been wondering——" said Hananiah, and, again, stopped.

"I don't know what's the matter with you!" She spoke jestingly, but her heart was heavy. What he needed, of course, was a long furlough; valiantly as he had striven, during the five years of their settlement in Charlestown, it had got him down at last; mentally and physically he was worn out with the battle against influences deriving, not only from pagan ignorance, and from the heathen cults he had patiently striven to eradicate among his native flock, but from the white and near-white element of the coastal belt. "You'd better wonder yourself to bed."

He answered her with the humility she sometimes found irritating in him; "Blessed are the meek," indeed, but it could be carried too far. She wondered, sometimes, if Hananiah would have been capable of scourging the moneylenders out of the temple—an act, which, she felt, with a sense of secret guilt, would have given her a considerable degree of pleasure. Hananiah would have been more likely to go on his knees and pray for them.

" Do you think I was right, in accepting our call to Charlestown ? " As she caught her breath, for indignant asseveration of her belief in him, he continued. " I sometimes feel that someone stronger, more versed in the ways of the world, would have made more headway than I."

She answered him sturdily.

" The heathen don't need the ways of the world ; that's what we're leading them away from, towards the Kingdom of God."

" That is true ; but we have to go along the world's way to find our wandering sheep." His voice was troubled ; she knew he was thinking of his former flock, of the little station up-country where, before the last Ashanti rising, they had been so happy, where the Lamp of the Lord shone bright, where, every morning, they stood together, men, women and children, with its brightness on their faces, to sing the morning hymn :

" Mu sunsum nsueri yi Nyami ayew ;
Mu sunsum nsueri yin' ayew——"

Arise my soul and praise the Lord, arise my soul and praise Him ! Happy days, among a tiny band of former cannibals, who, never having had contact with any other world, accepted with simplicity the message from a God greater than their own.

" It was easier up-country," she admitted ; " even that time when we thought we were going to be eaten. But we've never looked for ease, have we ? The heavier the cross, the greater the blessing ; isn't that what you've always told me ? Now drink that up, and let's take our troubles to the Lord in prayer."

" I don't deserve you, Charlotte. . . . It's a mercy the child died."

For a moment her hard, positive face was convulsed ; she made a quick movement, then snatched her hands to her, as though conscious they betrayed her.

" It was God's will. And it would have been hard work, bringing up a baby in Charlestown. It wasn't what we were sent here for, you and I ! "

He got up and wandered to the inner door, where he checked with a faint exclamation.

" I've neglected it again."

" What are you worrying about now ? " For once she allowed impatience to break out of her, at his continual preoccupation with sins of omission.

" I really meant to see to it to-day. We must appear sadly inhospitable."

" A lot of time you have for hospitalities ! I suppose you mean that young Flood ? Considering all things, he might have paid you his respects by now. He must know *we're* not people of leisure," she snorted.

" I hope there may always be leisure for a kindly thought." The mild reproach brought colour to her cheeks. " I've been thinking, Charlotte——"

"Oh, for mercy's sake, stop thinking! I simply must run over the accounts before I go to bed."

"Let me see to them in the morning." A likely thing; when had Hananiah's attempts to deal with accounts ever resulted in anything but chaos? "Could we not offer him lodging here?"

"Whatever for? You know the little space we have is kept for the sick, when the hospital's overcrowded, and for the brethren, if any of them happen to come this way."

"Your own kinsman, Charlotte," he reminded her.

She bit her tongue, to hold back the observation—self-evident to anyone but Hananiah—that consanguinity did not effect cubic content.

"I hear he has got Vickers'—a very unwholesome spot; you know what the Negroes say about the old Fort."

"Mercy upon us!" This time he had genuinely alarmed her. "You don't mean to say you're beginning to pay attention to Negro superstition?"

"Accursed ground." He spoke softly, but there was a spot of bright, purplish colour on the small section of his cheekbone that was not covered by beard. "Why should we doubt it, Charlotte? The past is ever with us. The question is, how long does evil endure?"

"Well, I suppose we—I mean, my people—contributed plenty to it, in the past," said Charlotte uncomfortably, "but we're doing our best to atone. I don't, however, see that atonement need take the shape of having young Flood here, in the mission. I don't doubt he's better off there—in his own opinion—than he'd be with us. From what one hears of the company he keeps he's not likely to feel at home in our society."

"We'd be to blame, if he fell into undesirable company for want of a welcoming hand." It was unusual for Hananiah to be so persistent.

"Oh, very well. I suppose," she pouted, "one of us will have to speak to him about Thomas."

"Charlotte." He came wandering back to her. Her heart contracted at the pain and bewilderment in his short-sighted eyes. That was what lay at the back of his mood of despondency; she had known it all the time. "Supposing—supposing we were wrong, about Thomas?"

Her strong hand lay on his shoulder, her voice was firm, but very kindly.

"How could we be wrong? You know it is our rule, which had to be made for cases like his."

She heard him moving clumsily about their bedroom, while she plugged the tampon of cotton-wool viciously out of the bottle of boiled water, poured out a glass and slipped into it the bit of iron which, red-hotted on the methylated stove, brought a faint, chalybeatic tang to the flatness of the sterile water. A small scorpion reared from the matting; she killed it dispassionately, conducted her usual methodical hunt for snakes, and, satisfied all was well, pulled the chain of the oil lamp and took her tired limbs to bed.

The two narrow military cots formed a white cenotaph under the mosquito net. Hananiah was already asleep, drawing the sharp, dry breaths of one whose heart is unsteady ; she paused to listen to him. Under the small sound went on the thudding of the drums.

She finished her undressing, and, with extreme caution, so as not to disturb him, insinuated her big body under the net. Always he awoke, and they knelt up, side by side, to say their prayers together. Dear God, let Hananiah sleep ; for once ; let my prayers do for the pair of us.

But there was the usual creak and rustle from the adjoining cot, and she felt the frail cage of his bones, under the pyjama suit, brush her arm ; felt his hand grope for hers, and moved to steady him with her shoulder. Outside the drums thudded, a shout, a shriek tore the tinselly web of sound woven by the mosquitoes. A party clattered past the mission, roaring light-hearted ribaldries, a woman screamed hysterically at the over-zealous attentions of a follower. Hananiah's voice rose steadily in the night prayer.

". . . O Lord, guide, protect and cherish Thine erring lamb, and bring him safely to Thy fold again. Amen."

" Amen," she echoed, and bent across his once more recumbent figure, to make sure the net was properly tucked in.

She slept, but he lay awake, anxious and troubled about many things. About the strange little flaws, like knots in a piece of wholesome wood, that interrupted the fine grain of her Christianity. About her young relative, alone and exposed to the temptations of a vicious environment, in a place where he was a stranger. And, last and most agonisingly, about a negro boy, driven from the House of God to the clanging of a bell. It was the prescribed punishment for his sin, and strictly in accordance with the rule of the mission. In earlier days, what stern, comminatory zeal he—Hananiah—would have brought to the ceremony ! With what righteousness he would have seized the opportunity of bringing home to his easy-going congregation the results of an offence against the purity of the body !

Now . . .

Was it that he had diminished in righteousness or in zeal ? Why was the image of the sinner brought to repentance persistently effaced in his memory by that of a dazed and trembling human creature, fleeing from a vast, incomprehensible Wrath—a helpless victim, driven into the jaws of its destroyers ? Was this the meaning of everlasting mercy, which he had tried for twenty years to drive into the minds of listeners to whom mercy was in itself an unintelligible quality ?

" For His mercy doth endure, ever faithful, ever sure." He himself had put the words of the hymn into four of the Ewe dialects, to be cheerfully bawled by little catechumens at the confirmation classes and chanted with fervour by adult communicants. Why should he doubt them ? Why should he accuse himself, by faithful adherence to a rule prescribed by the brethren, of putting doubt into another's heart ?

CHAPTER FOUR

I

"EVERYBODY complains of the food," Johnny wrote conscientiously, "but I have come to the conclusion that is mainly because the white can't get away from the idea of butcher's meat and poultry as the only basis for a square meal. Beef is certainly shocking, pork about as bad and an occasional fowl costs a fabulous sum and consists mainly of lengths of rubbery sinew with a little bit of tasteless flesh like an old kid glove here and there. In my experience you can eat really well on local vegetable and cereal. Bananas mashed into rice, with a couple of eggs on top, are both tasty and filling—providing the eggs aren't bad, which about seven in ten usually are ; you get used, however, to a whiff of sulphuretted hydrogen with your chop. Yams, grenadillas, sweet potatoes, avocada pears are plentiful in the market—but at prices prohibitive for the native.

"Suspension of local roadworks, etc., accounts for much unemployment and a lot of poverty ; tuberculosis seems general, and is, of course, increased by semi-starvation. Even rice is dearer than in some parts, owing to transport. The coastal native seems to have no notion of cultivation, and although he could no doubt live on yam and plantain, the trees are so neglected and maltreated that their yield is very poor. Rates of pay are very low indeed, and most people prefer to spend their earnings on liquor—i.e., palm wine or a villainous sort of doctored rum that some of the rascally dealers make up to sell to the natives. It does not seem surprising that the hospital—run by the missionaries—is full all the time."

He stopped, to dry his hands. The room was slipping into shadow ; in a very short while it would be dark. Blast that Tich ; what the devil was the fellow doing ? It was time for chop, but a conversation overheard at the Post Office put one off the idea of going back to Emma's.

"That mare of Clinton's got fly."

"Serve him bloody right. What's he want, fetching a mare down here ?"

"Wanted to run it next season at Accra."

"'Twasn't no fly killed Clinton's mare."

"Who says it wasn't ?"

"Betcha a dollar. Hammock boys."

"Could be. Say, did you hear ? When Clinton went to have it buried, there was a couple of legs missing."

"Hope they give the perishers bellyache."

"Hope they don't give us bellyache. Don't one of Emma's sons carry Clinton's hammock ?"

It might be just a bit of Coastal persiflage ; on the other hand, it might not. Better be on the safe side and open a box of emergency rations. Corn beef, wheatmeal and a pot of army issue jam went down better than Emma's ambiguous hash.

He found himself longing unspeakably for the clear English air: the sweet-scented, harmless air that poured over and cleansed you, instead of crusting you with a thousand impurities. And he longed sharply, as he had never done before, for the sight and company of women: gentle, formal women, enshrined in their natural modesty as their bodies were enshrined in soft, all-enveloping garments. He remembered some pictures, shown titteringly under cover of a desk lid, by one of the clerks, to himself and Joe; and Joe saying, later, when they were alone: "Did you ever see a woman—like that—with no clothes on?" He had answered gruffly: "Yes; plenty—niggers"—knowing as he spoke that there was a subtle difference between black and white nudity; knowing that in Joe's mind, as well as in his own, lingered the excited curiosity evoked by the prurient drawings. There were some fellows, he knew, who thought of nothing else; thought themselves into a fever, thought themselves limp and stupid and useless; a pity they could not have a few months on the Gold Coast! That would cure them, if nothing else did.

He was bored with the sight of female flesh—though he got pleasure out of the children and little girls who, though wanting in beauty according to any white standard, had a kittenish charm that was both amusing and appealing; but the older ones, with their little pear-shaped adolescent breasts degenerated into long, flabby flaps of flesh, their protuberant bellies and heavy buttocks nauseated, and even embarrassed him. There was one who persisted in squatting a few yards from the hut, displaying herself for his benefit; someone had told her that certain parts of her body had an exciting significance for white men, and she exhibited them with a business-like lack of coquetry.

It was indeed an alien world into which Fate—or Harcourt—had pitched him. How much did that old man know? And what was the motive that lay, deep-buried, beneath his imponderable actions? Perhaps time would show; meanwhile, the knowledge that he was on trial, that the whole of his future relationship with his uncle, and, possibly, the whole of his career, depended on the use he made of his present opportunities had begun to get on Johnny's nerves: for it seemed he had little to show, so far, for his five months on the Coast. It robbed him of sleep and woke him in the thin hours between night and morning, when time, like his watch, seemed to stand still. Curse that watch. It had stopped nearly a month ago, its works, like every other piece of mechanism on the Coast, clogged with sand. It was one of the first things he had meant to attend to, on his arrival in Charlestown; did his failure to do so mean that he, also, had become infected by the apathy of his surroundings?

He forced himself to think of other things: of Mark Kershaw and of the friendship that had started so queerly, by the grave of a stranger, in some far place along the coast: that had given one a jolt—and yet—it came to him with a start, how much of a commonplace death had come to be, during the months of his pilgrimage. It was not that he had grown callous, or that the dead were, in most cases, personally unknown to him; death had just—as Kershaw had told him—fallen into its place, as part of the cosmic design. One had no shock at the falling of a leaf, at the withering of grass—this, probably, because in their hidden roots was the secret of rebirth : in their end was their beginning. Could not this be true, also, of the human soul, with its roots deep-set in eternity ? The horror of the Gold Coast was not in its death, but in its life : its agonised, unwilling survival.

. . . It was a god-damned place, this hut of Vickers'. Pretty plain, why it had lain empty, since Vickers' death. Filled with the empty boom of the surf, there was something about it for which Johnny's limited vocabulary could only find the word " eery." As soon as night fell one was aware of the Fort, laying its shadow in black paper on the sand outside, and of the seaward darkness, cut into strips by the silver band of the calemma. A whispering went along the beach, where the blocks of stone lay scattered, forming, with their shadows, shapes oddly human, sprawling, disjointed, slain by the moonlight. A chill air moved ; but now and again, when its breath seemed suspended, the sand gave up, in a profound regurgitation, its burden of brine, of rotting coconuts, of a fetor composed of decay and of the mustiness that hangs about the scene of an exhumation.

He found, as he set the match to the wick of the lamp, and darkness drained back into the corners of the room, that his hand was shaking. Damn that Tich ! though it was a nice thing if the company of a black had come to be preferable to solitude.

Somewhere in the town they were having a conga—that meant somebody had found a job of work and earned enough for a bottle of gin. Wafts of disharmony came through the rhythmic crash of the surf, and the tapping of drums. Johnny slammed the door, which he had opened to look along the beach, and stood, listening to his own breathing. It came on him that he had never before, although often alone, known the true meaning of loneliness ; of a solitude which, calm and peaceful under an open sky, becomes grisly, pent between four walls. The kind of solitude that fastens on one, hampers one's movements, and ends by petrifying one into immobility.

It was true, what they said about the drums : there was devil in them. There was the other interpretation, of course, the practical one : African news machine, tapping out its leaders, its stop press, its special editions, across river and swamp. That was the lo-koli drummers. But not these. Deep, dark devil, stirring under African soil. Soul-sucking devil, fear devil, death devil : all dancing like mad in old top hats, prancing in white gaiters, clapping their thighs and leaping in the air and swinging capes of leopard skin in the bushlight, moonlight, blood light. . . .

It was several moments before he found that the noise he had taken for drums was the blood beating in his ears, and moved abruptly, to break the heavy rhythm which, like a clock, like a death-watch, went on measuring out time, Gold Coast time, in units of—what ? Of warning ? Of premonition ?

He forced himself to breathe evenly, and slowly to turn his head, as he felt the room losing its emptiness. Nothing but the small, square space, with its oddments of furniture, met his eyes : but he could feel it, filling itself with something that rose from the dank matting, that curled and churned between floor and roof-beams, and pressed on him like a living but invisible entity : pressed its pain, and its fear, and its loneliness into him until his body began to ache with it. Not one being, but many beings : now fusing, now breaking into separate elements, then fusing again. At one moment he had the impression that the lamp was smoking. He pressed his eyelids together, then opened them quickly. And it seemed that layers of thinning or thickening shadow crossed the space in wave-like formation ; he found himself balancing against them, as against a pressure of moving water. They came from one wall, and they passed out through the opposite wall, and, as they reached it, the waves assumed briefly a human shape, of heads and shoulders, and an occasional arm, tossing up ceiling-high. . . .

The back of his hand, which he had flung up to his forehead, was dripping. He cursed softly, drying his brow and his hand on the bandanna he jerked from the pocket of his pyjama coat.

This was Gold Coast jitters—of which he had heard tell, and had inwardly derided. Or it was the outcome—plus a fever bout—of all the hints, and the odd looks in people's eyes, which he had noticed each time he mentioned he was living out at Vickers' place. Or he was going cracked. (" Even the blacks are cracked ; haven't you noticed it ? ")

The strength had gone out of him like water, but he managed to stumble across to the wall and prop himself against it. He had been standing there for some time, with his palms against the wall above his head, and his head dropped forward between his shoulders, trying to conquer his faintness, when it struck him that the wall was tacky, as with dew. But when he brought his hands away, the stains on the palms were red.

II

" You carried all these things in here by yourself ? Nice work. So this is where the beggars were running them." The speaker squinted along the six-foot barrel of the weapon he held in his hand. " Had a go at firing one ? "

" No fear. I'd as soon try potting with a mediæval blunderbuss." Piled against the wall, the Danes gave out a dull glimmer of metal in the light of the kerosene lantern Johnny had brought down with him. " What's their range—one fifty ? "

" About two hundred. They're reckoned lethal, up to that."

" What about the charge ? "

" Couple o' dozen iron bars, chopped into cubes : that's the favourite. Old telegraph wire comes in handy—and makes a nasty mess : particularly if it happens to be rusty."

" Give me hold for a minute : I hadn't time to examine them the other day. Flintlock, by George : here's the powder chamber—what a hell of a thing ! You don't mean they're making these now ? "

" Making them in Brum." Kershaw nodded. " They sell out here for about sixteen bob—there's plenty of them about ; I'd have thought you'd have seen them before. We supply them ourselves—the blacks are whales for them at their big palavers and dance parties. Fifty of these, shot off together, makes a lovely big bang : very impressive !" Kershaw's teeth glittered in the crumpled rectangle of his face. " All very nice, so long as they keep 'em for parties," he murmured. " How many do you say—three dozen ? "

" That's it. Three cases—a dozen in each."

" Markings ? "

" ' Machinery,' and the Customs cross—furnished, no doubt, by my pal Komuntale. It 'ud be interesting to know how many he's got through, by his neat device of popping them among visitors' baggage, and collecting them later. What one would really like to know," said Johnny thoughtfully, " is the route they take afterwards."

" I bet there's enough stuff gone up-country in the last six months "—Kershaw bit his thumbnail, a trick of his, when he had something on his mind—" to arm the Protectorate and lay a railway line from here to Kumassi. Who's to stop it ? There's too many niggers like Komuntale in Customs, and too few whites to keep an eye on them. You can't run duplicated staffs from end to end of the Coast, and sooner or later some rascally clerk's bound to get his opportunity. They've all got tie-ups of some sort with the interior——"

" Well, what's the next thing ? " inquired Johnny, as Kershaw paused for reflection.

" You haven't reported it ? "

" I was waiting for you to turn up. I wasn't sure whose pigeon it was—civil police or military."

" No interest to the military. They use the .303 Martini-Metford and the Maxim ; these Mendi troops are no good with the heavy stuff. But this is going to raise a dickens of a stink for somebody." Kerhsaw, his hands in his pockets, had shifted along the passage from the cell in which Johnny had stowed the guns. He stood, scowling up through a hole in the flooring above, at a small blue patch of sky. " Who've they got now, in Customs ? " he asked, after a pause.

" Fellow called Cator—so I've heard."

" Heard ? Don't you know him ? "

" He's been in sick bay, ever since I got in. It used to be Cope ; but he packed up—a fortnight ago."

" Cope was a good scout. Look here." He turned his grotesque face, with the long snout and the small, piercing eyes on Johnny. " I've got a notion we'd better move carefully. It doesn't matter about that blasted nigger—but we don't want to bounce a good chap out of his job ; even in a dung-pit like Charlestown."

" There's surely plenty of this game up and down the coast ; they can't start firing our people for it—can they ? "

" I've got a bit of news for you. A tale's going round—I'm not vouching for it, but it's too general to be all hot air—about strengthening the Hausa battalions, and a general overhaul of ordnance at Cape Coast."

" That sounds like business." Johnny was startled.

" It sounds damn' well like business. If there's fighting in the air, the Up-Tops aren't going to take an easy view of any Customs wallah that lets unaccounted-for arms in through his department."

The appearance of the nonchalant figure at the head of a long line of carriers, with the sun-helmet on the back of its head, nothing but a fuzz of bleached hair on its mahogany-coloured upper parts, and bare knees showing between woven stockings of a sensational tartan and a pair of ancient khaki shorts had seemed like salvation.

It was a standing joke that Kershaw, who was always on the move, travelled enough junk to furnish a Residency, and Johnny avoided the dangerous emotionalism of welcome with a dry cackle at the familiar figure of the cook—hung with enamel household ware, like a travelling hardware store. A load of metal tubing, colander-like discs and tin cylinders of varying capacity, distributed among his assistants, was identifiable, to the initiated, as Kershaw's patent filter, his own invention, and superior, in its owner's opinion, to anything so far produced by the estimable Maignen. It was one of his eccentricities never to have these objects crated, but strung round the necks of chosen members of his retinue—by which means he claimed to be able to check them at a glance.

Stretched in the folding chair which had unexpectedly developed itself from sheaves of cast iron, Johnny watched drowsily the evolution of a music hall property in the corner of the room.

" Good old Maskelyne and Cook ; it's Home, Sweet Home, to see him again."

" Is Foxy Biddle here ? " Kershaw ignored the aspersion on his masterpiece. On receiving the affirmative—" Stopping at Prewett's, I suppose. We'll go and find Foxy ; he's the one to tell us what to do about these shooting irons. Here : where the hell's Tich ? "

" Bunked—hopped it—cleared out."

" Where to ? "

" How the hell do I know ? "

He felt Kershaw looking at him.

" Well—when do we start for Omo ?

" Permit ? You've gone crackers—or somebody has," was his reception of Johnny's explanation. The latter shrugged his shoulders.

" That's their line—at Endor."

" Huh." Kershaw had collapsed into the adjacent chair. The afternoon was heavy with heat and the humming of flies ; there was not a breath of air, though door and windows stood open. " I'll show 'em line, when I get after them. What have we got—a dictatorship ? So that's what Dorrien meant, when——"

" When what ? " inquired Johnny, as Kershaw stopped, biting his lip.

" Oh, there's a bagful of chatter on, back there. Listen, fella." Kershaw swung his bony knees over the arm of the chair and looked straight at his companion. " The rains will be starting any time now. Have you done anything about your passage ? "

"No. Why?"

"They're not so easy to get, when most of the Accra and Cape Coast crowd are off on furlough. Tt, tt, I forgot!" He broke off to grin. "You can get passage any time. What it is to belong to the elect!"

"Bunkum. I've got to fix it with the Accra office—like anyone else." There had been no malice in the tone, but Johnny scowled.

"Then fix it. How about packing up Omo—for now?"

"What are you getting at?" He heard his voice crackle.

"Keep your hair on. I was just wondering if you'd taken a look at yourself in the glass, since you got down here," was the calm rejoinder.

The red ray of the setting sun, chopping like a sabre along the beach, burned across his shoulder; Johnny staggered up to get a drink. He felt his temperature rising, and was disgusted to see the cup dither in his hand. He snapped: "I'm not in the habit of prinking."

"Nor of taking your five drops—by the look of it. You bloody ass, what have you been up to down here?"

"Oh, chuck it," exploded Johnny. "What do you think you are? My old nanny? Where d'you think you're going?" he snapped, as Kershaw, risen from his chair, was making for the door.

"To find Prewett and kick his backside."

"Would it be going too far, to ask what for?" Taken by surprise, Johnny gaped.

"No; nor to ask Prewett if he'd care to take a turn in Vickers'—as a change of air from his present domicile. I made sure, when I told you to look him up, that he'd put you up at his place. He's got room for a couple more—beside Foxy."

"I guess it's quite a while since you saw Prewett." Johnny had recovered his temper. "As a matter of fact, one or two people offered to take me in, but I thought I'd better look out for somewhere where there'd be room for the pair of us—dammit all, we've got thatch, and it's fairly cool at night. That tin roofing's like a blasted incinerator. As for the yarns——"

"Ah. You've heard them, have you?"

"As a matter of fact, I haven't; but of course I guessed there was something the matter—for a place like this to be lying empty, with people grilling away in those damn' tin shacks all over the town."

"Some day," said Kershaw, after a pause, "you'll have the sense to lay off places other people avoid. Well, well; live and learn. As a matter of fact"—his bull-terrier-like muzzle poked itself in Johnny's direction—"it wouldn't surprise me to hear you've been doing a little learning already."

"It was only a nightmare." As well give up the attempt to side-step Mark's pertinacity.

"Call it a nightmare." Kershaw had gone back to his chair with a tumbler of lime in his hand. Johnny noticed vaguely his narrow inspection of the glass, and the polishing he gave it with a clean handkerchief, before filling it. It was possibly owing to such niceties that Mark maintained his condition in circumstances that robbed most people of theirs. "Call it a temperature of one-o-one. Call it an extra gin-and-lime——"

"That it wasn't. I've gone easy on liquor all the time."

"What's it matter what you call it? There's a saying *autre temps, autre mœurs*; I'd paraphrase it—*autre pays, autre foi.* I've been here long enough to believe a great many things, in Africa, that I'd pooh-pooh at home. Believe enough, at any rate, not to meddle with them. The queerer the yarn is, the more I'm disposed to believe it. Except those ones that take a twist at the end which makes them reasonable from the white's point of view; then I'm ready to lay somebody's been tampering with them. The black's is an angle of sweet credulity; he doesn't care if you believe him or not; he knows it just *is.* And he organises his life on what *is*—which, of course, makes fetish a very paying proposition."

"In what way?"

The other shrugged his shoulders.

"The more the black believes, the more he's inclined to pay for his ju ju—not, mark you, to alter the thing that *is*, but to immunise himself from its effects. Moral—if you're looking for one: when in Rome do as Rome does."

"What? Take to ju ju?" Johnny laughed a little. The relief of Kershaw's company was very great; it was difficult not to be childish about it. When Kershaw raised his lips again from his tumbler, however, his expression was wholly serious.

"Lay off the inexplicable. See here—I'm going to say something. We've had a good many talks, since you and I set out together—and I won't deny I've thought, once or twice, you were cracked. You've got this bee in your bonnet about Africa, and some kind of a romantic notion about righting the wrongs of the African people. You needn't look sheepish; and you don't need to tell me what's there, behind all your curiosity about Negro conditions, and what goes on in the native quarters, and what form the customs take—and all that kind of thing."

"Well, what's the matter with that?" As well not waste one's breath in denial, although it was embarrassing to be accused of romanticism.

"Nothing, in a good many cases," allowed Kershaw, "though from what little I know of the Chairman of Flood's, I don't fancy it's what you were sent out here for. But that, as you're polite enough not to say, is no business of mine. I'll give you a tip, all the same—and remember that people who live at such close quarters as you and I've been doing, since Mappin introduced us, up at Dwana, get to know one another a lot sooner than when they meet in civilised circumstances. There's only one way for a white to live in Africa: that's by pretending—so far as the flies, and the fever, and a few other things will let him—it isn't there."

"That's in direct contradiction to what you were saying before," objected Johnny, after a pause for consideration. "What you said first was, virtually, adopted the attitude of the blacks to their own superstitions."

"Well, the two things dovetail, don't they? If you turn your back on a thing, you don't deny its existence. Only *turn your back*, fella. It's the best way for anybody with your disposition," said Kershaw earnestly. "Some people—like this man Morris—can take it all—the black and the white ; gulp it down and digest it and make a working proposition out of it. Others go——"

"Listen," said Johnny ; his lips felt tight. "I've had about enough of this going mad."

"All right ; let's call it eccentric." A grin twitched Kershaw's mouth awry over his improbable teeth. "Anyhow—they're liable to finish up like Vickers."

"Come on ; what's it about Vickers ?"

"Oh—he saw blood," was the nonchalant answer.

"Go on." His nails were biting into the palms of his hands. "I suppose you mean that witching business—fangaree, is it ? I didn't think it affected —whites."

"Never heard of it doing so. No, it's not fangaree ; that's another branch. 'Seeing blood' isn't uncommon ; I've come on cases of it, here and there—after they were over. An old woman in the Rivers gave me a fine lively account of it ! According to her, the hut dripped for twenty-four hours. And I've had boys who refused to go along certain paths——"

"What's it mean ? That there's been crime there ?"

Kershaw chuckled.

"There you go—trying to make it reasonable. That's how it would be, surely, if it was a white yarn. That's why I don't believe the end of Vickers' story. Give me a bit of paper."

He handed it back a moment later with some marks on it.

"Well—is it a puzzle ?" asked Johnny, after scrutiny.

"Doesn't convey anything to you ?"

"Not a thing."

"Try again."

"It might," he reflected, "be some sort of a brand ; an M, or a W upside down, and the two dots inside the angles. Don't they put that sort of thing on cattle——?" He stopped : his breath failed him suddenly at the look on the other's face.

Kershaw slowly tore the paper into small strips.

"Or slaves. That's what they found on his body, after he was dead. Chuck it !" Johnny staggered before a stinging slap in the face. "Sorry, fella." Kershaw was grinning. "I've never found anything to beat a slap on the mazzard for pulling a person together when he looks as if he's going to heel over.

"Don't you see," he went on, as Johnny dropped back in the chair, "that's what gives the lie to the whole thing—stamps it as an obvious white invention ? This place—all knitted up with the old slave-trade yarns, and the blacks' superstitions about the Fort, and Vickers 'seeing blood'—probably through a square bottle ? If there'd been a doctor about, I swear he'd have diagnosed heart failure ; as it was, his boy recognised the marks and rushed out of the place hollering blue murder, and of course it went round the cabins in no time, and blew up in Easy Emma's, and everyone went to have a look."

"Well—what's *your* answer ?"

" That's just it ; if it was a bona-fide sasabonsum case, or something of that sort, there wouldn't be an answer. Actually, it's as plain as a pike-staff. Vickers," said Kershaw, settling down comfortably, " was an unsavoury kind of fellow. Everybody knew he treated his blacks badly, and any one of them, if he'd had the guts, would have poisoned him. (Poisoning's simple, but it isn't popular with the D.C. It's a good mark to him, how, in the last few years, he's managed to work it out of the district.)

" Vickers died ; and one of his boys, who had always had it in for him, took a post mortem revenge, with one of the old branding irons—there's plenty of them still about. They mainly serve for pokers ; it's the first time I've heard of one being put to its proper use. Well, there you are ; and there's the explanation of the Vickers yarn—which everyone in his right mind accepts."

" It's a grand explanation." Johnny's teeth glittered briefly. " If one believed a word of it. I mean, if you believed it yourself. You see—last night——"

" Well ? "

" I saw blood."

III

As the door clanged behind them, the lamp slung from the ceiling gave out a sharp " ping," sputtered, shuddered a little and temporarily darkened, before resuming its orange glow. The men underneath it started beating the beetles out of their hair and off their shoulders. The air was so thick with tobacco that Johnny's eyes watered.

" If you two've come to cadge chop you're unlucky. The pork's gone ' off,' the ants have got at the jam and the solder's melted into the last tin of Maconochie." Loud cheers and an ironic flourish on the mouth organ interrupted the announcement. " Otherwise—welcome to our home."

" Foxy's in form." Various hands clapped Kershaw on the shoulder ; Johnny had a friendly wink or two that included him in the greeting.

" So it seems. Where's Prewett ? "

The absence of the host seemed to trouble nobody. In a good-humoured clatter of conversation, Foxy and four others were playing cards at a table on the corner of which a sixth seemed painstakingly to be trying to write a letter. The mate of a Runstable boat was the mouth organ artist ; a shy young factory clerk evidently with coloured blood in him, was accompanying him brilliantly on the banjo. Somebody shoved a tin of tobacco at Johnny, who helped himself and then propped himself against a wall to watch the performance of a little agent, called Milligan, who, with immense care and application, enforced by a piece of blue chalk, was inscribing something in handsome Latin uncials on the opposite wall.

" I reckon Prewett's had enough." Kershaw was chuckling at his elbow. " It's always like this when Foxy's around."

" Turn Foxy loose in a graveyard, and he'd have the corpses startin' a jack-pot," nodded someone on the other side.

" The banjo-merchant's pretty good value."

" Don't know him. There's some nigger blood there. By the way "—Kershaw dropped his voice—" have you seen any more of Komuntale, since your little game with his headman ? "

" Met the beggar on the front. All smiles and soft soap. Begged my pardon for the mistake—all the carriers' fault—and much obliged to me for teaching them a lesson ! I nearly laughed in his face."

" Could be he was laughing in yours. It 'ud be a good idea if we were up at Omo before he gets the other end of the story."

" Why ? What could he do ? "

" What's Batty up to ? " Kershaw had gone to look over the scribe's shoulder ; while he read the composition aloud, its author mopped a partly bald brow with a rag he used presently to entrap a spider with a body the size of a walnut, that was weaving its way towards the inkpot.

" ' Dear Madam,—I regret to inform you that your son—dash—died here on the—dash—inst., of yellow fever. His services are gratefully remembered by his colleagues who send you their respectful sympathy.' Who's had it this time ? "

" How the hell do I know ? " Batty killed the spider neatly and took a fresh dip of ink. " Take three to one, if you like, on Cator ; he's favourite for the cemetery stakes."

" Hot favourite. Takin' sixty grains a day and toppin' 'em off with calomel and colocynth. Give you evens," put in one of the card players, cutting the deck passed to him by his neighbour.

" You ain't pinning fever on Cator ? " The speaker, somewhere behind Johnny, sounded shocked.

" You don't want me to tell somebody's dear old white-haired mother how her ewe lamb managed to get himself a lovely case of the yaws, or burnt himself inside out with Van Hoytima ? " with indignation. Batty lifted his glass. " Yellow Jack ! "

" Yellow Jack." The company followed suit ; Foxy, slapping down a pair of twos, winked solemnly at Johnny.

" . . . That lets a man out decent, and stops folks askin' alotta awk'ard questions."

" What've you been having—a bloody holocaust ? " easily inquired Kershaw, as Batty added his page to a pile of others, took a fresh one and headed it " Dear Madam."

" Never seem to get these done at the office, and I like having half a dozen or so on hand—in case o' fire—you chaps," said Batty sourly, " having a way of picking the most inconvenient moments you can think of : when the boat's in, or we've got a fuss on with Customs."

" Damned unlucky service here, Customs ; Cope t'other day, and now Cator, getting ready to hand in his checks. Whole ruddy outfit's at sixes and sevens."

" That's how Komuntale manages to hang on to his billet. Men may come and men may go, but that blasted basalt image goes on for ever," grunted Foxy's *vis-à-vis*, pushing a pile of chips across the table.

"And gets more information than he ought into his dirty black paws."

Johnny's attempt to catch Kershaw's eye was thwarted by the sign-writer, who finished with a flourish, and stepped back to admire his work. "God Bless Our Home" stood out in a lively ultramarine from its dingy background. Somebody chortled.

"That'll go over big on Prewett!"

"S' a hobby o' mine." Little Milligan turned to Johnny for appreciation. "Uncials an' semi-uncial cursive. Them old seventh-century monks, they musta got fun out of it, eh?"

Before Johnny replied, the mouth organ artist swung into "Home, sweet home," with all the long-drawn-out lugubriousness of which only the sailor is capable; a chorus of whistles and semi-tuneful humming followed him. Johnny felt something in his throat.

What, exactly, was "home" to these men, gathered in squalor so far away from all that "home" implies? How many had homes—real homes—in England? Some had, and talked of them—usually under the influence of liquor—with a touching simplicity. There was a little clerk from Liverpool, who was always ready to babble about his "garden" in Bootle: were those damn' cats getting at the seed beds—supposing the missus had sown them? And them effing daisies on his strip of "lawn;" spent a fortune on weed-killer, but his Old Dutch wasn't the build for spudding up roots. The others listened, until somebody's patience cracked, and one of the mindless, formless squabbles of the Coast broke out. But the majority were silent; either they were homeless, and therefore untouched, or they dared not subject themselves to the emotions evoked by reminders of a world they had left behind.

Across the hut an oleograph of the Queen—a standard feature of interior decoration—dominated the scene. Johnny found himself staring at it, and wondering. Brought up, like every young Briton of his day, in the tradition of devotion to the Throne, he only—wondered. So, in all parts of the civilised globe, Englishmen were looking towards that image as the Elizabethans looked towards Gloriana: beholding in it, not only their Queen-Empress, but something more. Something read by wishful hearts into snow-white hair and a pouching bosom, something that stood to the majority for "mother" and "home." Misty eyed and with lumps in their throats, they raised their glasses to it. They died on the thought of it. Johnny was one of them.

Yet—because he was of the generation born in the ebb-tide of that tremendous reign, when already the surge and thrust of new traditions were beginning to make themselves felt—he wondered.

Had that old woman, sated with imperialism, ever reckoned the cost in human endurance of her country's conquest? Or was she too old to do more than acquiesce in what her statesmen told her? Surely Joe Chamberlain had spoken enough of the truth?

The door opened, and Prewett walked in upon his company. He stood by the door, swaying gently, looking with a faint air of puzzlement from face to face. Suddenly the puzzlement went—as though someone had taken a cloth and wiped it away. With the concentrated care of the unsober, he walked across to the banjo player ; took the instrument out of his hand and split it across the youth's head. With his expression of ludicrous dismay framed by the banjo, its strings in a tangle across his hair and teeth, the youth was hustled to the door and despatched by the toe of Prewett's boot into the alley.

The Runstable mate, whose eyes and jaw hung wide open during this unforeseen interlude, slid his mouth organ hastily in his pocket, as he drawled : " Say, cully, why didn't you say you jes don't like music ? " And had his fist swinging ready at his side. Prewett, however, showed no further disposition to aggression. Somebody said, " That's going to cost Bill something. Johnson was fond of his brand-new banjo," and picked up his cards again.

Johnny was aware of Prewett rocking towards him, and of Kershaw edging up on his left. Foxy, looking up across his hand, said, " If there's anybody else here you don't care for, Bill—I guess he'll go quiet."

There was a moment of acute attention. Prewett lifted up his hand and dropped it on Johnny's shoulder. He seemed surprised to find it had arrived there ; he stood, looking at it with admiration, and swaying quietly, before it occurred to him to speak to his supporter. His eyes had gone to slits of yellow, and his smile was benevolent.

" Dzhonny Flood. You're a goo' fellow. Y'know—firs' time I saw you —talkin' to that damn' black—I thought you were a nigger-fancier. Apolozhise. You're a goo' fellow. Hate the bloody niggers as much as we all do." He went on cursing the niggers in a gentle voice, then broke off, to assure himself of his ground. " You do hate the bloody niggers, don't you ? "

" Lord save us, Bill's off on his hobby horse," came resignedly from one of the company.

" When I'm looking for nigger "—in cosy tones from Milligan, once more engaged in his work of art, which he was now industriously occupied in ruining, by the addition of serifs to the original—" give me the old-fashioned, up-country sort, hung all over with ju ju, that keeps the Yam festivals and takes a fling at the blood rites once in a while. Something respectable about that lot—sort of superior."

" Oh, for Jesus' sake let's not talk about nigger. Who started talking about nigger ? "

" Johnson started it. Poor bloody Johnson. Bill went and picked on him, because his mother got scared by a black in her third month," piped up a ribald voice in the background.

" Put a sock in it." With a warning scowl at the speaker Foxy leaned back from the table to growl, " Can't you see Bill's bloodyminded ? " He tossed a handful of coins on the table. " An' that's the last you Israelites'll get out o' me. Hi, Bill——" He stopped, staring up at Prewett, straddling above him with his hands planted on his hips.

" I'll knock any bastard down," said Prewett softly, " that says he doesn't hate niggers."

" Sure," agreed Foxy, wall-eyed. " Everybody hates niggers." It was the kind of thing one did not argue about with Prewett.

" That's right." With the air of a gratified schoolmaster. Suddenly Prewett's forefinger stabbed at his audience. " And *why* do we hate niggers? " triumphantly.

" I guess I better go down to the bottom of the class." With an uneasy grin, little Milligan shifted. Johnny saw him work his way round the room and slip out. Milligan had a weak heart and was due for retirement ; no one thought less of him for avoiding a rough house. The others sat sullenly still under Prewett's diatribe.

" Every time we look at a nigger he reminds us of what we've done along this god-damned coast. That's why it's better "—the words came spaced with a dreadful deliberation—" to look the other way when somebody's taking out his personal and private hate on a nigger. You can't do any good and he can't do much harm."

Nobody seemed disposed to contradict. The sailor whistled softly, pulled a set of poker dice out of his pocket and rolled them on the table. The ruse did not succeed.

" Hate 'em—of course we hate 'em : as you'd hate a nasty, peeking ghost that keeps nudging your elbow : whispering its reminders of what it'll do one day when it gets its chance to pay you out."

" Say," came an injured whine from somebody who had had enough, " you're givin' us creeps."

" That's what's the matter with us." Prewett's voice, hardly above a whisper, rose to a shout. " That's what we've got back, for the smallpox, and the syphilis, and all the wasting diseases we've given 'em—for their oil, and their camwood and their rubber ! That's why we never get a chance to finish anything we begin, and why the swamp's still there, and the graveyard's full, and we pass on *and leave no ash* ! "

There was some restlessness, but no further interruption until he had finished.

" Africa's curse—that she put on the whites 450 B.C., in the time of Hanno. Africa herself's against us. Some folks say it's the Government." He gave a dry cackle. " To hell with the Government. It's ju ju. It's Tando. It's fangaree. It's all the stuff we push on one side, because it doesn't team up with our notions of Imperialism." His voice quietened again. " There's no god-damned Imperialism'll stop Africa visiting the sins of the father's to the third and fourth generation of the races that have exploited her in the past," said Prewett, on a note that spread hopelessness through the room.

. . . Kershaw said casually : " How's the Atabadi job going ? "

Prewett stared like a man just waking up : mumbled something, and a sharp-nosed little man put his spoke in.

" Pumps turned up yet, Bill ? "

Prewett started swearing, in a whisper. He lurched over to fill his mug, holding the bottle upside down to drain the last drops, before lifting the mug to his lips. Johnny thought : His guts must be like cinders.

"Seven blasted months since the chit went in for those mucking pumps. First they go to Takoradi, and lie about somebody's factory till there's half an inch of rust over them. Then after somebody else has helped himself to the odd parts, they're shipped for us. And dropped a quarter of a mile off-shore, where you can't take soundings because of the surf. You god-damned old bitch, why can't you see your country's run properly ? "

Johnny had barely time to duck as the mug flew across his head, to shatter on the portrait of the Queen. There was silence, then a whisper, as Prewett flung himself on the shards of glass, and sucked, and swore at the sting of the gin in his cuts. His chin and the front of his clothes were dabbled in blood. As though something in his brain had exploded, he clapped his hands to his head, brought them away again and smeared the bloody palms over the painted face.

The silence of the room brought him, at last, to his senses. His glance, as it went from one to another, was sly with humiliation. He crashed the door back on its hinges, and stumbled out into the darkness. Someone laughed. But the laughter was dead as a cracked bell.

IV

The others had gone down to Easy Emma's ; Foxy, accepting Kershaw's hint that the latter wanted to talk to him, called after them : " I'll be joining you ; tell Emma to wash me a plate," and shut the door.

For a moment or two, nobody spoke. Foxy was whistling through his teeth, shaving plug into the palm of his hand.

" Has the mail boat been in ? " said Kershaw.

Foxy nodded.

" He didn't get his letter."

Foxy snorted.

" Nor ever will. Jee-sus God ! There wasn't ever a chap waited for his sweetheart's letter like Bill waits for that letter from Accra. Every mail that comes, he's like a lad with the itch in his pants—ginnin' himself up to meet it, and ginnin' himself up again because there's nothin' for him."

" Still messing about in the swamp ? "

Again Foxy nodded.

" He's working out the costs, now, in pipeline, an' machinery, an' local material, an' labour. Nothin' wanted, but the cash an' the credit to go ahead. Pity, ain't it ? " Foxy grinned.

" That's what they were saying at Cape Coast. They said he hadn't given up ; he was working on it still."

" And will be," said Foxy, with conviction, " 'til he's dead—an' after. It's got him—like a bug. I wager, after Bill's gone, he'll come back an' flicker over that swamp like a bloody will o' the wisp."

" Suppose it's not there ? " Johnny felt that his silence was beginning to be conspicuous. " He told me swamps—move."

" It'll still be there." Foxy was packing his pipe. " And the carriers'll still be goin' thirty miles out of their way, an' the tsetse'll still be keepin' up the mortality figures. What the hell ? " He shrugged his shoulders. " It's all the same to the Colonial Office. Bill's plans'll never get past the table of some little bum-suckin' under-strapper, primed with the Big Tit's orders not to pass on ' anythin' tahsome ' from the Coast."

Kershaw grunted after a silence.

" And folks wonder why I go freelancing, sooner than pull down a nice, regular salary from the Civil Service ! " He made a prolonged and juicy noise, expressing succinctly his opinion of Whitehall. " Ain't it what you heard from Smythson at 'Mina ? " he added in parenthesis to Johnny.

" What he said was, that the Colonial Office never pays attention, on principle, to anything from down here."

" He ought to know ; he was in Whitehall two years." Foxy gave his dry titter. " We're a Crown Colony, chum—don't you forget it. And, what's more, we're a Crown Colony that *doesn't pay* ! "

" But why the dickens doesn't it ? "

It was what he had been trying to find out, all along the coast ; furthermore, he had a suspicion it was what Harcourt expected him to find out. Or, at least, to supply the information from which Harcourt, using his own shrewdness, could work out his deductions. He suspected his companions of despising his simplicity ; well, let them get on with it. He had done his best so far, to arrive at facts without asking questions, which he knew were unpopular, but, for once, popularity could go by the board. If they thought him a fool—so much the worse, for everybody ; but he had got to find out.

" Ay, why doesn't it ? " Foxy's head was on one side, his attitude faintly derisive. " If we were given a free hand, an' left to look after our own business, it wouldn't suit the wallahs that sits on their fat arses an' draws their pensions for dictatin' us our policy. Policy ! " He spat the word. " My old grandma had more sense of policy in turnin' the heel of a sock than Whitehall's got, in respect to the Gold Coast."

Careful ; Johnny felt the warning. Foxy was a trader, and sour on that account. He had been particularly cautioned against accepting the traders' views, without examination. He frowned.

" Who are you getting at ?—The Governors ? "

" Jee-sus—no ! " was the pious rejoinder. " Lord save us Charles, I'd sooner sweep a crossin' in the Strand than be Gov'nor of the Gold Coast. The poor, bloody sons of bitches can't blow their own noses without writin' to London to get a permit ! "

Kershaw had come to anchor in a chair, where he sat, nursing a bony knee. Glancing his way, Johnny got a glimmer of the reason of Kershaw's survival along the Coast ; his cheerful refusal to take it seriously, or to be shackled by the red tape that hampered departments. He went where there was " something to be done," and did it, not troubling how it fitted into the tangled web of local or territorial politics.

"I wouldn't mind having a pop at it for twelve months!" His big square teeth glittered in the brown mask of his face. "Cosy quarters at Accra, and a chance to put ginger under some of those muffin-heads in the clerking departments——"

"Then the next chap comes along, and starts grindin' *his* axe! That's just where they have you," scowled Foxy. "None of 'em stops long enough to finish anything he's started. It's sanitation with one an' education with another; then you get a chap that's stuck on missions and follow him up with another that don't give a damn for anythin' but drillin' the niggers into clerkin' jobs—I tell you, it's a madhouse! Lots of fun for the pen pushers an' sweet hell for the rest, that takes the blame for the waste an' the muddle, an' a state of affairs that's grown up because the 'uman brain won't stand up to conditions like these."

"Or the human body?" suggested Johnny.

"Oh, pish," said Foxy. "Look at me: fourteen years on the Coast, and it ain't got me down, has it?"

"How about the Tarquah business?" It seemed to amuse Kershaw to play on Foxy's indignation.

"Ay—there you've got a fair sample of it! Umpty-thousand pounds spent on runnin' a perm'nent way into thin air——"

"Well, you know the answer to that!" put in Johnny.

"I know their lordships' answer," grunted Foxy.

"Well, we ain't the Bank of England!" Though sweet reason might be unwelcome, Harcourt's training was too much for his nephew. "They say we can't afford to run the railway up into Ashanti until the Tarquah branch begins to pay."

"An' how in blazes can it pay"—Fox's voice rose to a shout as his fist pounded the table—"till it serves the big gold reefs? And how are chaps in the Public Works to keep their end up when machinery they wait twelve months for gets dropped in the roadstead, because the Gov'ment won't give us the landin' piers the French have got all along their coast?"

They were back at the old, fruitless argument to which Johnny seemed to have been listening in every station since his arrival. Probably because it had ceased to interest him, Kershaw said, "What's moving up-country, Foxy?"

The little trader's lips snapped together and his bright eyes shot sidelong, before he replied briefly, "Plenty."

"That means, too much, eh?" The light, almost indifferent grin had vanished from Kershaw's face; as he leaned forward, with his elbows on his knees and his hands dangling from his wrists, an unusual tensity in his position did not escape Johnny's attention. Foxy nodded, his lips still tightened, and Johnny guessed that it was his own presence that disinclined him to be more forthcoming.

"You don't have to be cautious." Kershaw spoke softly. "Maybe we both know something you don't know."

"What's that?" A spark of curiosity lit quickly in the other's eye.

"He'll tell you, presently." He jerked his head towards Johnny. "First

—what's the fuss on at barracks ? We came round by there, and they'd got them all out on the square, drilling like mad, and a bunch of new boys, tying themselves in knots, under the sergeant ! What's the blood-pressure about ? "

" Maybe the Colonel's expected," mumbled Foxy. He opened his mouth and closed it again. " Well—'t'ain't my place to tell you, but I suppose you know enough—both of you—to keep your mouths shut. The D.C. wrote a letter."

" What—Morris ? So it's true—phew ! " Kershaw's lifted eyebrows gave his face a comical expression of disconcertion.

" What have you heard ? " Foxy demanded suspiciously.

" Everybody's heard it ; it's all round the place."

" Well, don't say you got it from me," growled Foxy. " Morris told me himself he'd recommended the immediate strengthening of the Hausa battalions in this and all other districts of the Akim, Denkera and Adansi country——"

" And an overhaul of the depot. Good old Morris. That'll have made him a favourite with the high-ups ! "

" Any answer ? " asked Johnny, as Kershaw chuckled.

" A one-line chit, 'acknowledgin' receipt of.' He showed it me, and I told him what to do with it. He said he didn't require any suggestions "—it was Foxy's turn to laugh—" and he was lucky not to be on the mat for trying to teach them their business."

" So what came of it ? "

Foxy's grin vanished as his sandy brows drew together over his small blue eyes.

" Nothing'll come of it, till a couple of score of our chaps an' six or seven hundred decent niggers've been carved up by some of the up-country gentry that's just waitin' the tip-off from their well-informed pals on the coast that Kruger's got us busy down at the Cape. Then, if somebody's indiscreet enough to remember Morris's letter—well, you may bet he'll be found a quick job somewhere where his mem'ry won't have a chance of embarrassin' them responsible for the mess."

" But surely to goodness the Colonial Office——" began Johnny.

" The Colonial Office ? " For once Foxy's voice was weary. " It don't suit the Colonial Office to pay attention to what goes on in West Africa. If it pays attention, it doesn't believe it. Don't you forget, chum : it ain't the man on the spot who knows all about it, it's the Whitehall wallah. Instinct, or second sight, or maybe the voice of the Almighty tells him all he wants to know ! And if he doesn't quite catch what it says—well, what the hell ? It's only a few more British bones to manure African soil—and there's always the good old bottle of the widow at the jolly old club ! "

Johnny thought : It's preposterous, of course—but he's letting it get under his skin. If he doesn't look out he'll finish up as cracked as Prewett. It was, however, a disconcerting reflection that almost everybody one met had " got it under his skin." Was the whole Gold Coast mad ? Or on the way to madness ?

Kershaw was telling Foxy about the guns, and Foxy was cracking his finger joints and looking thoughtful.

" Morris is back."

" Back ? I thought he was up-country." Kershaw glanced at Johnny.

" Got back to-night. You know that fancy of his "—Foxy grimaced—" for catchin' us on the hop ? The niggers call him ' He that walks in darkness.' " He turned to Johnny to explain. " Half of 'em believe he ' witches ' himself from place to place, without 'uman agency : a handy accomplishment. I'd give a packet, to find out how he does it. Time and time again he's been known to beat the drums—and that takes a bit of doing."

" Well, what about it ? Had he better report the gun business to Morris ? " Kershaw was saying.

" I'll lay you a pound to a pippin he knows all about it already," said Foxy wisely. " The damn' flies tell him, or something. Yes, I think you should see Morris, chum. You can tell him if you like, I'll be going up to Omo one day this week, an' I've got no objection to taking a coupl'a passengers, if you two want to come alone."

" Thanks, that'll do me fine ! "

" Suits me ; I get tired of the comp'ny of niggers." Not to be outdone in courtesy, Foxy bobbed his head. His hand had fallen on the sheets of paper Batty had left behind him on the table ; sweat-stained, already fly-spotted, Foxy lifted one and murmured its first line aloud. " ' I regret to inform you that your son . . .' I wonder how many times he's written that since he came here ? I bet he writes it, sometimes, in his sleep." He sighed, pushed the papers aside and rose to his feet.

" 'Tain't the climate, chum ; and 'tain't the mosquitoes—whatever the medicos say. You can stand up to nat'ral disadvantages, when your spirit's sound. It's sheer, bloody discouragement, as time goes by, and the job you've given your life to is treated, back home, as if it don't matter to anybody. It's young ones, like Bill Prewett, that feels it the most : the ones that ought to be the life-blood of the country. You got to be an old stager, like me, before you can thumb your nose at the Gold Coast and call on your philosophy for what them as ought to know better don't give you."

" Yet "—Johnny hesitated—" I've heard my uncle say the Gold Coast is our richest potential."

Foxy snorted.

" You go back and tell your uncle what's happenin' to Britain's richest potential ! Tell him how ev'ry constructive job in the country goes to Crown nominees, and folks out here, that pay taxes, don't even get the chance of contractin' for the supply of local material. Maybe, as a business man, that'll appeal to him ? Tell him what the Government's refusal to industrialise agriculture's costin' us, and what it means to us traders to have to go fawnin' to niggers for what we ought to be able to command. Command it properly, mind you ; I'm no party to Belgian methods. Comes down to this ; have we conquered the nigger or have we not ? The answer is, we haven't, and somebody's goin' to know it pretty soon—or call me a turnip. Tell him why fellas like Prewett—the best chap the department's ever had—lose heart : go cracked, or native, and let down our prestige in the eyes of the blacks."

" God knows what my uncle can do "—Johnny spoke slowly, with a heavy, although—he could not help feeling—irrational sense of responsibility —" or whether he's got any pull with the Colonial Office. But I swear I'll pass on all you say, and, if once he gets it into his head to start a fuss—you can bet somebody's going to have to get busy ! "

Resting his short, gnarled body on his hands, Foxy leaned across the table.

" See here, chum : England's been takin' all she can get out of the Gold Coast for the last two centuries, and all she sends us are the goddam missionaries. When's it goin' to finish—eh ? "

CHAPTER FIVE

I

" CHRIST ! Where did you get them ? "

Kershaw looked down at a pyjama suit of bright yellow, with a dazzling criss-cross of magenta, with modest satisfaction.

" Had them made in Anamabu. A bit loud—eh ? But the mosquitoes don't like 'em."

" I bet they don't. Nor do I. Nigger cloth, isn't it ? "

" Why not ? I'd not be surprised if one reason the blacks don't get bitten is, they wear bright colours."

" How about the ones that wear nothing at all ? "

Kershaw was fiddling with a little box he had produced from somewhere.

" Give us your arm."

" What's this about ? " Johnny drew back, as he saw the hypodermic in the other's hand. " Damn you—what do you think you're doing ? "

His arm was imprisoned and the needle shot in ; Kershaw slowly compressed the piston.

" If you're seeing Morris to-morrow, you may as well cut a decent figure. Just now, you remind me of a seedy ticket-of-leaver at the end of a marijuana jag."

" What is the stuff, anyway ? "

" You wouldn't know if I told you." He withdrew the needle gently from Johnny's arm. " It's a new drug they're trying. I met the fellow who invented it last year, at Accra ; I let him use me as a guinea pig. Fetches the temperature down like billy-ho. The only thing—it's apt to give you funny dreams."

" I'll have them anyhow, after seeing your pyjamas. Who's your eech ?" asked Johnny, with some curiosity. "I met Glazebrook, but I houldn't think he's heard of a hypodermic. He's still back in the Stone Age, so far as drugs go."

"'But dear Dr. Glazebrook's such a gentleman!'" He was wiping the needle on a bit of medicated wool. "You wouldn't meet my friend in those circles. He's a black."

"Is he, now. Got his degree?"

"What do you suppose? M.D., Edinburgh. Just back, to practise on he Coast."

"He'll find plenty to practise on. Who goes to him?"

"Blacks, mainly. That's how he likes it. He'd sooner help his own people than be patronised by us!"

"What's his name?"

"Bofo. Got a younger brother at London University. You'd like them; very sound pair. Now—nip into bed."

Presently he heard Kershaw put out the light. He was cool—even chilly—and the fever had gone, but he was not particularly sleepy. A faint throbbing in the injected arm kept him conscious of it; he moved, so as not to press it against the mattress. The surf was very heavy, and the cracks in the shutters let the moonlight in in stripes. It was very different, with Kershaw there, from previous nights.

"I wonder where the devil that fellow is?"

"What fellow?"

"Tich."

A grunt came from Kershaw's bed.

"Why worry? He'll turn up. If he doesn't, we're all right, with my two. We don't want to pick up any of these local blacks: they're as dirty as sin and they'd steal your back teeth when you weren't looking." A yawn. "You've not paid him off, have you?"

"Gave him a bob or two. No, I'm not paying him off until I leave."

"He'll turn up," drowsily.

"Hope so."

"What the hell are you nattering about?"

"Oh—I suppose I'd got used to him. I liked the beggar." His brow knitted on the memory of an unblemished torso, with the gleam of dark plumage; a waist slender and supple as a girl's; flat buttocks and narrow hips, about which the ill-fitting cotton trousers were held up, as likely as not, by one of his master's neckties. Cock-a-hoop about his mission connections, but, in the main, simple—even in his cunning. Faithful. Eager to learn tricks and quick to forget them; disliking nothing more than routine, but performing a certain set of actions, useful to his master, mechanically. Wasteful, untidy. Odd mixture of vices and virtues, blended into a somehow likeable whole. You liked it as you liked a child, or a spaniel. . . .

"Well, if he's in trouble," Kershaw was saying, "the police will pick him up. If he's sick, he's probably gone to his family. And if it's 'woman palaver'—he'll be here in the morning, looking like a wet rag, and you can give yourself the pleasure of kicking his backside. Good night."

He heard the wire meshing screel as Kershaw rolled over. Presentl the darkness vibrated with long, satisfied snores.

It was nearly an hour later when, despairing of sleep, Johnny crawle from under the mosquito net to light a candle and get the notebook i which he was keeping his diary. Having dodged innumerable insects, an manœuvred the candlestick dangerously under the netting and on to hi pillow, he propped himself on his elbow and started to write. At least, h held the pencil and tried to marshal the thoughts whirling in his mind int sentences.

The conversation with Foxy. The arrival of Kershaw ; his views abou the guns. The evening at Prewett's. All these were disposed of in a fe trite words. Like many people, Johnny could express himself about th actual ; for things of the mind and spirit he had no more vocabulary tha the average young man of his type and upbringing, who concerns himsel more with doing than with thinking, and, in any case, believes in keepin his thoughts to himself ; whose opinions are decided for him by the con vention of his class and tradition, and whose attitude towards the exotic in any form, is of cautious disapproval. During the last four months however, all these comfortable foundations had been shaken, and it ha grown on him recently that he must by some means set the turmoil of hi mind in order. You might, as he had written to Joe, " fog it over" by tryin to set it down, but, later on, when one could look at the past in perspective it might make sense. The trouble was, one had not the faintest idea how t begin.

(Where the devil was that beggar Tich ? One minute knotted up wit bellyache on his mat, apparently unable to crawl—and the next, vanished His eagerness to get to Charlestown and see his family and his girl, and, afte the first evening, his reluctance to go into the town at all : his skulking i the cookhouse—as though he were scared of something. He didn't like th place, either ; there had been a flicker in his eye, when he was told they wer going to Vickers'. Then why had he waited the better part of a wee before bolting ? Had, possibly, his sickness anything to do with . . .)

He gripped his pencil and began to write : not thinking about the shap of the sentences, or whether they joined themselves together.

" You make a bed for your goat, or your dog. You see your horse has a stable. A nigger looks after himself. It's no business of yours where h sleeps, what he sleeps on, or if he has any rice in his bowl. The Negro ca see after those things for himself. So can the dog, but you don't leave hi to do it. You don't trouble about the black because you can easily replac him, and he is cheaper than a horse or a dog. You don't trouble because h is a black, and that absolves you of responsibility. A black has no importance, except to see to your comfort."

He stopped to read over what he had written, with a kind of horrified incredulity. Then he went grimly on.

" You do not think of the Negro who waits on you that he is an adult, with a private life of his own and some sort of dignity in his own family. If you do think of him that way, somebody says : Never mix yourself in nigger business. So you take away his private life and his dignity and you give him a nickname, because that helps to make you forget him as a human being. You call him Ally Sloper or Smoke or You-be-damned. He takes it as a compliment, so that proves he is subhuman. He makes it easy for you to treat him in this way because he is generally a fool, often a thief and can always be depended on to mistake your meaning, make muddles and be a nuisance. You would be much the same if you were shot into a strange environment among people with a different habit of mind. Don't let the colour question get on your mind. It's not a subject for the outsider and it is apt to make people do peculiar things. You've got to remember everyone is doing their best."

Another pause ; then :

" The black, like the higher apes, can be taught tricks, i.e., to weave cloth for clothes he does not wear and make boots that hurt his feet. This, of course, is more than the ape can do, but that's beside the point. You teach him these things so that he can be useful to you, but not to himself. Any form of making the Negro useful to himself is bad because it might end in his becoming independent. If a Negro happens to become useful to himself (Dr. Bofo at Accra, Akilagpa at Grand Bassam, Kojo, Kwesi Adoku Smith, Benjamin Mankesim, etc., etc.), you say good man, but you take care to leave the room if he happens to come in. Not because you know anything against him, but it creates an awkward situation. All Negroes are objectionable, but the educated or cultured Negro is objectionable in a very special way. So you must take care. . . ."

The pencil sagged in his hand ; he flung the notebook aside and blew out the candle. To hell with it all—with the heat and the darkness and Kershaw's infernal snoring : with Prewett and Charlestown and Foxy's jeremiads and the surf and something that had fallen on the mosquito netting from the thatch overhead. . . .

He was on the edge of sleep, when it came : a faint interruption to the rhythmical beat of the waves. He felt his body tense itself, and strained to listen. At last he was sure of it : thin and distant as it was, a human voice was calling, somewhere out of doors. His heart thumped at his breast bone as he jerked the net from under the edge of the mattress. There was no sign or sound from Kershaw's bed. Presently he had the door open, and was out in the rush of the night wind along the beach. He went a little way from the hut, and shouted :

" Tich. Hi, you—Tich ! "

The wind blew his voice back in his face, and only its echo went sobbing over the surf. He sent another shout, towards the Fort, and the sound rang back from the old, dishonoured stones. The dead lay round him on the sand—the dead ? It was as though the stones stirred, and became the dark, sentient flesh of thousands who had known living death in this very spot.

" Tich ; damn you, Tich."

Suddenly the boy's native name came back to him.

" Somilu ! "

The lovely, liquid syllables went racing away into the moonlight, like the ghost of their owner ; but he knew there would be no answer, no eager patter of feet, no flash of ivory.

"My God—I'm going mad : like everyone else. Of course he's not here—of course he wouldn't come back—at this time of night——"

"Shut up, for the love of Christ."

It was Kershaw, shaking his shoulder.

"I told you that stuff would give you bad dreams," he was saying, as he tucked the blankets and the disturbed net under the mattress.

Too much ashamed to reply, Johnny was silent ; he merely grunted, turned his back and drove his head down under the coverings.

Mark Kershaw stood for a moment, looking at the dim mound of the net in the moonlight ; put his hand absently in the pocket of his pyjama coat, pulled out a tin of cigarettes and lit one. As he dropped the match, he caught sight of something on the ground, beside the bed, and bent to pick it up. A notebook ; he recognised it by the feel. As he was about to push it under its owner's pillow, a thought struck him.

"Johnny," he said softly. "Johnny."

There was no answer.

After a moment's hesitation, he lit the lamp ; drew up his chair and, to avoid the unpleasant attentions of night crawlers, lifted his bare feet up on the table.

When he had finished reading, he swore under his breath. It was more than evident Johnny Flood had had enough of the Gold Coast—or, at any rate, of Charlestown. Cursing an obstinacy which he knew would refuse to accept deflection from its purpose, Kershaw made up his mind that, Morris or no Morris, they would leave for Omo within twenty-four hours. The greater part of the tin of cigarettes had been smoked when he went back to bed.

II

Mrs. Kaboha Komuntale's husband had bidden her write a letter. To write it she had put on her best dress—a three-flounced, starched muslin skirt with eyelet embroideries and a blouse with three similar flounces round the square yoke and puffed sleeves. In common with local fashion, the blouse was worn outside the skirt, for reasons of ventilation. She always dressed to deal with her correspondence, because this was in accordance with the illustrations in the *Sunday at Home*, *Church Weekly*, and other literature supplied by the mission ; in which the heroine, in spotless white, was usually depicted writing to the hero at a bobble-legged tripod table of which the principal adornments, apart from the inkwell, were a fringed tablecloth and a potted fern. Mrs. Komuntale, with her husband's concurrence, had gone so far as to provide herself with the table and the cloth ; a bottle of Stephen's Blue-Black did duty for the inkwell, and the shrivelled stump of some casual blossom, thrust into a pottery vase labelled "A Present from Aberystwyth" provided a symbol for the fern. Secure of her setting, Mrs. Komuntale blew the top layer of dust off the tablecloth, and drew a sheet of her notepaper towards her. Mrs. Komuntale's notepaper, brought her as a present by one of her husband's friends in Accra, was of a highly glazed candy pink, with a flourishing K in gold in the left hand top corner ; she fingered it with happy satisfaction. As one of the brightest of the mission pupils, she enjoyed writing letters.

"Dear Sir," she began, in a large, careful copy-book hand, spacing the words as she had been taught to do, and paying great attention to the thick and the thin strokes : she was proud of her writing and of her composition—subjects that very few of the mission girls managed to acquire.

> "My husband who is great man supernatural in Customs commands me to write you this letter which I beg to include in the volume of my correspondence."

Pleased with the final expression, culled in its entirety from a story entitled *Honour Where Honour Is Due*, read to the ladies' sewing group, she leaned back to admire it, before continuing.

> "I ask you please to peruse this note and give it your swift regard as it is our immoderate desire to exhibit brotherly welcome in consideration of vast affection in past. I therefore send you with bearer kind invitation to have tea with us and friends of notable degree to-morrow afternoon which you will much enjoy with best compliment.
>
> "Respectfully yours,
>
> "Mrs. Komuntale."

This missive, delivered by a piccanin to one of the house-boys, did not immediately reach its dedicatee, as Johnny was already on his way to the house of the Commissioner.

To most people making their first acquaintance of the garbage heap that went by the name of Charlestown, the Residency came as a surprise. Built in the early eighteenth century, by a merchant named Christie Doran, it stood originally in the outlying district of Endor, now absorbed within the sprawling radius of the town itself, and was acquired as local headquarters for British authority shortly after the forts were taken over by the Crown in 1843. Its pillared portico and the fact of its being built, unlike the majority of local dwellings, on two storeys, lent it dignity enhanced by its immediate surroundings—a spacious compound, some time maintained as gardens, but now a wilderness of vegetation, through which was periodically cut the drive that curved from an imposing gateway to the door opening at the head of a flight of stone steps. A fantastic sample, according to critics, of the methods of a Government cheese-paring in essentials, and one altogether out of proportion to the importance of the appointment.

For months on end—while the Commissioners did their duty up-country —the Residency lay empty : collecting mould on its floors and vermin in its handsome apartments. It was the envy of Commissioners' ladies, trying to uphold the prestige of their husbands' positions in tin-roofed bungalows, in stations of much greater importance and size than Charlestown. By some unwritten law, the Commissioner of the Charlestown district was always a bachelor—it being taken for granted that no one would bring a woman to a station whose mortality figures easily headed the lists of regions unfavourable to (white) expectation of survival.

The man who sat behind a table at the far end of a nobly proportioned room was slight and actively built ; his greying hair and moustache trimmed in military style, together with the knife-edge smartness of shirt and riding breeches, were the insignia of standard officialdom. But the effect of mass production was startlingly interrupted by a pair of almost colourless eyes, set between short black lashes, that dominated the expression of a well-cut, hard-bitten face. Those eyes, cold and direct, would spare no one ; Johnny was conscious of their examination, as he marched stiffly towards the table.

The Commissioner rose to shake hands, and immediately sat down again, pushing a tin of cigarettes towards Johnny, who refused them with a shake of the head.

" No, thanks, sir."

" You don't smoke ? "

" A pipe." He would not add, " or a cheroot " seeing none of the latter on the Commissioner's table. He noticed that Morris did not give him permission to light the pipe ; it was considered, perhaps, too informal for a strictly official interview. Morris's next words, however, dispersed the effect of formality.

" I'm sorry I was not here to welcome you on your arrival. I'm sure, however, you've found tolerable quarters ; your relatives would see to that."

" My—what, sir ? "

" You've surely met Mr. and Mrs. Gummeridge, by now ? "

" Oh—the missionaries." Not for the first time, he had a slight twinge of conscience. " He's no connection of ours I mean, apart from his marriage. And it was only by chance my father learned—you know he's interested in the missions——"

" That's common knowledge." Morris inclined his head ; his expression, to Johnny's fancy, was a little odd.

" Yes, sir. Well—well——" Under the glance from those cold eyes he found himself stammering a lit le. " Someone told him Mrs. Gummeridge is related to our family. It must be a very distant connection ; we don't even know what her maiden name was. I don't think it can have been Flood, as I believe we're the only ones left——"

" Through the Barbados branch, I understand."

" I dare say. Jonathan Flood of Barbados was my great-great-great-grandfather, and he had an enormous family. She may be descended from one of those."

" Very likely. Well, you must make her acquaintance. She's a great personality—and so is her husband, in a different way." He felt guiltily that Morris was over-emphasising it, and that he was being reproached for neglect of the courtesies. " You know they were prisoners of the Ashanti or two years."

" That must have been a tough experience, sir ! "

" Very tough. You must ask her about it, some time. We're very roud of them, in this district." Perhaps Johnny's expression, guarded as habitually was, betrayed some faint degree of disaffection, for Morris ontinued : " I know there's a good deal of prejudice against the missionaries, nd I won't say that some part of it isn't justified. But it's not a bad thing have an example before you of fortitude and endurance—even when they appen to be misdirected ! "

" That's one way of looking at it, certainly. But the general feeling "—e wondered if this was incautious—" seems to be that they do more harm han good."

The Commissioner shrugged his shoulders.

" If you teach the native Christianity, you must be prepared to grant im white rights ; he expects them. The missionaries aren't in a position give him these, and the other civilians see he's not fit for them. You've nade a self-respecting savage into a horrid hybrid, with all a hybrid's vices. 'm afraid the missionaries must carry the responsibility for that. But after ll "—a twinkle appeared in Morris's eye—" the results are not so very ar-reaching : not so far, indeed, as you might gather, from the devotees. You've seen a lot of it, of course, along the coastal trip, but don't forget the housands of miles to which mission teaching has never penetrated—and von't ; the climate will see to that."

" There's a lot of research going on, isn't there, sir, into the prevention nd cure of tropical disease ? " Johnny was constrained to observe.

Morris laughed outright.

" Come, you needn't grudge us that ! Nothing stands still," he mphasised ; " not even Christian dogma. By the time we've found out the erums that confer immunity from West African atmospherics, the missions lso, perhaps, will have learned their real function. And they'll find they've got plenty to do, without worrying about theologies. Now, Mr. Flood, perhaps you'll tell me how you come to be so remarkably fluent in our ocal vernacular."

This came as a jolt. Johnny hoped his expression did not give him away s he answered :

" Well, sir, I learned up a good deal of Hausa, before I came out. I've picked up the dialects mainly by talking to my house-boy and—and one or wo other people." As Morris did not immediately reply, he added : " I— thought it might come in useful—to know what people were talking about."

" I congratulate you on your industry—as well as on your memory. I'll give you a proverb, Mr. Flood. '*Ne to mesee oa, nku, mele ekpokpo dzige o.*' Can you translate that ? "

" It's Ewe, isn't it ? " Johnny knitted his brows. " ' If the ears do not hear, the eyes will not be inclined to see ; ' is that right, sir ? "

" Perfectly." Morris was smiling. " A useful principle to lay to mind. How long have you known Kaboha Komuntale ? "

A bit more of this, thought Johnny, and I'll be taking the count! H collected himself sufficiently to give Morris a short account of his previou visit to the Coast, at the end of which the latter nodded slowly.

" So it struck you as quite a coincidence, when you came across hin here, in Customs."

" It certainly did! I'd forgotten all about the fellow—and I wouldn' have known him, if he hadn't recognised me."

" With pleasure, I presume."

Johnny could not help laughing.

" To tell the truth, sir, I was confoundedly embarrassed by the fuss h made of me, and would have liked to give him the slip. But he made such a to-do about taking personal charge of my baggage—for very good reasons as it turned out——" He stopped; it had dawned on him that Morri already knew all he had come to tell him. " He that walks in darkness "— indeed!

Morris again was smiling.

" No 'witching' about it. I've seen Foxy Biddle. Go on."

" Well—I let him; I didn't want to make him lose face in front of hi —club pals!" Johnny grinned.

" And what form did your gratitude take?"

" Form——? Well, I was in a bit of a hole," confessed Johnny. " I couldn't make out how he came to have so much authority in Customs—I didn't know then, of course, that Mr. Cope was dead, and Mr. Cator ir hospital——"

" So you gave him a tip," suggested Morris.

" He was so good as to help me out by asking for ten shillings! I gave him five."

" And that was all?"

" Why—yes."

" Think again, Mr. Flood. Let me assist your memory," said Morris, as Johnny knitted his brows in the endeavour to produce that which, evidently, was expected of him. " He asked you, I suggest, if you had any English newspapers with you."

" As a matter of fact—he did."

" And you had, and handed them over."

With an uneasy sense that something had gone wrong, Johnny admitted it.

" There seemed no reason to refuse. They were several weeks old, and my boy had wrapped the washing in them."

" And Komuntale showed pleasure."

" He could hardly have made more fuss if I'd given him the Crown Jewels!"

" I believe you," was the dry rejoinder. " Well, Mr. Flood; you acted in good faith. You could hardly be expected to know that we've got Komuntale marked as one of a bunch of semi-Europeanised natives who make it their business to send news up-country. Thanks to him and his friends, the chiefs are as well informed as any of you in London about Cape politics and the discussions between the Transvaal and the Orange Free state."

Johnny maintained an abashed silence ; he had an impression that the pale-eyed man behind the table, without blaming, was despising him. Morris, however, spoke mildly.

"You may reasonably ask why such a person is allowed to hold a post as a Customs clerk. The answer is—it's easier to keep a check on Mr. Komuntale when we have him under our eye than leave him at liberty to run around, extending the scope of his activities."

"I see the point, sir." He was miserably sheepish.

"You know, Flood"—Morris swung one knee lightly over the arm of the chair—"these semi-educated blacks add appreciably to our problems out here. Kaboha's schooling made him dissatisfied with the life of his village, and he drifted at some moment to Accra. There, he's known to have got himself mixed up with the Aborigines' Society."

"I thought that was all right. Haven't they just sent a deputation to Chamberlain, and got the Lands Bill withdrawn?"

"Sarbah's a very fine fellow." Morris nodded. "I have a great personal respect for him. Unfortunately these organisations always acquire a fringe of young hotheads, quite incapable of appreciating the deeper issues involved in the movement. To Komuntale's friends the withdrawal of the Lands Bill was a triumph over British Government, and direct incitement to sedition among the natives."

"In spite of drawing his wages from us," Johnny was moved to interpolate.

"Not at the time of which I'm speaking. Nobody knew anything about him when he turned up here, with enough of the three R's to get himself a clerking job, and credentials we've since discovered were faked. Owing to circumstances for which nobody in particular is to blame, his wits—which are something above the average for a Negro—have put him in a position no native has any business to hold, in any of the public services."

"That trick, of shoving the guns in with my baggage, would have been smart, if it had come off," muttered Johnny, as the other paused.

"It certainly would. And if you hadn't taken the action you did, those cases would have been well on their way up-country by now, to reinforce somebody's private cache."

"They probably are, anyhow." He could not resist a grin. "Somebody, when he opens them is going to get a surprise ; and maybe it won't be so good for Komuntale with his partners."

"It doesn't appear to strike you that, 'maybe,' it won't be so good for you, either?" Morris was looking at him coldly.

"For me? I'm not worrying about that, sir." Off his guard, Johnny evinced a naïve surprise at the Commissioner's point of view.

"It's not your business to worry," rapped Morris. "You've done a smart thing in rather a foolish way. The trick you played on Mfabo made him look a fool, and also made a fool of Komuntale, who employs him. You 'put shame on him'—which, of course, you intended. You've also involved him in a packet of trouble with some person, unknown, up-country. And—this, from my point of view, is the most serious—you've given away the fact that we know about the gun-running, which, for our own reasons, we've tried to keep quiet in this district. I leave you to draw your own conclusions."

"I seem to have made a pretty bloody fool of myself all round." Johnny's ears were red with confusion.

The pale eyes twinkled as Morris replied.

"One does, you know, when one isn't in possession of all the facts. I do it myself; only, fortunately, I'm in a position to cover up my tracks. I'd like to have seen Mfabo with those cases. Idle slob; it must be the first honest job he's done since they made him headman." He chuckled.

"I suppose I ought to have reported the matter direct to police headquarters."

"The other was more amusing," conceded Morris. "Only—next time your sense of humour threatens to block your powers of discretion, there's another proverb you might remember: '*Hatsekaka hea avuwowo ve.*'"

"'Much joking brings on quarrelling.'" Johnny took courage of the more amiable expression on Morris's face to riposte: "'*Koko meagbe afeade me o*:' 'mockery is unavoidable in any house.' What about that one, sir?"

Morris laughed outright.

"Well—'*Medoa tefe wado hehe o*:' at this critical point it is useless to sob. One of these days we'll spend an evening swopping proverbs; I must find out if you're as good in the Kroo as you are on Ewe."

"I honestly do not know how to apologise, sir——"

Morris lifted his hand; evidently the subject was to be closed. He had risen.

"Well, I shall hope to see something more of you, before you go. You won't, of course, be stopping on into the rainy season. My sister, by the way"—he grimaced—"my sister's paying me a visit. And we're expecting some panjandrums. She told me to give you an invitation for to-morrow afternoon. I don't know what the programme is, but I see the tennis courts are being cleaned up"—he had strayed to the window—"so probably the whole town's expected——"

"I'm afraid I'm not much of a social light, sir." It was news that the "whole town" contained any society acceptable at the Residency.

"Nor am I," said Morris. "Remember, I'm counting on your support."

They had reached the door, when Morris said:

"You're a friend, aren't you, of Foxy's?"

"That would rather be to presume, sir. He's been very civil to me, since I came here."

"More civil than other people?"

Scenting a leading question, Johnny looked up quickly. Their eyes met, and Morris nodded slowly.

"Foxy's a very good fellow. But prejudiced—in some directions." There was a snap in the words he rightly interpreted as a warning.

"Don't pay too much attention to people who are sick, or discouraged in their work," said Morris, significantly. "We all get disgruntled at times."

"I'll remember what you say, sir."

"I wonder if you will? I wonder if I may be very direct with you, Mr. Flood?" A line had driven itself in, as though with a chisel, between the horizontal of Morris's brows. He straddled the threshold, with his hands in his pockets.

"You've visited Accra, and Cape Coast, and, I suppose, Sierra Leone. Not bad samples, do you think, of what can be done, in a few years of colonization?"

"Not bad at all," he stammered, wondering in what direction this might be leading.

"You've realised, of course, that three-quarters of our white population is periodically destroyed by epidemics; and that it's exceptional for any person to live to see the completion of the task he's begun—whether it's building, sanitation, medical service or communications. You've taken into account the natural obstacles which have to be surmounted before any constructive idea is put into practise."

"I—I hope I've taken in all that."

"And you'd say, considering all things, that we've not done a bad job after all?"

"I would say—that." The conclusion came lamely; was there something treacherous in the admission?

"I understand what is in your mind; it is always easier to see where people have failed than to give them credit for their successes." Morris paused. "You might remember that—when you hear us blackguarded for what we haven't achieved, and denied acknowledgment of the work that's been done. There are things that even governments can't alter—that just have to work themselves out.

"Above all, don't let what you've seen here wipe out the memory of pleasanter experiences. Charlestown is a curious place, Mr. Flood, and there are those who say we don't justify our existence. Whether we do or not—only time will tell. The answer won't come in your time or mine—that's a certainty! It's written somewhere back there." He pointed through the window to the tree-crusted hills blocking the horizon. "Sometimes, when I'm in there, among its own people, I seem to get a whisper; but it's probably no more than imagination. One can only go on believing one's job's worth while; so long as one holds on to that—the rest's no business of ours."

As he walked down the drive, one of the Commissioner's coloured staff ran after him, and pushed an envelope into his hand. Johnny put it in his pocket and promptly forgot about it.

III

Under cover of industry, a lot of matters were moving up-country. A flighty outburst of secret societies—frowned upon by the Government and suppressed wherever expedient—shook the social structure of communities previously tranquil. Some of the societies were good ones, and dealt with such useful matters as fishing rights, the preservation of female morality and the culture of yams ; others sprang up just, as it were, for the hell of it, reviving obsolete and quite unnecessary customs which had passed into desuetude with the coming of white rule along the rivers.

The representatives of white authority, with their usual thoroughness, had been at pains to establish the fact that, contrary to common opinion, there was no regulation in the constitution of the secret societies prescribing human sacrifice, and that those who practised it did it out of sheer devilment. It was a disappointing discovery for many, and a small faction immediately began agitating to have it incorporated in the by-laws. The majority, although depressed by a ruling which took so much of the old-time spirit out of the societies' meetings, bowed to the inevitable. Infringement of the exact constitution, they had been given to understand, was a penal offence, and the ways of British justice they knew, from experience, to be uncomfortable.

With the secret societies came, naturally, reports of an epidemic of witchcraft. Here a man, there a woman, was spoken of as possessing superhuman powers, and spread fear and disorder through the district. Little of this drifted down to the coast, because the coast is notoriously cynical about up-country magic, though not above calling in its own ju ju men in times of stress.

Then there was the trouble about the hut tax—a mild recrudescence of the resistance which had recently plunged the Sierra Leone district into a state of war. It was a tax cursed by all who had the unhappy duty of collecting it. Several of the chiefs, emboldened by the success of the appeal against the Lands Bill, dug in their heels, either by direct refusal to pay or by ingenious evasions.

All these things caused a fluttering in the bush. Traders and travellers were aware of it, but failed precisely to put their fingers on the source. Here and there an enterprising Commissioner, by exercising strategy, succeeded in swooping on offenders and catching them red-handed, but it would have taken an army of Commissioners, in perpetual motion, to keep up with the rapidity of bush movement. Always, ahead of the white men, the drums tapped out their warning, and it was by no means uncommon, on arrival in a suspected quarter, to find a whole village immobilised, in rapt attention to one of its own lay preachers.

Up at Omo, Akosua Ngomi was on tenterhooks. She had a mania for societies, for the atmosphere of excitement they engendered, the preparations, the mysteries, the drums, the dancing and the ritual. Her son Kufi irritated her by his refusal to encourage any of these diversions. He had a sluggish and not over-bold temperament, a tolerant disposition and a shrewd idea on which side his bread was buttered. His father had impressed on him that it paid to keep in with the British, but that one should make sure of the payment before committing oneself to a course of conduct that might not go well with the neighbours. A natural taste for running with the hare and hunting with the hounds kept Kufi observant of rules laid down by his white overlords, without preventing his assisting other people to break them. He was, in fact, quite triumphantly unsatisfactory, both as a British subject and as a tribal ally. His mother was not alone in regarding him as a worm, but, besides being the sleek and contented proprietor of a handsome tract of rubber country, he enjoyed the distinction of holding a territory of the utmost strategic importance in the event of tribal disagreements. His father had conquered and won it, and Kufi held it, because Omo men were good fighters, good river men as well as good land men ; and because, of course, of the Basin.

Akosua, however, had recently had a triumph which had gone right to her head. After years of obstinate endurance, the white men had at last removed their Wanga from the village. No amount of explanation would have persuaded Akosua that their departure was due to want of mission funds, and not to her own industry.

Moon after moon, with unabated perseverance, she had put evil on them, in small ways ; she had really worked at her witchcraft, had forced her memory to give up, a little at a time, the various charms practised by her grandmother, when she was a little girl, up at Bantama. The ground round the mission bungalow was littered, by Akosua, with fetish objects, ranging from bits of twig and rope, in fantastic knots, to the sexual parts of a young cockerel, all charged with lethal intent towards the inhabitants of the mission.

When these failed, she went scrambling through the bush in search of a certain root, which, forced into the ground to the accompaniment of a repetition of the name of the doomed person, is said surely to result in death. The missionary and his assistant flourished. Akosua, grinding her teeth, proceeded to more desperate measures. Indifferent to blasphemy, she actually took on herself certain offices supposed to be performed only by the priesthood ; she wound string round two sticks, mumbling the missionaries' names, laid them on the ground with a stone upon them—and was wakened next morning by the cheery sounds of :

> "Mu sunsum nsueri yin' ayew ;
> Nyhira onka Nyankupon nyi ni Ba,
> Ndasi onka Nyankupon hyi ni Ba"—

—just as if nothing whatever had happened.

The bitter knowledge, moreover, was hers, that her son Kufi, while not actually descending to taking part in these customs—he had tried it, and they had bored him—was quite capable of standing about with a patriarchal smile on his face, encouraging the renegades by his presence, if not by his participation.

So, on the morning when the missionaries' belongings were carried down to the river, she could not wait for the departure of their owners—with a few silly little crying children clinging on their coat-tails and about their knees—but, crazy with delight, went capering through the village, proclaiming the joyful tidings, and the village, always responsive to high spirits, soon was capering too. They capered for three days, by which time the gin had run out, all the powder had been used up and everyone was rather tired and peevish, like children after a party.

But Akosua, like many of the old, was insatiable. Every night, with descriptions of the scenes she had witnessed, the dances of the jackals, the dances of the leopards, the orgies of blood and terror at which she, in her youth, had assisted, she held the village spellbound.

Sometimes she talked to Kufi about them, but the utmost she got out of him was a chuckle ; he was not inclined to forfeit his standing with the Powers by humouring the old lady in her fancy for gore and guts. He was, however, uneasily conscious that she was making the people restless. He was, for the first time since his accession, conscious of public criticism, and knew something would have to be done about it.

It was obvious the people were set on a secret society, and, in their mood of growing dissatisfaction, repression was dangerous. It was equally dangerous to give them leave to form a society and hold himself aloof from it ; for it is a well-known thing that the object of secret societies is, sooner or later, to get rid of an unpopular chief, and to install a new one in his place.

So Kufi was in a cleft stick, and Akosua went shuffling and chittering among the huts, promising them all a fine time in the future.

She had another reason for being in high feather. The first consignment of guns had gone through successfully to Ya Ashantua, and the second was daily expected. Word had come from the coast that they were on the way, and she had decided, in agreement with Kufi, who, now knowing of it, and completely free from responsibility, was very pleased about a plan that secured him the goodwill of a powerful neighbour, to send half the consignment up to Ejesu and hold the remainder against emergency. Kufi had to admire his mother's ingenuity, and began to think it might be policy to reward her with a concession about the societies.

All these things, and more beside, had repercussions in the office of a tired man at Charlestown, who, having just returned from the round of his district, had now to decide in what direction to set off next, and how best to conceal his intentions so as to take his charges by surprise.

The decision was not simplified by the notification that he might expect a visit from a High Person, in connection with a letter received at Government House on the 12th ult. Whose letter ? And to what purpose ? The ambiguity was in itself suspicious. To Morris, as to the rest of his kind, Government snoopers were anathema, together with amateur scientists, self-styled authors and concession hunters : all of whom were to be classed as time-wasters, apt to involve one in a lot of troublesome correspondence, as well as getting themselves into trouble from which it was necessary, for the credit of the British flag, to rescue them. If they were not losing themselves up-country, and obliging one to send out salvage parties, they were writing letters home —letters which sometimes got into English newspapers and brought violent language from the Commissioner, and, occasionally, a pungent note of inquiry from Accra.

So he snapped at his sister and told her for pity's sake to make herself scarce, while he made up his mind whether the quick were of more importance than the dead: in other words, whether some eight hundred living souls in Omo called for more immediate attention than the murderers of a dead chief in Okomi.

IV

"What about Omo?"

"To tell you the truth—I hadn't the gall to mention it. Would you," grunted Johnny, "when he'd just made you feel all sizes of a fool?"

"Depends on how much I wanted to get there." Kershaw shrugged his shoulders. "Don't you know, fella? It's no use 'putting on dog' with a person like Morris."

"'Putting on dog!'" Johnny spluttered with rage. "If you'd like to know what I've got out of my interview with Morris," he produced, after a pause, "it's, a, the conviction that I'm a meddling busybody; b, that I've got a swelled head; c, that the sooner I clear out, the better it suits him."

"Jesus! The D.C. *has* been handing it to you."

"Well, in a way, he hasn't," truth compelled Johnny to admit. "As a matter of fact, he couldn't have been more agreeable."

"Oh, yes?" Kershaw whistled softly. "We know Morris, when he's agreeable. Something like a tiger that's just found a bone: try taking it away from him, and see what you get!"

"Hell's bells, I don't want his bone! And he *was* agreeable. I've taken plenty of plasterings from my father." Johnny smiled palely. "I've been, from time to time, a social disgrace, a mental deficient, something the Devil turns up his nose at and a candidate for the lowest grade in a reformatory. In polite language, of course; the parent is always choosy on his vocabulary. And I haven't given a damn."

"Laugh it off," advised Kershaw.

"That little man"—Johnny shook his head—"has got as much as he can carry, and I've added another chunk. It's not the sort of thing that builds up one's self-esteem."

"Somebody else is worrying about his self-esteem. Have you seen that?" He nodded towards Mrs. Komuntale's letter.

"Blasted cheek!" said Johnny, when he had read it.

"Interesting, though?"

"I don't find the idea of sitting down to a nigger tea-party interesting—thank you."

"You don't get the point. Komuntale's not found out, yet, what you did with the guns."

"No more he has. This, I suppose, is a feeler? Well, I'd like to see that black crook's face, when he gets what's coming to him."

"He's uneasy enough to want to stand in close with you," pointed out Kershaw. "You can bet he's had a pretty highly coloured account from

Mfabo. For all his soft soap and his wife's pink notepaper, that nigger's as sore as hell. I know his sort ; they're as touchy as sensitive plants when anything happens to upset their dignity."

" Be blowed to his dignity," said Johnny easily ; he flicked Mrs. Komuntale's missive across the room. The knowledge of having made someone else squirm took a little of the sting out of his interview with Morris. Suddenly his jaw dropped. " Now where the blazes do you think my washing's got to ? "

" What washing ? "

" God dammit—all my clothes ! There's a to-do at the Residency to-morrow and this is my last pair of bags. I suppose I'd better change 'em," mumbled Johnny, starting to undo buttons. " I'll be in a nice jam if the rest don't turn up——"

" What's got hold of Morris ? " Kershaw grimaced. " I've had a card myself, from ' the Honourable Mrs. Lever ; ' where does she come into the picture ? "

" Morris's sister, I suppose." He produced the duplicate of Kershaw's card from the envelope he remembered thrusting into his pocket. " 'Tea and tennis ; ' Jesus ! What's this—Accra ? "

Kershaw, who was looking across his shoulder, said, " Hallo." It was Foxy. He was mopping his brow as he stepped across the door ledge. He stared at them silently, before pulling a face.

" Well ; Bill's had it."

" What ; one of these ? " Kershaw waved his card inquiringly. " I may be a bit short on the side of imagination, but I don't see Bill capering about after a tennis ball——"

" He's laid out. Looks as if one of Batty's billets-doos is going to come in handy for our Bill. He cut himself up quite a lot, last night."

" What ? A few scratches—with glass splinters ? " Both were incredulous.

" Glass splinters—in a sac full o' poison. The sac's punctured and the poison's all over him. I'd sooner drink a pint mug o' prussic than a tea-spoonful of Bill's blood," grunted Foxy.

" What have they done—taken him to hospital ? "

Foxy still stared. His eyes went slowly from Kershaw to Johnny.

" I told you, didn't I ? Bill got his knife."

" Well, what about it ? " said Kershaw, as Foxy halted again.

" When he went out last night," said Foxy slowly, " he went to Maudie's."

" But——" It was Kershaw's turn to stop. " But Bill doesn't——"

" He went to Maudie's," repeated Foxy stubbornly. " And he handed it to Maudie."

" What—*knifed* her ? "

Silence. Johnny's mind jerked back to the morning at Emma's ; to the girl slung on the end of the counter, with her golden flesh showing through her tattered gown. . . .

" What did he do that for ? "

" Maybe he figured he'd got to. They found them in bed——"

Kershaw muttered something unintelligible, and turned away sharply.

"You see," added Foxy, for Johnny's benefit, "Bill never touched women."

"Where is he? In hospital?"

"Hospital's full. Batty come and tell me they got him in jail. We went up—and I fixed it—for the time being. They could see for themselves Bill wasn't goin' to put them to the trouble o' hangin' him. So we got him fetched home. And I've sent up for Mrs. Gummeridge," ended Foxy. "Gummeridge had got a pow-wow with Morris, and Batty's keepin' an eye on Bill. He wants to see you—Bill does."

"Is he—sane?" Johnny came out of his surprise to ask.

"Off and on. You better look sharp."

"The whole place is in a ferment," muttered Foxy, as they hurried through the dust. Johnny had already observed it; Charlestown's usual lethargy was broken up; an excited vibration came from motionless groups at street corners and flickered in eyes that watched the three white men along the street. A killing! Coloured girl killed by white man! It went through the cabins like a whistle. Everybody was out of doors; no one made any pretence of doing work. Charlestown watched, and waited. At last it had got a sensation. Charlestown watched and waited: knowing that if the position had been reversed, if one of its coloured population had killed a white, there would have been no waiting. Charlestown held its breath. It was the first white killing it had known since—since——?

There was a crowd round Prewett's hut, and one of the native police keeping it in order. Not that it was aggressive. It was merely eaten up with curiosity, and anxious not to miss the next move in the game. It contented itself with milling round quietly, occasionally flattening its nose against a window. It dared not, yet, take sides openly. It had, at any rate, a funeral to look forward to, because Maudie, in her off moments, had been a mission girl. The tale had gone round that Morris was coming down. And no one was particularly anxious to be caught misbehaving himself when the District Commissioner appeared.

Batty met them at the door.

"It's just about time for the bell to go on this round, but he won't go many more."

The four of them stood by the cot on which Prewett was lying. A Kroo was trying to keep away the flies which swarmed persistently on the bandages, and on the corners of ulcerated lips. Prewett's eyes were shut, his face a yellow wax mask under a bristle of neglected beard. The heat came off him and licked at the watchers. A continuous unintelligible babble ran from his lips, of which an occasional disjointed phrase detached itself with startling distinctness for the benefit of the listeners.

"Here, lend us a hand. He's going to hurt himself."

Between them they controlled, with pitiful easiness, the inconscient struggles of the dying man. As they laid him back on the mattress, Foxy, evidently accustomed to the routine, said:

"I guess that's the knock-out. He'll be round, after a bit."

They wet Prewett's lips, and Johnny tried with a damp towel to remove some of the crust that lay in a black rim round his mouth, but it had become part of the scalded flesh.

" How about giving that another poultice ? " He nodded at the swelling which, in the last hour, had run up Prewett's arm, and was spreading from the armpit across the upper chest and shoulder.

" Water—and boil 'um proper ; savvy ? "

The Kroo slouched across the matting. Prewett's eyes had opened.

" What cheer, chum ? " Foxy bent with clumsy tenderness over the bed. " Had a nice nap ? I could do with one myself—you lucky bastard ! " Foxy looked as if he could do with it ; the night's vigil was carved in grooves into his small, sun-peppered face.

The glaze on Prewett's eyes showed he had not heard, or not understood, what the other was saying. He opened his mouth, and his tongue showed, purple and swollen, in its evil-smelling cave.

" Give him a drop of lime juice, and keep that nigger out of the way ; we can manage, till Mother Gummeridge turns up." He picked up the palm-leaf fan and made a swipe at the flies humming across Prewett's face. Something made Johnny lay his hand on Prewett's. For several minutes, while the flies buzzed, and they were aware of the quiet restlessness of the crowd outside, there was silence.

" Tell Maudie . . . I didn't mean to hurt her. 'Noyed me. Got no bus'ness to be . . . nigger. Lost her . . . bloody . . . unities. . . ."

" Now, now—are we ready ? "

The four men started at the brisk interpolation. Johnny gaped at a gaunt female figure, which, followed by two hospital orderlies with a litter between them, trudged purposefully into the room : paying as little attention to himself and his companions as though they were non-existent. His shock was followed by embarrassment : a woman—in these indecent surroundings ! The Kroo had made some attempt at clearing up, but Johnny was about to make a screen of himself, when he was pushed briskly aside by a cross between a respectable and autocratic family nanny and the stalwart captain of a ladies' hockey eleven : this was the impression he received of the new arrival, who, commanding the orderlies in inaccurate but unflinching Hausa, drew back the soiled covers, nipped a roll of white calico under the helpless limbs and a blanket over them, and had the sick man transferred to the litter before any of the onlookers had time to offer their assistance.

" Now we'll soon be all right ! " Only when it was finished did she deign to turn to the others, pushing back a lank string of sandy hair that had plastered itself over her left eyebrow—the Flood eyebrow ! thought Johnny, straight, fierce, but in the case of Charlotte Gummeridge, rufous, not black, like the majority. A red Flood, by George, if there ever was one ! Her hard, noncommittal expression, and the sharpness of a greeny-grey eye, fixed on Foxy, produced in the latter an evident sheepishness.

" That's grand of you, ma'am. But there ain't any room at the hospital —so I been told," he mumbled.

She gave a practised look at the figure at their feet.

" It's not the first time our guest-room's served as hospital. We've not got any of the brethren stopping at present. I suppose you'd call that lucky? We say it's God's mercy." She gave a crisp order to the hospital boys, who bent to lift the stretcher.

" Wait a moment—if you please." Johnny had caught the appeal in Prewett's eyes; lucid for a moment, they turned to him with a painful urgency. He knelt quickly by the side of the stretcher and bent to catch the whispered words.

" My plans. For the swamp. They're at Whitehall."

" Yes. I know."

" Do . . . something . . . about them. Might come in useful . . . for the next chap."

" I'll get right on to them, as soon as I'm back. And I'll send you word——" Inwardly he prayed that Harcourt, or someone even more powerful, would help him to redeem his promise.

" You'll have to send word . . . a hell of a . . . long way!"

" Bunkum. Listen: when you're better "—he gulped, but forced himself to go on—" you can give me all the details. Then I'll get my uncle on the job. Don't you worry, Bill." He pressed the burning hand, and tried to return jest for jest. " Somebody's going to be sorry he's alive, when we get loose among the files!"

" Tell your uncle . . . tell him . . . plant as much cocoa as he wants . . . when they've cleared the swamp. No good . . . unless . . ."

He bent lower, so that the others should not hear.

" Hang on, Bill. We'll need your help, when we start to fight Whitehall."

There was a barely perceptible movement, negative, from the head on the pillow.

" Fought it for years. No good. No . . . more . . . fight . . . Time to go."

Kershaw's hand on his shoulder was drawing him back.

A tall, heavily-bearded figure had made its stooping appearance in the doorway, to the evident relief of the lady, who had been waiting, with poorly concealed impatience, for the conclusion of the conversation between Johnny and her patient.

" There you are, at last, Hananiah. Now you can see him up to the house. I'll be back as quickly as I can: I've got the senior girls waiting for me. Get those things from the hospital as you go past." She tore a leaf from a notebook in which she had been scribbling, and pushed it at her husband. A look passed between them; the situation was too familiar a one to call for words.

As the stretcher, with its trivial burden, jogged out into the sun, Foxy moved awkwardly forward.

" As friends of Bill's, we're much obliged to you, ma'am."

" Then I hope you'll all show your obligation by turning up at the service on Sunday," was the terse rejoinder, as the speaker held out her hand to Johnny. " Mr. Flood, isn't it? It's about time you and I'd met."

V

" It's a bit indistinct," she admitted, " but, so far as I remember, there was a Miss Flood of Barbados who married a Foxley, and one of their daughters married a Wilson ; that's my maiden name. And, for some reason, the Wilsons settled in Manchester—I'd have had it all pat, but what with the Bishop's visit and our last epidemic, and this and that, I never found time to write and ask them at home. Oh, yes, of course we'd heard you were here—somewhere on the Coast ; but we hardly thought you'd get as far as Charlestown. Most people stop short at Accra and Cape Coast Castle ; I might have known a Flood would be more adventurous than that ! " She frowned and smiled at him poutingly ; it was really ridiculously like Hacky !

He mumbled something polite ; it was hard to dismiss Prewett from his mind.

" Mamma was always talking about the Bristol Floods ; we might be old acquaintances ! So you'd better call me Cousin Charlotte ; that's near enough, to go on with, isn't it ? " she concluded, with a jolly laugh.

Johnny felt it might be quite near enough. The others having made the most of their opportunity to disappear, he marked with some misgiving that Cousin Charlotte united the Flood loftiness and breadth with something more than her sex's share of Flood muscularity. The first white woman he had met not to have surrendered her natural floridity to the climate, he was convinced, within a few minutes of their meeting, that Cousin Charlotte's blood was more than capable of keeping West Africa in its place.

He pulled himself together. Emotion and Cousin Charlotte were not compatible. Hard, capable, forthright—he reminded himself that phlegmaticism, in her case, must be almost a condition of survival. Anyone giving way to tenderness, to horror, to any of the more sensitive feelings must be torn to tatters. A good, hard-wearing, homespun compassion was, he decided, about the limit of Cousin Charlotte's emotionalism, and that she kept well under control. She probably—and reasonably—disapproved highly of Bill Prewett, but had the sense to know when disapprobation could be effective, and when it was sheer waste of breath. All the same, he wondered how much she knew of the truth ; what a Christian lady's reaction had been, when she heard of it, to murder in a prostitute's bed.

Whatever the reaction had been, it was hidden behind the large, stony façade of Cousin Charlotte's habitual serenity.

" Mamma always said we were a tall family ! " Little green eyes under bushy brows twinkled down on him. Resigning himself, Johnny admitted he was the runt of the family.

" Little but good, perhaps ? " She aimed an encouraging slap at his shoulder, and Johnny, feeling as though he had had a cuff from a playful she-bear, doubted that the Ashanti had had it all their own way, in trying conclusions with Cousin Charlotte. Remembering what Morris had told him, he proceeded to make up for his inward ribaldry with a respectful disclaimer of virtue, to which she nodded her head.

" No, not so good, either ! Nearly a week in Charlestown, and not a minute to call on your relations ! "

" I haven't had much time for calling, ma'am——"

" Nor have we," was the cheery response, " except on the Lord's errands. Never mind ; we'll turn over a new leaf, won't we ? You must come up for chop one night, and we'll have a good pow-wow about the Old Folks at Home." As he tried mentally to fit Dromore and Selina into the description, she added matter-of-factly : " Your friend is going to die, you know."

He could find no answer. What, indeed, else could one wish for one to whom life offered nothing but a postponement ?

" Don't worry," said Cousin Charlotte briskly. " He's safe in the arms of Jesus : Hananiah'll see to that. He's my husband—ought to have introduced you," she mumbled. " He's a true Christian ; I try to be. There's a difference. Well, and what do you think of Charlestown ? "

" Since you've been here considerably longer than I, ma'am "—he twinkled up at her—" what do *you* think of it ? "

She scowled, mistrusting him.

" We all think it a privilege to be called to Charlestown. Promotion, you know ; soldiers of Jesus. The stronger the fortress, the more satisfaction there is in taking it."

" I should think it's pretty tough—as fortresses go." He did his best politely to follow the metaphor.

" We're gaining ground, though ! Yes, we're well past the outposts now," she triumphed. " Considering it's our first experience on the Coast, we've had many blessings from the Lord. Naturally, we get our little set-backs. Mr. Gummeridge was deeply disappointed in Thomas."

" Thomas——? "

" I expect you call him Teapot, or Hot Cross Bun ! " She wagged her head in playful deprecation of lay ribaldry. " We always give them a Christian name, you know—after conversion."

" You're not, by any chance, talking about my Fan boy ? "

Charlotte nodded.

" Run away, I suppose ? They always do. But he'll turn up presently. And I hope you'll be very strict with him when he comes back," she ended on a note of severity which sounded a warning for Johnny.

" You'd better tell me about this, Mrs. Gummeridge." A more sensitive listener would have been put on his guard by the tone, but Charlotte, deaf to nuances, produced her information crisply.

" Thomas was one of our first converts—five years ago ; up in his own village, before the family moved down to the Coast. We do our best to keep in touch with them—naturally ; but it's difficult, after they leave the mission schools. We *were* delighted to find him here, among our first batch of communicants ! " She sighed, and rubbed away with her gloved hand the sweat that was pearling down her forehead. " Like the rest of them—I suppose he was led into temptation."

" I don't know about that ; but he was a very decent boy—as boys go. I've seen enough of the other sort to appreciate a good black when I get him," said Johnny.

" I'm glad to hear you say so." She scowled, her lips tightening, the under-lip jutting—as Dorset's jutted, in his evil moods. " You didn't know, I suppose, that he'd taken up with one of the local girls, before you engaged him ? "

" Well, ma'am "—it was diffcult to take this seriously—" you'll hardly pretend there's anything criminal in that ? As it happens, Tich—you call him Thomas—told me all about it. They're going to get married——"

" No, they're not," she snapped. " The girl's a heathen, and refuses to be married in church. Moreover, she's going to have a baby."

" His, or somebody else's ? "

" His, of course." For some reason, she appeared to take objection to the question.

" It must be—let's see—six months since he saw her. Tich was in service with one of the Civil Service bigwigs, at Accra, until I took him over," persisted Johnny. " Oh, well, I suppose it could be."

" It could," was the grim retort, " and it is. Of course, we had to ring him out."

" You had to—— ? Sorry ; I didn't quite get that."

" A convert who seduces one of the native girls is expelled from the services. There's a public ceremony, and we ring a bell after him as he leaves the church," she informed him, bridling.

" And what's the point in that ? " he asked, after a pause. She stared.

" Surely you know they're like children ? You've got to make them *all* feel their share in the disgrace."

" Well . . ." The thinning of her lips was repeated on his own. " I can only say—you've got an odd way of popularising the Christian religion, Cousin Charlotte."

The obstinate Flood pout, the intolerable droop of the Flood eyelid made him feel he had known her a very long time.

" One of these days we'll have a talk : shall we, Cousin John ? You'll remember, perhaps, that I've had eleven years of the Gold Coast. You've had—how many months ? "

" God damn it—don't be so superior ! I beg your pardon, but upon my soul, I don't know how to keep my temper with people like you," muttered Johnny.

" Now, now, now ! I know it's annoying to lose a good house-boy," said Cousin Charlotte soothingly, " and we'll do our best to find you a substitute ; I can't say fairer than that, can I ? They're not easy to find, I admit, but we've got a young boy, Peter, who might, I think——"

" Cousin Charlotte. I suppose you wouldn't believe me if I were to say I don't give a—row of pins for losing my house-boy ? "

" Then why do you lose your temper ? " she snapped.

" Answer me this : If Tich—Thomas—were white, would you think of him just as ' a house-boy ? ' "

"I don't know what you mean." She knitted her brows in irritable perplexity. "You don't have white 'boys,'" she mumbled.

"I'll try to explain. Has it ever occurred to you to wonder what happened to Tich, after you rang him out of church?"

"Oh, dear me!" She was plainly relieved. "They all do the same thing when they know they've been naughty! Run away and hide for a few days—and then come back and ask to be forgiven."

"And you forgive them?"

"Of course!" she answered, wide-eyed.

"Cousin Charlotte." He smiled palely. "How very nice it must be—to be God!"

The lowering of her eyelids showed that she was very angry. He went on deliberately.

"I don't pretend to know much—as much as you, for instance, of the native. I only know at second hand how he reacts to your mission teaching. I'm bound to say I haven't found its results very prepossessing. But there are certain things that strike me, not as matters of religion, but of pure justice. You take away his beliefs from the heathen, and put another set of beliefs in their place. Then you proceed to take those away."

"What nonsense!" she burst out.

"It's nothing of the sort," he retorted. "What do you think that bell-ringing means to Tich? That his mission God has gone back on him: that he's got nothing—nothing at all to protect him from all the evil spirits that every black goes on believing in, even after he's converted."

"Then he's got no business to," she snapped childishly.

"Why do you teach Christianity? For the sake of discipline, or do you really believe you're saving souls?" He tried to keep his voice colourless, not to sound as though he were sneering.

"Cousin John." She was shocked at last. "Do you mean—you are not a Christian?"

"What's that got to do with it? Cousin Charlotte: you know as well as I do that this town is stuffed with whites who are doing just what Tich has done, all the time, and getting away with it. Here we are—surrounded by a whole population that witnesses to white lust: and Tich, like every other black, knows it. He knows the race he is supposed to look up to—the great, white, Christian race!—is responsible for a breed that's despised and cold-shouldered, not only by whites, but by all the pure-bred people of his own race—wait a minute!" as she made a movement to interrupt. "People who talk this way get called nigger-fanciers, don't they? Well, I'm not a nigger-fancier. But it gets me on the raw when I'm obliged to be ashamed of my own race and its religion!"

"But what are you ashamed of?" Her voice quivered, whether with anger or dismay he could not determine.

"Tich has done something with a girl of his own colour, and, I don't for a minute doubt, with her full agreement, which white men are doing every day to coloured girls; often cruelly against their will."

"I've told you the girl's a heathen! Surely you can see the harm that does to a converted boy, who's trying to follow the way of Truth?"

"Oh, pish," snorted Johnny. "What's truth? Somebody wiser than you or I couldn't answer that. Every human being has his own truth, and Tich's, for some private reason of his own, is all knitted up with his girl. But because she's a heathen and he's supposed to have forsaken his own beliefs, you put shame on him in front of a churchful of mission smugs—and he bolts, because if there's one thing a decent Negro can't stand, it's being make a laughing stock of!" He paused to draw breath. "I don't know what you call that, Cousin Charlotte: but I'm damned if it's my notion of Christianity."

She had recovered her self-possession. Drawing herself up, she looked down on him from her superior height.

"I think we have gone quite far enough. I don't wish to be offensive, Cousin John; but I think the sooner you leave Charlestown, the better. Good day."

My God, I *am* a swine! For a moment he was tempted to rush after her and apologise. This woman—going steadily about what she believed to be her duty; devoting her life to the care of a people who failed her at every turn; eschewing all easy, pleasant living for Jesus' sake; labouring unceasingly among the basest forms of humanity; looking without flinching on the vile, the loathsome and the piteous, carrying healing in her big, firm hands; commanding respect even from men like Foxy Biddle—he, Johnny, had virtually insulted her.

He stood aghast, ashamed to put his first impulse into action. He watched her heavy figure go blundering away into the sun, the dust curling up about the hem of her shabby black alpaca skirt. Going to teach mission girls—girls like the unfortunate Maudie—to hem dusters and sing songs, translated from the English, half of the words of which conveyed nothing whatever to them, and to recite the catechism. Question: What is the inward and spiritual grace? Answer: A death unto sin and a new birth unto righteousness; for being by nature born in sin, and the children of wrath, we are hereby made the children of grace. Were they?

Cousin Charlotte believed so. And, with the same sturdy confidence she brought to convincing her mission girls of sin, she would presently tramp on to Bill Prewett; would minister to his physical needs, would perform, if necessary, the most revolting services that sickness exacts. She would not shudder away from a man whose tragedy was self-induced, or act the Pharisee to a grievous sinner. How did it come that such a one could not distinguish this, the true Christianity, from the other, the bogus kind, that consisted in brow-beating helpless human beings into the profession of faiths they were not capable of understanding, and punishing them for back-slidings which only their mission training had taught them to call sin?

When he got back to the hut, Kershaw and Foxy were rolling poker dice. Their reception was taciturn. Johnny sat down to watch them. Nobody talked. He thought of the next day's invitation to the Residency, and, by process of association, of his missing washing, which Tich had taken to the washwoman, somewhere in the town, the day after their arrival. He burst out:

"Damn that Tich!"

Kershaw swore, and scooped the dice into the palm of his hand. For once there was no glint of humour in his grotesque face.

"Look here, Flood: there's about seventy-five thousand Fan house-boys up and down the Coast. For Christ's sake stop bellyaching about one that happens to have gone off for a couple of nights with his girl."

Johnny was silent. The suggestion was a reasonable one. He was surprised not to have thought of it himself. Then he remembered that he had thought of it. And rejected it; knowing it was false.

CHAPTER SIX

I

"OH, dear, what a pity you're a bachelor!" sighed Arethusa Lever. "It's so bad for morale."

Her brother looked startled, as well he might.

"Whose? Mine, or the district's?"

"Both." She flicked her earrings with a toss of the head which Morris remembered as one of the prettiest heads in their Shropshire countryside. Now, alas, the soft curls were grizzled, the large blue eyes netted with wrinkles, the rose-petal skin gone to dust, and grained as with greyish sand. And Arethusa—it gave him a pang to remember—was only thirty-two. Stubbornly, year after year, she came back with her husband to the Coast; when his duty obliged him to cancel his furlough, she insisted on stopping on, through the rains. Arethusa was of the stuff heroes are made of: a point which did not appear to have occurred to herself.

"Thusy," said Morris quietly. "If Guy had been sent to Charlestown, would you have come with him?" And knew the answer before she flung it back at him with a flash of her eyes.

"Of course I would!"

"He wouldn't have let you," her brother contented himself with replying.

"I'd like to have seen him stop me!" cried Arethusa. "You men are very superior," she went on, "about our little tea parties and our amateur theatricals and all we do to amuse you—but those things are more important than you realise."

"I know they are." He paid her the compliment of being serious.

"Just think of the amount of entertaining you could do, in a beautiful house like this! Our place is a shack beside it!" said Arethusa enviously.

"I've got no time for entertaining, and you know it." His tone hardened. "As a matter of fact, I very much regret this confounded party of yours this afternoon. You know the place is in an uproar about that coloured girl, and

Bill Prewett and I were friends—once. I'm not in a mood for parties—or for entertaining Morison and his blasted staff! I'm not in his good books and he's not in mine—and I've got ten thousand things screaming for attention before I sit down to discuss local defence with a pompous tom-noddy from Headquarters——"

"You started it," pointed out Arethusa.

"I sent in a memorandum—as I was bound to do."

"Do you really think there's going to be trouble?"

"Of course not," he snapped. "What do you suppose we're here for? But if you don't report, they turn sour on you, and whatever happens is your fault. I suppose we'll waste five or six hours in a solemn overhaul of local resources——"

"Are there any?"

"Certainly not." He twinkled at her. "And, as I've told you before, you're too knowing for the sister of a District Commissioner. I must see if I can't find you a set of those little monkeys——"

"'See not, hear not, speak not?'" She pulled a face at him. "What a bore people would find me!" She sighed. "I'm afraid I'm not cut out for the rôle of Administrational memsahib. But—seriously, Henry: haven't you got any troops here, in Charlestown?"

"When I need the help of the military to run my district it will be time to get out the old carpet slippers and give notice to my present tenants at Church Stretton."

"I wish it were," muttered Arethusa, but took care her brother did not hear her. "Anyhow"—she brightened—"I mean to enjoy my party. I can't wait to see the Colonel's face, when he finds himself holding a teacup for Mrs. Kaboha Komuntale!"

"Great God!" Morris shot out of his chair. "You've not asked them?"

Arethusa arched her eyebrows.

"You said, all the members of the Christian Ladies' Guild, didn't you? She's Vice-Chairman, or something; I took it for granted her husband would be a Christian Gentleman."

"If he is, I'm a professed member of the Headhunters' Association," said her brother grimly. "I'm sorry, Thusy; your friends the Komuntales are out. Damn; that's another thing I've got to remember to tell the sentry."

"Oh, well." She was not to be depressed. "I don't doubt for a moment there'll be plenty of amusing people, without them."

She loved her annual Charlestown party—with its catholic flavour; its air, almost, of fancy dress: so refreshingly different from the formality of Government House, or even from her humbler but no less formal hospitalities on Guy's behalf. She agreed with her brother's dictum—that such entertaining as he did must be representative of all sections in his district. "White and black are obliged to work together; why shouldn't they play together?" was one of his sayings—highly disapproved in certain official circles, but earning him respect denied to many of his colleagues among educated members of the local councils. Apart from other considerations, there were not enough whites (of the presentable kind) in Charlestown to make up " a party," and, apart from missionaries' wives, no white women to be offended by finding themselves *vis-à-vis* with coloured fellow guests. Morris's sympathy for the coloured population was well known, and had brought him great unpopularity with most of his superiors, but this left him unmoved.

So beside the white contingent, uneasy in its freshly starched best, which moved about the space in the Residency compound which the persistence of Arethusa and the efforts of several gangs of labourers had succeeded in reclaiming from the wild—two local chiefs, wearing European shirts and jackets over their cloths and aggrey beads in their ears, spread their hands on their knees and viewed the shifting scene. Considering the chiefs were not used to garden parties, they bore themselves with an admirable imperturbability: showing none of that over-affability which betrayed several persons in excellent tussore coats into admission of their less positive standing. Under the too-bright smiles, the fulsome little gestures, ran, however, an undercurrent of satisfaction. Once a year, at the District Commissioner's party, certain people who normally made a point of ignoring their existence were constrained by politeness into acknowledgement. Mere acknowledgement; no more. " Ah—you, Mason." Nod, and pass on. Gradually, for all their smiles, their eager acclaiming of the few acquaintances who were unlikely to snub them—the social tide receded from their little band, until Arethusa took pity on them.

" Wouldn't you care for a game of tennis, Mr.—er——? "

A few minutes later, liberated from their social awe, they were leaping about the swish courts with the speed and grace of panthers. The white men looked, stared, and turned away. Niggers—playing tennis! What next? A handsome young Negro barrister, pausing in Charlestown on his way to conduct a complicated case at Sierra Leone, disassociated himself with a faint, cold smile from the gambols of his racial half-brothers and turned to take a glass of iced cup from a tray handed by a grinning boy in a red cummerbund—a touch of elegance imported by Arethusa, whose little wizened face smiled unceasingly across her collar-band of ruffled net; not even her assiduity, however, had succeeded in attaching the cummerbunds securely. They were always coming undone, falling off, or rolling themselves into a string round their wearers' middles. Nothing but tintacks, she reflected, would do it. Still—it was a festal touch.

Her welcome to Johnny and Kershaw was relieved to the point, almost, of effusiveness; her circus had begun slightly to bore her. Any amusement palls, when you have no one with whom to share the fun, and these hard-faced, shy men offered no fun. Henry, of course, was tied up with his military bigwigs. She met them by the tennis courts, from which the players, having finished their set in record time, were retiring.

" There; what do you think of that? " She indicated the nets and the rather straggly markings triumphantly. " The courts had practically gone back to bush, when I arrived! Of course they're in terrible condition, but I think it's just possible to pat a ball about, don't you? "

Kershaw agreed, and, terrified he might be required to go patting, saved himself dexterously by recognising an acquaintance in the middle distance. Arethusa looked after him amiably.

" What an interesting-looking person your friend is, Mr. Flood ! What department is he in ? "

" I don't think he's in any, ma'am. He likes describing himself as a jack of all trades—although, as a matter of fact, he qualified as an engineer," said Johnny, wondering a little at the ease with which one dropped back into the habit of small-talk—an accomplishment unpractised since his last trip to Cape Coast.

" Engineers are so intelligent," murmured Mrs. Lever. " Now I've got a great surprise for you. Look over there ! "

It was with a shock of incredulity that he recognised, in a group on the farther side of the room, his brother Gilbert. The astonishment on his face was not reflected on Gilbert's as it turned in his direction ; nor, it had to be admitted, was there any marked degree of pleasure in the stare with which Gilbert favoured his cadet. Still, if it came to that, there was never any marked degree of anything on Gilbert's face, blank as an egg, topping the long and seemingly boneless body that suggested a string of weed, wavering up from its anchorage in a shallow pool. The monocle driven in under a faint blond bristle of eyebrow emphasised Gilbert's departure from the paternal to his mother's side of the family.

" I thought you were stuck on the Frontier ! "

" Due for furlough, but it's been cancelled—the Lord knows why ! Nothin' but polo for the last six weeks ; a bit of racin' and a pot or two at hippos. Frightful grind. Now they talk of draftin' us down to the Cape. Beastly bore. Awful cads—South Africans."

Without troubling to inquire whether Gilbert's description was supposed to refer to Boers, to Basutos, or to the British colonial population, Johnny contented himself by asking what, in that case, accounted for Gilbert's presence in so unlikely a spot as Charlestown.

" Colonel's here : didn't you know ? " Gilbert's eyebrows expressed deprecation of his junior's social ignorance. " Old buffer over there—talkin' to the D.C. Some sort of pow-wow on about increasin' the native battalions." Johnny pricked his ears. So Foxy's information, then, was not a canard, and someone had taken notice of Morris's report after all.

" By gad, I hope I never get posted here ! " Panic flickered briefly behind the monocle. " Accra : one might rub along in Accra. But this—— ! Pahsitively frightful, my dear fella ! Pahsitively ghastly ! " Having dedicated a short pause to horror, Gilbert resumed : " Any news from home ? We missed the mail at Forcados."

" I had a letter from Grandmamma, and the usual screed from Miranda —a few days ago."

" Anythin' fresh ? Doss engaged yet ? "

" Not that I know of."

" Tscha ! If he doesn't look sharp," drawled Gilbert, " he'll be missin' Emily Temple. Frightful ass if he does—what ? Deuc'd attractive gel :

All the fellas after her—though my personal taste's for something a bit more dashin'. I don't suppose you agree with me ?"

. . . Emily. Emily, with the soft voice and soft movement, and skin so delicate it reflected the colour of a flower, of a leaf. Emily, bending over the lily-pond, with its green translucence lying in a band across her brows and gathered in the clear pools of her eyes. Sweet song translated into flesh. Dear, dearest Emily. . . . A rose-laden air stole through the sultry warmth of the room.

"I used to fancy you were a bit gone on her, you know," Gilbert was saying.

"Gammon. Emily's Doss's business."

"Quite." He had spoken a trifle too quickly, but nothing could have been more amiably vacuous than Gilbert's acceptance of his disclaimer. Then, recollecting something, Gilbert frowned.

"By the way—you've put me in the deuce of a corner !"

"How that ?" His voice, which he tried to keep casual, snapped.

"It's all over the place you've been livin' in native huts and mixin' with ticket-of-leave men and beachcombers. Damme, sir, what's come over you ?" rapped out Gilbert, with a fine assumption of his commanding officer's manner, that made Johnny's lips twitch, in spite of his irritation.

"I haven't been living in native huts, and it looks as if there's not much to choose, when it comes to scandal, between the Gold Coast and an old maids' sewing meeting."

"Pish. Everybody wants to know why you aren't stoppin' here. You know perfectly well the D.C. counts on puttin' up people like Us." Gilbert was pink with mortification.

"Very affable. He didn't say so, when I was talking to him."

"Surely you *see*," spluttered Gilbert, "that people like Us have a position to keep up—— !"

"The sort of position we were keeping up when we ran slavers from here ? Thanks, old boy. When I want to 'put on dog,' I don't think I'll choose to start it on the Gold Coast."

"When are you goin' home ? It strikes me you've had as much of the Coast as is good for you," scowled his brother.

"I'm supposed to be taking in some of the cocoa concessions for Uncle Hacky," Johnny told him mildly.

"Beastly stuff, cocoa. Well, I suppose you know your own business ; you might remember that in Our position——"

"I wish you'd tell me what that is ?"

"—we can't afford to get mixed up with a lot of riff-raff and small fry. Dammit all, you might remember it's hard on *me* !"

"I don't think my friends are likely to trouble you."

"Now, don't take it like that." Gilbert tapped him not unkindly on the shoulder. "I'm only speaking for your good. I know you, old boy ! Always ready to listen to somebody's hard-luck story—what ? As sure as somebody's got a grievance, he brings it to you—like a cat bringing a mouse —what ? Malcontents ! You needn't tell me ; I know all about it ; hear plenty of it—even in the service. Just bear one thing in mind : *we British hang together.* Nobody worth his salt pays attention to pin-pricks when the matter at stake is the old Empire. Damme, sir, what are you grinning at ? "

" I was only waiting to see the flag break behind your head. By George, Gil, I hope I live to see you in forty years' time. You'll be vintage, my boy —vintage," said Johnny, with conviction. He sobered himself to add : " So far as I'm concerned, the Empire's in no danger. All the same— things aren't as good, you know, as they look—well, at Accra."

" Colonial Office pigeon." Gilbert frowned, in grave disclaimer of responsibility.

" I wonder—— ? There's a man I wish you could have met : he's an engineer—crazy about swamps——"

" Oh, my dear chap ! " The monocle dropped, together with its wearer's jaw. " For mercy's sake don't talk about engineers. Most frightfully tahsome fellas, always chasin' some wild-cat scheme or other, and cussin' the Government for not lettin' them chuck public funds about like rotten apples——"

" Hold on a minute. Surely you, as a soldier, see the advantages of decent roads. And think what the drainage of swamps would do to the malaria figures."

" The swamps I grant you." From the manner of the speaker it was evidently a handsome concession. " But roads—good lord ! Give me five battalions of carriers—that's roughly five thousand niggers—ten companies to a battalion, each man carryin' fifty to sixty pounds. Send a couple of hundred pioneers ahead, to corduroy the bad ground, open up the bush and throw bridges where necessary—and I'll take care of your transport for you ! Must give these bally niggers something to do, damme, to keep them out of mischief."

" Well, why not set them to road-making ? It's a healthier job, after all, than shooting each other—and us—up ! "

" Got to have wars," said Gilbert solemnly. " Got to keep up Imperial prestige. And, incidentally, keep down the niggers. By gad, the beggars breed like rabbits ! Got to drive 'em now and again, to keep the ground clear."

Although it was not the first time he had heard the military point of view, Johnny felt himself sickening. The wanton waste of human life, the massacre and misery of another native rising—would we never learn ?— made him ill to contemplate. The mild social atmosphere around him was suddenly suffocating : scum over a bubbling cauldron.

And beyond it all—beyond the swamp, and the maggot-heap of humanity, white or black : offering, in its neglect and ignorance, hostage to all the evil, moral and physical, that the swamp belched forth—Africa, restless in her chains. Africa, stirring, fulminating, drawing in secretly, by her bush paths and her waterways, materials for rebellion.

" If you ask me," Gilbert was saying, " you look beastly off colour. Gad, the C.O.'s semaphoring me. See you later—and do take my tip :

if the D.C. invites you here—as he probably will, after I've talked to him—remember what you owe to the Family! I've really had a deuce of a time, explainin' to all and sundry that you're just one of these eccentric fellas—but quite pukka, underneath it all, don't you know, if it comes to the rub!"

"That's very kind of you." Johnny accepted this with a gravity he, himself, could not help admiring.

"And I wish you'd get yourself some decent kit. Candidly, my dear fella, those togs are a disgrace."

"I meant to order some things down from Accra, but I forgot—and my washing's gone astray." Johnny spoke with contrition. It was hard on the dapper Gilbert, to be obliged to acknowledge so ramshackle-looking a relative!

"Well, well—give Mrs. Lever a game or two of tennis. That's a damned plucky little woman: she's put on a dam' fine show, by Gad, for a hole like this!"

Setting aside his hostess's probable reaction to the compliment—of course, he thought humbly: Gilbert's right. Drinks, fans, flowery borders—it was just the British spirit, keeping its end up, in its own imponderable fashion, against the encroachment of the wild. Putting on a dam' fine show....

The crunch of go-carts on the gravel sweep, the splatter of bare feet, the small, social hubbub of departure animated the swift twilight. Johnny, looking for his host—whom he had barely seen—to bid farewell, found Arethusa Lever at his shoulder.

The compound seemed vast and ghostly in its sudden emptiness—as though the guests had taken fright, and bolted like a flock of sheep. Beyond its fringe the drums had taken up their faint, insistent reminder that the British, with their small civilities, their childlike pomps, were there on sufferance. Africa stirred, stretched, and resumed its habitual vigilance on the frail outposts of the invaders.

"You'll stay to supper, Mr. Flood. Nonsense"—as Johnny began vaguely to mumble a refusal. "Don't you know your manners?" Her eyes twinkled at him. "You can't leave, you know, without making your salaams to the Commissioner."

"I've been looking for him—I lost sight of him while I was talking to my brother. Can you tell me where to find him?"

She looked at him oddly, bit her lip, and, without replying, moved before him into the shadowy hall, beckoning him to follow her. They stood side by side beneath the portico, where the steps ran down to the drive, with its grove of trees, green-black against the flaming sunset.

"It's nearly time to strike the flag. Life's very strange here, isn't it? Life—and death." Small, drooping, it was as though she gathered to herself the melancholy of the sunset. Something to his surprise, he found himself thinking of her—not as one of the smart, metallic, Accra women, full of small tittle-tattle and fretful over questions of precedence: but rather as a younger version of his grandmother, gallant, enduring, looking proudly in the face of life—and, as she had said, of death. She turned her profile—which was very like her brother's—to him, as she said :

" They've been burying Mr. Cator. You wouldn't notice : my brother and a few of the others left about an hour ago. That's why the Gummeridges weren't here ; such a pity. She's one of my greatest *joys* ! I always feel as if I'd swallowed a dose of tonic after talking to Mrs. Gummeridge. Here he comes," said Arethusa, recovering herself. " And somebody else with him. Can you see who it is ? I suppose he'll stay for supper, so I'd better tell the house-boys."

The two figures on the drive—white against the dusk—the second of whom he recognised, by his walk, as Foxy, hastened their steps, and were joined by others, seemingly from under the porch on which Johnny stood. He saw them stop, and stiffen to attention, and the arms of the officers bend sharply to the salute. There was a pause, a hush, and he knew the flag, somewhere above where he was standing, was down.

II

Foxy was fidgeting uneasily at his elbow.

" This ain't in my line. I'm off."

" The dickens you are. Look here, I don't know any of these fellows ; you'll jolly well stop and back me up ! "

" You've got Kershaw." Foxy made an attempt to disengage himself from the grip Johnny had fastened on his arm. " Let go, I tell you ! You can tell the D.C. I'll be back later, if he wants me."

" He must want you ; or why did he bring you along ? "

" I ran into him when we were plantin' Cator—and we got talkin' about Komuntale——"

" What about Komuntale ? " Johnny's hand dropped ; it was not a welcome subject.

" Huh—that one's hopped it."

" Why ? Why ? "

" I reckon that nigger's got the wind up. There's been a fella from H.Q. ferretin' round the files this mornin'. Or maybe he's expectin' a visit from his up-country partner ! " Foxy gave his toothless grin.

Johnny swore under his breath.

" Can he do any harm ? "

" Who to ? " Foxy shrugged his shoulders. " I reckon our Mr. Komuntale'll will be too keen on avoidin' notice to make a nuisance of himself till the dust is settled."

" I didn't mean that." He gulped ; the question was hard to frame. " I know—Morris told me—we were wanting to lie low about the gun-running——"

Foxy shook his head.

" It looks as if you've blown that one, chum. The drums will have seen to it by now."

"You mean—they've had the tip-off—up-country?"

"What the hell? They'll try no more games round here, but the stuff will get in—plenty of it—by other routes. Komuntale's prob'ly skulkin' round the neighbourhood, waitin' till the clouds roll by. Makin' up his mind if it's safe to wait till pay day, or whether it 'ud be policy to seek fresh woods an' pastures new for his next little effort in double-crossin' his British overlords!"

A sick self-disgust settled at Johnny's stomach.

"I hope you're both ready for supper?" Arethusa had changed her gown; her small, scrawny neck and shoulders rose naked from a crushed fluff of black tulle, from which Foxy, after a glance, averted his eyes in panic. The spectacle of a woman in décolleté was not one to which the inhabitants of Charlestown were accustomed.

"I got to be going, ma'am," Johnny heard him mumble, and heard Arethusa's airy dismissal of the plea.

"Mr. Kershaw, look after Mr.—M'm'm—won't you? I know my brother wants to see you both after supper. And you are to sit beside me, Mr. Flood, and help me to support the Colonel!" she added, on a penetrating whisper. "The Colonel's a terrible old bore. He's only got one virtue—he goes early to bed! They say it's the only thing, so far, that's prevented his being murdered by his aides. Ah, Colonel!" tinkled Arethusa. "You *naughty* man! How dare you claim the privilege of your charm, to keep us all waiting for supper?" And sailed away on the arm of the small, parrot-beaked autocrat who, followed by his aide, had just made his entrance.

Wishing heartily that he had never accepted the invitation, Johnny felt impelled, each time he caught the Commissioner's eye, to crawl under the table. He saw Gilbert scowl at him, in deprecation of his social ineptitude, and Arethusa eyeing him, from time to time, with natural surprise at his monosyllabic contributions to the conversation she was gallantly maintaining with her partner. He knew he had earned the look of deep reproach she gave him when she rose to leave the gentlemen over their wine.

It was only after the Colonel had lived up to his reputation by retiring on the stroke of ten—evidently not to sleep, for Gilbert, with an air of long-suffering, obeyed a nod and followed him from the room—that the company thawed. The next half-hour was lively enough, and even Johnny found himself chuckling at some of the yarns with which Foxy—relieved from the embarrassment of the hostess's presence—was regaling the table.

The hands of the clock stood at eleven, and a prolonged burst of laughter had just died down, when Morris rose.

"If anyone wants a game of billiards, you know where to find the cues. Mr. Biddle and I have some business to discuss. If you care to join us, Mr. Flood——?"

Why couldn't he make a downright order of it? With sinking heart, Johnny prepared to follow the other two through the door behind the chair in which the Commissioner had been sitting.

"Kershaw—I think you'd better come as well; if you don't mind?" Pleasantly as Morris spoke, Johnny received, not for the first time, the impression that Kershaw was not one of his favourites. It was, perhaps, not unreasonable. To one who had sacrificed every personal inclination to the high conception of duty, someone who was known to thumb his nose at authority, and sedulously to reject any governance other than that of his inspiration, was hardly likely to be popular.

The room they passed into was small and cosy—evidently Arethusa found it so, for her sewing basket was on a carved Dahomey stool, although she herself was not to be seen—and filled with a pleasant, male disorder in contrast with the public rooms Johnny had already seen. Brief as were its periods of occupation, it had escaped, by some means, the atmosphere of mouldy disuse which lingered faintly in the rest of the Residency.

Morris flung aside bundles of papers and magazines to make room for his guests.

" Anyone having coffee ? I drink it to keep myself awake." His glance drew Johnny's attention to the coffee-pot that bubbled over a methylated flame on the hearth. " The spirits are over there ; help yourselves."

Johnny felt himself relaxing. This, surely, was not the preliminary to a rebuke, such as he had been dreading. The others were filling their glasses ; Johnny, deciding for coffee, occupied the time while Morris was pouring it into china cups in looking at a collection of terra-cottas on a shelf beside his chair.

" Do those interest you ? They're from Benin, '97 expedition. Pretty fine, aren't they, as samples of Negro art ? I don't know much about sculpture, but I should think that head would show up well in comparison with some of the early Greek work."

" I've never seen anything like it. It's—it's astonishing ! " The chaste profile, the smoothly chiselled features, the high pride of it took Johnny's breath away. " It certainly knocks out one's ideas of the uncultured savage ! "

Passing his cup, Morris laughed a little.

" I'd give most of the culture that's come my way to produce a thing like that." He dropped into a chair ; for a moment, while the lamplight ploughed furrows into his face, he closed his eyes. The others, summoned by Johnny, examined the head politely. Kershaw appeared to share his impression ; Foxy, after a glance, wagged his head.

" High class—but you ought to see some of the stuff they turn out in Dahomey ! "

Morris's lips twitched ; he opened his eyes quickly.

" Well, Sam." He was addressing Foxy ; there was no amusement in the pale discs of his eyes. " We've got three bags full this time. Beri-beri at Kumba. The Okomi have given a party, with that tiresome beggar, Efele, on the menu——"

" Hope he gave 'em the bellyache."

"—They've discovered a new god at Gyadodi, who is apparently telling all the people to set fire to each other's huts. The manioc crop's failed at Bingi, and the villagers are starving. The Diloli have just made a raid on the Bunsuru and taken ten of their women. They've got sleeping sickness at Tambo. And we've just had a report of a nasty case of fangaree up the Dufu river."

"Is that all?" Foxy yawned.

Morris smiled faintly.

"Take a cigar, Kershaw. These matters aren't in your line, are they?"

"Not in the ordinary way, Commissioner. I wouldn't say the Diloli are interested in sanitation, and the bush has got its own telegraphic system, hasn't it?" Kershaw's teeth flashed. "I've got plenty of 'lines'——"

"So I understand," put in Morris dryly.

"—But it's just too bad that most of them are too sophisticated for the tastes of the up-country."

"Too sophisticated for—that?" Morris pointed to the head. Remote and calm, its blind eye-sockets intent upon the invisible, it mocked with its dignity the pretensions of white wisdom. "The American Museum wanted it—but I decided not to part. I keep it around"—he spoke casually—"as a corrective."

"Corrective to what, sir?" It was Johnny who broke the silence.

"To the almost irresistible temptation to regard the Negro as a primitive form of life: not quite animal, not vegetable, but hardly human. When my black children"—the Commissioner smiled—"persist in behaving like a colony of rather vicious apes, it helps to readjust my outlook, when I come back and look at that."

"Doesn't it raise the question—which is the real Negro: that, or the apes?"

"Neither," said Morris promptly. "Something between the two. The important thing is, not to forget the one, in getting obsessed by the other."

Foxy, whom the conversation had stranded, and who had listened with dropping jaw to what, so far as he was concerned, was, to all intents and purposes, a foreign language, heaved himself forward in his chair.

"So you're urgently wanted in seven places at once, Chief?" A note of reproach suggested that it was high time the company stopped talking hot air and got down to essentials.

"Eight. There's Omo."

"What's Omo up to?"

"Nothing."

"You're right." Foxy spoke crisply, after a pause. "When Omo's up to nothing, it's high time somebody took a look round."

"There's nothing in particular," was the easy rejoinder. "The mission's pulled out—that's all; and they're always inclined to go on the binge for a few days after the missionary leaves—a sort of 'Hooray for the holidays!' don't you know? I generally manage to drop in and calm them down. However, for once, it looks as if they'll have to get over it without my assistance. I believe you were wanting to go up to Omo." He dropped the suggestion so casually that Johnny, still dominated by the Yoruba head, did not at first realise he was being addressed.

"I'm sorry, sir. Omo—well, I'd got Omo at the back of my mind. On account of the concessions," he put in quickly.

" How have you got on, as a whole, over the concessions ? "

" Not very well," he admitted.

" So that "—Morris appeared to muse—" is why you want to visit Omo."

" Yes, sir." Hope kindled in his mind.

" No personal reason whatever ? "

" Why—no, sir." The query was surprising. Morris was standing with his finger on a large-scale map on the wall.

" Come and look at this. You'll gather, from its boundaries, that Omo has had rather a chequered history."

" It's right on the borders of Ashanti, isn't it ? They must have seen a lot of fighting. I suppose," said Johnny apologetically, " I ought to know whose side they were on——"

" You'd know more than we do," was the dry rejoinder, as Morris resumed his chair. " Up to the early part of the century Omo was a kingdom—a very powerful one. It lost its Stool to the Ashanti in the risings of '64, but has maintained enough power, under successive chiefs, to be admitted as an ally state, rather than as a vassal. Since the fall of Prempeh its power is somewhat weakened, but as neighbouring territories are in the same situation, it's fairly secure."

" I suppose the river helps." He was scrutinising the map—wondering how nearly it approached to accuracy. No two maps of West Africa seemed to be alike ; he had long ago come to the conclusion that their makers, hopeless of arriving at truth, copied each other, added a few quirks for the sake of originality, sprinkled a few names around on the chance of not being more than sixty or seventy miles off the mark, and shrugged their shoulders on the possibilities of life or death involved in a map-reading. He and Kershaw—who had moved up behind his shoulder—comparing their own plans of the country, had discovered Prahsu, in two cases south-west of the sharp bend in the Prah river, in one north-east. This map of Morris's—corrected, he noticed, in various places by its owner—was probably the nearest to accuracy he had seen.

" And the ridge of high land between it and its hereditary enemies on the west." Morris was refilling his cup with coffee. " The nominal chief," he said thoughtfully, " 's a fellow called Kufi."

" Nominal's good ! " Foxy chuckled.

" What sort of a bloke's he ? " Kershaw had started to be interested.

" Ask him," Morris's thumb jerked towards Foxy. " He sees enough of Kufi—and his mamma !—on his up-country trips."

Foxy grunted.

" You can always start from scratch, when you're dealing with nigger. As big a liar as Ananias, as much of a thief as a jackdaw and as lazy as a sloth. Mr. Kufi fits nicely into the recipe."

" You're fond of them, aren't you ? " The Commissioner's faint smile lightened, briefly, his serious face.

" I'm not down on 'em like Bill Prewett—if that's what you mean."

" What about Bill ? "

Foxy turned down a short, spatulate thumb.

" He won't last through the night."

" Thank God for that. It would have been a hell of a thing to work out in court. Bill didn't mean it—of course."

" 'Course he didn't," affirmed Foxy stoutly. " Maudie—silly bitch—had been laying for Bill for months. And you know how he was about nigger ; never touched 'em. Johnny, here, will tell you he was blind when he went out, the other night. And when he found what had happened he lost his head ; that's all."

" Maudie's family won't see it that way."

" Nor the rest of the nigger push. They're all out for Bill's blood." Foxy paused. " Let 'em," he muttered. " The old chap that looks after the ferry'll save them their trouble ; Bill'll be catching the night tide."

After a silence Morris was the first to pull himself together.

" Well, now ; talking of our friends up at Omo——"

" They are friends ; are they ? " Johnny put in quickly. " I mean, well-disposed to the British ? "

" *All* the people in my district are well-disposed to the British." The Commissioner gave him a solemn look ; his cheeks wrinkled as he added : " Theoretically."

" Meaning to say," elucidated Foxy, for Johnny's benefit, " when the toe of the Chief's boot is behind them."

" They're not a bad lot—the Omos—considering," mused Morris. Considering what ? wondered Johnny ; but thought it wiser to let the point slide. Foxy, in an expository mood, chose to pick it up.

" Y' see," he said, turning to Johnny, " there's good nigger and bad nigger ; but good an' bad, if you get me, in a way that's got nothing to do with our moralities."

" I'm with you there." Kershaw was nodding. " There's blacks I'd trust—knowing they'd pinch the stopping out of my back teeth and lie their souls to hell as soon as look at me ; and there's others I wouldn't let within fifty yards—if they turned up with ' Good boy ' certificates round their necks."

Morris concurred.

" It's a thing you get to know only by living among them."

" Or you don't get to know it, and you're unlucky," said Foxy.

" Isn't it a pretty general rule," ventured Johnny, " that ' good ' nigger's thoroughbred ? I read somewhere that most of the trouble blows up among the bastard tribes—Bekwai, for instance : that's Ashanti-Adansi cross, isn't it ? "

The other three were smiling.

" I don't hold with armchair theories, and Bekwai happens to be in our good books at present," said Morris. " But one of our nice little problems is this Omo crowd. The chief's mother's from Bantama—she's pure-bred Ashanti. She married an Omo man, and they went and settled in Adansi country. Result—a beautiful hotch-potch of tribal squabbles, shows-down between rival fetishmen and hare-and-hounds with neighbouring powers, according to which happened to be topsides at the moment."

" Sounds lively. Do they find time for anything beside putting ju ju on each other and burning up each other's villages ? "

" They ain't so bad, from the trade point of view," allowed Foxy. " It's good rubber country, and the last chief, old Amoti, this chap's father, was a level-headed party—and keen on the bawbees. He got a lot of credit with us for stoppin' their larkin's around with the Ashanti——"

" But there was some gossip, wasn't there, about the head wife and the old Queen, up at Ejesu ? "

" Omo didn't come out on our side, the way that was expected." Morris answered Kershaw's interpolation. " Still, the Chief kept them at their rubber and oil——"

" And I take it they cleaned up in a big way when the shindy was over. Neutrality is a paying game," reflected Kershaw.

" It paid Amoti to the tune of forty wives, and settled the succession comfortably in favour of his eldest son "—Johnny felt the pale glint of Morris's eye—" with, of course, the help of the Basin."

" What's that, sir ? Some sort of geological formation ? "

" I was wondering how much you knew of your family's history," smiled the Commissioner.

" You mean, of the Gold Coast end of it ? Not much," he admitted. " You see, we weren't the Bristol branch——" He stopped. Rodríguez and Plant ; that wasn't the Bristol branch either. " I've got an old uncle who's something of an amateur of the slaving period—but it's not exactly a favourite topic with the rest of the family."

" Setting aside disagreeable matter—you probably don't know that your ancestor Matthew—later on the Abolition leader—concluded a trade treaty with the king of Omo, of sufficient importance to find its way into local records ? "

" No, I didn't know that, sir."

" I think his fellow traders looked on it as a bit of sharp practise, but it must have made a pile for somebody, before the slaving finished. So far as Omo's concerned, it made history. It gave them, incidentally, the Basin."

" An *actual* basin ? " Johnny was doubtful.

" Very actual." Morris's eyes twinkled. " Identical, in fact, with most of the iron pots used in native cooking. I've seen the thing ; I expect Sam has, too ? "

" I ain't on those terms with the fetish gentry ; all the same, no ill feelin'." Foxy bobbed his head in mimic respect ; the other returned the salute gravely.

" The point about this particular pot is, it contains a spirit which took up residence there after it was used for the blood brotherhood rites between your ancestor and the then king of Omo." He paused, to allow this to sink in. " As the story goes, this Matthew was something out of the ordinary in height and build, and the compact is supposed to have resulted in a great access of strength in the royal family."

" That sounds likely enough." Johnny considered it. " We've got a suit of clothes, supposed to have belonged to Matthew Flood. My Uncle

Harcourt's the only one who doesn't look like a clothes' moth when he gets into it."

"Well, it's a well-known tale round here, and the Basin's become a fetish object."

"That's a bit of a joke, isn't it?" Johnny was smiling broadly. "My Uncle Quentin will like that, when I tell him!"

"The thing that's puzzling is your not having heard of it before."

"It's not really a puzzle, sir," Johnny assured him. "Nobody's encouraged to talk about the Coast at home—I mean, apart from the missionary end of it. I certainly never heard we had any tie-up with Omo."

"You're the first Flood that's visited the Coast since 1764," Morris was saying, "and perhaps you'll understand why I was disposed against letting you loose in the district until I found out a little more about your intentions and—if I may put it this way, your character. You know—and the others will agree with me—in times like these, even well-meaning people can be responsible for a considerable amount of mischief: particularly, if, like yourself, they happen to have a backing of local superstition to lend authority to their actions. I heard of your arrival up at M'Bongo"—Johnny started; he knew vaguely that the village was nearly a hundred miles up-country—"and took a grave enough view of it to come down right away, to see what you were up to."

"You got a pretty bad jolt when you arrived, sir." His eyes were fixed on the floor, but Morris's voice, when he replied, sounded as if he were amused.

"My job hardens one to 'jolts.' Well, I take it you want to go up to Omo?"

A thought struck Johnny, but he hesitated before voicing it.

"I don't know what you think, sir; but—in view of what you've just told me—mightn't I, perhaps, have a chance of coming to terms with the chief? It would do me all sorts of good with my uncle, if I could hand him Omo—so to speak—on a plate."

"I'm afraid it's not likely to be quite so simple as that. What's your view, Sam?"

"They've had plenty of concession-hunters at Omo," said Foxy. "For his own private reasons, Kufi ain't inclined to play."

"I suppose the rubber brings him in a sufficient revenue to satisfy his tastes?"

"Or the old girl's. That's the nigger in the wood pile!" Foxy chuckled at the aptness of his metaphor, and neatly trapped a mosquito that went zinging past his ear. "That's the one you've got to reckon with."

"I may be talking out of my turn——"

"Come on; out with it."

Kershaw was standing, and the Commissioner had risen to face him. The two men eyed one another with a subtle antagonism obvious to the others, who sat silent.

"I dare say what I'm going to say won't be acceptable. It makes no difference to me if it isn't, because by God's mercy I've not got to trim my sails to any Government wind, and I'm dependent on nobody over here for my advancement. I'm free to go where I like, do what I like, and wag my tongue when I like—short of taking out extradition papers, people have got to take it."

"Well?" Morris remained impassive.

"I've got no interest in concessions, and this doesn't concern me. I'm just curious."

"I am perfectly prepared to satisfy your curiosity, so long as it does not involve the infringement of official discretion," was the smooth reply.

"It's said, by certain people, that in certain districts—this one was named among them—that concession seekers are being blocked, for a particular reason."

"Are you going to favour me with the reason?" as Kershaw paused.

"It's said that certain people—*privileged* people—have been informed of the Government's intention: the intention behind the hold-up of necessary material, the refusal to industrialise, the gradual transfer of power into the hands of the chiefs, the withdrawal of the Lands Bill—I could give you thirty or forty more examples of indifference to the welfare of the Coast——"

"I could give you, perhaps, twenty more examples," said Morris quietly. "But not of indifference; of—never mind. You were saying?"

"That the Government's getting ready to pull out. That we mean to pack it up—like the Portuguese and the Dutch have packed it up," the other flung at him. "The high-ups—those 'in the know'—will clear out with a packet, and the small fry—as usual, the small fry can sink or swim. If you know this to be unfounded, Mr. Morris, you'd better say it—or find somebody with a big voice to say it—because it's what about ten thousand people are saying, up and down the Coast."

There was a silence.

"Mr. Kershaw. It is not for me to answer those questions—if I knew the answers. It is not even for me to conjecture on them. I am concerned only with the proper performance of my duties—not with the length of their duration.

"So far as I am concerned, I can swear I've never obstructed any trading interests which I was convinced were concerned in the ultimate good of the district, and likely to turn out well for those who put them into effect. But do not forget"—the white blade of his glance cut across the other's—"I'm here to protect the coloured race, as well as the white. I am against any form of exploitation which infringes on the rights of well-organised communities and reduces the law-power of the chiefs over the lives of their subjects. The only way to govern the native is through his own law system. Anything else, in the long run, must lead to a state of affairs like they have on the Belgian Congo—or, alternatively, to the break down of British rule."

"A pity they don't see it that way in Whitehall," mumbled Foxy.

"I don't deny," continued Morris, "that, for the last six months, we've not been encouraging up-country expeditions. Whether they're after concessions, or bugs, or anthropological data—people are a confounded nuisance when they go down with sleeping sickness or snake-bite, in some unget-at-able corner of the district. We've got other things to occupy our minds. Are you answered, Mr. Kershaw?"

"Yes—and no." Kershaw's teeth flashed as he jangled the coins in his pockets. "What about a rising?"

"Please God, there'll be no rising!" The sharpness of the reply startled the room. "The temperature's jumpy. Secret societies are always a sign of unrest, and we've got a crop of them. There's a lot of witchcraft, under the rose, and, taking them by and large, the signs and portents aren't conducive to picnicking in the bush. What of it? We've had the same kind of thing a dozen times before, and it's died down."

"Then we take it the recruiting's to help it to die down?"

"That's the idea." Morris spoke shortly; he had evidently finished with Kershaw. "Well, Flood; I think we can arrange to send you up to Omo."

"That's very good of you, sir!"

"I'll only make one condition," said Morris. "That you look after my business as well as your own."

"I'm surprised you can find any use for me—after the exhibition I made of myself, over the guns." This was coals of fire.

"Quite a useful exhibition." The grim mouth relaxed. "It showed, among other things, that you've got some notion of handling natives, and it proved your fluency in the dialect. The version you used on Mfabo won't quite pass at Omo, but it will see you through, without too much dependence on a linguist. When do you leave, Sam?"

"I'm not partic'lar. I've done as much as I can do here; we could set out to-morrow—or next day. I'd have liked to have seen old Prewett out, before draggin' the anchor."

Morris was chewing his lip; they were surprised to hear him say, to Kershaw:

"What's your idea? To go up with them?"

"I wouldn't say no to a bit of shooting, upstream, Chief. What's it they say? 'Two men for the pot, one man for the shot?'" Kershaw's green twinkle spread in ripples over his face. "Meaning, I take it, that if you fall into the hands of cannibals, two of you may be for it, but the third's likely to get away and give the alarm."

"A nice little parable; is it your own invention?" The Commissioner smiled dryly. "How much of the language do you know?"

"Not enough to go preaching sedition to the natives!"

"You'd better not," was the grim reply. "Very well—you can go, so long as you do as you're told. You understand, this expedition is in charge of Biddle. He'll have my orders to turn the canoes round and start back, if he has any trouble with either of you." He nodded a curt good night. "Good night, Kershaw. Good night, Sam; I'll see you in the morning. You'll pardon me—both of you—for dismissing you; I want to talk to Mr. Flood."

The room became very small, very intimate, after the door closed behind them. Morris took a cigarette—the first he had lit that evening—and smoked it in an odd, detached manner : the way, thought Johnny, a monk might smoke for the first time ! Slowly, distastefully, almost disapprovingly. After a few puffs he laid it down. A dedicated man ; one who had deliberately put out of his life all that might prejudice the task to which it was devoted. The slow recognition of the fact that here was a man who inspired complete devotion in those who worked under him began to take possession of Johnny's mind. Long before the Commissioner spoke, he knew he was ready to assume any task Morris laid on him however onerous.

Kershaw and Foxy passed out on the portico : Foxy was saying :

" And, mind you, I'm takin' no fancy chiffoniers and stained-glass spittoons up in the canoes with me ! "

As their voices trailed away down the steps, Morris was frowning.

" Stupid fellow ! " And Johnny knew he was not referring to Foxy. " It's an astounding thing, that some people can't take discipline as part of their achievement. I'm sending one of the finest shots in the country with you. I need not add," said Morris, turning away, " that if there were the remotest question of Kershaw's gifts in that respect being called for, I wouldn't allow you to go."

Again silence fell. Morris had gone to the window, and inclined his head close to the dark pane, against which the moths were plastered in a pale confetti. Johnny thought he was looking out, then, from the angle of his head, knew he was listening to the drums.

" Now, what's all that about. . . . Be bothered to them, there's as much jabber going on as you'd hear in the news-room of *The Times* ! " He listened for a moment longer, and his lips were grim. Presently he returned to his chair opposite Johnny's.

" Sit down, my boy. I have a great many things to say to you."

CHAPTER SEVEN

I

THE whole of the following day was taken up with preparations. Kershaw's boys, used, by now, to the routine of departures, looked after the baggage, while Kershaw himself dismantled " Maskelyne and Cook "—the inanimate cause of a disagreement with Foxy. " Who d'you think drinks water where we're going ? Or coffee ? Or tea ? If that infernal machine gets in among my freight I'll have it sunk up-river." All their non-portable stuff was going up, for the present, to Prewett's ; one of the men who was moving in there—it being already taken for granted Prewett would have no more use for his domicile—had agreed to be responsible for it during their absence. It was noticeable that when Kershaw dropped casually, in Easy Emma's, a hint that the Vickers hut was available, temporarily, to anyone who cared to have a change from his present quarters, there were no offers. It was not only the blacks who shied away from the proximity of the Fort.

There were ammunition, stores, trading goods to be collected. As it was his first up-country trip, Johnny was interested to accompany Foxy on his excursions into the trading quarters scattered haphazard through the jumble of the town. Familiar as he was, by now, with the less presentable aspects of the coastal stations, he had inwardly to admit he had never seen anything like Charlestown : like the junk-heaps, the makeshifts, the crazy structures, less durable than card houses, puffing out their stenches with the clouds of flies that zoomed ceaselessly about them. Every alley was knee-deep in dust : it was easy to imagine them in the rainy season—turned to rivers of mud, to a crawling slime which, as it rose, slowly invaded the so-called " houses " in which human beings ate and slept, copulated and brought forth children. No wonder all the people were diseased : that a cloud of stupefaction lay upon them ; that every eye seemed glazed with blankness and every movement infused with an inexpressible lassitude.

On the fringe of this area of devastation, a row of perked-up, apparently newish dwellings was pointed out by Foxy as the houses of the " white-collar " workers : the negro clerks and office workers. " That's your pal Komuntale's. Wonder where that bastard's got himself to this morning ! " Johnny wondered, too, what had become of Mrs. Komuntale and her pink notepaper, as he glanced at the ramshackle façade, the window frames set in askew—though showing glimpses of Nottingham lace curtain. It was certainly a little smarter than the others, but the tin roof was slipping and part of the stoop was actually unfinished ; it was eloquent of local labour at its cheapest and most slipshod. The Komuntales', in common with the rest, was silted half-way up its sides with the residue of Mrs. Komuntale's efforts at house-keeping.

Their final visit was to the storehouse under the Residency, where they picked out the presents that were to sweeten their relationships with Kufi : a cloth for the head wife—striped plum-coloured and gold satin, with a binding of galloon, some necklaces of blue glass bugles, a parasol, whose rufflings of pink and buff taffetas suggested vicarage garden parties and the pomps of rural England. " For God's sake let's not forget the old woman," said Foxy, picking out the gaudiest items he could find, in a basket of imitation jewellery. For Kufi there were binoculars, which it appeared he had coveted for a long time—fully convinced that, with their assistance, he, like Morris, would see that which was hid from common people ; a case of gin ; various oddments of apparel—which included a top hat, a vintage specimen from the excellent Messrs. Lock of St. James's Street ; a set of paddles for the chief's canoe—very elaborately carved, and decorated with fetish symbols ; and a case of Sheffield cutlery, consisting of hunting knives, specially made for the coastal trade and mounted in Accra on ornate ivory handles. " Not that that'll satisfy old Greedy-guts," Foxy was saying, when they found Morris standing behind them.

" Well—good hunting, you men ! I'm sorry I shan't be here to see you off."

"You're not starting out again—already—sir?" Johnny's naïve surprise appeared to amuse the Commissioner.

"No rest for the wicked! I thought I'd remind you"—his eyes met Foxy's; the two men exchanged a glance of understanding—"that if, by any chance, you found you'd forgotten anything, we'll be on the look out. I'm taking the left bend of the river; you'll be going on, up the main stream. By the time you get there, we'll be at Diloli: not more than twenty miles away—as the crow flies. A rocket'll fetch us—if you run short of anything important."

He shook hands with the pair of them; as his slight, upright figure marched out into the sunlight, Johnny's sentiments broke from him in an involuntary exclamation.

"He's hundred caret—that little man!"

"Best Commissioner this district's ever had," grunted Foxy. "Knows the native as he knows his eye teeth. If Whitehall had a particle of common savvy, they'd put him in at Accra, in place of some of the stuffed dummies that come out for a couple o' years' tuft-huntin', and go back with a title and a chestful o' tinware an' ribbons to splash about at City dinners. The traders' best friend: that's Morris. I ain't biddable by nature"—he grimaced—"but what Morris says goes—with me."

Johnny felt it "went" with him, also. He went on with Foxy, to the barracks, where, in the magazine, they picked up a bundle of rockets, which, Foxy explained, would be called for later, and taken down to the canoes.

"First time I've carried fireworks! But you got to be fussy, when you're convoyin' quality." He smirked.

. . . Prewett died towards noon. At sunset, Johnny stood by the ready-dug grave, from which the diggers had removed its wooden lid, listening once more to the words of immortality—grown so familiar that he could recite them from memory. How many times since his arrival had he taken part in this last quiet scene? He had lost count. Like the rest, he had grown more attentive to a rustle in the long, surrounding grass, which might mean a snake, than to the ceremony itself. Yet one part of his mind caught at the words as they were spoken, and his memory went back to that grave of a stranger, by the side of which he had seemed, for the first time, to make contact with the true Africa.

"We shall not sleep, but we shall all be changed, in a moment, in the twinkling of an eye, at the last trump (for the trumpet shall sound), and the dead shall be raised incorruptible, and we shall all be changed. . . . Death is swallowed up in victory . . . forasmuch as ye know that your labour is not vain in the Lord."

Not vain in the Lord.

The western sky, blazoned with vermilion, with copper, with a hundred tones of rose and with a gold too brilliant for the eye to endure, spoke its asseveration to the group of men bare-headed about Prewett's grave. Not vain in the Lord; had Prewett found that out by now? Had he discovered, in a blaze of gold and rose, the meaning of his long ordeal, the waste of his hopes, the squandering of his talents and the moment of desperation that swept him to his end? Not vain in the Lord; were the words merely a piece of sonorous rhetoric, or was it true that that record of non-achievement meant something in the great, inapprehensible scheme of the universe?

Do I believe? asked Johnny Flood inwardly. It had never occurred to him before to question his beliefs, or the code on which they were founded. The slight bias against "religion," as such, which he had acquired through his father's melancholy pomposities and the enforced religious observance of his childhood and youth, had long given way to toleration. He could speak the Creed without embarrassment, without doubt—and without thought. The Christian doctrine was good because it provided a set of rules, which had proved valuable in the regulation of human relationships and affairs; and however many sects the followers of Christ chose to split themselves into, they all agreed on essentials. Himself agreeing with them, Johnny felt entitled (despite cousin Charlotte) to call himself a Christian. But he suddenly knew that this shallow acceptance of predetermined values was not enough, and it came to him, with a sense of blinding shock, that Belief could not stop short at Christianity.

The volume of his experiences during the last five months rushed over him like a wave; curled in on him; he felt it sapping his easy, accepted foundations. He thought of the government launch, bearing Morris away into the green hell of the bush, defenceless, but for his belief. Whether Morris "believed" in the articles of any set form of religion had, when one came to think, little to do with it. It came to Johnny, without words, more like a sensation than a thought, that Belief, in whatever god, whatever creed—even, possibly, in those dark plerophories of the bush, was a projection of Divine mind; a link between mutability and the Eternal, and that, without Belief, man was not man, but less than man. Belief: the unifying thing between man and man, between white and black. In one case shaped like a Cross, like a Crown of Thorns, like a Loving Face; in another like the tempest that rives the forest, like an iron vessel, like a Face of Fear. It struck him that it took more courage to accept the Fear belief than the Belief in love.

"O holy and merciful Saviour, thou most worthy Judge eternal, suffer us not, at our last hour, for any pains of death, to fall from Thee."

When it was over, he turned away sharply, not wishing to speak to the Gummeridges. He was a little ashamed of the evasion, but told himself he owed them no debt of gratitude; they had known Prewett longer than he. If friendship called for an acknowledgment, Foxy was there, to say or do whatever was necessary. Nor did he wish, immediately, to join his friends. His pledge to the dead man lay heavy on him: its reminder lay in each pair of eyes that met his, as he trudged from the cemetery grass on to the bare, sandy road; and in that area of dereliction which linked the small surviving patch of Charlestown itself with its own Golgotha. Go home and tell them this; it was as though Prewett walked beside him—that my end may not be vain in the Lord.

They were starting soon after dawn. He looked round the room, stark as when they arrived, and at the bundles lashed into their sheets of mackintosh, ready for the canoes. Kershaw came in while he stood, indecisive, surrounded by his belongings.

" What's biting you, fella ? "

" Nothing. I can't get out of my head there's something I've forgotten," Johnny contradicted himself.

" You'd better get it into your head, whatever it is ; you won't have any chances to make up for loss of memory after to-morrow. Now what the blazes—— ? " Kershaw broke off ; he was staring across Johnny's shoulder. " Take a look behind you ; looks as if your washing's turned up after all ! "

At some forty paces from the hut, down the slope of the beach, two women were standing : one, stout, middle-aged, dressed in the mission blouse and petticoat, with a bundle on her kerchiefed head. The other, young enough to be her daughter, was a " cloth-woman "—in place of Europeanised dress, she wore the cloth of a native, tucked up under her armpits. They stood in the twilight, with the off-shore breeze stirring their garments, evidently ill at ease, evidently consulting with one another as to the next step to be taken.

" Silly cows—they're scared to come closer. You'd better go down and claim your goods."

By the time Johnny reached them, the bundle had been deposited on the sand, and its bearer greeted him with a rich flow of trade English.

" Ha Daddy "—a term, he had discovered, not of impudence but of respect, along the coast—" I see you, Daddy. Yo' tink yo' loss all dem trousah, all dem shirt. Not ebry bit dat."

" You lib for washerwoman ? " inquired Johnny.

The speaker vigorously nodded her head.

" Dizzy Lou—dat's me. Lib nah Pos' hamfish oberside Missis Komuntale. Washum plenty, washum good. Lib fo' send yo' bwoy na narin—na pussin come ! Na sun-time—no come ! Na ebenin—no come ! Na, Daddy, how come yo' bwoy don' come fo' all dem shirt—— ? "

He was aware of a pair of eyes, dark as a stag's, that fixed themselves on him mournfully ; the tears that brimmed them gave the effect of a sheath of glass, set in between the upper and lower lids. The bulging of her cotton cloth betrayed pregnancy, and its fluttering her fear.

" What's the matter with her ? " he asked of the older woman, doubting that the girl could speak.

" Dem black gal, she po' stupid nigger." The initiative readiness of the Negro to accept his own kind at the valuation of his white masters spoke in the reply, but the anxious tenderness of a bitch for its young showed in the roll of the speaker's eyes towards Akiki. Dizzy Lou twisted her hands suddenly into a fold of her petticoat. " She come, beg yah, do nah, say—wheah dem wo-wo bwoy done put himseff ? He lib fo' sick ? He lib fo' drunk ? Do nah, Daddy, tell dem bwoy Tich he stop hide himself—— ! "

He questioned them, both in the dialect and in their own kind of English, and got the impression they were both too frightened properly to answer. From Akiki he got no words at all ; she was half-stunned, half-paralysed. Her feet dragged in the dust when her companion led her away, as though she were sleep-walking. He was satisfied that they knew nothing of Tich's whereabouts.

Kershaw's conjecture was possibly right—that Tich had run off into the bush. The incompatibility of Tich, with his taste for the lively existence of the Coast, his pride in his status as a house-boy to whites and his fancy for dressing up, with the existence of the bush families, was a point not to be dwelt upon. What other explanation was there to offer?

II

They had decided to turn in early, but neither was sleepy when Foxy left them, with the warning that the carriers would be there at crack of dawn to collect the baggage. Kershaw again gave Johnny the hypodermic, which seemed to have a miraculous effect in reducing the fever, and administered a shot to himself. The surf boomed, the moon staggered uncertainly between banks of cloud, the wind blew the sand against the shutters like fine rain; occasionally it rose to a shrill whine, and, somewhere in the black pile of the Fort, found the flagstaff and whistled in the flapping cords.

Under the mosquito netting, Johnny thought of the great elms at the end of the lower lawn, blocking themselves against a thin blue sky in masses of green, and of the girls in their white summer frocks, sitting in the shadow: Emily reading to Miranda, and Polly darning a sock, with a sweet, drowsy expression on her rosy face. Emily's voice . . . soft, slow, sometimes lingering on a word, as though she wished to make sure of extracting its utmost meaning; did anybody else read aloud, like that? It was queer, how she *obliged* one to listen to her—lying on one's back, with eyes closed and hands linked behind one's head.

Was there still a world where girls in white frocks—like water-lilies supported by their leaves—sat on green lawns, reading to each other in soft voices, and sometimes brushing away the soft, clean, silken hair that the breeze blew across their faces? Where streams flowed gently over brown trout and larks sang above the young corn? O fabulous world! No less fabulous than the one where the Sieur Guillaume crashed about among his gilliflowers of gold and Sir Peter Harpdon met his somewhat mawkish end at the hands of his cousin. Yes, it was Emily who, while still quite a little girl, had brought the red and the blue and the gold of chivalry into the bleak Guerdon schoolroom, where, certainly, no one had ever read poetry before. One could see Winkle, gulping it down, like someone tasting champagne for the first time: a little choked by the effervescence, a little bewildered, not quite sure whether she was liking it or not—and yet ravenous for more!

As for himself, most of it went over his head. He would have found other things to do, if it had been anyone but—Emily. And, even so, he had never admitted, even to himself, the sweet enchantment of that voice, that sometimes—it was not often—conquered his natural, boy's inclination to be about manlier things than listening, half-asleep, to a little girl reading poetry !

Half-ashamed of the surrender to sentiment, he allowed his mind to wander in those green pastures of a youth which he knew had not been so very happy at the time, but which, in retrospect seemed all sunlight and starlight—because it held Emily. Those snatched and happy moments, at week-ends, when the three—sometimes the four of them, for Polly was often of the party—went picnicking in summer, or, in winter, sat in the schoolroom, when Emily's delicate fingers would find occupations one would not have noticed, or would have jeered at, if it had been anyone but —Emily ! Sticking " specimens " into Winkle's albums—Miranda had inherited, with no particular enthusiasm, Vicky's flower collection ; but it was mainly Emily's industry that added to it from Guerdon hedgerows and pastures. Making " skeletons " of leaves. Building strange little landscapes, with earth, and rock plants, and shells, and bits of china, on big platters " borrowed " from the kitchen.

They played fewer games than most young people, because Winkle's hip troubled her, and Emily had not been brought up to play games ; yet there was an entrancing inventiveness about the occupations which Emily devised which brought light and amusement into the dull schoolroom, and even exerted the fascination of novelty over Johnny himself. " What nonsense have you girls been up to this week ? " was his excuse (to himself) for his invariable appearance in the schoolroom, at the hour the girls were supposed to have their tea. No one who appreciated manual dexterity could have been scornful about Emily's little landscapes, although one could hardly be expected to enter into the romances the girls wove about them.

Then came the holidays : with Dorset and Gilbert home from school, bringing their schoolfellows, and filling the house with a different atmosphere —grandly masculine ; with Dorset playing the young heir with a flourish, and showing off prodigiously for the benefit of his guests. Cricket matches, swimming contests, bicycle gymkhanas, skating parties, cubbing—according to the season : and Dorset glittering through all of them, admired and flattered to his heart's content—even by Gilbert, accustomed to basking in the reflected glory of his elder brother.

In all that, somehow, Emily vanished ; or, if there, shrank into herself, and was obviously discomposed by adolescent attempts at flirtation. Captive at Harcourt's chariot wheel, Johnny saw little of the festivities, and sometimes begrudged his brothers their freedom ; when at home, however, he marked and wondered at Emily's shyness—she, so free and easy with him and Winkle—in the company of strangers ; and tried not to be glad of it, and of her recoil from Dorset, which all her good manners could not wholly conceal. Doss was too swaggering, too thrusting, altogether too man-of-the-world for a simple girl like Emily : thus he explained it, to his own satisfaction. He got a thrill, sometimes, in protecting her from the other boys' too pressing attentions ; but it was good when the holidays were over, and the happy, normal rhythm of Guerdon life re-established itself.

Dorset's last term coincided with Lady Cullen's decision to send Emily to be " finished " in Paris : in no fashionable school, where she might be exposed to dangerous, Catholic influences, but in a good Protestant family, where she would perfect her language and get taken to all the galleries, museums and national monuments that a young English lady might visit without having her morals corrupted. And something happened in Paris. No one was told what it was, but Emily was back at the end of six months, or thereabouts, instead of the twelve months for which her guardian had stipulated.

He had not seen her until Christmas, at a ball at Clifton to which they were all invited. Johnny went—not because he felt he would be missed if he stayed away, but because he hoped to have one dance with Emily. He arrived late—later than the others, because it chanced, of course, to be one of the evenings when old Derbin kept them late at the office ; he had to scorch back on his bicycle, fling himself into his clothes, and persuade a reluctant groom to take him over in the dog cart. And the first thing he saw was Emily, dancing with Dorset.

For a moment he doubted whether it was she, or someone very like her. Her beautiful hair, which he had last seen in plaits down her back, was coiled on the crown of her little head, and her slim, still childish shoulders rose naked from a sparkling whiteness, like—like the surf when the sun was on it ! She was all in white, and the thin material of her gown swung out with her movements and clung like gossamer to the clothes of her partner. She was almost like a trail of mist in Dorset's arms.

When he had accepted that it was she, he tried to discover what—apart from the clothes, and the way she did her hair—was different about her, and suddenly realised what it was. She had lost her shyness. Her eyes luminous with the rapture of the music and the movement, her lips held the sweet, unconscious smile of one secure in her own loveliness. Dorset spoke to her, and she answered, and they laughed, as though she had said something witty ; and it was their laughter, as much as the look on Dorset's face, and on Emily's, as she lifted it towards his, that told Johnny that Emily was no longer any business of his. Dorset with his beauty and his arrogance had won her, as he won every woman he favoured with his regard.

Johnny turned and walked stiffly out of the ballroom. It is certain he had never, up to that moment, realised that he loved Emily Temple. Confused, flinching from the revelation, he tried to argue with himself. Emily had always *disliked* Doss ; Miranda had said so. Perfect as her manners were, she had never been " herself " when he was in the room ; she seemed to become cold, petrified, even at the sound of his voice.

Well—all that was over. And just as well. What had he—Johnny—to offer Emily, beside Doss, with Guerdon in his hand ?

He waited to make sure of his composure, before going and asking her for a dance. Her greeting was radiant ; she was " delighted " to see him. Of course she had kept a dance for him, on hearing he had been detained ; She handed him her programme, a little coquettishly, so that he might see what a favour he had been granted. He looked quickly to see whether there was another space, beside the one in which he scribbled his name. Not one—of course ; Gilbert's name down twice, and Dorset's initials no less than five times—including the supper dance.

" I say, Doss *has* been poaching ! I think, considering I couldn't help being late, he might let me have one of his."

" Ask him," said Emily, and smiled at him across the shoulder of her partner, as she was swept away. She knew he would not. Her look was not the look she had given Dorset, as they swung, in all the triumph of their youth and beauty, round the ballroom. To think of a miserable little runt like me ever thinking about Emily ! What a superb fellow Doss is. What a lucky devil.

Since that night, the times he had seen her could be counted on both hands. Well, almost. Eleven times in all ; he knew, for he had counted them. Sometimes he would pick out one moment, sometimes another, to console himself in his frequent longing for Emily. There was a year when he had gone about in constant dread of hearing they were engaged. A hint came along some channel or other—and was captured and passed on by Miranda—that Lady Cullen considered Emily too young for an engagement. " And so I should think ! " snorted Miranda. " Doss will fall in love with at least twenty girls in the next twelve months—and if Emily doesn't marry you I hope she'll marry a *complete* stranger. I'll certainly be disgusted if she marries Doss ! "

The Cullens had begun to spend a great deal of time in town, Sir Vaughn having become vice-chairman of one of his scientific circles ; Emily's visits to Guerdon became more and more brief, more widely spaced in the calendar. But Doss, of course, was seeing her in London. Considering his declared preference for the country, and that he was supposed to be in training for " the young squire," it was remarkable how many excuses he made to go up to town, and how bland Dromore—who had to foot the bills—was about his frequent and prolonged absences.

Emily, in seal-skin, stopping for a moment to smile in the snow-drifted porch, before stepping into church. Emily, all be-veiled and be-cloaked, in the Cullens' new Panhard, waving her hand as they flashed past across the Down. Emily, surrounded by half a dozen men, all anxious to see her to her carriage, after a concert of the Clifton Amateur Orchestra. With such flashes Johnny had to content himself, weaving into them all he could of emotion, of significance. Dorset could ride across the park at any time the Cullens were at home, and see his mistress. There was no question of inviting his haughty astonishment if he should find her entertaining his youngest brother.

Still no engagement was announced : but Johnny, like everyone else at Guerdon, accepted the " understanding " which gave Emily to Dorset : which even pressed her upon him—as though that should be needed !—a little to the embarrassment of two high-spirited young people, both capable of making up their own minds.

Lying in the darkness, he wondered if it had yet happened. Each letter from home that he opened he scanned to its conclusion in search of their names, before settling down to read it; not that he need do so—the betrothal of Dorset and Emily would certainly be front-page news, when it came! And sometimes when, owing to his changes of address, there was a longer gap than usual between letters, he hoped that it had happened, and that everyone was so excited, so taken up with the formalities, the correspondence, the preliminaries and arrangements for the marriage that they had no time to think of him. But that would not be so, in the case of Winkle. . . . If only it could have been settled and done with before he got back: that he might have been spared the first flush of Emily's radiance, Dorset's proud, patronising satisfaction!

He started, and almost shouted out with fright, as something pressed on him through the mosquito netting.

" What is it? Have I been bawling again?" he gasped as he grasped it was Kershaw.

" Shut up: there's somebody round the place."

III

The wind had gone down, and a dead hush lay along the beach. There was a grey light of the moon behind cloud.

" There's nothing here—not even fresh footmarks. It wouldn't be natives —and what would whites want here, at this time of night? You must have imagined it."

" Looks as if you're right." But the admission was grudging; Kershaw seemed reluctant to return to the hut. Circling in the greyness, his head thrust forward, his eyes on the ground, he reminded Johnny of some ghostly hound, trying to pick up a lost scent. He now went down towards the sand where it was wet, towards the band of the surf. Johnny saw him stop, bend down, and beckon.

" That's no ghosts, at any rate."

Johnny's observation of the object at which he was pointing was blurred by his surprise at the comment.

" Did you say ghosts? Have—have you seen any?"

" Every night," was the cheerful answer. " Stinkin' with 'em. You haven't met voodoo, have you? Well, when you do, you'll know the smell of it."

" Then the natives are right——?"

Kershaw shrugged his shoulders.

" I'd take a long bet there's been a pretty powerful voodoo merchant round here, at some moment of the place's history."

" It couldn't be collective mind, could it?" Johnny hesitated. " We're on the site, you know, of the old barracoons——"

" Call it what you like. The stuff gets down into the ground—and sticks. Until something happens to make it boil up. Prewett was the one to tell you——" He stopped, looking down at the sand, where the keel of a boat was visible, and a splather of footmarks, confused and half-inundated, but evidently of recent making, told of a landing. Kershaw followed the footprints a little way—they led off in the direction Johnny had taken on his first morning, in search of a bathing place—and returned.

" Come on. We'll get the Colts, and see what these fellows are up to. Nobody lands in a surf boat at this time of night, unless he's got particular and private business ! It'll be one hell of a joke, if we happen on the trail of another of Mr. Komuntale's little consignments."

The footprints continued along the line of the surf for some distance, then turned sharply inland.

" That's what I was expecting," muttered Kershaw.

" We're off Endor, aren't we ? "

" It's about three-quarters of a mile inland. Now you're going to see something," he promised.

They had reached a spectral region, which Johnny recognised as the remains of a mangrove swamp.

" It's a tongue of the Great Swamp," Kershaw was murmuring, " and the blacks don't like it, because it's supposed to be h'anted. But it's useful. You'll see. There's a bit of the stream comes down here, scooping round behind Endor, that joins on with main waterway half a dozen loops or so above the creek. If we go canny, we may learn something to our—and Morris's !—advantage."

Passing from the great, grey ribs of the prehistoric monster that was the dead swamp into the exuberant belt of screwpine and creeper that marked the line of the bush's encroachment on what had been the mangroves' domain, Johnny was aware of something unfamiliar. They had gone some distance before he realised it was the absence of sound.

He knew well the noises of the swamps by night : the sighing cough of crocodile, the rush and whirr of crabs, the sucking splash of mudfish in the slime, the innumerable grunts, whines and croakings of their denizens during the hours when, immune from human invasion, they gambolled in the dark. But now, save for the creaking of trees and the irrepressible chatter of frogs, it was as silent as by day. There could be but one explanation for so unnatural a state of affairs : there were others beside themselves near the stream.

The bank of clouds had moved away. The steady moonlight, reduced by the vegetation to a dark and smoky silver, concentrated itself ahead in a patch of dazzling white he knew to be water. Moving with caution, the two men saw what one of them, at least, expected to see : a small dugout, pulled half-way up on the beach, and four men busying themselves about it. Johnny had had, from childhood, the gift of silent movement ; it served him now, as, inch by inch, he worked himself into a position from which he could command, without being seen, the party on the beach. He could hear Kershaw, who, on account of his height, had more difficulty in moving noiselessly, breathing evenly at his shoulder.

All four were clothed only in loin-cloths ; three worked under the fourth's direction—a big, ebony figure, straddling the beach, which, hands on hips, dominated its companions : who, to the eyes of the observers, showed more than usual native ineptitude in their flustered and fumbling attempts to do its bidding. Clumsiness was to be taken for granted, but these three were scared to death, and unwilling : clearly only kept on their job by fear of the one who commanded them. Keeping up a shrill chatter of frightened birds, throwing scared glances over their shoulders, bunching together, they got in each other's way, dropped sections of the bulky loads they were in process of transferring from the beach to the canoe, and presented so ludicrous a spectacle of terrified disorder that Johnny felt Kershaw's chest shaking with laughter against his shoulder.

The cause of their fright was easy to conjecture ; it was less easy to determine what form of persuasion had brought them to the stream at an hour when all sorts of malignant shapes might be encountered on the edge of the swamp. It was only when the leader turned, taking the moonlight full on a face which looked as though it might be polished with black lead, that Johnny caught his breath. Turning his head across his shoulder to Kershaw, he mouthed the syllables—" Komuntale ! "

He felt Kershaw cautiously lifting his right hand, and guessed his finger was on the trigger of the Colt ; but, before he had time to press it, something —a twig, or a crab's shell—went off with a small, sharp report under Johnny's foot. Both held their breath as the men on the beach leapt round, as they were conscious of the glitter of four pairs of eyeballs, of four sets of ivory displayed as the jaws of the owners fell open in dismay. Johnny had shifted involuntarily ; he knew he was now blocking Kershaw's line of fire, and cursed under his breath as he tried to repair the effect of his own clumsiness. But an astonishing thing had happened.

The eyes of the four men were not fixed on him and his companion, but on a spot ten or twelve paces to the right of where they stood. An acute warning of danger from another source stiffened Johnny where he stood ; but while one of the men let out a howl and pointed, in that split second when he wondered whether to fire—all four, Komuntale included, had taken to their heels. Puzzled, they watched them and their shadows go leaping along the beach, saw the bright shafts of silver shoot up from a shallow water-splash as they crossed it, saw darkness swallow them at the foot of a clump of trees.

The dugout, half-loaded, lay deserted under the moon, but Johnny knew that he was not alone in his disinclination, immediately to go down and examine it. What had scared the four men—and even been enough to scare Komuntale, whose courage, or scepticism, or sheer desperation, was, no doubt, the thing responsible for being there ?

It was possible, of course, that they had glimpsed something, some effect of moonlight and shadow, and had taken it for a sasabonsum, an ombuiri, or one of those disquieting apparitions that walk in lonely places after nightfall. If so, and if Johnny and his companion were to remain hidden, it was probably they might return. Johnny had not availed himself of the Bristol library in vain : he knew that, when one has seen a spirit, it is important to examine the ground, to determine what class it belongs to— whether it is of the inferior grade that is amenable to a simple charm of the kind one has usually about one ; or whether for safety's sake it is better to make haste to the fetish practitioners, whose business it is to divert the greater evils. At least, one might as well give these authorities a chance of proving whether they were correct in their observations. He therefore stood still, and impressed stillness on Kershaw, with a clutch above the elbow. And the moments went by, and there was nothing beside the stream except the chatter of the tree-frogs and a brief rustle, which might be a snake, or might be a crab, trying to bury its unwieldy body deeper in slime.

A smothered grunt came from Kershaw.

" I've got a devil of a cramp—I can't help it—I've got to move ! "

Leaving the other rubbing the calf of his leg, Johnny moved cautiously towards the right. The feeling of danger, of being covered by an unseen watcher, increased, if anything, and he felt the sweat break out and roll in cold drops down his spine. His hand, with the Colt in it, felt as if it had gone dead at the wrist ; he doubted if he could, in crisis, make use of it. The sensation became, at last, so unbearable that he stood still, with the almost uncontrollable shudders running down into the earth at his feet.

When, slowly, he turned his head, his heart seemed to stop. A figure was standing within arm's length of his position at the foot of a pine.

For a second imagination flared, as it must, in such circumstances, flare in one whose experience, though small, is conditioned by his reading. He remembered the encounter, dreaded by Fan hunters, with the spirit whose one side is rotted away and the other sound ; and whether you see the dawn depends on which side of you he passes. . . .

And then he saw the figure was not standing. It was hanging motionless from a length of tie-tie, looped over a branch of the pine. Its legs had been eaten away—perhaps by a leopard—half-way up the thigh. It was Tich.

IV

" So—*Sur*. So—*Sur*. So—*Sur*. Ush !"

The canoe-boys' muscles fought the current, their grunting chant accompanied the swing of their bodies. The boys with the bamboo poles helped to keep the long, lightly-built craft away from the banks and the tree-root tangles that stretched out into midstream.

Under the grass-thatched cabin amidships, Johnny hung on to the bush-rope lacing that ran round the gunwale, as the canoe bucked, reared and threatened to pitch its occupants into the race. The others, nonchalantly lighting their pipes, seemed to have mastered the art of equilibrium in a craft which conformed to none of the rules governing water transport, and chuckled as Johnny, swearing, removed his ribs from painful contact with the chop-boxes which were stowed so as to afford some support for the passengers' spines.

Not that there was much of him to be damaged. Heat had pared from him such small reserves of flesh as had ever managed to accumulate on his meagre frame. The deep-yellowish veneer the sun had spread on his face had turned to near-black, and a doubtful bristle, crawling over the jawbone, supplemented a straggling, dust-coloured moustache. Foxy's eyes dwelt with approval on this youngster who took, with laconic toughness, the hazards of an exploit in sharp contrast with his former experiences.

"Sooner be on the old *Cariba*, eh ?"

"Remember Bob, the bar steward ? I could do with one of Bob's Planters now !" Kershaw puffed away a swarm of sandflies with a volume of smoke.

"All the same, I'd sooner this style o' travel than the Frogs' pattern. There's something in the smell of oil goes to my stomach. Know them French river steamers ?"

Picking himself off the shoulder-blades of the nearest rower, Johnny grunted a denial.

"Make you sweat oil forty-eight hours after comin' ashore. Lit me old pipe, and the whole of me bloody whiskers went up in a blaze, like a bunch o' cotton-waste," said Foxy, with the gravity in mendacity for which his profession is noted.

So suddenly that it seemed incredible, they were past the rapids ; the water ceased to run back flaked with white, and spread itself like oiled silk between the shallow banks. Johnny dragged his cramped limbs from under the awning, stretched and dropped his arms on the roof for support. The skin of hands and arms from knuckles to elbows was blistered raw ; it was a minor discomfort in the great sum of aches and pains that had accumulated since they started up-river.

Away ahead moved the string of canoes, sunk to the gunwales with trade goods and dash ; long and swift, they travelled swallow-like over their own reflections, down a spacious green channel which, holding out the direct rays of the sun, enclosed the heat and the swarms of insects that thrive on heat as in a tunnel. Looking up into the green web overhead, he experienced the faint, claustrophobic sensation of the unseasoned traveller through bush. A savage opulence of vegetation blotted out all but the broad architectural form of the channel along which they were progressing ; trunks, branches, the individual shape of a tree lost themselves in a close-knit fabric of vines which sucked up air, light and—but for the drip of the paddles and the occasional songs of the boys—sound. He had the overwhelming sense which, in such surroundings, comes to the untravelled, of being in a foreign land : foreign beyond the utmost resources of insular imagination. A land in which man is no longer the conqueror of nature, but its vassal ; where the plant has established a horrifying supremacy over every other form of life.

"Rubber." Foxy had crawled out at the other end of the cabin. "Grand rubber country, this."

"It would be better still if we'd get the handling of it." Kershaw's sour commentary came from beneath the awning. "It's cruel, the way the blacks murder the trees. By the time they've done grooving and gouging, most of them die off——"

"It doesn't exactly look as if they'd be missed." Johnny was trying to gauge the height of the specimen under which they were floating. Foxy became informative.

" Seven diff'rent varieties, I've heard tell of. There's sindura—and that's a funtum. They say there's male an' female, and the one dies if it hasn't got the other to keep it comp'ny. Nice thing, when sex gets goin' among the vegetable creation ! " Foxy spat disgustedly. " That's anomani —poor quality stuff : the blacks use it for linin' parrots. You'll see them at it, when we get up there."

The noiseless journey between the folds of green which, like an impenetrable tapestry, shut off from them the mysterious life of the bush, continued. Sometimes the boys sang, sometimes they were silent. A long and indelicate ballad about a turtle roused merriment, in which Johnny joined. Foxy grunted over the translation.

" Beats me, how you've picked it up. Here's me twenty years on an' off the Coast, and blest if I've got more than half a dozen sentences. It sets you back, if you got to do all your palaverin' in trade English, or depend on one of their rascally linguists."

" I was always rotten in Latin and French ; I don't know why this stuff comes easy to me." Johnny yawned. " I'm going to take a nap. Wake me—if the scenery changes."

. . . Foxy lifted his eyebrows, jerking his head towards the sleeping Johnny. " Got over his bellyachin' about last night ? "

Kershaw grimaced, then nodded.

" You done the right thing," confirmed Foxy. " What the hell ? The poor bugger was dead ; what's the good o' reportin' it ? A-top o' Maudie's business, it would be enough to set the place afire. Then there'd be all the pother in the court, a lot o' scandalisin' among the niggers, and, if any of the nigger-fancy got hold of it, a to-do for the Gummeridges. Sod missionaries, I say, but them two's too decent to be lumped in with the crowd. What did you do ? Cut him down ? And then what ? "

" Left it to the crocs," was the laconic answer.

Foxy nodded approval.

" 'T'ain't the first time them gentry's saved some poor devils the expense of a fun'ral. Folks shouldn't leave corpses about ; untidy," he disapproved.

They went into a mumbling conversation about a case expected to come up at Accra, over instance of outrage on a mine worker ; the first which had actually been traced and pinned down to a white overseer.

" I lay you five to two he gets off ; he's got a good line of defence," said Kershaw.

" What's his line ? "

The other shrugged.

" The usual : medical report, and the fact he missed his last furlough, owing to the proxy not turning up. They're holding up the case for depositions from England—good husband and father, kind to dumb animals, and so forth ? You know the form."

" They got a tough bunch at that mine," nodded Foxy. " Ain't that where they beat up the coloured headman and raped his wife ? "

" And a couple of fellows broke jail, with about two hundred pounds worth of dust : went on the binge at Dixcove and finished up in a row with some sailors——"

" Considering the workings are under water half the year, they're rottenly underpaid, aren't they ? "

" I thought you was supposed to be asleep." Foxy looked round at the figure under the awning.

" Not much sleep, with you two jabbering like old magpies." Johnny sat up ; he looked very thin and yellow. " You know what I've been wondering ? " he was beginning, when Foxy's hand fell on his forearm.

" St-t ; lie back—the pair o' you. Pretend you're asleep, but pull yer hats down and use yer eyes. D'you see ? Are these, by any chance, your pals of the other night ? "

A native dugout was coming downstream. It contained, beside the rowers, two passengers whose heads turned with curiosity towards the string of canoes. Foxy paid no attention ; he appeared to be lighting his pipe. It was doubtful whether the strangers could see under the awning, into the bottom of the canoe, where Johnny and Kershaw were lying.

" It's them, all right ! And the big chap, sitting in the stern's my old school friend Mfabo. Wonder if he spotted me."

" A pity, if he did," grunted Foxy.

Pulling his gun up beside him, Kershaw had turned over on his chest, to watch the dugout on its journey downstream. He had barely done so, when a crack broke from the stern of the dugout : something, zinging through the air, ploughed into the grass thatch directly over their heads. In the split second before Kershaw's Martini-Metford had spoken, the race of the water had swept their assailant into safety, round the bend of the stream.

" Nice timing ! " snarled Kershaw.

The canoe-boys, losing their stroke, were chattering profusely. Foxy roared them into order. Johnny was grinning at the lump of metal he had picked out of the thatch.

" Nice little present ! Which of us do you suppose it was meant for ? "

" Pah ! There'd have been some more, most likely, if the dirty geezer hadn't miscalculated the speed of the tide. So that's the set-up." A vexed gravity replaced anger in Foxy's face.

" A sort of hint we're not popular—isn't it ? " It was hard to prevent a kind of schoolboy exultancy breaking through respectable nonchalance. " What's that lot been up to, I wonder."

" You can take your Bible oath they been up to no good." Foxy was chawing his beard ; presently he broke into a swearing bout to which Johnny paid respectful attention. " We'd turn round and sink 'em, if there was anything to gain by it. But the damage is done by now—or call me a turnip. That bunch of skunks—I bet they left their stink somewheres, and we're coming in for it." He sounded sober and anxious.

There was an odd expression in Kershaw's green eye as he turned it on Foxy.

" What price Komuntale ? He wasn't in the party, was he ? "

" No, he wasn't in the party ! " Johnny was clear on this issue.

" You bet your sweet souls he wasn't," was the sour rejoinder. " You can bet by now he's rubbin' noses with some of his pals at Omo——"

" You think they've come from Omo.

" I'm goddam certain they've come from Omo. Where else 'ud they have been, up this stretch of the river ? "

" But—surely—they've not had time—— ? "

" What was in that dugout, when you saw it up the creek ? " Foxy interrupted.

" Not guns," said Johnny, misunderstanding the drift of the question. " Fishing tackle ; a bundle that looked like clothes ; domestic stuff——"

" Ah. So the beggar was flittin'." Foxy chewed his thumb-nail.

" All the same," persisted Johnny, " I don't see how they could get up to Omo, and back, in this time. Didn't you say it's another couple of days on from here ? Starting at daylight, they can't have had more than an hour's advantage of us——"

" You know how this river is : like a corkscrew. There ain't nothing to prevent 'em beachin' up one of the creeks and cuttin' across a coupl'a loops by bush-path. It 'ud prob'ly save 'em a day."

" All right ; but what's the hurry ? "

" It's dawned on our Mr. Komuntale," growled Foxy, after a pause, " that there might be healthier spots than Charlestown for a nigger that runs with Her Majesty's Gov'ment an' hunts with the gun-running bunch. Your bit o' fun down at the Fort gave him a warning ; Morris's arrival's fairly put the wind up him ; he wasn't expectin' that ! Our Kommy knows he's just about as dear to the D.C. as a lump of cow dung. I shouldn't wonder, either, if we was to run into a little informal reception, organised by Mr. Komuntale and his friends, somewhere between here and Omo."

" In Morris's district ? Rubbish ! " from Kershaw.

" Don't you make no mistake." There was no answering lightness in Foxy's rejoinder. " That nigger's stabbin'-mad. You can take it for granted he was watchin' the pair of you nosin' around his dugout, and if he's on the run he won't stop to reason. He's the sort that likes gettin' his own back, and he's in for you two—Johnny in partic'lar—for scotchin' his lucrative little game."

" It's a bit quaint, all the same, that he should bolt to Omo. I thought Kufi's lot were Morris's good boys ? "

" Yeah ? " said Foxy dryly. " They're all ' good boys '—till it pays 'em to be something else."

Johnny stretched himself and yawned. It seemed, for once, as though Foxy were making a mountain out of a molehill.

" Well—what of it ? Morris himself will only be about twenty miles away, at Diloli. What's that, in a Government launch ? "

" About thirty-two miles by waterway, my bright lad. Morris may walk in darkness, but he ain't taken to flyin', that I know of. For two pins," muttered Foxy, " I'd pack up the whole shootin' match and plank you two back at the startin' point——"

" Like hell you will ! " Johnny sat up, stiffening. It was Harcourt Flood in miniature who leaned forward, with jutting underlip and brows drawn down over eyes that said, for once and all, their owner was going to have his own way. " I haven't come up-country to admire the landscape, Biddle. I'm here on business, and I'm under orders from the Commissioner. You know that. And he expects me to carry the orders out. I'd sooner explain any trouble we get into on the way up than fail in my duty. And I'm perfectly prepared to take the responsibility if things don't pan out exactly according to schedule."

There was a brief hesitation before Kershaw said :

" That goes for me too, Foxy."

The little trader gave the pair of them an exasperated look.

" Well—I reckon the Basin's going to work overtime, if it gets us three out of this trip without any sort of interference from that damn' black nigger."

CHAPTER EIGHT

I

THE routine, carefully worked out between Morris and Foxy, and memorised by Johnny, was to be as follows :

The trading post was two and a half bends farther upstream than the chief's village, which, normally, Foxy would have missed. They were to go straight up to the post, leave the trading goods temporarily in charge of the agent and work their way back by bush-path—this being much shorter than the waterway—using the hammock boys and as many carriers as were needed for the chief's " dash." Their arrival in this style would create a certain impression of formality, especially as a salute of guns was to be fired for which Kershaw was to hold himself responsible, and which he had already rehearsed with the dozen or more boys who could be trusted with firearms.

" We'll hear that from the launch, and know you've arrived and all's well," explained the Commissioner, and went on to say that a messenger was to be sent in advance of the party, to order the chief and the villagers to prepare themselves for the reception of their visitors. " That'll give them a chance to pull themselves together if they're misbehaving ! " The Commissioner's eyelid flickered : at the same time he explained that this matter of the messenger was of sufficient importance for him to detach one of his own Hausa guard, a man of great stature and dignity, army trained and soberly educated, whom Morris himself employed on occasion to lend pomp to his own appearance. " Igolo's a fine fellow ; he's used to this kind of job. His way of walking down the village street's enough in itself to convince the people that he's an emissary of royalty—if not royalty itself ! "

The next part of the programme lay in Johnny's hands, and he did all in his power to forget about it. Save in charades, where improvisation was everything, he was nothing of an actor : being afflicted with all the more painful symptoms of stage fright when called upon to give a set performance. It would be followed, if all went well, by suitable jubilations, during, or after, which Foxy, using his own discretion, might take his departure. If Kufi was pressing, and the signs seemed propitious—Foxy to be the judge of this—Kershaw and Johnny might, if they chose, spend the night in the guest house—" You'll find it no more uncomfortable than the shack you've been living in, and Kufi will take your presence as a compliment."

If Foxy decided that discretion was the better part of valour, or if, by any chance, Johnny's share in the proceedings had failed, in the former's opinion, to carry full conviction, they were to set off, all three, well before moonset, and spend the night at the factory.

In either case, Foxy would be well through his business by the following evening and ready to pick them up for the return journey. When the canoes were ready, with all aboard, three rockets were to be sent up, as a sign that the business was successfully concluded. " Remember," said Morris, " I'll post a look out from the time we hear the guns. If any difficulties arise "—his casual tone lent no importance to the words, but each of his listeners was conscious of the implications that might lie behind them—" one rocket will be enough. Have fun—in moderation !—with Kufi—he's really a very pleasant fellow, with a nice taste in ladies ; the head wife is a most striking creature. But be careful of the old woman—old Akosua ; let Kufi see you expect him to keep his mother in order."

It all sounded beautifully simple, thought Johnny—excepting his part of it, from which his mind shied away. All the same, he was determined to carry it through ; this was the least return he could make to Morris for the latter's generosity. And, up to the time of their arrival at the village itself, everything went perfectly to schedule. There was nothing to cause unease, no indication that they were deep in a savage and only partly conquered land, among people who, only a few short years ago, would have used the arrow, or the deadly blowpipe, at sight, upon any white invader of their secret territory. Now and again, at long intervals, they came on a solitary fisherman, or heard, deep in the bush, the tap-tap of the rubber gang. A little way up one of the creeks they glimpsed a young mother, washing and scouring her numerous family with flat pancakes of the hard, dry river clay which serves the bush dweller for soap ; the purified offspring skipped about in the sun like kittens ; Johnny noticed their small, hard, shining limbs, the straight little bodies—inwardly contrasting them with the pot-bellied, rickety children of the Coast.

" Where every prospect pleases, and only flies are vile." Kershaw, a connoisseur in the combination of comfort with utility, had actually produced a length of mosquito netting from somewhere and festooned it from the brim of his hat—looking so like Vicky going out for her periodical inspection of the bee-hives that Johnny burst out laughing. But, as the chatter of the boys told them they were getting near their destination, and Foxy became preoccupied with his freight, both laughter and conversation died. Each felt in himself, and was conscious of in his companion, the prickle of apprehension of the unknown—increased in Johnny by his anxiety to acquit himself to the approval of Morris.

Kershaw had had the stiffest interview before their departure. He had been sent for while the other two were in the town, and with him the Commissioner had minced no words.

" This is not a pleasure trip, Mr. Kershaw—though I hope it may turn out that way for you all. For the other two it is a matter of grave business, and I have a stake in it myself. I want to make this perfectly clear——" He paused.

" It's not my first up-country trip—if that's what you mean ! " Kershaw lifted his eyebrows, as to remind the Commissioner that he had no taste for admonitions. Morris stared at him.

" I know your record pretty well. I know about your road work, and the way you took the telegraph through that bad patch at the back of N'Sumi, and your useful work in the Police Force. I have heard you spoken of as courageous, enterprising, resourceful, a fine disciplinarian——"

" But—— ? " Kershaw was grinning.

" I'm glad you realise there's a ' but.' " Morris's lips twitched faintly.

" There's always a ' but,' " was the flippant rejoinder. " I'd have gone on with road and rail, *but* the fun of that palls when you run out of material. I'd have stuck to the Police, *but*—oh, well, you know all the answers. The fact is "—hands in pockets, Kershaw allowed his shoulders to drop against the wall behind him, and smiled at the Commissioner—" I came to the conclusion long ago there's nothing to do on the Gold Coast, except put in time. We're just a lot of kids, playing with boxes of bricks. We start one thing, then another kid knocks it down and begins another. There aren't enough bricks to finish anything, and if there are, we've got no cement to stick them together and make it permanent. What the hell ? Until the Government's decided what it means to do about West Africa—why not call it a hobby, and let it slide ? "

" It's a pity," said Morris, after a pause, " that a man of your ability, Kershaw, should not have a higher conception of duty than you seem to have."

" 'Theirs but to do and die ? ' " Kershaw grimaced. " Not I—sorry. That's Bill Prewett's line of country. He got a bug in his brain, and it's killed him—or will have done, before the day's out. I don't mind puttering around—doing a bit here and a bit there, helping out poor boobs who've got it into their heads that their job really *matters* : but as for taking it seriously, or running a temperature when a theodolite, despatched in answer to yours of the 7th Jan., arrives on the 2nd Aug., in the thick of the rainy season, having got itself changed into five gallons kerosene and a fretsaw on the way—not this man." He shook his head. " Laugh it off. Variety's the spice of life : I will say there's plenty of variety out here—if you go and look for it."

" I think you do yourself an injustice." Morris spoke coldly, wondering, as he spoke, if too many years in the same district had begun to blur his sense of humour. "There's such a thing as seeing a job through. However, I don't want you swashbucklering about the bush! I've only got one reason for sending you out with the party: to keep yourself out of the way of the others and, if it's necessary, to shoot dam' quick and dam' straight. Have you understood me?"

"Yes." Kershaw looked at him curiously. An odd fellow, Morris. His bark was said to be worse than his bite, but Kershaw was not the only one who, after meeting the Commissioner, decided that only a fool would put the aphorism to the test. "Yes." And for once, the habitual levity was absent from his voice. "I think we don't see eye to eye on many things, Mr. Morris; but we'll agree on one. It would be a pity if anything—uncomfortable happened to young Johnny Flood, among your protégés at Omo."

"Don't talk balderdash." Morris's patience snapped. "Nothing will—so long as you behave yourselves and don't try to improve on the perfectly straightforward plan of action that Flood understands—if you don't. I wish I felt more certain of you, Kershaw." He sounded a little fretful. "Your stock in obedience to authority doesn't stand high. I hope you realise that originality, on this occasion, would mean, not merely a breach of discipline—which, of course, you don't recognise—but might bring disaster."

"You don't need to worry—this time."

"I'm not worrying." Morris rose sharply. "I've got more to worry about than an up-country expedition to a trading post in a so-far respectable part of my district. I'm only reminding you, for your own good, that these are tricky times, and that if anything gets in the way of my purpose in allowing young Flood to take this trip—notwithstanding your gifts, Mr. Kershaw, and your usefulness, of which I've heard more than I've experienced, I'll have you run, not merely out of my own district, but out of the Colony. That's not a threat, but a promise. And now—good day to you, and good hunting."

"I'm quite one of your favourites—aren't I?" Kershaw did not speak the words, but they were in the unsmiling glint of his eye, as he saluted smartly and removed himself from the Commissioner's presence. He told himself he knew how it was: he and his kind—the few professionals who, out of curiosity or just for the hell of it—were freelancing about the districts—were anathema to the red tape brigade, who could not forgive them for not binding themselves to one or another of the services: for not giving up their liberty of conduct and action "just for a ribbon to pin on their coats;" who cocked metaphorical snooks at the sacred initials of Civil Service, having sufficient of independent means not to be dependent on their country's pay; who were supposed to foment dissatisfaction among the regulars—and were invariably called in when local, technical or administerial difficulties had reduced the regulars to despair, or melancholia, or madness. Why can't they see we'd be batty like the rest, if we were forced, day in, day out, to dance to the tune of Whitehall—played on a tin whistle instead of a brass band? Half of them can't hear it; have to pick up the tune from their companions. But they all know they're bloody well for it if they march out of step! It took Civil Service to get me out here—he grinned as he remembered his six months in Public Works—but it'd take all Tophet to send me back into Civil Service now I'm out of it. God bless my uncle's legacy. I wonder, ruminated Kershaw, as he accepted with a nod, the salute of the Hausa sentry under the arch of the Residency drive, why fellows are called rebels who prefer making their own mistakes, to having those of other people foisted on them?

II

Nervous as he was, Johnny had to give credit to Foxy for his stage management; even Morris, he felt, would have approved of it.

After an hour's jog-trot in the hammocks, the carrier line halted, and a salute of twenty-five guns was—somewhat raggedly—fired, scattering the screaming flocks of parrots and spreading a pall of smoke under the leafy boughs and a stench of gunpowder over the clearing. Someone, inevitably, had managed to get himself peppered, and a couple of his friends were left behind to see to the victim, while the rest of the procession moved on towards the village—which, by now, was signalling, with a sporadic outburst of shots and noises described by Foxy as a first-rate Kilkenny concert, its jubilance at the approach of the visitors.

The bush came to an end about two hundred yards from the stockade of the village, where Johnny, bearing in mind Morris's admonition to use his eyes, saw, to his surprise, a broad slope of much trodden grass, running up to the north, on which, midway, was perched what he conjectured to be the mission building: now a shell, bearing traces of Omo's having lost no time in helping itself to whatever structural or other oddments struck it as desirable for the improvement of its own properties. Still farther up the slope, where the clearing rejoined the bush, an isolated thatched tenement, with no visible inlet, but some form of decoration round the eaves, suggested the fetish house: an impression strengthened when Johnny's eyes, accustoming themselves to the strong light after the green of the forest, recognised in the decoration a collection of skulls—mementos, no doubt, of Omo's stormy past, for it was long since Omo, discreet under British rule, had made frank display of its differences with its neighbours.

On the left the grass slope dropped back into bush, and, no doubt, to water; for, according to the compass, the river itself could be at no great distance, and there was the opening to a well-worn path—used by the villagers on their way to the landing beach and the canoes.

The spectacle the travellers presented was not unimpressive as, under Foxy's orders, they collected at the edge of the clearing. An imposing assembly of carriers and hammock boys, and the four gun-carriers, who, each with a couple of rifles across his shoulders and others slung on his back, presented the appearance of walking arsenals, formed a background to the figures of the white men—of whom Kershaw alone, by the gravity and pomp of his demeanour, might have passed for one of the higher magnates of the Administrative service. On his left breast a row of decorations dazzled the eye and inspired respect for the wearer—until they proved, on inspection, to bear the inscriptions : "First, Hundred Yards, 1881." "Buxton Road Sunday School, Recitation." "Freehand Drawing, First Prize." And other evidence of a past as varied as Kershaw's present.

"I sent for them after a dinner at Accra," volunteered their wearer, "where everyone was wearing such a chestful of fancyware I felt I was letting the company down. Used to have a Crimean one, but I lost it. Nothing like 'em for impressing the niggers. You ought to pick up a handful, next time you're passing a pawnshop."

"You'd better pass them on to Johnny ; you ain't supposed to be the star turn in this concert party," growled Foxy—who, however, admitted that his suit of khaki drill would be as good as fancy dress to Omo, which had never before seen him in anything but an old singlet and a pair of striped pyjama trousers. Johnny, who wished to God he could join in the levity of his companions, but who had been sick in his stomach for the last hour, would have been outshone but for the umbrella which, by Foxy's directions, was supported over his head—and occasionally poked into his eye—by a Kroo, afflicted with St. Vitus' Dance by his elevation to this office of dignity.

The final touch was also Foxy's inspiration. When they had waited a short while—Omo, apparently, being so transported by its preparations for company that it forgot the reason for them—the headman of the canoes lifted his horn, and sent the whooping, hollow low of a mystical cow across the clearing.

A certain amount of tumult and excitement that Johnny had accepted as normal to their arrival now swelled into a veritable uproar, suddenly dominated by a jubilant drubbing on the drums. The opening to the stockade became the entrance to a beehive, with the bees about to swarm, and the entire population spilled itself into the clearing, while over the stockade itself bobbed, like a sudden growth of fabulous mushrooms, the state umbrellas.

"Looks as if Omo means to do us proud !" He forced the words through his chattering teeth, wishing the sweat would stop pouring into his eyes. This was terror of a different brand from that which he had experienced on the night alone in the hut : terror of failing to justify Morris's confidence in him—all mixed up with the excitement of coming face to face with an aspect of the native so far unknown to him. His brain hummed with the effort to remember all Morris had said to him in their long *tête-à-tête* at the Residency : the words which, coached by Morris, he was bidden to speak. He felt the sweat icy in the palms of his hands when he remembered that, whenever he had been required, in amateur theatricals, to speak a single line, stage fright had robbed him of his memory, had descended on him in a pall of blankness, paralysed his organs of speech, and, on more than one occasion, driven him headlong from the stage.

"It means the advance publicity's worked." Foxy's hand had fallen on his shoulder, and he realised, with a tremor of incredulity that Foxy was nervous too. The knowledge shocked him into steadiness. A nice pack of

messengers Morris had sent out! Somebody had to keep his head. . . .
"I wasn't sure if they'd swallow it, but—by Jesus! Here's Kufi himself, at the head of his menagerie. Steady, now. Mind you play up. And if either of you bastards laugh—by Jesus, I'll blow your brains out, when we get back, if Kufi's lads haven't saved me the trouble!"

He had never felt less like laughing, as, half-dazed, he took a step forward into the unspeakable loneliness of the sunlight.

The procession, although hurriedly convened, was impressive enough to command respect, even from a connoisseur in royalty. Stubbornly tenacious of its historic privileges, Omo, even after its annexation by Ashanti, had clung with a grimness of determination to all the pomp and ceremony surrounding its now extinct Stool.

In the wake of the horn-blowers and drummers, from whose instruments swung a notable collection of human skulls, came Kufi's executioners, the twin swords slung round their necks slapping their thighs at each step; these functionaries, always a popular note in any festive occasion, were surrounded by a noise as of heavy rain—the noise of the calabash rattles shaken by the youths who pranced at their sides. A curious rabble swept with them, for such a parade attracted all elements, and among the young and old who, knotting their loin-cloths or their girdles of dried grass hurriedly about them, had hastened to join the procession, were a few who defied the reactionary spirit of the village in calico shirts of mission origin.

On the tail of the hubbub, surrounded by his "souls"—the comrades of his youth and adolescence on whom had been conferred the privilege, when the time came, of dying with him—came Kufi Kaboha: moving, it is true, with unkingly speed, but clothed, apart from his hastily assumed ceremonial vestments, in something of the dignity that is royal, and from which no eccentricity of bearing or garment can detract. Behind him, his fourteen wives, their small, shaven heads bobbing with excitement, maintained a clucking of agitated guinea fowl. Then there were some councillors, court functionaries, big-wigs of the occult and medical departments, who, somewhat hampered by the insignia of their calling, jostled each other and Kufi as they scrambled on the heels of the crowd.

Kufi thrust himself to the front of his subjects, his ribs and belly heaving with the unaccustomed speed of his progress, his fine eyes rolling on their balls of amber in search of their objective. Whatever he had expected, it was assuredly not the spectacle of an insignificant white man, in mould-speckled white cotton, under a common, trader's umbrella, and, as the truth dawned on him, a slow swelling of his features proclaimed to the audience his resentment of what he took for a hoax.

Johnny felt a drop of ice slip down his backbone. He was unaware that the other two were sweating, or of anything but the extreme delicacy, of which every nerve in his body informed him, of their position, and he heard a groan from Foxy—"For Christ's sake!" A terrible moment of unbelief came to him—in Morris's judgment and in his own mission; yet while he was wondering how long it took, in an African village, to die, and how far the Colts Foxy and Kershaw and he carried might go, in postponing the Moment of Truth—a tall figure, detaching itself from the milling horde in front, crossed the short space between the hard-breathing chief and the three white men, paused long enough for him to recognise Morris's Hausa, Igolo, and knelt, surrendering its pride, as it had been bidden by its master, to the Messenger of the Queen.

He was suddenly unlocked from his paralysis. He knew, in that moment, that he must make no use of the linguist, who had shuffled to his elbow; and his short spine clicked into stiffness, as he raised his head and his hand, and, in a voice louder than that which was habitually his own, spoke the words which Morris had bidden him. He heard his own voice go out into a silence which had fallen like death on the people in front of him.

" Hail to the Chief. Here am I, who was dead, and am come again to bring my goodwill to you. For I am of the blood of him who gave you the Basin, and his spirit lives again in me. I come to you bearing the word of Morrissi, who walks in darkness, and who bids me tell you his will : which is that you and I shall make blood brothership, for the renewal of that spirit, and for the continuance of your tribe in power and in duty to the Great Queen."

Kufi Kaboha looked round wildly. Omo had always been respectful to its " well-disposed ones ; " to the ancestors who, acting in conjunction with the tribal of family fetish, give the family its cohesion, its discipline and its superiority in politics or warfare over other tribes. Its beliefs had, however, been a little shaken over the Ashanti business, when, as a few of the bolder had murmured, their ancestors had let them down. It was this hour of disappointment, resulting in a temporary scepticism which, in the opinion of the elders of the community, had weakened the fetish, and rendered Omo vulnerable to the magic of missionaries.

Kufi knew he was not a great fetishman, and he suffered from a slight guilt complex. He had, in fact, been neglecting the Basin, and part of his agitation was due to his efforts, during his rush to obey the summons, to compute what he actually owed it, in goats' flesh, rum, calico and replenishments of its bedding. Was it angry ? Was it likely to transfer its benefits elsewhere ? Could he venture to reproach it for its inattention at the time of the Ashanti trouble, in extenuation of any complaints it might have to make of his recent negligence ?

His heart was beating too fast for comfort, and he wished, as he confusedly scanned the faces in front of him, that his mother was there : but his royal blood helped him to conceal these evidences of weakness as he stood forth in front of his people, with the long, sleeved robe of woven silk and gold falling open over the damask loin-cloth, and the heavy crown of gold alloy studded with nuggets (which had replaced the Manchester tin one of his famous ancestor) pushing out his ears on either side of his good-looking, arrogant face.

" *Go on, fella, go on.*" Kershaw and Foxy, their eyes boring like gimlets into his face, were breathing heavily behind Johnny.

Under less of an emotional stress, Omo's credulity might have failed him. A small, white man, in crumpled cotton suiting, is not, in the face of it, a likely shell for the reincarnated spirit of a colossus. But there was Biddli Daddy, whom he knew, and who had always treated him as a man of honour ; there was the tall stranger, bearing on his chest gold and silver, such as were worn only by the great, by the kings and princes of the white people.

Kufi was anxious to put himself on the right side, and his mother was not there to advise him. His brain whirled with recollections of his younger brother's rivalry, and of the unrest among his people. Here, surely, was the way to safety, and to the settlement of all those vexed questions of precedence that not only Quabina, but, he recently suspected, Akosua had been raising. The Basin should fix for ever his rulership of Omo.

He gave a shout and plunged on his hands and knees, and his subjects followed his example. His abiakok, who had been delayed by the completion of a toilet of which the salient properties were mud and blood, charged through the kneeling multitude with something wrapped in leopard skins under his arm. He reached Johnny. He flung back the skins to exhibit the object they concealed, and Johnny, with hysteria gripping his throat, wondering if it was all a rather childish thing, did the right thing. He stepped forward, drawing the sleeve up from the wrist of his right arm.

Foxy, primed by Morris, was also prepared. As Kufi scrambled to his feet, he handed him a knife presented by the Commissioner, of which the handle was of horn, set in a metal convincing enough to pass for gold. Kufi was so pleased with this that he forgot for a moment its purpose, waving it about, making passes with it at his nearest neighbours, for the pleasure of seeing the blade flash in the sun, and even executing a few steps of a dance with an indubitably sanguinary motif, that drew howls of applause from his appreciative audience. Feeling, however, that there had been enough of this anticking about, his abiakok drew his attention, with a sharp nudge, to the business in hand. Kufi sobered down ; a wholesome smile broke across his face, as he took firm hold of Johnny's wrist and held it with his own across the rim of the sacred vessel. Raising the knife, he drew it, with a sharp, experienced stroke, across the black and the white flesh.

They stood there for a moment, the black man and the white, watching the bright drops mingle, as they rolled into its scoured bottom. Someone came forward with the calabash of palm wine, into which the blood would be drained, for the participants to drink at the conclusion of the rite.

As a joyful howl went up from the spectators, fourteen young women solemnly broke eggs round the feet of the blood brothers. Kufi bent forward, gravely to rub noses with his *vis-à-vis*.

The next move was the parade to the guest-house—situated at the farther extreme of the village street and looking down it, across its own neat palisade of slender stakes, profusely hung with ju ju, no doubt to assure the security of the visitor. This being evidently the exclusive residential quarter, they had as nearest neighbour the mansion of the chief, set in its own compound and dotted about with the thatched huts of his personal staff and attendants. The village was more extensive than appeared on first entering : there was nearly a quarter of a mile of curving street, lined with dwellings of various sizes and degree, before one reached the farther stockade, from which not more than twenty paces took one back into the bush.

"An interestin' layout." Foxy was nodding, as he looked round their temporary domicile. "I've visited Lord Tom Noddy in his own domain, but it's the first time I've been privileged to view his accommodation for comp'ny." He turned to clap Johnny on the shoulder. "Good work, chum. And I hope you feel better for bein' brother to a six-foot nigger!"

Johnny grinned; Foxy's speech was hardly audible, for Omo had settled down to its business of serenading its visitors in style. Drums, rattles and the yappings of the general public made pandemonium on the other side of the palisade, while a constant stream of the bolder spirits kept coming up to the clay stoop for a peek at the strangers, and going away, to return again. Kershaw's boys kept chasing them out of the house with expressions of contempt for their rustic ignorance, which obliged Kershaw eventually to box his henchmen's ears.

The guest-house was roomy, although it consisted only of one apartment; its furniture consisted of four or five beds, made roughly of branches, but well padded with skins, and a number of small plaited mats, which Foxy explained were for squatting on. Though thatched it was, for a native hut, estimably free from vermin, and someone had thoughtfully set fire to the oil which, running in a little channel at the base of the stoop, prevented the access of local fauna—snakes, scorpions and tarantulas—to the interior. Kufi had departed in high spirits, to prepare for further celebrations.

"We're off on the right foot with Kufi. Wonder what he's done with the old girl. Ought to be cosy enough here to-night, for the pair o' you—if all goes well."

If all goes well. Johnny, dabbing the cut on his wrist with iodine, smiled wanly. So far as he was concerned, the worst part was yet to come. And it all depended on him.

III

Akosua Ngomi had lost her temper, and the bad blood had broken out, as usual, in boils. Knowing all about boils, she made two of her step-daughters sit down and chew nchechi, mix it with the red and the white earth, and sputter it over the infected places. This home treatment was the cause of a quarrel with the local doctor; cheated of his dues, he sulked, went into conference with his confrère, the abiakok, and Akosua, in due course, was visited with a sharp onset of rheumatism.

Conservative in other ways, Akosua liked an adventure in medicine. Pooh-poohing the local man, with his fancy for the knife and the clay poultice, she sent for a bright young graduate of the Mpongwe school. This one, sharp to seize his advantage, made great parade of his preparations; Akosua, knotted up with her pains, almost forgot them in watching. First there was the digging of a hollow, like a grave; then the to-do of choosing he seven necessary herbs which, plentifully mixed with cardamum and the peppers, made a mattress in the earth. The women in Akosua's household displayed an altogether unheard-of alacrity in soaking this with boiling water.

Getting the old woman stripped and into the vegetable purée took perseverance ; Akosua yelled, as her scrawny buttocks met the scalding mess, and yelled more when they packed it over her. Working fast, the young man from Mpongwe and his assistants built up the framework of twigs, clayed it up hastily, and left Akosua literally to stew in her own juice. When they had finished, nothing was to be seen but her old, angry head, sticking like a turtle's out of its shell. A couple of great grandchildren were left to look after her pipe, push it in her mouth and take it out again, according to her requirements ; while her household, delighted with their brief respite from Akosua's tempers, her meddling and her unalterable persuasion that no one but she was qualified to give an opinion on anything whatever, made a fuss of the new doctor and filled him so full of palm wine that he executed, free of charge, a neat piece of kid's horn surgery on an old, unvaluable member of the community, whose death, if it occurred, was not going to make much difference to anybody.

Oh, yes, declared the doctor ; Akosua could bake for a day—or longer, if it were more convenient for her family. She had managed to get herself a very severe attack of the *tanta ki tanta*. The family capered with glee—and Akosua lay there, making more and more bad blood, as the original cause of her anger boiled in her mind, and the children, bored with lighting her pipe, gambolled off from time to time in search of beetles.

When the news came of her old acquaintance Biddli Daddy's arrival, no doubt with a new batch of trade goods, she yelped to be let out ; but the doctor, aware that his credit was at stake, remained adamant. Akosua must go through with the cure ; she was not properly cooked. The parboiled state was a very dangerous one, laying the patient open to all sorts of invasions from undesirable spirits. Supposing Akosua got a *sisa* into her ? No reputable practitioner would hear of exposing his patient to a *sisa*, the expulsion of which was not his province at all, but meant the summoning of the specialist, and the performance of a most difficult and risky operation.

So she lay in her clay and twig and vegetable coffin, while a veritable hurricane of rumour gathered over her head : rumour which, despite her threats, her objurgations and, eventually, her all but apoplectic raving, no one could be bothered to explain to her. The froth ran out of her lips, as they rushed round, over and past her, all but treading on her face, in their wild and inexplicable frenzy, through which she caught the word Basin, Basin, Basin, repeated again and again, as though the whole community had gone mad.

She wailed, she implored them to tell her whether any harm had come to the Basin : if it had been stolen, lost or if some fearful calamity had fallen upon it. The Basin was the only thing in which Akosua truly believed ; sceptical of all other forms of religion, although practising them for safety, she had brought up her family in the creed of the Basin, and at the mere thought of danger to the Basin, panic drove deep into her corrupt old heart.

Was it not by virtue of the Basin that Omo, although technically a vassal state, had maintained its glory and independence? Did not the sons of Omo draw their strength from the Basin? Did the Basin not figure in the rites of puberty, by which each Omo youth attained to his manhood? Had it not, at certain dark ceremonies which she could remember, and whose suppression she deplored, held the draught of blood which none but rulers could drink or rulers furnish? From it, far back into time, the kings and after them the chiefs of Omo had drunk the blood of the ones they supplanted: so that the strength of Omo was kept in the blood-stream of its rulers, and no single precious drop was squandered on the earth that received their bones.

She began to gibber those appeals to Tando which her mother had taught her, as a little girl in Bantama: Tando the Hater, who uses the driver ants as his dire messengers. Send the driver ants on those who threatened the Basin! For, without the Basin, Omo was lost and the seed of its rulers spilt strengthless on the ground. And through her distracted prayers went the thought of her son Quabina, who was her favourite, because, unlike his elder brother Kufi, he always listened to what she said, and was as eager as she was herself for the revival of the secret societies and all the blood rites which would reinstate Omo in its proper position as a governing state—Quabina, who had gone off, by her instructions, to receive the last consignment of guns and to see to the despatch of Ya Ashantua's quota and the conveyance of the surplus to his own village: a matter which Kufi preferred not to handle, although perfectly satisfied to turn a blind eye on his mother's little schemes for increasing the village arsenal. If Quabina had been there, he would not have left her, helpless and derelict, with something exciting going on. . . .

Then the drums broke out, and the horns, and she lay, half-smothered in dust, while the whole village swept by her, and her son, Kufi Kaboha, that child of Tando, that ingrate fruit of her womb, went forth from the Chief's compound, with the umbrellas and the music and the swords, to a palaver of which she—the true ruler of Omo—knew less than the sandfly at present sitting on the top of her nose.

IV

It was the sort of dream one had in boyhood, after reading too many adventure stories.

He was standing in smoky semi-darkness, alone, but aware of a hushed multitude that waited for the sound of his voice. Over his own clothes was a robe of woven material, trimmed with the tails of wild cat; it had a yoke, or collar, of coarse netting, and each point of the net was finished with a tooth; it smelt of carrion and of stale fish.

On his head, incredibly heavy, was a bowl of iron. This, mainly, was what convinced him he was dreaming: how should the bowl get there, and what was the silly idea of it? He was back in the dormitory, at Curbham, and he had somehow got his head jammed up against the bed-head, so that the iron bars gripped the top of his skull. He had only to wake himself up, and move . . . but he would drop the bowl. That was certain. That disposed of the theory of a dream.

They had killed a hen, allowing the blood to run into the bowl; then they had taken certain parts of the carcase and poured palm oil over them, before putting them into the pot: all this to an accompaniment of drumming, and a bobbing, stamping kind of a march round a fire. After which they had actually proposed to strip him, for what probably was some sort of a ritual cleansing. It had taken long argument to persuade them that the souls of Those Who Had Passed On needed no cleansing, but were purified throughout eternity: and that to uncover such a one was to shed the virtue which, accumulating down the ages, attached not only to their limbs and to their flesh, but to the garments that enabled them to manifest themselves to the eyes of the living. This statement created a sensation, and led to a committee among the priesthood, none of whom had ever heard anything like it before. With the help, however, of Biddli Daddy, whose word, given through the linguist, was accepted for the sake of old times, they were convinced. There were some antics in masks, there was some daubing with a stickiness, the names of whose component parts it was better not to inquire, and he was led into an empty hut and left alone, to speak with the voice of the oracle, which is the voice of the Basin, and to give Omo its message from the departed.

The perturbed faces of Kershaw and Foxy, as he was led away, had tempted him to giggle, but he knew—both from Morris and from his reading—that this was no time for levity. Childlike and foolish as all these actions were, to the sophisticated mind, they were the projection of an orthodoxy older than any church; rising like steam from the tree-roots, the depths of swamps, the darkness of jungles, the nameless lights that flicker along a bush-path on a moonless night. He made a conscious act of respect to that orthodoxy, lifting his hands to the Basin, to steady it, and moistened his dry lips.

Omo, squatting in circles in the darkness—the moon had hardly risen—stopped hunting its lice, scratching after its fleas and digging the ticks out of its calves, and held its breath, as the Basin spoke.

"This is the Voice of the Basin, and the Voice of the lord Matti that is in the Basin, and the Voice of Amoti and his grandfather, and Efeli and his grandfather, and N'Kema and his grandfather, and so on, back to the beginning of Time."

"Wa!" breathed Omo, on an assembled note of awe: for Morris had taken pains to get the names right, and there were among the listeners at least a couple who professed to vouch for them.

"Tell the people of Omo it is the Basin's will they should in all things and at all times obey the will of Morrissi, which is the will of the Great Queen:

"Whose servants, like Morrissi, walk in darkness:

" Who see everything and hear everything, and from whom it is not possible to hide the falling of a leaf.

" Tell the people of Omo that the times are evil, and that there are evil men who scheme against the Great Queen. And for them there is surely destruction.

" Tell the people of Omo that as the lord Matti loved them, so shall be the love of the Great Queen and her servants, including Morrissi, to those who love her and keep her law.

" Tell the people of Omo that they shall in time of trouble rise to the defence of the Queen and her servants; for these are people of the lord Matti, and it is his voice that calls on them for support.

" Then Omo shall be strong in the land.

" Tell the people of Omo their chief shall be Kufi, and to no other shall they pay heed.

" And this is the Voice of the Basin. The palaver is finished."

. . . They had built a temporary hut round Akosua and given her a bush-light; then they had squabbled over who was to stop with her. The prospect, although unattractive, offered no particular penalty, as Akosua, long ago, had bawled herself dumb. A barely audible croak came from her cracked lips. If pity had been in them, some might have pitied her. Tears had made long streaks in the furrows of her face and neck. Her eyes were bloodshot and clotted with rheum. The very old, imbecile sister-in-law who finally agreed to invigilate paid no more attention to her than if she were dead; it was a matter of moments before—having seen to the proper disposal of those little bundles of rubbish that keep evil spirits out of the way—she was asleep herself.

The bush-light, untended, had sunk to a glowing stump when a figure stole into the hut. Warned by a startled hiss not to tread on her face, it went on its haunches and started to whisper. The whispering went on a very long while. The moon rose full, cresting the forest with silver. When the matting that formed the walls of the hut began to reveal its web-like texture against the dazzling moonlight, there was a hole in the ground, and a great litter of broken clay and twigs.

" We're eatin' monkey, my boy! and monkey's reserved for visitin' royalty. Wait till Morris hears about this." Foxy leaned back, wiping his mouth with the back of his hand. He beamed with the respect that is so nearly akin, in simple natures, to affection that the two are almost inseparable, upon Johnny. Kershaw saluted him with the spoon which, in the formal rotation prescribed by etiquette, he was plunging into the savoury pot.

" You ought to be a parson, fella," he leaned over to say seriously. " I hadn't more than a dim notion what it was all about, but I damn well found myself saying Amen when you finished!"

" Amen and amen. If you don't get those cocoa concessions to-morrow, call me a turnip! You ought to have seen Kufi's face—he was fit to burst with gratification."

" Smart way of spiking the old woman's guns: saying Kufi was to be chief, and they weren't to pay attention to anyone else. Whose idea—yours or Morris's ?"

"Came to me at the last moment," admitted Johnny. "I wasn't sure—then I thought I'd chance it."

Outside the chief's compound, Omo was letting itself go, and Kufi, on his clay platform, a little apart from his guests, smiled benevolently at the sound of his people's rejoicing, in which, later on, when the liberal potations he was allowing himself had produced the supermanhood they always achieved, he and his guests would join. He surrendered his spoon to one of the wives who moved quietly behind the mats, filling cups and offering wooden bowls in which were heaped the small, silver bananas which everyone ate, complete with skin and pulp. Kufi sipped rum from the cup handed to him by his youngest wife, squirted it through his front teeth and, leaning over, passed the cup to Johnny, who courteously followed suit. Kufi smiled. He liked guests with good manners.

Handsome and vain, his tall frame, in his late thirties, had surrendered some of its original splendour to the fat which was beginning to encroach on his belly and breasts. His short, broad nose and full but by no means grotesque lips were admirably proportioned, and he looked better now he had taken off the crown. Although his mother was Ashanti, he had, fortunately, not inherited the exaggeratedly regressive forehead and narrow, pointed skull of her people ; his head was the round, well-shaped dome of the male line, set on a massive neck. Apart from his colour, he could have passed, in a West End club, for a 'Varsity ex-athlete ; his manner was slow, surfeited, yet pleasant, and his movements infused with that leisurely self-confidence that betokens unchallenged authority. No one, in fact, had ever challenged it, save his mother, and she only in private.

It was agreeable, for once to hold a palaver without the old lady, who had the mischievous habit of stealing his thunder. Nor was her manner propitiating ; she was always rude to whites, and Kufi was at last convinced it paid to be on good terms with the whites. That attack of hers was a sure sign the Basin was on his side ! He must really have a word with the doctor, and make it well worth his while to prolong the treatment—at least until the visitors had quitted the village. He grinned at Kershaw, and made signs to him to come once again and show him how to manage his binoculars, with which he was delighted, though he had not quite got command over their magic, and was forgetful about putting the small end to his eyes.

"All serene, chum ?"

"All serene," said Johnny, smiling, although he was very tired.

"O.K. about stopping the night ?"

"Good grief, yes. Though I can't see us getting any sleep, at this rate !"

"They'll keep this caterwauling up till morning," Foxy assured him ; "and Kufi'll have such a thick head he won't be fit to talk turkey until the afternoon. Anyhow, try an' get through with your cocoa palaver before the canoes come down ; we can make another night of it, if it's strictly necessary, but they'll be wondering, at Diloli, if they don't hear the rockets."

" Are you off, now ? "

" I'll be pushing along." Foxy strangled a yawn. " I've got to beat up those boys of ours before Kufi's pals have started to get them blind. And, by the way, I'm taking those two of Kershaw's."

" Have you told him ? "

" You can tell him after we've gone—I don't want those coast niggers gettin' tough with any of the village maidens ; it's just the sort of thing to start a row, when everybody's had the half-gallon or so more than he can carry. 'Lookee plenty, no touchee : ' that's Omo's motto, so far as its women go. I'll leave the head man and a couple of hammock boys, to sleep on the stoop. It's just a formality—doesn't look well for distinguished visitors to have no attendants." Foxy heaved himself from the mat, with groans of anguish for his stiffened limbs, and dropped his hand on Johnny's shoulder. " You've done a dam' good job of work, chum—and I won't say we've not been lucky : hitting the town when the old woman was laid up with collywobbles ! Kufi's a good chap, but keep your eyes skinned for that slick brother of his. It's queer, his not turning up : in a pet, most likely, because Kufi's gettin' all the limelight."

Foxy went up to make his farewell to Kufi, then the three of them strolled down to the palisade round the chief's compound, on the other side of which Omo was letting rip in a style worthy of its reputation as the best party-givers in the district.

" Talk of a witches' sabbath ! " Foxy had to put his ear to Kershaw's mouth to hear. He nodded in reply.

" I bet that caterwaulin' 'll keep us awake at the fact'ry. Well, good night, chums, and sweet dreams. I'd sooner it was you than me ! "

They went back into the chief's house, and Kufi, grown expansive, invited them to sit beside him on the platform.

The bush-lights, propped on their stones, filled the hut with a smoky amber and with the aromatic oiliness of resin ; they flickered on the company, mostly sunk back in attitudes of repletion. Kufi's " souls," distinguishable by the plaques of gold slung round their necks, were drunk on a mixture of gin and palm wine and were inclined to be quarrelsome, but most of the chatter had subsided, temporarily, into snores, and an occasional deep belch of satisfaction.

Johnny watched the decent and orderly scene—inwardly comparing it with dives he had been in along the Coast. The women had retired, led by the head wife : a tall, grave creature whose air of modest reserve compensated for her lack of beauty. He had noticed that, when feminine chatter threatened to become obstreperous, a look from her was enough to quell it. She had not raised her eyes when Kufi introduced her : drooping her head towards her breasts, while laying a hand of inconceivable delicacy and narrowness in Johnny's, as she had evidently been taught to do. He hated Kershaw briefly, for a momentary glint that came into his eyes, as they looked upon her quiet nakedness.

None of the chief's women covered themselves above the waist ; Akosua would not hear of it. The indecency of wrapping the upper body in cloth was a form of degeneration deriving from the white races. Nor would the matriarch tolerate the adornments most of the girls expected to indulge, when privileged to marry the chief. The innumerable strings of dark-red coral that lay on the shoulders and bosom of each were the only marks of favour permitted ; and, whether she liked it or not, each was obliged to follow tribal custom in shaving her head, leaving only a small, circular patch of fuzz, high between crown and left temple. It was only by the will of the chief that the head wife wore, in each exquisitely shaped ear, twin knobs of gold, joined by a short length of filigree chain : in which Johnny recognised the famous aggrey beads—now almost fabulous in the markets, and falling only to the wealthiest collectors. He wished he could have bought such a set, for Emily.

Kufi leaned towards him, his polished belly pushing up towards the almost feminine bulge of his breasts ; and his smile and his eyes were dim with liquor and good feeling.

"There are those," he said, "who hold with war. Omo has done much fighting, with the spear and with the arrow. By war, in those days, a man grew rich. Now war makes poor, peace makes rich. Peace with riches is good. I say it."

Johnny nodded amiably, although he felt that the conclusion, in some fashion he was too sleepy to analyse, had gone astray.

Then the musicians invaded the compound, with the drums, and the ripple of the orchid-stringed harp, and the liquid clucking of the marimbas, for word had gone forth that the Chief had eaten, and was ready to join in the diversions of his subjects, and the hut was suddenly a smoky confusion of men springing to their feet and shadows leaping about the walls.

CHAPTER NINE

I

KABOHA KOMUNTALE was saying for the fiftieth time : "It is no devil that turns guns into stones," and cursing the hill-billy mentality of Quabina which was apparently incapable of assimilating this self-evident fact.

Like all coastal Negroes, he had gone far, mentally as well as in geographical distance, from the bush ; he had nearly forgotten how up-country Negroes thought and lived. What he remembered he despised.

He had passed an uneasy night on a mat that kept him in uncomfortable remembrance of his bedstead and mattress in Charlestown. He would have made straight for Omo, but was put off by not meeting his friend, Quabina —the latter having gone off in another direction to meet the carriers, whose arrival by bush-path had, unfortunately, coincided with Kaboha's swifter arrival by water. This, on the face of it, looked like a bad omen, and kept

Kaboha biting his nails and fidgeting for close on twenty-four hours. For, although he was on a perfectly legitimate errand, he was fully aware that his kind, the coast nigger, who wore white men's clothes, and even, on occasion, shoes, was not in good odour at Omo. He wanted to find out the lie of the land from Quabina, who was green enough to be rather impressed by him, before claiming the hospitality of relatives whose ignorance was such that they did not realise the privilege implied in entertaining so high-class a visitor as Kaboha Komuntale.

Mr. Komuntale was, in fact, seeking a temporary retreat, from which, while out of the immediate and inconvenient range of the District Commissioner's eye, he could keep a hand on his gun-running arrangements, which, up to now, had put a nice little sum in his pocket—quite enough to pay for Mrs. Komuntale's muslin dresses and her pink notepaper, while leaving enough over for an occasional large Havana cigar and a case of gin for himself: luxuries to which the pay of a Customs clerk was not equal. Much as he objected to working for it, and would have preferred to borrow it, money was essential to Mr. Komuntale, and loans were increasingly difficult to come by and even more impossible to repay. Money would be even rarer, if he were to lose his (official) employment, for, to put it plainly, Mr. Komuntale knew he had left a dirty trail along the coast, and was unlikely to get another job carrying the opportunities he had found in Charlestown.

It was only since the arrival of Johnny Flood, and the peculiar incident of Mfabo and the gun cases that a certain uneasiness which had troubled him whenever Morris was down at the coast came to a head. Although he had tried to persuade himself that Johnny could not possibly have guessed the contents of the cases, and, if he had done so, would surely have come and spoken to his old friend Kaboha about it, before reporting it to authority, he remained uneasy. And when the news reached him that Morris had come back, he panicked. A little trip up-country, a quick revision of his plans, was a far, far better thing than remaining to face the curiosity of Morris—only too clearly indicated by the person who had arrived, without previous notice, to look through the files of Mr. Cope and Mr. Cator, both deceased.

Contemptuous as he was of up-country superstition, he had just started to be terrified at the prospect of another night alone in the bush, when Quabina turned up: goggling with excitement over the cases, which had just been opened, yielding up their extraordinary contents. Komuntale's heart stood still. He saw in a flash—but did not find it necessary to tell Quabina—the meaning of Mfabo's dolorous pilgrimage, and knew it was Johnny who had played the trick on him. The question was, would Akosua, seeking to preserve her face with the Ejesu end by pinning the blame on any handy person, believe him?

The news, said Quabina, had not yet reached Akosua: he then—having poor powers of concentration—went off into hyperbolic descriptions of the festivities at Omo; bemoaned the part he was missing, and besought Komuntale to waste no more time in havering over a few missing guns, but to come along and join the fun. Sourly biting his nails, Kaboha demanded what all the fuss was about.

" It is on account of One who has come, with the name of the lord Morrissi in his mouth, to say that our Basin is his, and that the strength of it lies in his hands."

" Has he taken away the Basin ? " Despite his scepticism of Basins, or of any other barbaric customs, Kaboha was startled.

" The Basin is still there, and his blood is in it, and the blood of my brother Kufi, whom it is plain he favours. And this," said Quabina simply, " is displeasing to myself and to my mother ; for, as you know, I am her favourite, and we have often talked of Kufi being dead, and of my becoming chief in his place."

" That is good talk," grunted Kaboha, on thinking it over—for, with Kufi out of the way, there would be no need to carry on the gun-running in this half-hearted sort of fashion : the old woman always clamouring for supplies, and Kufi always on the dither for fear he was caught, and beating one down over the money, into the bargain. " It would be good if Kufi were dead, for I think he is afraid of Morris, and what sort of a chief is it that carries fear in his heart ? " concluded Kaboha scornfully—having himself a stone-cold fear of the District Commissioner, and no small degree of relief at having, for the moment, moved himself out of that officer's vicinity.

He had never got so far as killing a man himself, but suspected, rightly, that it would be a mere bagatelle to Quabina ; he therefore hinted :

" There are many ways in which a man may die." And paused for Quabina to contribute his views on the subject. Quabina, however, shrugged his shoulders under their elaborate mantle of cicatrisations.

" How may a man die who is under the protection of the spirits ? For he who is found with such a one's blood on his hands shall surely perish, and in no pleasant fashion."

" Under whose protection is Kufi ? " scoffed Kaboha, and Quabina stuck out his lower lip.

" Under that of the lord Matti, who has come among us again under the name of Fludi : a little man, and white, who wears hair on his lip, after the fashion of white men. And," added Quabina, while Kaboha's brain rocked, " it is as though he had a fishing spear in place of the bones of his back."

In nine cases out of ten, among his kind, the reaction would have been horror, followed by stampede. Kaboha, after that one reeling moment, stood his ground. He had his education to thank for it : that education which, although so brief, so limited in its effects on his achievements, had at least taught him to use his brain in a way no primitive Negro uses it.

His was the by no means uncommon case of the semi-Europeanised savage who, despising his own race, loathed the whites with an explicit loathing built up from his early schooling and subsequent experience. Such loathing, while not rare, was usually fluctuating, at the mercy of the capricious temperament of the primitive Negro. But Kaboha was no longer primitive, and, although chancy and undependable in his moods, his hatred was the one steady factor which so to speak polarised his nature.

On his return to the Coast, prepared to be cock of his native village, his ambitions were set back by the obstinate refusal of his elders to yield him and his opinions any sort of precedence. Disappointed and rebuffed, he shook the dust from his feet, and sought the prestige to which he considered himself entitled in the coastal towns. But here, also, he failed to achieve that equality with his white colleagues that had been taken for granted in his English school, and, out of wounded vanity, built up a hatred he was cunning enough to disguise. Outwardly bland and amenable, every snub he received, every real or imagined injustice that came to him as a Negro working among whites was pigeon-holed in his mind and added to the sum of vindictiveness it had become his mission to diffuse, and to foment, wherever he came across it.

He had not precisely hated Johnny Flood : in fact, he had drawn a considerable satisfaction from the fact that, at their first meeting, he had been a cabin passenger and Johnny a ship's boy. But under all that fawning friendliness he had found expedient to employ, when he wanted to get something out of white men, he had sensed Johnny's repudiation of the past. He was perfectly aware of the moment when Johnny shook his arm loose from the clasp Kaboha, wishing to advertise their intimacy to the onlookers, had fastened upon it ; and he would have liked to yell with laughter and point to the scar on Johnny's cheekbone—the permanent witness to what a black could do to a white, when it came to a showdown.

It was this smothered hatred, no less than the desire for financial gain, which had got him ten days in Elmina jail, mixed him up with a crazy bunch in Accra—none of whom had the least idea what they had joined together for, apart from their slogan, "Africa for the Africans"—and accounted for the gun-running : the fleer at the authority he was obliged overtly to accept, or forfeit his house and food.

It was this smothered hatred, which, blotting out all discretion, seized, almost with relief, upon Johnny, as its focussing point, as the symbol of all he believed himself to have suffered at the hands of his white employers, and of Morris, and of the British in general. He would go with Quabina : he would strip from Johnny all his pretensions, show up the trick he had played upon an ignorant people, in pretending to be the reincarnated "Matti," their fetish spirit : and would reveal him for what he was—Morris's spy, come up to Omo to catch them red-handed at their gun-running and bring down the vengeance of the British upon them.

It was, indeed, the most unfortunate thing for Kaboha that he had so completely forgotten the mind of his people and that, in the pleasure of his villainy, he lost that wariness he had so far preserved in dealings with Akosua.

Pulled out of her clay coffin, scraped down, dusted off and twisted into a cloth, the old woman was at first too jitteringly mad with her tormentors to take in the full implication of what Quabina, with the assistance of Komuntale, told her. Somebody, however, was thoughtful enough to go and warn the doctor that she was at large again, and the young man from Mpongwe thought it expedient to remove himself and his paraphernalia while the going was good ; not even waiting to collect his fee, he made hell for leather for the bush—his going rendered erratic by the generosity of his hosts in the matter of palm wine.

Restored to some part of her normal self, Akosua took a look at Komuntale, who had never been one of her favourites. Although he had had the forethought to arrive in a loin-cloth, and—the night being chilly—had borrowed a skin from Quabina, she knew by the look and the feel of his flesh, which she poked maliciously, that he was in the habit of wearing white people's clothing, and sneered at him for it. So far as the substitution of stones for guns was concerned, she did not believe a word of his story. Kaboha, of course, had stolen the guns himself and double-crossed her with Ya Ashantua—selling them direct to her rival at Ejesu and pocketing the difference which should come to Akosua. The other part—that they had a traitor in the village, a desecrator of the fetish, and that Omo itself, and the Basin, were in danger—she chose to believe. Having chewed the matter over, she despatched a messenger to her son Kufi.

The messenger came back, saying that Kufi, wearing a hat that was like a log covered with the skin of the puma, was leading a dance of the young men on the space in front of the palace of justice.

The second messenger reported that Kufi, with the help of his magic eyes, which Morrissi had sent him, had the whole village flabbergasted with a demonstration of his visionary powers : that half the people were already hailing him as a supernatural being, and that the former adherents to Akosua's party and that of her favourite, Quabina, were seriously shaken.

The third messenger, who returned in a condition of flustered dishevelment, and had obviously been through an unpleasant experience, brought message that Akosua would please cease making a nuisance of herself, as the chief was making love with one of his wives, and deprecated the repeated assaults on his privacy.

Akosua's jaw tightened. If that was the tune, she would dance her own measure to it. But she also had a little matter of business to attend to first.

By her instructions, they took Kaboha Komuntale, removed his eyelids and other sensitive superstructure, and spatch-cocked him in full moonlight on the top of an ant-heap. It was an old Ashanti custom : she felt like a girl again in Bantama as she summoned her bearer, clambered up on his shoulders and, smoking her pipe, set forth to teach Kufi, whose rank stupidity and crass vanity had allowed these interlopers to invade their citadel and violate their fetish, his place in the internal economy of Omo.

II

Johnny sat hugging his knees. He hugged them so tightly that his arms ached, his spine ached and an aching ball of tightness in the middle of his body felt as though it would either burst or end by suffocating him. The air was thick with layer upon layer of noise, of which the drums provided the basic texture, stabbed from time to time by the squeal of a flute or torn by the blare of a trumpet : and woven into it, embroidering it, lending it riches, came the bush noises—the barks, shrieks and long, flesh-creeping wails of the four-footed.

He did not know how long he had been watching the phantasmagoria of whirling shapes, of beast-heads and bird-heads worn by the dancers. Something was going on that threatened the very core of humanity itself; something was taking possession—something that came seething like black smoke out of the bush, that involved them all, even himself and Kershaw, sweeping them back to the animal. He gave one glance at Kershaw, and hurriedly looked away.

Kershaw was half-crouched, half-lying, in a queer, knotted position; his eyes were glittering and now and again he grunted. He appeared quite unaware of anything but the swaying, snake-like line of the women, the hard, purposeful bodies of the men, that the firelight painted with grey and ochre and the glowing red of mahogany. About them the tree columns took on a priapic significance, seemed to swell and palpitate about the figure of a young girl who, bearing the tribal phallus, appeared suddenly in the middle of the ring. A smothering stench of sweat, like rotting bamboo, poured from the wet bodies of the dancers, the faces of the women were blank with abandonment and there was vicious purpose in the jerking loins of the males. All the loin-cloths were dropped and, with them, the last vestiges of humanity.

There was a twitching in Kershaw's limbs and a blind, almost naked look about him that identified him with the orgy. It flashed into Johnny's mind, with a pang of sick horror, that Kershaw was being sucked away, sucked into the black African womb that now prepared, with its expansions and its contractions to usher into the world some unspeakable fœtus implanted by one of its antique gods. He found himself gasping, hammering on Kershaw's shoulder.

"For God's sake—come; let's get out."

Kershaw's only answer was a shrill laugh. Johnny leapt on him, shook him, rolled him over on his back, and Kershaw lay there, laughing at the sky like an idiot. Suddenly the laughter stopped. His vision withdrew itself from indescribable distance to focus slowly on Johnny. Then he rubbed his hands over his face, as though ashamed of what was written there.

"What——? Sure; I've had enough—if you have."

But he reeled as he walked, and the laughter continued to squirt out of him hysterically, as though he could not control it. At last he managed to mutter:

"I've never been in on anything like that before—though I've been out here seven years!"

Johnny felt drained, incapable of answering. Stumbling along the street, empty save for a few stragglers from the main centre of festivity, he was stupid with noise and fatigue. The day that lay behind them seemed to have been endless—eternity stretched between their present situation and the quiet reaches of the river.

They went into the dark hut, Johnny plunging for the nearest bed, while Kershaw pulled the mats over the door, shutting out the moonlight. He heard a stumble, a crash, and Kershaw swearing.

" What's up now ? " His voice sounded thick, unused.

" Those perishing Kroos of mine ! They might have been using umbrella stands all their lives ! "

He waited with a kind of bored impatience for Kershaw's facetiousness to expend itself.

" There was a sort of calabash thing standing just inside the door, and they shoved the rockets into it. I caught them with my elbow——"

" Christ—it's a wonder we weren't blown sky high ! "—Startled out of boredom, Johnny heaved himself up on an elbow to remark. The incident had banished Kershaw's hysteria, for the chuckle that came through the darkness was normal.

" That's where the laugh comes in. I didn't tell you before—in case you got uneasy. The damn' pot was full of water—it's all over my feet—and those rockets——"

" They're done for ! " It was Johnny's turn to break out in a dry cackle. " Pity Igolo didn't know, before he set off for Diloli. The D.C. will wonder what's up—unless we can find some way of letting him know. Oh, what the hell. Time enough to start worrying, in the morning."

" If you can sleep in this you're a freak," Kershaw was complaining, an hour later. " Just listen to it. Sounds as if somebody's turning nasty. And can you wonder ? After all that palm wine. What muck it is. Oh, well. As we used to be told as children, 'This'll all end in a good cry.' Let's hope Kufi will be over his crying in time to talk sense to-morrow afternoon. Omo's certainly hot on its hospitalities, but I doubt if my system will stand up to another night of this ! "

Johnny was silent : wondering what had happened to his sense of humour. Wondering why Kershaw's was suddenly offensive. Feeling that his own irritability was childish. Omo *was* funny—in its present mood : as a flock of mischievous apes is funny, as children playing a grown-up game are funny . . . as the Yoruba head in Morris's room was *not* funny. " Something between the two." Something dark, incalculable as African night. Something knitted into the very entrails of Time itself . . . one did not laugh at these things. Yet—he had already reached the point of wondering whether he had really seen the things he had seen that night : things too esoteric for the ordinary mind to grasp, though in some way related to the dreams which visited all youths—it was said—on the threshold of manhood ; dreams of which, on waking, one was ashamed. Only here, in the bush, there was no shame. Shame was a thing that attached only to some physical shortcoming, to the evidences of senility, to the failure of the body to carry out its normal functions. . . .

A cry shot him upright on the bed of skins. It went through the drums, and the stamping, and the howls, through the rattle, the shuffle and the clonk, like a sword. With these it had nothing in common, It was a sound or mortal anguish. It was, in fact, the cry of Kaboha Komuntale, as the ants got at his mutilated parts. And it was repeated many times.

III

From the moment that Kufi caught the change in the note of his people's revelry, and hurried out of the women's hut to find out the cause of it, he knew trouble had broken. He could feel it in the air, even in his "souls," in whose attention he sensed something mechanical. There were other signs—not blatant ones, but unmistakable in their implication: that the going forth of the Chief was of less significance than some new motive that engaged his flitter-headed subjects—who, like moths in a storm, were now whirling and bobbing about the palaver house.

To the astonishment of Kufi, it now appeared that his mother, or his brother, or both, had actually taken advantage of his own preoccupation to call a palaver in the official precincts themselves. Kufi gave a shout of anger—and partly of fear. Then he remembered himself: he had for backing not only his chieftainship, but the spirits of the lord Matti and of all the long line of rulers whose blood had flowed into the Basin; he had the lord Morrissi, and beyond him the Great Queen, and the great and the small guns that stood for defence to her loyal subjects and for ruin to her enemies.

Kufi gulped. While he padded along between his "souls" he had to make up his mind, and the Basin must be his inspiration. Omo held, by tradition, a reputation for great ingenuity and resource in the disposal of weak or unpopular leaders; it was only of recent years that prejudice had made itself felt, in a few punitive expeditions against villages which persisted in managing their own affairs in a fashion displeasing to the white interpreters of the penal code.

Between the pair of them, Akosua and Quabina had got the palaver house humming like a hive of bees about to swarm. From the moment she had disposed of Kaboha Komuntale, the old lady had snatched the initiative from the hands of a few who were disposed to treat the matter in a more constitutional fashion, and who now, squatting in corners, hunting their fleas and chewing beans, listened to Akosua and reserved judgment.

Kufi was a fool—was a dupe—was in no way fitted to lead so important a tribe as Omo. This went down in a big way with the supporters of Quabina, who, setting the words to a rhythm, proceeded to dance them—partly because this was their custom, and partly in compliment to Quabina, himself a great dancer: who, by way of showing his appreciation of the tribute, leapt into the middle of the palaver house and held up proceedings for a full twenty minutes with a song and dance commemorating the great feats of Omo in the past. This created an impression; for what, indeed, had Omo done, of latter years, but produce rubber and act as a buffer between small surrounding states? A faint gleam of reminiscent gratification crossed the faces of the flea-hunting elders, and some of the small fry which had crawled in between their knees set up a sympathetic capering, until smacked into decorous behaviour by those with a finer conception of the sancity of the building.

When Kufi and his bodyguard appeared, behind their shields and fully armed, taking the palaver by surprise, most of the company felt embarrassed. Kufi was not a spectacular chief, but he was popular, except with the juvenile hotheads. Under his rule Omo had prospered, life had been easy, if dull, and justice had been administered in a way satisfactory to all but a few congenital troublemakers who, naturally, were loudest in support of the more irresponsible Quabina.

So when Kufi stalked into the heart of the assembly, well protected from every angle by the shields—a hush fell, and, apart from Akosua, there was no undue eagerness on the part of anyone to obey his command, and speak. Akosua, however, seized her son Quabina by the back of his neck and hurled him before his brother, and, the two of them speaking, for the most part, together, Kufi heard for the first time the story of Kaboha Komuntale.

Kufi was a slow-witted man. Battered by the waves of public opinion —for, one having spoken, there was no longer any self-consciousness on the part of the rest—the first thing he grasped was that, however divided the company might be on other points it was unanimous about a killing. While he chewed this over uncomfortably, cursing his own bad luck that such a situation should have arisen through his own credulity, Akosua was hobbling round, clutching first this and then that influential member of the assembly, pouring out her views, and hammering them home with shrewd allusions to tribal prestige, and the importance of keeping well in with Ejesu.

The man Fludi was an enemy, and must die ; that first. There was no telling what mischief might follow an affront to the fetish, unless the affront were wiped out in blood.

With this everyone, including Kufi himself, was in agreement ; an offended fetish was the most damaging thing a community could harbour, and the purification formulæ were specific. Nevertheless . . . supposing it were a mistake ? Kufi's brother-in-law, a sober-minded young man who had been named as in the running for the chieftainship, had considerable backing when he pointed out that the self-identification of the man Fludi with the lord Matti had been accepted, not merely by the irresponsible and impressionable rabble, but by such alumni as the fetish priest and by all the witchcraft fraternity : all of whom must lose face if the identification were proved to be a hoax, and would cause the name of Omo to be a laughing stock up and down the river.

" Where is he who brought this story ? "

A general outcry was answered, perforce, by Quabina, who admitted that his mother had looked after him. Akosua was dancing with impatience ; she had set her heart on a good, old-fashioned killing, and a killing she was going to have. Someone put forth the nervous reminder that if the man Fludi were to be killed, and if it turned out after all that he was not an imposter, there would be the devil to pay ; and Akosua's retort that if this were so, his hand at least could be kept as ju ju was not received well by those who lacked the old woman's scornful independence of spirit.

Kufi sat silent in the midst of it all ; looking round the palaver house, he could tell at a glance which were his friends and which his enemies, and it seemed to him that the latter were far in the majority. He could not hear, but he could guess what they were saying : Why not kill Kufi ? For it is he who has landed us in this predicament, through his anxiety to keep in with the British. And what have the British done for us, except upset our traditions, interfere with our law system and send their God-men to us to teach our children disregard of our old beliefs ? There are men here, old men, who remember Omo as a great kingdom ; what have the British done to help us defend our Stool against our enemies ?

Yes, it would be good to kill Kufi. And when Quabina is chief, there need be no more fear of Morrissi and his guns and his soldiers, for Quabina will immediately make treaty with Ejesu, and Omo with the Ashanti will lead the rising against the white people, and we shall be great again, as we were in the days of our kings.

Kufi read all this in the faces around him, as plainly as though the words were spoken aloud, and his heart within him was as water. Only anger and pride reminded him that he was still chief of Omo, and he was sure of the support of his " souls " who would certainly be no less disinclined than he to render up their lives—as tribal law would compel them to do, if their chief were killed : for it is the duty of all souls to accompany their master into the house of death, in order that he may not want for companionship and congenial entertainment.

So Kufi spoke plainly. His face was the colour of dust and his eyes rolled like black cherries on the amber syrup of the eyeballs, but his jaw thrust itself forward and his voice was steady. His feet, planted wide apart and his head lowered like a bull's on its thick shoulders and neck lent him a sufficiently formidable aspect to drive his brother Quabina a couple of sharp paces back, and to dry up, for a moment, the babble on Akosua's lips. He said :

" This is bad palaver, and it will be no matter for surprise if those who began it see blood before the end of the moon." Most of the audience took this without emotion ; it was what they were hoping for. " But since you plan evil, the man Fludi shall answer for himself. There shall be a palaver, and the tests shall be put on him. I say it ; though he is my brother and well beloved of Morrissi, who is my brother also, and loves me as he loves Fludi. And it will be bad for Omo when I say to Morrissi, ' This, lord, I did, because the people willed it.' "

This swung public opinion heavily to Kufi's side, for the tests were varied, and there was much blood in them. Delighted at the prospect of the entertainment—fitting crown to an exciting day—no one cared a brass button for Morrissi, or for any remote reprisals that might follow a witchcraft trial—which was what it amounted to.

Had Fludi or had he not the spirit of the lord Matti, which was the spirit of the Basin, within him? If he had, the tests would fail. If he had not, the mutilated but still living body of a white man, pegged out to await death on one of the big ant heaps which had already served Kaboha Komuntale, would be a useful object lesson to any person who took it into his head to interfere with the private business of Omo.

Kufi sucked the sweat from his upper lip. He had gained a brief respite: captured, for a little while, his uncertain popularity. There was nothing for it now—but to get really drunk.

IV

The palaver house was at the opposite end of the village, and all Omo had drained itself towards it. Under the moon, which stared cherry-coloured through a bank of mist, the empty huts were like squatting hedgehogs.

"Come on," said Kershaw, and with one accord they flung themselves towards the stockade.

"Look out for those perishing bells!"

While Johnny was frantically trying to decide which section of the stockade it was wise to attempt—for, like most villages of the district, Omo surrounded itself with an alarum system they knew it would be fatal to set in operation—some empty-headed Omo youth, too half-witted to realise the momentous events that were going forward, ran out gaping to see what the guests were up to. Before he could let out the yell which, obviously, trembled on his lips, Kershaw planted his hunting knife deep in his throat. As the youth fell, Johnny let out a gasp—and the next moment felt himself flying through the air; Kershaw, with his shoulder under the other's buttocks, had put all his muscle into a heave. Before he had time to recover his breath, Kershaw had crashed on top of him—having taken the chance before which Johnny had hesitated: of scaling that piece of the stockade immediately facing him, and behind the guest house.

Neither daring to speak, they picked themselves up: their fall had been broken by the offal heap which—again, as in most villages—formed the base of the stockade. A few yards, and they were in the bush.

"Nice going," observed Kershaw, "and none too soon." From where they were hiding, spears and bush-lights could already be seen, jogging up towards the guest house. The militant intention of their bearers was not to be mistaken, even by those who had never heard Omo hell-bent for trouble before. "Nuisance, we had to get out on this side. That means we've got to work right round at the back of the village, to hit Foxy's trail again."

"How if they cut us off?"

"Ten to one they will; and that'll mean a night in the bush; *not* so cosy a prospect," ruminated Kershaw. "I'd like to know what the leopard incidence is round here."

"There won't be any swamp incidence; that's one good thing," observed Johnny. "We're too high for that." He was surprised to find in himself no fear—only a kind of high excitement, mingled with a gratitude that he was sharing this adventure with Kershaw.

" Come on : our only chance is to make it before they find out we've gone," Kershaw was saying.

" Then," said Johnny, " we've lost our chance. Listen to that."

A long, concerted howling went up to the red moon, punctuated by screams.

" Oh, hell, won't Morris be mad."

" To hell with Morris. We're in a pickle : a father and mother of a pickle." He had never heard Kershaw undilutedly serious before, Johnny was thinking. He said, with a vainglory intended to bolster his own courage :

" They're drunk as lords—the whole lot of them ! I bet you and I could have walked straight down the village street, and not one of 'em would have noticed anything, until they got to the hut and found the birds flown !"

" You're cracked," said Kershaw calmly. " Don't you know the only time a nigger's really dangerous is when he's roaring drunk ? The blacks don't go in for gentlemanly blinds, you know, as we do. This is a damned odd do. I'd like to find out what's at the back of it."

" Have you forgotten what Foxy said, about the nigger in the wood-pile ? I bet you a pound to a coconut Akosua's the one that's put the match to the fuse—the blasted old busybody ! " He found himself catching Kershaw's flippancy, and felt cheerful about it.

" She had to get her match from somewhere, hadn't she ? I guess our friends who took the pot-shot at us yesterday could supply it."

" And Komuntale." A sudden thought struck Johnny. " Do you suppose the old woman's in on the gun-running ? "

" Wouldn't put anything past that old danger-signal—from all that's known of her." His face, clear under the red moon, turned from side to side. " By God, I'd like to see them trying this on, if Morris was here, with a brace of his Hausas." Johnny thought of the rockets, and knew Kershaw was thinking the same. " Come on, we'd better be making tracks. There's nothing to fluster about." He wouldn't have said it, if he believed it, thought Johnny. " Foxy's bound to have heard the din, and you can be pretty sure he's started back by now. Won't we be popular, for spoiling his beauty sleep ! "

Won't we be popular, Johnny was thinking bitterly, with Morris, for being the cause of this set-up !

They began, with no particular attempt at silence, to trudge through the outer fringe of the bush ; the noise from the village was loud enough to drown any sound their feet might make, or their bodies, thrusting against the heavy tangle of the vines. Shallow as the forest was at this part, the going was heavy ; the vegetation that the natives were continually chopping back lay thick at its edge, some shrivelled, giving off reports like musketry at each step, some sodden with heavy dews : all harbourage for snakes and for the deadlier insects that Omo drove from its thresholds. The tortuous stems of plants, the ubiquitous tie-tie held them back from time to time ;

now and again they came on patches of rag tied to a stump—Omo's preventive measures against devil-invasion.

They had not gone a quarter of a mile when Johnny heard a grunt, and a crash. There was no answer, when he spoke Kershaw's name.

V

Among Harcourt Flood's papers, after his death in that summer of 1910 which, with the passing of Edward the Seventh, marked the end of the Age of Opulence, was found a big manila envelope inscribed in Harcourt's crabbed hand : *Log kept by John Flood, West Africa*, 1898-99. Between the pages of the thick, typewritten wad it contained were a few sheets torn, evidently, from a notebook. Scribbled in pencil, they begin suddenly, as though they might be the continuation of some former passages, lost or destroyed on the writer's return to England :

" When Kershaw told me to leave him " (the notes begin) " and get on, in the hope of meeting Foxy, I realised what a tight corner we were in. To make matters worse, the moon, which was now very low, had disappeared, and we were in pitch darkness, with nothing but the lie of the land to tell us how we were going. In short, we'd got to go uphill, and then we had to turn sharp right and start going downhill : but where the turn came neither of us had the slightest idea.

" There was now a devil of a row going on inside the village, to which we were a lot too close to be comfortable. I could only drag Kershaw a few yards at a time, and, careful as I tried to be, he fainted twice with the pain of his broken leg. He kept cursing at me and telling me to leave him, but I remembered his remark about the leopard incidence. When we found ourselves up against something like a fence, it looked like being the end, because I could never have hauled Kershaw over it—he being pretty near the six-foot mark and a good twelve or thirteen stone. However, patting round with my hands in the dark, I felt thatch, and realised it was a hut, and empty. So this seemed to be our only hope, and there was a chance if they found out where we were we could hold them up with our Colts for a little while.

" It was now I started to feel sick with myself, and pretty desperate, for I knew the whole thing was, in a way, my own fault. It all stemmed back to that business with Mfabo, when I thought myself so smart at handling a bad nigger ; and it was going to finish with gunboats and a full-scale punitive raid on Omo—the very thing Morris wanted, above all, to avoid. I was mad, too, at getting Kufi into a jam with the D.C., because I liked him, and that blood brotherhood business, although most people take it as a joke, stuck in my throat.

" The place we were in smelt unbelievable, even for an African village. I daren't strike a light, for fear anyone was looking our way, but I felt about, and there seemed to be hides. There were other things—disgusting.

It took me quite a while to find out we were in the fetish house, and when I told Kershaw I thought he would never stop laughing. With all the pain he was in, he laughed until he had hiccups. I suppose it was just the silliness of it. Trying to escape, we'd run ourselves straight into the worst trap we could have found if we'd spent our time looking for one. It flashed across us both that something might have been done if the Basin had been there, but there wasn't any hope of that. Anything so precious as the tribal fetish wouldn't be left in an unprotected hut, outside the village boundary; it had probably gone back, after its airing, to a hole in the ground, that only the priests knew about.

"The worst part was that we now couldn't get away; the moon had come out again, and Kershaw was too heavy and too helpless to risk it.

"There were drums and horns and as much yelling and hallooing as if all hell was let loose. Kershaw was hiccuping somewhere back of me. Then there was a shadow across the doorway, shaped rather like a haycock. While I was wondering where it came from, it ducked in towards me, and almost without thinking I let it have it with my Colt. It fell in with a crash like a ton of bricks, and I remember thinking I could deal with three more and there would still be a couple of shots left for us. But nobody else turned up and the shindy was still in full swing, so I took a chance and struck a match and it was the witch doctor, all got up in his fancy dress. I suppose he had come to look for some of his tricks. Anyhow, he was as dead as mutton.

"It sounds silly, but I got into his clothes. I think I must have gone a little crazy, for I didn't seem to care what I did, so long as it wasn't just crouching in that fetish hut, waiting for Omo to get through its hunt inside the village and extend the area of its operations. The clothes were alive with vermin, and I was nearly stifled with the heat and the smell. It was sheer luck I had managed to hit him in a vital part, because the costume or whatever you call it had a thick padding of straw. It was shaped like a wigwam, and went high up into a head, with eyes and real teeth in it, that scraped the roof of the fetish house: a really smart piece of work, that children would enjoy dressing up in! I'd seen plenty of them and always wanted to try one on—but not in circumstances like these.

"I'd just discovered that there was a hole in front, to look through, and that my arms inside the wigwam thing were free, and I could bend them a little, when we heard the rest of the party arriving, and at the very same minute the 'head' wedged itself somehow into the thatch above, and there I was, jammed between the floor and the ceiling, practically in the doorway, but unable to move in or out.

"I couldn't see much, but it looked as if the whole clearing was covered with people howling like wild cats and leaping about like kangaroos. There was a lot of stamping. We could feel the ground shaking. I couldn't see Kufi, or any of his friends. All this time I was trying to twist that infernal headpiece loose from the thatch that was holding it overhead, and Kershaw was cursing like a navvy. He couldn't shoot, because of me, but I'd managed to jab the barrel of the Colt through the skirt, or cage, or whatever you call the lower part of the witch doctor's costume, and found I could move it around a bit. Luckily the moon was behind the hut, so I was in shadow, just far enough inside not to be seen unless anyone came right up to the door.

" Lower down the clearing was the empty mission house, and when I saw some people prancing around with torches, I made sure they were going to fire it, which of course would have been the best thing they could have done from our point of view, as the light and the smoke would have brought Foxy like a shot, and would probably have been seen at Diloli. But evidently the same thought struck some of the leaders, because the torches were put out, and the whole gang started to shape themselves into a rough kind of semi-circle, facing towards us, but twenty or twenty-five yards away. The moon was fairly steady by now. They all had spears or swords, and some were stark naked and others had on costumes that made one think of schoolroom charades when we were children. But there was nothing childish about this set-out, and it made one feel sick, to see these Omo people, who, a few hours ago, had been as merry as grigs, transformed into a horde of beastly, bloodthirsty savages, some in full war paint, striped like zebras and hung with the most disgusting objects which I suppose were ' killing ' charms.

" They had all started to bawl and shout towards the fetish house. I thought, *This is it*, and I was just going to tell Kershaw to be ready, when there was a scuffle at the back of the crowd, and six or eight big fellows pushed their way through with something they threw on the ground, and it was Kufi.

" The poor fellow was covered with blood from head to foot and I couldn't make out if he was dead or alive. I guessed dead, because there was a lot more noise, and Quabina came strutting through, with people beating drums and shaking rattles all round him. He had got the Chief's crown on his head, and the robe Kufi was wearing when he received us. After him, on the back of a carrier, came the old woman ; I knew it was she, though I was seeing her for the first time—all gewgawed up and shrieking with excitement. Then there was a lot more yelling and tossing of spears, which Quabina took to himself like a peacock.

" Presently Quabina gave a kind of cross-eyed look up at the fetish house and said something to two of his followers, who came trotting up the hill—no doubt to order the witch doctor to be sharp, and come and pay his respects to the new chief.

" I didn't like Quabina. Apart from Foxy's warning, I'd caught only a glimpse of him, at a moment during the dancing, but he struck me as a treacherous, dangerous sort of beast—a different breed from Kufi, who, poor fellow, was a decent sort of chap in his way, and might have been valuable to us, if we'd been in a position to give him the backing he needed.

" Anyhow, I guessed we were done for. So when the messengers arrived, and stood gaping at what they took for the witch doctor wedged top and toe inside the sacred building, I took a chance. Just then something went crack above my head and I found I could move : some of the stays, or cage-work, inside the headpiece had given, and as I shuffled into the opening, I could feel it lolling and nodding above me. Pretty grim it must have looked, with its four rows of grinning teeth which I'm nearly sure were human.

" The two niggers jumped back and I thought they were going to bolt. I made my voice as hollow and unnatural as I could when I said it was the will of the fetish that Quabina should come himself. When he walked up towards me, wagging his buttocks and looking every bit of the conceited, cowardly rascal he was, I shot him in the belly.

" I don't know why I hadn't realised the effect it would make—Quabina's falling like that in the moonlight, right in front of everybody, without a gun or a human soul in sight except the members of his tribe, who, a moment before, had been bawling their heads off in honour of the new chief.

" I don't believe it took more than sixty seconds to empty that clearing. They vanished like smoke. There was nobody there except Quabina, rolling and screaming and clutching his belly, old Akosua, howling over him—one had to admire the old vixen's guts, stopping with her dying son—and the dead body of Kufi, with its awful mutilations, which I examined later on, lying there in a sort of grandeur of moonlight and blood."

The writing, which had been steadily growing weaker and more indistinct, ends there, but is followed by a line in Harcourt's hand:

" *Written by J. F. in hospital. A brave record.*"

CHAPTER TEN

I

TO spare his further sufferings, Johnny shot Quabina in the head, as he would have shot a mortally wounded animal. Acting on Kershaw's advice, he had taken the previous precaution of securing Akosua. " We don't want that old she-scorpion starting up something fresh before we get away. Don't forget," grunted Kershaw, his teeth set against the pain of his broken femur, " she's the only one, so far, that knows for certain what killed Quabina. It may be another couple of hours before some bright spirit recovers the use of what he might possibly call his brains, and remembers that fetish doesn't kill its victims with a Colt."

It was easy to talk of catching Akosua, hard to do it. Old as she was, she could double like a ferret, and she was off from the moment she caught sight of Johnny emerging from the witch doctor's teguments—her bare feet gripping the dry, sandy earth on which Johnny's boots slid and scuffled. At one moment he had hold of her cloth, at the next, to his horror, he was clutching the cloth and Akosua, a grotesque in skin and bone, was skipping across the clearing at a pace which drew a warning shout from Kershaw, afraid to use his Colt in case of hitting the wrong person, as they dodged in an antic pattern of moonlight and shadow round the corner of the mission house.

"Wing her, Johnny, wing her!" Concentrating on keeping between the old woman and her get-away behind the stockade, Johnny was too breathless to shoot, but he managed at last to head her back towards the fetish hut, outside of which Kershaw had dragged himself on his forearms and the undamaged leg. Johnny's flesh crept as his hands closed on the skinny body, with the breasts that swung like pointed bags of dried leather far down over that part of her abdomen her cloth was supposed to cover. He let out a yelp that was as much surprise as pain, when, ducking her head, she sank her fangs into his flesh—and thought he had lost her; it was Kershaw who, with a sudden lunge along the ground, caught the old woman's ankle and, by jerking it in the air, brought her down crashing, spitting and squealing, almost on top of him.

"Shut up, you disreputable old varmint." With a dispassionate clip on the head, he put a temporary end to Akosua's activities. "For the love of Pete, fetch her peignoir and put it over her. I can't abide raw woman flesh, unless it's young and wholesome. Did you ever see the play of *Hamlet*?" he was inquiring, when Johnny returned with the length of striped plush that was Akosua's best cloth, put on for the dramatic occasion. "This scene's beginning to remind me of it—the last act, with dead bodies three a penny."

"Let's have a look at that leg of yours." He did not want to look at the empty, moonlit space, with the two still shapes in it: shapes from which manhood and the gladness of living had drained away, as their blood drained into the dry earth.

"Never mind my leg. There's a hell of a lot of things to do, fella; it's a pity I can't help you."

"Go on; tell me what to do and I'll get on with it the best I can."

"Those bodies have to be got out of the way, before the blood-smell fetches the cats down. Also, they may send out a party to reconnoitre and collect the remains. The sooner we get the evidence removed the more chance we have of playing up the 'mystery' end. Nothing frightens the nigger like something he can't find a reason for, and, with luck, we'll put such a wind up these beggars, they'll clear out, lock, stock and barrel, before Morrissi gets here to see what they've been up to."

"Do you mean, bury them?" He kicked the ground, iron-hard below its sandy substrata, doubtfully. "It'd take a crowbar to break this earth." Johnny shook his head.

Kershaw said, after a brief consideration:

"There's only one thing for it. . . . Here; give me a pull."

Sweat was running down both their faces, when Johnny had dragged Kershaw down the hill to Quabina's side.

"Now help me off with my coat. I'll keep my gat handy—thank you." Johnny wondered what was coming next. "Now my hunting knife." The moonlight ran in a streak of blue along the blade as Kershaw pulled it from the sheath strapped to his belt. He felt its edge reflectively, before looking up at Johnny with a smile of curious tranquillity. "Now, fella, you'd better clear out—if you don't want nightmares for the rest of your life. Just bear in mind that what we're going to do isn't pretty, but it's necessary——"

Between sickness and incredulity, Johnny stammered :

"Gammon. I'll lend you a hand."

"Go on—do as you're told ! Cut off back to the fetish house, and see what you can find that'll make a splint for this leg of mine. I'll call when I'm ready—and if that old vampire comes to, knock her across the head again ; we don't want any caterwauling from her at this point. Johnny !" he called, when the latter had gone a few reluctant paces. "Fetch me down the old geezer's dressing-gown ; I guess this is one of the times it doesn't pay to be fussy about female modesty."

By Kershaw's directions, they sliced the seven-yard cloth into pieces ; then Johnny went away again. Ferreting about in the unspeakable contents of the fetish hut, he could find nothing that would conceivably serve for a splint for a broken limb. It struck him that the missionaries might, in their departure, have left some odds and ends of furniture that might do, if the ants had not been at it—and that to go down to their house meant passing Kershaw at his grisly task. He pulled himself angrily together, and, as he was setting out, remembered Akosua.

The old woman lay there, to all appearances still unconscious from Kershaw's tap on the temple, but just as likely foxing ; in any case, a potential danger. He knew what had to be done, and forced himself to do it, although the thought of touching her again made him shudder. But as he drove the gag of rolled-up palm fibre between her jaws, the rightness of his suspicions were proved ; she fought him like a cat until he got the tie-tie round her wrists and ankles. Rolled into a corner, the potential danger had become a useful hostage ; his satisfaction inured him to the ordeal of seeing that which he must see, as he went to look for Kershaw's splint.

. . . When the call came, there was nothing but dark patches and several knotted bundles. Kershaw kept his hands concealed ; he had parted not only with his coat but with his shirt, and there were splashes here and there on his hairy torso that Johnny's eyes avoided.

"Your job now." He was grinning. "I fancy that's "—he jerked his head towards the knife, stuck into the earth at his side—" set up a record to-night. We've got none too much time if what I think I hear's correct. Some of those heroes are getting over their fright, and it won't be long before curiosity sets in. Pull me back to the hut, and I'll tell you what to do next."

. . . The first journey was agony, for the trees held out all that there was of light, and he was constantly hitting or tearing himself on some obstacle in the narrow track. It was one of those creeks formed by the main stream's spreading its fingers through the fibrous soil netted by the tree roots : the one to which he had noticed the track on his initial inspection of their surroundings. But the fifth journey he made, and the subsequent ones, with his loathsome burden, were accomplished almost at a run ; he no-longer cared, he only wanted it to be over. Suffocated by the pounding of his heart and past any coherent thought, he swung his last load out into the creek and heard, as before, the splathering rush and clash—this time so near that he was sprayed with water before he had time to leap back out of reach of the jaws that fought over their unwonted feast.

He stood for a moment, shivering and sweating, trying to hear above the obscene sounds the noises of the canoes coming downstream. They had both agreed that Foxy, if he got the alarm, would be more likely to arrive by water than by the bush path, which, although shorter, might be ambushed. But there was no such heartening sign, and he realised that they had to face the possibility of Foxy, worn out with a hard day and Omo's hospitality, not catching, in his drowsiness, that note which betrayed the change in the temperature of the night's rumpus.

" What I'd give for a couple of drums of kerosene ! " Kershaw was saying, when he fell, rather than walked, into the fetish house. " It would keep the cats away and give Foxy a hint that somethin's gone wrong. We're a long way from out of the wood yet—though it can't be far off dawn."

Then there was a silence, broken only by groans, as Kershaw forced the broken ends of bone back through the jagged flesh, and, when they seemed to be aligned, made Johnny lay the strips of wood he had found in the mission house along the line of the break and bind them from knee to ankle with the ever-useful tie-tie. When this was done, and Kershaw had collapsed for the moment in a stupor of pain, it occurred to Johnny that, with the long drought and the inflammable material to hand, it should be easy to fire the mission house.

It was a risk, because it was bound to fetch the people out to see what was going on, but there was the chance that they would have such a shock, on finding the bodies of Kufi and Quabina vanished that they would think the spirits had been at it again, and would take to their heels.

Alone with Kershaw, Akosua kept to herself the fact that her hands had been free for the last ten minutes, Johnny, in his haste, having failed properly to secure the binding round her wrists. She amused herself for some time, thinking what she could do with those horny thumb nails of hers, but devious herself, she seldom fell into the error of underrating other people's powers of duplicity. For all her companion's stillness, she was not sure he was sleeping, and the fact that he had, under his hand, the very weapon which had killed her son, her Benjamin, her well-beloved one, Quabina, made her cautious. Quabina—her treasure—who had gone unaccompanied into the house of death, not having even had time to appoint his " souls ! " Akosua's face wrinkled up and she was about to let out a howl of mourning but thought better of it.

Instead, she trapped a little lizard which had stolen unwisely from the matting of the wall by her side. She looked quickly to see whether her action had been noticed. No. The eyes of her enemy were still closed. She turned carefully on her side, so as to have her back to him, and drew, thoughtfully, a few twigs and shreds of fibre from the wall. The little lizard tickled the palm of her hand. Very carefully, so as not to injure it, she pegged it to the ground with a forked stick. The little lizard struggled weakly, and was still.

When Johnny returned, his body showed in the entrance to the hut against a faint, rosy flicker. He was about to say, "I've done it!" when the sharp crack of a breaking twig startled him and made him look towards the corner where Akosua, now careless of her captors, was squatting on her haunches. "You—old——" he was beginning, and saw her lift her hand and bring it down as though she were striking something. A blinding pain shot through his head.

II

"Great God in heaven!" breathed Morris, as the sky over Omo turned from the dark steel of just before dawn to a restless crimson. It might have been sunrise, but for the fact that the sun does not rise in the south. The smoke had started to belch above the trees when the launch went chug-chugging down the waterway, with Morris muttering: "God damn them, why can't they give us some sort of efficient transport?" It was not often the District Commissioner forgot himself so far as to swear at the unspeakable "They" which focussed most of the Gold Coast bad language; but a man who knows he has to cover thirty-odd miles of land and water at an average speed of forty minutes to the mile may be forgiven for losing his sense of loyalty, when ten minutes might make "all the difference."

This was the last thing he had expected, when the drum message despatched by Igolo came through, to say that all was in order. And yet . . . a man who has spent the better part of nine years in the bush develops a sensitivity to vibrations not given to the ordinary. He might have known it was not for nothing—that impulse which had bidden him, before turning in, give orders to keep steam up, just in case Diloli's complicated affairs should settle themselves in time to make an early start for those disgraceful fellows, the Okomi.

He had just got to the point of persuading himself that some Omo idiot, at the height of celebration, had set accidental fire to his hut, when the bush, and the waterway, and the launch itself were rocked by an explosion that sent the parrots screaming over the tree tops and landed a small, hysterical monkey at Morris's elbow.

"That'll teach 'em," Foxy was muttering, as he scrambled to his feet.

He, too, had seen the red light in the sky; he, like Morris, had thought that Omo was carrying skylarking to an extreme; but he had seen enough of junketings in the bush to take no chances. He wondered, guiltily, if he had missed the rocket, as he shook his companion's shoulder and brought him out of a sound sleep.

Lewin, the factory agent, had spent enough time within earshot of Omo to be sceptical of scaremongering.

"Hell fire, you know what Omo is like when it goes on the bottle! A bonfire's just part of the fun and games, and I've been waiting for them to fire the mission house ever since the Bible-merchants pulled out."

"How much gunpowder have you got?" Foxy demanded grimly.

"I dunno: two-three kegs—hey! Where are you going?"

When they were rolling the drums to what Foxy considered a safe distance from the factory building, Lewin became uneasy.

"Who's paying for this lot? I got orders, I tell you, and my customers ain't going to take it in good part if they've got to wait another three weeks or a month for their supplies!"

"To hell with their supplies," said Foxy, and, yelling to the ring of canoe-boys drowsing round their fires to duck, threw the bush-light he had snatched from the Kroo who, in some trepidation, had obeyed the order to follow him.

There was a dead hush on Omo when the white morning light found it. The mission building was a pile of smouldering ash buried in the waist-high ground mist that curdled about the eaves of the deserted huts and clung to the stockade broken in Omo's wild bolt for the bush.

The message had got through that Morris was on the way, and it was Foxy's idea that they awaited his coming. A canoe, bucking through the rapids, was no suitable conveyance for a man with a broken leg: Kershaw might as well have the chance of coming down on the launch—unless the Commissioner had business which took him urgently in the opposite direction. And there was Johnny Flood. . . .

It was late dusk when the launch arrived. Even Kershaw, propped up on his bed in the guest house, had nothing to say when Morris walked in; made a few terse inquiries about the broken leg, and, having had his answers, walked out. He asked for no explanations, and was offered none; those would come later. It was enough, for now, that a village in his district was laid waste, its people scattered.

In the hut where Johnny lay—Foxy, with some vague idea of hospital proprieties, was responsible for the segregation—there was silence. Morris's brows knitted as he looked down at the short figure, with a blank, obliging smile on its face. There was no recognition in the level look he fixed upon Morris; no response when Morris, pressing the palm of his hand over those uninterested eyes, carried it up over the untroubled brow to the roots of Johnny's hair.

"I can't make it out," Foxy was saying. "He's either like that, or he's twisting his head about and bashing it as if it was hurting him. I seen plenty of Yellow Jack, Chief, but I've not seen anybody taken that way before."

Morris made no answer, turning on his heel and walking out of the hut. His attendant, Igolo, went with him; walking at his heels and carrying one of the launch's lanterns, whose pale-orange light flickered over the huts and into the dark mouths of their empty doorways. Through the village he went, leisurely, not keeping to the street, but looking behind the huts, occasionally entering one and looking with pity on its emptiness. So this was the end of Omo; and there were many other colonies he would sooner have seen eliminated.

He had almost reached the stockade. Close to it, dark against its silvery pallor, were the mounds he knew for the great citadels of the bush ants. He directed the light of the lantern towards them, one after another, and what he saw on the last one made him stand still.

He passed out through the opening of the stockade, and mounted the hill to the fetish house.

"We left the old bitch there," Foxy had told him. "I got her roped up and left her to think things over. I lay a pound to a potato, from Kershaw's account, this is all her doin'. So I saved her up for you, Chief. If anybody's got to answer for Omo—I reckon she's the one."

Akosua was there—in mummified condition. They had found her a cloth, and over it, from feet to neck, she was bound with tie-tie. Propped against the wall, like the corpse at a wake, her old eyes glinted a deathless malice at the Commissioner.

"You have done evil, Akosua." Morris spoke evenly. "You have brought wrath upon Omo and on its Basin. For the spirit of the Great Queen is stronger than any of your spirits, and there is no Basin, save by her Yea or Nay. This I am come to tell you: that before the sun rises I and those who are with me will find the Basin, where it is hidden, and this shall be the end of Omo, because of your evil doing."

Akosua made no answer, and, this being unusual, he went nearer, to look at her with curiosity, taking the lantern from his attendant's hand so that he could see clearly the expression on her old mask. He had always had a sour degree of respect for this black sheep of his district—for the dauntless way in which she had kept her end up against the various assaults of civilisation on her way of life and her way of thinking. And he wished to heaven he could push her out—across the border of his district—to be someone else's headache for a change. But there was Johnny Flood, lying in a hut with a sickness upon him which Morris had seen once—and only once—before, and for which someone had got to answer.

"What have you been doing, Akosua?" he asked softly, and her face met his like a piece of worn granite, but something moved—was it triumph?—under the thin film that time had drawn across her eyes.

Morris looked at her, and his face was as relentless as hers, and he slowly lowered the lantern. It took him little time to find what he was expecting, and he stood looking down at it: at a little lizard, pegged across its back and under its forelegs with a piece of forked twig; and by its side was a dry stick snapped in half, and a heavier one that lay still, where it had struck, across the lizard's head.

Morris straightened his back, slowly slipping the revolver out of its holster at his side. He spoke evenly.

"Thou knowest, Akosua, that the payment for witchcraft is death." And shot her between the eyes.

III

" *To Harcourt Flood, Esqre.,* 10 *Berkeley Square, Bristol.*

" DEAR MR. FLOOD,

" You will have heard from your nephew that he is sailing on the 23rd, instead of on the 2nd, as originally arranged. I felt it my duty to tell you that this postponement of plans is due to me, and in some degree to his medical adviser. As you know, we take malaria for granted in this part of the world, and you were no doubt prepared for the likelihood of his collecting a dose of the coaster's old enemy, 'Yellow Jack.' Thanks, however, to his excellent physique and, probably, to his temperate habits, the attacks have not been unduly serious. It takes time for the microbe to work its way out of the system, and this, together with some small complications which have been inclined to slow down his recovery, influenced me in suggesting, in concurrence with the doctor who has been in attendance, that he should spend a fortnight in sanatorium as a break between the extremes of climate here and those he will meet on the voyage. I hope that this will meet with your approval ; I can assure you that I have had hard work in getting John to agree to it.

" May I, in conclusion, pay a tribute to the remarkable qualities of this young man—he is in many respects hardly more than a boy !—whom you, for your own reasons, sent out to our colony. On a community in which character counts for fully as much as experience, he has left an impression of integrity that goes far to counterbalance his want of the latter. He seems to have an instinctive sympathy for the problems involved in the administration of our piebald community, together with a sense of justice in dealings with both black and white, which it is possible to spend years on the Coast without acquiring. I am especially struck by his modesty and his readiness to defer to people of greater experience than himself ; at the same time, it is obvious he has formed his own opinions, and is prepared to stand by them. With all of them I may not be in agreement ; youth is a period of exaggeration—or it should be : since to exaggerate is to have ideals, and to be impatient with those who are unable, either through circumstances or lack of inclination, to live up to them.

" I hope I am not presumptuous in admitting that I am persuaded that the matter of the cocoa concessions is the least part of your motive in sending your nephew out here. In any case, pray accept my assurance that any report he may bring to you is worthy, at least, of consideration. It is not for me to offer criticisms of a policy to which, by virtue of my appointment, I subscribe ; at the same time I admit, as every person of common intelligence must admit, that it is high time that an exhaustive inquiry into the affairs of the Gold Coast Colony was instituted by some person of authority, such as yourself. Let me assure you, Mr. Flood, that we are both better and worse than we are represented ! But that, until a balance is struck between the two extremes, and our needs recognised by those who are in a position to satisfy them, there is little prospect of our fulfilling the high expectations of those who have chosen to identify their fortunes with ours.

" I hope I have not exhausted your patience by this long disquisition —of which the main impression I would like to leave with you is my personal affection for your nephew John, and my high regard for the spirit he represents.

" I remain,

" Faithfully yours,

" D. J. MORRIS,

" District Commissioner."

(This letter was found among Harcourt's papers, with his comment: " Received after J. Flood's visit to the Gold Coast in 1899. The kind of thing that makes one feel one's backing the right horse.")

Johnny pushed it back across the Commissioner's table with a smothered exclamation.

" What's that you say? "

" I can't believe I deserve it, sir. But I'm very grateful. It certainly starts me off on the right foot with Uncle Hacky."

" Well—enjoy yourself in Accra "—Morris held out his hand—" and forget this last patch as soon as you can."

They stood, side by side, looking at the rain which drenched the compound and rose in steam from the parched earth. Morris smiled and stretched his arms above his head.

" I suppose we're the only people who are thankful when the rainy season starts! There's nothing like rain for damping down misbehaviour up-country."

" What about furlough? "

" Oh—I'll go up and stay with my sister presently; I'm thankful of the chance to get even with my clerking. A tribe like Omo can't exactly vanish into thin air, and ' leave no wrack behind,' " said the Commissioner wryly.

" I can't understand why you're not sick with me——" blurted Johnny

" Sick with you—for a miscalculation of my own? Get along," said Morris curtly, " and if you have any more bother with those pains in the head, see a Harley Street man; don't potter about with local fellows. There's a man called Whittick—a specialist in West African troubles——" His thin, hard hand gripped Johnny's. " We'll see you back here—one day."

" Well, sir, I suppose that will depend on my uncle."

Morris shook his head, as his other hand dropped on Johnny's shoulder

" The Gold Coast's put its mark on you, Johnny. You'll be back."

CHAPTER ELEVEN

I

IN his cabin on the *Baraka*, one of the smaller passenger steamships of the Flood-West African line, Johnny groaned and wished for death. The surgeon had a look at him, diagnosed him casually and gave him the usual dose ; there was a more interesting case on hand—a labour which looked as if it might present complications before it was over. The surgeon went away, whistling cheerfully, to brush up his obstetrics.

Johnny groaned. The grinding squeak of casemates scraped on a raw nerve. Something had got loose inside the washstand and clinked with every roll of the ship. She was a middle-aged ship and stank fearsomely in every quarter of oil. As the Chairman's nephew, Johnny had a state-room ; he wondered what the steerage was like. He kept his eyes closed tightly because, if he opened them, there was the Face.

The next time he groaned, he was aware of a figure bending over him.

" Excuse me. My cabin is next to yours and I heard you ; can I be of any help ? "

" Oh—get to hell," he groaned, and plunged for the enamel pan.

A hand came on his head and steadied it, and a very hard muscular body seemed in some miraculous fashion to control the roll of the ship. Presently he was laid back on the pillow and something damp and aromatic was passed over his brow and face. A glass was held to his lips. He swallowed mechanically.

He did not know how long he had been sleeping when he opened his eyes. He had the light, swimming sensation that follows acute pain, but no sensation of sickness. The porthole and a corner of the cabin swung before him, waterily white ; a grey line of sea rode half-way up the porthole and dropped away again ; a seabird screamed.

A figure was sitting near the door. Turned partly with its back to Johnny, so as to catch the light on a printed page, a pair of immensely broad shoulders in an immaculately fitted coat were presented to him. The farther extremities of a pair of long legs appeared, for their owner's convenience, to be accommodated in the gangway. As the reader turned his head, a face of ebony was illuminated by the flash of a resplendent set of teeth.

" Excuse me. I hope you are better. Perhaps I can get you something. Then I will go." As the speaker rose, he was obliged slightly to bend his head, to avoid the metal beams above.

" I guess I'm all right—sorry I disturbed you—much obliged," mumbled Johnny.

The Negro bowed ; he was a magnificent type—well dressed, Europeanised, yet devoid of the subtle aggressiveness that is apt to characterise a class continually on the defensive against real or imagined slights.

"It was no trouble. I happened to be in my cabin. I am gratified if I was able to be of assistance." Except for the formality of the phrasing, the English was as pure as Johnny's own.

"See you later, I hope," said Johnny.

"It would give me much pleasure."

The door closed noiselessly.

Very carefully Johnny looked round the cabin, from corner to corner; managed, after a pause, to find his feet; opened the wardrobe. Presently, very carefully, he closed it again. There were no signs of the Face.

"Brudders an' sisters, ain' you lucky to be sailing on de sea! All dis great ole water, an' de Lawd pushing de boat along. Less gib de Lawd a big clap, for de way He's pushing de boat along! Hallelujah, Lawd!"

Sunday, and the Negro evangelist addressing a white and coloured steerage congregation, with a few of the first and second-class passengers looking on amusedly. Pink palms beating together, and "Hallelujah!" and "Glory, glory!" and big belly laughs at the preacher, giving a realistic imitation of physical effort. Most of them had seen it—the boys pushing the boats off the beach, following them into the water, letting the waves lift them like seaweed and starting to swim as the rhythm of the paddles set in.

"De Lawd—He don' need to swim! His foots is on de flo' of de ocean, way down 'mong de little fishes an' de crabs an' de big momma turtles, an' His haid is way up in de sky, so He can keep His eye on de way de angels is behaving while He looks after His chillun heah below. Praise de Lawd, for He sho' is a great—big—man!"

No signs here of his visitor; Johnny made for the smoke-room.

Barely ten, but the air already thick; most of the tables taken over by poker-dice players; Goanese steward serving champagne to three Waff officers on leave and straight gins to a couple of flash mulattos with mouths full of gold stopping—working hard against the barrier of ostracism set up by the whites. A few grey-faced, elderly Civil Servants, keeping themselves ostentatiously to themselves. Thin, multiferous layers of racial and social distinction making themselves felt through fumes of tobacco and alcohol, puffing from woodwork and leatherwork and the smartly laundered mess jackets of the stewards.

Not here either.

Apart from meals—when Johnny, at the captain's table, had no opportunities for contacting one at the farther end of the saloon—the ship was off Grand Canary before he saw his friend again. Although most of the passengers were going ashore, he decided to stay on board. The heat was excessive and he had had one or two small shivering fits that put him on his guard against inviting worse by the exercise of energies he had only just begun to be able to depend on. There were two deck-chairs in a patch of shadow behind one of the ventilators, and one was empty; as he dropped into it he received the impression that it had been reserved for him. He shot a quick glance at his neighbour, who smiled courteously and noncommittally, as he lowered the book he was reading to the thin silken rug that covered his knees.

"I hope you have quite recovered from your illness."

"Oh, I'm all right; it was only—well, you know; eight months on the Coast!" He asked, to change the subject, "What's your book—George—Meredith. Oh, yes; I've never read any of him. It looks pretty tough!" said Johnny naïvely.

"It is 'tough.'" The other smiled. "A very curious, complicated vocabulary," he added reflectively. "I have never—actually—met anyone who talked in this manner. But I find it very interesting. It is, of course, more interesting to converse"—as Johnny made some deprecatory sign of not interrupting his reading.

"You yourself talk English very well—don't you?"

"I have studied for two years in the University of London. Yes, of course I have a longer acquaintance than that with England! First, I spent a year in an English family, with a tutor, and then went to one of your public schools—not a very important one," he admitted, with a smile. "It was, in fact, a grammar school, in the Midlands. It was considered better that I should have the advantage of living with a family than that I should go to boarding school. Myself, I should have preferred the school—for some reasons."

"Then you know England almost as well as you know your own country?"

"I would not say that," was the modest reply.

"How long have you been back?"

"Do you mean, in West Africa? I have been back constantly, during the last four years. I have always kept close touch with my family—not only the Europeanised branch, in Accra, but the older branch, in the interior." The amused look in his eyes betrayed his appreciation of what his companion was thinking: How did this grave and sophisticated figure fit into the thatched huts and the primitive society of his people?

"You don't mind my asking—what made you leave the Coast?"

"My father, and my grandfather before him, were very wise men." The answer came reflectively, after a short pause. "They knew the world does not stand still. They knew there were many inventions, many forms of progress, which might benefit us. It is better that these things should come to us through our own people, than in a translation. I do not know if I make myself clear?"

"Yes, of course. You were to get the education and pass it on in a form your people would be likely to understand," nodded Johnny.

"It is that we really felt that our people would accept more in the way of education from their own kind than they will—or can—take from foreigners, who have every sort of handicap in dealing with them."

"So what's your idea? To start a school?"

"Something of the kind; perhaps a little more—ambitious!" He laughed, as though the word amused him. "A college, should one say, for native graduates who wish to enter the teaching profession. Actually, it would be little more than a school, to begin with, but college sounds better!" His eyelids lowered themselves to hide the twinkle. Johnny felt greatly drawn to this happy giant, who seemed to find the world an agreeable place.

"Is there really a demand for—anything like that?"

"More than you would think. There is a great will to learn among a certain section of our people; there are many who would like to do as I have done—go to England and study in the colleges and universities." He had become grave again. "But you will understand there are a great many obstacles."

"I wish you would tell me some more about them, Mr.—I'm afraid I don't know your name: mine's Flood, John Flood."

"I know your name. Mine is Osei Bofo." As he bowed to Johnny, the deck-chair creaked under his weight. "Yes, there is a good deal of opposition," he went on, "particularly from people who, although they are willing to educate their sons, are disinclined to send them away from home—into surroundings where they may meet influences that would weaken their racial and family ties. That is reasonable, is it not?" He seemed anxious to have Johnny's approval.

"It sounds so," the latter agreed.

"So you see, there is really nothing but for us more fortunate ones to bring home all we can of learning and share it with the others," said Osei simply. "And at present there are not enough of us, and it is all rather disorganised," he admitted. "The trouble is, of course, that those of us who get away want to stop away, in an environment that offers us more opportunities. There are, unfortunately, very few of the ones who 'make good' over there who are content to come back."

"Would you have any trouble in financing your—college?"

The Negro's brows rose.

"Why? We are not a poor people!"

"And of course you'd have British support," suggested Johnny.

"No, no; we wouldn't want that." The other spoke quickly, and immediately made a gesture of apology. "Please do not be offended! I only mean that the acceptance of help entails also the acceptance of an authority which must, of necessity, be at cross purposes with some of our aims."

"'Africa for the Africans;' is that what you mean?" He wondered if Osei would take offence, but could not resist putting the question.

Osei chuckled.

"It's a great, big world, isn't it? And there ought to be plenty of room for all of us." Johnny had noticed that his vocabulary simplified itself as he became more confident of his companion. "Shall I tell you something? Africa has got to be a much better country before it is fit for Africans to live in!"

"And what about white people?"

"Ah!" Osei spread out his big hands, then allowed them to drop from the wrists. The gesture said volumes. As their eyes met, a strong current of liking passed from man to man.

The conversation—which then turned to trivialities—was the first of many, each marked by an advance in intimacy ; they got into the habit of going to each other's cabins, of walking together—followed always by a half-contemptuous kind of curiosity, of which Johnny was aware, and hoped Osei was not. Whether he was or not, he ignored it.

Presently they were on the chaffing terms which, between young men, stand for friendship—Johnny extracting a half-affected humour out of Osei's smartness, his addiction to finery which, in his case, came out, not in the grotesque or the flamboyant, but in the finest materials, and in a wardrobe whose extensiveness took Johnny's breath away.

" What on earth do you want with all these things ? You've got enough to rig out a ship's company ! "

Osei, a dignified figure in a dressing-gown of rich, plum-coloured silk, bearing, Johnny had previously been amused to see, the label of a Jermyn Street outfitter, bubbled with laughter, as he replied :

" What on earth do you want with the English climate ? What is one supposed to do when it's summer in the morning, winter by midday, and there may be a heat wave or a hailstorm any time before you go to bed ! "

" You have awfully swell things." Even Dorset, in all his glory, was not arrayed as one of these ! thought Johnny, fingering a morocco case whose soft sides bulged with its contents of monogrammed silk.

" I like handsome things," said Osei simply. " There is no point, is there, in having poor stuff if one can afford the others ? " There was no boastfulness in the comment ; it was the plain statement of one whose background had always been one of wealth. Osei had told him quite simply of the almost fabulous hoards in gold and precious stones amassed by his grandfather, an up-country prince, which his father, moving with the times, had converted into specie on the advice of an English trader. A handsome account with Coutts provided for Osei's requirements during his sojourns in England. " A friend I have was so kind as to recommend me to his tailor in London——"

And I bet the cutter enjoyed himself ! Johnny glanced with friendly envy at the Praxitilean proportions, whose smooth flow of bone and muscle were, if anything, emphasised by the perfectly fitting material that covered them.

A voracious eater, like most of his race, Osei's drinking habits, he had discovered, were as moderate as his own, and were inclined to make the pair of them conspicuous in company that made a virtue of its capacity for hard liquor. After their gin sling, or the rum and lime that Osei favoured, they usually left the saloon and walked round the decks, chatting about Johnny's experiences on the Coast, or about " home," in which Osei took a tremendous interest.

" You'll have to pay us a visit." The invitation was out, and accepted, before either remembered what it involved. Johnny found he had not the slightest idea what the family reaction might be to entertaining a Negro at Guerdon ; it might be amusing—but not for Osei. He made a mental note to make sure of the lie of the land, before confirming his offer, which now rather embarrassed him—on Osei's account, not on his own. A stubborn resolution took possession of his mind : that, given Dromore's concurrence —how, indeed, holding his convictions of the universal brotherhood, in God—of man, could he withhold it?—he would stand for no nonsense from Dorset. Doss could behave himself, or, temporarily, get out.

A drunk, reeling out of the saloon, thrust Osei aside with a mutter of: "Bloody niggers ! Pity there's not a few Virginians on this boat, to keep 'em in their places." As Osei was the only Negro travelling in the first-class, the speaker appeared to be seeing double ; but Johnny was furious.

He had instinctively swung his clenched fist up when Osei caught and held it, shaking his head.

"No, no. Let it alone."

"I don't know why you don't knock bastards like that down ! "

Osei winked ; he appeared to be amused.

"No, Johnny." They had suddenly arrived at Christian names. "Black against white—that's a bad idea. Only makes trouble—for everybody."

"But don't you *want* to ? "

"Of course I do." He chuckled. "But, like every Negro who looks ahead, I save that pleasure for my sons, or my grandsons, or may be my great-great-grandsons ! At present, a 'nigger' has no standing among white people, so whatever he does to the whites goes against him. We can't start knocking them down until we've made them accept us as equals. Otherwise we're only pushing ourselves farther down."

II

In the nights, Osei stood by him ; when he awoke, sweating and gasping with pain, as though someone were driving a nail through his temple with an iron mallet, there was the tall, calm, plum-coloured column ; there were the two big, strong hands, ready to grip his head, to blot out in their cool palms the thing that grinned from the corner of the cabin. He would have liked to tell Osei about the Face ; he could never quite bring himself to do so. All sorts of things involved themselves in the admission—the events at Omo, of which he did not want to think, in detail, and some obscure lowering of racial pride. The subjects of fetish and witchcraft had never been raised between them ; nor had they ever touched on West African politics. It was no matter of taboo, but, on Johnny's side, of a profound exhaustion—of putting off, for as long as possible, things which, sooner or later, would have to be considered.

Recurrent fever bouts kept snatching at the small reserve of strength he had managed to build up during his brief rest in the sanatorium at Accra, and he found himself with little inclination for the social life which had developed among the passengers while the *Baraka* ploughed her leisurely way across the ocean : the poker schools, drinking schools, the flirtations to which a few resorted to wile away the tedium of the voyage.

The faint cloud of disapproval which (as he was aware) overhung his persistent companionship with Osei was put into words one night by an elderly military pundit, the father of his fair *vis-à-vis* at the Captain's table: who invited him to a game of nap, and when Johnny politely excused himself, pulled down his brows, puffed out his moustache, and was delivered of an evidently premeditated speech.

"Will you accept a hint, young man, from one old enough to be your father? It's not 'done,' in the first-class, to associate with niggers. Some of the passengers, especially, the ladies, find it offensive."

"I'm sorry if my conduct is offensive to anybody, sir; but, even in the first-class, I suppose one's free to choose one's own company?"

The other's head jerked up and he turned sharply on his heel. In the dining saloon Johnny discovered that a young lady who had previously been lavish with her smiles persistently presented him with a view of her ear. After dinner, he sought Osei.

"Do you mind if I have my cover moved to your table?"

Osei, first startled, smiled.

"You can't do that, Johnny. It wouldn't be polite to the Captain."

"Blow the Captain. I can say I want to be near the port—that all the chatter over there addles me."

But Osei shook his head.

"What would the ladies say to your desertion?" was, Johnny guessed, only a pretext covering Osei's more delicate perception, his dignified disclaimer of an act planned blatantly to advertise their friendliness.

To be near Osei was like living under the shadow of a great tree. One looked at Osei and saw infinity behind him: deep forests seeding, being born and dying. Deepness and darkness and distance. Something immeasurably antique that formed itself now and again behind the shining ophidian of his eyes. Once, looking into his eyes, Johnny saw it distinctly: the minute figure, exquisite as an intaglio, of a naked female: and once it was there like a snake; and on each occasion Osei himself appeared to be unaware of it, and went chatting in, in his deep, slow voice, infinitely benevolent and easy, as though there were nothing there at all.

In spite of this background of antiquity, of which Johnny never lost sight, Osei, like most young people, took a keen interest in the modern.

"Did you ever see the Bioscope, Johnny? There's something with a great future before it! It would do a lot for our educational scheme, if it were developed further. It is much easier to teach people through pictures than through books," he pointed out gravely. "I think, as an invention, it is even more significant than the horseless carriage. I was trying to describe that to one of my uncles." He broke off to chuckle. "We didn't get much farther than admitting it was some sort of witchcraft—which, when you come to think of it, is as good an explanation as most for the harnessing of electrical power."

When they passed into the cold waters, and he laid away his tropical suit and pulled out the old and crumpled tweeds which, with their patches of mould and crumbling edges, were hardly decent, a sudden premonition of what the future held for him descended on Johnny like a pall of lead.

The *Baraka* was rolling like an old cow and there were many empty places in the saloon at midday. Johnny took advantage of the Captain's absence to have his cover removed to Osei's table, whose occupant, more than ever immaculate in a Norfolk jacket of Harris tweed, its opening filled in with a heavy silk scarf, Paisley-patterned on a chestnut ground, was eating his way with his usual heartiness through a third helping of roast beef.

"We'll be having the fiddles on to-night," said Johnny gloomily, as the steward handed him the bread basket—his own roll having careered across the saloon, to rest under a distant table. Of the pea soup, about a spoonful survived in the plate the boy slipped over his shoulder. With vivid recollections of his own experiences as cabin waiter, Johnny forbore complaint. Although he had no sensation of sickness and his temperature was normal, he felt little inclination for food.

"We've made good time," Osei informed him. "They say, unless we meet bad weather off the Welsh coast, we'll be in soon after midnight to-morrow."

"Where are you making for first?" He pushed his untouched plate aside.

"London. I've got to pick up my instructions——"

"You've never said what you're over for, this time."

Osei smiled with modest pride.

"Last time I was here I promised to give some lectures: at my own University, for one, and then at several of the smaller ones in the provinces."

"You *are* a swell." The thought crossed his mind that, whereas the introduction of an unclassified Negro to the hospitalities of Guerdon might present difficulties, that of presenting a distinguished coloured lecturer was quite a different matter. "You're not coming to Bristol, by any chance?"

"I've not seen my schedule yet; but, as a matter of fact, I believe I am."

"What a fellow you are—not mentioning it before! Of course you'll stop at Guerdon—and we'll all turn out to support you."

"Excuse me." For the first time Osei was not looking at him; his big hand, coloured like dark-brown satin, was crumbling the roll on his plate. "I don't wish to make any trouble for you. There is sure to be some hotel——"

"What are you talking about? I asked you before and you said you'd come."

"I thought you were being polite," admitted Osei. "I don't know how your people feel about my people. I should not like to put you in an awkward position."

While Johnny made spluttering denial of "politeness," and indignantly scouted Osei's proposal to stop in a hotel, the thought had come into his mind, What kind of a hotel would be likely to take in Osei in Bristol? The Royal might; indeed it should. But it was by no means unlikely that a Negro guest would be exposed to unpleasant attention from some of its regular and influential patrons, a word of complaint from whom would be enough to furnish the management with an excuse to get rid of him. With this in his mind, Johnny redoubled his insistence on Osei's staying at

Guerdon, dismissing any misgivings about his being welcome there. A sudden wave of anger, that so simple a matter should be beset by so many obstacles, silenced him. He sat for a moment, staring at his hands, then abruptly spun his chair away from the table.

"Are you feeling ill?"

"No. I don't want anything to eat. I'm going to my cabin."

Osei found him lying on his bunk. A squall had come up and the stateroom was almost in darkness.

"Are you sick, Johnny?"

"No. I want to be by myself—that's all." His ungraciousness struck him as Osei was preparing noiselessly to depart. "I didn't mean it that way. Sit down and read—if you want to. I'm thinking about something."

"I'd better leave you to think."

"You don't need to. I might want to do some thinking aloud." He laughed shortly.

"I will get a cigar. Will you have one?"

"No, thanks."

When Osei returned he had a small box in his hand.

"I thought you might have someone you would like to give these to." Johnny found himself looking at four of the famous aggrey beads.

"By George, Osei, they're fine! But I'm afraid I can't afford them." Emily would love them. They would look wonderful, hanging from her small, delicate ears.

"They are a present." Osei sounded a little offended.

"Dash it—I can't take a thing like that."

Osei laid them down on the edge of the bunk.

"No one else will have them, if you refuse. I think something is worrying you, Johnny," he said, as the cabin filled itself slowly with the scent of the cigar.

Suddenly it was pouring out of him, and he left it to Osei to make sense out of the disconnected sentences.

"After I left Accra . . . nothing working out the way it should . . ." He babbled on for a while; Osei, leaning back in the only chair the cabin contained, bracing himself with his feet on the edge of the bunk against the roll of the ship, while the smoke curled from his thick, flexible lips. From time to time he nodded, to show that he was following the incoherent argument.

"Tell me something straight, Osei: do you, and people like you—the intelligent Negroes—wish the British out of West Africa?"

"Now, that's foolish question, Johnny. What would we do without British trade? Without British shipping?"

"Well—what do you really think of us?" he persisted. "I don't mean you—who have had opportunities of knowing us apart from your country and your climate. What does the average Negro think of the people who have conquered his race?"

"What is 'the average Negro?'" There was a tolerance in the question that convicted Johnny of naïvete, but he clung doggedly to his point. " You might as well speak of ' the average white man.' It would be a mighty fine mathematician who managed to strike an average, in your race or mine."

There was a moment when Johnny felt Osei seeking some phrase of evasion ; when he felt sure that, had the darkness permitted him to see it, the symbol of the eternal Africa floated on the dark glass of his eyes.

" I can only tell you what I know. In the big towns, and in up-country districts where they have a fine Commissioner, like your Mr. Morris, they think the British are a great and powerful people, to be respected and given their dues for trying to do their best under very difficult conditions. They see, for the most part, only the best British types : the Governor and his staff, the Resident, the military, what you call the ' high-ups ' of the Civil Service."

" And along the coast—where we have our thickest population ? "

Osei's eyes were on the tip of the cigar he held between his strong fingers. He lifted his shoulders and allowed them to drop, gently.

" Do you think the Negroes are better off, now, under British rule ? "

" Well, no, Johnny, I don't," was the frank reply. " That's just what lies at the back of my mind when I try to plan for my college. It is right we Negroes should be governed by our own leaders ; but we have no leaders, yet, who are capable of evolving a collective system of government, such as the British are trying to establish. We are split into groups, or tribes, with no sense of unity between one and another, and you know that does not make for a powerful nation, or for progress in any important degree. It's very easy, isn't it, to be iconoclastic ? " he broke off to observe. " I am sure you, as well as I, have many constructive ideas—— ? "

" Everyone seems to admit," said Johnny, shelving for the moment the question of constructive ideas, " that the mixing of black and white is bad for both. What's your view about that ? "

" I think you are speaking in the sociological, not the biological sense," said Osei, after a pause. " Along the coastal belt both whites and blacks are subjected to very violent influences, of which the worst, from the whites' point of view, is the climate. It's a kind of vicious circle : climate reacts on whites, whites react on blacks, and blacks react back on the whites again. So you see us at our worst and we see you at your worst. And that, naturally," concluded Osei, " makes for a lot of trouble."

" You can't alter the climate," muttered Johnny.

" No ; but you can make it tolerable for a white man to live in."

" Oh—you mean, better housing conditions——"

" How many of you live in little wooden sheds, with tin roofs, in your own country ? Surely you need more, not less, comfort, when you come out to a country like ours," the Negro protested.

" That's perfectly true. Better housing, better sanitation, some sort of provision for cold storage," nodded Johnny.

" Better medical service and—isn't this more important than anything ? A much fuller preparation for the kind of living out there. I've heard of people arriving without the slightest idea of what to expect : imagining the whole of the coast to be like Accra and the whole of the interior inhabited by raging savages—to be shot on the slightest pretext!" Osei's laugh roared out, but, for the first time, Johnny caught a bitter note in it.

"When are the scientists going to discover something that will clear vermin out of the houses? When is the serum for the prevention of malaria going to be ready? How long will it be before your Government realises that it takes something more than a fine character and a good bill of health to qualify for a post on the Gold Coast? Well, there you are, Johnny; you have asked me a great many questions; there are a few for you to answer." He beamed on his companion.

"Is that what you're going to lecture about?"

Osei shook his head regretfully.

"One must be very careful not to give offence, when talking to a white audience. But why don't you say it?"

"Me? Lecture? I could no more lecture than fly," grimaced Johnny.

"I think it is best not to look on it as 'lecturing;' take it as an important message that you have to get to as many people in as short a time as you can," advised Osei. He rose; to stretch himself he had to press his hands against the ceiling and let his head drop back between his great shoulders. He shook his coat into place as he bent forward to smile at Johnny.

"Don't mistake what I said about wanting the country to be governed by our own people, Johnny. Nobody wishes the British out of West Africa except the Ashanti—and they are a crazy people, very greedy, and annoyed because they don't get the revenue they expected out of their trade routes. We must have the British, to teach us how to govern ourselves."

"And then? After you've learned?"

Again he was conscious of a slight withdrawal, of something that was not quite candour, in Osei's reply.

"We shall always need the British—but we would like them as an asset, not as a liability, which they threaten to become, unless their Government realises its duty to them."

The door closed gently.

A buzzing in the brain—a vision seen darkly—a tangled web of immature thought. How was any of this to be conveyed to Harcourt—in a form that was not already stale from over-familiarity?

The sea had flattened a little, but the ship still rolled and cracked; a running tide of pale reflections raced ceaselessly across the deck head over the bunk. The dusk had lifted, but a pallor of sunset made pockets of shadow in the corners of the cabin. The oil stank. It was clammily cold.

The last thing he saw, as the pain in his head rose to its by now familiar crisis, was the Face, in the angle of the bulkhead and the door. He forced himself to look steadily towards it, until it was blotted out by the film which pain had brought across his eyes.

the whole of the coast is like Accra and the whole of the interior is filled with savages—we get shot on the slightest pretext?" Osei's laugh rang out, but, for the first time, Johnny caught a bitter note in it.

"When are the scientists going to discover something that will clear women out of the houses? When is the serum for the prevention of malaria going to be ready? How long will it be before your Government realises that it takes something more than a fine character and a good bill of health to qualify for a post on the Gold Coast? Well, there you are, Johnny; you have asked me a great many questions; there are a few for you to answer." He beamed on his companion.

"Is that what you're going to lecture about?"

Osei shook his head regretfully.

"One must be very careful not to give offence, when talking to a white audience. But why don't you say it?"

"Me? Because I could no more lecture than fly," grinned Johnny.

"I think it's best not to look on it as 'lecturing'; take it as an important message that you have to get to as many people in as short a time as you can," advised Osei. He rose; to stretch himself he had to press his hands against the ceiling and let his head drop back between his great shoulders. He shook his coat into place as he bent forward to smile at Johnny.

"Don't mistake what I said about wanting the country to be governed by our own people, Johnny. Nobody wishes the British out of West Africa except the [illegible]—and they are a crazy people, very greedy and annoyed because they don't get the revenue they expected out of their trade routes. We must have the British, to teach us how to govern ourselves."

"And then? After you've learned?"

Again he was conscious of a slight withdrawal, of something that was not quite candour, in Osei's reply.

"We shall always need the British—but we would like them as an asset, not as a liability, which they threaten to become, unless their Government realises its duty to them."

The door closed gently.

A buzzing in the brain—a vision seen darkly—a tangled web of immature thought. How was any of this to be conveyed to Harcourt—in a form that was not utterly stale from over-familiarity?

The sea had flattened a little, but the ship still rolled and creaked; a [illegible] tide of pale reflections raced ceaselessly across the deck head over the bunks. The dusk had lifted, but a pallor of sunset made pockets of shadow in the corners of the cabin. The oil stank. It was clammily cold.

The last thing he saw, as the pain in his head rose to its by now familiar crisis, was the [illegible], in the angle of the bulkhead and the door. He forced himself to look steadily towards it, until it was blotted out by the film which pain had brought across his eyes.

T.P.

BOOK THREE

Bristol and Guerdon

1899-1900

CHAPTER ONE

I

"THERE's the dressing gong."

Miss Victoria Flood rose and folded her needlework neatly.

"Coming, Emily?" She spoke kindly to the girl who, with her small, pointed chin resting in her hand, continued, unheeding, to look down the broad slope of pasture that ended in the stream.

Her eyes, heavy-lidded, were beautiful and melancholy in shape. From a broad forehead deep waves of dusky-coloured hair were drawn back into an elaborate knot that overweighted the small head, and emphasised the fragility of a long, flexible neck. A type, thought Vicky Flood, produced by in-breeding; fine, sensitive, rare—and oddly touching. Although this was purely fancy! Orphan or not, few young women could have had a happier life than Emily Temple, cherished ward of elderly, wealthy guardians, heiress in her own right, to a considerable fortune, and—consideration above all others, in the mind of a doting aunt!—the intended of Dorset Flood.

Why, then, had Emily that disconcerting, that *unhappy* air; that touch, occasionally, of an uncomfortable exoticism, vaguely irritating, for all her partiality, to so forthright a person as Vicky Flood?

She made her voice deliberately bracing.

"And Dorset will be waiting to see how his camellias look on that green gown! You mustn't leave yourself short of time to do yourself justice in it."

A flash of irony, glimmering in the long grey eyes, was instantly blotted out. Graceful, blank, well mannered, Emily rose, and the two ladies stepped from the gazebo out on the bridle-path which ran, between its iron hurdles, to the end of the lawns.

The sun was low; the Elizabethan manor dropped its shadow across the terrace, across the clipped box hedges, across the short flight of steps that joined the terrace with the lawns. Then came the ha-ha, and the wooden bridge that spanned it—the bridge Dromore had built, for his mother's convenience, to shorten the distance between Guerdon and the Dower House. A ripeness of age lay on the house, a mellowness of light and shadow that was a mellowness of fruit in vintage. Coloured like the grape, the design of the pointed gables spread itself on the turf, which gave off summer sweetness in gusts of warmth. Striped by the mower in bands of light and darker green, the lawns offered themselves to the feet of the women like a deep carpet, as they had offered themselves to wearers of the ruff and farthingale, to the diaphanous nymphs in their little satin slippers of the Regency. Involuntarily, Victoria checked her steps.

It was beautiful—so very beautiful; her heart filled with a warm contentment. What a fortunate, what a happy old maid she was. An irresistible impulse to share her happiness with her companion turned her towards Emily, whose eyes questioned her politely.

" Remind me, sometime, to show you Venetia's picture of it. Such a pity there are no children, to inherit their mother's gift for drawing. It's so pretty ; is it not ? "

" Yes, it's very striking."

Vicky was conscious of a little chill. Was it unreasonable, she wondered, to have expected a more positive note of appreciation from Guerdon's future mistress ? Some day, not so very far ahead, she would have—she hoped with good grace—to resign the authority poor, anæmic Selina had been content to transfer to her hands, to Dorset's wife. It would have helped, to know that the hands were loving, like her own.

Something, however, had distracted Emily's attention. Following the direction of her eyes, Vicky's comely, unhandsome face stiffened a little.

The young woman hurrying towards them seemed unconscious of observation, as she swung her basket at an occasional tall head of cow parsley, leaning outwards from the hurdles. Half humming, half singing to herself, her voice carried easily on the still air—a strong, confident soprano, which seemed to please the singer ; for now and again she threw back her head and launched a note of lucid rivalry at the larks, suspended overhead, and followed it with a full-throated chuckle and the flirt of a frilled petticoat, as though for the benefit of an imaginary audience.

Her dress was a painstaking travesty of current mode : immense " leg of mutton " sleeves broadened her shoulders and emphasised the slimness of a waist from which sprang the arches of voluptuous hips and the swinging fullness of a fluted skirt. From the high-boned collar to the tips of fingers discreetly covered in netted gloves, there was nothing that was not completely modest and correct in such an outfit ; yet something about the wearer evoked irresistibly an image which, to a Victorian spinster, was shocking. Those Old Masters—all those breasts and thighs and haunches : dear me, why was one reminded of them, each time one met Polly Bowling crossing the park ?

Suddenly aware of the watching ladies, her little song was cut short and her gait became all but affectedly prim ; but when she drew level with Victoria and Emily, it was she who spoke first, in a rich, easy voice, with a little air that might have been pert or defiant, but was redeemed by the abounding spirits of which it was evidently the natural expression.

" Good evening, Miss Flood ! "

Her mother would have said " ma'am," thought Victoria, as she returned the greeting courteously, but with a coolness meant to remind the other of her proper station, of which she appeared to be unconscious. The eyes of the two girls met with a shy friendliness which showed itself, on Emily's part, in an all but imperceptible quiver of the lips, too faint to be called a smile, and, on Polly's, in a flash of teeth dazzling in their whiteness and perfection. A radiance of health and vitality, of thoughtless good humour and easy benevolence came out in the soft curves of a face too plump to be pretty, but alive with animal spirit and gaiety.

"Polly! How gay you look!" The younger girl spoke involuntarily.

"I *feel* gay! I guess it's just the sun; it seems as if it goes to my head."

"... She's grown so pretty!"

Vicky pulled herself out of the unpleasant mental turbulence into which encounters with Polly always plunged her, to answer shortly:

"Absurdly over-dressed, for a young person of her class." She was not often acrimonious. "They ruined the girl with sending her to boarding school, and having her taught French and the piano. Such nonsense! Instead of putting her into service, and making a useful woman of her. I'm afraid Polly Bowling looks on herself as—well, as quite a person of consequence!" ended Vicky, on a short laugh.

"Yes? . . . I suppose there is something a little—superior about her. Elphinstone is getting married. You don't think it would be any use asking Polly if she would like to come to me, as my maid?"

"No, I'm afraid it wouldn't. Silly girl!" frowned Vicky. "A great many would be grateful for the opportunity——"

"Oh, it doesn't matter," murmured Emily.

Vicky looked at the watch she had drawn from her belt.

"My dear, we must hurry. Is your head better?" She turned her head sharply towards her companion.

"No . . . it isn't . . . really."

Vicky's brow creased. Such a pity, if Emily turned out to be delicate. There had been too many puny wives in the last two generations; Vicky, ignorant of eugenics, felt all the same that what the family needed was stamina. She was annoyed to find herself thinking of Polly Bowling; oh, dear, why couldn't the upper classes produce that type of hearty, exuberant young womanhood? And why, on the few occasions they did, couldn't Floods meet and fall in love with them? And she had another source of worry. . . . If Emily were but simpler—less reserved—and she, Vicky, less nervous of violating some delicacy in a situation which surely, by now, should have lost its ambiguity? . .

"Emily; please don't think me impertinent. But—you and Dorset haven't quarrelled, have you?"

"Oh, no. Not," she added, to Vicky's shocked astonishment, "that it would make any difference."

"My dear child! Believe me"—she was almost stammering—"it would make the very *greatest* difference—to us *all*—if Dorset did anything to make you unhappy. I don't think you realise"—she sought for words; chose carefully those which came—"how very fond of you we have grown. You know," floundered Vicky, "we all look on you—already—as quite one of the family!"

"I know." Her lips twitched. "Aunt Vicky—I feel I should tell you: if there is any—any misunderstanding between Dorset and me, it is entirely my fault; not his."

"That is very generous of you. I really don't know what to say to that, my dear. So far as I know, you have always been charming." (Oh, dear, am I saying the wrong thing ? Mama would handle this so much better than I.)

" Perhaps—too charming." The colour that ran up into Emily's cheeks was reflected, morbidly, in Vicky's.

" Oh, no ! You two have known each other so many years : there's bound to be a certain informality ! But Dorset would never presume—I mean, he wouldn't—— ! " Vicky's jaw dropped ; she stood for a moment, gaping at Emily ; then, as though in flight from her own embarrassment, started stumblingly towards the house.

At the head of the steps her brother Dromore was waiting, with a look which, for her, was reproachful, and, for Emily, whom he favoured, tempered tolerance with deprecation of unpunctuality. The handsome, heavy build of the master of Guerdon fitted so well into its architecture that Vicky paused instinctively for a small act of homage.

" I am afraid you have not left yourself very much time."

" Give us an extra ten minutes," pleaded Vicky. " I must make sure Miranda is tidy, before I start to dress——"

" Miranda," boomed Dromore, " is not dining with us."

" Why ? What's the matter ? "

He gave her the look of icy displeasure which had been known to quell even Dorset.

" My dear Victoria, dinner will be more than ten minutes late, if we stop to discuss a matter which is of no further importance, since I have already dealt with it ! "

This was the moment chosen by Uncle Quentin, fruity, polychromatic and irascible, as he was wont to be, before being mellowed by his second bottle of port, to appear, glass in hand, on the threshold of the library.

" God damme, Drummy, does one have to drink alone in your blasted mausoleum ? "

Dromore turned, with a faint, forced thawing of the ice, and Vicky, grateful, as she often was, despite her disapproval, to Uncle Quentin, turned towards the stairs, down which her nephew Dorset was sumptuously advancing.

Yes, " sumptuous " was indeed the word for Dorset. As he stood aside, to make room for his aunt, and for Emily, who passed him with a cool little nod that earned Vicky's approval, there was that air of satisfaction and of an amused kind of self-indulgence about him that betrayed his conception of himself as the excellent animal, entitled to all the pampering its owners choose to bestow on it.

Heavily built, the breadth of his shoulders tended to reduce his height —the average one for an Englishman of his type and class. Hard riding, and indulgence in his favourite forms of exercise, which were racquets and boxing, held back the thickening with which, already, he was threatened, but which immaculate tailoring disguised. There was something glossy, and, to the ascetic, faintly repugnant, about Dorset ; yet his face, hard, high-coloured, and, where the razor had polished it, faintly shining, passed easily enough for the face of a " good fellow," and his portrait—an early

Sargent, which came under the hammer in 1939—stands, with its hunting pink, the rakish cant of the topper over good-humoured, lecherous eyes, and its background of pasture land and grazing hunters, for the quintessence of the sporting squire. Only his mouth, full-lipped and treacherous, the mouth of all the Floods, supported the whispers of the few who disliked him.

While Vicky halted, confused, as her nephew always managed, in some inexplicable fashion, to confuse her, he said to her, in that voice which, even to a woman who held, for him, no sexual significance, was like the purr of a tiger :

" Well, Aunt Vicky ? I hope you had a pleasant afternoon. Is Emily's headache better ? "

He knows he is responsible for the headache, she thought. God help the poor child ; what does he *not* know ?

" Oh, yes—you'll see her at dinner." A foolish observation ; he had already seen her, and not at her best. Vicky, who associated herself completely with the Throne's deprecation of the assertion of women's rights, felt a sudden partisanship, primarily for Emily, but for every member of her own sex engaged in the losing battle against mankind, as represented by the Dorsets of this world.

" I hope so." He gave her his special smile of complicity—the smile which deluded every woman, with its inference that she was the sole object of his attention—and continued on his progress to the library.

" You're not starting a chill, ma'am, are you ? " The woman, who had been with her ever since she left the schoolroom, felt Vicky shiver, as she unhooked her bodice. " You'd better take a glass of sherry before you go down, Miss Vicky ; you know what you're like with them nasty summer colds of yours ! "

" There's nothing the matter with me whatever," snapped Vicky, surprised to find she had a headache, but resolved to die, sooner than admit it. There was nothing the matter, except that she felt *worried* : a state of mind so unusual in her that she was inclined to pay more attention to it than a less placid person would have done.

Dromore's mood was already sufficiently tetchy not to provoke him further by being late for dinner. And what had Miranda done to annoy him ? She ought to slip through to the schoolroom and find out, but that would certainly make her late, and she must be down to look after Emily.

" Will you have the pearls to-night, miss ? Or do you want the filigree set ? "

Was it possible she had been wrong, all these years, in looking on Guerdon as a happy house ? Was there something, moving beneath its sunshine, that accounted for Uncle Quentin, drinking himself into confusion every night ? For Miranda, limping on the stairs ? For Selina's languor, Dromore's cold abstraction and Dorset's Judas charm ? Was it something her mother had known of, that had driven her to the sanctuary of the Dower House ? Something from which Hacky and Roan had retreated, as soon as marriage furnished them with an excuse? Something that had warped Johnny's childhood, and now reached out its dark tendrils towards poor little Emily Temple?

"You're pinching me!" She twitched herself angrily out of her serving woman's hand.

"You're not so slim as you were!" was the ruthless answer of one who considered that long service entitled her to truth, however unpalatable.

Vicky looked at her reflection with dissatisfaction. Clothes were not what they had been in her girlhood; she missed the billowing folds, the apron tiers, the confidence that whalebone and horse hair gave one. How beautiful those swelling draperies had been, and how they enabled a woman to take command of a situation! These broad-shouldered, umbrella-skirted styles might suit the young and frivolous, but they added nothing to the dignity of a middle-aged woman, whose figure, as her maid had been so tactless as to point out, was not what it had been.

What a fool of an old woman I am getting! thought Vicky at dinner: glancing between the candles at her sister-in-law Selina, who, bulky but placid, smiled wanly at Uncle Quentin's fuddled attempts at gallantry. At Dromore, pompously but pleasantly criticising Lord Milner's handling of the situation at Bloemfontein, and humouring Dorset's impatient strictures on the Chamberlain policy. At Emily, sprinkling her smiles and her comments like diamonds, and pretending to be unconscious of Dorset's eyes smouldering upon her. She had recovered from her mood—whatever that meant—and how that curious green became her! They spent a fortune on dressing her, and she was worth it. Dorset was no fool; and there was no question, Vicky decided happily, of his infatuation.

I really must not allow myself to become fantastical, she reproved herself sharply. We are what we have always been—a most happy and united family.

II

Mrs. Harriet Flood poised her coffee cup above its saucer and raised her head in an attitude of attention, as her clock struck its third silvery quarter. Up at the house they were dining. It was too late for evening callers, too early for the formal *pour prendre congé* visit she expected from her grandson Dorset. Had she been mistaken, in hearing, through the chiming of the clock, the distant tinkle of a bell? A victim of routine, Mrs. Flood took a lively pleasure in the unexpected; she had had so few opportunities of enjoying it during her married life.

The door opened, and her butler stood there. She gave him a sharp look of inspection, under which the man stiffened like a ranker on parade, his eyeballs glassy, his forefingers seeking the side-seams of his trousers. A new broom, she decided contemptuously; still, young—and passably good looking.

"Is that the jacket?"

"Yes, madam."

"It drags at the left shoulder. Take it back and have it seen to."

"Yes, madam. Mr. John Flood, madam."

"What?"

She rose, incredulous. The tea-gown of dark ivory lace, falling about her, revealed her small, slight figure, erect as a spear, for all her seventy-four years. In her youth she had been a pretty woman; with old age something better than beauty had descended on her, something disturbing, on which her grandchildren, sensing it vaguely, were a little alarmed. Grandmamma's eyes, coloured like a moss agate, the flare of her nostrils, her pointed, ironic mouth held something the family found uncomfortable, although they would never have admitted it. And she was careful to give them no grounds on which to found their uneasiness.

"My dear Johnny!"

She held out her hand, and smiled as he bent over it. He was the only one of the grandchildren sufficiently civilised to kiss her hand, a form of salutation to which she was partial; the only "gentleman," according to her reading, that the family had produced—which, apart from the question of good manners, meant that he was honourable, kindly and given to that form of imagination that instinctively respects the feelings of other people. Nothing to look at, of course; none of the flaring charm of that imperial bounder, his brother Dorset, or of Gilbert's etiolated elegance, deriving from his mother's line! Her eye flickered over him, missing nothing: the shocking colour of his skin, his thinness. No, she would not forgive them for packing him off, a mere cog in Flood machinery, to serve their interests at the West African end of their commercial web. For all their vanity and social pretension—not above making capital out of their own flesh and blood! To her horror, she felt her chin beginning to quiver: furious with this sign of old-womanish weakness, she dug her nails into his arms.

"How are you? All right?" she muttered hoarsely.

"Fit as a fiddle!" His grin dared her to challenge the obvious lie.

She dropped her hands and straightened her spine, giving him back smile for smile.

"So I see. You're ahead of your schedule," she pointed out, as she returned to her chair.

"I had a piece of luck and got passage on the *Baraka*, instead of having to wait for the *Benina*," he told her.

"Well. I suppose your mother is gratified."

"I hope she'll be! I haven't been up to 'the house' yet; I thought I'd drop in and see you, on my way."

"I suppose you've not dined?" Her hand went out to the bell. "They can grill you a cutlet—with which, no doubt, you'd like a pint of champagne. Or have you lost your palate for such civilisations, since living among savages?"

"Try me and see." He heaved a sigh of pleasure, stretching himself in the chair she indicated, beside the fire. For a moment he closed his eyes; a look of sodden exhaustion drained the life from his face, in which the bones, rising through the thin flesh, made caverns of the eye-sockets and under the cheekbones. With a quickness of movement that belied her age she unlocked a cabinet and, presently, brought him a tumbler, quarter full.

"You had better drink this, while you are waiting."

"Scotch?" He inhaled it appreciatively. "I thought you never had anything but ginger beer for your visitors! Where on earth did you get this?"

"Ask your uncles. You don't suppose I keep liqueur whisky for scrubby little shipping clerks who have just left school?"

"It's something like a drink, after old Van Hoytima!" He smacked his lips. "Sorry, Grandmamma! I expect I ought to feed in private for a few days, until I've got back to the drill again. Bother all that. Tell me what's been happening at home. It's going to take me some time, you know, to cover the last few months."

An hour went by. She was smiling at him across a shallow shell of crystal, the diamonds in her small, half-hidden ears catching the firelight and sending it out in minute sparks of crimson and blue. She had ordered the fire to be lit, guessing that, even on the June evening, he would be cold; and she noticed—but concealed her observation—that the hand he stretched mechanically towards the flames vibrated a little.

"How nice you've made it all, Grandmamma! You've changed this room, haven't you? I suppose Papa has seen it; I hope he's complimented you on your taste."

"Our tastes differ." She considered privately that Dromore had no taste at all; taste was not a Flood quality. Apart from the "state" rooms, sedulously preserved as show pieces, open to the public twice a year and otherwise used only on grand occasions, successive Floods had swamped the beautiful old rooms with the worst products of the Victorian decadence. Selina's boudoir, a jackdaw's nest of brackets and cosy corners, of ball fringe, peacocks' feathers and questionable willow pattern, she had never been able to enter without a sensation of nausea. Dromore, fortunately, had made no objection when she asked to be allowed to explore the attics, in search of the Georgian treasures expelled to make room for "fashionable" atrocities.

"What are you smiling at, Grandmamma?"

"Never you mind." She gritted her even little teeth at him, like a naughty child. "What have you come home for?"

He stared, flung himself back in his chair and shouted with laughter. "Of all the questions? When I've been sweating my soul out among the heathen ever since last December——!"

"There's no need to be coarse. And if you were pining to see your family, you wouldn't have come here first," she retorted astutely.

"I'm sorry, if I've done the wrong thing."

Knowing she had hurt him, she leaned forward, quickly to lay her small fingers over the knuckles of his hand, clenched on the table's edge.

"Don't be absurd. How much leave have you?"

"It depends on what Uncle Hacky has in mind."

Slumped in his chair, his brow knitted, he reminded her of the small boy who, when plagued by his brothers or outlawed from their company, had brought his mute resentment to her for comfort. She, who had not the habit of caresses—her children had never known them—remembered stroking the smooth, childish brow, with a curious pleasure in its softness and the feathery submission of the eyebrows to her fingers. The brow was no longer smooth, but furrowed and yellowed by tropical sun to the band where the topee cut across below the hair-line, and the eyes were netted about with wrinkles, as she remembered her father's eyes, when he was an old man. It was as though the veneer of age, like a fine, semi-transparent wax, had been laid across the youth of Johnny's face.

What, she thought, with a rush of anger, was this mania for money-making, that took boys like Johnny and robbed them of their youth? While Dorset and Gilbert enjoyed all the privileges of their father's indulgence, and jeered (albeit good naturedly) at "poor old Johnny, who had been fool enough to go into the business!" They had always sneered at him, she remembered indignantly; and he was the only one of the three who was worth a farthing. She waited, impatient of her own tenderness, until he said slowly:

"You've been telling me all about everybody—except Dorset."

"Your brother Dorset"—she took her time from his—"is like a sleek tomcat which has just swallowed a pan of cream, and is now engaged——"

"Engaged?" like a shot, as she paused.

"Engaged, in mesmerising a sparrow. Without labouring the metaphor—it seems unlikely: for a cream-fed cat, to be interested in a sparrow."

He rejected this, with a quick movement of his hand.

"I rather thought, from something Mamma wrote——"

"Selina," said Harriet Flood, "is given to taking the will for the deed; especially when it happens to be the will of your Papa. But"—she looked at him directly—"Emily Temple is staying at Guerdon. She goes home—according to present plans—on Saturday. Selina—which means Vicky—has been looking after her. And—you may as well have it now—both families are determined on the match." She turned her head quickly aside, to avoid the sight of a muscle twitching in his cheek.

"Well"—his voice reached her out of a short silence—"I think they should be very well—suited. Emily has always thought a great deal of Dorset."

"And Dorset, flattered, no doubt, by the 'thoughts' of so charming and effective a young woman as Emily Temple, basks like—as I said, like a tomcat in the sun."

"I don't know that I should describe Emily as 'effective.'" The word appeared to trouble him. "'Effective' is a bit showy, isn't it? As I see her, Emily's a particularly modest, simple kind of girl."

"Perhaps I meant 'attractive;' you mustn't criticise my English!" She tapped him reprovingly with her fan. "Of course she's modest; so she should be, with her breeding. She is, in fact, an exceptionally good girl—much too good for Dorset! As for simplicity—my dear boy, there's no such thing, among young woman of to-day. Don't mistake us ; we're a devious sex—it's our form of self-protection. You won't give us votes, and although in law we're entitled to handle our own property, you don't consider us capable of doing it ; so we have to defend ourselves as best we can, against your overbearing behaviour ! "

The glimmer of a smile, for which she was hoping, relaxed his drawn face.

" Well, I suppose I must prepare my congratulations. Do you suppose Doss has ' popped the question ' yet ? "

She shrugged her shoulders.

" Who's to know ? I can only say that, in his place, with the girl going home at the week-end, I should not be going to town to-morrow, unless I had some very urgent reason."

" Probably he has one," said Johnny loyally.

" Fiddlesticks. His tailor or some low music hall are the only excuses that ever take Dorset to town. If I were Emily Temple I should be very cool indeed about it ! "

" They probably understand each other very well, Grandmamma. And it must be rather embarrassing for both of them, to have the family sitting around, waiting for them to make an announcement ! I dare say Emily feels shy about it ; she may even have asked Doss not to say anything until she goes home. He'd be bound to respect her feelings in the matter."

She stared at him with exasperation.

" I am more than touched by your affecting assumption of Dorset's delicacy ! I can only assume that you've been away so long that you see everything, included your brother's character, *couleur de rose*. Let me tell you "—her small, pointed nails rapped the arm of the chair in which she was sitting—" that his conduct is that of a prima donna who takes liberties under the impression that she is indispensable to the performance ! "

" No, no, Grandmamma ! " Johnny's smile glittered in his sallow face. " You can't mix your metaphors like that. You had Doss a tomcat a minute ago——"

She glared at him.

" Don't be impudent ! And when, may I ask, are you going to get married yourself ? "

" I ?—I ? " he stammered. " Good heavens, I'll be in no sort of a position to marry for years—perhaps ever," he muttered.

" Nonsense. You know perfectly well your father would increase your allowance—as he will do for the others."

Johnny's lips twitched wryly. His grandmother—his mother—his Aunt Vicky—they were all the same : all persuaded that Flood and Company was a bottomless purse, into which each and all could carelessly dip their hands, whenever it pleased them.

" I'm not quite a free agent, you know, like Doss and Gilbert ; I've got Uncle Hacky to consider."

" In what way ? "

" He hasn't told you anything about his plans, then ? "

" My dear John, your uncles have never paid me the compliment of considering me capable of an intelligent interest in their plans."

" Wait until I'm a director ; I'll never move an inch without consulting you ! But I don't think I should say anything for the present."

" By all means keep your information to yourself ! I'm only a tattling old fool," retorted his grandmother, with asperity.

" You're a dangerous witch, and I wouldn't put it past you to put a ju ju on me ! You know as much as we all do about Uncle Hacky's mania for getting back into the West Africa trade."

" Oh—*that* ! "

" ' That ' "—he mimicked her—" may have considerable bearing on my future—unfortunately."

" *What are you saying ?* " He raised his head, startled, to meet the concentrated darkness of her eyes.

" Grandmamma—— ? "

She had risen, to stand beside him ; he could see the light shivering down her gown, which palpitated like the wings of a moth.

" You are not telling me that Harcourt will send you back to the Gold Coast ? "

Rising quickly, he took her in his arms.

" Grandmamma—darling——"

" I won't have it ! " Her clenched fists beat his chest. " Harcourt is mad—they're all mad—mad with their lust for money. As though they haven't enough—enough to damn them to all eternity ! And now they make you—make you——"

" Hush, dear." He tried to calm her. " Deuce take it, this is all my fault ; what a fool I am ! Listen : everything's unsettled—in the air—and may well remain so, if Uncle Hacky acts on the information I've brought back for him. I oughtn't to have said anything about it—I was only trying to explain that until—until my future seems a bit more settled, I couldn't even begin to think of marrying. You know Uncle Hacky ; he's never satisfied unless he's got a bunch of irons in the fire. I might be sent to Liverpool, to work under Mary's husband ; or, if we open the London branch he's always talking about, I might go there—which I'd much prefer, because a new venture always offers more opportunities than something that's already running smoothly on established lines——"

" You needn't treat me like a child." She touched her eyelids quickly, seeming to press the tears back from them, before saying fiercely, " I know my son Harcourt. If this West African folly materialises—— ? "

" Oh, I might get sent out there for a year or two "—he made deliberate light of it—" because, naturally, I've picked up a bit of useful knowledge, here and there—but it wouldn't be a permanency. Nothing's permanent on the Gold Coast ! "

" I will not hear of it."

" Right, darling. I'll leave you to handle the old boy." He glanced at his watch. " By George, it's getting on for eleven ! We've rattled all the family skeletons, haven't we ? Let's make sure I've got it all straight." He spread out the fingers of his left hand and started counting with mock solemnity.

She made no reply. He found himself looking down into her lovely, angry eyes.

" You may be an excellent servant of the Company ; you may, on occasion, be capable of ' great forethought, initiative and responsibility——' "

" Good lord, what on earth nonsense have you been listening to ? "

"—but in the management of your own affairs you are an utter nincompoop ! "

There was a short silence before, manlike, he changed the subject. Putting his hand in his pocket, he produced a small object, which he gave to her.

" I brought you something—it's ivory ; French Gaboon. I don't suppose you'll like it, but it was the best bit I could find."

" That was thoughtful of you." It was thanks to Quentin that she could appreciate the beauty and rarity of the piece he had given her ; but her gratitude was cut short by the faint peal of a bell. His look questioned her.

" That will be Dorset," she informed him, not without malice. " Come to inquire whether I have any commissions for him in London. He will probably have Emily Temple with him. Well ? You may get the answer to your questions, if you stay to meet them."

" I'll go," said Johnny abruptly. " I'll be seeing them later on, but I'd better not let the news of my arrival get to ' the house ' before I put in an appearance."

" Your best way," said his grandmother, perfectly understanding him, " is through here."

She crossed the room and drew back the curtain that masked the door of the conservatory.

" Mind you don't knock over any of my plants in the dark ! "

She felt the soft brush of his moustache on the back of her hand, waited until the outer door had closed, and came back as her butler was saying : " Miss Temple and Mr. Dorset," into what, from his disconcerted expression, he had evidently taken for an empty room.

CHAPTER TWO

I

"YOU can take my supper things away," mumbled Miranda, without looking up from her occupation.

"Yes, miss."

The unexpected voice flung her head back and her body forward in clumsy concealment of that which lay at her knees ; she stared for a moment through ugly, steel-rimmed glasses, incredulity shimmering slowly into rapture across her plain little face.

"*Johnny!*"

He was lifting her, she was hugging him warmly—yet in a guarded fashion, having been taught, both by precept and example, that demonstrativeness was "bad manners." A sudden access of shyness made her disengage herself ; she gave him a quick, prim smile, as she slid back to the floor ; blinking rapidly, as though to banish the indecent joy that had poured into her eyes, at the sight of the brother she adored.

"You—you've grown a moustache!"

"And, by George, Winkle, you've—grown!" He twirled the adornment on which her admiration centred.

She wriggled, flung into embarrassment, as always, by any reference to her appearance, and plunged at her handiwork, to create a diversion.

"What—are you and Emily *still* making dish-gardens?" He laughed, leaning over her. Then, because of what he saw, checked the laughter.

"Look : that's the hall where the people are judged, and those are palaver huts ; there's going to be lots more of them."

"You are a rum Winkle." He crouched on his heels to follow the pointing of her skinny little hand. "How do you know about these things?"

"I got some of Papa's books, out of the library."

On a large tin tray was a perfect representation in miniature of a West African village ; trees, buildings—some no larger than a thimble—and stockades, executed with a remarkable skill ; roofs neatly thatched, clay pillars ornamented with intricate designs. She showed him one with pride —no mere rolling pin of dough, but a carefully cut and levelled bundle of thin reeds, ligatured with cotton, over which she had begun to smear the clay.

"There's the sacred grove. I don't think those beads are much good as skulls ; do you? I tried peanuts, but they split after you peel them. I believe I'll try dried peas ; they're wrinkly—more like faces, aren't they?"

Taken aback, he tried to disguise it in his reply.

"It's dev'lish good. What are you going to do with it?"

She hunched her shoulder, giving him across it what was known as "Miranda's deceitful look :" the expression of her profound mistrust of adult questioning.

"It's my best—so far." The wistfulness of the unappreciated artist sounded in the reply.

"What—what does Emily think of it?"

"Pooh—Emily doesn't play these sort of games any longer. They've eaten the missionary," chanted Miranda gruesomely, "and they're just getting ready for the big palaver that's to settle how the white men shall be driven out of their land for ever——"

"We'll soon settle that," said Johnny easily, "with a couple of Maxims and the good old Martini-Metford. You'd better warn your gentleman in the sacred grove to pack up his fetish and tell the king the palaver's off."

Secretly he was shocked: sufficient of a Flood to feel that such an occupation was unsuitable for a young lady who would shortly be lengthening her skirts and pinning up the hair which, at present, straggled in untidy plaits over her rounded shoulders.

"Look here: where's The Grim?—and what are you doing out of bed at this time of night?"

"Me?" She appeared to make an effort to remember. "Oh, yes; I'm being punished. I'd forgotten all about it, until you reminded me."

"And what have you been up to this time?"

She took off her glasses to wipe them; the lenses were covered with clay. As she looked blindly past him, he thought, It's too bad. Her eyes are really beautiful.

"I've got to be 'up to' something." She evaded the question. "I can't sit here all day, listening to what the men talk about in the yard."

Johnny strode to the window; he was angry, but not with Miranda. He knew the old night-nursery, which had been made into Miranda's schoolroom, overlooking the stables—that, nominally, was its outlook. Actually, little was visible from its windows but the roofs of the lofts, with the clock tower rising above them. On wet days, a certain amount of entertainment was to be had from watching the rain washing down the slopes and making miniature cascades where the tiling had slipped. On fine ones, a rich smell of manure and sewage rose from the concealed yard. Governesses had complained, both of the smell and of the chequered language of the grooms, and had been told either to close the windows, or to take themselves and their pupil, temporarily, into the adjacent sewing-room. Miranda liked both the smell and the language, as she liked the clatter of pails in the early morning, and the scrape and thud and cronk of the loose boxes, when the horses were being bedded down for the night.

The room itself was square: of that squalid ugliness that often obtain in the concealed apartments of fine houses: with a brownish wallpaper, patched with damp, and an old red carpet, in which a three-cornered tear had been carelessly repaired with twine. Its oddments of furniture had individual handsomeness, but no coherence, of arrangement or design. It was a room no one had troubled about, a room that existed only as a convenience, with regard neither for appearance nor comfort.

Johnny, who had as little æsthetic perception as the average young man of his upbringing, felt, none the less, that it was an unsuitable room for his sister Miranda. Vicky—to whom his thoughts inevitably went—was not to blame. She, after all, had maintained her status at Guerdon—fortunately for them all—by knowing better than to interfere in any major issues of household policy. Selina, since the birth of her last child, had been too languid, too listless, to concern herself in any deviation from the routine, she, with Vicky's help, had established ; " Mamma must not be troubled " had been a by-word from Johnny's youth. And Dromore . . .

He stood still, telling himself that he admired and respected his father. But he, with all his loyalty, could not blind himself to the truth : that if Miranda had been beautiful and dashing, a fearless horsewoman, socially promising, and likely to attract the sort of young man Dromore would like for a son-in-law, she would not, in her fifteenth year, be languishing in a dark room on a back staircase.

She had clambered to her feet and was looking down at her African village with the fixity of a young diviner who reads the future in a tray of sand. Her crumpled cotton frock, daubed with clay, lost its " hang " over the hip she clasped habitually with a hand brown and icy as a bird's claw. She had lost the ribbon from one of her plaits, which scattered itself like a nest of young snakes over the smocking on her narrow little chest.

" Well—you haven't told me about The Grim."

" I did tell you—in one of my letters. I suppose you didn't get it. She got married. Last February. To the curate from Frenchay." Mockery glittered in Miranda's eye.

" Then who looks after you ? "

" I'm not supposed to do lessons. Mytton dresses me, and I read, sometimes, with Mamma—or with Aunt Vicky, when she's not too busy."

" Who says you're not to do lessons ? "

" That last old doctor," she mumbled. " I don't care. I'm writing the family history. That's what I'm being punished for."

He chewed his lip, frowning ; then pulled her suddenly down on his knee.

" It's jolly well time I came back to keep an eye on you—by the look of things ! Now, come on, Winkle : what's all this about ? "

It came out, in brief, matter-of-fact sentences. Miranda had left her exercise book, in which she was writing the " history," in the library, and Dromore had found it. There had been a " scene," based on what Papa was pleased to call her false, scandalous and improper statements about matters on which she was wickedly misinformed.

" Who informed you ? "

" Well, if you want to know—Polly," was the surprising answer.

" You should have the sense not to pay attention to Polly's chatter ! " What had possessed Polly, to open so queasy a subject with Miranda ?

" Well, then I asked Uncle Quentin."

" Uncle Quentin's in his dotage ; nobody listens to him."

" He wasn't in his dotage ; he was in his bottles," said Miranda simply, " when I asked him. All about us, and the slave trade, and the black woman that Matthew Flood married," she concluded, on a note of satisfaction.

"Well, I don't wonder you caught it from the Pater. My stars, I bet he was rampageous!" A whistle broke from Johnny's lips. "You're nothing but a little scavenger, Winkle! I think you might humour him by not digging up a particularly smelly carcase out of our past——! What did you do? Write it all down in your 'history'?"

She nodded; he could not help laughing, although his sympathies, for once, were with Dromore. Encouraged by the laughter, Miranda sidled up, to rub her head against his sleeve.

"Now—tell me all about it."

"All about—what?"

"All the thing you didn't put in your letters. All about——" She was looking up; he down. Something leapt into her eyes; something that tightened the clasp of his arm about her body. "What are you looking at?"

"Me? Nothing."

"You were. Something——" She turned her head, to fling a quick look behind her. Go on: tell me—tell me!"

"Oh, shut up, Winkle." For once he was brusque with her. "Do you know what the time is? Do you know it's nearly midnight? You're going to bed now, this minute. Can you manage, or do I ring for Mytton—or someone?"

"You—can't—fool—me." She was pushing her face close to his: screwing up her eyes to peer at him. "People can't, you know: they're always thinking they do, but, really it's silly to try."

"You're crazy." He gave her a little shake, pushing her off his knee. "If you're not going to bed, I am; and to-morrow——" He stopped; to-morrow—what? To-morrow something must be started: something that would get Miranda out of this queer, unhealthy state—make a normal, cheerful, little girl of her. What in the name of goodness had they been doing—or not been doing—with her? And who would be the one to speak to, Selina, or Vicky? He would have to be very careful; any assumption of authority would surely, if it had any effect at all, be attended with unpleasant consequences for the one he desired to help. "To-morrow," he began, and stopped again.

The lamplight on her face made it like a little, bleached skull; puzzled, he watched her lift her finger slowly and lay it to her lips. The melodrama of the gesture, it's deadly seriousness, made him want to laugh—and yet not to laugh; it was like a child's performance of one of the witches in *Macbeth*.

"*There's something going on.* I don't know what it is, but it's happening—*now!*"

His jaw dropped; he gaped at her. No; Winkle's not acting; what the——?

She had lurched to the window, the sash of which, with difficulty, she threw up, and leaned out, her nostrils flickering, into the night.

"Can't you *smell* it?" She drew her head in, and faced him accusingly.

"No, Winkle ; I can't say I can."

She shed occultism abruptly, like a mantle, and was the sullen schoolgirl gain.

"Well—it's about time you came back. To look after Emily."

II

The park stretched in milky waves between the fringing woods and the istant orange beacons of Guerdon ; overhead, the stars quivered like notes haken from the thin white tambourine of the moon. A faint, invisible tirring in the grass suggested the presence of the white Guerdon herd of attle, blotted out against its silvery background. A nightjar chirred. A abbit made a minute crackle, as it lolloped into the brushwood.

"Emily."

She turned her head of a victim towards him helplessly : as a lady of he Terror might have turned it towards her executioner. Dorset said, in is sultry voice, his voice of a purring tiger :

"I am going to kiss you, Emily. Do you mind ?"

She felt herself dissolving. Emotionally, she was already in his arms, vhile the artificial side of her, the veneer which training had laid like a atin gloss over the primitive Emily, put up a faint, confused resistance.)id girls—girls of her own class—allow men to kiss them before they were ngaged ? Would not her guardian, and Dorset's mother as well, be shocked t the idea of his bringing her out, to kiss her, like a housemaid, in the park ?

Dorset was smiling at her. His eyes, clear and ice-grey between their ong lashes, were full of moonlight, and his closed, smiling lips filled her— he did not know why—with sudden terror.

For seven years she had been completely, fatally in love with Dorset ; he had schooled herself towards this moment—whenever it should come : he moment which was to crown her with joy and make her the happiest of women. Such innocent experience as had come her way—and she had ad much admiration—she had cherished and woven into the garland of er love for him : glad that others should find her desirable, for his sake. She had *prayed* for this moment. And, now it was here, she knew with a hocking certainty, that prayer had nothing to do with the emotions he evoked in her : that if Dorset were the Devil, and she herself about to become the damned, nothing could save her from the embrace towards which her flesh moved, while her spirit recoiled.

"My dear Emily," he was murmuring, as his lips took hers.

It was over, and she was lying against him, half-fainting, with the terror gone. So that was being kissed—by Dorset. Ignorant as most girls of her class and upbringing of the meaning of passion, she was stunned by the reality. Dorset's mouth, travelling softly from her lips to her eyes, to the curve of her ear and down the tremulous column of her throat, had completed the surrender of her youthful, serious conventions. She was his at last ! She could feel his body trembling too, as he held her against him, and this was, of all things, the most marvellous: that she, Emily Temple, so shy and doubtful of herself, had shaken his careless assurance. This, she thought blissfully, is when he's going to ask me to marry him.

He muttered: "Kiss me again," as he curved his hand under her chin and lifted her mouth to his. This time she responded frankly, and felt him start, and his hand slip lower, to her bosom. For a few seconds there was nothing but their joined mouths and a whirling of stars overhead. Then, at a too intimate touch, awareness rushed back, and she leapt involuntarily from his embrace.

Her teeth were chattering and her fingers trembling as they thrust back the pins in her heavy coil of hair, which had slipped to her shoulders. Dorset was stopping, to pick up her cape, which had fallen to the ground and when he rose, his face was curiously dark and his breath audible. He replaced the cape, faintly wet with dew, on her naked shoulders, gripped them briefly, and let them go. She heard, confusedly, his short laugh as he stood aside for her to pass.

"I think—perhaps—you're right!"

What did he mean?

A wild weakness passed through Emily and she felt herself sway, as her eyes closed. He must catch her, he must hold her, or she would fall, and break to pieces. . . .

"Well?" he was murmuring. "I suppose we'd better go in; Aunt Vicky will be wondering what's become of you! You know, Emily," he was saying, when they had travelled a few yards over the lace-like pattern which the young elms had laid upon the moonlight of the avenue, and she had stumbled a few times, and he had put his hand quickly to her elbow, but had shown no disposition to leave it there—"nobody has any right to be as beautiful—and as nice—as you!"

What was the answer to that? It did not sound like the beginning of a proposal! But Dorset had his own way of doing everything. Speak! Speak! her heart cried to him; it doesn't matter what you say, only stroke me with that voice of yours, which is almost as wonderful as stroking me with your hand. She shivered, and her head turned towards him as though it were dragged: her mouth, which had just learned the magic of his. Another kiss—before saying good night?

His leisurely voice went on.

"I suppose you know why I'm going to town to-morrow?"

"You're playing polo, aren't you?" She was glad to hear that her own voice was light and steady; there was something in being taught to control one's feelings.

He laughed shortly.

"This isn't the best preparation for polo! I expect I'll play an abominable game." He paused. "There's no point in beating about the bush. I'm going away because we've seen as much of one another as is good for either of us."

". . . I don't think I understand."

"Oh—come." He was smiling, but there was a faint, metallic ring in his voice. "That won't do, Emily! You know, you're a terribly intelligent girl. You quite alarm me sometimes!"

"Nonsense," said Emily faintly.

"Oh, yes, you do." He gave his short, disgraceful chuckle. "In fact, you've got a shocking hold on me. If I were to stay here another twenty-four hours, I should probably lose my head and ask you to marry me."

It was at this moment that another woman slipped inside Emily Temple's skin, driving out the sensitive girl, ready to deliver an adoring heart into a lover's keeping. Someone hard, wary, sceptical had usurped the place of that tender Emily. He had cut her open with a sword, but she was too proud to let him see the bleeding.

"What a disaster!" said the woman who wore the outward shape of Emily.

"Yes, it would be." He was serious. "In fact, I can hardly imagine a worse one."

"For yourself, or for me?"

He had stopped, to gaze at her.

"Emily, you're terribly nice: but you're—terrible. I don't suppose you know what I am talking about," he muttered. "But, for a fellow like me, you're"—he made an impatient gesture—"you're—impossible."

"I quite understand—that you had to kiss me first, to find out how 'impossible' and 'terrible' I am!" she heard the other woman say; and gave a little laugh at what she could not help admiring, as an apt and witty retort.

"By God——!" His sudden fury had her by the throat again, with terror. "If you say that kind of thing, I'll kiss you again. I'll kiss you—until there is nothing left for either of us but to—go—on—kissing——!"

Some unknown force drew her back from the movement he made towards her.

"Please——!"

Presently he muttered:

"I shan't forget kissing you, Emily." And something, some hint of weakness in him, brought back the girl who, a moment ago, had fled from Emily Temple. She said, with a hopeless childishness:

"I'm glad you enjoyed it." Which might have touched anyone less pitiless than Dorset Flood. He turned to smile at her, again secure of his ascendancy.

"What wonderful times we might have had, if you weren't—you!" He said it lightly, but something, some dark undercurrent beneath the words which, to her innocence, were enigmatic, froze her again. "I see you're puzzled, and, just now, a little upset," said Dorset kindly. "There's nothing to worry about, my dear. In spite of all they say, there's nothing criminal in being kissed on a beautiful moonlight night!"

She was speechless. Looking at her profile, fine and delicate as glass in the curious light, he was tempted to ask her if she had never been kissed before. But the point seemed, in the circumstances, immaterial. Besides, he had had his answer—in that one wild moment when her lips clung to his ; no man of experience could mistake their virginity.

" I'll tell you something, Emily." He was now quite sure of himself, as well as of her. " When Mamma told me you were coming to spend the summer at Guerdon, I very nearly went straight off to the Highlands."

" I'm sorry my visit upset you—like that."

" Don't be foolish. I knew it would spoil things—as it has done, of course."

" Of course," she agreed, obediently.

" I should have proposed to you while we were seeing each other in your own home, and at balls, before our families had the precious idea of mewing us up together for eight weeks——"

Why didn't you ? He answered the question as though she had spoken it aloud.

" I always meant to do it," said Dorset, for him a little clumsily, " but—well, I suppose a man hangs on to his freedom ; I wanted to wait a little longer, before tying myself up——"

" I quite understand." The hard, wise woman had resumed possession. " Please don't take so much trouble to explain——! "

" I wouldn't—to anyone but you. But you're different from other girls, and—you know I'm madly in love with you."

She made a helpless gesture. He was incredible !

" If you had ever cared for me a little—which, of course, is impossible ! " —his smile cajoled her—" it would have been finished off by these busybodies, intent on flinging us into each other's arms."

" Of course." She despised herself for yielding to his persuasion.

" Quite naturally, the last thing a girl of pride and spirit wants is to be handed over like a parcel." He seemed determined to labour the point. " And I'll never forgive the family for ruining what might have been wonderful—for us both. Now—won't you give me credit for being honest ? A nice mess we would have been in, if I hadn't acted like what most people would call a ' cad,' and faced up to it ! The truth is, that although I'm completely crazy about you, we're completely unsuited to each other—and I can only hope, for my own sake," concluded Dorset, on the note of one who feels he has handled a delicate situation very creditably, " that the time will come when we're both thankful to have realised it before it was too late ! "

" Oh, yes, no doubt it will," she hastened to assure him.

" You don't hate me, do you, Emily ? " He could not resist the characteristic appeal.

She heard, incredulously, herself give a little laugh.

" What an absurd idea ! "

" And do you realise," he persisted, " that I've done this for the good of us both—your good, as much as my own ? "

Past speech, she made a little gesture with her hands.

" Well." He drew a deep breath and spoke happily. " You are a darling, Emily ! . . . Let's go the long way round, shall we ? We shan't be seeing much of one another for a while, and we may as well make the most of it." As they turned back to the avenue, the moonlight struck full on her bosom. "You've dropped your camellias; do you want to go back and look for them?"

"Go back? Why?" She was sincerely puzzled.

He smiled in his secret fashion.

"That's one of the nice things about you; you're so unsentimental!"

Her pride raised its battered head.

"What have I to be sentimental about?"

This was a little too much, even for Dorset.

"Oh, come! I gave them to you, didn't I? Some girls would have kept them—in remembrance!"

"Oh, God! she was praying; help me to forget this night.

"Shall we have one more kiss?" He was drawing her into the shadow of the rhododendrons—the rhododendrons which, that afternoon, had sheltered her tears. "Oh, Emily, Emily!" He pulled her to him. "And you don't even know what a kiss means! All that I could have taught you——"

"Don't—someone may be looking—one of the servants—going back to the house."

"As you please." She was right, and it was dangerous; but he was hot with the desire once more to take her lips with his. Still, his mind was made up, and it was wiser to leave things as they were. "I've just been thinking——"

Looking down, she saw stains on the striped hem of her gown, which the moonlight turned from green to grey. She would never wear it again.

"What were you thinking?"

"It might make it easier for you—with our families, I mean—if I told Papa I had proposed to you, and you had turned me down."

"Oh, dear!" She drew in a quick breath. "He'll be furious with me——!"

"Nothing of the sort; he's bound to think I've made a blunder of it. They've all been sitting round like amiable vultures," said Dorset savagely, "and perhaps this will teach them to mind their own business in future! Anyhow—it looks better; and my going away to-morrow will clinch it."

"Unfortunately, I'm not going away to-morrow, and I'm very bad at telling lies," she whispered.

"Well, what do you want me to do?" He scowled at her; it had gone off well, up to the present; was she now going to spoil it by turning difficult?

"I think—I think," said Emily faintly, "—you had better propose to me, and I'll refuse you; and then, at any rate, I shan't have to make up a story about it."

He looked at her, with deep, animal-like mistrust of her motive. Then:

"Very well. Will you marry me?" he muttered.

Emily closed her eyes. Behind the deep lids she saw the scene as she had a hundred times imagined it: his eyes smouldering into hers, as they had done a dozen times a day ; the shocking sweetness of his mouth ; all the flippancy stripped from him—just for this one moment. His hand sought hers gently—perhaps raised it to his lips, before they pressed the chaste salute of betrothal on hers. She knew clearly, in this moment, that the Dorset of the picture was not the true Dorset, but a schoolgirl's dream. But it was the dream Dorset she addressed, as she opened her eyes on his anxious, angry face.

" My dear Dorset—my sweet Dorset—don't be afraid. I would not marry you if there were no one else left on earth."

He bloomed into glossiness under her eyes.

" By God, Emily, I shall always adore you ! And now your conscience is clear, and you can have a good laugh when you remember the way you turned me down ! "

" I doubt if your father will be so much amused—— ! "

" Oh, he'll get over it," said Dorset cheerfully. " You haven't caught cold, have you ? I believe you're shivering ! It's extraordinary, how you hot-house girls can be chilly, even on a summer's night." He linked his arm fraternally in hers and walked her briskly towards the terrace. " I shall get a frightful wigging from Aunt Vicky, if you're sick to-morrow ! "

" My feet are wet." Her teeth were chattering. " I'll go straight to my room. Please say good night to the others for me."

" I will. Emily ! "

She turned towards him from the foot of the stairs ; her face was the colour of paper, and the deep hollows of her eyes so aged her that her face was the face of a woman of thirty.

" Good night—Emily—my darling ! "

Her lips parted, and she put her hand to her throat.

Johnny came down the stairs behind her.

" Good—God ! Look at this," said Dorset.

She turned quickly. Johnny's eyes met hers, and he stood aside, to allow her to pass.

" Johnny ! I'll see you in the morning." She had fled past him ; his eyes followed her up the stairs.

Dorset had taken his cigarette case from his pocket, and was striking a match. He had blown it out, tossing it away and set a ring of smoke spiring upwards, before Johnny moved from his position against the banister rail. Dorset's eyes dwelt reflectively on his younger brother.

" Where've you come from ? "

Johnny resumed his descent of the stairs. Dorset was smiling, as though something amused him.

" You've arrived at quite a dramatic moment, old fellow ! You see before you "—he grimaced, tapping the ash of his cigarette on the rug at his feet—" Emily Temple's rejected suitor."

Johnny, like all Englishmen, had been schooled in the repression of emotion ; but, at Dorset's words, it was as if a mask had been torn off. His hand went automatically to the recently acquired moustache. Then the mask dropped back : the mask he had opposed in childhood to Gilbert's arm-twisting, and the more poignant, although less physically painful, torments of his brother Dorset. He said gruffly :

" Taking all into consideration, you look pretty damn' satisfied ! "

Dorset laughed ; naturally he was bluffing. How much had Dorset cared, really ? It must have come as a shock ; he was putting a good face on it, considering. . .

" You'd better help me break the news to the Pater ! " He flung an arm casually round Johnny's shoulder. " I rather fancy he'll take the satisfaction out of me ! You know, old fellow "—Johnny looked up into the handsome, candid, brilliant face—" women are astoundin' ; positively they are."

" You know more about them than I do."

" Putting all conceit, and that sort of thing, aside—wouldn't you have said Emily was pretty fond of me ? "

" I wouldn't know. I haven't seen as much of her as—the rest of you."

" Do you know what she said, when she refused me ? "

" It's no business of mine." He moved restlessly away from the purposeful grip on his lapel.

" No—but listen." Dorset spoke slowly, deliberately, as though determined that each syllable should register on his unwilling listener. " She said : '*I wouldn't marry you if there was nobody else left on earth.*' What do you think of that ? I tell you, old boy, it gave me a jolt ! To put it plainly, it's not the sort of thing a fellow expects, after——"

" Don't you hear what I say ? It's no business of mine."

Dorset stood still, with narrowed eyes, for a few moments, before following him into the library.

III

He must get married quickly ; just for the sake of peace. Some tough, sensible girl who, after marriage, would be satisfied to go her own way and let him go his ; the kind who would either sink herself in the children or find her own diversions—he had no desire to act as a dog in the manger about those, so long as she was discreet !

Only—blast the family, and blast Emily Temple.

The whole business was damnable, and no one but the family was to blame. Set on the match, what they had actually done was to work up a tension between the two people concerned, making it virtually impossible for either of them to think of the other in terms of normal companionship. There had, in fact, been a period when he had almost disliked Emily : a period which came—unfortunately, as things turned out—to an end with the rumour of her engagement to a boy in the Guards, the most sedulous of a group that had danced attendance on her throughout the season. The Cullens were said to approve of the match.

It had been amusing to return, to cut out Emily's aspirant by the simple means of not appearing to take him seriously ; to scatter a largesse of charm about the bedazzled girl, and gracefully to regain one's status, as her accredited cavalier—without committing oneself. For—it was curious, but he was quick to perceive it—a certain kudos did attach itself to those whom Emily favoured. There were girls in society more elegant, more dashing and certainly more beautiful, with larger fortunes and a background of titles and armorial bearings—who did not cut the ice Emily did with people of discrimination : of whom, of course, the foremost, in his own estimation, was Dorset Flood. Actually, in his case, discrimination consisted in noticing what other people admired, desired and were enthusiastic about, and acquiring it promptly for himself. Having acquired it he was likely as promptly to relinquish it—with a little of its glamour gone. There was, he had discovered, an even subtler thrill in ex-ownership than in actual possession : something very gratifying in being able to say, when someone praised a horse, a set of sporting prints, a gun—" Yes ; it used to be mine " —the implication being, of course, that the speaker had now found something better. In the case of a woman, one just—smiled. But Dorset was wise enough to realise that it would not do, to smile, in the case of Emily Temple.

Because she was, in her delicate way, inaccessible—that is, inaccessible in the way he would have liked to have had her—she had begun to haunt him. It took him a little while to perceive that that disturbing loveliness, that gossamer-like shimmer were responsible for the break up of the *affaire* with Edy Lane-Fox, for the fading out of Mabel Barron, for the sharp conclusion of the Silverton episode, and for a general sense of tasteless dissatisfaction with life which had made him wonder, seriously, whether he were sufficiently off-colour to see a doctor about it.

His appetite for women had always been well in the family tradition : fierce, greedy and insatiable ; an aspect of the superabundant physical energy which had earned him distinction in the field of sport. He had seldom known rebuff, because instinct led him, always, to the type of woman who was prepared to give him what he wanted without troublesome exactions : women older than himself, skilled in intrigue, young, married women of the raffish set which was just beginning to gain ground in society : a professional or two—out of bravado—and the usual quota of pretty thespians regarded by a young man of fashion as indispensable to his social background. Laughter and levity were for Dorset, necessary adjuncts of passion ; a hint of wistfulness, of tears was, for him, enough to bring any affair to a ruthless conclusion, to change partiality to a dislike which, should the offender be guilty of insistence, turned quickly to disgust.

And there was something about Emily which scared, and put him on the defensive : some underlying hint of seriousness beneath her gaiety that warned him of danger ; something in her which told him—for all her gentleness, her unconcealed response to his advances—even more surely than her own background, that he could not play fast and loose with Emily Temple.

He was mad for her—and knew exactly what his passion would do to her : how it would first intoxicate, then crush, overwhelm and, finally, annihilate her ; and that, in marriage, there would be no escape from the effects of his act of destruction. She would shackle him for ever with her fidelity, would hold him chained to the prospect of her suffering—a damnable prospect for one, like Dorset Flood, who hated the sight of pain : especially pain of his own creating.

It was none the less damnable to be obliged to forgo her. Who would have expected, in a girl of her type, to meet so authentic a response to that experimental embrace ? A good many fellows, he thought, with some pride, would have allowed themselves to be carried away ! There was that much to be said for experience.

At least he had had her lips ! He groaned at the recollection. Yes : too soft, too sensitive, too complicated and clinging. He had known it all, in the moment of their embrace. A ravishing mistress—as a wife she would be ruin, to a man of his temperament. So far as he was concerned, Emily Temple was forbidden fruit—which, of course, quickened his desire for her—was poison, was destruction, was future misery in return for present rapture. The acute self-protectiveness of the male—in Dorset's case stronger than in the majority—rose in his defence.

For a very little he could have hated her, because she had wounded him in his self-esteeem. She had obliged him to act abominably to her—and bad behaviour, to a woman like Emily, was outside Dorset's code. He knew there was not a man who, like himself, had been favoured with her acquaintance, who would not condemn him outright for it, and he knew they would be right in doing so. His popularity among his own sex was very dear to Dorset, and he disliked the idea of forfeiting it ; he disliked Emily, for putting it in jeopardy. He had always prided himself on his scrupulosity in his dealings with women ; on knowing the kind with whom one need not be " particular," and on respecting those who, by their ignorance, or innocence, or the principles of their upbringing, had claims on his consideration.

A fellow was a " cad," in Dorset's estimation, who " took advantage " of what he and his kind were pleased to call a " nice girl," and it was not pleasant to find oneself falling into the same category—on account of Emily Temple.

Yes ; he must marry quickly—before the family had time to recover from the shock and start their disgraceful plotting again. And no doubt Emily would marry as well. The pair of them settled, the element of danger would be removed ; they might even . . . It would depend, of course, on whom Emily married. One thing was plain : she was as much infatuated by him as he by her. In those circumstances, her fidelity might serve them. It was not a matter to bank on ; there was something indecent even, in considering it. But . . .

Oh, God, I want you, Emily ! And there is nothing in my life that I have wanted, and haven't got, sooner or later.

His hand shook, as he lit a cigarette, and every desirous corpuscle in his body was aware of her, within call, actually within a few paces of the room wherein he sat. It was not the first time he had thought of Emily in this way, but his torment was increased by the persuasion that, after the episode in the park, she also was thinking, in the same way of him. The idea made him hold his breath. . . .

IV

" ' And like a dying lady, lean and pale,
Who totters forth . . .
. . . led by the insane
And feeble wanderings of her faded brain. . . .' "

Something had happened to her which was never supposed to happen to girls of her class, carefully brought up, guarded girls, with traditions to protect them and secure their futures. She had been offered—so much she understood—not love, but something that such girls were taught to hold in abhorrence. Even now incredulous, she stared into the looking glass at that stark mask, that shell of the slain Emily, the terrible, impossible Emily, who was to be desired, but not loved ; to be kissed, but not married ; the Emily who had gone through her short life enamoured of a phantom, dedicated to a hero who existed only in her fond, foolish imagination.

. . . From the confusion of her mind she snatched, at random, a memory of her father, whom everyone had expected to marry again after her mother's death. Instead, there had been his " friend "—the Madame de Séguin who was the unwitting cause of the abrupt curtailment of her " finishing " interlude in the establishment of Madame Larpentier : Madame de Séguin, who, on the occasion when the young ladies from Madame Larpentier's were taken to a performance of Molière at the Théâtre Français, was standing in the foyer with a radiant incredulity in every line of her charming little face.

" *Pas possible ! Ce n'est pas toi, Emilie !* "

What memories of the past rushed into the minds of both, as they clung together : of a whole volume of sweet scents, sweet moments, sweet sights and sounds and blithe adventures, centring round the debonair figure of papa. Madame de Séguin was gasping a little, opening her eyes very wide, so as not to spoil her mascara'd lashes ; apologising for the involuntary *tutoiement* which had risen from the past to her lips.

" Say ' *toi* '—please ! Never call me anything but ' *toi*.' "

The other girls, with the little, elderly *promeneuse* who accompanied them on such outings, had drawn tactfully aside ; she cared nothing for their curiosity, for their veiled glances of inquiry.

" I must see you again. We're allowed to ' receive ' once a fortnight—tea and coffee and little cakes and best frocks : Sunday afternoon—*numèro quinze*, rue des Belles Feuilles. Say you'll come ; oh, please say you'll come ! "

" Of course I will come ; and you must come and visit me."

" Promise ! " she cried, still clinging to the hand, as to the beloved past.

" I promise." Madame de Séguin was laughing as she turned away, but her eyes still glittered with tears.

Then there was Sunday : the *salon*, with its striped lemon and white Empire furniture, imposing Empire manners on the young hostesses—conscious of their gowns and their coiffures, anxious about the impressions made on each other by their guests : sporting fathers, on their way back from Longchamps, mammas still exhausted from the *couturiers*, a dashing brother or two, in Paris for a " spree," reluctantly obeying parental injunction to " look up " Isobel, or Joyce, or Violet ; a few formal young Frenchmen, hand-picked for correctness by Madame Larpentier—all perched on uneasy-chairs, making stiff conversation, respectfully deferential to *les jeunes anglaises*, and to Mademoiselle Angèle Larpentier, who, responsible for the musical education, summoned, now the Neilson twins, for their pianoforte duet, now the younger Miss Cotter, for her rendering of *Connais-tu le pays*.

She sat a little withdrawn ; pale, abstracted, looking at her watch. How had she ever been so careless as to lose touch with this friend, so dear, so admired, so kind to a shy little girl, lost in the forest of an adult world ?

Had Madame de Séguin forgotten ? Had she lost the address ? How stupid not to have written it down, and sent it to her. . . . Then the door opened ; the blood rushed to her cheeks, and she sprang to her feet.

Not by a day, not by an hour had she aged, since those always legendary times her presence recalled. Emily was amused, and pleased to see, in the glances of the other women, that *nuance* of acidity which accompanies unwilling deference to one of their own sex. The men's interest was inevitable—and the clumsy attempts of the anglo-Saxon element, to disguise it. Why, in England, was it a mark of ill-breeding, to allow a woman to see you admired her ?

" A race of boors and schoolboys, my dear. I hope you will never waste yourself on one of them—although," added Everard Temple regretfully, " I should be sorry if you married away from your own countrymen." Talk of marriage—to a little girl in a bonnet, with a pelisse down to the pom-poms on her slippers ; strange, that memory should revive it now.

" You are looking at me, darling ; you do not like my *toilette* ? " Madame de Séguin was saying gently.

" I adore it ; it is perfection. I was thinking of Papa. Do you remember——"

A spasm crossed the other's face ; she rose quickly.

" And you will take lunch with me, next week ? It is a little depressing here." She seemed faintly to shiver. " *Tu t'ennuies un peu—n'est ce pas—chèrie ?* "

" Evidently," said Emily seriously, " it is not the Paris of old times."

" *Depuis le mort de ton père—ca n'éxiste plus.*" The elder woman's lips tightened ; she put her hand lightly through Emily's arm. " *A la recherche du temps perdu !* We shall find them again, perhaps, on Wednesday next ? "

They went down the long room together, Emily, in her happiness, not noticing that backs were turned, or the dropped jaw of Madame Larpentier's nephew, whom Emily very much disliked. The French boys had been edging nearer and nearer, hoping for a presentation, which Emily ignored. For to-day, she would share her friend with nobody. Particularly not that detestable Henri St. Jules, whose staring was, actually, insolent. Madame de Séguin and Madame Larpentier exchanged the frosty civilities of hostess and unfamiliar guest.

" I will send the carriage for you, on Wednesday, a little before one."

Henri St. Jules was waiting for her, on her return.

" Madame de Séguin is a friend of yours ? " His English accent was shocking—no less than his insistence upon speaking English on every possible occasion. Emily answered coldly, in French :

" A very old friend," and passed on.

. . . A night of happy dreams, a brief rapture of anticipation : then :

" I am not empowered, as you know, *mademoiselle*, to make a prisoner of you ; but I must warn you that if you insist on keeping your appointment, I shall be obliged to write to your guardian."

" Pray write to Lady Cullen," said Emily haughtily. " You will no doubt be told, *madame*, that she has never assumed it her duty to interfere with any of the friendships I made before she adopted me."

She thought of telling Sophie de Séguin ; but why bring shadow into the sheer sunshine of the afternoon they spent together ? Time rolled back in the little pavilion at Auteuil ; tinier than she remembered it, from childhood, but even more beautiful. She found herself comparing it instinctively with the tasteless pomp of her English home ; the London house and the big country place in Gloucestershire seemed in a flash to epitomise the profound want of sympathy which, for all the latter's kindness, existed between her and her parents by adoption.

" Tell me about *your* home, *chèrie* ; I should like to be able to picture you in it—when you go back to England."

She caught her breath ; it seemed, in that moment, indescribable—at all events to Sophie de Séguin ; yet some flash of Everard's humour came to her rescue, and she laughed as she replied :

" Did you know that some kinds of architecture, and some kinds of furniture, are moral, and others aren't ? Mamma—I call her Mamma, you know—is very Victorian ; Balmoral—Victorian—if you know what that means ? She wouldn't approve of any of this ! "

" *Tiens*," observed Sophie mildly.

" The Gothic is moral," Emily told her solemnly. " Anything Empire—in fact, anything French, of whatever period, is rather improper. Mamma has only once been to Paris—on her honeymoon : and I think perhaps Sir Vaughn was a little bit indiscreet——"

" Sir Vaughn ? Then you do not call him ' Papa ' ? "

" Oh . . . no." There was only one Papa.

In Sophie's bedroom—they were on Christian-name terms by then—a painting of her father ; not very good, but so alive ! As though the spirit of its subject lingered in the canvas, to smile down on Everard Temple's daughter, and on his. . . .

For the first time, she knew what Sophie de Séguin had been to her father. The knowledge came to her naturally and gently, without shock, without anything but gladness that these two, so near and so dear to her, had found a happiness that might, some day, be hers. Their eyes, and then their lips, met silently ; the little room, the great urn of carnations—his favourite flower—under the portrait, held the perfume of a love each knew to be everlasting. Something told Emily that no other foot had crossed the threshold since her father died.

At the end of the week, Lady Cullen arrived, and she was taken back to England. Very little was said ; Emily guessed that her guardian had not regretted an excuse for terminating an experience which only Emily's urgent and repeated appeals had induced her reluctantly to concede. Paris —even under the unexceptionable roof of Madame Larpentier—was no place for a young English girl ; and, in Emily's case, particularly undesirable, since it must revive memories much better forgotten. Paris was all very well for a bride on her honeymoon—with an attentive husband to keep at bay all those unsettling influences which no future matron of a British household can afford to entertain.

Emily cried herself to sleep for many nights. Although she could, and would, write to Sophie, Sophie, on her own admission, was no correspondent. " What is the use of letters, *chèrie* ? " She had gently set aside Emily's attempt to wring a promise from her, to write. " Between lovers, they are an indulgence ; between women—folly. *A plus forte raison*," she concluded, with her charming smile, " they are very indiscreet ! " So there had only been a card, for her birthday and for New Year, and no letters, from Sophie, to lighten Emily's darkness. One thing remained to comfort her : Sophie's words at parting—was it possible, Emily wondered, that she had foreseen the swift conclusion of their brief delight ?

" Remember, *chèrie* : if you are ever alone, or if ever in grief—I am here, waiting. So much, I think, your father would wish : that the two he loved most dearly should share each other's sorrows."

Had the time come, now ? Something told Emily that it had not ; that a broken love affair was a humiliating kind of thing to trail across the Channel ; that Sophie, tender as she was, would deprecate the loss of dignity involved in flight, on such a pretext. And the return—oh, that would be intolerable ! with everyone knowing what one had done, and why one had done it. Sophie, when her lover died, had not fled from Paris, but, after the little pause allowed for mourning, had gone steadfastly about those occupations which, since so many had been shared with him, must each have plunged a thorn into her heart. Yet—was not death the easiest way to lose the one you loved ?

It was the kind of thing one found ridiculous—in novels, or when one came across it in life : the foolish girl, " giving her heart " where it was not wanted. There had been such a case in Emily's first season—the Cotter girl, she who sang *Connais-tu le pays*, crawling around, dripping devotion for one of the Sax boys, who was obliged eventually to bolt for Switzerland, where he broke a number of limbs, and appeared to find the hazards of the new and highly dangerous sport of ski-ing preferable to that of being obliged, for the sake of peace, to marry Joyce Cotter. So embarrassing for everyone and so lowering to self-esteem ! Emily winced, remembering all the cruel little jests, the witticisms, to which—she was thankful to remember—she had not contributed.

It had not been she who pursued Dorset ; she had been so careful to give no grounds for that accusation ! Why, why had he not left her in peace, to marry Winty Ingram—with whom, in time, she might have been quite contented—if he did not mean to make her his wife ? Too late, now, to talk of discretion ; the dismissal of Winty, coinciding with Dorset's re-appearance on the scene, had let loose the hounds of gossip. Not only Guerdon and Champion Court, but all London, were sitting, with their mouths open, waiting for the announcement.

They say . . . let them say. What did anything matter ? She had lost him.

Her mind went wandering back, to the days of her strange—her inexplicable fear of Dorset. Was it some unrecognised, childish premonition of the blow he would deal her ? Had it been instinct, trying to give her the warning that was swept into limbo on that first night they danced together, at the Clifton ball ?

" You never came to say good night to me."

She gasped, dragging the folds of her silk dressing-gown about her, as she lept to face the door.

" Did I make you jump ? I knocked, twice," said Miranda, " and I saw your light was on, so I thought you'd forgotten to put it out before you went to sleep."

" Oh, Winkle, why aren't you in bed ? "

" Johnny's come home ! "

" I know—I've seen him." How many hours ago ? She tried to recover the sense of time and place—deploring her carelessness in forgetting to lock her door.

Miranda limped across the room and stood by the dressing-table, myopically fingering Emily's brushes. In her shabby red dressing-gown, without her spectacles, she looked a very little girl.

" You ought to be asleep," said Emily helplessly.

" I wanted something to read. It's such a long way down to the library."

" There are some books—on the table, by my bed ; what do you want —a story, or poetry ? "

" I think poetry's best, for this time of night," observed Miranda, as she held the print almost to her nose ; she lowered it, to smile shyly at Emily. " If it hadn't been for you I'd never have known about poetry ! Do you remember ' See where she sits upon the grassie greene,' and the ' five sweet symphonies,' and your song ' Greensleeves is my heart of gold ' ? "

" Yes, darling ; yes."

" What good times we had, after you came ! Are you coming back to live with us ? "

" To live—with—— ? "

" When you and Dorset get married."

The voice dried in her throat. The minute tick of the travelling clock on the mantelpiece was all the sound the room contained. Miranda knocked a pair of scissors on the floor, apologised profusely, and stooped to grope for them. Her voice came, muffled, from the level of her knees.

"I suppose I'm too young to be told things any longer."

"Why—Winkle—what do you mean? I tell you everything—almost——"

"It's very odd." She shook her head sagely. "When we were children, we seemed to be the same age, but now it's different."

"Don't!" cried Emily suddenly.

Stuffing her fists into the pockets of her dressing-gown, Miranda had found her spectacles; pushing the ear-pieces behind her ears, she stared with a mild astonishment of one coming from darkness into light, at Emily.

"I mean, you're so much prettier without them!" stammered the latter uncertainly.

Miranda shrugged aside the idea of prettiness; there was no point in being pretty, and blind.

"You're getting like other grown-up people: all closed up and secret. Why do you, Emily? It was so nice—before."

"Darling, I've got a headache—that's all; I'm always the same—to you. Come"—she caught Miranda's small, cold hand and drew it against her side—"have you got your book? I'll tuck you up in bed."

"Why—you've got nothing on! And you're shivering! Where's your nighty?" demanded Miranda, suddenly maternal. "*I'm* going to tuck *you* up," she decided, thrusting Emily towards the bed, on which she sank without protest; strength had suddenly deserted her. The pillows seemed to rise to meet her; she was surely not capable of the volition to lie down.

Miranda, breathing hard, full of importance, was pulling the coverlet from under her, was drawing the sheet, and the blanket up to her chin; with a flap of air the eiderdown settled somewhere round her shoulders.

"Now I'm going to ring for them to bring you a bottle!"

"No, Winkle—for pity's sake! Do you know what the time is?"

"Twenty minutes to three. What's that got to do with it? What are servants for?" asserted the child of the slave trade, lurching towards the bell.

"If you ring for a bottle, I shall throw it out of the window! I'm absolutely burning!" The protest brought Emily to a sitting position, with the silken gown falling from her shoulders.

"Cover yourself up," said Miranda primly. "I should think you're going to have influenza. Oh, well—I don't know what to give you. I should think you'd better just lie down and go to sleep. I know! I'll read to you, like you used to do to me, when I had headaches. Would you like that, Emily—darling Emily?"

Oh, to be alone. But the old habit of tenderness for Miranda held good.

"Thank you, Winkle darling; it won't be long, before I'm—asleep."

There was a rustle of pages, then the light—perceptible even through aching eyelids—sinking suddenly, and Miranda's voice, soft and slow, half-muffled by the book in which her face was sunk.

"I cannot see what flowers are at my feet,
Nor what soft incense hangs upon the boughs,
But in embalméd darkness——"

Embalméd darkness! Ah, never again embalméd darkness, with its sweet, sweet dreams, its lovely memories and lovelier visions, its voyages to Cytherea. . . .

"Fast-fading violets covered up in leaves,
And mid-May's eldest child—
The coming musk-rose, full of dewy wine——"

. . . and gush of prisoned tears, that cool and innocent lips were brushing away—oh, Winkle, Winkle. . . .

She started against the soft, caressing hand.

"There's someone at the door!"

"No, there isn't; you're imagining," said Miranda, after a pause. But they were still, alert like young fawns, listening, until Miranda, at least, was satisfied.

"I can't see to read properly; but I've remembered something else. Listen:

"Weep no more, nor sigh, nor groan,
Sorrow calls no time that's gone;
Violets plucked, the sweetest rain
Makes not fresh nor grow again.
Trim thy locks, look cheerfully;
Fate's hid ends eyes cannot see.
Joys as wingéd dreams fly fast,
Why should sadness longer last?
Grief is but a wound to woe;
Gentlest fair, mourn, mourn no moe."

Mourn, mourn no moe.

His hand trembled on the door knob; anger rose, and died on the cadence of a girl's voice; then rose again in recognition of defeat. He turned, and groped his way back unsteadily, along the gallery. As he entered his room, the draught from the open window snatched the door from his hand, slammed it behind him—and brought him to his senses.

He stumbled to a chair and let himself drop into it. In front of him was a figure—his own; he looked at it with an incredulous horror. Had he really meant——? He must have gone raving mad! His hands were shaking, his brow dripping with sweat. By God, if that was the kind of thing a girl like Emily Temple could do to one——! To-morrow night—Kitty, or Edie, or Vi; get oneself pulled together and then—no more fooling around! Get on with it—get down to it; the longer one put it off, the worse . . .

"There *was* somebody!" Emily's fingers were clasped round Miranda's wrist. "Didn't you hear the door slam?"

"It's only the dawn wind rising," murmured Miranda, on the edge of sleep.

Le vent qui vient à travers le montagne me rendra fou.

CHAPTER THREE

I

IN the hot little parlour, smelling of musk and verbena, crowded with the small lares and penates of a simple family, Polly Bowling struck the amber keys of the piano and challenged the low ceiling, the heavy furniture and the multitude of tinkling oddments that quivered on shelves and cabinets with an exuberant C in alt; then spun round on the stool to face her companion.

"How's that—eh?"

"I reckon they could hear it on Colston Avenue," was the glum reply.

Polly, in whom the elements of touchiness were absent, nodded happily. Her face, flushed geranium pink with her effort, and round with the puppy flesh, which, to her mortification, still clung to her indeterminate features, grew soft and absent, her eyes dim with a vision beyond that of the youth who watched her, with a kind of bitter tenderness, under his dark brows.

"I reckon it's like a brass band," he amplified. "I reckon the Salvation Army could use that voice."

Polly let out a yip of laughter, seized a knitted antimacassar from the back of a chair and flung it over the speaker's head.

"Salvation Army!" Straightening her spine, she clasped her hands in her lap, set her feet together and swung them from side to side, tapping the ground lightly with her toes at the end of each swing. Confident, happy, she smiled at the young Guerdon footman. "The Salvation Army won't catch me, Bob! But something else might." Mysterious, important, she giggled at his expression of sour mistrust.

"What are you getting at?"

"Joe Prior says"—vanity outrode discretion—"I'm as good as Lottie Collins—if you know who she is!" A delicate note of mockery made allowance for bumpkin ignorance, and brought a flush to the youth's face.

"I know, well enough—and if your dad heard you, I bet he'd tan the hide off you!"

"He'd better try!" She giggled again.

"And if I come across that Prior, I'll give him a piece of my mind, for putting notions into your head."

"Oh, don't be unnatural. I'm only teasing." She sighed, and patted a few disconnected notes. "The nearest I'll ever get to the stage will be singing

'Nazareth' for the Young Women's Christian. Cheer up—and for goodness' sake don't look as if I was headed for the bottomless pit!"

"I don't like hearing you talk that way; it doesn't sound like you," he persisted.

"How do you know what's like me? We've hardly seen each other since we were children; and I never come up to 'the house' since Miss Vicky took against me—the lord knows why!" she grimaced.

"That's what I was thinking. . . . Are you going to marry Joe Prior?"

"Of all the questions——!"

"You've grown too grand for me, haven't you?"

"Oh, stop being such a goose, and listen to this." Her agile fingers rattled into a prelude.

> "'The Stilton, sir, the cheese, the O.K. thing to do
> On Sunday afternoon is to toddle in the Zoo.
> Week days may do for cads, but not for me and you,
> So dressed right down the road, we'll show them who is who!'

"Come on, Bob:

> "'Walking in the Zoo,
> Yes, walking in the Zoo,
> The O.K. thing on Sunday is the walking in the Zoo!'"

"Polly Bowling, stop that caterwauling and come and give me a hand with the butter!"

"Oh, Ma. It's my singing lesson to-morrow. You know I've got to practise." A wink invited her companion's complicity.

"Don't you call that practice, my girl! If you put in a bit of practice with the churn, it would be better for everybody."

"Bob Ames is here; he wants cheering up."

The tall, spare figure of a middle-aged woman appeared in the doorway. With freckles and labour-lines in a thick fretwork over her leaden skin, it was still evident that she had been, in her youth, a much better-looking woman than her daughter. A certain nobility of modelling in the brow and eyelids gave her that permanence of beauty of which there was no promise in Polly's plump features.

Her eyes, silver-rimmed, darted, hawk-like, from Polly to her companion. "Why does he want cheering up?" The average woman of her class would have said: "What does he want cheering up for?" There were curious small refinements in Ellen Bowling's speech and manner that derived from a different society from that into which she was born. She was spoken of, respectfully, or jealously, according to the speaker, as a "superior" woman. The youth's discomfiture was patently increased by her appearance.

"He's got the glooms," said Polly cheerfully.

"What about?" came the uncompromising demand.

"I came to ask Polly if she's going to marry that Prior chap that's always hanging round here on Sundays." He blurted it out with a defiant look at Polly, who murmured :

"Did you ever hear such impudence ?" and batted her short, thick eyelashes at a butterfly.

"What's that got to do with you ?" snapped the mother.

"Polly knows I've never looked at anybody but her, since we was in school together," he stammered miserably.

"Well, I can't stop his looking, can I, Ma ? If it comes to that, you're not the only 'looker,' you know !" beamed Polly.

"I know—well enough ! And it's all very fine, if it stops at looking——"

"What's that you say, Bob Ames ?"

"Oh, don't take any notice of him. He's got out of bed the wrong side this morning," murmured Polly, relenting, as usual, as soon as she felt someone was getting the worst of it.

"Hold your tongue. Now, then : what's this about 'stopping at looking ?'" pursued the elder woman inexorably. Polly heaved a sigh of exaggerated patience.

"I didn't mean no wrong," stammered the youth. "There's a lot of fellows that's got their eyes on Polly—that's all I meant—and I—I'd like to know where I am."

"I'll tell you where you are." Mrs. Bowling came forward to stand by the table, with its crochet centre mat and its Staffordshire bowl filled with faint, lilac-coloured auricula ; bending across it, she rested her weight on her dark, work-warped knuckles. Blinking up at her mother, one of the odd thoughts that occasionally floated into Polly's by no means reflective mind came there, as she noticed the contrast between her mother's hands and the satin-like surface in which they were reflected. Years afterwards, the beauty of the old walnut table stood to Polly for the sacrifice of her mother's hands.

"You're my cousin's son, Bob Ames, and blood's thicker than water ; but I've been meaning to speak for some time, and I'm glad to have the pair of you in front of me now. We've not given Polly her good education to hand her over to a fellow who hasn't got a shilling saved up, or a decent prospect in front of him."

"I'm a footman—and you get raises ! You get chances, now and again," he defended himself, "if you work for the gentry."

"Ay ; for the *gentry*." Her lip curled. "Your grandma was in service with the Centlivres ; you'd have learned the difference between *gentry* and those that buy themselves into places they'd not have dared lift their eyes to, in the days when breeding talked louder than money."

"Now Ma's off," said Polly resignedly. "You're silly, Ma !" As usual, when impudent, her voice was like a caress. "Times are changing, and people like the Floods are the gentry of the future." She paused, to give her suitor an encouraging nod. "You've got to own, Ma, you always said Miss Vicky's quite a lady, and Mr. Flood's a gentleman in his way, and as for old Mrs. Flood—she's a real grandee : the old vixen !"

" Don't be saucy, and don't show your ignorance. Gentry of the future ? Gone up like a rocket and they'll come down like the stick ; you mark my words ! "

" Pretty slow-falling stick." The youth took heart of Polly's levity to grin. " Floods was here in my grandad's time, you know, mum——"

" And Bowlings were here when George the First was king. And Bowlings don't marry their daughters to Guerdon flunkeys."

Again the purple raced up his thin cheeks.

" Maybe they marry them to a trollop's come-by-chance ? "

" Now that'll do from you, Bob ! " Polly sprang to her feet. " You needn't start ' calling ' Joe, just because you don't get your own way. And I'll tell you something—and you too, Ma." She included Ellen Bowling in a toss of the head. " Bowlings don't ' marry ' their daughters anywhere : at least, not when the daughter's me ! I'll do my own marrying, thank you —and the sooner you mind your own business, the quicker I'll look after mine ! "

" So that's it ? " Ames also had risen clumsily ; the ugly thrust of his mouth showed that he was goaded past discretion. " And maybe we could guess who you mean by your ' business ' ? Maybe we've seen some of your bloody ' business ' ? "

" You say another word, Bob Ames, and I'll never speak to you again ! " Her face was no less crimson than his.

There was a silence, broken only by the buzzing of the bluebottles against the window pane. Mrs. Bowling said quietly :

" You'd best be going." And Ames turned on his heel.

Avoiding each other's eyes, the two women listened to his footsteps retreating down the box-edged path which led to the gate on the main road.

" You needn't have been so hard on him, Ma. We've always been friends, and I know he's soft about me ; but—bless my heart ! I'd no more think about marrying Bob than the man in the moon."

" Then you should be ashamed of yourself, letting him hang around the way you do."

" It's easier to be kind than hurt people's feelings. Bob knows I don't feel ' that way ' about him," she murmured.

" You're too free, Polly." The disillusioned eyes of middle age dwelt with wistfulness on the girl's glowing face. " That ' kindness ' of yours will get you into trouble some day."

" I wonder if it will ? " She was twisting a sprig of verbena into a buttonhole of the print bodice that broke into a modest ruffling over her full young breasts.

" Why don't you take Joe Prior and have done with it ? He's a good, steady fellow and his heart's set on you ; he's spoken out honestly to your father——"

Polly moved restlessly.

" Oh, Ma, I wish you wouldn't bother me. You can't make up your mind about a thing like that, all in a rush——"

" You've been rushing, as you call it, for getting on three years, and it's high time you knew your mind by now. Don't you talk about kindness, while you keep a poor fellow in misery—as you keep Joe Prior. And it's no laughing matter, Polly!" as an irrepressible gurgle came from her daughter's lips. "You'll be getting yourself a bad name——"

"That doesn't take much doing! When folks are jealous they'll say anything," said Polly scornfully. She flung an arm about her mother's shoulder. "What an old worrit you are! Come on; we'll work it off in the dairy."

"Sit down, Polly." Ellen Bowling withdrew from the embrace. "I've been wanting a talk with you for a long time."

"What about the butter?" Disconcerted, Polly made an evasive movement towards the door.

"The butter's come. I've been worrying a lot about you lately. There are plenty of loose tongues about," said her mother slowly, "and it doesn't please me, to have them making free with your name."

"And who's been 'making free,' pray?" The tone was a little too jaunty to be convincing.

"I'd like to have heard the young fellow that would have spoken to me as Bob Ames spoke to you—when I was your age!"

A note of relief sounded in Polly's ready bubble of laughter.

"Oh—*Bob!* When a fellow's got his complaint, he doesn't know what he's saying; you ought to know that, Ma!"

"He knows when he's being respectful or not," insisted Ellen Bowling. "I'm not joking, Polly; it upset me properly, to hear a young man speak to my daughter as though—as though she was no better than she should be. It's a mercy your father wasn't here! He'd have thrown Bob out of the house——"

"Oh, fiddlesticks," said Polly easily. "Bob's got a quick temper; he doesn't mean half he says——"

"He didn't say what he said without something at the back of his mind; and, what's more, my girl, you know what that something is."

"Upon my word, Ma——!" Polly's eyes were wide with so genuine an innocence that the other's drawn face relaxed.

"If you'd only be a bit more careful, Polly——"

"Well, what am I *supposed* to have done?" Temper showed now, in her knitted brows.

"When you've learned more sense, you'll know it's not what people *do* that hangs them," was the grim reply. "Eh, Polly! " Her voice softened on a sigh. "I know you're what they call a comely girl——"

"Well, you needn't sound so mortified about it, Ma! If I hadn't been pretty, they wouldn't have chosen me for the May Queen. What do you want me to do? Cut off my eyebrows and black my teeth?"

"Don't trifle; I'm serious. You know as well as I do the kind of things people say, if a girl's good looking, and lively—and a bit careless how she looks at the men."

"Bother what they say." Angry now, Polly stamped her foot. "Who've I been looking at? Who? Who? Who?"

" Stop hooting like an owl," said Ellen Bowling calmly. " You can answer that question better than I. You're my daughter, and I've tried to do the best for you. I may have been foolish. But they think so much of education nowadays, and I wanted you to have a better chance than either your father or I had, when we were young. You've learned things no girl in your station was taught, in my young days. But there's one thing I can tell you. No good's ever come from stepping out of your own class, and no girl's ever been happy that's let a man persuade her out of the honest ways that belong to her own people."

" Well, after all, it was your idea, bringing me up like a lady——" She showed confusion in her stammer.

" *Never.*" Ellen Bowling's work-worn hand came down heavily on the table. " I've got none of your kind of learning, Polly, but there are things I know which I doubt your education will ever teach you. Those words, ' lady ' and ' gentleman,' are used too freely in these days. Nothing will every make you a lady, my girl—no, not if you married a lord : which God forbid."

" Well, Ma——! "

" Your father is a tenant farmer," Ellen Bowling pursued relentlessly, " and your grandfather herded cattle for Mildenhalls at Paragon. My father farmed his father's land, and you're born of generations that dealt honestly by the earth and received the earth's bounty in return. That's what you've got to be proud of ; not any fancied fine ladyship, laid on like butter over the good bread baked by your ancestors."

" You can't say butter doesn't improve bread ! " Polly's essential good nature was not proof against the elder woman's gravity. She stooped quickly to kiss her mother. " I'm only teasing, Ma ! Of course you're right, and I've got no high-flown notions—I haven't, truly. All the same, I don't know why you had me taught *O sole mio !* and made me chatter French at Miss Fleming's, if you meant to make a dairymaid of me."

" When did you last see Dorset Flood ? "

The girl's lips dropped open ; visibly she held her breath. Then she flung up her head, and the look she turned on her mother was insolent in its defiance.

" So that's what you've been getting round to ! Upon my word, I'm about sick of this village, and all its nattering old women. So now one can't so much as say, ' How do you do '——"

" That's enough. I'm no fool, my girl. There are ways and ways of saying, ' How do you do,' and I know his—and yours."

" Pooh ! Dorset Flood—he's—well, he's—oh, for pity's sake stop nagging me ! I don't know what's come over you—I've never known you like this in my life. You—he—oh, *damn* ! " exploded Polly in exasperation. " You know perfectly well he wouldn't——"

" Wouldn't he ? " said Ellen Bowling bitterly. " I know what he wouldn't do : and that is act honestly by any silly girl who gave him encouragement. You've got no call to make yourself easy to Floods, Polly Bowling ! *Floods !* They may be all right in their place : but their place isn't Guerdon, where the greatest in the land have been made welcome in the past, and the rest were shown where they belonged."

"Oh, what a snob you are!"

"I'm this much of a snob: that Bowlings are as good as Floods any day, and they don't accept Flood patronage. I know you, Polly; you're so vain, you're flattered every time someone takes off his hat to you."

"Well—manners make the man, don't they?" was the glib retort.

"Manners don't make the husband."

"Husbands!" with the confident scorn of youth. "You've got husbands on the brain, Ma. Bless your silly heart, can't you wait until I choose one for myself?"

"I'm not worrying about husbands. You're not a schoolroom miss, and you know when a man takes notice of a pretty girl in a lower class than his own, he's not thinking of marriage. I'm only reminding you. But if ever there's any gossip about you and one of those young Floods, and it comes to your Dad's ears, you'll never cross this doorstep again."

At last she was frightened. The blood was crimson in her ears, and she began to cry—loud, bawling, childish sobs—partly of anger, partly of fear born of the desperation behind her mother's words.

"I'll leave home! That's what I'll do! I might just as well—the way you treat me. I might just as well be *really* bad—instead—instead——"

"Instead of what? Polly!" Ellen Bowling's hand shot across the table and gripped her daughter's wrist. "What were you starting to say? What have you got to tell me?"

"Nothing—nothing. Not a thing! I don't know what you're scolding me about!"

Not a few kisses, stolen in the spinney; not a caress—exciting, alarming, but, oh, so delicious while it lasted; so delirious, to dream about in bed at night; not a meeting or two, carefully "accidental," and a jesting assignation. . . . It was only fun; part of the fun of being grown-up, and pretty, and making curious discoveries about oneself which no rustic flirtations, previously, had revealed; and the attraction of a well-groomed male body and a voice which said amusing things in a way that made them—well, not amusing at all, but thrilling and deeply significant; although significant of what one could not be sure. . . . Polly sniffed, jerking her hand away to rub it across her eyes, and groped for her handkerchief.

"It's too silly for words—as if everybody doesn't know he's going to marry Miss Temple!"

The arrested clip of a horse's hooves drew Ellen past her whimpering daughter to the window. Across the small yellow blossoms of the musk she saw the Guerdon dog-cart halted at the gate, with three people in it: the Guerdon groom hurrying up the path, with a letter in his hand. Without waiting for the knock, she went to open the door.

"Is there supposed to be an answer?" Ignoring the occupants of the dog-cart, she gave the missive a disdainful glance. There was no need to make out that communications from Guerdon were welcome.

"If there is, you'd better be sharp; they're waiting."

Her hawk eyes put the speaker in his place, before she returned to the parlour with deliberate leisure.

" There's no need to go out." Polly, with the traces of tears already blotted from her cheeks, was leaping for the door. Her mother's figure, blocking it, frustrated her. " It's only Mr. John and the two young ladies," added Ellen on a note of quiet malice, " and the letter's for you." She held it out reluctantly.

" For *me* ! " Polly whooped with incredulous pleasure, tearing it open and mastering at a glance the half-dozen lines of Vicky's stiff, old-fashioned script, that filled a side below the engraved pictorial letter-heading. " Well, did you ever ? They must have been in a hole ! " The reflection gave her evident satisfaction. " It's Miss Vicky ; she wants to know if I'll play the piano for the hymns at the missionary fête ! Well, I dare say I might manage——"

" So I should hope, considering what's been spent on your piano lessons," said Emily dryly.

" I'd do better with *Ta-ra-ra-Boom-de-day* ! Let me pass, Ma, please——"

" There's no need to get excited. You sit down and show you can write as good a letter as Miss Flood," was the remorseless reply, to which, after some passionate protestations, Polly was obliged to surrender.

At the expense of two spoiled sheets the note was written—by which time there was no one at the door or at the gate. Polly took the matter with exemplary calmness.

" There ! Now I'll have to run up after supper and let Miss Vicky know. Goodness, it's nearly dinner time. I'll lay the table, if you like, Ma."

" Wait a minute. I've not finished talking to you," said Ellen Bowling.

II

" ' Greensleeves was all my joy,
Greensleeves was my delight,
Greensleeves was my heart of gold,
And who but Lady Greensleeves.' "

" Here—hold the candles. No, put it down, there. Take care, she'll rape you." He quickly drew back his gloved hand, into which the tercel was digging her pounces. " Can you tie these, Winkle ? "

As Miranda drew the braces, the young merlin, lulled by darkness, subsided into tremulous immobility on Johnny's fist.

They were in the little thatched mews, where, according to history, an Elizabethan Centlivre had established his cast of jerfalcons, which he had matched against those of the queen, for a wager of two hundred guineas. It was used as a toolshed, until Gilbert, on leave from India, infected the family with a brief craze for falconry, which ran its course, and, on the departure of its instigator, was abandoned.

" It's a damned shame." Johnny, on entering, had peered round the hut, at the dejected birds on their perches. " Who's supposed to be looking after them ? "

" One of the gardeners. But I believe he's scared. He says they're lousy."

" I bet they're lousy ! " He swore under his breath, as he cast the nearest bird, and lifted it to look at the jesses. " Take a look here ; these haven't had a spot of grease on them for a month ; the poor thing's crocked." He passed a compassionate hand over the mailes, drew out a wing and found a shattered primary. " Go on, Winkle : get me a needle, and some oil—and keep out of the range of that damned gos ! " he warned as she started across the hut.

He had lit a candle-end which he found among the litter of the bench—though it was hardly needed ; the birds were too lifeless to bob when he hooded them. The goshawk he left alone ; it was too far gone. From the slits of its dying eyes it fixed on him its dying gaze of an imperishable malevolence—reminding him, for a moment, of Akosua. Poor old chap ; it wasn't I. Nothing to be done, there, but, later on, when Winkle was out of the way, to put it out of its misery. Like Doss, to leave the birds untended. Although he enjoyed the swagger of riding out on a fine morning, with the silver-belled hawk on his gauntlet : thrilled at the *volée*, and glowed with pride when his bird, with closed pinions and the wind whining through her bells, dropped on her prey—he would not be troubled to keep her, like a true falconer, continually on his fist.

He set to work quietly, while Miranda, squatting on the bench, sorted, at his direction, a bag full of feathers, and, presently, showed her the delicate process of imping, which delighted her.

" Oh, let me do one—please let me ! " she begged, as he taught her how to smooth the quill-fibres into a silken ribbon after the shaft was mended, so that no sign of the join remained.

" Bravo ! " as she thrust the brine-steeped " needle " into the stump and looked proudly up for his approval. " You're better at it than I am. We'll have her on the bow-perch in a week, and you can try your hand at reclaiming her. Then she'll be yours," said Johnny.

" Really mine—to have about with me ? "

" ' The Tiercel of a Jerfalcon for a king,
The Gentle-falcon for a prince,
The Falcon of the rock for a duke,
The Peregrine for an earl,
The perky Merlin for milady— '

There's not much perk about this one, but it will soon cheer up, when you start to man it," he assured her.

" Poor little thing." She touched the hackles tenderly. " Yes, this one's mine. It's lame—like me."

" It's only lame because the jesses have shrunk ; you must remember to keep them soft——"

" ' Greensleeves was my heart of gold—— ' "

"Oh, chuck that damned tune!"

"So this is where you were hiding, my boy!" Dromore's conscious geniality broke down in a grimace, as he hastily drew out his handkerchief. "Dear me—very malodorous!"

"It stinks a bit, sir; whoever's supposed to look after it has been lacking."

"No place for a young lady." Dromore scowled on Miranda—mopping, with more zeal than tact, a patch of mutings from her skirt, with an oil rag snatched from the bench. "My dear——! Pray go instantly—instantly! —and ring for your maid——!"

As Miranda scuttled across the flagged yard between the mews and the stables, he turned, to see Johnny picking up his pipe, and feeling in his pocket for matches. Alas, alas for Dromore! It was evidently to be his day of penance—for what or how many sins he had not the slightest idea, but felt, like Job, that he was not in safety, neither had he rest, neither was he quiet; and yet trouble came.

"I'm sorry—very sorry indeed—to see you have acquired that pernicious habit, John!" He looked sorry; he had an actor's mobility of features—an actor, not of the first rank: inclined to labour his effects.

Johnny raised a startled head; the pipe had become so much of a habit that he had forgotten it was new to Dromore, and wondered for a moment, to what his father was referring. The other's sorrowful gaze enlightened him.

"Oh—this. Well, it can't be blamed for stopping my growth, sir!" He cracked the wry little joke with a grin, looking up at the towering figure beside him. "It's almost an inevitability on the Coast; you've got to discourage the flies."

"You are not on the Coast now, my boy," Dromore pointed out, with reason. "I hope I need not remind you not to produce that unpleasant object in the company of ladies."

"Of course not." He smothered a smile. Nothing had made him feel more completely "at home" again than Dromore's reprimand. Dromore was puzzled to find his son regarding him with a curious kindliness.

"You know it is very bad for your health." He stopped aghast. It almost sounded as though he were *excusing* himself. "I suppose"—he pecked fretfully with the ferrule of his stick at a plantain which had forced itself up through a crack in the threshold—"I suppose, it is too much to hope that you paid any attention to our missions, during your travels."

"As a matter of fact, sir"—he grasped gratefully at the change of subject—"I met your—our—relatives, the Gummeridges, in Charlestown. They sent all kinds of messages——"

"I am glad to hear it. Sometime, when I have less on my mind, you must give me a full account of the meeting. This morning, unhappily, I have many things to distract me. You know, of course, that your brother——' For once, Dromore's admirable vocabulary failed him; he turned his head quickly, presenting his handsome, melancholic profile to his companion.

"Yes," said Johnny.

" A misunderstanding—obviously a misunderstanding. Your mother is having a talk to Emily, now." A spasm crossed Dromore's face, at the thought of the conversation now in progress in Selina's room. Had he been wise, to depute so delicate a mission to one who . . . He hesitated to admit it, but there had been recent moments when Selina had caused him uneasiness ; to put it even more plainly, doubt. *Was* Selina handling the matter properly ? Had it, perhaps, been an exaggerated sense of propriety, on his part, which had left to her a matter with which, in all essentials, he was better qualified to deal ? Might he not, in the course of a paternal talk, have won Emily's confidence ? Whatever motive, of caprice or of coquetry she had produced, in justification of her conduct, he at least would have found the right words. For the last hour, his imagination had dwelt on the scene—not without some melancholy enjoyment. He would, actually, have been shocked beyond measure, had anyone pointed out to him the pleasure he derived from the picture of himself, wooing Emily Temple, on behalf of his eldest son.

" Are you feeling—ill, sir ? "

" It is of no consequence." Softened, nevertheless, by the solicitude, Dromore allowed his hand to drop on Johnny's shoulder. " Well, my boy, it is good to have you home again. You and I must have a long talk—when our present trouble is over."

" There's something I would like to mention now, sir—as we happen to be together."

" I hope it is nothing painful, John." Dromore's tone was fretful, suggesting that Johnny was taking an unfair advantage.

" Oh, lord, no. I've asked a friend to stay with us—that's all. He's going to let me know when he's able to come."

" Indeed ? " was the cold rejoinder.

" Well—that's all," said Johnny lamely. " Except—I think you'll like Osei."

" I hope so," with pessimism. " I have not met your friend, Mr. Ozay—have I ? A curious name ; a foreigner, I assume ? "

" O-S-E-I." Johnny spelled it. " A West African Negro," he said, deliberately.

". . . I don't think . . . I can have heard you correctly."

Hands in his pockets, Johnny allowed his weight to drop back against the door ; his eyes, fixed on Dromore's were steady.

" Osei is the son of a prince who owns one of the largest oil concessions. He has taken a degree at London University, and he's over here, lecturing to some of the colleges on West African sociology. He's a most delightful fellow, and, knowing your interest in the West African races, I thought you would like to meet him."

Dromore was nonplussed.

" My dear boy—I hope you do not think—we—I——" He paused, to collect his scattered periods. " As you know, I have always maintained an open mind on the colour question. I am, I hope, the last to disclaim the noble work of our missionaries, whose zeal has enabled many—h'm—

savages to attain positions of respect—I will even go so far as to say distinction—which entitle them to consideration in our social scheme. Nevertheless——

"*Really*, John!" spluttered Dromore; his face was congested. "You must recognise the difference between meeting the coloured people on their native soil, or on some common, public ground, and introducing them into your own home—into the company of your mother and sister!"

"May I tell you, sir, that the term 'coloured people,' on the Coast, stands for the bastard offspring of white and black parents, and is usually regarded—even when not intended—as an insult? Osei is a full-blooded Negro, of good family and education: and I don't see why the colour of his skin should be used to exclude him from our society."

"Don't be—preposterous! Would you—would you, for instance, present this—this black man to your sister Miranda?—to—to Emily Temple?"

"I don't want to draw what they call invidious comparisons"—there was a slight edge of irony on Johnny's voice—"but I'd rather introduce Osei to my sister, or to Emily, than several people who've already been made welcome at Guerdon. You don't suggest, do you, sir, that there are two standards—one for black and the other for white?"

"Of course—of course. The law of Christianity is the law of brotherhood." It evidently cost him an effort to admit it; Dromore was struggling for equanimity. "That, I imagine, is accepted by all who profess to follow the Galilean teaching." He took a few agitated paces about the yard and returned to Johnny. "I am astonished—I may say I am aghast—at one thing. Can you really have forgotten——?"

"That one of our ancestors married a Negress?" he returned coolly. "No, sir, I haven't forgotten. I've often wondered what their descendants are like—the Cuban branch——"

"That disaster has already visited our house, through a member of the Negro race?" corrected Dromore, awfully.

"The cases are not at all similar." But, pitying his father, Johnny spoke gently. "You've got nothing to dread—I give you my word, Father—from meeting Osei. As regards race, he's no less proud than we are——"

"Is he a Christian?" solemnly interrupted Dromore.

"We don't discuss religion," said Johnny shortly. "From point of view of breeding—the Bofos are probably our superiors! Osei's certainly our superior in education. And, so far as manners go—he's Europeanised: if that's an advantage!"

"I must have time for reflection. It is impossible for me to give you an answer now."

"Answer to what?" He had unhooked his shoulders from their support against the door, and, still with his hands in his pockets, faced his father. There was something ruthless in the attitude which Dromore recognised, and, recognising, hated. Each was conscious of the old antagonism, leaping like flame under the bellows. "I've given an invitation, Father, and it's been accepted. I'm afraid there's only one answer to that."

"What do you mean? This house is mine, and your mother is its hostess," blustered Dromore.

"I know—and so does Doss, when he fills the house with his friends—half of whose names you don't even know until you meet them in the hall! This is the first time I've ever invited a guest of my own, and—I'll be quite candid with you, sir—if you turn him out, I go with him. Some day, perhaps, I'll tell you—what I owe to Osei. For the present—you'd better take my word for it: you'll be 'putting shame' on the family, not only on me, if you oblige me to withdraw my invitation."

Dromore said, after a long silence:

"I find your opinions, no less than your conduct—outrageous."

"I wonder why?" said Johnny quietly. "You've spent thousands on converting and educating the 'heathen.' What do you think becomes of them, after they've taken in your teaching? Are they to be confined to the company of their moral and social inferiors? Or are they to be allowed the privileges—I suppose that's what you'd call them?—of the civilisation they've been taught to appreciate?"

"At least spare me these parrot-like generalisations!" trumpeted Dromore.

"I know the soundest generalisation breaks down, when it's applied to the particular; but surely it's the *principle* that forms the basis of our relationship with what cousin Charlotte Gummeridge would no doubt call our 'coloured brethren'——?"

"I shall have to talk it over with your mother. Your aunt also must be consulted——"

"What about Uncle Quentin? What about Hacky and Roan? Why not call a committee on it?" said Johnny flippantly. "Can we, a slaving family, suitably entertain a Negro under our roof? So far as I'm concerned, the boot's on the other foot: can a Negro accept our hospitality, without losing face among his own people? If you ask me, that's the reasonable way of looking at it. And if Osei can stand it, there's not much left for us to make a fuss about."

"Your levity does nothing to advance your argument," pointed out Dromore.

"I know; I apologise, Father. But, since it all seems to boil down to a question of colour——"

"A most superficial statement. You should know better than I, that the difference between the races is not confined to their skin. I repeat, I will think the matter over. You, of course, are at liberty to choose your friends; I have never interfered with your freedom in that respect. But when it touches the women of our family, I have a right to exercise my own judgment; and you, my son, must abide by it."

"I've told you exactly what form my abiding will take," said Johnny, steadily.

"That you must decide for yourself," was the cold rejoinder, as Dromore turned on his heel.

Watching his father's figure retreating across the yard, his fists for a moment clenched themselves.

" Was Osei a Christian ! "

How many of Dorset's friends, the light-hearted occupants of the bachelor wing, had been subjected to the highly personal inquiry ? What would Dromore say to some of the diversions indulged behind double doors ; to the roulette wheel that relieved the pompous note of Guerdon Sundays ; to the footmen called on, to convey roisterers to their beds, as a sequel to some of Dorset's hospitalities ?

Oh, well—it was the guv'nor's way ; no use making heavy weather about it. He pulled out his watch ; might as well ride into Bristol, for a word or two with Joe.

The appearance of Vicky, under the stable clock-tower, checked his progress to the coach-house in search of his bicycle.

" Oh—Johnny ! " Even Vicky showed traces of agitation ; her skin looked grey, her eyes puffy underneath, her gesture, slightly dazed, of one hand to her temple, betrayed that Miss Flood was not in possession of her usual abundant self-possession. " Oh, Johnny "—she blinked, as her mind shot off at a tangent from her original purpose—" what a terrible state your clothes are in ! Ames has just called me to look at them. You careless boy ; you must have been leaving them in the damp for weeks ! "

" That's too bad, Aunt Vicky," he said, with gravity.

" Even your whipcord suits : a mass of mould ! "

" Tell Ames to get rid of them. I'll have to pay a call on Cole. I'm going into Bristol now ; is there anything you'd like me to do for you ? "

" Oh—I suppose you're going to see your uncle——"

" He's in Liverpool—coming down on the afternoon train. I'm commanded to The Presence to-night. No ; I was just going to have a look round——"

" If you're not in any hurry——" Vicky hesitated. Suddenly she sat on the edge of the horse-trough. " It's all such a *muddle*," she said plaintively. " Dorset going away like this—and Emily—and Emily——"

He felt the muscles in his face tighten, as he answered shortly :

" Well, if I'm not wanted for anything in particular——"

" I was going to ask if you'd drive the girls down to the farm, with a note for Polly Bowling. It's really too provoking," said Vicky, pulling herself together. " That tiresome Mrs. Cary has broken her wrist, and I'm certainly too much out of practice to take her place."

" Place ? What in ? "

" Good gracious, boy, I keep forgetting you've been away. The missionary *fête*," snapped Vicky. " Somebody's got to play for the hymns. I don't like giving Polly an opportunity for showing off—she's quite forward enough already : but it's a case of needs must—— ! " She gave her quick, humourless smile. " Take the dog-cart, will you ? The drive will do Miranda good, and I'm sure Emily will be glad to get away from us all for an hour. I suppose Dorset hasn't said anything to you, has he ? " she leaned forward eagerly to inquire.

"I haven't seen Doss since last night. He'd gone before I was up."

"Well, goodness knows what it all means," shrugged Vicky. "And just think of the scandal—— !"

"Rubbish, Aunt Vicky. They weren't engaged, were they?" He spoke roughly. "Why on earth can't you all stop fussing? It must be pure hell for Emily!"

"She's shown a great want of consideration." Vicky's lips were pinched; she tossed her head resentfully. Johnny smothered an exclamation.

"Well, you'd better tell the girls to get their things on, if they want to come," he muttered, and beckoned to one of the grooms who was crossing the yard.

They were waiting for him on the steps, when he took the mare round; Miranda in a clean print dress and cotton gloves; Emily . . . He took one look, and glanced quickly away. From Emily's clothes—her pleated summer frock, the broad hat with its bows of tulle—a slim sawdust doll gave him a waxen smile. It was like seeing Emily in effigy: Emily, who for so long had been tacitly Dorset's; had lived in a glass cage contrived from Dorset's open intention and her no less open acquiescence. And now the glass was broken, and Emily was there, within reach of anyone. Broken by herself. Why, then, Emily, are you so dismayed? Why have you shrivelled, in the air you yourself have invited?

He touched up the mare. As they swung through the park gates on to the highroad, Miranda, who, up to that moment, had been strangely silent, began shrilly to sing:

> "'Greensleeves was my heart of gold,
> And who but Lady Greensleeves.'"

III

"I've had a rise," Joe produced, among other trivialities of information.

"Thought you'd been up to something of the sort!" Johnny could not forbear a grimace. Joe's sartorial development had caught in his eye in the first moment of their meeting.

The bright red hair had not merely darkened under a heavy coating of pomade, but was coaxed into a "quiff" which occupied a good deal of his owner's anxious attention, over Joe's left eye, while a flourishing moustache, its ends fiercely waxed into points, had made disconcerting appearance on his upper lip. An imposing, if doubtful, "gold ring" confined the bright purple tie round a three-inch collar, and was supplemented by an apparently massive cable strung between a buttonhole and (ostensibly) his watch pocket; but the latter was flat, and, when he wanted the time, Johnny noticed that Joe's eye went to the clock over the bar; he made a mental note not to embarrass Joe by asking him for the time when they were out of range of a timepiece from which he could conveniently glean the information.

" You're a hell of a swell! What's it all about?" inquired Johnny innocently.

Joe's cheeks empurpled themselves; his eye went sidelong to a couple of girls who, at the counter, were eyeing the two young men across their glasses of ale. While Joe winked at them, Johnny eyed him curiously: sensing beneath his companion's swagger some kind of discomfort that his assumption of ease belied.

" How about it?" Joe's elbow was in his ribs.

" How about what?"

" We could take them to the Empire——?"

" Not me, I'm afraid. I've got to dine with Uncle Hacky." After a pause, during which Joe, leaning back, jingling a handful of coins in his pockets, avoiding the giggles of the girls, had a slight air of disappointment: " Don't let me cramp your style. Go ahead—if you want to fix something up with them."

But this, it appeared, was a little beyond Joe's sang-froid, in present company.

" How about a breath of air?" he suggested, after a few moments of fidgeting.

The evening air, lying soft along the wharves, the quiet slap and suck of the water, disturbed by a passing barge, caught Johnny's breath, and brought a lump into his throat. They had so often shared the delight of the river that he turned with confidence to Joe—only to realise that the latter had discovered other interests during his absence. Joe was eyeing a full-blown young woman who, taking advantage of the litter along the Back, lifted her skirts to display a more than generous view of a pair of ankles which were riveting Joe's attention.

Well—that was that. It was not until they went back, to collect Johnny's bicycle from Queen Square, that he broached the subject which had risen to his mind, while watching, with concealed amusement, Joe's new-found mastery over the feminine sex.

" You know—I was wondering, when I came back, if I'd find you engaged to Polly."

Joe, engaged now in ogling a girl in a straw boater, started as though shot; all the rakishness, the masculine complacency vanished from his face and his bearing—so completely that Johnny was filled with compunction. He would rather have cut out his tongue than evoked the humble, shamefaced Joe who looked out, as though asking pardon, through the grey eyes of Kitty Prior's son.

" It's all off, Johnny. I'm not good enough for her."

" Gammon! You know Polly: she's a dev'lish little flirt, but she's as sound as a bell at heart. You still go there, don't you, at week-ends?" demanded Johnny indignantly.

" Every blessed Sunday," he confessed. " I've tried to stop away, but —it's just too much. 'Tisn't as if she doesn't make me welcome—and I know the old folks are on my side. Only whenever I try to talk about getting married, she turns it into a joke. It seems like she's made up her mind not to take me in earnest.

"You wait until I see that young woman!" Johnny spoke with the confidence of the unaffected. "I'll give her such a talking to——"

"No, don't, Johnny. You see"—he turned his head away; Johnny could barely catch the mumble—"I believe—I've got a kind of notion—there's somebody else."

"I'll tell you what's the matter, Joe," said Johnny, after a pause. "You've been too patient with her. She gets so much fun out of having you on a string that she doesn't want to give it up," he concluded, with frowning, masculine wisdom.

"Oh, I find my own fun, if it comes to that. She can't lead a fellow on, and expect him to behave like a saint," muttered Joe. Ashamed, yet proud of the oblique admission, he stole a look to see whether its implications had registered on his companion.

"Oh, well—look out; that's all," mumbled Johnny. He paused with his foot on the bracket, before taking off. "I'll lay you a pound to a shilling, if you like, that I'll be godfather to half a dozen kids, for you and Polly, in the next few years!" he rallied him.

"How about your own?" Joe rose valiantly to the jest.

"Mine? I shan't be having any kids, at this rate!"

Joe had laid his hand on the handlebars; he spoke simply—not at all like the masher, with the bowler hat cocked over one eye, and the waxed moustaches, which, suddenly, to Johnny's fancy, lent him the aspect of a small boy, tricked out for the Fifth of November: "Please, mister, a penny for the guy!"

"Haven't you ever thought about getting married?"

"Well—yes, if you want to know; sometimes."

"Have you got a girl?"

"No." It seemed an abrupt note on which to end their conversation; although it meant delay, and he was already late, he found he could not resist the mute appeal behind Joe's questioning. "Well—are you going to walk up Park Street with me?"

They crossed the Broad Quay and St. Augustine's Parade. On College Green couples were strolling arm in arm; there was plenty of uniform about, and some coquettish bids for the attentions of moustachio-ed warriors whose pill-boxes and scarlet tunics gave them unfair advantage over their scowling rivals. But Joe's interest in the fair sex was evidently in abeyance; tramping along by Johnny's side, with his eyes on his feet, he ignored in silence the many inviting glances which, to Johnny's amusement, were directed towards him.

"I sometimes wonder——" he began, and stopped. Johnny stood still to look at him.

"Wonder—what?"

"How it'll be"—he brought it out with a rush—"when we're both married—with families of our own."

" How d'you mean—' how it'll be ? ' It won't be any different, will it, between you and me ? "

Joe nodded, with a sad wisdom.

" It's bound to. The women'll alter it—if we don't."

" Why should they ? Polly likes me, I think, nearly as much as she likes you ; I'll be mightily injured if the pair of you don't make me welcome, after you're married ! "

" You jolly well know we will ! But you "—it came out at last, clumsily —" your wife'll be a—a lady."

" The sort of lady I'll marry—if I ever get married," said Johnny, after a moment's silence, " won't be the kind to separate me from my friends." Was it true ? He caught his breath, realising that he had actually, for a moment, visualised Emily as his wife. " For the love of Mike ! " he burst out impatiently. " What are we chewing this over for ? You're bursting to get married ; take my advice and have it out with Polly. I bet she'll change her tune, when you let her see you are standing no more nonsense. But, so far as I'm concerned—Hell's bells ! Life's too short, and there are too many things to be done, to start crossing one's bridges before one comes to them."

Life is too short. There was the very shape of eternity in the long sweep of the sky over the downs, and eternity in the calm, meany-breasted earth. Can eternity itself be long enough, wondered Johnny, swooping towards Northcote, for all that's required of a man, before his task is done ?

A church clock was striking, while he pedalled through the village : six—he was barely going to make it : changing his clothes, and getting back for his appointment with Harcourt. And he was done in. It was the first time, for months, that he had taken any exercise, beyond the casual strolling of the tropics. Must get myself in condition——

" Oh, my—oh, goodness—oh, I'm sorry, Mr. Johnny ! "

He was dizzily conscious of being pulled to his feet, of the bicycle sagging down into the undergrowth of the narrow track through the shrubbery, from which he had been knocked by a flying figure.

" Oh, Mr. Johnny, have I hurt you ? "

" Where's the fire ? " The clasp of a strong, young female arm round one's shoulders was too much for human pride. He evaded it by bending for his cap, which Polly found, bent and handed to him quickly.

" Isn't that just like me ? " Her pink, flustered face was full of compunction ; she was struggling for decorum. " It's—it's nice to see you back ! " Then, native warmth breaking through formality : " But you aren't looking well ! I believe you caught that nasty fever ; did you ? "

" You look fit enough for two, anyhow ! You've grown—in all directions," he teased her.

" You don't need to rub it in," she pouted. " Honestly, though "—her hand, kind, concerned, lay for a moment on his arm—" I never saw anyone so thin ! You must come and drink some of our Jersey milk ; it's much better than Guerdon ! " she told him impudently.

" What's this about your playing at our *fête* ? I hope you're going to sing as well ; I suppose you're about in the Patti class, by now !" It was refreshing, to talk unwitty nonsense to Polly.

" Oh, I don't suppose I'll be asked to sing. But it's a pity I couldn't have given you ' Grandfather's clock,' for ' positively my last appearance.' " She grimaced at him.

" What do you mean ? You're not going away ? "

" Not very far ; only to Bristol. Oh, Mr. Johnny, isn't it fun ? "

" I know somebody who'll think it's fun. When are you going to fix it up with Joe ? It's high time I was looking for a wedding present, you know." He said it soberly, glad of the opportunity to put in a word for his friend.

" No, there's no hurry for that. They've got me a job in a shop : I guess it's to keep me out of mischief ! " A beguiling flash of the teeth followed the admission.

" What form's the mischief been taking ? " He tried to make the inquiry sound light, but it brought him a quick look, and an unexpectedly serious reply.

" You've changed a lot, haven't you, Mr. Johnny ? You said that so strangely—as though you were older than me. Girls are supposed to be older than men—you know what I mean," she added confusedly. " Did you have a bad time—out there on the Gold Coast ; did you ? "

" As a matter of fact, I had a grand time—in lots of ways." He was surprised, and rather touched, by the urgency of her inquiry. She nodded slowly, her eyes still fixed on his.

" Something's upset you." It was an assertion, rather than a question. " I'm sorry. You know I'd help, if I could ; but I expect I'm too stupid to be any use to anyone like you."

It was as though a mantle of age and experience had fallen on both, through the green dusk of the trees. They were both to remember that moment, so grave, so grey, that dropped with the unexpectedness of a summer shower into their sunshine. Years later, Polly was to say, with a sniff of sentimental remembrance, " It was the first time I'd felt really grown up ; felt I ought to act sensibly, and begin thinking about something besides having a good time."

" You're very sweet, Polly." It was with no surprise that he found her small, strong hand lying in his. She gave her hand as readily as she gave her smiles. She was a little—a very little—taller than he, and, for once, there was no humiliation in looking up to a woman. There was something —he sought for a word—sheltering about Polly ; something, for all her levity, deep and warm and generous, that drew from him the comment, " What a lucky fellow Joe is. You are going to marry him, aren't you ? "

She drew her hand away quickly.

" Oh—we'll see."

" He's a grand fellow, and he worships the ground you walk on." It was important, for Joe's sake, to emphasise these things.

She made a little movement of impatience.

" Never mind about me. I'm so glad I met you, Mr. Johnny—and I'm sorry I knocked you down—and you must get well, now you've come home." She gave an oddly maternal little nod. "You mustn't *worry* so! Everything comes right, you know, if you give it time."

He smiled at the naïve philosophy.

"That's a good way of looking at things, anyhow."

"How's—how's——" He wondered what had brought the crimson into her face. "How's Miss Emily?"

"She's—all right." He was conscious that his own voice had stiffened. "You've seen her, haven't you, while she's been staying at 'the house?'"

"Not—not to talk to." Her head was bent, her fingers twisted the buckle of her belt.

"She's going home on Saturday."

"On Saturday? But—but——"

He understood, suddenly, what was in her mind; the village gossip which, for months, must persistently have linked Emily with Dorset: which must carry particular significance for one who, only a few years ago, had been a playmate; almost like one of the family. Emily, and Polly, and Miranda; of course; they were constantly together.

"Something's gone wrong with—that, Polly," he heard himself saying, in a queer, stiff voice.

"Oh-h-h. I must fly, or I'll be in trouble when I get home," she said, on a kind of gasp, that made him look at her quickly.

"Well, I shall count on you to cheer us up, when you come to Bristol! I'll come and buy—what can I buy in your shop, Polly?" He strove to lighten the tension which, for some reason, had come into the air.

"You won't be coming in my department!" She recovered her laughter. "It's not my notion of the gay life: helping old ladies to buy stays! Still—it's better than growing moss, out here."

"I won't risk the stays; but I'll certainly ask you to tea one day—if you'll do me the honour."

"Will you—truly?" Her eyes sparkled. "I'm going to live in; all the girls do, at Mercer's. I don't know what they'll say—to me, going out to tea with—a gentleman!"

"That will be all right; Joe will be there, and you can bring a friend, if you like." Had she imagined she was coming to a *tête-à-tête*? It would have been rather amusing; but there must be no question of putting Polly in a false position. Girls in her class, he reminded himself, were much more conventional than those of his own; and, lively as she was, he felt Polly would be decorous enough, when it came to challenging the manners of her own kind.

"Don't break your neck!" he teased her, as, with a wave of the hand, she was lost in the maze of the shrubbery.

CHAPTER FOUR

I

"I MAY have missed some small points, but that's the bulk of my findings, sir. Gentlemen!" Johnny corrected himself hastily, as he looked round the table.

The circle of men, half-blotted out by the smoke of their cigars, was silent, as Johnny ended. It was the first time in his life he had made a speech, and it was the last thing he had anticipated, when he received his summons to Berkeley Square.

After the first few minutes, no one had interrupted him. He stole a surreptitious glance at the clock; good God! They were surely asleep. He started slightly as Roan, leaning forward, replenished his glass.

"Good work, Johnny." He was so tired that the murmur hardly registered. He drank thirstily.

The mutter of approbation ran round the table, but he knew it was to Harcourt, and not to him, they were paying tribute: Harcourt, who, wall-eyed at the head, suffered neither satisfaction nor pleasure to appear on his face. But all heads turned towards the Chairman, when, grudgingly, he spoke.

"Well; you've all heard what he's got to say. I take it we'll chew this over, and I don't doubt you'll want, as I do, to check up on some of the facts we've been given. There's nothing to gain, at this point, from discussion; we'll leave that to the next meeting. So I propose, gentlemen——"

"Just a minute, Harcourt!" It was Joe Lloyd, as Harcourt half-rose from his chair. "I've got a notion it's the wish of everybody here—I know it's mine—to say a word of thanks to young Johnny——"

"Balderdash." Harcourt's face was purple. "He was given a job to do, and he's done it; that's sufficient."

"Maybe sufficient for his uncle!" Samson Killick had risen, and, much to Johnny's embarrassment, gripped him by the hand. "Good work, Johnny. We'll have a lunch on it, one of these days."

Johnny's thanks were tempered with misgiving, for it would certainly not sweeten his relations with the office staff, if he were reported lunching with one of the directors. He looked across at Harcourt, hoping he would move; before, however, he had opportunity to do so, Lloyd spoke again.

"We'd just like to hear whether Johnny's got any general observations. Maybe there's something rising out of his trip that's struck him in particular?"

What the hell are his observations worth? The words were not spoken, but were visible in the curl of Harcourt's lip, as, with averted eyes, he gave Johnny his permission to speak.

"Well, sir"—he found it necessary to moisten his lips—"I've been taken a bit by surprise; I hadn't expected to give you my report—verbally——"

" Go on, Johnny." The invitation encouraged him to feel that one at least of the listeners round the table was in his favour. He straightened his shoulders.

" Since I got back, I've been reading your Journal of Commerce ; and it seems that one of your speakers had my point in his mind. This was the piece that struck me." He paused for a moment to recall the wording. " ' It should be made a condition of a seat on the Board of a West African gold mine, that the directors should in rotation visit the Coast, as an incentive to good work and a check on maladministration.' "

Someone laughed. Johnny's jaw stiffened ; he continued :

" What applies to the mines holds good for all British interests in West Africa to-day. There's far too big a cleavage between this country and the one we're colonising. The effect of that's bad, on the white and the black population—equally. I'd like to add, that's not only my opinion, but that of Mr. Hobbs, who's just taken up his job as District Commissioner in Ashanti."

" That's Government business, not ours," sneered the fox-faced man opposite Johnny. Johnny rapped back at him :

" There's only one way of getting the Government to do its business : that is, for there to be so much come and go between here and the Gold Coast that the Colonial Office can't go on sticking its head in the sand any longer. There's a lot of things going on that need looking into, and a devil of a lot of money coming out of West Africa that should be going back into the country for the betterment of local conditions. And that's a matter for private interest—interest strong enough to beat the Government and operate independently of a policy that's not only strangling trade but wasting human lives by the thousand."

" What, exactly, do you mean by private interest ? " Roan's detached manner suggested, as usual, that his own interest was purely academic.

" I mean—sir—whoever wants to make a good thing, now, out of West Africa, must be prepared to spend millions—and in despite of the Government. Take the cocoa trade : all the stuff's coming down in head loads, and a thousand loads have to be tested before you can buy a hundred bags of cocoa. No doubt some way will be found of speeding that up : but you're still up against transport and communication."

" And what's the answer—to your way of thinking ? " Harcourt's tone jeered, but his eyes, resting on Johnny, were reflective. Johnny shrugged his shoulders.

" I don't pretend to have one. We've got this cock-eyed notion of leaving the natives to work their own land : which is one way of washing our hands of what would be, undoubtedly, a very tricky business. It looks as if that ought to be altered. I don't say we'd have the kings and chiefs with us to begin with ; but I've come across one or two of the brighter ones who seem to have a glimmer of the advantages to be gained by putting labour under direct British control. Naturally, they'd expect to retain some sort of authority——"

" What ? Have white men taking orders from niggers ? "

Johnny turned quickly towards his fox-faced *vis-à-vis*.

"I don't say that, Mr. Cruikshank—though I've met Negroes I'd just as soon take orders from as some white men I know." *Careful*, he thought: and suppressed the latter part of his sentence.

"Now, see here." Joe Lloyd was leaning across the table. "You had plenty of time, I take it, for looking round—apart from the firm's business. Have you got any black marks, in particular, against anybody—department or individual?"

"If I had, I wouldn't specify them." He faced the speaker squarely. "I've seen too much of local conditions to set up as a critic of the departments. So far as I've seen, there isn't a man, from the Governor to the sub-agents, who isn't sweating his guts out on his individual job. It's not their fault there's no cohesion, that Administration scotches everything they try to do——"

"We've been listening to this for years." Cruikshank spoke contemptuously. "And we know the gains are substantial and the prospects encouraging——"

"Encouraging to whom?" It was the silent partisanship from the rest of the table that emboldened him. "I know you've heard these things before: heard them so often that they've ceased to affect you. I've just come back from *seeing* it," said Johnny. "It's not old wives' tales to me: it's fact—and damned ugly fact, at that. You say the gains are substantial, sir. Do you know they're not a third of what they ought to be, if the traders had their proper backing? Do you know the Crown Colony system is costing us twenty-five per cent of the entire bulk of white trade in West Africa?"

"Steady. Are you sure of your figures?" came from the head of the table.

"I wouldn't quote them if I weren't, sir," muttered Johnny.

"Well, Flood." It was Samson Killick who spoke, after a heavy silence. "What's your answer to that?"

"Ask him." Harcourt jerked an ironic thumb at Johnny, and lowered his eyelids to conceal his satisfaction. The boy was making his impression.

"Isn't it a matter for the Chambers of Commerce?" A cautious voice spoke into the silence.

"Be damned to the Chambers!" Killick exploded. "It took nine years and cost the shirts off our backs, to get action on the French monopolies, after Salisbury's bloody lie about the Assinee tariffs! No offence, Walter; you weren't in office then." His fist smote the table. "All my capital's tied up, as my father's was before me, in West Africa; and I'll see 'em in hell if I'll part with twenty-five per cent of my profits to a Government that doesn't look after my interests."

"I take it we're all in the same boat." Joe Lloyd spoke in his heavy manner. "But, as Sam's just asked—what's the answer? I don't mind allowing I, for one, have too much in the pot to sell out, without a loss."

A rumble of acquiescence followed his declaration. Johnny nerved himself for the first time, directly to address his Uncle Harcourt.

" Mr. Chairman ; our name's carried weight on the Coast for a century and a half. Isn't it possible to bring pressure to bear through direct representation ? "

". . . What do you mean, boy ? "

" If the Chambers of Commerce can't get action, can't we go over their heads ? Can't you, or someone representing the firm, get at the Colonial Minister, and lay down some sort of an ultimatum ? "

" *What* sort of an ultimatum ? " sneered Cruikshank, before Harcourt had formulated his reply.

" That's hardly for me to say, as I'm not in a position to know the extent of our—of the firm's commitments," answered Johnny levelly. " Perhaps ' ultimatum's ' the wrong word. Perhaps we'd do better to throw out some kind of bait——"

" That's enough for now." Harcourt had risen. Roan, politely smothering a yawn, was looking at his watch. The others had plainly had enough, and were easing themselves from their chairs. A sudden feeling of helplessness and futility swept over Johnny ; had he undone the good impression he had made, by airing his own opinions ?

" You can have a bed, if you want it," Harcourt grunted.

" Thanks very much, sir ; I've ordered a fly," said Johnny wearily. As he stumbled towards the door of the hall, held open by Harcourt's footman, he reflected dimly on what his elation would have been, twelve months ago, on being called before the Board, to make a report on his own enterprise ! It was rarely the Board met in Berkeley Square, and only on portentous occasions. He wondered what the opinions of its members would have been had they known that the big, stately house was nearly as unfamiliar to the Chairman's nephew as it was to themselves ! And more vaguely, what sort of a time Mary and Bell had had in their childhood, shut up in their virgin chamber, out of range of their father's activities. And, once in the fly, which waited on the corner of the Square—he had decided it looked pretentious to have it wait at the door, beside the broughams of Harcourt's other visitors—he slept like a log throughout the long drive to Guerdon.

II

" You're a cunning old fox, Hacky ! What made you send young Johnny to the Coast ? "

Roan had yawned himself to bed—when the Board met at night it was his custom to avail himself of Harcourt's hospitality. It was Samson Killick who had stayed behind the others to share Harcourt's nightcap. The latter cocked a bleary eye.

" Why not ? Do him good to have a look round, before settling into the business. Too damn' pampered, those lads of Drummy's. Never see my nephew Dorset without wanting to take my foot to him. Gilbert the same."

Killick wagged a knowing head.

"What are you looking so cunning about? For the rest, I wanted a bit of information from somebody that hadn't got an axe to grind," muttered Harcourt, testing the brew that simmered on the trivet.

"And you wanted to show us what Johnny's worth—eh? Tee-hee! Cruikshank's face was as good as a play; he ain't forgiven you for not taking that gangling lad of his into the business. Baffin, Elder, Watkins." The speaker enumerated the names on his fingers. "You could have sent any of 'em: experienced fellows, and Elder, at any rate, with some working knowledge behind him. Not a bit of it; you elect to send—Johnny. I repeat; you're a fox, Harcourt! And, by gad, you've caught your goose this time."

"You're making a fool of yourself, Sam. Say I'd sent Baffin; the brokerage would have been at sixes and sevens by the time he got back. Elder—Liverpool 'ud have howled blue murder at losing him for six months. Watkins—he's a ninny. I sent Johnny, if you want to know, because his absence wouldn't make a ha'porth of difference, for better or worse. He's under Derbin; he doesn't even make out an invoice on his own responsibility. He's of no more importance, actually, than one of the office boys."

"And when do you propose to make him a director?" came the cunning inquiry. Harcourt's face purpled.

"Have you lost your wits?"

"Nay, keep your temper; I was only joking. At the same time, let me give you a warning: Cruikshank's place on the Board is going to be vacant, by the end of the year."

"Who told you this?"

"Never mind. I got it in confidence—from a source of information I've found useful, from time to time. Just you wait; you'll get his resignation, one of these days: reason—ill-health. 'Tisn't the first time Alfred's liver's come in handy!" snickered Killick.

"What's at the back of it?" asked Harcourt, after a pause.

"Might be this, might be t'other." Killick turned cautious. "One version is, he's been offered managing directorship of Runstables."

"Those—bumboat runners!" Harcourt snorted his scorn. "He must be out of his mind." But the veins swelled on his temples. Look at it as one pleased, it was no good advertisement for Floods, to have a member of their Board quitting it for Runstables.

"Ain't you ever heard the old saying, Hacky—about reigning in hell or serving in heaven? Cruikshank's only a member of the Board, here; at Runstables he'll be cock o' the walk—and a precious twisty walk it is too, if one's to believe all one hears. Ah, well; it may be the whole thing's a mare's nest, but I warn you to keep your eyes open. 'Twon't be so good, if some of our business finds its way, through Alfred, on to Runstables' files."

"Aye," said Harcourt, but it was as though he were not listening. He wafted the subject aside, with the smoke from his cigar.

"What do you make of the lad's report?"

Killick eyed him warily.

" Between ourselves ? "

Harcourt ducked his head in assent.

" Well—it's not what you'd call enlivening, is it ? But, if it means anything at all—there's one thing hits you in the eye ; this ain't the moment to open up a new venture in African trade."

Harcourt nodded again slowly. He had long suspected it, but had not chosen, unsupported, to force his suspicions on a Board eager to get in on the cocoa.

" I'd say keep the Guineamen moving, and the rest fetching the oil into Liverpool. That's a counsel of prudence," Killick admitted, with a nod, half of apology, to his companion, " and I know you, Hacky ; prudence and you keep bad company."

" Not in this case. Well, Sam." Harcourt had risen ; his towering figure cast its shadow half-way across the ceiling. " I'm going to fight 'em."

" Fight the Government ? " Killick wagged his head. " Others have tried it and learned their lesson. Most of us shy at involving ourselves in disputes with Whitehall." He chewed his thumb nail for a moment or two in silence. " There's another matter to be taken into consideration. You can't fight an enemy that won't put up his fists. This Boer business has got 'em with wet towels round their heads. It's as plain as the nose on your face Kruger's only playing for time, while the beggars pile up armaments. Do you know what I heard the other day ? That they've got eighty of the new-fangled Krupps field-pieces. Can you believe it—our letting 'em get through ? " Killick sighed, passing his hands over his bald head, and Harcourt, looking down on him, was startled to see that this man—this friend, who had grown up with him from boyhood—was old ; did that mean he was old himself?

" It's bad luck for the Queen—this turn up, at the end of her reign."

" Not only the Queen, Sam." Harcourt's voice was unwontedly mild. " We're lucky, you and I."

" Lucky ? How ? "

" We've enjoyed all the benefits of imperialism ; our children may continue to enjoy them—yours, I should say ; I don't know that it makes much difference to women. But this trouble in South Africa's only the beginning of something—something——" Words seemed to fail him ; he was silent, staring at the end of his cigar.

Killick spoke simply, with the deference he had always paid to Harcourt, that started on Clifton playing fields.

" What's there to do ? "

" Nothing—but leave things as safe as we can for those who come after. We're on the edge of a new century." Again he paused, and, like Killick, he sighed. " ' In my end lies my beginning ' . . . one of those damn' silly lines that annoy you because they don't make sense, and yet—and yet there's something at the back of them. Beginning of *what* ? It won't concern you or me, Sam ; but what of our children ? We've had the sunshine ; they're going on—into the rain and wind."

The clocks were striking midnight when Killick got into his brougham and was driven away to his fine house in Clifton. Harcourt stood on the doorstep, looking upwards, where the trees of Brandon Hill made a fringe of greater darkness to the dark sky. Presently he put out his hand, and the waiting manservant, accustomed to the formula, put his hat into it. The pavement of the square rang under the steady tramp of his feet, as he made down towards the river.

The Avon ; the precious heart, the life of Bristol, the mistress of Harcourt's soul. In every mood he loved her : when she sank to a grey snake, a mere trickle between her banks of mud, and when she rose, imperious and strong, sweeping her freight of ships along on her proud bosom ; angrily swelling after the rains, to mount the stonework of her locks and drown the Marsh of St. Philip's and all that part adjoining her Cumberland Basin. Dimpled with showers, sparkling with sun, sullen under her burden of sediment, mischievously curling before the skimming breeze that brushed her as the wings of a swallow—subtle, sly and unpredictable as a woman : he loved her with a love he had given to no human creature—certainly to none of the female sex.

A little boy, he had ridden his pony across Westbury Common and Durdham Downs, only to look down on her ; had begged for picnics to Leigh Woods and Nightingale Valley, just for the sake of the brief crossing ; and, while Drummy and Roan went bird-nesting, and Vicky, with her specimen box, sought mosses for her " collection," had crouched for hours in still contemplation of the water's ebb and flow.

" Where does it come from ? "

" Out of the sea."

" And where does it go to ? "

" Into the Bristol Channel—and then out to sea again, of course," Vicky, proud of superior knowledge.

Geographical instruction was later to correct this topsy-turvy version of the evolution of a river, but not its mystical impression on a little boy's mind. It was many years before Hacky saw the Avon other than as a grey riband, mysteriously weaving and waving through the uncharted oceans, collecting its own ships and bringing them back safely to Bristol town.

A smattering of mythology endowed it with a goddess : the Nile had one ; why not the Avon ? History, and a few volumes of old prints, peopled it with romantic craft—with snows and brigantines, many, as he came to know, built in Flood shipyards. As they grew older, the boys were allowed to sail their boats down at Pill, and finally, when a Clifton scholar—Dromore and Roan had gone to Charterhouse ; there is no clear explanation of Harcourt's entrance on the Clifton roster—the record of its commerce took possession of his imagination, and it became for him a roadway to adventure whose only boundaries were the periphery of the globe itself.

As a grown man, there were nights of high tide when, restless in Berkeley Square, he rose, dressed and tramped down the steep incline of Park Street, seeking—he knew not what : surely no phantom brigantine, no pearly-breasted nereidic deity rising from the still waters, with the red and the green shafts of the riding lights across her swan-like shoulders. He knew not what he sought ; was it, perchance, reassurance from the past?

That Avon, lapping quietly on her wharves, had carried the hopes and fortunes of his forefathers ; it was the magic link between the past, from which derived his strength, and the future, for which he was jealous. Quietly he laid his dreams (and, odd as it may appear, Harcourt Flood was a man of dreams), or his problems, or his frustrations on its bosom and returned, tranquil, as a child is tranquil, after its mother's night blessing.

He looked on it now. In my end is my beginning. That which has no beginning has no end. Like the flotsam of the river, such tags of thought drifted on the surface of his mind. That Avon, flowing gently through the centuries. . . . He knew suddenly that he wanted to go out on her tide ; that when he was dead, he wanted his body to be taken down the river, on the *Rembwe*, or perhaps one of the newer ships, and slipped quietly in the water, somewhere where Avon meets the sea. . . .

And then he told himself it was a sentimental, silly idea, which would cause a lot of commotion and inconvenience for somebody, and relinquished it. Soothed, his spirit calm, he went back to Berkeley Square.

III

Saturday. The grimy vaulting pinned down on the travellers' heads a sour stench of soot and steam, and a grey drizzle falling between the rails and spreading the platforms with a film of blackened mucus, added to the discomforts of passengers waiting for the Penzance to Paddington " corridor " train.

Emily's maid, Elphinstone, discreetly withdrawn, mounted guard over her mistress's luggage, staring primly past one of the Guerdon grooms, whose wooden expression and attitude of detachment belied certain " passages " which had left Miss Elphinstone pensive, if unconvinced of her admirer's motives.

" *The Queen* and *Country Life* ; is there anything else you would like, Emily ? " Johnny, at the bookstall, consulted his companion's taste. Behind the chenille-spotted veil which converted her head into a little bird-cage, Emily blinked acceptance.

" That will do quite well, thank you." She wondered what sophisticated women read in trains ; looked wistfully at the ornate backs of a few " yellow-backs " and decided she had better not risk one. " I wonder if the train will be late."

" I hope so," he told her, smiling, then turning to glower at a flashy person who, in the course of his platform-pacing, never failed to trail a pair of bold eyes over Emily in her pale-grey travelling costume. " That's too bad of me," said Johnny with compunction, " for this is a beastly place for you to have to wait in. Are you sure you wouldn't rather go to the ladies' room ? "

She shook her head.

"I hate waiting-rooms; they *smell*." He caught the glitter of her teeth behind the mist of her veil. "Railway platforms are always amusing—one sees such odd people. Look at that man with string tied round below his knees; he looks like a farm labourer. Do you suppose he's going to London?"

"Emily—I wish you were not going."

"How kind of you, Johnny. But, really, I've quite outstayed my welcome!" She spoke on a high, artificial note, that made him look at her quickly.

"You know that's not true. We all love having you—and I've hardly seen you, since I came back."

"But if you had come by the other ship, you wouldn't have seen me at all! Why not look at it that way?"

She was different; there was something crisp and crystalline about her that puzzled him. All that grey and white—she usually wore colours—made him, for the first time since their childhood, a little shy of her. She seemed aloof—perhaps it was the veil—and a flicker of unfamiliar frivolity disturbed the soft seriousness he loved in her. But this, he told himself, was due to their uncongenial surroundings; people were always a little false on railway stations—forcing their gaiety, bridging with trite jokes the awkward interval that, with everything said, delays their departure. Yet between him and her, there was so much to be said. . . .

"When am I going to see you again?"

"Why—I suppose you will be coming to town, sometime?"

"Do you mean, I may call on you?"

In her clear laughter he imagined a faint note of mockery.

"Do we say 'calling' now? You know that you, and—and the others—are always welcome in Brook Street."

"It's a little different." The inflection in his voice forced her to look at him. "You are a grown-up young lady, Emily, and I shall be calling on *you*." Was this going too far?

"Oh, yes—I hadn't thought of that."

"Well; you will receive me?"

"Of course." But she was a little shaken. "Only—you must let me know when you are coming. I expect I shall have a great many engagements, when the season begins."

"I'm sure you will," he said gravely. "But I hope you'll find a few minutes to spare for an old friend. Damn! I *beg* your pardon, Emily!"

"What's the matter?" The expletive seemed to have amused, rather than offended, her.

"It's Uncle Roan; I didn't expect to see him on this train."

Here, indeed, was a situation. Uncle Roan was—well, he was Uncle Roan; but, according to the rules that governed people like Emily Temple, he was no suitable companion for a strictly brought-up young girl, whose guardians—this had from time to time been impressed on the young Floods—were extremely particular about the society she kept. It was the most unutterable twaddle, of course, and Uncle Roan was a prince of good fellows;

but it took little imagination to picture the reactions of Selina and Vicky, not to mention Lady Cullen, if he were to make the pair acquainted, at the outset of a journey which would give plenty of opportunity, if Roan were so minded—and who would not be?—to pursue the acquaintance.

"Your Uncle Roan?" Emily was looking about her curiously; fortunately Roan, in confabulation with a porter, was at the farther end of the platform. "Oh—I should like to meet him! It seems so odd"—her voice vibrated with an eagerness she forgot to control—"I've never met him since I was a little girl; I've almost forgotten what he was like."

"You know what the Roans are." He put his hand to her elbow, in an awkward attempt to pilot her even farther from the danger spot. "The firsts are generally a bit lower down. They're quite gadabouts—Aix, Biarritz and all that kind of thing. My uncle only comes to Bristol for directors' meetings." With a little luck, Roan would have ploys of his own; and, in any case, Johnny remembered with relief, he always travelled in a smoker. If there were only some way of avoiding the introduction. An idea seized him. "Emily, will you excuse me for a moment?" He tried in vain to attract the attention of Elphinstone, gazing, apparently, into futurity, across the groom's shoulder. "I'd like to have a word with my uncle before the train comes in——"

"He's coming towards us," said Emily calmly.

Yes, there was no doubt about it; Roan was the "show Flood." The silvering of his hair on the temples was an added distinction to one in whom—Johnny wryly reflected—distinction had never been lacking! To the charms with which he was born, Roan, typically, had added a flourish of his own; some slight nervous affection—a product, no doubt, of those roses and raptures on which Venetia raised a cynical brow—had made the left eyelid droop; it hooded the blue-grey eye of the Dorsets with an effect—not of raffishness, as might easily have been, but of profound toleration for other people's follies.

He came up the platform leisurely: a handsome, middle-aged man of a type sufficiently rare in Bristol to attract attention. An aura of West End clubs, of continental travel, of intimate acquaintance with all that makes up the sum of sophisticated living, a light touch of cosmopolitanism—were all in Roan. Emily turned aside; perhaps, in this last moment, she was shy. Her brief experience had not, yet, prepared her for anything like Roan Flood.

"Hallo, Uncle Roan." Johnny hoped his voice was more welcoming than he felt. With a lifting of the heart, he saw the engine appear at the bend of the line. Only a moment, thank goodness! But Roan, damn him, had spoilt his farewell to Emily.

"Well, Johnny; are you also making a bolt for civilisation?"

"No, I'm only seeing Emily off. Emily, may I? My Uncle Roan, Miss Emily Temple."

. . . It could not be; it simply was not true. That voice—like the purr of a tiger; the voice, like a hand laid on one's heart—Dorset's voice; Dorset's voice, like Dorset's ghost, risen to torment her!

The engine and the first coaches rushed past her. She felt herself sway, felt herself caught by an arm that steadied her ; saw Elphinstone's surprised, stupid face, and the woman hurrying towards her.

" It's all right, I'm looking after Miss Emily. Does she go second, or travel with you ? " muttered Johnny, in Emily's ear.

It was a strict rule that, whenever she travelled alone, Elphinstone shared the compartment. A stupid, childish, old-fashioned rule ! And Elphinstone was such a bore, with her ripple of genteel conversation. She had not yet acquired the art of snubbing servants ; Elphinstone would not have dared to open her mouth if Lady Cullen had been present.

Helplessly, she surrendered to the inevitable. The compartment selected by Johnny was empty ; she submitted in a stupor to being placed in a corner, to having the shantung wrap laid over her knees. Elphinstone placed herself in the farther corner and stared discreetly out of the window.

" Good-bye, Emily ; I hope you'll have a pleasant journey."

Roan had vanished, to look after his own comforts. And the farewell to Emily was ruined. Not, thought Johnny, striving for justice, that that could be blamed on Roan. She had hardly spoken. But she seemed hardly to hear when one spoke to her. Was it that she was suddenly sorry to leave Guerdon ? Or had the attractions of her home in London presented themselves to her in such glowing colours that she was eager to be gone ?

The train drew out of the station, and a sick sensation of cleavage came over Emily. She closed her eyes, so as not to see the familiar, squalid approach, the glimpse of the river : stations, in the past, to Paradise. There would be no more visits to Guerdon—nor, if invited, could she accept the invitation. A choking lump formed in her throat, and tears gushed to her eyes. The past was being torn from her in bleeding strips, and, in her agony, she longed, as young creatures long, for death. Seized with panic at the prospect of the long, desolate years ahead, a little whine broke from her—that she caught back in dismay, but not before it had turned Elphinstone's head towards her.

" Did you speak, miss ? "

She shook her head. Damn Elphinstone ; she could not even push up her veil to use her handkerchief. Abruptly she snatched up *The Queen* and held it between her and her companion.

" The rain is doing the country good," observed Elphinstone chattily. " Quite green—I'm shaw ! " Cockney, patronising the rural landscape. In spite of the groom, Elphinstone was very glad to be returning to town. There was a groom also at Brook Street—she had always had a taste for horsy men. One of those little loft-dwellings in the mews ; so central—and you did see life ! No ; she would not care to settle in the country. . . .

" Oh, miss, are you ill ? "

Emily, flinging the wrap aside, rushed through the door into the corridor ; Elphinstone, following her, received the slam of the lavatory door in her face. Well, what next ? She retraced her steps doubtfully along the narrow, swaying gangway.

What her ladyship would say when she saw Miss Emily was none of Elphinstone's business. Not much " holiday in the country " in that face !

White as a ghost, and all mouth and eyes. Elphinstone had had to alter the hooks on her skirt, and as for her stay-bones—they were overlapping at the back. And no engagement to report ! A nice to-do for the servants' hall, where they had been discussing the wedding present for months. Elphinstone was injured ; she had been bent on getting her " young lady " off before taking her own affairs in hand, and had counted on certain perquisites from the bride's discarded wardrobe to enrich her own bottom drawer.

In the lavatory Emily was quietly but copiously sick. Then she sat for a while on the seat, with her head back, hoping she was not going to faint. She felt quite numb, as though for the moment she had sicked away all her heartache. She was light and empty as a shell.

" Are you all right, miss ? " Elphinstone was tapping on the door. Presently she unbolted it, and had her face and hands sponged with eau-de-Cologne and her veil retied.

" Oh, miss, you did give me a fright ! It wasn't your breakfast, I'm shaw, for you don't eat enough for a sparrow. Oh, mercy, I was wondering if I'd find you in a heap on the floor. What I'd have done I'm shaw I don't know, if you hadn't opened the door ! I was wondering if I'd have to ask the gentleman——"

" What gentleman ? " She had forgotten Roan.

" The gentleman that was speaking to Mr. Johnny when the train came in : that caught you in his arms ! It's wicked the way these trains rush in—I thought for a minute you was going to be swep' off your feet——"

Caught you in his arms ? *Not* Johnny—— ?

Her veiled face met her in the glass with the immobility of marble.

" Will you put your hand on my shoulder, miss ? It's terribly rocky in the corridor ! "

" No—go on ahead of me."

In the corner of his smoker, Roan Flood read *The Times*.

> " Two companies of Royal Engineers and departmental corps with reserves of supplies and ammunition are being despatched to South Africa."

The tiny paragraph was almost lost in columns of diplomatic and political reports, but Roan pursed his lips for a whistle. His eyes, skilled in detection, pursued the close lines of print until they found what he sought.

> " The General Officer Commanding in South Africa has been authorised to complete the transport arrangements for the troops of his command, and the following special service officers have been ordered to proceed to South Africa."

Names of his friends ; men he met every day, and lunched with at the club ; Baden-Powell, Cecil, Hanbury-Tracy, Plumer, Jenner, Pilson, MacMicking, Bird. He murmured them aloud, raising his head, and lowered the paper abruptly.

The glimpse of a grey costume, of an ivory-gloved hand, quickly withdrawn, reminded him of the girl to whom Johnny had introduced him on the platform. Emily Temple: the girl who was *not* going to marry Dorset. H'm; that would take the young peacock down a peg. Roan turned to consideration of more serious matters than those of his nephew. A door slammed farther along the corridor.

IV

"You're late!"

"I'm sorry, sir! I didn't know you were expecting me."

Johnny was genuinely taken aback. It had seemed reasonable to assume that his duties would not start before the beginning of the week; Ricketts, his deputy, was at the desk which belonged to Johnny, and Johnny had just told him easily "not to fuss about clearing," as he had only dropped in to have a look round, and, incidentally, to make sure of Joe for a trip down to Avonmouth, when the office closed, as was the custom on Saturdays, at midday.

Nor was it a common thing, at this hour of a Saturday morning, for the Chairman to appear in the general office. Harcourt turned on his heel and stumped out; there was silence, and then winks along the desks.

"Welcome to our city!" grinned Ricketts, a sharp-faced youth a year or so Johnny's senior.

"Looks like it, don't it?" He shrugged his shoulders. "Well, I'd better see what's biting the old boy."

"What it is to be the Chairman's nephew!" mocked the other.

"I'm sorry, Uncle Hacky; it was a misunderstanding. I've been seeing Emily off at Temple Meads." He had caught Harcourt on the landing. The latter ignored him, marching into his room. Johnny, hesitating, wondered if he was expected to follow.

"Don't hang about there! Come in and shut the door!" His uncle's bellow disposed of his doubts.

He wondered, as he did Harcourt's bidding, whether the beauty of the room had become a commonplace to its occupant: the high Adam fireplace and pilastered doorways—each pillar carved to represent a sheaf of slender reeds, crossbound with ribbons that rippled into an elaborate design of bows and knots above the lintels. Were he master of such a room as this . . .

"I don't care for people who abuse privilege."

"I take exception to that, sir!" Johnny's lips had tightened, his spine stiffened itself, as it invariably did, when up against injustice. "Apart from the question of privilege—and I don't know what you mean by that, as I've never come across any 'privilege,' so far, in this office!—it never occurred to me you'd expect me before Monday. There isn't even a desk for me, until Ricketts has cleared up!"

"That'll do. You'd got plenty to say for yourself last night," grunted Harcourt.

" I wasn't expecting to say it. My report's written out ; Farren's typing it. It's pretty lengthy. I thought you'd find it easier to go through, in typescript."

" So you don't think much of the Coast."

" If that's the impression I gave——" He shrugged his shoulders.

" That's too bad," sneered Harcourt, " as you'll be going out again."

The expression blotted itself from his face.

" When ? " was all he asked.

" When it pleases me to send you." But the acidity had gone from Harcourt's voice. He moved to the window, his great shoulders, blocking out the light, turned towards Johnny, his hands in the pockets of his trousers. Old swine ! But he's an outsize—in character, as well as in build. The thought forced itself against the sinking of Johnny's reluctant heart.

" Where do we start ? "

" I—I don't think I understand—sir ! "

" You heard what I said : where do we start ? " repeated Harcourt. " You'd got enough to say last night about the mess we're in out there. Any ninny can see a thing's wrong ; it takes intelligence to tell *where* it's wrong, and something more than intelligence "—he laughed sourly—" to set it right. Have you got any intelligence ? Or are you one of the gas-bags that want to run the world from an armchair ? "

Words whirled in his brain ; words—ideas—none of which he knew would answer Harcourt's question. Give up the Interior. Confine the British Protectorate to a trading belt along the coast. Pour money and material into a scheme for making the trading zone commercially profitable. Rationalise the lives of the white population. Wild suggestions—and chimerical. For how could one man, or group of men, however powerful, put into practice a scheme that controverted the entire policy of the Coast ?

" Beaten ? " sneered Harcourt.

" No. But it's no good suggesting things without knowing the lie of the land. How far do you propose to go ? "

" You mean, how much do I propose to lose ? " Harcourt scowled at him. " As my hopeful nephew, you naturally want to know what it's going to cost *you*, if I start pulling the West African chestnuts out of the fire ! I'll tell you." His thick forefinger described a circle in the air. " See that ? Nothing. Because, as far as this business is concerned, you'll get nothing anyway."

Controlling his fury, Johnny spoke icily.

" I haven't worked for you for six years without learning not to expect anything but bare justice. I'm bound to say there's not been much of that about, so far, this morning ! "

" Keep your temper," said Harcourt easily. He was always good-tempered himself, when he had forced other people to lose theirs. He let himself drop into a chair and set about clipping a cigar. " Johnny. Listen. A man's work doesn't end with his generation. A man builds for his sons—if he has them. Or he builds for personal ambition. Or—just now and again—he builds for humanity. In my case, the building was started for me : close on two centuries ago. I picked it up when it had been at a standstill for a generation, but the foundations were there. They were here "—he tapped his chest—" in myself : running like corpuscles in my blood, alongside of the character that's come down to me—for good or evil —from Bristol men who shaped their lives round that water down below ; who gave the best and the worst of themselves to bringing prosperity to this town. Now——"

He sat silent, staring before him through the smoke of the cigar. Johnny also was still.

" A fat, white grub."

" What did you say, Uncle Hacky ? " Johnny was startled.

" I said, a fat, white grub," repeated Harcourt distinctly. " Sucking the good out of us ; sucking us dry, like flies in a spider's web ; feeding on our profits, that ought to be the profits of every man that draws his living out of Bristol's trade. . . . *You know what I mean.*"

" Guerdon ? "

" Damn it ! Blast it to hell—may it rot with the old fool who saddled us with it ! What's Guerdon got, for a Bristol Flood ? " His voice shook with contempt. " Here's our place—here in the town that made us : not playing at gentry over in Henbury ! Yer precious brothers—yer precious Gilbert, and yer popinjay Dorset—living like lords on money that's never cost them a hand's turn nor a drop of sweat from their lily-white brows ! Great Jesus—what's the matter with us ? Have we all got worm in our brains ? "

" I don't see you can blame Doss and Gilbert. Grandfather set the pace, Father keeps it up—after his fashion—and they naturally fall into it. And I dare say Mamma's side has something to do with it. There's a lot of Westermain in Gilbert."

" Pish ! Skim milk and dill-water : that's Westermain. How much of my mother d'you think there is in me ? "

Johnny grinned.

" Plenty—I'd say. Grandmamma's a great woman ! "

" She's a damn' nuisance," snorted Harcourt, " and as spendthrift as a Gaiety girl." Johnny licked his lips at this description of his grandmother ; if only Harriet could have heard it ! " Look at her—putting us to the expense of keeping up the Dower House all these years ! Why couldn't she wait till Doss got married and she was obliged to turn out ? God knows there's room enough for her in that damned Elizabethan barrack ! And I dare say Doss 'ud sooner set up on the other side of the park, to begin with, than share quarters with Drummy and Selina—I've done ! I tell you, I've done ! " He flung the butt of the half-smoked cigar into the empty grate, and sat with a hand clenched on his desk, a lonely and dissatisfied man.

" There's the almshouses, wanting a further endowment, because the sum we settled on 'em in 1760's not worth a third its value in 1899. There's the school—tumbling down an' crawling with livestock : nice thing, isn't it, to get a complaint from the sanitary inspector about your own property ?

Here's our city, stinking with poverty and vice, and the river, neglected by a pack of time-servers that can't see water for mud. And all of 'em paying for Drummy playing the squire, and Gilbert playing at soldiering, and Dorset playing at——" Harcourt used a word which, although Johnny had become used to the sound of it in Easy Emma's, left a curious echo in a fine Georgian chamber. "Dorset, turning the house into a Hotel Cecil for all the smart riff-raff that likes to cling on the petticoats of Guerdon, because they fancy they're lined with gold! They'll get their shock, one day. Let's hope," muttered Harcourt, "the Temple girl'll bring him to his senses——"

"That's all off." Johnny's voice cut harshly into his uncle's maunderings.

"Eh? What?" The thick brows twitched upwards, the prune-coloured eyes stared at Johnny.

"Doss proposed to Emily, and she refused him."

"Hey—hey—hey." For once Harcourt's vocabulary failed him. "Serve him right. Damn' good thing for the girl," were phrases scattered about the surface of his unintelligibility. "I wager that's made Drummy's hair stand on end?" emerged slyly from the medley.

"They're upset—naturally."

"I'll be bound they are! Well, let them get on with their playing," said Harcourt grimly, "for the game's nearly up."

What did he mean? Had the firm been having losses? Suspecting there was wisdom in silence, Johnny held his peace.

"Twilight on the Floods," Harcourt was mumbling. "Twilight, and time to draw the stumps. Aye; but I've seen some grand play at twilight" —his eye was on the distant spire of the Redcliff—"with the sun just settling down behind there and the clouds all bloodshot at their edges: no more than light enough to see the batsman——"

Incalculable old man. Where did he learn that trick of changing his voice—the domineering Flood voice—so that it seemed to caress his words, to stroke them, as a gentle finger might stroke the ruffled plumage of a bird?

"I've given my blood and my guts," Harcourt was saying, "to support a bunch of parasites that sneer at me for it. But I've found a better use for my energies, and I suppose I've got you to thank——" His mouth curled grudgingly. "I'm going to hand over the Managing Directorship to Sam Killick."

"Good God!" The words jerked themselves out of Johnny. "But—but you'll still be Chairman?"

"Maybe, maybe." He sounded uninterested. "There'll be changes. . . . Sam's all right; he's not as sharp as I am, but he's got vision. He'll stand by me when the rumpus starts. And rumpus there'll be!" Jingling the keys in his pockets, Harcourt appeared to find the prospect agreeable. "The howl'll go up from here to the Coast when Flood dividends start falling! When the Bank rings up about Drummy's last cheque for foreign missions, and Mamma takes a look at her pass-book! When the Belgravia landlords receive their polite notification that we withdraw our backing for Roan's cheques, and Selina hears she's got to choose between giving up her brougham and dismissing a couple of servants ! Do 'em damn' well good ! " Suddenly he smote the desk in front of him. " If I ruin the lot of 'em—if Guerdon goes under the hammer—I'm going to stop this drainage. I'm going to direct my energy where it'll profit better people than those fribbles at Henbury ! "

He seemed to hear Foxy's voice : " They've taken everything out of the Coast, and all they send us are the god-damned missionaries. Where's it going to stop—eh ? "

" The luck of the family and the luck of Bristol has always been bound up with the Gold Coast. While I'm Chairman of Floods, we're going to back our luck. It'll take time and money, and cut our profits to the bilge-line for the next twenty years ; but at the end of it the West African trade'll be sound. Twenty years ; and then—it's up to your lot. At any rate, I'll have done my best."

" What do you mean ? Force them to abandon the Crown Colony system, and make the Gold Coast into a chartered company, like Nigeria ? " Johnny's eyes sparkled.

Harcourt glowered.

" You're talking like a simpleton—like a child that wants to run before it can walk ! "

Johnny pulled himself together.

" Of course. The thing's on my brain," he admitted. As how could it not be ? Long discussions in skippers' cabins, in trading posts, in the fly-infested huts of men whose living was conditioned by scraps of paper pushed carelessly across Whitehall desks by people with nothing to gain and possibly something to lose by too close inquiry into affairs at so convenient a distance from British shores had crystallised in that one brief outburst ; he knew there must be no more.

" Give me a minute——"

His short, compact figure, with its oddly military bearing, crossed the room, to stand with folded arms where Harcourt had previously stood. But it was not the still water, the huddled roofs between the wharf and the Redcliff that spread below him : it was bleached sand silted across the ruins of barracoons, a welter of sick and hopeless faces, white and black, in narrow alleys ; it was the belt of disease and corruption that stood for " civilisation " along the West African Coast.

" Well ? "

He turned.

" We've got to find a wedge."

" Go on," muttered Harcourt, as Johnny sought for words. They came at last.

" Thousands of people in this country—people like ourselves and the Liverpool shippers—know what's going on on the Gold Coast. It's talked about in societies, and now and again something leaks out in a public lecture. But it's never taken up by the Press, and nothing's done, because the general public hasn't got hold of it. And it wasn't until the general public got hold of it that anything was done about the slave trade."

Harcourt nodded. His pencil was describing a network of squares on the pad in front of him.

" The public, takin' it by and large, is an ass," was his contribution to Johnny's statement.

" Yes—but an ass has enough sense to follow a carrot if it's dangled in front of its nose, hasn't it ? "

" Puzzle : find the carrot ! " sardonically. " One person in a hundred thousand has got sense to see what West African trade means to the nation. Apart from flag-waving, and bawling the Anthem, the common Briton doesn't think nationally."

" But if the same point's put to him in terms of humanity—call it sentiment if you like—wouldn't you be likely to get a response ? "

" Generalisation," growled Harcourt, adding a big black square to five pale ones.

" I'm coming to the particular. Take the swamp at the back of Charlestown. Knit it up with the mortality figures, and the importance of Charlestown as a trade outlet. Show the connection between disease and vice among the coastal population."

" Too abstract." Harcourt wagged his head. " Can't you see it's no use preaching to these muttonheads about something nine out of ten can't imagine ? There's no swamps in England ; the English mosquito raises a pimple that itches and is gone in twenty-four hours ; the nigger twangs a banjo, wears striped pants and calls everybody Massa——"

" Half a minute." Johnny thought quickly. " Tell them about Bill Prewett's plan for draining the swamp, that was approved at Accra and got lost in the Colonial Office. *Where's Prewett's plan ?* There's our wedge, Uncle Hacky. There's nothing the public enjoy so much as a hint of official slackness ! Get a few questions like that rolling, and we'll bust the show wide open."

There was a silence, during which the pencil was busy.

Suddenly the sultry eyes under the black brows lifted themselves to settle on Johnny.

" Now you're talking," said Harcourt, grudgingly.

" You'd better lunch with me," he said. Two hours had gone by, and the hands of the gilt sunburst clock over the fireplace pointed to ten minutes to one.

Johnny accepted the invitation, not without some slight degree of alarm. He had been, once or twice, to the Constitutional Club, but it was well understood that the dining-room, at lunch-time, was reserved for the commercial aristocracy, and that the smaller fry, squeezed into corners, were expected not to intrude their insignificant presence on the panjandrums. Lunching with Harcourt was equivalent to lunching with royalty, and Johnny was glad that, thanks to his earlier appointment with Emily, he was more or less dressed for the part.

He waited while the head clerk came in for the Chairman's parting instructions : a thin, harassed-looking individual, his anxious over-deference was reflected in the contempt of Harcourt's manner. Johnny wanted to say,

" For God's sake, can't you be a man, and not a worm? Don't you see it would pay you, with Uncle Hacky?"

But he was gone, and Harcourt turned, hatted, gloves in hand, leaning on his great malacca, polished like a ripe chestnut and topped by a Turk's head in gold. He looked down at his nephew—a long way down. Johnny straightened himself, but it was no use; the top of his head reached barely to Harcourt's shoulder. For some reason, Harcourt chuckled.

" I don't know how you come to be such a miserable little runt"—but it was kindly spoken—" but damme if you're not a Flood—and what the devil do you mean, sir, by keeping me waiting?"

Uncle Hacky was satisfied; so much was clear. But there had been no word of the future. As he followed his uncle's broad shoulders down the curve of the stair, Johnny's mind was on Emily, in the train, trundling on her way to London.

CHAPTER FIVE

I

"WELL——! I can't imagine where we're going to sleep him," was Vicky's reception—in the vein of " *Il ne manquait que ça!*" —of Dromore's announcement, which was also his tacit admission of defeat.

Dromore's face, handsome and nul as a sculpture, gave no indication of his feelings. It had gradually and painfully been borne in on him that to blackball the unwelcome guest was to commit himself, in an unpleasant and possibly conspicuous manner, to colour prejudice: an uncomfortable situation for a professed Christian and supporter of the missions.

" To *sleep* him——?" Johnny looked up with a frown.

" I know about his being a friend of yours, and all that," nodded Vicky. " But it's really rather awkward! What are the servants going to think—about a Negro, in one of the spare rooms?"

With an enormous effort of self-control, Johnny refrained from wishing the servants to hell.

" What do you suggest? Putting him on a mat?" He managed to force a laugh. " In case anyone imagines"—he addressed the company at large —" that our style of living is likely to impress Osei, you'd probably find him, at home, sleeping on a carved wood bedstead with gold and ivory inlay, and a couple of mattresses by Maple." His impatience crackled into a sudden outburst of anger. " Unless you can get it out of your heads, that I've invited a savage to Guerdon, I should think I'd better write and ask Osei to postpone his visit until I've had time to educate my family in the kind of reception to which he's accustomed."

" John!" His father's voice followed him to the door. " I will speak to you in the library."

" Well—— ! " Left by themselves, the eyes of the ladies met. Miranda yawned, and swung a bored foot. How long would it be before she heard from Emily ?

" Did he say the twenty-first ? " asked Vicky, with sudden interest ; her worried brow cleared. " But that's excellent ! I wonder if Drummy realises ? It's the day before the *fête*. How seldom it is that things work out so well ! " she beamed. " This Mr. Boko—what a terrible name ! Oh, dear, all the village will be funny about it—Mr. Boko can give us an address."

" Bofo," murmured Selina ; she had a better ear for names than Vicky. " A Negro ! " Her soft, detached smile swept over her delicate face. " Eighteen ninety-nine ! " Her sister-in-law stared at her. " I shall always remember eighteen ninety-nine," said Selina reflectively, " for the number of odd things that happened in it."

While Vicky pondered this ambiguous remark, Dromore was saying :

" And remember, I shall hold you wholly responsible for your friend's conduct while he is staying here."

" I don't think I'll find the responsibility a heavy one, sir." He would have liked to add that he wished he could be as confident of the conduct of his family, but there was no point in straining good will for the sake of a slick retort. On the principle of returning good for good, he added, " I appreciate your kindness very much, Father, and I think you'll find Osei a good fellow, and enjoy talking to him."

" I am sure I hope it may be so," was the gloomy response, as Dromore inclined his head in dismissal.

" There's just one more thing. I think it would look well, sir, as Osei is our guest, for some of us to go to his lecture. I think your presence "—he gulped, but, as much aware as the rest of the family that the one way to manage Dromore was to flatter him, forced himself to continue—" would be taken as a compliment, not only by Osei, but by the University itself."

" We'll see, my boy, we'll see." Some such thought had been, actually, in Dromore's mind ; it would be interesting to see what the missions produced—of course, in exceptional instances.

Not a few passengers turned to stare at the meeting between the tall Negro, well dressed to the point of dandyism, and the short, slight figure of Johnny, who had driven his way through the crowds on the narrow platform, to meet his friend.

For a moment they forgot they were not alone ; they stood laughing, with their hands on each other's arms, holding on to one another, laughing with pleasure.

" By George, Osei, it's good to see you ! "

" Is it a castle ? " Osei showed his first surprise when the hired cab turned from the bend of the avenue into full view of the house. He bent forward with interest in the long, golden façade, the pointed gables, the twisted chimneys that were the beauty of Guerdon.

" Good lord, no. But it's old—seventeenth century."

" It would hold—how many ? A hundred—a hundred and fifty people ? One of our villages "—Osei's teeth flashed—" or a school of students.

Yes ; a good place for study, in the middle of all this bush and clearing. As good as one of the Oxford colleges. Perhaps, some day, we might have a place like this."

" ' Bofo College ! ' " A vision flashed through Johnny's mind. " That's a thought—my word ! Guerdon—a University for Negro students ; my God, what a turn of the wheel ? "

" It will take a long time, for the wheel to turn so far," was the tranquil reply.

" Where's everybody ? " Dromore, he knew, was out ; Selina, of course, in her boudoir. Vicky ? She should have been there, to do the honours. He realised, with a rush of shame, that they had deliberately absented themselves to postpone an awkward meeting. Of one person at least he was sure.

" Come and meet my sister Miranda ; she's longing to know you."

He flung open a door eagerly.

" Winkle ! "

He remembered it later : Miranda limping across the room—she never went to strangers ; waiting, as a rule, for them to come to her—and laying her hand in Osei's, with a faint, upward-peering smile. The small white girl and the tall black man stood, hand in hand, with no self-consciousness in either.

" Mind my hawk," she said, in her little, hoarse voice. " It'll be all right, when she knows you."

" I think it is all right now." Osei laid a tender finger on the hackles. " Will she let me hold her ? "

" Without the glove ? She'd lay your hand open." She proceeded efficiently to transfer her pet to the cage, for which Johnny had made a stand in a small, dark alcove in a corner of the room. The merlin fluttered a little ; it was seen still to be lame, as it sought its grip on the padded cross-bars. Miranda returned to them, stripping the gauntlet from her left hand ; the oyster whiteness of her face was faintly flushed as she turned to Johnny. " Well ? What shall we show him first ? "

Luncheon passed off with gratifying smoothness—thanks mainly to Osei's composure. Selina and Vicky, having got over their (well-concealed) astonishment that a West African Negro should understand the conventions of the table, were almost embarrassingly cordial, before they found it possible to relax into normal behaviour. Dromore, as usual, assumed control of the conversation, directing it along those channels of courteous neutrality that well-bred people adopt in converse with strangers, and evidently agreeably surprised by his guest's ability in following such gambits as he chose to introduce.

Uncle Quentin, alone, managed to supply his customary element of uncertainty : mainly by puffing out his lips, pulling down his brows, and fixing Osei with an unblinking stare, which the latter accepted, when he happened to notice it, with a slight but courteous inclination of the head, as who should say : " Please don't hesitate to satisfy your interest to the full." And it was left to Uncle Quentin to produce the *gaffe* which smote the breath, not merely out of his neighbours, but out of the footman who happened at that moment to be passing a dish of peas across Selina's shoulder.

It has to be admitted that Uncle Quentin's reactions had become more and more spontaneous, as age absolved him of the conventions that govern society. Osei was lifting the fork to his lips when, from the other side of the table, the old gentleman shot at him :

" Jou eat 'umans in your part of the country ? "

The silence of petrifaction which settled on the company was broken by an extraordinary sound from the young footman, who, turning the colour of pickled cabbage, managed by an act of sleight of hand to save all but a spoonful of the peas, then, banished by a glare from his superior at the sideboard, vanished precipitately from the room. The only person unaffected was Osei, across whose face broke a smile of the simplest and most genuine amusement.

" Well, it is not among the customs of my own family. But I believe it is practised—occasionally—by some of our relatives along the rivers."

" Miranda ! Leave the table ! " gasped Selina, as Miranda's sudden ripple of laughter pulverised the listeners.

" No—please ! She is not to blame. It is I who should go." Osei had half-risen from his chair. It was Uncle Quentin who saved the situation he himself had created.

" Siddown, siddown. What's the fuss about—perf'ly nach'ral question," mumbled the old gentleman.

Vicky spoke on a high, twittering note.

" Pray have some more vegetable, Mr. Boko." And, with a flick of an eyelash, recalled the young footman, restored but still quivering in every limb, to his duties.

" I like your Uncle Quentin," chuckled Osei, when, after lunch was over, the pair of them were on their way to the fives court.

" I call that pretty big-minded of you—considering ! " grinned Johnny.

" There are times when one gets discouraged, and there seems no good reason for going on, because one is getting no further," was the simple rejoinder. " Then something happens which gives one back one's historical perspective."

" Something like—Uncle Quentin ? " He found this puzzling, but Osei nodded, with glittering teeth.

" Being weighed up like that, in terms of poundage, of height and muscle and temper ! Fifteen guineas, or thirty guineas worth of prime nigger ? I think he'd have bought me, Johnny ; I think he would ! " He flung back his head and guffawed, then, in his sudden way, sobered, to add, " And he can't. Neither he nor any other white man can buy Negro, ever again. So there *is* progress, and we've only to to be steadfast, and go on."

" Can I go to the lecture to-night ? " Miranda was asking Vicky.

Taken by surprise, her aunt could think of no reason for refusal. Miranda had lately begun to evade public appearances—a development which disquieted her family and which all agreed was to be resisted. So she took sherry and sandwiches with the lecture party—Dromore, Johnny, Vicky, herself and Osei : the lecture itself being arranged, with the usual disregard for the dinner hour of a select audience, for half-past seven.

The small lecture theatre was crowded, an address by an African Negro attracting more than the usual student group, which was packed into the gallery and round the sides and back of the hall. The Guerdon party was conducted to the platform : a form of conspicuousness which annoyed Johnny, and which he would have resisted, but for the opportunity it afforded of observing the reactions of the public to Osei's address. But as he looked down on row upon row of fatuous, slightly smiling faces, interest swelled into resentment, and into a smouldering anger on the speaker's behalf.

To about a third of the audience, he calculated, Osei was a performing animal, a spectacle rather than a voice ; a diversion, rather than a serious claimant on their attention. And, for the intellectual minority, his discourse was too simple—as though he had in mind the students of his visionary college rather than people with an educational tradition behind him. Johnny bit his lip, as he saw the exchange of smiles, or glances of amusement. Osei's manner was admirable, his bearing full of dignity and authority. . . . If he could only have talked as he talked on the ship !

II

The next day dawned in a flutter of excitement. The estate carpenters had set up the refreshment marquee, had strung up the bunting which defined that section of the meadow to which the proletariat was to be admitted, and the small, shady part of the lawn where the gentry were to take their tea. Timber was hammered into a platform, and tested to make sure it would take the weight of the piano.

Vicky, for a few fretful moments, had pondered the possibility of having the piano down on the grass : the prospect of Polly Bowling raised up, the cynosure of all eyes, was a disagreeable one. However, it was bad for the piano, and the alternative, of placing Polly with her back to the audience, was, when one came to think of it, nearly as good as having her out of sight. Provokingly slim waist the girl had got ! Vicky turned from such tiresome considerations to commendation of the head gardener, whose contributions in floral garlands and scarlet butter muslin to the decorations of the platform brought a gratifying touch of gala to the occasion, and would set off her own and Selina's summer frocks. (What would the Bowling girl be wearing ? A note : " P.B. to dress quietly "—went down on Vicky's tablets.)

Almost with dawn, the farm wagon was on its way up the avenue, with chairs borrowed for the occasion from the village hall. These—hardly inviting, with their stiff, wooden seats—were placed in a semi-circle before the platform ; it was only the elderly who would require them ; the younger element could seat itself on the grass.

Vicky fled from the breakfast table to supervise the arrangement of the stalls, at which her appointed bevy of helpers rushed, on their arrival, to seize the most advantageous positions for the display of their ware. By mid-morning footmen were carrying sherry and biscuits to revive the exhausted toilers ; the lawn had blossomed with small, decorated tables, and chairs of a very superior standard of comfort to those down in the meadow. It was at this moment when, even to Vicky's anxious eye, every prospect was pleasing, that things began to go wrong.

" Miranda—where's Miranda's village ? "

It was not for an incredulous half-hour that Vicky accepted the shock that a tin tray, with a few grains of dried earth and some withered grass, forced on her.

" I broke it up." Behind the glasses, Miranda's eyes were blank. Distracted questioning, scolding, even a threat of punishment brought no further explanation. Vicky, ready to weep for her own beautiful lettering—" African Village, One Penny a Peep "—nailed to the woodwork of the gazebo, turned to meet the lightly ironical smile of her mother. She had forgotten that Harriet was invited to lunch.

" Well, Victoria." " Old " Mrs. Flood presented her cheek to her daughter's distracted kiss. " You seem to have been very industrious." The tip of her parasol indicated negligently the animation of the outdoor scene. " You are losing a hairpin. Miranda, my child—— ? "

" She's destroyed her village ! " burst out Vicky.

Harriet raised her fine eyebrows. She knew nothing about Miranda's village, and showed by her expression she could not care less.

" And now it's lunch-time, and nobody seems to have seen Johnny and Mr.—Mr. Boko——"

" I have seen them," said Harriet calmly. " Down by the lodge."

" The lodge ? But——"

" Johnny and Osei have gone to lunch in Bristol," Miranda now took it upon herself to announce.

" In—— ? Oh, this is *too* bad ! " Vicky collapsed. Harriet directed an expert look at her daughter.

" I think you had better have a short rest after lunch."

" Rest ! " gasped Vicky. She remembered the hymn-sheets—as yet unpacked, on the library table ; and the gardener's little boy, who, dressed as a piccaninny, was to sell tickets for the raffle—had somebody remembered to snip the astrakhan wig ? The size of that child's head was incredible ; probably water on the brain. Who was in charge of the collection boxes ? Had that parcel of garments, sent up tiresomely late from the Mothers' Meeting, been priced? Was Lady Gannet's crimson satin tea-cosy adequately displayed ?

" The Reverend Septimus and Mrs. Spalding," intoned the butler at her elbow. The Reverend . . . oh, dear, yes : the clergyman who was opening the *fête*. He and his wife were lunching, also—" Lady Gannet and the Misses Gannet. The Misses de Winter. Mr. and Miss Wix."

Harriet looked thoughtfully after her daughter, as Vicky fled, with a smothered moan. The second boom of the gong travelled in waves along halls and galleries. Lunch was in the Great Hall. There were thirty places.

Harriet sent up one of her periodic thanksgivings for having quitted Guerdon.

The opening ceremony took place at two o'clock, the speaker exhorting an audience reluctantly drawn from the stalls around which they were already prowling (several, defiant of the summons, remained to clutch items of which they were not going to be cheated by any slavish deference to ceremonies) to remember that, although the occasion was one of pleasure, it had a deeper purpose ; to think of the benighted souls to whom their pleasure brought spiritual, and, as a secondary consideration, material profit—those poor, dark brethren waiting for the Lamp of the Lord to be borne to them by our patient toilers in the mission field—and so forth, and on on.

Toilers on Guerdon earth swallowed their impatience as best they could, mumbled their way through the first hymn on the sheet—*Souls of men, why will ye scatter*—and scattered like scalded cats for the rummage and the bran-tub, while Polly was concluding the second chord of a demure Amen. A few asked for the "African Village," the notice of which Vicky had forgotten to remove ; irritably she sent a servant to see to it.

But as the afternoon wore on, and pockets grew lighter and string bags full, it was evident that another motive than charity held the gathering together. Word had gone forth that "a black man" was actually stopping at Guerdon. Someone eventually plucked up courage to put a direct question.

"Where do you suppose Mr. Bofo is, Victoria ?"

"I told you : lunching in Bristol with Johnny."

"But surely by now they have returned ?"

Vicky shrugged her shoulders ; she was near the end of her tether. The *fête* had not—it was no use blinking the truth—been its usual success : and yet it was difficult to find a reason. It was an atmosphere, more than anything, she had come to the conclusion : some sort of an attitude of dissatisfaction—almost as though people felt they had not had value for their money ! And the smaller children had started to be very naughty—and there was far too much giggling and foolish behaviour between the older boys and girls.

"You told Bofo that we wished him to say a few words to our guests ?"

Vicky's jaw dropped in horror.

"Oh, Drummy ! I thought that you——!"

Dromore's eyebrows rose ; on the point of saying to Vicky that it was her *fête*, he desisted, after a glance at her exhausted face. An unfortunate lapse ; but Victoria had had much on her mind, and others had not been helpful.

"I will use the telephone," he said solemnly.

The telephone—an innovation for which Dorset was responsible—was generally avoided, except in emergency. Clamped to the wall of the gun-room, it was regarded by most people as a type of infernal machine ; Vicky had never conquered its procedure.

Approaching it with an air of calm resolution, Dromore lifted the receiver, adjusted the vulcanite mouthpiece to his own height and turned the little, crackling handle exactly ten times. He liked dealing in numerals; they lent him confidence. A series of miniature explosions, pops, clicks and whines went off in his ear, before an all but inaudible voice, the thin, eery voice of a disembodied soul, informed him that Mr. John Flood was not in the office.

III

It was a very hot night. She had come to bed early, because she was tired—like everybody else after the *fête*—and because she wanted to write to Emily. Because her hip ached, and because . . . because . . . because . . .

There were stars, but no moon. From the window of her new bedroom—the room which had been The Grim's, before she married her Frenchay curate: which had, somewhat astonishingly, been made over to her, about a week after Johnny's return—she could see the stars. She liked the new room, which had two windows, instead of one, and was nearly twice as large as her old one: possessing, moreover, the advantage of not being close to the water cistern, which gurgled and bubbled most of the night. Actually, she missed the tank, which suggested something alive; companionship.

The new room had gas—Dorset's ambition for electricity had not yet been gratified—instead of an oil lamp; a bell rope which, in conjunction with a metal ring and a wire, near the ceiling, actually functioned in some remote domestic quarter, and an almost new carpet on the floor. The hangings were of a pleasant, faded chintz, with bobble fringe, and the furniture included a bookcase, inadequate to the library Miranda had begun, by lawful or illicit means, to collect.

But best of all, and overlooked, she was sure, by Aunt Vicky, was the door at the end of the small back landing on which this room opened: which led to a staircase seldom, if ever used, on account of its steepness and narrowness—too steep and narrow even for the servants, with their buckets of coal, cans of hot water and housemaids' boxes; which, in its turn, led to a side door, and so into the sunk garden. It was hard to come up, and even harder to go down, but, by taking time, it was negotiable, even by someone with a weak hip.

The dew soaked through the soft woollen soles of her bedroom slippers, and a shimmering band of silver on her right stood, she knew, for a border of pinks; she snuffed up the scent luxuriously. Somewhere hereabouts were the two little box trees: one clipped into the shape of a cock, and the other a hen; and between them ran the path to the lily pond. As she shuffled along it, a heavier, more exotic perfume blended itself with that of the pinks, and a red star appeared by the pond. A tall figure was smoking its cigar in the starlight.

"What—what are you doing here?"

"I'm waiting for Johnny, Miss Miranda." The deep voice was like an organ note. "Your father called for him."

"Oh!" Her heart, which had leapt a little with surprise, steadied itself, and her breath ran out on a sigh—of pleasure. The darkness in which they stood seemed very kind, very safe. "Do you like it here?"

"Very much. It is a beautiful house. A beautiful garden."

"And us. Do you like us?"

"Why, Miss Miranda! How could I not, when you have all been so kind to me?"

"Johnny's very fond of you. Johnny and I always like the same people——" She stopped, astounded by the sound of the words; even more astounded, and puzzled, by her own embarrassment. Frustrated in her impulse to run away, she stood rigid, mute with shyness.

"I do appreciate that, Miss Miranda," Osei was saying gravely. "I'll remember it, after I've gone."

"When have you got to go?" she muttered.

"To-morrow morning."

"Why?"

"I've got some work to do. I have some more lectures—and then I am going to be secretary to a friend of mine who is a writer, and is going to work in Paris," he told her simply.

"Shall you like that?"

"Very much. Paris is a very good place for writers, and for people like—us." His voice sounded as though he were smiling.

"Do you write too?" she inquired breathlessly.

"A little, when I have time. Do you?" asked Osei.

She ducked her head in embarrassment.

"What sort of things do you write? Stories?"

"No, not stories." He sounded regretful. "I try to write poetry sometimes."

"I'd like to read your poems," mumbled Miranda. She had perched herself, by habit, on the curved curb of the pond. On their dark leaves and the darker water, the lily buds were like pale candle-flame, immobilised by the still air.

Squatted on his heels, the cigar dangling between his long fingers, Osei was talking: telling a fairy tale of that strange land of which she sometimes dreamed—but not in terms like these.

"You would waken to a strange world! To a moon the colour of fresh blood, and to a sun pale like a silver apple. There are curtains of leaves so straight and fine, they look like water pouring over the lip of a waterfall. And there is a plant with starry flowers, you could pin in your hair——"

As he paused to rekindle the fiery heart of the Havana leaves, as the tip of the cigar turned to a rosy star again and its smoke, like a little wraith, floated between them and across the pond, she cried in a voice of pain:

"Why did you have to spoil it?"

"To spoil—what?"

"Who do you think is going to pin flowers in *my* hair?" scoffed Miranda bitterly.

"Why not?"

She was silent.

Osei said :

" You think too much about being lame."

Her breath, as she caught it in through her teeth, made a little whistling noise. No one but Johnny had ever been frank about her lameness ; certainly no one had ever used the word " lame " in front of her before. Not even the dear, the understanding Emily had ever ventured to lift the veil of reticence which, by tacit agreement, was flung over all reference to Miranda's " weakness."

Very early in her short life it had been decided that she was not to be encouraged to " brood " on her physical defects, and that the best way of preventing " brooding " was to preserve a bright, astringent manner ; not to pet the child unduly, or to single her out for more attention than was given to healthy people. Had it been suggested that she was savagely self-conscious of her plainness, her lameness and her dependence on other people, they would have pooh-poohed it. She was " used to it," as people about her were used to it—and at all events, nothing was to be gained by discussion of a painful and tiresome defect which the poor child must endure, since medical opinion agreed it was not to be cured.

" Don't you know, Miss Miranda, that nearly everybody is lame, in some way or other ? If not in their bodies, in their souls ? "

" Souls don't show ; and—anyhow—you're neither," she accused him.

" I used to be."

" Which ? " Her tone showed that she did not believe him.

Instead of answering, he put out his hand and touched her head very gently. She stiffened ; then, slowly, her head drooped, in acceptance of the caress.

" Some people would say I am, still." He touched his own face. " This —my colour, you know. Some people look on that as—as an affliction ! "

" Is that how *you* feel ? "

Osei's chuckle came comfortably out of the dark.

" Of course I don't. It's sometimes a little—nuisance, in white countries : because it makes one conspicuous. But why should one mind about that, unless one's got something to conceal ? "

" You don't mind—when people stare at you ? "

" Why should I ? Staring doesn't do any harm. People who stare can't take away the things that belong to one—the things that are hidden inside. You know what I mean : all one's thoughts, the kind of person one is— no staring can alter that, Miss Miranda ! "

The simple words—above all, the source from which they came—were strangely convincing. For years she had suffered in silence the swelling of a spiritual tumour even more agonising than her diseased pelvis, and it was as though Osei's honesty, his frank acceptance of something everyone else conspired to ignore—although there could be no real ignoring—had acted like a surgeon's knife. Poison was running out of the lanced tumour ; a sense of relief so overwhelming that she felt as though she might be going to faint made Miranda's head swim. She swayed a little on the edge of the pond, and felt Osei catch her hand.

" I shall spoil the flowers, Miss Miranda, if I have to go swimming ! " he said, with mock gravity intended to make her laugh. So she laughed, obligingly.

" Please pull me up." She could not remember ever asking anyone, except Johnny, to help her before. " I'm getting pins and needles, with sitting on this stone."

" Do you think we ought to go and find Johnny ? " he asked, as he drew her carefully to her feet.

" Yes. Osei—can I call you Osei ? "

" Of course. It is much nicer than ' Mr. Boko ' ! " He let out a roar of laughter, in which she joined.

" Please will you write to me when you go away ? "

" Yes, I will."

" Will you send me some of your poems ? "

" If you like ; but I think you will find them rather queer. There aren't any rhymes," confessed Osei, as he took her arm, and they went back towards the terrace. Everyone must be upstairs by now, and it was easier going up the front stairs than her own narrow flight. She laid her finger to her lips, enjoining silence, as they tiptoed beneath the library windows. Above them, the windows of Dromore's and Selina's rooms, and of the dressing-room, were lighted ; below, the stacked chairs and trestles of the *fête* waited to be cleared away. Voices fell clearly through the quiet air.

" . . . most thoughtless of you. You know how much importance your aunt attaches to her yearly effort."

" Well, I'm very sorry, but it never occurred to me that Aunt Vicky would mind whether I turned up or not. Of course we'd have come back earlier, if I'd known."

" Johnny—getting into trouble with Papa ! " Miranda bestowed a sharp pinch on her companion's arm.

" I am not referring to your absence, but to your friend's," came from on high in Dromore's voice.

" Osei ? I don't think the *fête* would have been much of an entertainment for him ! "

" There was not much ' entertainment ' for any of the people who spent the afternoon in exerting themselves for a worthy cause ! " his father rebuked him. " It is a pity that you two should be the only members of the household to contribute nothing to your Aunt Victoria's achievement ! "

" I must go upstairs." Osei was trying to loose himself from the clutch on his arm. " It is too bad Johnny should get into trouble on my account——"

" Sh : listen." She continued to hold him.

" I don't know what you expected Osei to do ; guess the weight of a bun-loaf, or buy woollen kettle-holders to take home as presents for his family ? "

" Your tone is exceedingly unbecoming. You must see the value, at a function in aid of our West African missions, of the presence of a person whose very appearance helps, in a village as remote as this, to bring home to the people the cause we are striving to support. Your aunt had expected Mr. Bofo to say a few words."

"I thought as much." Johnny's voice had risen. "Well, sir, you happen to hold one view of hospitality ; I've got another. And I'm damned if any guest of mine is going to provide a penny gaff for the village ! "

There was the sound of a slamming door. As they came guiltily into the hall, Johnny was running down the stairs.

"What the blazes—Winkle ! What the dickens are you up to—at this time of night—— ? " Fraternal disapproval took in Miranda's companion, her dressing-gown, the grass stains on the hem of her nightdress. Osei said quickly :

"Johnny—I'm sorry—— ! "

"It's all right." But his uneasy eye followed the small figure hoisting itself up hurriedly by the banister rail. What would Aunt Vicky, or Mamma, say, if they caught Miranda, out in her dressing-gown, with Osei ? "I hope she wasn't plaguing you," he muttered.

"No, of course not. Johnny, of course I'd have spoken to the people, if you had told me ! "

"Oh, gammon." His face cleared. "We don't expect visitors to pay for their board and lodging ! At least, I don't. Do you mean to say you heard us—the Pater and me ? Jesus—we must have been bawling ! "

"Was that why you took me to Bristol ? " persisted Osei.

"I wanted to show you round—well, it was partly that," Johnny admitted, and changed the subject. "Look here : have you really got to go, in the morning ? "

"I think, after this, it is just as well I have ! " smiled Osei. He dropped his arm across Johnny's shoulder, looking down on him with concern. "You look sick, Johnny. You look as if you ought to be in bed."

"I'm going. It's only my damned temperature—it always dodges up at night." He avoided the other's anxious look.

But he was sick next day—too sick to go to the office, and therefore too sick to see Osei off at Temple Meads. Osei was standing, watching the carters clearing away the *débris* of the *fête*, when he crawled to the door. A thin veil of rain clothed the park in melancholy. They gripped each other's hands, saying little.

"I'll keep you posted—how we get on."

There was a strange glitter in the Negro's eyes, and a note in his voice almost of despair, as he said good-bye.

"Don't let them send us war—and don't send us any more missionaries, Johnny ; it comes to the same thing ! "

"Aren't you going to come and have some breakfast ? " It was Vicky behind him, as he stood, watching the carriage down the drive.

"No, thanks—I'll just keep quiet—for a bit."

"I believe you ought to be in bed."

No, not in bed. There was just a chance that, in the library, the Face would not be waiting for him.

CHAPTER SIX

I

JUST at the end of the summer, Miranda was confirmed. They had her in Selina's room to dress her ; the full, white muslin gown was slipped over her head and hooked down her back, the tulle cap placed on her head and held in position by the elastic under her plaits, and the veil drawn carefully over her shoulder.

"You look very pretty, dear." Selina, from her sofa, commended her kindly.

" I think I look like an earwig in tissue paper." She vetoed gruffly the unwonted tribute to her vanity.

" Silly child. Such a pity about the glasses, isn't it ? " Selina murmured to Vicky, who was thinking the same.

" Do you think you could manage without them, for once ? "

Silently, she took them off. Her reflection in the cheval glass blurred into a patch of silver, then cleared a little, into the full, white spread of the gown, the mist of the veil about it—almost like a little bride's. She found herself gazing at it impersonally—admiring this strange Miranda Flood, all in white, slim and romantic. Like a bride—or like a swan, floating on quiet water. Never before—never again—had Miranda that conception of herself, which curved her lips into a little smile and lifted her hands unconsciously towards the lovely vision of herself : herself as she might be, with a curtain of dripping leaves behind her, and starry blossoms in her hair.

The thought crossed her mind, and was gone as soon as it came—that it would have been nice for Osei to have seen her.

It was, in a sense, typical of Uncle Quentin to steal the thunder of the first opportunity that had ever come Miranda's way of focusing the interest of her family.

True to himself in death, Uncle Quentin elected to shuffle off his mortal coil at a moment calculated to cause the utmost possible embarrassment to everybody. With the Bishop staying in the house, and the drawing-rooms stiff with gaiters, with the sober splendour of clerical ladies, with young chaplains agog to catch The Eye, and a hand-picked selection of local gentry, guaranteed to preserve the punctilio of so important an occasion—Uncle Quentin, who had announced that he was damned if he'd dine with a clutter of parsons, and, to everyone's satisfaction, had had dinner served in his room—either became bored, restive, or the devil entered into him. He had, in short, an attack of pottering.

Uncle Quentin's pottering attacks had become a trial of latter years. They carried him into the most unlikely places and sometimes entailed search parties, as the mere suspicion of being followed was enough to plunge the old gentleman in an apoplexy. He appeared to have no motive in his wanderings beyond a raging curiosity ; it was not unnatural, therefore, that his wanderings had taken him into the Bishop's bedchamber.

His Lordship on this occasion was on his way between two ceremonial appearances. His valet, a conscientious fellow, was worried about the lining of a cope which, at its last wearing, had shown signs of disintegration at the hem. Knowing that his friend, Miss Mytton, was adept at the needle, he had had a word with her, and had received her instructions to lay the consecrated garment out on His Lordship's bed, when, having performed her duties to her mistress, she would see to it.

Uncle Quentin loved anything that glittered, shone or was jewelled. To cut short a painful story, he was discovered, comatose, on the Bishop's bed, folded in the cope, with—most heinous of all—the mitre, which, for some reason that was never satisfactorily explained, the valet had lifted from its box and placed on the corner of the dressing-table, cocked over one eye. His catalepsy was explained by the bottle of Napoleon brandy—his invariable companion on these jaunts—which was discovered, empty, lolling against the valance of the bed. Vicky, who had had previous experience, insisted that he must not be touched before the arrival of the doctor—a discreet man, and sufficiently aware of his dependence on the good will of Guerdon to hold his tongue. Dromore's head was in the dust ; he was convinced that this spelt *finis* to his secret hopes of receiving, one day, the peerage to which—under a Throne to which virtue appealed—his public good works entitled him. He had borne much ; the time had come for a clear understanding with Uncle Quentin.

Uncle Quentin's understanding had, for once, outrun his nephew's ; he had already reached that bourne where, presumably, there are no misunderstandings. When his will was read—proving to his outraged family that he was much better off than any of the surviving generation—they learned that he had scattered his money round in the most deplorable fashion : leaving legacies, here of five thousand, here of ten thousand, to a number of people the family had never heard of. The unheard-of sum of twenty-five thousand pounds was left to someone of the name of Santiago Maria Xavier Jaime Mateo de los Flujos Rodríguez y Torrevelludo Baviera, of San Juan de Remedios, on the island of Cuba ; a name nobody believed in, and which would have been seized on as proof that Uncle Quentin was not in his right mind at the time of the making of the will, had not the date—some five years previous—happened to coincide with that of one of his periods of marked lucidity. It was, actually, Dorset who pointed out that to make out that Uncle Quentin was crackers when he made his will was not very gracious to Johnny, the only member of the family who benefited under the old gentleman's depositions.

Johnny was to enjoy the income on three thousand pounds for life, after which the capital reverted to the inconceivable individual in Cuba. Not to be counted as a fortune, but enough to lend the recipient the dignity of a man of modest independence. Sobered by the unexpected stroke of fortune, he went to break the good news to Harriet—and found it was no news to her.

"He should have left you more!" She bit her lip with annoyance. "He promised me——"

"So you're at the back of it!"

"It seems time for somebody to look after your interests," she told him tartly, "since you appear quite incapable of doing so for yourself! A hundred and fifty—at the utmost two hundred—a year," she muttered. "Scandalous! I had thought better of him." Her eyes dwelt with a mixture of love and disparagement on Johnny, slouched smilingly across the back of a chair.

"And I have as much again from Uncle Hacky, and, since I came home, Father's opened an account for me with the Capital and Counties——!"

"For how much?" She interrupted him ruthlessly.

"Oh—fifteen pounds a quarter." He tossed it lightly in the face of her disgust. "Well, hang it, Grandmamma, that makes nearly four hundred a year! I'm a man of means; I'll be buying you diamonds before I've done."

"It is absolutely disgraceful—and you're a fool." Her beautiful eyes were smouldering.

"A good many fellows have less—and it's not as if we were millionaries." He hesitated, wondering how much Harcourt had told her.

"A good many fellows have more," she muttered. "When are you going to propose to Emily Temple?"

He stood, petrified. As she glared at him, awaiting his anger, he began to stammer:

"I didn't—there's no chance of my getting married—yet. I don't know if she—cares for me. She's got—dozens of fellows to choose from—and she turned Doss down!"

"Sit down," said Harriet gently.

"When did you last see Emily?" she presently asked him. He would have told anyone else to mind her own business; he answered her grudgingly.

"Not since she left us, in the summer."

"Is that your doing, or hers?"

"I've called twice," he muttered. "Each time she was out. I left a note for her, the second time."

"Well? Has she answered it?"

"There wasn't anything—in particular—to answer. When she wrote to Miranda she thanked me—and said she was sorry to have missed me. Well, what do you expect?" His eyes were as fierce as hers. "I've got none of Doss's advantages; if she refused him, she's not likely to want me."

"*If she refused him.*" It was a moment before, shocked, he realised what she was saying. "Who says she refused him?"

"Why—why—Doss; and—and, of course, Emily. She told Mamma herself——"

Yes, there was no answer to that mystery, which Harriet had, from the first, discredited. It was, of course, going too far to say to Johnny that the girl he loved was lying; but she was prepared to take her oath before heaven that it was Dorset, the smiling traitor, who had wearied of a devotion that bound too many obligations upon him, and had—by what demoniac means Harriet's imagination fell short of supplying—contrived the situation. She spoke carefully, choosing her words.

"Yes, my dear, we know all that. But, like all young men in love, you don't know very much about the feminine mind. Dorset and Emily have been—shall we say—attached to one another for many years; a woman is apt to become possessive about someone who, for that long period of time has shown her, in every way, that she comes first in his regard. Although, by the time he had made up his mind to propose, she found that she did not, after all, want Dorset as a husband, I think we would not be mistaken in assuming that his sudden change of affections and the announcement of his marriage have come as a shock to her."

"I don't see why they should." Male logic refused to accept this. "There isn't a trace of dog in the manger about Emily, Grandmamma, and I'm sure she would be the first to be glad that Doss had found someone to make up for her—her letting him down. I know she felt terribly about it——"

Praying heaven to send her patience, Harriet leaned forward to touch his hand.

"I am quite sure Emily will hold all the proper sentiments," she said, a little dryly. "All the same, my dear, you can surely imagine that the gossip and excitement about Dorset's wedding must have been painful to a sensitive person, who—it was their own faults, of course—had been tacitly accepted as Dorset's future bride? It must, at any rate, be a time of poignant memory for Emily, whose devotion to your brother no one, up till a few weeks ago, has questioned. She cannot fail to be conscious of the vulgar conjecture that gathers about a young woman in her position——"

"Do we need to talk about it, Grandmamma?" Her heart was wrung by his tormented look, but she answered firmly.

"Yes. Don't you realise that the consolation Dorset has found is also open to Emily? In her situation, she will be especially grateful to someone who helps to restore the dignity which Dorset's conduct (in her own imagination, at least) has hurt."

"Good God, I don't want Emily's gratitude!" he answered her roughly. "Nor—I've known her all my life, and, I assure you, she's not the kind of girl to think about her offended dignity."

"You misunderstand me," said Harriet quietly. "I mean that Emily would be very glad, just now, of an old friend who is prepared to put her happiness before his own——"

"She's at no loss for friends," was the bitter rejoinder. "Winkle gives me her letters to read: she never seems to stop tearing round to balls and theatres and concerts——"

"I said, an *old* friend. Balls, theatres, concerts:" her voice dwelt on the words. "You know better than I; does that reflect Emily Temple, according to your acquaintance with her?"

He said, after a pause:

"It's no use, Grandmamma. Even if I were in a position, immediately, to offer Emily a home, I'm too tied up with Uncle Hacky's business to embark on—on a courtship ! " He apologised, with a laugh, for the old-fashioned flavour of the word. " I'm a good deal in London, it's true, but I'm supposed to be there on his business, not my own ; I'm not free to fit myself into the engagement calendar of a young lady in Society ! "

How deeply she has hurt him ! thought Harriet, with the bitter inflection of his words ringing in her ears. But she had a preoccupation of her own ; her voice was sharp with misgiving as she asked him : " He's not sending you back to the Coast ? "

" Not for the present, at any rate. Well, Grandmamma, bless you for the way you trouble about me ! " He had risen, and had taken her hand, as usual, to kiss it. " You shall be the first to know, when I've made my fortune——! "

" Stop ! " The fierce grip of her little fingers round his own took him by surprise, although it was not the first time that he had thought her handclasp was like her character, strong and tenacious, belying the fragility of her appearance. " John. I am seventy-four ; I haven't much longer to live—within reasonable expectation. And I am not, by the standards of your family "—she dissociated herself, as usual, with a grimace, from her late husband's kin—" a wealthy woman, although," she added proudly, " I have ample for my personal needs." Had she ? he wondered, trying to repress a grin at Harcourt's description—" Spendthrift as a Gaiety girl." " What are you grinning at ? " His effort, then, had not been successful. " I could very well have maintained myself, if I had chosen, without recourse to the jointure, but I happened to have other views for the disposal of my means."

He wondered what was coming ; another shock for them all, no doubt, when it transpired that not only Quentin, but Harriet, had been preserving their own nest-eggs at the expense of Guerdon ! Quentin, probably, had been advising her ; like the other males of the family, Johnny found it hard to believe that a woman would know how to organise her private fortune. He was conscious of a distinct feeling of sympathy for Harcourt, watching the estate being milked by the pair of them.

" It's yours," she was saying. " *All* yours—do you understand ?—when I am gone." She laughed a little grimly. " Oh, I know well enough that Guerdon's not as sound as it should be, in spite of Miss Ethel Phillipson's money ! " She spoke the name with a little dry emphasis, as though deprecating its plebeian syllables. " How amusing it will be, if you, in the end, are better off than all the rest of them ! "

" I don't give a damn about being better off. Dear Grandmamma—I don't know how to say it—how touched I am——" His voice failed him.

" Let that go," she told him shortly. " There's something else. On the day you come and tell me you're engaged to Emily Temple, I'll instruct my lawyers to look after you. You understand what that means ? I'm removing any ridiculous notions you may have about not being able to support a wife. It was your father's duty to do it, but—well, perhaps Dromore's not as comfortable about the future as he was a few years ago. When do you go to town again ? "

"I think—probably—next week."

They looked at one another in silence—a deep, profoundly understanding silence—before he laid his lips to the back of her hand.

II

But for Vicky's diary—conscientiously kept from her schoolroom days—the events of the following twelve months might well defeat the chronologist. Terse, factual, and concerned wholly with affairs of the family, the diary gives little idea of the background against which those affairs were conducted. The departure of the Second Gloucesters, "Good-bye, Dolly, I must leave you" and "The Absent-Minded Beggar," although whistled by every errand boy who tramped up the long avenue to Guerdon, leaves no trace on those genteel pages ; the outbreak of the South African War appears as "Gilbert's regiment ordered to the front," and an event which plastered the streets with golden eagles, slung imperial crowns and floral emblems from Venetian masts and brought 80,000 country visitors streaming into Bristol is dismissed as "Queen's visit. *Very moving.*" We are not told what Selina and Vicky wore, for the reception at the Victoria Rooms ; there was nothing of the coquette in Miss Victoria Flood.

The utmost Vicky does is to provide a stark pointer, here and there ; there is no indication of the upheaval behind the entry, on September 10th —"Dorset engaged to be married," followed, in due course, by "Dorset's wedding." "Gilbert wounded" and "Gilbert brought home" give no picture of the warrior's return, and, of course, no hint of Selina's emotions at the spectacle of her fondling with, to use Gilbert's own words, "enough lath and plaster about him to build a henhouse." Apart from the fact that Vicky would have considered it an impropriety to commit emotions, her own or other people's, to paper, it is safe to say that the proximity of two brothers (Dromore was too scrupulous to come into the category) had taught her early discretion in the keeping of a diary.

So it is from other sources that we glean information on Dorset's marriage —an event rushed on for the convenience of the bride's father, who, having marketed his daughter successfully through her first season, was impatient to return to his diamond mines. It is from the family photograph album that we get the picture of the bride herself—*plus reine que reine* in her bridal gown by Worth : a pale girl with heavy but not bad features and a determined chin : beautiful in a commonplace fashion enhanced into something a little more than commonplace by excellent dressing. Harriet Flood, on her first meeting with Miss Ethel Phillipson, is recorded to have said that she felt quite put in her place—"as one is put in one's place by someone's *very* superior parlourmaid !" "I'd like to see the parlourmaid who would put *you* in your place," Harcourt had chuckled.

"Finished" in Paris, cheek by jowl with princesses, archduchesses and the cream of the British *haut ton*, Miss Phillipson's poise was impeccable. She was (at this period of her upbringing) exceedingly biddable, and the chaperon (she was motherless) who saw her through her first season had no difficulty in persuading her to put away the *parure* of diamonds, emerald clusters and other furnishings of her jewel case until after she was married. In Chantilly over rose-pink chiffon, with a single string of pearls, she received four proposals, and accepted Dorset's. Public opinion said she could have done better for herself, but Miss Phillipson was no fool. She was shrewd enough not to wish to marry into a family which would patronise her for lack of breeding, and she meant to take an important place in the "new society" which, thanks to the Heir-Apparent's taste for Jews, was beginning to exercise a power of its own. Montagu Phillipson's daughter knew plenty of rich Jews ; she was quite equal to creating a circle for herself.

It is more difficult to imagine why Dorset chose her ; he had gone, in the main, for the small, dark, brilliant type, and Ethel, at her first Drawing-room, is said to have looked like Mont Blanc in white satin. She knew every rule in the book of etiquette by heart, and obeyed the lot of them : Dromore, after the first shock of astonishment, rather liked her. He liked formality, and felt she was dependable. The bride's father presented her with a mansion in the country, as part of her dowry, and it was understood that, while this was being got ready, the young couple would make their home at Guerdon : an infliction on Vicky, for Mrs. Dorset had no mean conception of what was due to her, and required accommodation, not only for herself and the innumerable items of her trousseau, but for her secretary, her maid and an old governess from whom it appeared she had never been separated since her childhood. The governess came as a shock to Dorset, but he was given to understand that she was part of the bargain ; he could take it or leave it.

It was said, inevitably, that he had married her on the rebound, and there can be no doubt that Dorset's choice was in part conditioned by his determination to find a complete contrast to Emily Temple. He had *cared* —after his fashion—and he wished in every way to be made to forget his caring. Ethel was handsome, and wealthy, and beautifully mannered ; her physical stamina was almost equal to his own ; she was not troubled with the sensibilities. He was in the strong position of being loved, and of giving no love in return ; he was prepared to treat her well—which, in Dorset's calculations, meant concealing his infidelities from her. If she found him out, he had both her pride and her faultless sense of behaviour to depend on ; neither would allow her to "make scenes," or to do what was no less detestable to a man of Dorset's temperament—break her heart.

So, almost before the Guerdon family had regained its breath from the announcement, they were married, and departed on their honeymoon a week or two before Dromore went down to Southampton to meet his second son, and to travel back in a special ambulance coach with the supine Gilbert.

Of these situations the sparse entries in the diary are mere shadows ; they stand out like peaks, dominating a period of uneasiness and tension which, in greater or less degree, involved every member of the household. It was almost a relief to have these major trials on which to peg the multitudinous irritations, spleens and tantrums that affected everyone, from the head of the family down to the outdoor staff : a relief for Dromore to turn from some very disquieting communications from his bank manager to his daughter-in-law's demands on his attention : for Selina to stop grizzling over complaints from the steward's room, about the curtailment of kitchen staff, and to focus on the problem of Gilbert's future ; for Miranda temporarily to cease fretting about Emily's continued absence from Champion Court, to indulge in sardonic conjecture on the kind of dance Ethel was likely to lead Dorset.

Unentered, also, in the diary was Vicky's dismay when, at the end of the summer, she was faced by an unexpected deficit in her missionary accounts.

" Oh, Johnny, would you just have a look at this ? " It was unusual for Miss Flood, proudly confident of her ability in financial matters, to appeal for assistance.

" What's the matter ? Have you got your sums in a mess ? " He relieved her good-humouredly of the account-book, and raised his eyebrows over the balance. " That's pretty handsome, isn't it ? "

" It's *not* handsome," said Vicky, " in comparison with last year. You see "—she brought her pencil to the elucidation of the columns—" that's for the churches ; it's not so bad. But the schools are terribly in debt ; they may even have to close the one at—I forget where, but I've got the Bishop's letter somewhere ; I'd like you to read it."

" Thanks." He laid the book back on her table, in a drawer of which she was fumbling for the letter. " Don't bother ; I don't want to see it. And there's nothing wrong with your adding up, so far as I see."

" Of course there isn't ! " said Vicky indignantly. " I only wanted you to realise how badly we need help. I thought that perhaps—perhaps—knowing how generous you are——! "

The insinuation was lost on her nephew. His hands in his pockets, Johnny shook his head.

" Not this time, Aunt Vicky. For all I care, you can close down the whole lot of the schools to-morrow."

" Well——! " She bridled. " I *would* have thought, considering all your—your Negro friends, your friend Mr. Boko——"

" Bofo. For goodness' sake, can't you remember one little ' F ? ' "

" It seems to make very little difference. And it's surely not unreasonable to assume, after all you've seen of the natives in West Africa, that you'd take some interest in their education."

" I don't give a hoot for it. We've only got one object in educating the blacks : so that they can take our orders. Anything more and it's ' Down, you nigger ! ' That may be your notion of education, Aunt Vicky. It isn't mine."

" Really, Johnny ! " She gasped her astonishment. " I'd no idea you felt—you've quite startled me—after all, your friend Mr——"

" Bofo," put in Johnny warningly.

" I'm sure he was very glad of an opportunity to show his gratitude to our noble work in the schools ! " said Vicky, tossing her head.

" You don't mean to say you asked him—— ? "

" I drew his attention to the collecting box in the hall," was the defiant reply. " Why not? Everyone who stays with us——"

" You ought to be ashamed of yourself ! " he cried at her, as the meaning of Osei's parting words flashed into his mind : " Don't let them send us any more missionaries. . . ."

" You're being very extraordinary," his aunt told him coldly. " Your friend didn't appear to find anything unusual about it. In fact," announced Vicky, " he put in a sovereign, which I thought very handsome of him."

The idea of Osei's being constrained, through courtesy, to contribute to a cause that outraged his every principle so nauseated Johnny that he found himself unable to speak. Triumphant at having gained her point, Vicky continued :

" And as for what you say about ' Down, you nigger,' how do you suppose, in a black and white society, we are going to maintain our authority, unless the ordinary natives are put in their places ? "

" One day, Aunt Vicky "—the answer came chokingly—" they may put us in our places. It's only a matter of time."

Her astonished gaze followed him to the door. He stood for a moment, holding the handle, as though he were trying to remember something. Presently he raised his head and looked at her across his shoulder.

" Has it ever struck you——? "

" Has *what* ever struck me ? " she demanded petulantly, as he paused.

" ' Black and white : ' it's always in that order, isn't it ? No one says ' white and black.' Just a coincidence—perhaps."

She sat staring after the closed door.

Johnny wasn't well. He couldn't possibly be well ! Somebody ought to take his temperature—but men were so difficult when they had anything the matter with them.

It was one more thing for Vicky to worry about ; another breath of the prevalent bad wind whose currents brushed the Dower House, and were already curling round Uncle Quentin in his den.

III

" We can't do much for the present," Harcourt told him, on the outbreak of the war, " but we can get in some spadework. There's a lot of ground to be cleared before we're sure of our foundations."

Leaning back, a little tired at the end of a long day, Johnny gazed at the dark old shipping prints, in their frames of birds'-eye maple, on the wall of his uncle's study.

" What are you starin' at ? "

" The river must have been a picture, in those days."

" It 'ud be a picture to-day," grunted Harcourt, " if we'd got a live Dock Board, instead of a bench of graven images. Those belonged to Hercules—the first Hercules : five times your grandfather. Young Fred Elson brought them to me ; picked 'em up in some sale. I've told him to keep his eye open for any of our early stuff. . . . Damme, sir, you're yawning!"

"Only because I'm comfortable. It's queer, how much more like 'us' this house seems, than Guerdon."

"So it should. It's a product of honest industry, instead of parasitism."

"Well—it's high time I was going." He stood up, stretched, and smiled at his uncle.

"You needn't go, you know." Harcourt was looking at him oddly. "There's plenty of room here for two people."

"Thank you very much——" He hesitated, wondering if he had mistaken the other's meaning.

"Well? What about it? Stubbs can go down to that kennel of yours—where is it?—in Ship Lane; pack up your traps and bring them up here." Harcourt spoke gruffly, to conceal his immense eagerness. It had suddenly come over him like a wave—the perception of the emptiness and loneliness of his existence in the big house in Berkeley Square.

"It's very kind of you, sir, but—there's Joe."

"Joe? Ah, Joe Prior." He took it like a slap in the face. "How d'you get on with him?"

"Very well. Joe's a grand fellow."

"He is—is he?" sardonically.

"Yes, he is." There were evidently to be no doubts about it. "I've got a lot to thank Joe for. It wasn't easy, you know—seven years ago—oiling myself into Queen Square! I'd have got myself into plenty of holes, if it hadn't been for Joe.

His son—or not his son? The old question, long lulled to sleep, raised itself like a snake in Harcourt's bosom. His son—perhaps; making the way easy for the one who was to supplant him. When he could speak, he said:

"So you won't leave Joe?"

"No, sir—thanks all the same." With some idea of palliating the refusal, he stammered, "He's got nobody—really—except me."

The man who had no friends rose heavily; his hand dropped with all the weight of the heavy body behind it, on Johnny's shoulder.

"That's right, my boy. Never let down your friends."

It was long before the short, crisp footsteps, traversing the Square, ceased to echo in the loft hall, up the broad staircase and even to the door of the Master's chamber. My empty house, thought Harcourt. My empty house . . .

Not all their contacts, however, were of this mellifluous nature, and it was only a few days later that a storm threatened to shatter a precariously established relationship.

In the little spare time at his disposal, the docks exerted their old spell over Johnny, and there were few days or nights when he did not walk, alone or with Joe, along the familiar waterfront. There was something that warmed his heart in rough voices calling "Good night, Jake," out of the darkness. The owners of those voices would have said "Mr. Johnny" by daylight—if they had claimed acquaintanceship at all; but it was Jake

Waters who trod the rain-sleek cobbles by night, or sought a star in the black mirror of Cumberland Basin. It was Jake Waters who ordered his pint of beer in little taverns where Johnny Flood would not have been welcome, and drank it from a mug that tasted of oil and tar and brine ; and paid his round when he won at shoveha'penny, and now and again, picked up some precious bit of news about places and people who were seldom far from his mind.

Usually he was alone. Joe's interests had narrowed themselves to a channel in which there was no place for Johnny. He felt that Joe's girls, unlike the men, never accepted him simply for himself ; that, to the former, he was *a Flood*, whose use for them and their kind was, by tradition, specific. The few who acquitted him of ulterior motive in sharing their society despised him for failing to live up to the tradition.

On the night the trouble blew up he was in the Three Queens, with a bunch of lads newly off the *Runstable* that had just tied up in Bathurst Basin. The " Queens " was no favourite resort of Johnny's, being too freely patronised by the female riff-raff of the dockside and too closely under observation by the dock police for peace-loving citizens. But it was popular with the lower deck as a handy place for the disposal of small contraband, and, seeing the *Runstable* in dock, Johnny knew where to look for his friends.

It was wearing on towards midnight, and he was thinking of taking his leave, when a squabble which, for the last half-hour, had been going on in mutters at the farther end of the tap room broke suddenly into uproar : into crashing of glass and splintering of wood. Over the faces of Johnny's companions spread the pleased anticipation of a brawl that should fittingly celebrate their homecoming ; hitching themselves from benches and edging towards the scene of the combat they got ready to participate, while Johnny, draining his mug, made towards the door. The half-scream he gave, as he came face to face with Somilu, was drowned in the din.

. . . It was not Somilu, of course, that broke from the crowd, with blood streaming from claw-marks down his frightened face. The coloured youth collided with Johnny, and the two of them half-stumbled, half-fell through the swing-door. Then the others were rolling over them, the air was full of flailing fists, a boot caught Johnny in the ribs—probably unintentionally ; but it made him fighting mad, and he swung round with doubled fists to find the culprit. He had launched a few haphazard blows before he became aware that the Negro boy was the centre of a savage onslaught. The " Queens " customers were rough, at times, but seldom savage. The instigator of the attack he localised in a big, drunken stevedore, who had one of the waterfront trulls clinging to him, egging him on.

The boy, by this time covered with blood, was staggering : reeling from punch to punch. Some of the men who hit him were laughing, treating it as a game—seeing " how much the nigger could take." Swearing between his teeth, Johnny tried to force his way into the circle ; somebody pulled him back. Then there was a shout and a sudden gap, through which Johnny plunged. The stevedore stood with his back to him, an ape-like figure in the light from the open door. Johnny looked at the spot behind his ear and packed all he had into it. He could not understand it when his fist seemed to go right through the stevedore, into space—he was falling—something stopped him—and he swung his left up—crash !—into someone's face.

" Now, then—you ; that'll do ! "

". . . Uncle Hacky." They had allowed him, after some persuasion, to ring up from the police station ; an impressive figure in blue stood by the wall box as he used it. " I say—I'm sorry to tell you—I'm in quod."

A rumble of imprecation was distorted by the instrument to squeals.

" I'm in for obstructing the law," roared Johnny. " You'd better come down if you can. They won't listen to me."

" You must have taken leave of your senses." In no previous mood of anger, he realised, had Harcourt ever spoken to him in that tone of freezing contempt. Consciousness of a torn sleeve and a promising lump under one eye made it difficult to meet the attack with dignity. He stood in sullen silence while Harcourt paid over the sum of money that prevented his spending the night in a cell and followed his uncle silently into the street.

" I don't want to look at you ! I don't want to speak to you ! "

" I'm sorry," he muttered.

" I'll see to it you're sorry ! So that's the sort of company you keep. By God, no wonder you didn't want to come and live in Berkeley Square ! "

" I'll tell you all about it—to-morrow."

There was something in the whisper that, enraged as he was, took the edge off Harcourt's fury. He struck the ferrule of his stick on the pavement.

" If you were a couple of years younger I'd beat the lights out of you, with my stick—with my stick ! " But as they walked towards Park Street he got some version of the story out of his crestfallen companion.

" They said he hadn't paid for his lodging. His tale is she went through his pockets, and he'd got nothing left to pay with. Then it seems she set her pimp on him——"

" Jesus God, what had it got to do with you ? " exploded Harcourt.

" What would you do, if you saw a chap being murdered ? Stand by with your hands in your pockets ? "

" Don't talk such twaddle. You can't ' murder ' a nigger ! " sneered his uncle disgustedly. " Whenever a nigger comes ashore he makes for a whore shop ; do you need *me* to tell you that ? "

" The reason they make for the whore shop is they've got nowhere else to go. He says he'd tried all the lodgings ; they wouldn't take him in. God dammit—there's not supposed to be discrimination here ! But it looks as if we're as bad as the United States."

" The United States know what they're doing. We've got houses over here, as they have there, that cater for the blacks. If they try pushing themselves where they're not wanted, they know what to expect. What do you think the Seamen's Missions for ? "

" Supposing the houses are full ? "

" There are plenty of honest poor devils sleeping down there." He lifted his stick and pointed to where, beyond the pitch darkness, the tongue of the river lapped St. Augustine's Back.

"On a night like this?" Ever since dusk the rain had been falling heavily. At every other step they took, puddles shot their cold content up into the cuffs of both men's trousers. "Choose between pneumonia and the clap; is that the idea—if you're a nigger?"

". . . Good night," said Harcourt, after a long silence. Neither saw fit to comment on the fact that their uneasy companionship had led them to Harcourt's doorstep. He raised his hand to the bell—he would never be troubled to carry house keys—touching his hat to Johnny, as to a stranger. Silently returning the salute, Johnny swung on his heel. The rain plastered his torn coat to his shoulders and chest, as he beat his way back to the lower town.

IV

He felt the great room cold and antagonistic, like its occupant. He had just returned from another encounter, as little warranted to raise his sense of personal dignity. It happened to be Alfred Cruikshank's turn on the Bench. Johnny was not the only one conscious of the malicious satisfaction an ex-director of Floods derived from sentencing the nephew of his former Chairman for "an act against the preservation of law and order within the City boundary"—having failed, despite vicious cross-examination of the young policeman Johnny had hit in the face, to pin a charge of "drunk and disorderly" on him. Wall-eyed, Johnny paid his fine, and was not surprised, on arriving in Queen Square, to receive a summons to his uncle's presence.

Harcourt had his elbows spread on the desk, his head down like a charging rhinoceros.

"I don't want nigger fanciers in my business."

The accusation, so unexpected, so doubly hateful from Harcourt's lips, smote the breath from his lungs and drove the blood to his head. He began to stammer, "I'm not——" And Harcourt, with an extraordinary gesture, as though he tore the words from Johnny's mouth and flung them aside, roared:

"Nigger, nigger, nigger! I'm sick of hearing 'nigger' from you."

His head spun, as he tried to remember on how many occasions the evidently opprobious topic had entered into his conversations with Harcourt. Those friendly, unguarded conversations, interrupted by chuckles, by questions from Harcourt that he answered freely and as fully as he could—was it conceivable Harcourt had been trapping him? It was a sickening thought; he found himself unable to speak.

"You hobnob with nigger on the Coast; you ask a nigger to your home; you get into a disgraceful street brawl on account of a nigger; you talk nigger to whoever will listen to you." (Who, he wondered bitterly, had been betraying him?) "D'you ever stop to think of the harm you're doing?"

" Harm to whom ? " He opposed ice to the other's fire.

" To most people who know anything about the Gold Coast the word ' nigger's ' like a red rag to a bull."

" It happens to be a word I never use. I call them Negroes."

" What do you want to call them anything at all for ? Don't you realise, you loose-tongued young fool, that for one person who tolerates your prattle about the blacks, a dozen are antagonised into packin' up our West African scheme altogether ? "

" How do you propose to keep the two separate ? " asked Johnny, after a pause in which he tried to keep control of his temper. Harcourt chose to ignore the question.

" I tell you, you're betraying us ! "

" By dragging out our dirty linen—is that it ? " He failed, this time, to keep the note of irony out of his voice. " I'm afraid it's inevitable, Uncle Hacky. Dirt breeds vermin, you know ; you've got to get rid of it—some time."

" Some time—ay ; and it's not for young upstarts like you to say when the time comes ! So far as I'm concerned," said Harcourt savagely, " the niggers can *burn*. They've done enough harm to us, and we owe 'em nothing. We've got to make the Gold Coast *pay* "—he thumped the word home with his fist on the desk before him—" in *spite* of the niggers ! In spite of their idleness, their filth and their immorality. We've got to exterminate them, if necessary, like a disease—a disease that menaces every white man who goes out to work in their god-damned country——"

" And when you've exterminated them, what do you propose to do for labour ? They say along the Coast," said Johnny slowly, " that the blacks are bad for us. But we're a million times worse for them, because we hold before their eyes a Promised Land that not one in ten thousand can ever hope to reach."

" I suppose you got that from your nigger pal ? " sneered Harcourt. " By God, if I were Drummy, you'd not have brought that black buck into my house ! "

Some dangerous look on the grey young face opposite modified the violence of his attack.

" For God's sake, boy, can't you see you're muddling the issue ? Let's get our own end right, first, then, if you've got to, tackle the nigger's. We've got to find people enough, and money enough "—again he was beating the words out with his fist—" to launch our attack on the Government : to float our private company that'll tip the scale once and for all in favour of prosperity, instead of the poor, mean grubbing-along that's been our record up to now." He waited for a moment, then, when no answer came, spoke in a voice that had lost its former truculence.

" I want you with me all the way, boy : not half of you given to our scheme and the other half-grinding some private, sentimental axe of vour own, to do with niggers' rights and niggers' wrongs—maybe there are plenty of 'em : of the latter. But this ain't the moment for considering them."

" But the one's part of the other, Uncle Hacky." He felt a great misery, a kind of shame before the older man's appeal; a passionate longing to explain, coupled with the conviction that no explanation could ever satisfy Harcourt, deep-sunk in ancient prejudice.

"Listen, Johnny," Harcourt was saying, with a patience that would have astonished any of his associates, that even astonished himself, and of which he was half-contemptuous. "We're out, both of us, after big game. But I'm the old hunter, and you're the youngster that's yet got to be blooded. Follow me, and we'll mark our quarry; go off on your own, and the whole god-dam' herd will be plunging over the edge of the horizon before we've glimpsed as much as a shadow."

It was not long after the above conversation, which, although it left Johnny miserable, and not wholly contrite, tightened the bond between them, that he paid one of many visits to London—that bright London of the end of the century: where motor vehicles brought chaos among the horse-drawn traffic, where elderly coachmen, from the elevation of their boxes, cursed the impudence of chauffeurs, and the chariot of a Die-Hard peeress was already, with its footman swinging from the straps in the rear, an anachronism in the park; where ladies took their engagement books together with their prayer-books to matins on Sunday morning and checked up on the week's functions between the Stanley Gate and the base of the Achilles statue; where social distinctions were so clearly marked that "improperly-dressed persons" could still be removed from certain purlieus reserved by tradition, although not by law, for the upper classes, and no gentleman would appear West of Piccadilly Circus save in the frockcoat and silk hat prescribed by the arbiters of masculine fashion.

Not that that world had much to say to Johnny, though, on Roan's advice, he visited the latter's tailor, and, thanks to the influence of a distinguished patron, found to his surprise that he had only a couple of days to wait before blossoming forth in a style of which, to begin with, he was distinctly self-conscious. It was, in fact, a pocket Crichton who, by way of Clifford and Burlington Streets, to give himself time to get used to the new dandyism, joined Roan at the Bristol for a glass of sherry. Roan graciously approved of the general effect, criticised a pair of gloves, led him down the Burlington Arcade to repair the defect, and mentioned, *en passant*, that the house in Halkin Street was abandoned.

"Your aunt has gone down to Wiltshire. I," said Roan, with evident satisfaction, "am in Albany: delightfully convenient." He did not say, for what. "You must dine one night."

"Thanks; I'd like that." The prospect of escape for an evening from the staid family hotel at which, by Harcourt's instructions, he was staying, with its staid, elderly waiters, its elderly, pompous patrons, was agreeable.

"By the way," said Roan, "Dorset's little ex-inamorata"—the description applied to a dozen young women, but Johnny's heart missed a beat—"is creating quite a furore this season!"

"Have you seen her?" He made his voice wooden.

"Here and there." Roan smiled, as at some satisfactory although slightly amusing memory. "She is much prettier than she gave me the impression of being, that morning, on the platform. Quite a beauty, in fact !"

" Yes," seemed to be the only suitable reply.

" I was favoured with a dance, the other night, at the Litherlands' ; quite a privilege, for an old quiz like me !" Under the dropped eyelid gleamed for an instant the coquetry of one so sure of himself that he could afford to jest about his age.

Roan's arm round Emily's slim waist. Her hand on his shoulder. Roan, with his slightly—although, one had to admit, not unbecomingly—damaged reputation, touching Emily. Sharing with her the intimate magic of the waltz.

" That was jolly for both of you. Is she still in town ?"

Roan's lifted eyebrow was evidently intended to convey to his nephew that Emily Temple's movements were no concern of his.

" My dear fellow, how should I know ? Does she hunt ? It hardly seems likely that a pretty and popular young lady should waste much of her time in our deserted metropolis, now that the season is over."

He realised how little he knew of the fashionable calendar that dictated the movements of people like Roan, and Emily Temple.

" What's this," Roan was saying, with the faint, ironical curiosity he always brought to bear on the activities of the family, " what's this about Hacky buying a newspaper ?"

Johnny thought quickly before answering ; his smile was nearly as *rusé* as the other's.

" I'm not in his confidence to that extent, sir !"

Roan's smile took on a slightly respectful nuance, as he gravely placed two fingers to the brim of one of Messrs. Lock's finest creations, and nodded his nephew good day.

V

He talked to men in offices, to men in clubs, to men in the solid, respectable taverns round the London docks, where good English meals were served in darkish rooms that smelt of beef, Yorkshire pudding and Stilton, blended with the scent of spirits each time the door to the taproom was opened. Now and again he had an appointment—usually after dinner—in a panelled library, or in some atrium reached along furlongs of empty corridor, where only the tread of the night watchman echoed : the name of Harcourt Flood opening doors hermetically sealed to less illustrious callers. He was listened to patiently, impatiently, with respect, with scepticism ; he was humoured, ridiculed, once in a while encouraged. He made the discovery that the name of Flood, theoretically all-powerful, would not, when it was put to the test, work miracles. Yes ; it was undeniable, that Gold Coast affairs needed looking into ; but when it came to fighting the Government—— ! Lips were pursed, brows knitted, heads wagged. Patiently, wearily, on his return, he recorded such interviews ; slowly and painfully the truth was borne in on him : that of fifty people he had striven to enlist to their cause, forty admitted, under pressure, to a tepid interest ; thirty-nine shrugged their shoulders and refused to commit themselves to what they allowed it to be seen they regarded as a wild-goose chase. Forty-eight out of fifty wanted to know, more or less directly, what they, individually, got out of it. The majority made it plain that, with affairs at sixes and sevens in South Africa, it was something of a presumption to expect people to spare time for the interests of the Gold Coast.

Sometimes he found himself sharply aware of things he had formerly ignored, or to which he had accorded a mere sharp, mechanical act of pity : the solicitation of a shabby whore, the bare feet of a newspaper lad in the icy slime of the gutter, bundles of rag and paper with a human, or half-human, core, in archways, or crouched behind dustbins in the entrances to shops ; a woman with a child wrapped in her shawl begging for coppers outside a tavern, an old man raking through a garbage pail in search of scraps of food, a ragged child snatching the skin of a rotten banana from the pavement and avidly devouring it. Could, indeed, a Government with these things on its hands, and under its nose—the great, crimson, Victorian nose ! —be expected to sympathise with the plight of a few subjects it had—luckily—got out of its way, into one of its distanter outposts ? He felt, at such moments, the rising of a wave of discouragement, which he set his teeth to resist. For the sake of Osei and his people, they must go on. The vicious circle must be broken—whatever went into the breaking.

Back again to Bristol, with nothing very definite to report ; no successes to boast of ; no notable names to add to the list of those who would be interested in a scheme urgently affecting the commercial future of the Gold Coast. He marvelled, sometimes, at Harcourt's patience ; at the stubborn philosophy with which he brushed aside disappointments and set about devising another approach. Would they have made more progress if Harcourt had set in person about these preliminaries ? Was it that the people they desired to interest were offset by being approached by so unimportant an emissary ? Harcourt shook his head on the suggestion, when Johnny put it forward.

" They know as well as we do that you're my mouthpiece. When they're ready to talk, I'll be there to do the talking. You ain't suggesting I waste my time going round hat in hand, begging for a hearing ? " he snorted, and cursed South Africa violently. " Those damned Boers have ditched us, for the time being." It was then he told Johnny he had bought the *Diorama* —familiarly known as the " Old Di," a weekly much respected by the soberer element of the public for the soundness of its democratic views, whose small but steady circulation had recently suffered from the competition of its more sensational rivals.

" That'll be our spearhead. We'll not have our stuff cut down by some blasted sub-editor whose notion of front-page layout's an East End murder and a Gaiety girl's wedding ! We'll give 'em West African stuff, and we'll hold their noses in it till they sneeze," said Harcourt, with satisfaction.

" They say it's social news sells the papers to-day." Johnny was thoughtful. "I don't know what sort of a kick they'll get out of hearing that Mrs. Kaboha Komuntale cut a hell of a dash in a puce sateen that set off her Cross and Blackwell's complexion to perfection, at the missionary bun-fight on Tuesday the twenty-second——"

"Don't be an ass." But Harcourt chuckled. The more difficult it was the more he enjoyed it; his obstinacy, as well as his confidence, inspired Johnny on his next visit to town.

The same dispiriting round; the same search for someone with sufficient imagination, as well as sympathy, to pledge himself to what Johnny now saw as a declaration of war on the Government. At least the Colonial Office was aware of them; a couple of Harcourt's pungent letters had set up a fluster in Whitehall. Where *was* that document which one or two people dimly remembered having seen? Which had something to do with drainage of swamps—a score of such, at least, having reached Authority, and been pigeon-holed, during the last decade. "Dear Sir, We are fully aware of the importance of the matter you call to our attention, and can give you our assurance." No assurance was going to satisfy Harcourt Flood: that fact was impressed on clerks, agitatedly riffling through files of dusty correspondence, on under-secretaries whose business it was to know what the clerks were doing, on secretaries who, having received tacit instructions to forget, were now aggrieved at being required to remember matters most untimely raised by that annoying old trouble-maker down in Bristol.

He found some compensation for the many setbacks, for the brooding sense of ineffectuality which threatened at times to sap all his energies, in being able to pay regular visits to Harley Street, and to get to know Morris's friend, Whittick, not only as a doctor, but as a friend. The malarial condition was not under control, though he still had occasional bouts, at lengthening intervals, of the tremors which the most pernicious of all diseases leaves as a reminder with all who have succumbed to "Yellow Jack;" but the pains in his head, which Whittick was treating with a drug, still, he admitted, in its experimental stages, had subsided from hours of torture to brief, though none the less agonising stabs, which passed quickly, leaving only a sensation of weakness and exhaustion that vanished within the hour. As for the Face . . .

"Been seeing it lately?" Whittick inquired, in his usual matter-of-fact way, when Johnny went in.

He nodded. The Face was there—most of the time. It was just that he was getting experienced in dodging it. He had begun to know by instinct where not to look: and it was only when the wretched Thing managed to slip in between him and the book or paper he happened to be reading—as it had once or twice succeeded in doing—that he was unable to ignore it. It had been a great deal better—in the sense of being more endurable—since discovering how completely Whittick took it for granted, as an acknowledged symptom of a disease which might reasonably be expected, in time, to surrender to treatment. Whittick, a little, wizened, toothless man, incorrigibly untidy and shabby in his clothing—at their first meeting, Johnny had marvelled that a great Harley Street name should be accompanied by such indifference to appearances—had practised for two years in Accra, to get his hand in—so he said—on tropical pathologies.

"I'd like you to see Dietrich."

"Who's he? Never heard of him."

Whittick grinned a little. He kept his eyes away from his patient—thin, grey-faced, much too old for his years: yes, this Johnny Flood had a worse dose of West Africa than any he had treated for the last decade.

"Didn't suppose you would have. He lives in Salzburg."

"Oh; a German." After a pause: "What's his line? Mental?"

Whittick clicked his tongue impatiently against his gums.

"I wish you'd get out of the way of looking on yourself as an asylum case."

"Isn't that where most people would put me?" Johnny had forced himself to this conclusion, in preference to the possibility of having it forced on him. In one cell of his brain—the cell that the Face inhabited—he was mad. Why not accept it? Whittick's denials were the only thing that irritated him about the little doctor.

"Most people are damn' fools. I've told you until I'm tired that you're a victim of very powerful, very highly cultivated suggestion, which, though it only acts, as a rule, on primitive minds, can, in a moment of unpreparedness, gain hold on a product of a cultured society." Whittick sighed. "I can't put it any more plainly, without resorting to a vocabulary that would leave you no wiser than you were before I started. You've either got to wait for it to wear off, or—in my opinion you'd better go and see Dietrich."

"What? To Salzburg? Not likely," said Johnny. Capering off to Salzburg, to see a doctor! A pretty thing to explain to the family—to Harcourt—considering that none of them knew anything about it, nor should, so long as he had power to prevent it.

"He's in London, every now and then," said Whittick, as though he had had enough of the subject. "I'd have to write to him and fix an appointment for you——"

"And what would *he* do?"

"Hypnotise you," said Whittick calmly.

"You're joking."

"Hypnosis—witchcraft; synonyms, aren't they?" Whittick's toothless grin made mock of the other's ignorance. "'Set a witch to catch a witch'—eh? Ah, well; I wonder how long it will be before the muttonheaded public—in which category I'm pleased to put you, my friend—has progressed to the point of recognising the power of mind over mind as an exact science? Look here, Johnny: if you want to drive out one suggestion, you've got to put another in its place. That's common sense, isn't it?"

"Sounds like it—except it just boils down to 'think about something else,' doesn't it?"

Whittick groaned; the fondness of the lay mind for inventing a *cliché* to express the result of generations of scientific thought was no novelty to him.

"I'm all for simplicity," was his dry response, "except when it runs over the edge, into a plane of sheer imbecility. Neither you nor I can get rid of this bee—we'll call it, this Face—in your bonnet until we've got something strong enough to lever it out and keep it out, where it belongs. That, my bright lad, is a specialist's job, and Dietrich's your man. He'll charge you anything over a hundred guineas. In your place, I'd think it worth it."

"Yes; but do I go and tell Dietrich I've been witched? You know, Whittick, I've been thinking this business over; and, candidly, I'm beginning to lose belief in it myself. Couldn't it be some sort of hallucinatory bug—picked up very likely in the village——?"

Whittick sighed again.

"The first part of your remark," he said plaintively, "encouraged me in the impression that you're making progress; the second leaves me with the very poorest opinion of your general intelligence. *a*, There's no such thing as a 'hallucinatory bug;' *b*, I wish to God you'd not talk balderdash; I'm a busy man, and I haven't got time to listen to your gug-gug-gug—like a four months' child in its bassinet."

"Sorry. I was only trying to rationalise myself," grinned Johnny.

"Leave the rationalising to me—and to Dietrich, if you've got any sense. Now listen to me." Leaning back in his chair, Whittick ticked off a point on an iodine-stained thumb. "God knows we've been over this time and time again, but it's vital enough to bear repetition. First, as regards credulity.

"You say you are beginning to lose belief in your own past experience. Good—in a way; it shows that the mind is getting ready to receive help; in other words, that we're no longer up against that obstinate resistance which was an earlier stage of the disease. Candidly, I don't believe my dope has got much to do with that. You've got yourself to thank, for your insistence on living an absolutely normal life. I've seen other people settle down into the rôle of 'the haunted man;' it's very difficult to do much with those cases.

"In another way, it's bad; because what I—or Dietrich—hope to do for you is in a way conditional upon your absolute acceptance of the fact that you have, as you call it, been witched. You've got to take that, Johnny, whether you like it or not, and look it straight in the face—"

Johnny burst out laughing; even Whittick smirked a little—impatiently—at the appositeness of his metaphor. Waving a dismissive hand, he continued:

"Another point to be taken into consideration is, you're a sensitive."

"I suppose you wouldn't let me have that, in writing, to present to our Chairman, would you?"

For once, Whittick lost his temper.

"That's enough of your smart-alecking. Unless you're prepared to take this seriously—get out. I'm a little too old to appreciate schoolboy wit."

Inwardly grateful for his promotion from the bassinet to the schoolroom, Johnny apologised, and was serious.

"Your sensitivity," continued Whittick, ignoring the apology, "operates for and against you. It exposes you to influences which don't affect the majority of people ; at the same time, it may facilitate the discovery of counter-influences, and so provide its own anti-toxin to the poison already absorbed into the system."

" I take it you mean mental poison," ventured Johnny.

Whittick nodded grudgingly. It was not worth while troubling to correct people who persisted in translating every statement into their own idiom. He went on groping for words that would not need translation, even for the elementary understanding of a non-scientific young man.

" You got your first dose," he continued, " down on the coast. You are, incidentally, the only first-hand case I've ever come across, of a white person ' seeing blood.' "

" I suppose it was blood ; it was pinkish, and sticky—and it hadn't been there before."

" And, allowing for the fact you'd got a temperature, and your head was chock-a-block with old slaving yarns, and the place had a bad reputation —we might put a question mark to that," nodded Whittick. " But not dismiss it completely. Personally, I've not the least doubt you made contact, that night, in some shape or form, with fetish. They say fetish is only operative to the degree one lends credence to it ; I wouldn't agree. There's an enormous projective force behind it, which, when properly directed, can affect, in my opinion, almost anyone at whom it is aimed. To varying degrees, of course. You're a natural for it."

" But why ? "

" How should I know ? " Whittick shrugged. " Something in your occult make-up ; possibly something in heredity—there's no point in conjecturing. The fact remains that, of twenty people who come into the range of fetish, or witchcraft—keep the two distinct in your mind—though all may be affected, only one may produce a conscious reaction : and the explanation for that lies down Dietrich's street, not mine.

" The working of the ' Face ' charm "—he hunched himself deeper into his chair—" is not known, so far as I'm aware, to any white person. It is, however, known to be only the prerogative of very skilled and experienced practitioners in witchcraft, and is said to be handed down in families. It's the worst form of curse you can put on anybody, and any black who gets it invariably goes mad, before he dies. The comic feature in your case is the mixture of the ' Face ' with that bit of old-fashioned fangaree with the lizard." Whittick grinned and folded his hands cosily over his stomach. " Now, that suggests to me that the person doing the witching wasn't quite sure of herself. A kind of ' Morton's Fork ! ' Missing you on one prong, she wanted to make certain of not missing you on the other."

" I can't give you any help over that." Johnny shook his head. " I never saw the old party until we got up to Omo, and I don't actually remember a thing after hearing the crack, and turning round, and feeling as if somebody'd driven a pickaxe into the front of my skull—the rest's what Morris told me."

Whittick nodded again.

" Yes, yes—that's the form it takes. The trick consists, so far as 'mechanics' go, of striking a living animal, with intent to affect, in the place where the blow falls, the human object of ill-will. Could be an arm or a leg—see? Or a nasty rap across the kidneys. Akosua's blow fell, evidently, across the head. The operative factors are, actually, will-power, comprising absolute belief, of the subject, and the unpreparedness of the object: the latter being secured, of course, by the snapping of the twig."

"You mean, if the crack hadn't taken me by surprise——?"

"That's it. Your personal guard"—Whittick emphasised this—"was absent. What that is"—he hunched his shoulders—"I can't say; intellect, or religion, or a habit of mind—might be any of them. The point is, it was disturbed, made void, robbed of its effective quality. Assailed by an enormous conviction, highly centralised, it permitted the infection of a brain-cell—in fact," Whittick chuckled, "if she hadn't made a mull of it, by trying to crowd one charm on top of another, the chances are about ten to one that, instead of sitting here, having a cosy chat about it, you'd be in a strait-jacket, or in one of those handy holes you described to me up on the hillside. Teaches you a lesson—not to be venomous," concluded Whittick.

"Maybe she was feeling venomous. She'd just had two of her sons killed."

"Sounds fair. Well—if the average Christian had one-tenth as much belief in his own fetish that the Negroes have in theirs—'black magic,' as we call it, would have no power over us. The effect of culture is, however, to reduce credulity, and you can take it as a generalisation that, the higher the degree of culture in the individual, the more prone he is to scepticism. Unfortunate, but true. Not," added Whittick with a grimace, "that you're in danger—from culture. You're one of the people who are sympathetic to the coloured races, aren't you, Johnny?"

"Yes. I suppose I am."

"So am I. Do you know what I think? That civilisation—our sort, I mean—'s the damnedest thing we ever forced on them."

"But a great many are asking for it——"

"Give it them, give it them!" cried Whittick. "Great God—who wants to stop them having it, if they ask? But the majority *don't* ask—or don't know what they're asking for. And, I tell you, it's murder, giving it to them. It's like pumping strychnine into a man with a normal heart-beat: setting up a palpitation that'll end by killing him."

"We've gone too far now. It's too late to draw back."

"You're right—unfortunately. But they'll get over it," said Whittick cheerfully. "Like John Brown's body, they'll go marching on! Pah—it 'd take more than civilisation to destroy the virility of a race that's not only survived its environment but its own in-breeding, since the beginning of time."

"Yes—they'll go marching on——" The Face was so clear that it seemed incredible Whittick did not see it too. "Marching to glory—across red-hot cinders—for the next century—or three—or four—or five—— What's that for?"

Whittick was pushing a glass into his hand.

" Knock it back. And for pity's sake, clear out! Do you know you've kept me yammering three-quarters of an hour? God knows how many people there are in the waiting-room."

Johnny drank. When he set the glass down, the Face had faded, and he had the odd sensation of coming out of a stupor, or a sleep.

" I say "—doubtfully—" did I—was I—I haven't been saying—or doing—anything peculiar, have I? " he asked, with suspicion.

" Not a thing," Whittick assured him gravely. " Now get along, and think over the trip to Germany. Johnny! " he called, as his patient reached the door.

Whittick came down the room slowly—a grand room, a typical Harley Street room—much the smallest and shabbiest object in it.

" I've got no desire to pry into your private affairs. But, if I were you, I wouldn't get married without seeing Dietrich."

" I'm not thinking of getting married," he said sharply.

" Good. Good." Whittick turned away.

" Do you mean, it might affect—the children? "

" Nonsense—balderdash—blether! " Whittick spluttered into rage. It was a moment or two before he recovered his equanimity. " Nothing whatever to do with the children," he brought out eventually. As though regretting he had spoken, he turned on his heel, and paced furiously up and down the carpet several times.

" If you want to know—I was only thinking—it would be rather hard on a nice girl—to find her husband—looking away past her shoulder—on her wedding night."

". . . You'd better fix it up with Dietrich," said Johnny.

Towards Christmas, Johnny was placed in a position of great difficulty. On his return from the Coast, he had not rejoined the Volunteers. His decision not to do so—which caused him much heart-burning—was partly independent, partly the outcome of Harcourt's plainly expressed wishes. The cause of South Africa—Harcourt pointed out—was not going to be seriously prejudiced by the loss of one amateur soldier; whereas the cause of West Africa, while it would be a pity if Johnny got it into his head it in any way depended on him—needed as much attention as anyone could find time to give it. Johnny had taken upon himself the position, for the moment, of a key man at the Bristol end of it; his uncle made it sufficiently plain that he would take a poor view of Johnny's giving up a task of undoubted drudgery for a couple of months' sport, Boer-chivvying in the Transvaal.

It was made harder because Joe had just got his sergeant's stripes; and it was from Joe that he learned that the earnest plea of the Second Gloucesters to be sent out to the Cape had had a favourable reception, and that a number of members of the Rifle Volunteers and Yeomanry Corps and Engine Volunteers were offering their services, which were not likely to be refused.

" I've made up my mind to go, Johnny."

It was hard, not to be envious; not to betray one's envy.

"Have you told the Chairman?"

"Not yet; I'm going to see him to-morrow." The set of Joe's jaw made it clear that with or without the Chairman's approval, he was going to carry out his resolution.

"And—Polly?"

Joe's good, plain face wrinkled into a wry smile.

"She was tickled by my stripe; but I reckon I'll just be a plain Tommy, if they'll have me in the Gloucesters."

"She's not given you her answer? She is a little—bitch! I can't imagine what she's up to," said Johnny vexedly.

"Perhaps if I get wounded she'll think more of me," was the simple answer.

"Well—you can depend on me to keep an eye on her for you; and if she gets up to any pranks, I'll make Miss Polly ashamed of herself!"

No one knows what passed between Harcourt Flood and the boy who may have been his son, in the brief interview that passed behind the closed door of the Chairman's room. Harcourt was called away immediately afterwards, and Johnny, summoned to hold the fort in his absence, noticed a scribble on the corner of a blotting-pad: a woman's name, and an address in Chicago. They conveyed nothing to him, for Joe never spoke of his mother. In case, however, they should be important he entered them in the firm's address book. He was glad of such small ways of employing himself, when Harcourt left him with no specified instructions for the disposal of his time.

VI

This was the winter when a little breath of something too faint to be called gossip began to steal through the drawing-rooms of Mayfair.

"Emily Temple . . ."

"Emily is much more amusing than she used to be; supposing we ask her and Buff to make another couple?"

Emily at a studio dance in Chelsea, Emily in a "farewell" party at Romano's, Emily as the "mascot" of a racing-car, on the road to Brighton, Emily in the Row at seven o'clock in the morning, with her ex-swain, Winty Ingram—and only a groom in attendance! Emily at Tattersall's, Emily in fancy dress at Covent Garden . . . all very harmless diversions, and —apart from the outing with Winty—no absence of chaperons! Young Mrs. Winty Ingram, most dashing of the season's brides, was in high favour; she and Emily appeared to be inseparable. If not Mrs. Winty, the young Countess of Mexford was in the somewhat ludicrous position of chaperoning a girl twelve months older than herself. *Was Emily Temple on the shelf?*

"Is Lady Cullen loosening up? Or has Emily got the bit in her teeth?"

Emily at the opera, Emily at the new and fashionable ice-rink, Emily even so far afield as St. Moritz, and up in Scotland at somebody's castle. . . . Emily, in fact, everywhere excepting at those sedate gatherings, those stately receptions, the dinner parties whose guests appeared next morning in the Court Circular—where once she had bloomed, at her guardian's side. " Where is your charming daughter, Lady Cullen ? " Few people now put the word " daughter " into inverted commas. " It is so disappointing, to see so little of her. I hope she is not becoming quite a recluse ! "

" Oh, not at all ! " What mother, whether by birth or adoption, would brook the insinuation that her daughter is out of the social running? " Emily has her own circle of friends, now, you know. Indeed, her engagement book is even fuller than mine."

Emily, " skirt-dancing," on behalf of charity, before an exalted audience. Emily on the Jockey Club stand—where, it was rumoured, she caught a very exalted Eye.

" Lady Russell said she saw you at Newmarket, with some *very conspicuous* people ! "

She caught her breath. Was she beginning to be " talked about ? " Had she won her way into that bright galaxy of dashing Society girls who lightly captured, and as lightly flung away, the devotions of the hunting male—like Dorset Flood ?

CHAPTER SEVEN

I

THE old century died, to the strains of *The Absent-Minded Beggar*, to *The Honeysuckle and the Bee*, to Black Week—Stormberg, Magersfontein, Colenso, in rapid succession : an ominous conclusion. In a sleety, wind-swept February, Johnny's landlady gave permission to her young gentlemen to have two young ladies to tea.

The only day possible was Sunday—which meant the cancellation of the week-end at Guerdon—because it was the only day on which the female assistants at Mercer's drapery store (all of whom, according to the custom of the day, lived in) were at liberty to indulge in social diversions. Polly and her friend—a pretty little dark girl, introduced as Miss Livingstone from the haberdashery—arrived in a downpour of rain ; there was enough to do about getting the girls' capes dried, their umbrellas sent to drip in the kitchen sink and their feet—Polly's in Joe's, Miss Livingstone's in Johnny's slippers—disposed on the bright fender, to eliminate any stiffness at the beginning. Coquettish jokes, relating to the smallness of the girls' feet and the inappropriate size of the slippers filled in time until the serving of a lavish tea, to which three of the party did ample justice. It was unusual to see Polly failing of her appreciation of the luxuries of the table.

" Polly, I believe you've been stuffing already ! " Johnny tried to relieve the situation with a clumsy jest.

" I believe she's caught a chill," Miss Livingstone offered, in support of her friend.

" Feed a cold and starve a fever, isn't it? Come, Polly, you must do your share!"

" I don't know what it is, I don't seem to fancy anything; I must be fretting, because Joe's going away!"

The flash of light that overspread Joe's face died on her grimace. Johnny felt it would have been a pleasure to have taken Polly Bowling and spanked her.

The tea party tailed away rather dismally in an exhibition of good manners, the gay Miss Livingstone doing her best not to show boredom when the conversation fell back on reminiscences which she could not share, Johnny exerting himself to his utmost to cover the gloom of Joe. It would have been something of a relief if Polly had indulged in her habitual teasing; instead, she was quiet, even wistful. Johnny wondered if this might be a good sign, and if she cared more about Joe's going than she chose to admit.

But when the bells started for evensong, and the girls said they must be going—not because either was going to church, but because it was unheard of, to prolong an invitation to Sunday tea beyond " church-time"—he was taken aback to see Joe hurry ahead with Miss Livingstone, leaving him to follow with Polly.

The rain had stopped, and although the cobbles were sleek with mud, and patched with the reflections of the lamps, the air was fresh and clean. He felt that, for Joe's sake, here was an opportunity which must not be neglected.

" Polly, have you given Joe his answer yet?"

She did not reply, and, for a moment, he wondered if she had heard—preoccupied in holding her long skirt out of the puddles that made a series of hazards of the uneven pavement. Feeling a little foolish, he tried again.

" Polly—I know it's none of my business; but I do think you should tell Joe, you know, before he leaves for South Africa."

She stopped under a lamp. Its shadows, flung into the plump curves of her face, aged, and, in some strange way, beautified it. She had altered, since being in Bristol; it struck him that she was more refined, quieter in her dress and bearing; that anyone, seeing them together, might take her for a girl of his own class. Ashamed of the snobbery of the thought, he felt himself colouring. She said quietly:

" I shall never marry Joe, Johnny."

It was the first time she had ever called him by his Christian name, without the respectful prefix, but it seemed natural to both. Her eyes, deeper and sadder than he had ever known them, begged his understanding.

" Does he know?" asked Johnny, after a pause, in which his heart ached for his friend.

She shrugged her shoulders wearily.

" He should. We've not spoken of it, for a long time. Not this year."

" Is there . . . somebody else?"

There was a pause, before she bent her head in an acquiescence so complete that no words were necessary.

"I'm glad, Polly, for your sake. You'll let me know, won't you—before it happens?"

"There'll never be anything to know." She had laid her hand on his arm; her forlorn eyes looked into his. "I mean—there's no question of marriage—or anything like that."

"Polly. That's too bad." He did not know what to say, to comfort her.

She forced the old, frivolous smile to her lips.

"Serves me right, doesn't it? It's the biter bit—though, truly, I never did much biting. I flirted with lots of boys—but I'd begun to think I'd never fall in love. That's why I kept Joe waiting; it didn't seem fair to marry him, while he was so fond of me, and I'd got nothing to give him, but—liking."

"Are you sure? Joe's such a splendid fellow; he'd make you a good husband, Polly. I'm sure he'd do anything—for your sake."

She shook her head with melancholy decision.

"It would have been different, if I'd said 'Yes' at the beginning—when there wasn't anybody else. But now"—she stammered a little, and he had to bend his head forward to catch her words—"I'm no more use to Joe—or anybody." His silence—during which he wondered if he could possibly have mistaken the implication of her words—made her look up quickly. "I don't mean that; I'm still 'good,' if that's what you're wondering." Her face had crimsoned.

"Of course you are. You'll get over it, dear; and perhaps, when Joe comes back——"

"I shall never marry Joe Prior." She stamped her foot, as though she had had enough of this partisanship. "I wish you'd get that into your head, and put it into his!" she said, petulantly. "Whoever I marry—if ever I do marry—it won't be Joe. So please let's talk about something else."

"All right, we will. But do tell me, Polly, what's set you against Joe? I can't understand it—he's so devoted to you," blundered Johnny, conscious that he was overdoing it, but unable, for Joe's sake, to relinquish the struggle.

"That's—just—why." Her lips closed with a snap, and it was evident that she would allow no more.

She walked on rapidly, and Johnny had to hurry to keep up with her until they arrived at Mercer's side door, which the assistants used for their private comings and goings. Joe had disappeared, and when Polly rang the bell, the door was opened by Miss Livingstone, who had evidently been waiting for the purpose on the other side. Polly bade him a brusque good night and ran up the dimly lighted stairs. They heard her heels tap along an oil-clothed landing; the downstairs lobby, with its one unshaded gas burner, smelt of calico and beeswax. Little Miss Livingstone was looking at Johnny, as if she were not quite sure if it would be polite to close the door in his face. He said, to break the abruptness of their parting:

"I hope she's not ill. She doesn't seem to be quite—herself."

The girl's bright eyes measured him before replying.

"You won't say I told—if I tell you something?"

" No, indeed." He was a little afraid of what he might be going to hear. She stood on tiptoe to whisper :

" She cries—every night. We sleep in the same room, you know—eight of us : but Polly has the next bed to mine. I can't help hearing her."

" Is she unhappy—in the shop ? " It was difficult to conceive, of the light-hearted Polly.

" Oh, I don't think so ; she's a great favourite with the customers, and we all like her—she's so lively."

" You aren't—I mean, it's not bad, living here, is it ? " He tried, but found he could not imagine, the kind of life led by the " young ladies " of Mercer's store.

Miss Livingstone made a *moue.*

" Not bad—as these places go ! They give us plenty to eat, and we've not got a bad room to sit in. But it's awfully strict ! You're dismissed, if you're out after half-past nine."

" Perhaps she misses her freedom at home." He wanted to find out if she knew anything about Polly's unfortunate attachment, but it was obviously impossible to question her outright. She shook her pretty head, seemed inclined to say something, but evidently decided for discretion.

" Well, good night, sir, and thank you very much for the lovely tea party ! " The door closed gently.

Some married Bristol blade, taking advantage of a lively young country girl's ignorance and prudently retiring to the safety of the conjugal hearth on finding the affair threatened to be serious ?

When he got back to Ship Lane, Joe was sitting over the fire. He did not look round or speak when Johnny came in. He found he did not know what to say. There was a heavy silence. Presently Joe said :

" I'd like her to have my watch chain, if I don't come back."

" Rot ; of course you'll come back."

" I'd just as soon not."

" Don't talk such perishing rubbish." Because he was touched, Johnny lost his temper.

" She doesn't love me, that's plain," said Joe stoically.

For the first time, Johnny noticed some torn pieces of paper on the hearth.

" What have you been tearing up ? "

Joe looked foolish ; he bent hurriedly and put the scraps on the fire.

" I had my photo done to give her before I left. I gave it to her while you were in the kitchen." He looked up, and Johnny saw that his eyes were red, his ugly mouth twisted into a smile. " I found it here when I got in, on the mantelpiece. She'd forgotten it."

Johnny thought, Damn Polly Bowling. Aloud he said :

" Come on out and have a drink."

II

The *Diorama* was running a new series on the Crown Colony system in West Africa, to which a number of distinguished people had been asked to contribute ; unfortunately, many of the best informed on this vexed topic had little or no gift for expressing their views on paper. It was therefore arranged that they should be interviewed in turn, and the interviews written up into articles by a member of the reporting staff. It was the suggestion of the new proprietor that a good deal of time and trouble might be saved if the interviewing was handed over to his nephew, whose personal experience would enable him to pick up many points and put questions which might not occur to a layman.

So Johnny, something to his alarm, found himself, at least temporarily, a special reporter on *The Diorama*, with a corner of his own in the newsroom, where he endeavoured laboriously to decipher his own notes, scribbled—he had not the advantage of shorthand—on the leaves of writing blocks which always seemed to have a way of disintegrating and getting screwed into balls in one or another of his pockets.

There was a period—just after Joe left with the regiment for the Cape—when he saw almost nothing of Bristol. Like every other paper, *The Diorama* devoted the whole of its front page space to the war ; it was on the leader page that there began to appear that series of articles, signed by august names, but written in the newsroom by an experienced journalist, for which Johnny was responsible—articles which were read, to begin with, only by a limited number of subscribers, but which gradually began to gain a public through the correspondence they provoked. Much of it, of course, was concocted in the editorial office ; Johnny had the pleasure of acting as part-author of a scurrilous attack on one of his own articles, in the course of which he damned himself thoroughly as an anti-Imperialist, a traitor to the British cause and an arm-chair critic of matters of which he knew nothing. A paragraph adroitly slipped into one of the leaders themselves, sub-headed *Ball-and-Chain Tactics*, and revealing the obstructiveness of Colonial Office methods on trade development, brought a volume of bona fide correspondence—all, however, in tune with the paragraph itself, so abusive that Johnny was obliged to sit down and think out a defence of the entire system : which, in its turn, lit such a bonfire that it was a wonder Whitehall itself did not burst into flame.

The editor of *The Diorama*, anxious to increase his paper's circulation, took a leaf out of the books of most of his rivals and started a gossip column, the editress of which—an anxious, hard-working young woman—having gleaned, along the mysterious channels of newsroom tattle, that Johnny had "connections in Society," frequently approached him for titbits to furbish her column.

The first time she did so, he was completely taken aback.

"Me—I mean, I ? Good heavens, Miss Roper, I don't know a thing about 'Society,' as you call it !"

"But Mr. and Mrs. Roan Flood—aren't they relatives of yours?"

"Yes—but I never see——" He stopped.

"And your brother—wasn't it your brother who married the South African heiress? And Miss Temple: I'm sure you know the lovely Miss Temple! Wasn't she engaged to your brother, before he married Miss Phillipson?" she persisted.

That the private affairs of his family should be known to a little, ferreting woman journalist was a revelation to Johnny: he felt a gust of anger. Then—something about the anxiously intrusive eye, the attempt at smartness—Miss Roper had just come from a fashionable wedding—the cheap veil twisted into a little knob under a nervous chin—touched him. He said quietly:

"I'm afraid I'm quite out of touch, these days, with that side of my family. You know, I'm only a Bristol business man." The description gave him an unexpected thrill of pride.

But a Fleet Street woman was not to be defeated by such disclaimers; she not only continued to importune him for news but insisted that he should read her column, and even criticise it, despite his protestations that she knew her own job a great deal better than he knew his. Gradually he got in the way of memorising harmless bits of information which he brought her, somewhat as a bird brings back worms for a greedy nestling.

"What do you suppose old Fratton was up to, when I saw him to-day? Sitting for his portrait! If I'd got ears like kites and a nose like a strawberry, I wouldn't let a painter loose on me!"

He chuckled to see the form in which this appeared in the column the following day:

"A little bird tells me"—he could usually identify his own contributions under the coy ornithological metaphor—"that Academy-lovers have a treat in store: one of the most distinguished members of our House of Peers being at present engaged in sitting for his portrait by Sir Vesey Marvell. A Marvell portrait is always an event" (computing the output of the most prolific of contemporary portraitists, Johnny felt he was living, without having realised it, in eventful times) "and, given such a subject and such a painter, the private view at Burlington House will present a more than usually dazzling spectacle for those anxious to get a first glimpse of Sir Vesey's latest masterpiece."

Who, he wondered, would be interested in such a piece of twaddle? The smile faded from his lips as he read farther down the column.

"Among a bevy of beauty at the Shellingden ball last night, Miss Emily Temple easily maintained her pride of place. Wearing one of Worth's most exquisite creations in flowered pink and pale yellow mousseline-de-soie, the corsage outlined with ostrich tips, Miss Temple was seen chatting merrily with a group of guests, which included, among others, the master of a well-known Hunt and a popular young *Chargé d'Affaires*."

He flung the paper down and stamped out of the newsroom, unable to decide on the spur of the moment whether his anger was aimed at the painstaking Miss Roper or at the " Master of a well-known Hunt " and a " popular young *Chargé d'Affaires*."

" Would you like to come to the Haymarket, Flood ? " He was caught in the passage by *The Diorama's* dramatic critic. Usually too tired to indulge in evening diversions with his colleagues—such diversions being apt, as he knew, to develop into sessions in the Fleet Street taverns, at the Savage, or in one or another of the billiard saloons favoured by sportsmen—he had previously refused such invitations. On this occasion, probably because he was already tired, disgruntled and he wanted to thrust the too-vivid thought of Emily from his mind, he accepted.

The Diorama was not a sufficiently important Paper—*yet*, thought Johnny grimly—to command the best seats for its critics ; they found themselves at the back of the stalls, uncomfortably situated behind a side pillar. Johnny, whose tastes, like those of most people of his age, were for music and dancing, speedily lost interest in the play, and was not surprised when his companion, with a nudge and a jerk of the head, indicated his intention of going out to the Press bar. In order, however, to avoid being drawn into a drinking group, against which Whittick had cautioned him, he pretended an interest he was far from feeling, and, giving the other to understand, with a nod, that he would join him in the interval, waited, comatose, for the fall of the curtain.

When the lights went up, and most of the masculine element of the audience was crowding towards the exits, he strolled down towards the orchestra pit, to see whether, by chance, there were any people of his acquaintance in the house. He was standing with his back to the boxes, looking across the stalls, when a laugh broke on his ears.

" By George ! " thought Johnny. " That's Doss ! "

Experience warned him not to turn too quickly, to identify his brother ; Doss might be paying an unexpected visit to London with his wife, on the other hand, knowing Doss, it was quite on the cards that he might be cutting loose for an evening with one of the beguilers of his bachelor leisure—in which case it would be embarrassing for him to be recognised by his younger brother. Having allowed what he considered a discreet time to elapse, Johnny turned slowly, and scanned the boxes above him. The lowest one, on a level with his own head, was empty ; on the padded ledge of the one above lay a woman's gloved arm and hand, holding a fan. In the corner of the box, standing, with his handsome head and amused smile lowered towards his unseen companion, was Roan.

Of course it was Roan, not Dorset, who had laughed ; the similarity between the two voices, the misunderstandings it had caused in the past, came back to him in a flash. He had just decided that he was not in a mood for his uncle's persiflage, and was about to move away, when Roan looked down and saw him. There was nothing to do, but raise a hand and smile.

A look of mild surprise came over Roan's face ; he murmured something to his companion—and Emily leaned her small, jewelled head, her eager and astonished face over the balustrade.

" Johnny ! Come up—please come up at once ! " The sound of the orchestra and the hum of voices all round him made her voice inaudible, but her gesture was unmistakable. He went, in a stupor, through the nearest door, and up the stairs behind the boxes ; Roan had the door open, and was waiting for him.

"I didn't know you were a patron of the serious drama !"

The four chairs in the box were occupied ; Roan was evidently a visitor, like himself. For some reason this gave him an inexplicable satisfaction.

"Johnny !" Emily's welcome was radiant ; her hand held his, as she performed the introductions quickly. "I thought I was never going to see you."

The reply, that the fault was hers and not his, rose to Johnny's lips and was dismissed in the almost unbearable joy of meeting her.

"They keep me very busy, you know, on the paper."

"The paper ? What paper ?"

Her complete ignorance of his actions silenced him for a moment ; one could hardly begin an account of one's occupations in front of three strangers. Roan said, in his soft, ironic voice—Dorset's voice :

"They haven't given you the leader column yet."

"Not quite : only next door to it—in a manner of speaking." He answered Roan, but his smile was for Emily. She was more utterly beautiful than he remembered her—but more remote : remote from that small Emily who had stood beside him in the gazebo with her rain-sodden hat plastered round her little, pale face. Her skin had the same dewy freshness, and had not lost its exquisite texture under the powder that some of the smarter young women were beginning to wear. But that endearing suggestion of shyness, which had clung to her like a veil of gossamer, was quite gone. Her eyes met his—not boldly, but with a clear confidence, as though Emily, by now, had fully learned how to manage her own affairs and was prepared, in any situation, to maintain her own independence of thought and action.

"When are you coming to see me ?"

While Johnny hesitated :

"You had better join us for luncheon on Sunday," Roan said, including the other occupants of the box in what was evidently a general invitation. Emily spoke quickly :

"Oh, no. I mean, one can't really *talk*, at a party like that. To-morrow, Johnny ? For tea, in my sitting-room ; and I'll be 'not at home' to anyone else who happens to come."

"Thank you, Emily, that will be delightful." Whatever claims the paper might make on his time, they must wait, while this dearer summons was obeyed.

The warning bell went, and Roan left the box with him. In his elation, he hardly noticed Roan's conventional inquiry after the family, until the latter repeated it.

"No, I haven't been home for nearly three weeks, sir."

"Nor down to Hampshire, I suppose ? I fancy," said Roan with his wise smile, "that will turn out a success. The other would never have done, you know."

" The other—— ? "

" Emily Temple." A slight note of impatience sharpened the speaker's tone. " Our Dorset—a charming fellow. But too heavy-handed for a girl of that temperament. The little Temple "—the smile had returned—" has a will of her own ! "

What should Roan know of Emily's " will ? " A faint resentment of Roan's assumption of intimacy coloured Johnny's reply, and his farewell to his uncle.

" By the way, sir, I'm afraid I can't accept your invitation for Sunday —if it still stands ? Uncle Hacky wants me to go down to Bristol at the week-end."

" Pity," murmured Roan. His interest in the play seemed to be no greater than Johnny's, for, although the curtain had risen, and, through the *œil-de-bœuf* window of the swing-door they could see the figures on the stage, he showed no haste to regain his seat. Was he, by any chance, thinking of returning to the box ? Johnny swung the door open.

" After you," he said crisply.

" My dear fellow." Roan's hand gently restored the door to its former position. " This is really an amazingly dull play, is it not ? Shall we have a cigarette, and walk a little ? "

They paced the crimson carpet together, and, presently, on Roan's suggestion, got their hats and overcoats and stepped out into the empty Haymarket. Crossing over, they strolled towards St. James's Square, where Roan, who hated walking, hailed a hansom cab.

" I enjoy a short turn round the Park at this time of night ; do you care to accompany me ? "

Feeling it would be ungracious to refuse, considering how little he saw of his uncle, Johnny mounted to the seat. It seemed an odd occupation, to be driving round in a hansom with Roan, going nowhere in particular, when people were in the theatre, at their clubs, in their own drawing-rooms !

" Your Aunt Venetia used to say," Roan was chuckling, " that Dorset ought to have been shut up in a monastery, as soon as they breached him. Amazing thing—the way women lose their heads, over cads ! "

" Look here——" burst from Johnny. " Do we have to talk about all that ? It's over and done with—and Emily's affairs are her own business, after all."

" My dear fellow—of course ! I hope," said Roan formally, " that I'm not guilty of indiscretion, in voicing a curiosity which is felt, it appears, by practically everyone in Miss Temple's circle."

" Well, I can't satisfy it," growled Johnny. " If Emily's contented, I don't see what it's got to do with anybody else." His scowl on the lights brushing the darkness on either side their course, he did not see the slight lift of Roan's brows, as the latter settled himself more comfortably in his corner.

" To change the subject—I've asked your aunt if she would like her divorce."

" What did she say ? " asked Johnny, after a pause in which he wondered whether this subject was any improvement on the former. He, Gilbert and Doss—especially Doss—had always had a *tendresse* for Aunt Venetia, based, probably, on her recognition of the kind of presents schoolboys like to receive on their birthdays.

" She was most kind ; most kind and considerate," said Roan, with evident sincerity. " She said that, on her part, she had nothing to gain, and would much prefer things to remain on their present footing. Of course I agreed with her. I don't want to go through all that fuss and public to-do—and I would very much deprecate it on Venetia's account. I mention the matter to you, because I suppose they're on tenterhooks at Guerdon ? "

Johnny muttered that he supposed they were on something of the kind. Harriet had informed him on the night of his arrival that the subject of " the Roans " was one to be avoided. " One is at a loss to know what is coming to the young couples of the present day "—with a shrug of her elegant shoulders. " In my time we knew how to manage our incompatibilities ! " And he had heard, through Gilbert, some rumour of a separation. " No legal twaddle, old boy—just an amicable arrangement ! " In their matrimonial differences, no Flood ever went in for " legal twaddle ; " that was a matter of understanding in the family. Johnny wondered what had possessed his uncle to drag him in on the matter, but agreed to pass on his information, if anyone raised the subject in his hearing at home.

When they parted, he was disconcerted, and a little aghast, at the discovery, that his feeling towards Uncle Roan—who had been as much of a favourite with the boys as Aunt Venetia—had undergone a change. I do not like thee, Doctor Fell !

He strove to thrust the thought aside, but it accompanied him, like an elegant, mocking ghost, to the door of his hotel.

III

His hat freshly ironed, his boots polished, his hands discreetly covered in lavender suède, a very smart young man presented himself in Brook Street, at four of the following afternoon. At the head of the broad staircase, Emily sprang past the footman to greet him.

" Oh, Johnny—at last ! " She caught both his hands impulsively. Her sweet, artificial manner suggested that she had been waiting hours for this very moment.

A little dazed by the warmth of the welcome, he allowed himself to be drawn into a sitting-room filled with the scent of hyacinths, with *bibelots* and small bookcases and little china lamps with frilled shades ; with photographs in silver frames—mainly of girls in presentation gowns, and *jardinières* filled with potted plants. A ribboned mandoline lay on a sofa. Pinned to a corner of the draped mantelshelf was a sheaf of dance programmes, with their pink and white and blue tasselled pencils. It was so exactly the room of her age and social position—a young and popular member of what vulgar people called " the Smart Set "—that Johnny felt himself an intruder. He could not have said what he had expected ; it only seemed strange that Emily, so rare, so different from every other girl in the world, should bend her rareness to the acceptance of a universal pattern.

" Will you smoke ? " She was holding cigarettes—gold-tipped, feminine—towards him, in a china box.

" Are—are you sure you don't mind ? " he stammered.

" Mind ? " She laughed, taking one which she held delicately between the narrow tips of her fingers. " Won't you give me a light—please ? "

He tried to make a commonplace act of it ; actually, the flame, as it bit on the slim cylinder of tobacco, burned up something more than the cigarette. He found her looking at him curiously.

" You're not shocked, are you ? "

He hastened to disclaim so clownish a sentiment.

" You forget what a bumpkin I am ! I haven't had much time to get into the—the fashion, since I've been in London." Yet Miss Roper took a cigarette with her cup of afternoon tea, and it had never occurred to him to do other than take it for granted.

" I don't very often," she admitted. " Mamma disapproves—naturally ! —and I—I usually do it to make people feel at home. Not that you count as a visitor, Johnny ! " She gave him the sweetness of her smile. " Now—tell me everything about yourself."

She was attentive and kind—too kind. She might have been encouraging an awkward schoolboy. Beneath the seemingly smooth current of their conversation, each was aware of a whole lifetime of unspoken experience, a broad flood that swept between them and the past. Neither mentioned Guerdon ; for Emily the curtain was down on that—for ever. Even Miranda's name evoked no more than a gasp of, " I must write ; I owe her a letter," and was dismissed with a hurried and obviously conventional inquiry after Harriet, Selina and Vicky.

" What busy people we are—you, with your newspaper, and I, with all my nonsense ! But, seriously, Johnny, we mustn't lose each other again, as we seem to have done, ever since last—last summer." She stumbled a little on the words, and hurried on, as though to escape the memories they evoked. " It's absurd that, with both of us in London, we should not see a great deal of each other, if—if you care for the idea ! " She seemed to avoid his sober gaze : a strange, although ever to be adored Emily, for whom, indeed, much water had flowed, since their last meeting on the platform at Temple Meads.

" I'm not sure that I'm not a little hurt," she told him, " that you should not have taken more trouble to come and see me, before now ! "

" But, Emily——" He could not admit this reproach. " I did take trouble. Only a few weeks ago—"

" *What ?* " Her brows puckered.

" Have you forgotten ? You sent down a message you were dressing to go out." He remembered the palliative conclusion of the message—" Very disappointed to miss you—hopes you will call again "—and, through an open door, another voice speaking in the hall, with the assurance of privilege: " Is Miss Temple ready ? "

He remembered the leap of his heart, the sensation of blood clotting in his temples, as he followed the servant from the small back drawing-room, where, he supposed, people who called without appointments, or were unknown to the staff, were shown, to wait its mistress's pleasure. A figure was mounting the stairs, with its back to him ; beside the open street door, a footman was holding a man's evening cape, and a gibus. Johnny passed him blindly.

There was a brougham, with another servant by the wheel. He caught a glimpse of two figures : of a man, leaning forward to light his companion's cigarette, and of the flame briefly catching a girl's jewels, her uncovered bosom. He walked a few paces and halted, fighting the almost uncontrollable impulse to go back ; to snatch the gibus out of the hand of the man in the hall and read the name stamped on its silk lining. " *Is Miss Temple ready ?* " Were there two—no, three—such voices in the world ?—or was it just hallucination, born of a disgraceful envy ?

All this he had forced into the back of his mind—he had made himself forget it—until this moment, when he looked into Emily's burning face.

" Oh, yes. Yes—I do remember," she was gasping, as though the words threatened to choke her. " But you mustn't be offended—I have scores of visitors—and I wasn't expecting you ! "

" Of course I wasn't offended, and it was all my fault," he told her, with compunction for her agitation.

" Oh, well—*passons l'éponge là-dessus* ! " She had recovered her self-possession. " And, to make up for it, how would you like to take me to a *matinée* ? "

" I'd love it. Do you think Lady Cullen would let us ? "

She gave him a wide-eyed look of astonishment, that ended in a nervous little laugh.

" Oh, Johnny, doesn't that prove how long it is since we saw one another ? I'm an independent person now." She sighed, leaning back in the chair. " It's been a tussle ! But I've *almost* convinced Mamma that things are rather different from the days when she was a girl. I'm allowed to make up my own engagement book, and though she doesn't approve of all of my friends—well, I suppose she feels it is better not to interfere. After all—one must live one's own life : mustn't one ? "

He agreed, gravely, with the youthful *cliché*. Their eyes met ; she brought out suddenly—breathlessly :

" Do you think I've altered—much ? " And bit her lip, as though regretting she had spoken.

" Very much."

" Not for the worse, I hope ! " He felt her mocking him through her flippancy. " Don't let's be solemn ! " she begged. " I don't like solemn people : they frighten me. And I think the war has made everything very gay, don't you ? That sounds shocking, I know ; but when people are going to South Africa, they expect to have a good time before they leave, and, naturally, one tries to make it as amusing as possible. Oh—excuse me!" She strangled a little yawn with her fingertips. "I was dancing until four o'clock this morning. I'm sure you weren't doing anything so frivolous."

Did it mean that she was finding him a bore? A pang went through him. Did she ever think of their Christmas parties? Of hopping round in the polka, passing under the mistletoe—of which he was too shy to take advantage?

"Oh, Johnny," she was saying, "I'm terribly glad you haven't gone to South Africa."

"Are you? I feel a shirker, sometimes," he added, on so low a note that she had to bend forward to catch the words.

"Do you? *That*"—it was the old Emily who spoke, stressing her words in the old, sweet, childish way—"is the very last thing anyone could call *you*, Johnny."

Then, as though gravity scared her, she flung the subject aside, and, for the next hour, chattered of people and places of which he knew nothing, but in which he tried to take an interest, for her sake.

"Do you know Candleby? I've been asked there, after Goodwood. I'm terribly thrilled! Very few girls get invited; it's mostly the very gay married set and one or two important actresses. It's an enormous compliment, to be asked to Candleby—why are you looking at me?" she broke off to ask.

"I was thinking," he said, "that it would do you good to go somewhere—to the sea—or—or anywhere where you can just laze about and not do anything in particular—after you've got all this racket over."

"How very ungallant of you, Johnny, to suggest that I'm not looking my best!" Her hands had flown to her face, but the indignation rang false; he got the impression that she was pleading with him, begging him for something, behind it.

"You always look your best, to me," he told her stubbornly. "But a fortnight of the kind of times you've been describing would slay me—and you never were very strong, were you, Emily?"

"Oh—the past, the past; why can't you let it alone?" The cry of impatience took him by surprise; when had they spoken of the past? Then he knew that all her animation, the spate of her chatter had been intended deliberately to hold the past at bay, and he felt for her an agonising tenderness, less simple than the old love and much less happy.

"Is the present better than the past?"

"What do you mean?" she asked him, as though she resented the question.

"You used to enjoy our quiet times, down in the country."

A spasm not far removed from horror crossed her face.

"I loathe 'quiet times'—and I can't bear places where there's nothing to do but think."

. . . The artificial light of the theatre, her own gaiety and the rapture of meeting her after their long separation had concealed from him things that haunted Johnny's mind when he left Brook Street. She was very thin;

there were faint hollows in her cheeks, and under the fine lace of her blouse her collar-bones made a distinct ridge that displaced the thin gold chain of a pendant she wore. She who used to be still and, even as a child, reposeful, was now full of nervous little gestures, of tricks copied from older women ; her beautiful eyes slid constantly to one of her several mirrors ; she touched her hair, or a bracelet, or arranged a fold of her gown, as though perpetually conscious of an effect she wished to produce ; and these were not gestures that belonged to a spirit at peace. With one hand she offered him friendship, with the other she warned him to lay no trust in the intimacies of yesterday, to base no claims for the future on those of the past. . . .

Harriet's exhortation buzzed in his mind like a gadfly. At one moment he had almost decided to act upon it ; at the next, a horror of ruining his chances by premature action made him thrust it aside. Yet how, unless he proposed to her, and was accepted, could he protect her as—he made no doubt of it—she needed to be protected ? How rescue her from this vortex in which she was spinning ? How exorcise Emily's ghosts, that came and went in the shadow of her smiles and lent their hollow echoes to her laughter ? And how achieve all these things and continue to do his duty to Harcourt, to the work which, day after day, claimed more of his thought and energies ?

Dawn was sliding through a slit in the curtains of his hotel bedroom before Johnny fell into exhausted sleep. He had reached no conclusions—save that he was, for ever and ever, for better or worse, Emily's, and that some day, God willing, she would, in accepting his love, lose her horror of places " where there was nothing to do but think."

CHAPTER EIGHT

I

"WE'VE had a slap in the face," Harcourt greeted him, as he walked into the dining-room. " They've found Prewett's scheme."

" Never ! "

Harcourt picked up the letter lying at his elbow.

" ' Dear Sir,' " he read aloud. " ' The documents which form the subject of our previous correspondence are now available for your inspection at any time convenient to yourself. In order, however, that you should not be put to unnecessary inconvenience, the report of the Chief Engineer is herewith enclosed, for perusal at your leisure.' "

" Which means exactly—what ? " He caught the thick envelope that Harcourt tossed towards him.

" I'm not a technician," grunted his uncle, " and two-thirds of the jargon conveys nothing to me. Summed up, however, it means the scheme's no good."

" No good ? But it was approved by Accra." Frowning, he ran his eye down the typewritten sheets. Harcourt gave him time to read them ; when Johnny looked up, he was grinning.

" Well, how much wiser are you ? "

" I suppose one's got to admit they've been examined—not just shoved in a pigeon-hole. I see the report's dated eighteen months back." He said it grudgingly. " Well—they've spiked that gun for us : damn them ! "

" Take it easy," Harcourt advised. " One thing stands out a mile—our articles have been getting under their hide. I lay that's created hell for a few people ! " He chuckled.

" All the same," said Johnny, after reflection, " I don't see that we've got to accept this report, just as it stands. They aren't fools, in Accra—and the view they take is likely to be a lot more practical than that of some fellow over here with a string of letters after his name, and no more experience of local conditions than I have of the North Pole ! What about getting hold of the plans themselves and having an independent opinion ? "

" And then what ? " There was a note of irony in the speaker's voice that Johnny challenged with his reply.

" Well—I suppose the next step would be to see whether sufficient money could be raised privately to float the scheme, independently of the Government."

" Wait a minute, wait a minute. You young hounds," said Harcourt, not ill-temperedly—" you're all the same ! You will go after the hares, while the fox gets away under your noses ! What was the idea of going in after these plans, anyway ? Wasn't it to give the public something to bite on—something that might rouse 'em to the state of affairs at the Colonial Office ? "

" That was our idea ; but——"

" The Colonial Office has done its job, for once : so that's no good to us." Harcourt hammered home the point with two fingers on the edge of the table. " Wash it out, my boy, wash it out. We've got to find a bigger faggot than that, if we mean to start a blaze."

" But, hang it all, Uncle Hacky, I gave Prewett my word——"

" Prewett's dead, and, so far as we're concerned, his plans died with him." The heavy, ruthless face met Johnny's eyes across the silver and glass. " Bring me a thousand Prewetts, ten thousand Prewetts, dead or living, and they'll serve our purpose : what do you suppose one miserable, crawling ant of a person is in the organisation of a colonial system ? "

" But you yourself agreed——"

" I agreed that we might get something out of an individual case that would appeal to the imbecile imaginations of the British public ! We've got precedent, haven't we, in the parables ? If you've got a truth you want to ram home, wrap it up in a nursery tale—but see that your tale rings true. Thank God we got this straightened out," grunted Harcourt, " before we plastered it in the paper ! There's nothing does more harm to circulation than starting a hue and cry after something that peters out."

" I suppose you're right," he admitted reluctantly.

" I'm damn' well right," was the quiet answer. " We're after a big thing, Johnny : much bigger—this time—than anti-slavery. If we bring it off "—he stopped, to laugh—" we may finish up, the pair of us, in marble, down there on the Parade ! You know—where they wanted to put old Matt. And, if we don't "—again came the pause, but there was no laughter this time to fill it—" we'll die, perhaps, knowing that we've done our best to help our fellow men."

" It's all right dying—if you know you've started something that's going on."

" No need for you to talk about dying ; you'll have your hands full when I'm gone, if this comes to anything. Keep the big map in front of you, and the little ones where you know where to find them if they're needed : that's what you've got to remember," said Harcourt. " The Charlestown swamp —all the swamps in West Africa—are just a postage-stamp-sized bit of the problem that has to be tackled. And another thing you've got to take care of : never allow personalities or sentiments to come in, when you're following a cause."

He got up, and took the pages of the report from Johnny's hand.

" I was joking, just now, when I talked about us, in marble. Immortality isn't marble ; it's a million souls, like this "—he tapped the report with his fingernail, but Johnny knew it was not of that he was speaking— " crying out for justice, down the long, empty passage of eternity."

He bent to lay the papers on the fire, and, as the flame mounted, and the ash fell with a tiny crackle to the hearth, Johnny heard in it, and in Harcourt's words, the funeral oration for Prewett.

One more failure to report to Osei—whose reply to his last letter lay on the table in the bedroom to which he mounted because it was necessary, in decency, to conceal from Harcourt one's bitterness of discouragement.

When Joe had gone out with the regiment, there was no longer any good reason for Johnny to continue to occupy his shabby little lodging in Ship Lane, and it needed no pressure on the part of Harcourt to make him remove his few belongings into Berkeley Square. The satisfaction—concealed by Harcourt, overt on the part of Johnny—was mutual ; for one it meant the end of a solitude stoically accepted, but none the less distasteful, and, for the other, luxuries as novel as they were agreeable. The Constitutional Club saw less of one of its leading members, and the Llandoger Trow missed a regular (though moderate) patron ; the cook at Berkeley Square was obliged to exchange well-paid idleness for the preparation of regular meals, and the housekeeper—virtually pensioned off, since the young ladies got married—to bustle about her duties again.

It was pleasant, after sojourn in London, to return to the handsome house, with its atmosphere of tradition that went far back beyond the actual structure ; which contained so much—far more than Guerdon—of the fabric of his people. Harcourt's mania for the acquisition of family relics was known to all the antique dealers in Bristol, and there were few pieces of the old Triton furnishings which—provided their authenticity was established—did not find their way to Berkeley Square, as the deaths or departures of later owners brought them on the market. It was pleasant to waken in a room whose walls were lined with the old maps of Hoffnægel,

Millard, Donn and Roque which hung in the study of the first Hercules ; to look up at a tester from which a black fighting cock had launched its triumphant valediction for a departing soul—unregenerate as that soul might be !

There was little Harcourt did not know of those early histories, woven into the legend of his city : little he did not impart to his nephew, in drowsy sessions over the port. Hercules's globes, on which he plotted the fortunes of his ships, stood now in the bay of the dining-room ; a saddle-bag, oiled and polished to the darkness of mahogany, into which they stuffed newspapers that were not to fall into the firelighters' hands, was said to have belonged to the Abolitionist Matthew—slung at his saddle-bow on the day of that disgraceful arrival in Bristol, when, with all hell behind him in the shape of creditors, he came to seek sanctuary of his grandfather, and found—not sanctuary alone, but a fortune.

They drawing together meant happiness for both : for the elder, the discovery in his companion of qualities, hope of which he had cynically abandoned in the rising generation ; for the younger, the sense of being the object of a personal interest he had never so far—except from his grandmother—enjoyed. The household—in the way of all households—was quick to perceive the alteration in Mr. Johnny's status, and it was only the natural simplicity of Johnny's disposition that prevented his recognition of the fact that he was accorded, in Berkeley Square, very much the same position that Dorset occupied at Guerdon.

He picked up Osei's letter and read it through again. The last paragraph he read several times :

> " Don't take me amiss if I say you are expecting too much, too quickly. At this rate you will wear yourself out with disappointments, long before we come in sight of the goal. Perhaps it is the difference in time sense between us and you which makes it easier for me to be philosophic. I don't quite know how to put it, but I feel that this great change upon which we are set has to be *lived* as well as *made*. It is not a simple and straightforward thing, like stopping the Slave Trade. It may not come about in your life time or mine ; but why should that distress us ?
>
> " I understand, of course, the difference of your uncle's point of view ; his is the commercial one. Well, why not ? "

(Here Osei had drawn a triangle, mounting to its lofty apex from a very narrow base.)

> " You see what I mean : two lines, travelling together, closer and closer, until they meet. A wedge accomplishes more than a flat implement."

II

" Why don't you take the machine ? " growled Harcourt, on a day when Johnny was setting out, as usual, on his bicycle, on a visit to Guerdon.

" What—do you mean the motor car ? " his nephew gaped.

" You can drive the thing, can't you ? "

" As a matter of fact, I can." He concealed, behind a grin, the guilt of moments spent, under the tuition of Harcourt's chauffeur, in mastering the mechanics of the Panhard.

" Take that—or a cab. I don't want my horses wasted on the hills. It's time you stopped going about like some tooting little counter-jumper."

The implication of promotion that the words contained was lost on Johnny—sweeping grandly past the Dower House, with a blare of the horn (Grandmamma should have a demonstration later), and drawing up negligently, in a cloud of steam, just, as luck had it, when Gilbert, on his crutches, happened to appear on the steps. The latter goggled.

" Isn't that Uncle Hacky's ? "

" What ho—it is." It was not quite so slick and shining as the Guerdon De Dion, but the fact of arriving, self-conducted, in a vehicle still sufficiently rare to terrify horses and old country people in the lanes, was enough to confer a distinction which evidently left its impression on Gilbert.

" Johnny ! " Miranda, hanging out of a window, was waving to him joyfully.

" Come on down ; I've got something for you."

" Where are we going ? " she demanded, as he pulled her up into the seat beside his own.

" To the stables, first," he answered, enjoying her excited anticipation. He made her sit still, while he lifted a large, canvas-covered object out of the back of the car. She caught her breath as she saw gleaming, chestnut-coloured leather.

" A saddle ? But——"

" Look at the way it's made ; you can be almost as cosy as you were in your old basket."

" But it's much too heavy for Fenella," she demurred.

" Of course it is. I've coaxed father ; he says you can have the cob."

" What—Marcella ? "

" She's got too fat for the governess cart, and she's used to the saddle. She's to be yours, in future."

" Oh, *Johnny* ! " Her eyes filled ; she clung briefly to his arm. " Nobody but you thinks of things like that," she muttered. And no one knew how she loathed the wheel-chair she was obliged to use for expeditions beyond the range of the park : the humiliation of going about like a baby in a perambulator ! She was too big, now, for the basket saddle, and Fenella was getting old.

" Gammon. It's your own fault ; you don't make enough fuss," he told her gruffly. " Here, Pat : saddle up the cob for Miss Miranda."

The car was forgotten, and time went by, while Miranda got the sense of her new means of locomotion. The small, stolid cob plodded seriously, as though aware of her responsibility, the thickly padded saddle absorbing the jar of her movement before it could touch Miranda's sensitive spine. He showed her how to spread her petticoats, so that nothing was seen of the eccentric shape of the saddle ; a girl riding a pony evoked none of the vulgar interest and curiosity from which she shrank in her wheel-chair.

" Stand away ; let her manage by herself," were Johnny's orders to the groom, who thereupon loosed Marcella's bridle, giving her rider the ecstasy of independence, for the first time in her life. She sat there, holding the reins, feeling the cob's tough mouth. Marcella was as steady as a rock, as she had been between the shafts of the governess cart. Before he lifted her down, Johnny showed the groom the art of mounting her, so that she should be independent of the ministrations of the family.

Those were happy days for both of them, when they drove, or sometimes rode, along lanes which already held the mystery of the sap quickening towards Spring ; days which Miranda was to remember for the rest of her life—less for their intrinsic pleasure than for the relationship which they established between herself and her dearest brother.

Miranda—no one appeared to notice it except Johnny—was growing up, and clutched at the one person she trusted, for reassurance in that unhappy standing water between child and maidenhood. Her reading had given her an adult outlook which her still childish vocabulary denied, and there were times when he felt her intelligence outpacing his own. It was to Miranda he confided, one day, his misgivings about Polly.

" Perhaps," said Miranda calmly, " she's going to have a baby."

" Good God, Winkle, what a suggestion ! "

" Girls do," was the unruffled rejoinder. " Dairymaids, and laundry-maids, and that little Ellen—the shepherd's eldest. It seems to happen, as a rule, if they're pretty, and go for walks a good deal with the village boys : though goodness knows, Ellen's the dirtiest little thing and really ugly, when you come to look at her. I often think it's odd it doesn't happen to ladies. But Polly's not quite a lady, is she ? Rather betwixt and between. It might be that, I suppose."

" Of course it's nothing of the kind ! Really, Winkle, you must know that's a shocking thing to say about anyone ; what on earth do you suppose Aunt Vicky would think, if she were to hear you ? " reproached Johnny, remembering his duty as elder brother.

" Never mind Aunt Vicky ; let's talk about Polly. Do you think it's an unhappy love affair ? "

" That's what I'm afraid of. You haven't got any idea who it might be, have you ? "

" Not the dimmest. All the grooms and indoor servants were in love with Polly, but she turned up her nose at all of them," declared Miranda.

" It looks as if she's got herself into some trouble in Bristol," said Johnny ruefully. " Poor Joe went off in a sad state about her."

" She won't marry *him*." She shook her head decidedly.

" How on earth do you know ? "

" I'll bet you, if you like," said Miranda, in an off-hand manner. " To begin with, Joe is too humble. You don't get anywhere by being humble with a girl like Polly."

" My word, you *are* growing up ! " he mocked her, but tenderly. He wondered if she knew how lovely she looked, in the loose cape she wore for riding, the crimson felt tam-o'-shanter pushed to the back of her head and the dark hair blown into little flakes about her broad brow. Even the glasses could not spoil her, when freedom and happiness brought colour into her lips and cheeks. " At this rate, I shall soon be too shy to talk to you at all."

" I've had a letter from Osei," ignoring the foregoing, she startled him by announcing.

" Have you ? What did he write to you about ? "

" He sent me some poetry." She produced the thin sheets of foreign notepaper from her pocket. He read it, leaning against Marcella's shoulder while she peacefully munched grass. It was hard to know what to make of it.

" It is good to be a black man in Paris,
And to be proud and walk in gardens where kings have walked
And there are statues in white marble.
I am tall like a tree, like the cocoa palms on my beach,
I pluck the lights and make crowns out of them,
I take strings of them and wind them round my body,
I tread them under my feet.
All the lights jingle together with a noise of bells,
Like the fountains I wear like a scarf round my body.
I sit at a table and am proud
Because I am a black man in Paris
But most of all because I am a man in Paris. . ."

" I say—it's a bit cracked, isn't it ? You can't call that poetry," scowled Johnny. Privately, he was disconcerted by an aspect of Osei hitherto unrevealed to him. Surely Osei had not been " on the binge ? " And yet——

" He's only saying he likes Paris," said Miranda flatly. " Yes, I suppose it's poetry—of a sort. It's queer, isn't it ? " she had the candour to admit. " But I'm sure it must be poetry, because it gives me the poetry feeling."

" I think it's absolute crackers," said Johnny, with equal candour. " Of course I'm no judge of poetry ; as a matter of fact, I can't read the stuff——"

" You used to listen, when Emily read it," she said astutely.

" That was different." For once, he was cold with Miranda.

" Do you ever see Osei ? " She had sufficient tact to change the subject.

" Only once, since he stayed with us. He's only been back here for a week, since he went to Paris."

" Isn't it odd—that somebody so big, and so *very* black, should be so gentle, and so *warm*. His voice makes me think of Mamma's old Shetland shawl, that she used to lend me when I had earache. When are you going to ask him again?"

"I don't know. You see—it's not very easy——"

"There isn't Uncle Quentin," pointed out Miranda.

Johnny chuckled.

"Oh—Osei liked Uncle Quentin. Tell me something, Winkle: when you think about Osei, do you think of him, first, as a black man, and then like him, in spite of it?"

"I think I like him because of it," she answered, after consideration. "Because it puts him apart from everyone else. You feel he isn't governed by other people's ideas; he's just—himself. So few people are themselves!" said Miranda. "They seem to accept a pattern, or invent one for themselves, and that satisfies them."

"And you don't think about his being black at all?" This was the important point; he harped on it.

"Only in a nice way. I like his *bones*, and the loose sort of way he moves: like a cat. I suppose his nose is rather funny, and he's got rather a lot of mouth," she reflected. "But they suit him. They go with his eyes and his hair. It must be wonderful to have hair that fits like that: just like a very fine crochet cap," she ended, on a note of envy.

He tried to think of a way of putting it.

"Have you ever examined any white person—in the way you seem to have examined Osei?"

"I—don't—think—so. White faces are so much alike, aren't they? They aren't really interesting," said Miranda.

"Are you going to write back to him?"

"I have done," she told him promptly. "And I sent your love; that was right, wasn't it? I knew it wasn't correct, to send mine, writing to a gentleman; but I wanted him to feel that we're fond of him, and we'd like to see him again."

"That was quite right. Don't they ever look at your letters?"

"They used to," she admitted. "But I've rather put down my foot about that! I told Aunt Vicky it wasn't really fair to you and Emily—and you're the most important people who write to me—and you know what an enormous post we get here; I don't suppose Papa has time to look at it very closely, when he's sorting our letters."

"And what about your own letters—that you send yourself?"

"I get one of the servants to take them down to the village, after the bag has gone."

There is no one I trust, more than I trust Osei, he was thinking; but—what's the good of blinking it? This means hell, if it ever gets out. Miranda writing to a man—that would be viewed askance, by Vicky, by Selina, and most certainly by Dromore. Miranda, writing to a *black* man——! He set his jaw. It was like Osei, busy, successful, full of his own projects, to make time to write to a little lame girl. No; Winkle should not, if he had anything to do with it, be done out of her pleasure.

"You'd better let me have your letters to post in future," he ended his perfunctory reprimand. This was a sop to his conscience—not wholly easy in being party to an act, on Miranda's part, of deceit. Every girl did it. He himself had many a time acted postman for Penderel's sisters; Dorset received, and, with chuckles, had even shown him, on occasion, epistles which had certainly never passed the scrutiny of their writers' fond mammas. And who was the worse for it? Who, in his right mind, would take exception to the kind of letter Winkle would write, or Osei, to the sister of his great friend?

"When are you going to see Emily again?"

"Emily——?" He started, then pulled himself together. "Will you come to London with me one day, Winkle?"

"Me?" She was incredulous. How could such a thing be, or the family be persuaded to assent to it?

He began to explain: not looking at her face, from which the colour had faded; holding tightly to the hand, which had grown cold within his own.

"But what's the good?" she muttered. "They said, last time, it's no good. Nobody can do anything."

"You're not going to let them get away with that, are you?" he rallied her. "Now, listen: I know a man called Whittick, a very big name indeed in Harley Street; and he told me the man we ought to go to. I spoke to Grandmamma, and she'll back us up with the others. We could take her old Venables, to look after you, and spend a night, or even two, in a hotel. Only think what a time we could have! Will you face it, just once more, to please me?"

It was long before Miranda could be persuaded; but at last she gave in, and, with lips set tight, allowed herself to be driven in silence back to the house.

When he left Guerdon, Selina and her idolised Gilbert were sitting in her window, Gilbert obligingly holding wool for his mother to wind. They both started as the Panhard took the clutch with its usual series of explosions.

"Only Johnny. It looks as if he's well in with the Old Boy—what?"

Selina nodded absently. She was more interested in whether Gilbert's foot-rest was comfortable, and whether he would like another cushion in his back, than in the relationship between her brother-in-law and her youngest son.

III

"I'm either mad, a fool, or a villain." Thus, to himself, Roan Flood, resting a shoe of patent leather on the polished fender, and looking round, as though he might find the answer to his proposition in the brocaded panels, outlined in gilt *boiseries*; in dubious Louis Quinze *bibelots*, in a small, round table, bunched with hothouse flowers, in the gold-foiled neck of a bottle protruding at an elegantly abandoned angle from the pail of ice.

He knew it all; as he knew, presently, the rustle of a woman's gown outside the door, the waiter, averting his eyes with cynical tact from the veiled figure hurriedly entering and waiting for the door to be closed before advancing towards her host. As he helped to remove the veiling, and the enshrouding folds of a taffeta cape whose lining of ermine was warm from its wearer's bosom, Roan had a pang of regret. He was none of those three things that he had accused himself of being ; he was simply, for the moment, a very sad man—a weak man ; yes, that was true—in the grip of circumstances too strong for him.

" How *thrilling* ! "

She looked round her with the entranced delight of a child at its first party, and he found an intolerable pathos in her pleasure in all these stale manifestations of manufactured romance.

" I feel as if I were in a play ! It's *quite* incredible."

" Come and warm your hands." They were cold, and trembled a little in his. He suspected that she was as much frightened, now the thing was done, as excited. Poor child ! The thought flashed into his mind, " Should I ask her if she would like me to take her home ? "

To voice such a query would have been to make mock of the gay—a little too gay—smile, the proud little head, the swift decisive grace with which she moved to the fire. His blood ran cold at the thought that she was " ruined " if they were discovered here ; then he reminded himself angrily of the impossibility of such a disaster, and told himself that his fear was far more foolish, and a thousand times more irrational, than hers. It was not Roan Flood's first *tête-à-tête* in a private room !

Her movements scattered perfume, and a spray of diamonds nestled between the heavy coil of her hair and the soft mound that rose above her brow. Had it been anyone else, he would have been amused by her evident dressing up to her conception of the part—of the daring Society girl, coming to a secret assignation with a—— Was it possible that she had thought of him, perhaps, for an instant, as her lover ? The only play that occurred to his mind, as providing a similar parallel, was *Lady Windermere's Fan* : she could hardly visualise herself as Mrs. Erlynne ! The thought brought a faint smile to his lips, but he was conscious of a quickening of his heart, that was partly horror and partly—he dismissed it guiltily—pleasure.

" So this is it ! I've always longed to know what a private room was like." She sounded awed. Suddenly she laughed. " Isn't it divinely absurd ! All that imitation Sèvres, and the ridiculous little gilt chairs, that look as if no one had ever sat on them ! " There was no need to tell her that, in all probability, no one ever had : that the significant feature of the apartment, plush-covered, and heaped with cushions, was drawn across in front of the fire. That it had caught her attention was proved by her next remark. " It really would be quite pretty, but for that terrible couch ! How extraordinary to put a thing like that in here : like putting a bath-tub in a drawing-room."

He filled a glass with champagne and took it to her. She was still wearing her gloves, that went into soft folds, like cream, over her narrow hands. He watched her lower her head, and sip it delicately, like a doe by an alien stream.

" I hope it's not too dry for you ? "

" Delicious. *How* kind you are ! "

" Kind ? " As he fetched his own glass, he had a premonition that the evening was not going to be an easy one. Her youth. . . . Youth was a quality that appealed sharply to Roan Flood, and he had paid highly for it ; but he was sufficiently fastidious to be keenly—even shamefully—aware of the distinction between this youth, sheltered, innocent, gently bred, and the kind of youth which, in the main, had come his way of latter years. How old did he seem to her ? He shot a covert glance towards the glass, and was glad to find the reflection reassuring. He had worn well ; better, for his age, than his nephew Dorset, who, from an Adonis-like youth, threatened, unless he mended his habits, to be gross in the middle forties.

He had chosen the supper with care—complimenting her taste, as well as his own : caviare, a *mousse* of game, individual ices, each shaped like a great white orchid, laid on a spray of real foliage. The very food of love ! An irony, when one came to think of it.

" All my life I've longed to have supper in a private room ! " She raised her eyes, a little dim with champagne, from the orchid, to give him an enraptured smile.

" You funny child ! Well, now you've had your wish." He wondered if it had fulfilled her expectations. Suddenly she held out her hand to him, with the palm downwards, and, realising what was expected of him, he kissed it ; then he laid it back gently on the edge of the table. His own hand was not quite steady.

She had risen, and was going towards the couch. He realised, with a shock, that there was no other place—comfortable—for her to sit upon. He watched her make herself comfortable—against the abominable cushions, and found it impossible to go and help her—as he would have done any other woman, in her place. He saw her profile turned dreamily towards the fire.

" Are you bored ? " She startled him with the question.

" There is surely no need to ask me that ! Do I seem bored ? "

" You've been silent such a long time."

" Because—I'm getting ready to scold you."

" Scold *me* ? " She sounded astonished, as though she were not accustomed to being scolded.

" You know, Emily, this is breaking all the rules."

" Whose rules, pray ? " a little haughtily.

" The rules," he persisted, " that govern well-behaved people—in your society, and in mine."

" Aren't they the same ? " She gave him a flippant little smile. " We seem to know a great many of the same people. We seem to have been meeting everywhere, for months ! "

" An odd thing—considering that, up to last June, we had not met at all," he could not refrain from reminding her.

" Very odd," she agreed demurely. She turned her head suddenly to face him. " Not so odd—as I arranged it myself."

An indescribable sensation shot through him. It passed as he set aside the implication of her words.

" You must have noticed, yourself, that one meets a person, unexpectedly—perhaps after years : and then it seems as though some fate takes you to the same places, time after time."

" What a charming explanation. Fate ! " He felt her mocking him with her raised eyebrows. " Is Fate masculine or feminine—do you suppose ? "

" I should say—hermaphrodite." He matched his mood to hers. She looked at him gravely for a moment, then shook her head.

" They say that Fate's a woman. The spinner of webs."

" The mischief-maker ! " It was his turn to mock. Something prompted him to add, " ' The Fates will find a way—— ! ' "

" Ah—that was one of Papa's favourite sayings : isn't it the Æneid ? "

" *Fata viam invenient.*" Roan nodded.

" And, you see—I did."

" Are you—by any chance—pretending to be my Fate ? " He forced himself to smile. " Because, if you are, dear Emily, may I remind you you have dressed the part very badly ? Don't you know that Fate is a hag in grey tatters—— ? "

" *Vous êtes bien arrièrré*, monsieur ! " She sparkled at him. " Don't you know that Twentieth Century Fate is dressed exclusively by Worth ? "

" *Tiens*—the old minx ! "

" Do you really think I'm—very—minxish ? " He had robbed her, for a moment, of her aplomb.

Astride the chair, his elbows on its back, his chin resting on his clasped hands, Roan allowed her to wait before answering.

" I think . . . that you're a very sweet person. And I shall presently exercise my elderly prerogative and call you a cab." It cost something to say it ; he found he could not meet her eyes. When the silence had grown unendurable, he broke it roughly. " Why did you do it ? "

She did not even pretend to misunderstand him.

" I wanted to see you."

He was startled into a short laugh.

" That's absurd ! You lunched with me on Sunday last ; during the previous week we met at least half a dozen times—and next week-end we're invited to the same house-party."

" Where we'll never be surrounded by less than a dozen people ! Where you'll speak to me across a table, and I'll have to lean forward and say, ' I beg your pardon ? ' because the chatter on my right and my left will not let me quite catch what you say. Where we'll play ' chemmy,' and be much too interested in our winnings and losings to pay one another any attention. Where—oh, you know the sort of thing as well as I do. You know how it was at your luncheon party : Mrs. Arbuthnot on your right and I on your left—oh, you are always scrupulous as a host ! I sometimes wonder if you've got your watch hidden under the edge of your plate : five minutes—left, *turn* ! Five minutes—right, *turn* ! " She mimicked a parade-ground voice. " Don't think I don't love good manners," said the daughter of Everard Temple, sweetly, " but it is just a little mortifying, for—friends, to have to accept the same ration as acquaintances."

" You are right, of course. Isn't it the folly of all rules, that they usually end up by penalising the people they're intended to benefit ? "

" The rules are altering," she told him. " Do you know that a party of us went to the Alhambra last night ? " She laughed softly. " And on to supper at Romano's ! What a shock for Society that would have been a few years ago, when no ' lady ' was seen at a music hall."

He wondered who her companions had been. So this was the younger generation—taking the bit in its teeth. He doubted whether Venetia—with all her daring, too astute to risk her reputation for fastidiousness—would allow herself to be seen at the Alhambra. Surely Lady Cullen did not know of this escapade ?

" Surely one must make one's own kind of life ? " was her retort, faintly edged with impatience, to a hint to this effect. " For us all to behave as our grandmothers did would be almost as ridiculous as wearing their clothes ! *Autre temps, autre mœurs :* every generation has its own manners—surely ? "

" I'm going to ask you something." She was already regarding him as a fogey ; the humiliating suspicion robbed him, for once, of his natural ease in conversation. The words that came sounded impossible in their clumsiness. " As a mere matter of curiosity, Miss Emily—is it part of the *mœurs* of the younger set—to have supper *à deux* in a hired room ? "

" It is part of our ' *mœurs* '—as you call them—to try to be a little more—more original than our parents were, in amusing ourselves ! " she stammered.

Oh, Emily, Emily ! He had not known himself capable of the tenderness evoked by her folly. Oh, Emily, my poor, silly darling, if you only knew how pitifully unoriginal you are ! Momentarily baffled, he leaned back, to the length of his long arms, and his wrists crossed on the chair back.

" Yes ? " Her whisper reached him from the couch.

" What made me the partner of your ' originality ? ' " The question was out at last. It seemed as though, across the space between them, she must hear the ticking of his heart. " You know you have done me a great honour : but surely, from your point of view, my dear, the adventure would have been better shared with someone of your own age ? "

" Would you rather it had been ? " she petrified him by retorting.

Roan got up suddenly.

" We'll have another glass of wine before I order your cab. You haven't answered my question," he said, as he brought it to her.

" Nor you mine."

He stood looking down on her long, uplifted throat, her heavy eyes that lent exoticism to the delicate face ; on her hand which, trembling, had spilled a little of the champagne. He thought how disgraceful it was—that he and Emily Temple should be together, in this vulgar temple to vulgar loves.

" Didn't it ever strike you that there were many ways in which we might enjoy each other's company, without placing yourself—and me, although that is not of the least importance—in a very dubious situation? That's to put it mildly!" he ended, on a short laugh.

"Why should it be 'dubious?'"

"Come." Roan set his teeth; it was time to apply the lash. "Even girls as innocent as yourself know what it means—from the world's point of view—to arrive at this hour of night, in a hired cab, to have supper alone with a man; even a man old enough"—he loathed saying it, but it was out—"to be your father!"

"In this case"—he could not but admire her proud detachment—"'the world' has not a point of view. 'The world' is not concerned."

"But why——?" He gave it up; she was making him into a prig, a hypocrite.

"Why——?" Her small teeth glimmered in her stark smile. "Have you forgotten what we were saying about Fate? It's never wise, is it, to question the workings of Fate?"

"Fate has been very kind to us"—he hardly knew what he was saying—"in making us fellow-guests next week-end at Candleby; surely it would have been better to wait for that?"

He heard her say:

"I wanted to make sure that it would be—better."

Moments went by, while Roan Flood fought a battle with himself, such as he had never experienced before. Many women had offered themselves to him, and he had accepted lightly, never feeling any principle involved in the indulgence of an impulse pleasurable on both sides. But this was different. It had nothing to do with Emily Temple's background, or with the fact that she was a young unmarried girl, of a class that raised its daughters strictly. He was sufficiently man of the world not to discount such considerations, but he knew that it was not they that weighed in the present dilemma. Selfish and self-indulgent as Roan had always been, he had never, like his brothers Dromore and Harcourt, been impervious to the sentiments of others.

"Emily——" He hesitated, and cleared his throat. It was plainly of no use to beat about the bush. "Before we say, or do, anything that we—most certainly you—might bitterly regret, will you answer a serious question?"

"I'm sorry if I've appeared flippant, up to the present!"

"Do you think," he said, ignoring this, "that two people who are not very—satisfied with their present circumstances, are likely to improve them by taking a step which will complicate matters even more than they are complicated already?"

"What a cold-blooded way of putting it!" She had flushed brightly: for the first time she let him see he had embarrassed her.

"You oblige me to be cold-blooded——" He held back the end of the sentence: "Or to pretend to be!"

After a moment of utter stillness, she picked up her gloves; the colour had faded from her cheeks.

" There seems to have been a misunderstanding ; I thought you—liked me."

" Emily ! " He checked her attempt to rise. " You are a charming, cultivated woman, with many devoted friends who ask no greater privilege than to make you happy."

" What a pity they don't succeed ! " she mocked, waving him aside. Roan ignored the gesture.

" Then—why should you imagine I could ? "

" Wasn't it worth trying ? "

" Oh, my dear, what a way to try ! "

" There's such a thing as ' leaving no stone unturned ! ' " she reminded him.

His imagination went to the lifting of a stone, to the things crawling from beneath it, grey abominations her desperate act might bring upon them both. A sudden and explicit detestation of the one responsible filled him with a pity he knew to be fatal, and against which, to his credit, he continued to struggle : knowing himself weakened by many things—by her youth, her beauty and her appeal to his understanding, and the susceptibility of his vanity to all three.

" Will you please order the cab ? " she was saying.

He knew suddenly that he had humiliated her, and that he had no right to let her go in such a fashion.

" When shall I see you again ? "

" At Candleby—surely ? " She raised her eyebrows.

" No, that's no use." He frowned. Suddenly he laid his hands over hers, that were occupied with her gloves. " Have you any idea how careful we shall have to be ? "

Her lips parted, with a genuine astonishment.

" Careful ? Of what have we to be careful ? "

He could not restrain a smile.

" No, Emily ; I'm afraid we've gone too far. It's too late now, my dear, to sound the retreat ! "

" But I don't understand——"

" I love you," said Roan deliberately. " Foolish, and wrong, and completely undesirable as it may be—that's how it is. It's particularly foolish on my part, because—you are not in love with me."

" But—— ! " Her bewilderment, in other circumstances, would have made him laugh. " Please—— ! You must really let me explain——" She moistened her lips.

" What can you explain, Emily "—it was his turn to mock her—" that I don't understand already ?

" ' Ah Love ! Could thou and I with Fate conspire
To grasp this sorry Scheme of Things entire,
Would we not shatter it to bits—and then
Remould it nearer to the Heart's Desire ? ' "

He was struck by her closed eyes, her expression of almost fanatical attention, the slight inclination of her head, as though she were listening to a voice in the distance.

"Go on—please go on," she breathed.

"I can't," said Roan practically.

"Don't you know any more? Oh, you must, you must!" She shocked him by sounding slightly hysterical. He took her hand to calm her.

"Come, dear. We shall have to see what we can do about the 're-moulding.' But you must promise there'll be no more escapades like to-night's. It's the end for both of us, you know," he told her gravely, "if anyone were to hear of this."

"I promise." She lifted her head like a child's, and he drew back, shuddering a little, from the offering of her lips. Whatever Emily Temple might be to him, or he to her, in the unwritten future, it should not begin in their present surroundings. He lifted both her hands and pressed his face into the soft palms that quivered against his flesh.

"*Roan!*"

. . . Presently he helped her into her wrap.

"Will you come and have tea with me to-morrow?"

"At Brook Street? No, that I won't!" said Roan.

"Why not? How absurd!" she pouted. "You've dined with us, you've fetched me for parties at the theatre——"

He realised how foolish his abstention might appear; how it might even draw upon them attention which, for Emily's sake, must, at all costs, be avoided.

"Very well," he said reluctantly. He thought of warning her not to give instructions that she was "not at home" to other callers, but did not care to run the risk of a misunderstanding. Emily, who, for the last six months, had been "running" with the most sophisticated of the younger sets, must surely have some notion of how to conduct a clandestine flirtation?

She was smiling at him, with the black mist of her veil held above her head like a canopy.

"And, if you care to know, I don't repent in the least of having made you bring me here! We should never, never have got these things said in—any of the usual places."

"Certainly not at Candleby!" Should he warn her that, of all houses they might have visited together, none was more dangerous than Candleby? Be thou as chaste as ice, as pure as snow—at Candleby thou shalt not escape calumny! He tried to remember who would be there, of the smart, scabrous crowd that, preserving always its veneer of convention, kept up a diamond-cut-diamond competition for daring. An amusing place, Candleby—but surely, oh surely not a setting for Emily Temple? She had told him it was her first visit there; he must certainly put her on her guard. . . .

"I know a girl who always makes her appointments at the Wallace Collection," Emily was saying, with her soft chuckle. "She knows all the miniatures by heart—from the catalogue! Her mother is terribly pleased about her interest in art."

. . . Those things could be said later—when one had had time to think : to meditate upon this fantastic situation of which the wildest imagination could hardly foresee the progression, since it could not hope to develop on accepted lines.

How, to put it bluntly, could he and Emily become lovers in a Society which preserved the virtue of its unmarried girls no less assiduously than it connived at dissipation among the married ranks ? Yet the absurdity of a platonic romance was not merely out of the question, it was an affront to the dignity of both. Moreover, he knew himself incapable of it. To attempt to run it on such lines was courting disaster—for both.

In different men, chivalry takes different forms. In Roan Flood, a cynic and a materialist, it took the form of a a profound disapprobation of any unconsummated attachment between a man and a woman. Not applying such standards to the light loves—the *passades*—that star the path of a man of his nature, he had not expected, within so short a time of separating from Venetia, to meet a woman whose claim on his regard was serious : serious in a sense that he and Venetia had never been serious. They had played a complicated game successfully, for a number of years, and, suddenly, it had palled : that was all. Venetia had wanted a change of opponent—someone whose technique she had still to master ; and, like a good player, he had accepted her decision.

But with Emily it was different ; so different that he found himself a little stunned by it. He had tried, all along, to ignore the attraction she had for him : bearing in mind the difference in their ages, to realise the folly of imagining that such attraction could be reciprocal. Yet it had happened—and he found himself, for the first time, in that incredible state known as " being in love." Sensitive, doubtful, half-ashamed, he wondered if it was senility, or Indian summer. At all events, being Roan, he could conceive of but one outcome of it.

There was nothing to be done but to approach Venetia again, about the divorce ; and, meanwhile, to go softly as Agag, and impress on Emily the need for an impeccable discretion. It is not to be doubted that Roan, as his hansom bore him back to Albany, was keenly alive to the risks implied in their present situation. So much alive, that dawn still found him wondering if there was any way in which, without giving offence to his hosts, he could get out of the week-end at Candleby.

CHAPTER NINE

I

LIKE swarming hives on the beating of a gong, the villages gave np their people ; by the small paths and the large, by the great Patassi-Terrebum-N'Kwanta road, by swamp and river, by the live lands and the dead lands and by mountains that have no name, the hordes converged on that spot of which word had gone forth, Ye shall be there. Mampon, Bekwai, Kokofu, Juabin, Adansi, Aguna, N'Kwanta, Bompata, Omo—the last, under its new young chief, inclined to be assertive, but speedily put in its place by those who agreed that, considering what had gone before, Omo's duty was to be seen but not heard. N'Koranza was having trouble with his bush soul, and the Queen of Ofinsu sent word she was too old to travel—which drew much ribaldry from Ya Ashantua, undaunted after a journey in the course of which she had been dropped head first (and who shall say it was by accident ?) into a pondful of leeches, a couple of her carriers had been snatched away by leopards and, her sight not being what it was, she had sat carelessly on a slab of stone that turned out to be a hippopotamus.

Behind these kings and lords flowed each his stream of retainers, and each had so many warriors to lend him prestige—though this was strictly a peaceful gathering ; and, naturally, each brought his priests and his sorcerers, and they had their assistants—and so it went on ; Kumassi rocked, bulged and staggered under the invasion. While squabbles for precedence went on among couriers in charge of the parties, the less responsible proceeded to treat the expedition as a sightseeing tour. Many had never seen, some had not seen for years, the palace and the great hall of justice that, in days gone by, embodied the pomp and majesty of the rulers of Ashanti. All viewed with awe, some with misgiving, the big square fort from which, once and for all, the paramount power of the Great Queen was to be proclaimed by her emissary, the Governor : now on his way from Accra for the great palaver that was to confirm the submission of the tribes to British rule.

The sun poured its heat over a forest of state umbrellas, of canopies ; over Mampon's drum and fife band, over old Aguna, dancing like David before the Ark of the Government—Aguna, a famous expressionist in dance forms, having been warned, on account of white prejudices, to curb his ardours ; over the triumphal arch with "Welcome" inscribed on it, under which Their Excellencies drove, to be received by the members of the Confederation and the Native Committee ; over the gubernorial staff sweltering in its uniforms, and over Ya Ashantua, elbowing her way to the front—where she had no business—to shake hands with her opposite number. Over a ruined glove, Her Excellency's smile was a model of diplomatic graciousness. The air was syruppy with diplomacy and stank to high heaven of Mampon, Bekwai, Kokofu, Juabin, Adansi, Aguna, N'Kwanta, Compata and Omo, all settled on their haunches, and, in certain cases, in their chairs of state, to hear the proclamation of the Great Queen.

It came in a thin white voice from under the central canopy and was translated into the vernacular by an interpreter whose final words were almost lost in the babble that ensued : because many of the listeners did not speak that language, and had to turn to their neighbours for elucidation.

Ashanti must accept the paramount power of Great Britain, as vested in the speaker and in his representative, from now on resident in Kumassi. Apart from a few congenital grumblers, this was favourably received. The memory of Ashanti was notoriously short : Prempeh was already a forgotten man, and the few old chiefs who, mainly out of pique, had been backing Atcheribonda's candidature, had not sufficient supporters to implement their objections.

His Excellency then, however, proceeded to make another call, and a more inconvenient one, on Ashanti's memory. What about that fifty thousand ounces of gold, that was settled as indemnity for the '74 rising, and the expenses of the '96 expedition ? Ashanti hitched its shoulders. These debts were accumulating interest, the speaker pointed out ; and Ashanti went glassy-eyed. Ducking their heads, some of the young war captains pulled faces at one another ; why should they be expected to pay up on debts contracted before they were born ? There was a perceptible division among the tribes ; some sulking, others taking refuge in self-righteousness from a problem that was no affair of theirs ; *they* had not taken part in the '76 or the '96 risings ; let those who had settle the matter. The air cleared slightly when it was explained that the Great Queen was not pressing for lump settlement, but was prepared to take it in instalments, and—here the clouds descended again—they would get the benefit in local development.

For the first time one could have heard a pin drop. Ashanti sat petrified, in rows like waves of lava. Local development meant stone-breaking, tree-felling, hauling, and a host of menial occupations offensive to people with royal blood in their veins.

Over its cups of tea, when the first day's palaver was over, authority voiced its general satisfaction ; its opinion that " H.E. had made a very neat job of it," while, in their quarters, the correspondents who had come up from the coast with the Government party let themselves go in ecstasies of description, regardless of the fact that little more than their headings would survive the sub-editors' blue pencils.

" The *real* fun starts to-morrow ; over the Nsuta Stool."

" What's that about ? "

The first speaker turned to the second, and spoke in the rather frosty accents of minor officialdom.

" Excuse me—are you the Press ? I didn't quite catch——"

" Oh, lord, no, I'm not the Press." He appeared to be amused by the suggestion, rolling the chewed stub of a cigar from left to right across a barricade of improbable ivory with a practised movement of his lips. He directed a grin of tolerance at the mess-jacketted figure which had drifted across the compound, nodded its acknowledgment of his greeting and, apparently out of courtesy, passed a casual remark on the success of the day's proceedings. "Not the *Press*," he repeated, on a note of faint irony. "I just dropped in—to watch the circus."

"Really?" Something—perhaps the incompatibility between an educated accent and a disgraceful pair of cotton shorts that partnered the remains of a diamond-patterned pyjama jacket which time had mercifully deprived of its violent colouring—seemed to puzzle the speaker; he returned a frown to the other's grin. The frown, which he understood referred to the unseemliness, on an occasion of high official importance, of his attire, was ignored by Kershaw, repeating his inquiry about the Nsuta Stool.

"Oh—there are two claimants; His Excellency will decide the matter to-morrow." The curiosity of an ambiguous stranger was, evidently, not to be satisfied. The subject, however, appeared to have lost interest for the inquirer.

"Looks as if somebody's pulling out, doesn't it?"

A little string of people was making off along the high road. It was perhaps the dusk, added to the speed at which it was travelling, that lent it an air of furtiveness; in all events, there was too much going on in Kumassi for its departure to attract attention.

The next day's palaver opened in a turmoil of excitement. British rule over Ashanti was a distant, political affair, but the Nsuta Stool was a highly personal matter, a pie in which almost every person of importance wanted to have a finger. On the fringe of the assembly, all the rag-tag of Kumassi scuffled for a glimpse of the candidates and their supporters, as they made stately entrance and took up their positions respectively to right and left of the dais. Owing to the excitement, it was some time before the empty seats allotted to the chiefs of the Confederation and the Native Committee were noticed; and by that time, the onlookers had too much interesting matter to occupy their minds to worry about a defection which, in other circumstances, would have been considered highly significant.

Squatted on his haunches in the front row of the ranks reserved for the general public, Kershaw amused himself with conjecture on the outcome of the palaver.

The tall, fat, luxurious-looking youth on the Governor's right was said to be the rightful heir to the Stool, Quasi Berekum; confidently, if prematurely, draped in the robes of chieftainship, he stared about him from small almond eyes under puffy eyelids, while his sorcerer hung him with innumerable small fetish objects, presumably intended to ward off the ill-will of his rival, Quabina Ntem, similarly bedecked. To the lay eye there was little to choose between them. In the rear of Berekum skirmished and squabbled the rabble of his supporters, whose antics held the attention of the spectators, and focused them on his side of the ring.

Behind Ntem, in a slender bronze forest, stood about a score of men, neither young nor old. There were two or three, older than the rest, who wore beards, and whose bodies, above their loin-cloths, had fallen in with age. And all these stood silently, gravely, their eyes fixed upon the dais with an urgency that could surely hardly fail to communicate itself, even to the official mind. The situation was plain—to Kershaw, as to the sober-minded among the onlookers ; that here, ranged behind Berekum's rival, were the responsible minds of Nsuta, its elders and its sages : disclaiming, by their support of Ntem, the hereditary rights of one they did not consider worthy to sit on the Nsuta Stool.

They stood there silently, and it was as though the mantle of their dignity slowly spread itself over the youth before them, so that he began to glow with it. Gradually he lost his preoccupation with the finery they had loaded on to him ; his face lost the childish fatuousness it had worn on his entrance to the assembly and assumed an expression of pride and intelligence that beautified it, and raised its owner into another category from that in which Kershaw had mentally placed him. Obviously, the Stool was Ntem's.

He saw, while they waited for the arrival of the Governor, this impression spreading among the gathering ; saw Berekum's backers increasing their demonstrations, and Berekum himself strutting and showing off, demanding this and that from his retainers, displaying his authority. . . .

Then the dais filled slowly with the white British uniforms, and a hush fell on Ashanti, as the voice of the Great Queen went forth through its mouthpiece. And the name it spoke was that of Yow Mafu.

II

" Dear Mr. Johnny,

" I hope you won't mind having a letter from me, but we are giving a Social Evening and Concert next Saturday at the Hamilton Rooms in aid of the Shipwrecked Mariners, and I thought you might like to know, as I am singing and you used to like my voice ! If you can't manage Saturday there is a rehearsal on Friday night at eight, and I'm sure nobody would mind if you just dropped in. Do come if you can. It may be the last time I sing in Bristol, as Mother is ill and I am giving up my work and going home to look after her and Father. I am taking the liberty of enclosing tickets for Saturday night, in case you are able to use them. If you don't want them perhaps you will be so kind as to drop them at the caretaker's. I hope you are very well.

" Yours sincerely,

" Polly Bowling."

" P.S.—I am singing Tosti's *Goodbye*. I thought it would be appropriate ! "

Saturday, he knew, was impossible ; Samson Killick's daughter was having her twenty-first birthday party and he had promised to be there. Harcourt—also invited—would not stay longer than to drink Linda's health, and the preservation of amenities between Flood and Killick households rested with him. Ten o'clock would be the earliest he could hope to escape from the hearty hospitalities of Cotham Road.

So he made a note of the rehearsal, slightly amused at the tragic note on which Polly had chosen to end her career in the entertainment world. The " nice cheerful girl from Mercers " had become quite a figure in amateur circles—and had actually parted with her amateur status, having on a couple of occasions received payment for appearing at " smokers." Bristol was strong in its support for local talent—and not averse from securing the services of a pretty and accomplished local singer at a third of the fee claimed by a " real professional." Joe never missed any of Polly's public appearances, but his visits to London had, so far, prevented Johnny from verifying his friend's enthusiasm. He was determined now to repair the omission.

He nearly forgot about it all the same, for the London newspapers, carrying the news that the Governor of the Gold Coast, with his wife and staff, were besieged in Kumassi, smote all else temporarily from his mind. He and Harcourt were discussing its possible repercussions on the firm's business when the clerk who had replaced Joe in the general office announced a name that brought Johnny leaping to his feet.

" Biddle ? By George, sir, it's Foxy ! Can we have him in here ? "

An unrecognisable Foxy, with smartly trimmed beard, a new suit, obviously off the peg, and a bowler hat uneasily in hand, bobbed acknowledgment of superiority in the person of Harcourt, while Johnny was pumping his hand.

" No intention of buttin' in : but I just got in, off the *Neaba*, and I thought you might like to hear what's movin'."

" A pretty set-out ! " Harcourt came back from the corner cupboard with the ingredients of hospitality, which Foxy politely ignored. " Taken us nicely on the hop—the beggars ! "

" Taken 'oo on the hop ? " The short figure of Foxy straightened indignantly. Johnny was amused to see the pair of them eyeing each other, sizing up each other's qualities. " You will excuse me ! But when you find a dead hen pegged out in the middle of the road ; when you meet a chicken painted bright red with a string o' cowries round its neck ; when a couple o' blacks that hates work worse'n poison starts sweating themselves to make a war-drum out of a four-foot tree trunk—nobody's taken on the hop except a few gentlemen in Accra, that gets their game o' lawn tennis interrupted."

Harcourt's big head tipped sideways to wink at Johnny.

" We'll get something out of him for the paper."

" Paper ? Me ? Not much." Foxy went wary.

" When did you quit ? "

" The seventh ; after gettin' word of a couple of our chaps bein' chopped up by Adansi, and Ashanti detachments friskin' around, workin' up their spirits with a raid here an' there. Gave me a sort o' taste for Home, Sweet

Home. Very kind, I'm sure." Foxy affected surprise at the sight of a tumbler, observed briefly, "Chin-chin," and sank its contents absentmindedly. Harcourt signed to Johnny to replenish it.

"So the palaver at Kumassi went phut."

Foxy cocked a cautious eyebrow.

"What are they sayin' over here?"

The two Floods exchanged glances; Johnny laughed.

"'Triumphant visit to Kumassi—State reception for the Governor—God Save the Queen!' That's about all we got, for *The Diorama*."

"Huh. Kershaw oughta hear that one——"

"Kershaw? Have you seen him?" put in Johnny eagerly.

"He larked his way up to see the fun. On the face of it," reflected Foxy, "it oughta've been funny: the blacks, all in full fig, bustin' themselves over the establishment of a British fort, practically on the site of Prempeh's palace!" He broke off, to wag his head. "It seems like these political wallahs, when they gets into office, has a dose of somethink that paralyses their brains. They see the State umbrellas an' hear the National Anthem and shake hands with a lot o' niggers, and think God's in his heaven, be blowed to a coupla million chiefs and captains that wasn't in on the handshaking."

"They gave the Governor a good reception—surely?" Harcourt interrupted Foxy's persiflage with a frown.

"Oh, ay," said Foxy airily. "And you can depend there was plenty goin' on under all the kiss-an'-make-friends that started when they got tired of listenin' to the linguists, and thought it was time the drinks was comin' round."

"You think the trouble was brewing there—at the palaver?"

Foxy shrugged his shoulders.

"That's what Kershaw said. But it was the Nsuta Stool that properly popped the cat among the pigeons."

"What did they do? Give it to Berekum?" asked Harcourt, when Foxy had given them Kershaw's version of the contest for the Stool.

"Better if they had." Foxy snorted. "The way I see it—from what I was told—things had been goin' too smooth. Either His Jills got a rush o' confidence to the head, or he couldn't resist showin' off to the chiefs. Now, it's a very tricky business," said Foxy carefully, "showin' off to niggers."

Johnny found it suddenly politic to study a carved bow on the architrave opposite him.

"Unless you've got all the cards, better play it straight: see what I mean? The Gov'nor thought he'd play it fancy, an' pulls in another candidate—fella called Yow Mafo: hands him the Stool—and Ntem and his buddies, all strong, sharp-witted fellas (for niggers) goes slap over to the anti-British faction represented by Adansi, that old cow Ya Ashantua and half a dozen tribes that's tired o' the taste of humble-pie and are ready to take a fling as soon as Ashanti gives them the lead."

"And what happened then?"

"That's where Kershaw cleared out. He don't care for being about when niggers get arguin'," said Foxy discreetly.

"So it's war." Harcourt's words fell heavily into a silence.

Foxy disclaimed opinion with the hitch of a shoulder.

"When I left we were scoutin' around, lookin' for arms dumps. There was a row at Bali and another at Atchiassi, and it was all round the bush that the Ashanti lib for fight. All the niggers on the Coast were runnin' about squawkin' like a henhouse with a fox in it—you'd think the Ashanti were at Akroful, just gettin' ready to wipe out Fort William!"

"What about us?" asked Johnny, as he paused.

"You know what we are. But the shipping offices will have their work cut out," was the significant reply. Foxy looked thoughtfully at the palms of his hands, which he patted one against the other. "After all—there's other ways of dyin' for your country, besides gettin' an Ashanti knife through your face."

"You mean—we're bolting?" Outrage empurpled Harcourt's face.

"Who says we're bolting?" came the fierce rejoinder. "There happens to be some nice rag-tag up round the minefields and in places like Charlestown that'll furnish the niggers with a funny sample of British behaviour if anything happens to scare 'em; that's all."

"They've got the military organised, of course." They'd *better* have them organised! was in Harcourt's voice.

"I wouldn't know. They hadn't got that far when I jumped the Coast."

"What about trade?"

"Trade?" He looked up quickly. "There ain't any trade. It stopped, bang, on the day the Ashanti opened fire, somewhere near Kumassi. Well, I won't keep you any longer——"

Harcourt looked at his watch.

"I've got an appointment—out. If you two want to go on talking, I'll not want anything for a couple of hours." As he went past the back of the chair, he dropped his hands heavily for a moment on Johnny's shoulders; the latter, deeply sunk in thought, barely noticed the rare demonstration.

"What does Morris say?"

"Dunno. Haven't seen him." Foxy sat down again, feeling in his pocket for his pipe, which, although he preferred it to cigars, he had not liked to produce in Harcourt's presence. "Haven't been in Charlestown for weeks; it's no favourite resort o' mine!"

"I'll have to write to him," muttered Johnny.

"Write; but there's no knowing when mails'ull get through. I bet he's got his hands full with the Omo crowd. Their affairs ain't settled yet, you know, since our little circus. There's been four chaps hanged for the murder of Kufi, and about thirty still on trial for participation. Morris has set 'em up under a new chief, but he don't appear to be much good. Some of 'em are flirtin' round with those nasty beggars the Akim, and some have flown the coop, up to Ejesu. You know Akosua was always thick as thieves with the Queen Mother. It looks as if the Ashanti blood in the tribe's comin' out ; I shouldn't wonder if Omo wasn't a particularly warm corner, if the fighting breaks that way."

" Ought I to go back ? "

" What the hell for ? " Foxy gaped.

" They'll need linguists, won't they ? And people to help on the hospital staffs ? And won't they put whites—if they can get 'em—in charge of carrier lines ? There's bound to be jobs going, too, at the Base——"

" Take it easy, chum. Who says we got a Base ? For all we know, it may clear up yet, with a few skirmishes. Somebody's got to get the Gov'nor out of Kumassi—but that's Accra's headache ; Denton's Actin' Gov'nor —accordin' to the papers—much good may it do him ! Take my tip and hold your hosses ; they'll have to let out some more news if this goes on, and it'll be time enough then to decide whether you'll ' rally to the flag ' "— Foxy winked—" or do your bit this end, by keeping the Colonial Office up to the mark. Wait till the cables start flyin' around," advised Foxy, " and don't forget the newspapers can do a lot by workin' on public opinion, when it comes to puttin' the skids on political machinery. You ain't told me yet," he added, " how you're gettin' on. They ain't made you editor yet ? "

" I didn't know you knew I was on a paper. My stuff's not signed— I don't even write it : not the version you see in print. Do you mean to say ' The Di ' gets out there ? "

" Those leader-page articles are the talk of the Coast." Foxy chuckled. " I spotted your hand first time ; good work, chum ! That's the stuff to give 'em. Though it don't make you pop'lar with some of the stiff-collar crowd ! "

" Well, there's one thing we'll have a shot at doing : we'll see that the Gold Coast news gets its proper share of space—instead of being shunted off into corners—as you'll find it in the rest of the Press. The first thing to do will be to get our own correspondent out there—not have to depend on the agencies.

The same thought shot through both their minds.

" That could be a job for you, Johnny ! "

" I'll have a talk to my uncle about it." His heart leapt at the prospect.

" I've been talking to Samson," said Harcourt, on his return, " and we've been on the wire to London. You may as well take a holiday," he threw across his shoulder at Johnny.

" A holiday—— ? "

" I've told Marshall to hold up that new series ; there's no point in wasting ammunition on a blank wall. Nobody's going to bother about politics, with two wars to read about."

" That's what I've been thinking. All the other papers are crammed with Boer stuff ; considering our policy, surely we ought to arrange for special representation on the Coast ? "

Harcourt's eyes narrowed.

" With you as special representative, I suppose ? I thought that 'ud be coming."

" Well, is there anything wrong with the idea ? "

" Wait a bit, wait a bit. It takes a fortnight to get out there ; in a fortnight's time they'll either have Hodgson out of the Fort or the show'll be on—and no mistake about it."

" And we'll have missed the start," pointed out Johnny.

" Pish," said Harcourt. " What's the agencies for ? Now, get this into your head : you're not going gallivanting off for a month or six weeks because of a nigger-rising. There's people on the spot to look after that, and the whole thing may be over by the time you get out there."

" Supposing it isn't ? "

" Don't be childish," said Harcourt fretfully. " We'll see what the cables say, and I'll get in touch with the Colonial Office. If there's anything serious in it "—he paused ; Johnny's eyes were on him. " Surely," they were saying, " the imprisonment of the Queen's representative in an isolated fort of the interior is serious ? "

Harcourt spoke with a rough kindliness.

" The *Seahawk's* down at Pill ; why don't you get Bugle to give her an overhaul, and take a bit of sailing ? "

Johnny thanked him for the offer—an even greater compliment than the previous one of the Panhard. The thirty-foot *Seahawk* was the pride of Harcourt's heart, which no one save he and its crew, ex-mariner of the Flood Line, was permitted to handle. For one week in August—his only holiday—Harcourt and Bugle were to be seen chasing the tides between Pill and the mouth of the Channel. It was difficult to explain that, with one's friends along the Coast probably in mortal danger, one did not feel like enacting the Halcyon rôle. With the arrival of Foxy, Africa had drawn very near : *how* near it seemed impossible to convey to Harcourt.

II

The Face now took up its permanent habitation with him. It was not so intrusive during the daylight hours, but from the first oncoming of dusk it was there, just on the edge of vision ; seldom directly in the line of the eye, but haunting a corner of the retina.

After dark it developed assurance—sometimes as distinct as his own face in a mirror, but in the most curious places. One opened a cupboard, and the Face was there ; bent down to pick up a pair of shoes, and there it was, lying on the back of its skull, looking up impassively ; it was waiting on a stair newell when one went quickly out of a room. As a face, there was nothing particularly horrific about it, save its quality of all-pervasion. It was sometimes incredible that other people did not see it as clearly as oneself. Once or twice he tried staring it out—without effect ; for its eyes, which appeared, when his own were not fixed directly upon them, to be looking at him, had a way of infinitesimally shifting their focus, the moment his sought them.

He found Harcourt gaping at him one night across the hearth-rug.

" What in blazes are you goggling at ? "

A sickly smile was the only possible response to the challenge. Harcourt grumbled :

" It's about time you saw a vet. When are you going to get that fever bug out of your system ? "

The one thing the Face did not care for, apparently, was company ; it seldom plagued him in public places—although he had once or twice the suspicion it was floating somewhere among the crowds along Baldwin Street. When only two or three people were about it was there, serene, remote as the Yoruba head, but not so lofty. It was perfectly recognisable, with its low brow, its broad though well-shaped nose, its thick, flattened lips and the aggrey bead it wore in one ear : except that it had a dignity in its living death, that life had not bestowed on it.

On the Friday night he kept his word to Polly, and slipped into the Hamilton Rooms, staying at the back, so as not to disturb the performers with his presence.

The usual farce was rehearsed, with so keen an appreciation of its witticisms that it was doubtful if the audience would gather, through the giggles of the actors, the point of most of the dialogue. A spirited young lady with a moustache burnt-corked on to her features, a Phil May bowler and a man's riding-coat over her costume, acted and sang, with great *brio*, *The Tin Gee-Gee*, and a young man recited a long and lugubrious temperance poem with a seriousness which, to Johnny, was more exquisitely humorous than all the rest of the performance ; Polly, who had found her way to him at the back of the hall, had to implore him not to disgrace her. " He won't be nearly so funny to-morrow night," she assured him, " because he nearly dies of stage fright and forgets half his words."

He was glad to see that she seemed to have recovered her spirits, and thought it better not to damp them by inquiring after her mother.

" Now it'll be me," she whispered presently. " I come in both halves of the programme, but they're letting me do all my part now, so I'm not late getting back. I do my proper songs first and the ' comics ' after," he heard her chuckle. " I tell them they've got to take the rough with the smooth ! And if they behave themselves through the first part, I'll give them a good laugh after."

" I hope you're well prepared for encores," he told her, and she flicked her eyelashes at him and ran towards the platform.

He knew, while she was whispering to her accompanist, that the many times, as children, they had listened to Polly's singing had not prepared him for what was to come. From the moment she took her place, there was silence : excited chatter among her fellow performers abated ; they found seats, or stood about in knots, their faces turned expectantly towards the platform. There were none of the anxious giggles, the smirks and air of nervous apology of the other soloists ; Polly stood there calmly, taking possession of a visionary audience her manner of grave authority evoked.

She had taken off her hat and coat ; on the badly lighted stage, the comely column of her throat, the proud shelf of her bosom over which the muslin blouse was drawn down tightly and tucked into a trim belt, became statuesque. The only sign she gave of discomposure was a slight screwing up of her eyes over the glare of the footlights. Her hands were clasped in front of her, and she raised them a very little way, still clasped, as the prelude began.

Johnny Flood did not know enough of music to appreciate the full grandeur of that voice of Polly's, which, half-trained though it was, filled the empty hall with a burst of song. Later to be known as a coloratura soprano, that night it ranged effortless through three and a half octaves of one of those showy " drawing-room pieces " taught by ambitious singing masters to their more promising pupils : pseudo-operatic, artistically worthless, and, in fact, dangerous to the tender young voice, not yet " placed " by sufficient training. Now and again sounded, probably without the knowledge of the singer, the pure clarion note that is the true soprano.

She sang as one who loves singing, independent of an audience, and yet is fully aware of her audience, and of the effect her singing produces on it. It was a rich, a *wholesome* voice : guiltless of trick or evasion, of the fashionable minauderies of the concert hall—hitting each note plumb in the middle and giving it its full value of crotchet or quaver, and its just degree of *forte* or of *piano* ; the kind of voice that goes with profound, yet naïve emotions—that takes a simple audience by the throat and brings to the surface all the sentimentality shallowly embedded in British phlegm. It would have taken someone much less responsive than Johnny not to have recognised in Polly's singing those qualities that have made the great popular singers of the past.

As she finished there was a spontaneous patter of applause from her fellow performers, taken by Polly with her slow, bonny smile, with a hand raised casually to adjust a hairpin, with a laconic, " All right—eh ? " and with a nod to the pianist, followed by a wink and a mischievous " Got your handkerchiefs ready ? " to the group nearest the platform.

. . . The room blurred before Johnny. Not *Polly's* voice ?—that smothered, tearing thing that poured its importunacy into the words not yet hackneyed—and faintly shocking to an unsophisticated audience.

" What are we waiting for, O my heart ?
Kiss me once on the brow—and part.
Again . . . again . . . My heart, my heart !
What are we waiting for, you and I . . . ? "

He wanted to shout at her : " Polly, shut *up* ! " and felt that he must have imagined the whole thing when, while the air still trembled with the last " Good-bye ! " she turned happily towards the piano.

" That'll do, won't it ? Now let's have a run through *Daisy, Daisy* ! "

Miss Ethel Phillipson, now Mrs. Dorset Flood, ruffled the pages of her song album, strummed with her right hand the air of *Home from our Mountains*, and turned to find her husband smiling.

" Is something amusing you ? "

" We had a girl—one of the tenants' daughters—who used to sing that. She had rather a good voice. It just reminded me."

Ethel yawned. She was not interested in tenants' daughters ; she thought it was rather tasteless of Dorset to introduce them into the conversation.

III

A Dower House footman arrived at the office with a note which he said he had been told to deliver immediately to Mr. Harcourt. He had been to Berkeley Square, but was told its master had gone to business. Search revealing that the Chairman's room was empty, the footman's jaw dropped ; he knew from experience the result of failure to carry out his mistress's orders.

" What's that ? What's that ? " Old Derbin came tottering to the door of the general office ; whenever anything slipped up in Queen Square organisation, he seemed, by instinct, to get wind of it. He peered at the superscription in Harriet's handwriting, which he knew. " Here—you ! " He beckoned to one of the junior clerks. " Take that to the Chairman—he and Mr. Killick have gone down to the new caisson "—pronounced " cassoon " in local speech. " The *Sampa's* in there : go into Number 19 and get a pass." He looked doubtfully over the tops of his spectacles at Harriet's messenger. " Urgent ? " he snapped. The footman nodded his head.

" Looks like it. She sent me down with the baroosh."

" ' She's ' the cat's mother. Speak properly of your mistress, young man. Look sharp," he enjoined on his subordinate, and grudgingly produced a handful of change from which he picked the necessary coins and handed them to the other. " Since it's for madam, you'd better take a cab." Only the Dower House commanded this attention from Derbin ; Manor affairs could look after themselves, or await the Chairman's convenience.

A junior clerk, vastly enjoying a cab ride on a fine April morning, was to get into trouble later, for failing to recognise the Killick brougham, which passed it, travelling in the opposite direction, somewhere on the Stoke Bishop Road. Harcourt and Samson—also, possibly, affected by the Spring, though heavily laden with the cares of office—agreed on a break with precedent and directed the coachman to the Mall, where they lunched agreeably at the Clifton Club and sat with their cheroots until Samson made a move.

" I'm going down to the Chamber ; are you coming with me ? "

Harcourt shook his head ; he had had enough, recently, of the Chamber of Commerce ; he found it depressing, to watch a body of honest men, doggedly pursuing a Sisyphus task without any apparent hope of reaching an objective.

" I'll walk down ; I could do with a breath of air."

" See you to-night, then, Hacky ? "

" I'll be there," nodded Harcourt, " though I'm getting too old for young folk's parties."

" Gammon ! You'll be giving parties of your own, when Johnny gets married ! "

" More fool he, if he does."

It occurred to Harcourt, after the other was gone, that he owed Samson the courtesy of a birthday present for his daughter, and he turned his steps towards Elson's, then in York Buildings. As usual, when surrounded by the treasure-trove of the small, dark store, he lost count of time. Harcourt had a genuine sense of the beauty of antiquity, and sufficient knowledge to command respect from the dealers he patronised. He pooh-poohed a set of Georgian silver he was offered, beating down the contention that he was missing a bargain. " I've got enough of the stuff to fit out a Mansion House. Show me some Bateman—if you've got any. You ain't ; of course you ain't. Then don't plague me with that pot-bellied stuff." He haggled over the price of a Champion jug and abandoned it, saying he was not interested. Old Elson and his son Fred exchanged winks ; they knew it paid to humour Hacky. The jug was manœuvred out of sight, to wait until their customer had come to his senses.

Harcourt went on his usual way : poking here and poking there—picking up, among other unconsidered trifles, a silver theatre token of 1766, an early Bristol tobacco jar, a glass paper-weight crammed with multi-coloured flowers, for all of which he gravely tendered a half-sovereign in payment. It was one of his favourite jokes, to see what he could pick up out of Elson's " rubbish," for ten shillings. The money was accepted without comment ; throw a sprat to catch a whale. The longer Harcourt could be detained among his " rubbish," the better it was for business.

The greater part of the afternoon had worn away, before he decided, grudgingly, on a pair of candlesticks in dark-blue glass, with pendant lustres, for Linda Killick's present. Miss might not appreciate them, but Samson collected Bristol blue, and it would be a pretty compliment to him. It was one of Harcourt's grudges against the young, that they had no veneration for the beauty of age ; their craving for " the latest thing," no matter if it were pretty or hideous, disgusted and infuriated him ; he would have liked to have taken it out of them with the cane ! Even while young Fred was boxing them, he still deliberated whether he was dishonouring the beautiful pieces, by wasting them on a fashionable flibbertigibbet, who would rather have for her dressing-table some ornate atrocity of her own period. Well—let it go. He directed the package to be sent to Cotham Road, and strolled back to the Saturday afternoon quiet of Queen Square.

All of which foregoing explains why it was four in the afternoon before Harriet's note reached Harcourt : handed to him by old Derbin, who, although it was Saturday afternoon, had stopped behind to perform what he regarded as his duty.

He read it, and cursed her refusal to have the telephone at the Dower House.

" My dear Harcourt,

" Please come to see me on a matter of importance. If your morning engagements prevent you, you will perhaps do me the favour of taking luncheon with me. And if that is impossible, I would be much obliged if you would let me know at what hour of to-day I may expect you. You will appreciate that I would not make this claim on your time and effort for any trivial reason.

" Your affect. Mother,

" H. Flood."

There was nothing for it but order the car. What mischief was she in this time? He had seen her pass-book a few days ago, and this, for once, was in order. It could hardly be any domestic difficulty, with the Manor at hand to lend support or assistance, if either were needed. Shrugging his shoulders, Harcourt abandoned conjecture, as the Panhard chugged its way up from the crawling suburbs into open country. If the damned thing broke down, he would not be at Samson Killick's. It struck him there were a good many people in black about. South Africa—of course. The thought of a red-haired young man stabbed him—and he thrust it angrily aside. Why the devil should anything happen to Joe Prior?

It was an exquisite afternoon, with the shadows of small clouds chasing lightly across the Common. He wondered what Johnny was doing—and, as though in answer to the thought, a figure appeared on a bicycle on the road ahead. Recognising the Panhard, Johnny lifted a hand; the two vehicles drew up alongside each other. After a brief exchange—Johnny, it appeared, had been showing Miranda the use of the bow-perch, in training her hobby—it struck Harcourt to say to him:

" Did you go to the Dower House? "

Johnny gave him, he thought, rather a peculiar look, as he replied:

" As a matter of fact I did."

" Well—how's your grandmother? "

" She sent down word she wasn't well."

" You didn't see her—has she ever done that before? " asked Harcourt, after a pause.

Johnny shook his head.

" She's been all right, I think, since I came back. In the old days, she often had me up to her bedroom."

Damn, thought Harcourt. This was evidently more serious than appeared.

" If I'm not back before you go to Samson's, tell them I'll be over later," he called from the window, as his chauffeur let the clutch in.

Harriet's drawing-room had the cold atmosphere of an apartment which has not been occupied all day. He had been standing for nearly ten minutes in the bay window, looking towards Guerdon, wondering why on earth Drummy did not have some of the timber down—it was worth money—when he heard her enter behind him.

Harcourt, not as a rule sensitive to people's appearances, was shocked by his mother's. She seemed to have shrunk, to have lost the arrow-like uprightness of her carriage, in the few days that had elapsed since last he saw her. Her face was the colour of grey paper. Although she wore her usual elegant attire, it seemed hardly to fit her, but hung loosely on her attenuated frame.

Without speaking, she handed him a letter. Harcourt's face crimsoned as he read it with growing incredulity.

" The *confounded* idiot ! Does Drummy know of this ? "

IV

" My dear Mamma,

" I fear I am about to deal you a heavy blow, but there is nothing to be gained by beating about the bush.

" I am taking Emily Temple to Paris, and later, I hope, to the South of France. We were both guests last week-end at Candleby, and something happened. The details do not matter, but I should like you to believe that, incriminating as the circumstances indeed are, we are not guilty of what has been attributed to us. This is the exact truth, which, however, is impossible to give the world without covering ourselves with the ridicule which seems to be the lot of those who try to maintain their dignity without prevarication. There is, of course, a great scandal, which Emily cannot be left to face alone.

" I have written to Lady Cullen, but as we are virtually strangers, I cannot feel that any letter of mine can convey what I would wish to make clear—that Emily and I are deeply in love, and that my utmost solicitude will always be directed to her comfort and happiness. I realise it is asking a great deal, but we would both be eternally grateful if you could bring yourself to see her ladyship, and to add your assurances to mine. Emily has been trying to write to her guardian for the last twenty-four hours, but the task is too much for her. She is now prostrate, and I much doubt if she will be equal to travelling, as we had planned, in the morning.

" I am asking Venetia for a divorce, and if she grants it me I shall marry Emily at once. If not, believe me, I shall do all in my power to make up for the great sacrifice she has made on my behalf. You will appreciate that we have not taken this irrevocable step without grave reflection.

" I am afraid it will be long before you see me again. This will depend, in some degree, on Venetia's verdict and on that of the law. I shall never in any circumstances allow Emily to be subjected to the slights and worse which are the lot, in our society, of women in her position.

" Tell Hacky I shall be writing to him, but that he may take this as notification that my position on his Board of Directors is vacant. I obviously cannot fulfil my obligations to the Company from the other side of the Channel. Letters forwarded to Lloyds Bank, 19 rue Scribe, will reach me ; Emily, for the present, will be staying with a Madame de Séguin, an old friend of her family, in Passy.

" In conclusion, dear Mamma, may I most sincerely and from the bottom of my heart ask your forgiveness for the pain this letter will cause you.

" I am, as always, your affectionate son,

" ROAN FLOOD."

" He should be ashamed of himself ; a dastardly trick ! "

" I agree with you."

" Good God, the girl's hardly in her twenties, is she ? "

" I don't feel like thinking about Emily Temple, for the present." Harriet lowered herself into a chair, as though the action were painful.

" Well, look at it as you please, the girl's ruined." He used the old-fashioned term distastefully.

" She's not the only one," said Harriet bitterly.

" H'uh, a man can live that sort of thing down easily enough—and you know it ! Though there's plenty of people who'll hold their noses at Roan's performance—of running off with a girl young enough to be his daughter ! " grunted Harcourt. " By God—I suppose Drummy's out of his mind ? "

" I have not yet shown him the letter."

He looked at her compassionately.

" You'd better leave that to me. You've had quite enough loaded on to you, by the look of things."

She drew her shoulders up slightly, as though disclaiming the accusation of weakness.

" I don't mind about that." Suddenly she crumpled, and, for the first time in his life, Harcourt saw his mother's face hidden in her hands. " There is one thing—cowardly though it must seem—you've got to do it for me."

" Of course I will, Mamma," said Harcourt uncomfortably. He hesitated, then bent down and patted her clumsily on the shoulder ; he could not remember ever doing such a thing before. " What is it ? "

" Tell John."

" Johnny ? " he gaped. " What the devil's it got to do with him ? "

" He's in love with her."

" Don't be ridiculous ! "

" If you don't know it, you're the only person who doesn't." Her wan smile suddenly twisted into an expression of such malevolence that he felt himself recoil. " *She* knows it ; Roan must have known. . . . May they both burn in hell for it."

" *Mamma.*" Of course the shock had sent her, for the time, out of her mind. At a loss for words, he paced the room. At the far end he stopped ; he turned ; his big face showed a ludicrous expression of bafflement. " What in the world's come over us ? What *is* there about the girl ? Dorset—Johnny—now Roan ! " He made a gesture which almost made her laugh, with its futility. " Is she—— ? "

Harriet had partly recovered herself ; she sat upright in her high-backed chair, with a fine, ironical smile on her lips.

"My dear Harcourt ! Emily Temple is all there is of good breeding, good manners, and, up to now, good morals. It just happens to be her misfortune that she is what Venetia once described as the Flood 'type.' I don't suppose it has ever occurred to you that we are all very much alike—Selina, Venetia, Emily and I ?—and even poor Isabel. It is just too bad that you are all, as a family, drawn towards something which is, essentially, bad for you all."

"Pish !" said Harcourt. She knew he detested this kind of conversation.

"In the case of Emily, the attraction is peculiarly unfortunate, since it seems to be reciprocal. Oh, why are we wasting words ?" She pressed her thin palms together. "Harcourt, how will you tell John ?"

"Goodness knows. It's a pretty kettle of fish, I must say," he mumbled.

"But it will come better from you than from me," she urged. "Men can say things to one another that are impossible between a man and a woman. I couldn't hide my pity—and he would be humiliated ; I couldn't hide my pain—and it would add to his own——"

"All right, all right, Mamma, don't upset yourself." He spoke irascibly, because she took him aback, in this mood of emotionalism. He had never known her anything but direct, steely, uncompromising in her attitude towards sentiment. "You know, you've always been soft about Johnny. Great heavens, he's not the first fellow who's lost the young woman he's fond of—— !"

"Not in such circumstances of treachery ! She had him to tea, last time he was in town ; he came back radiant about it."

"More fool he. He doesn't suppose he's the only one Emily Temple has given a cup of tea to, does he ? H'uh !" Some wisp of gossip, gleaned in London, detached itself like a cobweb from a remote corner of his mind. "Anybody but a fool 'ud know there were plenty of pebbles on *that* beach !"

"Allow me to advise you, Harcourt, that you will not do much with John, by proceeding on those lines," said Harriet dryly. "Would you care for a whisky and soda before you go ?"

It would take more than one whisky and soda, thought Harcourt, as the car took him back to Berkeley Square, to get the pair of them through this entanglement. Long before the Whiteladies Road was reached, the disgust with Roan which had been dominant in his mind had given way to a vast, bewildered concern for Johnny. The shallowness of the intimacy, on which, secretly, he had prided himself, was revealed by his own ignorance of the boy's sentiments. He told himself that Harriet was probably making too much of the thing altogether ; that it was just "a young man's fancy," magnified by a doting grandmother into a three-act drama of passion. And remained unconvinced. Johnny—it was no use not facing it—was the kind in whom still waters run deep ; the kind that takes things hard. He did not appear to run about with girls ; he never indulged in those gamey little jokes about women with which most young men vaunt, indirectly, their experience of "the sex." Though equal to roaring with laughter when

Harcourt and Samson together swopped an occasional bawdy story, he did not contribute to the symposium.

Harcourt, who had never known delicacy in regard to women, whose amorous experiences had never been anything but of the *ventre à terre* variety, and who had known nothing but boredom in the company of women of his own class, liked less and less the prospect that lay before him. In fact, by the time he tramped up to his dressing-room to wash his hands—having forgotten all about Samson Killick's party—it was thoroughly on his nerves.

The sight of his evening clothes laid in readiness on the chairs jolted his memory unpleasantly. The manservant who told him that Mr. John had gone on received his sourest look.

" Shall I draw your bath, sir ? "

" Get out. I'll ring when I want you."

He sat down ; trying, among other things, to remember if he had ever been young, and simple, and in love. He absolutely failed to discover any trace of it, in those grimy memories which alone rose, to shame him, from the past. He had, he supposed, loved Isabel : and a nice thing that turned out ! Even then—he was ruthless with himself—his emotions, on finding the packet of letters that proved her faithlessness, had not been those of wounded love, but of anger at his betrayal. He had, in fact, hated her, as he was, later, to hate Kitty Prior, for making a fool of him. Casual affairs of the countryside, with the girls of Trenchard Street, with an actress or two on visits to town—what had these taught him of love ? And how was such a one as he to talk of love to a young man, wrung and twisted by emotions he could not even imagine ?

He had known love of a dog and love of a horse, and known those loves returned ; love of a human being was a folly on his immunity to which he prided himself. It had not occurred to Harcourt, secure in his citadel of non-loving, that a red-haired small boy had been the first to weaken his defences, had prepared the way for the one who was to complete their ruin. He sat, gripping the arms of the chair, his white head dropping, his dark eyes staring, his heavy lower lip relaxed like a child's about to cry—aghast before the fact of his love for Johnny.

He did not know how long he sat there ; he only knew that solitude, and the thing which had to be done, suddenly became intolerable. He pushed himself up from the chair and went downstairs to the telephone.

CHAPTER TEN

I

A PARTY in a house full of young people, all of whom have known each other from childhood, is apt to be a formidable experience for a stranger. Johnny was not a stranger, but there had been no exchange of hospitalities in his youth between Guerdon and the Bristol mercantile families, and it was only since he had come into the business that he had made acquaintance of the families of his uncle's colleagues.

He was young enough to enter full-heartedly into the robust merriment, the homely atmosphere, the casual mixture of games and dancing, the cheerful uproar that swung around three generations—all of whom made no bones about enjoying themselves and were insistent that their guests should have no less lively a time. There were none of the assumptions of sophistication that stiffened such functions at Guerdon; no haughty youths or patronising girls, aping the manners of their elders. The lack of "style," which Gilbert would have deprecated, was amply atoned for by a good, briney element of sea-salt supplied by young men in the running for their "ticket," and by the antics of schoolboy and schoolgirl friends of Linda's younger brothers and sisters.

Beamed upon by aunts, elderly cousins and the grandparents of both sides, Johnny found himself capering through the Lancers with the best: playing "forfeits," chasing a spry young Killick along upstairs landings in the course of Hide and Seek; turning the pages of Mrs. Killick's music while Samson roared *Maid of Athens*, his invariable contribution to the evening's entertainment on such occasions—received with the rapturous applause accorded to the tone-deaf and leather-lunged when enjoyment has reached the pitch of the more noise, the more fun.

"I wonder what has happened to your uncle?" he had been asked when they all trouped in to supper—served at seven-thirty for the benefit of the more juvenile members of the company. Johnny explained that he had had to go out to the Dower House, but that he would no doubt be coming later. He looked at the clock with something like astonishment when, at a quarter to nine, Samson came to his side.

"Your uncle's on the telephone, Johnny; he wants to speak to you."

Harcourt's voice, distorted by the instrument, reached him through the crash of a polka, the jangle of laughter and singing. Johnny, who had automatically snatched a yellow paper boater trimmed with red and purple feathers from his head, on receiving his uncle's summons, had to press his ear closer to the receiver to make out what he was saying.

"Come on home. I've got something to say to you."

"Right, sir." He paused; was he to be given any inkling of what lay behind the order? "I'll come—now."

He heard Harcourt fumble the receiver back on its hook. He found Samson standing at his elbow.

" Nothing wrong, is there, Johnny ? "

" I shouldn't think so." The disclaimer was as much for his own re-assurance as for Samson's. " He'd have said if there were—wouldn't he ? But I'm afraid I've got to say good night, sir. He wants me."

" Be damned to the old bashaw ! " said Samson good-humouredly. " Would you like me to ring back, and ask him what he means by not turning up to Lindy's party ? "

" No, I think I'd better go," said Johnny.

Harcourt was waiting for him ; on the walnut stand at his elbow was a bottle of Napoleon brandy and two glasses. It was evident that he had been putting on time for Johnny's arrival.

" Well—did you enjoy yourself ? " he grunted. Avoiding Johnny's eyes, he filled the second glass.

" Famously ; I like old Samson. He's a good sort."

" All the family there ? "

" I should think so ; it looked like about a hundred people ! " He laughed. But what was Harcourt beating about the bush for ? " Is Grand-mamma all right ? " he asked, as a sudden possibility struck him.

" Yes. Go on—have your brandy."

" I say—this is a bit tough for me ! " He eyed the glass, as he lifted it doubtfully. " I'm rather off spirits just now, you know, sir. Vet's orders."

" Go on," said Harcourt ; refilled his own glass, and drained it.

Johnny stood watching him, his own glass still in his hand. Presently he lifted it and took a sip. Still Harcourt had not spoken.

" It strikes me, sir "—he made his voice deliberately steady—" you've got some pretty bad news for me—when you offer me about a quarter of a pint of your best brandy."

Harcourt turned his face towards him slowly ; it was purple, and seemed to have lost its drawing.

" Emily Temple has gone to Paris with your Uncle Roan."

He heard himself say :

" *What ?* "

He saw Harcourt looking at him, saw the big shoulders lift, saw his right hand go out, with the palm open, and drop again to his side. He felt a queer sensation round his lips, as though, without any volition of his own, they were smiling.

" Well——" said Johnny. " That's that." He lifted the glass and drank slowly. When he set it down, like Harcourt's, it was empty. After a moment, Harcourt leaned forward and filled it again.

. . . Later on, when the pain in his head was no longer to be borne, he said :

" I'll go out for a bit and get some air."

" Do you want me to come with you ? "

" No, thanks. I'll not be more'n a quarter 'f 'n hour. Jus' down to the

Backs—an' back." He repeated it, as though he liked the sound of it. "The Baxanback!"

The door slammed. Harcourt remained slumped, scowling at the bottle. Ought he to follow him? No; no. Leave the boy alone—to pull himself together in his own way. Damn' good boy. Taken it like a trump—like a brick—like a *Flood*. He knew the panacea he would have found, at Johnny's age—in Johnny's place. So much the better if he found it; there was no shortage of that kind of medicine in Bristol. Fuddled himself, he tried to remember in which murky chambers of the past he had delved, in search of the philosophy to which his nephew had listened, with a polite, attentive smile plastered across his face.

II

The Park Street pavement rose and fell in waves, the street lamps coiled up like gnarled trees, rocking in the wind. It was surprising to find so many people about: people of all sorts and sizes, giants and dwarfs, with faces on different levels; and why were they dancing? Up and down Park Street—dancing and dancing; on the kerbstone and in the gutters and sidling across the cobbles. Lights everywhere—square boxes of light, crashing down the hill emitting blue and lilac-coloured sparks, square boxes crawling up as though drawn by invisible pulleys; lights in windows, chains of lights strung out over the dizzy pit towards which his feet—slip, lurch, jostle—were carrying him. Dancing and dancing—bodies. Bodies jerked on strings. Swinging their arms and their legs absurdly and making grimaces with their pink faces. Coming up close—collision? No; swinging away; swinging their heads and their legs and their arms in their silly dance. Pavement gone soft. Feet going to sleep. Too much dancing. Too many lights. Body coming now—getting in the way—now for it—*bump*. Sorry—beg pardon. Tiny faces scattered like hawthorn blossom on a dark night tide. Tide going out . . . Good-bye for ever. . . . What are we waiting for? . . . I beg your pardon, ma'am. . . .

"Why—Mr. Johnny!"

Soft pink face—fuzz of gold about it—lamp behind—must be a body somewhere——

"Why—did you come to the concert after all?"

Did he? The wind made an eddy of the dancing figures and the hawthorn blossom and the lights on their curious stalks.

"Mr. Johnny—are you ill?"

The muscles of his mouth felt stiff with smiling, but he forced them again into the pattern which, he seemed to remember, was the pattern of politeness, and his hand went to his head but came away empty. He looked at his empty hand in surprise; surely there ought to have been a hat in it?

"Mercy on me!" whispered Polly Bowling.

A church clock was striking eleven, and she was only a few steps from her own door. "Not a minute later than eleven, young ladies." Concession made to the Shipwrecked Mariners. Was any mariner nearer shipwreck than this wanderer down the stream of night?

"Mr. Johnny——?" She touched his hand timidly, felt its deadness, grasped it and drew it through her arm. Suddenly a glow of strength poured through her, of protectiveness, of maternity. "It's all right, Mr. Johnny; I'll look after you; lean on me."

Another clock was striking. "Don't be silly," muttered Polly, to the strokes quivering against the starry gong overhead. "I can't leave him in this state, can I?" What about getting in? Suppose they lock you out? "I can go to the Y.W.—or the Salvation!" You'll lose your job. "Oh, pooh to that—I'm quitting, anyhow. That's right; you lean on me. Mercy goodness, he's *tipsy*! Whatever sort of a party can it have been—at the Killicks', of all people!"

All that long way—across Colston Avenue—and along Baldwin Street—and then the Bridge—and Redcliff Street: was it possible, without help, at this time of night? And coming back—alone—past the empty warehouses, with all the trumps and derelicts crouching in the doorways, and the drunken men coming out of the pubs, and the women waiting for them—goodness; she felt her spirit quail. It would almost be better to spend the night in the porch of the Redcliff—in a holy place like that one was sure to be safe. The Redcliff . . . J. R. Bowling, faithful servant, good friend. Her arm tightened more closely on the limp one through her own; she pressed it closely against her waist, halting for a moment to get her breath. The wind had scattered her hair about her face; she tried to find a hairpin with her free hand, to make herself more respectable. What would his landlady think? Supposing she thought they had been out together—on the razzle? Oh, dear, that would make things awkward. . . .

But she must know Mr. Johnny wasn't that kind of gentleman. If only he would manage to keep on walking. Every now and again they had to stop; people looked at them with amusement, with sneers, and she felt her face burning. A drunk, being taken home by a girl! She felt the tears starting to her eyes, for all the decency of her traditions was offended by the thought expressed by the sniggers, by one or two lewd jests she could not help overhearing. His weight was getting heavier and heavier on her arm, his ankles kept turning over, twice the pair of them nearly fell. In despair she flung her arm round his waist and drew his arm across her shoulder.

The space between the end of Baldwin Street and the Bridge brought the encounter she was dreading: the portentous figure of a policeman slowly advancing with purpose in his tread. He was within a few paces of them when Johnny gave a lurch that obliged Polly to throw both her arms round him.

"Oh, please, officer!" She lifted her face, bathed in tears, to the impassive one of the law; oh, please God let him see she was a decent girl. "Please could you help us? We've got to get home—to Ship Lane." A faint glimmer of hope had come into her mind, that Johnny's landlady would let her spend the night in the sitting-room: followed by the sinking knowledge that to arrive with a policeman at the door would be to create the worst sort of impression. But it was that or nothing ; if Johnny became completely helpless, she knew she could not manage him alone.

"Now then—what's all this ?" He caught Johnny roughly under the armpit ; she felt, and instantly resented, the brutality of the movement.

"There's no need to be so rough with him—can't you see he's ill ?"

"We know this sort of illness ! Come on, now—you !"

It was useless to protest ; there was nothing to gain by setting him against them. She bit her lip, doing her best, on the other side, to make up for the policeman's handling ; she found his hand and pressed it, clammy, against her breast.

"What number, Ship Lane ?"

She muttered it.

"That where you live too ?"

"Of course. I—I'm his wife," gulped Polly. It had come to her in a flash that this was the only way to get rid of the policeman when they arrived at the door. She had a moment of panic, for fear he had noticed her unringed left hand, and hid it in the folds of her skirt.

"We—we can manage now, thank you." After a seeming eternity they had reached the narrow street, with its squalid little brick houses, one exactly the same as the other. The windows were sheets of black glass, the lace curtains showing smokily behind them. Whoever was in had gone to bed. "That's all right—thank you very much," she gasped. He must be got away, before ringing the bell ! The little street was badly lighted, with only a bracket-lamp at the end. Johnny stood there, swaying a little, staring at the door as if he had never seen it before ; she clutched him to steady him. So long as he did not fall down before they managed to wake the landlady. . . .

"Please !" said Polly desperately. "I don't want them to see—that a policeman—brought my husband home !"

The appeal succeeded—by good fortune. Policemen are human beings ; Ship Lane had, as such places go, a decent reputation, and the representative of the law's majesty knew well enough the stigma that attaches, in the eyes of a censorious neighbourhood, to his uniform. Experience had taught him enough to enable him to size Polly up as a respectable girl, very much upset by her companion's lapse from the path of rectitude. With a muttered "Good night, mum," he paced away down the street ; Polly waited for him to reach the end before putting her trembling hand to the bell. She held Johnny propped between her body and the wall.

She had rung four times before it dawned on her quivering consciousness that there was no one at home. Oh, dear God, what are we to do now ?

Suddenly her heart gave a bound of relief.

"Why, Mr. Johnny—haven't you got your key ?"

He did not seem at first to understand what she was saying.

"*Key !*" repeated Polly urgently. "You've got a key, haven't you ? Oh, do find it——"

The word seemed to have penetrated his understanding, but his movements were so weak and motiveless that, impatient, she plunged her hand into the pocket of his trousers and gave a gasp of thankfulness as her fingers closed on the key-ring. She fumbled them wildly, trying one after another in the lock. It did not seem possible that one of the six or seven should not fit. At the end of palpitating moments she turned to him trembling.

" I can't make it open. Will you try? Oh, please do try!"

He tried to oblige her. The keys fell clattering on the step.

Baffled, she bent to grope for them. He had never told her, and, in his present state, he did not remember, that it was more than a fortnight since he had given up the Ship Lane key, on his removal to Berkeley Square. It was Polly who, with her experience of humble homes, knew it was possible, if the owners of the house were out, or away, that the key was hidden somewhere—in some cranny or chink that her distracted fingers, exploring up and down the brickwork on each side of the door frame tried to discover. *Nowhere.* Smooth and solid brick and mortar met her fingertips wherever they moved.

Her sobbing penetrated the remote world into which Johnny was withdrawn.

" What is it, Polly? Polly, why are you crying?"

Without answering, she dropped on her knees. The top step hollowed slightly under the palms of her hands. But the framework of the door itself, at the bottom, was straight. She gave a sobbing gasp as her fingers touched metal. A moment later the door swung in.

" Where's your room? Where's your room, Johnny?"

Ancient custom directed his steps. There was no light, but Joe and he had too often crept up those dark stairs, not to find, automatically, the way.

" Haven't you got any matches?"

Of course he had matches; they were there, in the pocket where the keys were kept. She struck one, shivering. The gas bracket thrust out its gaunt arm, almost exactly above where she was standing.

" But—the bed's not made up!"

Not made up? Even the sight of a bare mattress was grateful to Johnny. He staggered across the room and let himself drop. A moment's ecstasy. . . . Then up and down, up and down in waves, like being tossed in a blanket. But worse. Hammer, hammer, inside his skull: something like a gimlet, driving through his temples; agony—that relieved itself a very little when he sat up—if he could sit up. . . .

" Help me—help me. . . ."

" Oh, Johnny!"

" That's better—your shoulder—yes, that's better—don't go away, will you?"

" Of course I won't——" Suppose his landlady returned? Whatever would she think—a girl—in Mr. Johnny's bedroom? Why wasn't the bed made up? Why was it all so uncomfortable?

" Polly—how kind you are——"

His poor face—all altered—with pain. Nobody ought to suffer like that. It wasn't drink. People didn't shiver, with drink. And yet he was burning.

Blankets? Something to prop him up? My shoulder. My cape across him. Dorset's brother. Mr. Johnny. Always so sweet. Always so good. Johnny.

Johnny. In trouble. Wanting somebody to comfort him.

"Do you see it?"

"See what?" Her gaze went negligently about the room.

Fancy not having his bed made up for him. These landladies! Out somewhere—having a good time.

"You won't leave me alone with it, Polly?"

"Of course . . . I'd never leave you . . . alone, Johnny . . . darling."

III

On two walking-sticks, which had replaced the crutches, and the nurse's arm, Gilbert negotiated the broad, shallow stairs of the Royal Hotel, to the first floor. Outside, a green haze of Spring blurred College Green, and spattered its shadows on the Victorian effigy which, fifty years previously, had usurped the position of the beautiful stone cross, now banished to Stourhead.

"Well, so much for your fussin', nurse! Nobody here?"

"Not yet, sir—captain!" the page corrected himself, under the cold glitter of Gilbert's monocle.

"Send a waiter. Damn' queer business—eh?" as the page left the room.

"I'm sure I don't know," said the nurse discreetly.

"What? No; nach'rally not." Gilbert recollected himself. "Well, nurse—wait downstairs, will yeh? I expect my brother'll be—ah! Here we are. Well, Doss, old boy——?"

"What the devil's all this about?" Dorset, glossy, agreeably redolent of Mr. Penhaligon's Hammam Bouquet, divested himself of a belted travelling coat and cap.

"By Gad, you look as if marriage agrees with you!"

"It does. Have you any notion at all why we're here?"

"Not the dimmest." Gilbert shrugged his shoulders.

"Huh! Pretty cool of young Johnny, whistling us up——!"

"Johnny's quite a fella, nowadays!" Gilbert gave his pleasantly vacuous smile. "Tell you something, old boy; young Johnny's in the runnin' for the money, doncherknow!"

"Whose—Hacky's?"

Gilbert nodded.

"Devil of a joke—what?—if Hacky made him his heir?"

"And cut out Mary and Isabel?"

Gilbert shrugged.

"You know how Hacky is about them. Dashed uninterestin' gels—ain't they? Got husbands to provide for them."

His hands in his pockets, Dorset paced the room. Marriage, as Gilbert had observed, agreed with him ; it had also, to a surprising degree, steadied him. Ethel was a gratifying and (so far) not too exigent wife, with all the right Flood principles : church, children and *cuisine*—balanced by a nice regard for social observations. She liked entertaining and being entertained : was witty enough to hold her place as a hostess, without the faintest glimmer of that dangerous kind of intelligence which is anathema to the male. Her morals were impeccable, and she knew just what allowance to make for the less perfect morals of other people, without appearing to be aware of it. Although it was a matter of common knowledge that certain guests expected rope for their aberrations, nothing could ever take place under the young Dorsets' roof like that shameful affair at Candleby—which had shaken Dorset more than he admitted. He sweated, occasionally, in the night, to think what a narrow escape he had had from marrying Emily Temple.

" I only hope the young idiot hasn't got himself into trouble. My God, we've had about enough, for the present ! "

" Uncle Roan ? Nasty business," concurred Gilbert.

" Damned unpleasant for Ethel. Not so good, when you've just got married, to find yourself in the thick of a particularly dirty scandal." Dorset consulted his watch. " This is going a bit far—upon my soul, it is ! The least he can do's to be punctual—— ! "

" Here he is."

Neither Dorset nor Gilbert Flood were young men of imagination ; neither realised, as they turned towards the door, that they accepted the authority of the short figure that walked into the room. In comparison with them, their young brother had an air of middle age. Grey-faced, sallow, provincially dressed, the indifference of his bearing made nothing of them and the years of their domination over a junior.

" Sorry to have kept you waiting."

" Hacky on the war-path ? " Gilbert offered the excuse which the other did not appear to find necessary.

" No, he's in Liverpool. Sit down, won't you ? What are you drinking ? " He walked sharply to the bell and rang it. A waiter appeared, with surprising alacrity.

" Yes, sir ? "

Neither the tone nor the manner were lost on the other two, unaccustomed to seeing Johnny as a recipient of deference.

" . . . I'm sorry to put you to this trouble. I thought I'd better see you, before going away."

" Going—where ? "

" Back to the Coast." His eyebrows flickered, as though to say, " Where else ? " " This Ashanti business. They'll want white men. I think I might be useful."

" What's Hacky's view on that ? " asked Dorset, after a pause.

" One has one's own view "—he shrugged his shoulders—" doesn't one ? "

" Obviously. All the same—what the devil's the idea ? You're not a soldier ; do you mean you're going to fight niggers ? " came sharply from Gilbert.

" I'd rather not ; it depends on what comes along. What I actually wanted," said Johnny slowly, " was for you both to witness my will."

The other two exchanged glances.

" Look here," said Dorset. " Aren't you being a damn' fool ? You came back last summer with a man-sized dose of fever ; you look as sick as a dog, now——"

" All right. We'll let that go. I've married Polly Bowling."

" You're out of your mind——" came on a dry whisper from Dorset.

" We were married by special licence the day before yesterday. If you want the proof you'd better go and look at the register at Easton in Gordano."

" My—Christ ! "

Gilbert yammered :

" Does Mamma know ? "

" Nobody knows. Except yourselves. And for the present," said Johnny, " nobody has to know. I leave that to your honour—both of you." His glance, red-rimmed with weariness, went from one to the other. " Polly's mother is ill—probably dying——"

" I should think it would revive her pretty quickly—to know she's got that pretty slut of a girl of hers married off to a son of the squire's—— ! " Dorset gave a short, bitter laugh.

" That's enough," said Johnny quietly.

" It's too bad of you ; by Gad, it *is* too bad of you ! " Gilbert was mumbling. " This'll about break Mamma's heart, you know. And right on top of that rotten Candleby affair—— ! "

" Cut that right out." Johnny's voice crackled across the uneasy sentences. " You used a very offensive word just now, Doss—and if we were at home I'd knock you down for it. You seem to forget—both of you—that Polly grew up with us ; that we all played together as children ; that her family and ours have been linked together for more than a century——"

" Don't talk such blistering rubbish ! I withdraw the word I used," muttered Dorset, " but you can't expect Mamma and Aunt Vicky—not to mention Ethel—to accept Polly Bowling as——"

" Polly Flood."

Dorset snorted. For the love of heaven, whatever sort of a family would Ethel Phillipson think she had married into ? A cruel twist came on the corners of his lips. Let her think. Let anyone think that money gave them a right to criticise the Floods.

" Hang it, Doss—you always liked Polly."

This was carrying war into the enemy camp—with a vengeance ! A sudden fury—with himself, and for Johnny, for so allowing himself to be gulled—deprived Dorset of words ; he made a gesture of futility. A sudden thought smote him.

" When is the child to be born ? "

Johnny's face was like granite.

" It takes nine months, doesn't it ? "

An extraordinary sound came from Gilbert.

" With luck, I'll be back. If I'm not—it would seem the natural thing, wouldn't it, to ask you—between you—to look after my wife ? "

" ' Don't let poor Polly starve ! ' " A laugh broke from Dorset. " My God—who's mad in this outfit ? You're not, by any chance, asking me, a married man, or Gilbert, who will certainly be married some day, to support your widow and child, are you ? "

" I've got a bit of Uncle Quentin's legacy, that I'm settling on the child : the rest, of course, reverts to the Cuba family. There'll be a few pounds in the bank, for Polly ; she can't be left with nothing but that."

" She has her parents, hasn't she ? "

" She has. And they'll turn her out, for marrying a Flood."

" Balderdash."

" I can only tell you what I know to be true. Other people besides ourselves, Doss, have their pride," said Johnny wearily. " Let's cut the money question out of it, shall we ? I don't think any of you are ever likely to be troubled—by Polly. She's the last person to ask for charity ! "

" There's no need to drag in sentiment. It's all very well—but a woman entitled to call herself Flood can't be allowed to go about sayin' she's unprovided for : can she ? " Gilbert appealed fretfully to Dorset. " Looks confoundedly bad ; puts the fam'ly in a rotten light——"

" And what, may one ask, has Harcourt to say to this ? "

" He has not been told about it," said Johnny, after a pause.

" Huh ! Just as well, I should think. Well, we've had a few scandals in our time, but you've certainly topped them. It's the first time, to my knowledge, that a Flood's married his mistress." Dorset gave a short, unpleasant laugh.

" You think that does us credit, do you ? "

" I don't think it does *you* credit—to involve us in a mess like this."

" Will you leave my credit out of it ? " He had been looking out on the Green ; he turned now from the window, to face them both. " Can't we cut out all this stuff about family ? There'll be time enough to worry about that later on. I didn't get you here for the sake of hearing your opinions on the right or wrong of what Polly and I have done. There's one thing I want to get clearly into your minds : that there's no question of my being ' caught ' by a designing young woman. That, of course, will be Mamma's view, and Aunt Vicky's, and probably your wife's, Doss ; but it isn't true.

" I had the hardest job in the world to get Polly to marry me. She only gave in, in the end, for the sake of the child—if there is one——"

" Do you mean to say you don't *know* ? "

" How the hell should we know ? It's only—five days ago."

" You must be out of your senses." Dorset spoke incredulously.

" It's not the sort of thing one takes chances on, is it ? Supposing I'm killed—is my son to be a bastard ? "

" Supposing it isn't your son ? For God's sake," said Dorset, intercepting Johnny's look. His bitterness and rage alike had gone ; only remained a profound concern for this fool of a young brother for whom—he was surprised to discover—he had always cared. " For God's sake, Johnny! Don't lose your temper again; the only thing we can now do is to try and consider this—this disaster as dispassionately as we can. Can't you see that—even as Polly's husband—you won't get one person in fifty round here to accept you as the father of her child?"

" What in hell do you mean?" His lips whitened.

" You don't seem to realise the spotlessness of your own reputation!" Dorset's lips parted, but there was no mirth in his smile. " Unfortunately, old fellow, Polly's been no miser of her charms; you know that as well as we all do. They'd be more likely to put me down as the person responsible——"

" Behave yourselves!" Gilbert's heavy right-hand stick crashed down on Johnny's forearm as the latter struck.

" Damn you—let me get at him——!"

Dorset's hands, pinioning his wrists, held him helpless.

" Listen; and don't be a fool. I've kissed Polly—twice—in the park. That's all—before heaven."

" So that's why you try to dirty her credit?"

" I'm not dirtying her credit! You know what they all say about Polly —and it's probably nothing but local malice. But do, for God's sake, old boy, try to remember there's no smoke without fire. Even if Polly has never gone over the mark with any of her flirtations, nobody about Guerdon's going to believe it. *Now* can't you see why we're so put out about what you've let yourself in for?"

The strength drained out of him as Dorset let go of his wrists. A chair stood behind him, and Dorset's hand on his shoulder pressed him down into it. There was silence for a long time: silence broken only by Dorset's pacing up and down the broad room with his hands behind him, the back of one clenched hand beating into the palm of the other.

" The first thing you've got to realise," Dorset was saying, " is that Gilbert and I are backing you—naturally."

" Nach'rally." The monocle twinkled blankly across the room.

" Wait a minute. It's all very well for you to say that—and, of course, I appreciate it. But I can only accept your 'backing'—the moral kind; I'll look after the material myself—on one condition."

" Well——" Dorset's brows arched themselves at Gilbert. " I must say, in your place, I wouldn't have much to say about conditions. Go on."

" That you accept Polly's child, without any reservations, as mine. Unless you do that, both of you, there's no more to be said."

" That's a pretty tall order—what?" came from Gilbert, after a pause.

" Only because you've let Doss talk you into another point of view."

" It's all very well to say that. What do you say, Doss?"

Dorset was standing still; his handsome, high-coloured face wore a strange expression. He snapped at Johnny:

" I suppose you know what you're talking about?"

" I do."

Dorset lifted his broad shoulders and allowed them to drop.

"That finishes it, then." He looked at Gilbert, who nodded.

"You see—the only person to be considered is—the child. I'm talking about it as a certainty, but of course—anything may happen. If I come back, all safe and sound, this is a waste of breath! And if there—isn't—a child——"

"What'll you do? Get a divorce?"

"That will be for Polly to decide. I should consider myself very fortunate, if she chose to let things rest as they are. But if her future happiness is bound up in any other person—I'd certainly have no right to stand in her way."

Dorset was staring at him.

"What an extraordinary fellow you are. I'm damned if I know where you get these chivalric notions. They certainly aren't in the blood!"

"Chivalry be blowed. There's such a thing as plain justice, isn't there? That's all I'm trying to bargain for now; I want justice for my son, if he's born, and if I'm not here to see he gets it. It sounds a poor thing to say—but I've got a pretty shrewd notion that father's emotions, when he hears about my marriage, are going—at any rate for a time—to wash out his sense of justice. That's why I want you two to back me up. The Bowlings mustn't suffer for this. As a matter of fact, Polly thinks her mother is going to die, and she is quite positive her father will turn her out, for marrying a Flood!"

"Pish! That old-fashioned stuff——"

"It's no good, Gilbert; people like the Bowlings are old fashioned, and the lives they live are the lives of the middle of last century. Bowling, I suppose, knows his daughter would never be accepted by us; he'd be humiliated by Polly's marrying 'out of her station.' So who's to look after the child?"

"Well, what do you mean? Do you want it separated from its mother?"

"My God, no. That would break Polly's heart. But she's got to be helped over the education. She's been educated herself—in a way; but it's not the way that's of any use in bringing up my son. She can't do anything, for instance, about getting him into a good school, and, obviously, she can't give him the discipline a boy needs—especially a boy with our blood in him! I—well, naturally, I'd like him to go into the business——"

"I can't see why you haven't taken Hacky into your confidence over this. Aren't you his favourite—by now?"

"I'll tell you why I haven't bothered Uncle Hacky," said Johnny. "To start with, you two are my contemporaries. By the time my son grows up, Hacky's going to be an old man—and I don't believe he's a good life. I'll tell him—naturally; but I wanted to make sure of you, first. You belong, like myself, to the age we're living in; Uncle Hacky belongs to an age that is dead, or, at least, is dying so fast that people like Hacky can't keep pace with it. I don't want my son to be shackled with the ideas that belonged to that age: I want him to be free to make the most of the times he's born into. He's not going to find it easy, because he's not going to have the one thing that seems to count to-day: money. He won't have the advantages we've had—if I say, *you've* had, you won't misunderstand me; I'm a kind of misfit. I've not used the advantages I suppose I might have done: Guerdon; an influential background; 'connections,' through Mamma, with important families. My son will have none of those—through my fault. So he's got to have all the best we can give him in other directions."

"Well?" from Dorset, as Johnny paused.

"I want you to allow me to appoint the pair of you as guardians—so that, if anything goes wrong, when I'm in West Africa, I'll know his interests, and Polly's, are being looked after. The legacy will be payable to Polly, until he comes of age; incumbent, of course, on her seeing he gets a proper education. I think it ought to just do that—though it will mean a pretty narrow shave for her. Afterwards, it should be up to him to provide for her—if she needs it. Uncle Hacky's advice will be invaluable; I'd like you to consult him over any alteration in the disposition of the funds."

"What the devil made you do it?" burst from Dorset; he had sat silent, with his head in his hands, through the foregoing.

"That's my business," rapped Johnny. "Have you been listening to what I was saying?"

An hour later the car was taking Dorset and Gilbert back to Guerdon. The nurse sat in front, with the chauffeur, separated from the others by a sheet of glass.

"There's one thing," Gilbert was saying, "that nobody seems to have thought about."

"What's that?"

"Supposing it's not—a boy?"

"Oh—in that case——" In the manner of all Floods, Dorset swept the suggestion aside. He was calculating that his own son should be born, if all went well, a good six months before Johnny's. "There's no need to bother, if it's not a boy," he added, as an afterthought. "I'll tell you what, Gil." He turned heavily towards his brother. "I'm not going to let this damn' thing lie. I'm not going to let them make a mug out of Johnny! An infernal piece of trickery—that's what it is!"

"Looks like it," admitted Gilbert. "Same time," he mumbled, "I wouldn't have said she was smart enough, to pull a fast one, like that. 'f you ask me, there's something confoundedly fishy—somewhere."

"For two pins—I'd go to Hacky!"

"Shouldn't do that," counselled his brother. "Don't want to make a mess of the young 'un's prospects."

"Blast his prospects!" exploded Dorset. "What sort of prospects has he got, do you suppose—after marrying Polly Bowling?"

CHAPTER ELEVEN

I

"NATURALLY, you must follow the dictates of your conscience, John. What is Harcourt's feeling about the matter?"

"I've got his permission to go, sir. A great deal of our business is at a standstill, with this trouble on the Coast."

"One can but hope for a definite settlement, this time. It seems extraordinary our punitive measures were not more effective under Scott," said Dromore fretfully. He lifted a paper-weight, put it down again, and was delivered of—for him—an astonishing remark, "I wish you were not going."

Johnny found himself at a loss for a reply: knowing silence to be ungracious, he could think of no phrase which, in sincerity, met his father's unexpected overture.

"I'll not be away long," was all he could find to say.

"You must let me know if you require any—assistance."

"Thanks very much. I will."

The scene with Selina was brief, and followed a classic pattern. Selina was standing in front of her looking-glass, patting the sleek coils which Mytton had redressed; the opalescent gleam of her broad, naked shoulders was very handsome by the light of the candles on her dressing-table, and she was engaged, with serious absorption, in coaxing a curl towards her left eyebrow.

"I've already sacrificed one son! It seems hard I should have to go through all the strain and worry again—on your account, Johnny!"

"Try not to look at it that way, Mamma. For all we know—the whole thing may be over, by the time I get out to the Coast."

"I simply can't imagine why you want to meddle in matters that haven't anything to do with you. It's not as if you were in the Army!"

"It's mere chance I'm not with the Volunteers, in South Africa," he reminded her.

"Well——" Selina shrugged her superb shoulders. "All I can say is, you're all very selfish. Roan, with his ridiculous behaviour—and now you." She returned his kiss grudgingly. "I suppose we shall be seeing you, before you leave."

"I'm afraid not, Mamma. I'm sailing to-morrow."

"To-morrow!" came in a cry from Vicky, silent spectator of the scene.

"It's rather sudden, Aunt Vicky—but it's a matter of getting passage. Our own ships are all on the move—I missed the *Sampa*; she sailed yesterday. The *Cetus* leaves to-morrow, with a lot of rations and hospital stuff——"

"The *Cetus*? Not one of Runstables?" incredulously.

"With my old pal Wildblood. Comic, isn't it? Comic, isn't it?"

he repeated. There was something unbearable in the look on Vicky's face. She seemed dazed when he kissed her.

When the latch of the door clicked, she found Selina standing beside her with a glass.

"You had better have a few sips of this ; I'm just taking a little myself."

"Good gracious, what is it ?" Vicky sipped, had a brief convulsion, and lowered her nose to the glass. "*Spirits*, Selina ? I thought the doctor had forbidden——"

"I feel," said Selina calmly, "I need a little pick-me-up before dinner."

"Oh—are you coming down ?"

"Oh, yes, I'll come down." Absently Selina was refilling the glass she had left on her dressing-table ; absently she tilted it to her lips. Fascinated, Vicky watched the thick white columnar throat swell and contract, as she swallowed her second dose—neat. Great God ! thought Vicky : is this the next thing ? Roan—a social outcast ; Selina—an inebriate ? She lifted her own glass to her lips mechanically, shuddered a little—but was obliged to admit the brandy helped to steady one.

Oh, God ; Miranda—and then Harriet. He had to fight, for a moment, against the cowardly instinct to run away. In the end, he slammed open the schoolroom door and walked in. She lifted her face, bright with welcome —then, suddenly, it went dead.

"When do you go ?"

"How—how did you know ?" he stammered.

She gave a scornful little laugh.

"I've been expecting it, ever since the war started, with the Ashanti."

"I'm going out as *The Diorama* correspondent—not to fight," he told her quickly. She turned her head away, hunching her shoulders. "Don't be a little beast, Winkle," he tried to coax her.

"When are you going ?"

"To-morrow morning."

"So it's got you," she muttered bitterly.

"What's got me ?"

"The Coast. Oh, how could you be such a fool ?" she wailed. Puzzled, he took her quickly in his arms. "You got away twice," she was sobbing, "and now—and now——"

"Don't be a duffer, Winkle. I shall count on your letters, to cheer me up," he reminded her.

He held her for a little while, to comfort her ; but it was a strange emptiness of comfort. It was almost like being gone already ; like a dream of holding Miranda's little body and feeling her soft hair brushing his chin. He wondered if she felt the same ; she kept her eyes closed and said nothing ; after the one outburst she did not even weep.

When, an hour later, he left the Dower House, his limbs would hardly carry him. For a while he found it better to wheel his bicycle, his shoulders bowed like an old man's, than try, with swimming head, to keep his balance over the wheels. The curious part was, that there had been no sort of scene, no clutch at his emotions, such as he had dreaded, in telling his grandmother.

Arm in arm, they had walked quietly about the garden, looking at the early summer flowers. " I'm glad you've seen my antirrhinums ; they will be over, by the time you are back." He was passionately grateful for her calm, for her acceptance of his decision as an inevitable thing—little guessing at the stormy way by which she had reached her present quietude. It struck him that she had become very small, that there was something more frail and brittle about her than he had found on his last visit.

" You'll take care of yourself, won't you, Grandmamma, until I come back ? "

" Of course." She gave him her proud, distinguished smile.

There was only one moment when her spirit failed them : when she suggested—carefully casual—that, if he had nothing better to do, he might dine with her that night.

" I'm awfully sorry—I'm afraid I can't manage it. I've got a lot of things to go over with the Chairman to-night."

" This *is* your home, you know," she told him, in her pain ; then, quickly recovering herself, " Of course you will have many things to see to—in so short a time."

I ought to let her see how much I care, he was thinking ; but all power of expressing emotion seemed muffled. Even the familiar scene—the tender English pastoral, to which he was saying farewell (for how long ?)—could not break through the stupor which had grown upon him during the past twenty-four hours. The peaceful sweep of the landscape ; a cow voluptuously rubbing itself against a hurdle ; the long grass brushed to silver by the fingers of the breeze, then green again, as the breeze died down : these things, which once had thrilled, now woke no response in him ; he had no share in them any longer, or in the life they represented. The same sensation of dream, that he had felt in his good-bye to Miranda, blurred his parting with Harriet ; he only knew that he felt weak, and suspected his temperature had risen. It was a nuisance there was no time to see Whittick—and to let him know the appointment with Dietrich, fixed for the end of the month, must be postponed.

II

He packed a few books, to read on shipboard ; one bore on its title page the inscription, " With birthday greetings to Johnny from Emily." He looked at it with indifference. Emily. The name stood for a pattern in flesh and blood, for a voice and some gestures, for a string of incidents as clear and complete as a row of beads, but unrelated to each other or to him. He found it quite impossible to associate them with any part of his former life, or even to recall the set of emotions for which they once were symbols. Emily. A hieroglyph petrified in some sealed chamber of past existence.

His mental and emotional numbness had so increased, by this time, that he actually found himself asking, " What am I doing this for, anyway ? "

And it seemed a foolish, melodramatic thing to do, calculated to draw an altogether undesirable and certainly inconvenient attention to himself. Several times, while collecting his belongings, he stood, undecided whether or not to go down to Harcourt and tell him he had abandoned the whole project of going to the Coast. And, each time, he was driven to continue by clearer perception of something which had been forming itself in his mind for the last forty-eight hours : that the incidents leading to his decision were no more than instruments of a deeper purpose, and that it was intended he should go back to the Coast—perhaps to play out another small scene of the sombre drama which linked him to its soil.

He looked at his watch and saw it was nearly half-past nine : went downstairs, past Harcourt's closed door, found his bicycle and set out, for the second time that day, to Guerdon.

Polly met him where they had planned ; her caped figure detached itself from the hedge into which she appeared to have been shrinking, and he propped the bicycle against a stile and lit a cigarette. It was several minutes before he remembered that he ought to have kissed her. It did not seem to matter.

" I thought I wasn't going to be able to come. Mother's very bad to-night."

Mother. Mrs. Bowling. My mother-in-law.

" I'm sorry. Well—are you all right ? " They were both stiff and embarrassed.

" Yes, thank you. But I mustn't stop long."

" Listen." He told her, speaking quickly, of the plans he had made on her behalf. Before he had finished she was sobbing quietly. " And, if you're in any sort of trouble, write to Doss."

" Oh, no ; I couldn't do that."

" Well, write to Gilbert, if you'd sooner ; only Doss has got more sense. And—Polly, dear—here's some money." He thrust a wadded envelope into her hand, which resisted it.

" No—no ! What are you thinking about ? I don't want money ! " Her voice was rough with pain.

" Don't be silly ; you're my wife. Take it—and look after it for me, if you like ! But you're to use it, if you need it. You might want it for your mother." Ignoring her resistance, he found the pocket in the folds of her cape and pushed the money into it. She was now crying openly.

" Oh, God, I wish we hadn't done it ! "

" Do you mean—hadn't got married ? "

" Everything," she muttered.

His arm went round her, and he felt the shy stiffening of her body, disclaiming all its previous tenderness. He was filled with pity for her—and for himself : knowing he had no true comfort to offer her.

" I'll try to make it up to you. And I'll write to you—where shall I address the letters ? "

" Oh, I don't know—I've not had time to think. Don't send them home, for heaven's sake ! "

" That's what I thought. Damn." He bit his lip. " I tell you what I can do : send them through Miranda."

" Does *she* know ? "

" No, not yet. But I'll fix it, somehow. You might want to collect Gold Coast stamps, you know ! " He tried to make her smile.

" You'd better not write," said Polly suddenly. " Letters are dangerous things—you never know—they get opened by the wrong people. Oh, dear, what on earth am I to do if—if——? "

" If you find you're going to have a baby ? " he ended for her gently. " I thought of that. It's partly why I gave you the money. Inside the envelope you'll find the address of a doctor, in Harley Street—in London. He's a great friend of mine. You must go and tell him who you are ; I promise he'll help you. You're not scared, are you ? "

" A lot of good it will do, being scared, when the time comes ! " It was the old Polly, struggling for ascendancy over her trembling shadow. " Anyhow, I've got my lines," she asserted, as she blew her nose. It was a moment or two before he understood that she meant her marriage lines.

" Are you going to fight niggers ? " she asked, when their hysterical giggling had subsided.

" I hope not. And don't call them niggers, will you ? "

" I forgot. I'll have to remember to speak properly now, shan't I ? " she answered gravely.

" No, don't, Polly ; I don't want anything about you altered. But it's got nothing to do with 'speaking properly.' 'Nigger' 's a beastly word, and the Negroes hate it."

" Well—keep out of the Negroes' way, won't you, Johnny ? I wouldn't know what to do—I couldn't——" She stammered into silence ; he saw her eyes, widened by her unspoken thought, plead with him for reassurance. " Oh, God—I wish you weren't going—leaving me all alone——"

For the first time he felt his numbness lift ; instead of being something dead, incapable of feeling or caring, he was agonisingly alive—stabbed, suddenly, by a thousand needle points of memory, of realisation, misgiving, apprehension and of frightful compunction for what he had done to her. Up to this moment it had all been thinking ; it seemed easy to plan, to build up a smooth sequence of practical detail, that took in, one hoped, every possible contingency. But her cry of helplessness, her arm, that trembled against him in the dark, her fear, fluttering like a moth between them, made dust of his planning.

" Oh, Polly—Polly ! "

In an instant she had changed, as the maternal, so powerful and so fatal in her, sprang to his own admission of weakness. He felt her strong young arm about his neck.

" It's all right, Mr. Johnny—Johnny ! You don't need to take any notice of my silliness. Of course I'll be all right—and I'll just be waiting for you to come home—and we'll—well, we'll see how it all turns out," she concluded, a little lamely. " Anyhow, there's nothing for you to worry about—except looking after yourself, and not getting sick again. And if you do, I'll have to nurse you ! "

He found himself turning towards her, as a child towards its mother. " Polly—you've got no business to be so sweet to me ! "

" What—after all these years ? After the way you used to be so rude to me about my darning ? " She twinkled at him. " After all the games we used to play—you, and me, and Miss Miranda ? Why, I even used to save you a piece of my birthday cake ; I don't suppose you remember that ! "

" Of course I do." He tried to tune himself to her gallant note. " When is your birthday, Polly ? I've forgotten."

" I nearly forgot it myself this year," she confessed, " with mother being ill—and—and everything. It's in May—right at the beginning——"

" Only a week or two ago ? I ought to have remembered."

" Born under Taurus ; that's my trouble ! " smiled Polly.

" Taurus ? Look ; come here." He made her climb on the stile, supporting her with his arm. " Right over there—low down—west-nor'-west : do you see it ? The big, pink star ? "

" Is that Taurus ? "

" It's Aldebaran—part of Taurus. It's just going to sink below the horizon, together with that lovely bunch beside it—the Pleiades. Presently I'll be catching up with them—after we cross the Equator. So we'll be together—your star and me—and I shan't be leaving you behind."

" When do they—do we—come back ? " she whispered.

" There was an old boy called Hesiod, about three thousand years ago, who wrote :

> ' There is a time when forty days they lie
> And forty nights, concealed from human eye,
> But in the course of the revolving year,
> When the swain sharps the scythe, again appear.' "

" Forty days." She drew a sharp breath. " Oh, well—I'll manage : for forty days."

" It's longer, really ; he took ' poetic licence.' Taurus disappears completely at the end of May and doesn't rise again on this hemisphere till the beginning of September. But if all goes well, I'll be back in time to ' sharp the scythe.' You'll have to teach me to be a farmer ! "

" I must go." She half-stumbled in coming down from the stile, and caught her skirt in a splinter on the lower step. As he helped her to loosen it, their hands touched, clasped and clung. They stood dumbly, face to face, stunned, for the moment, by a sharp realisation of parting.

" Good-bye—dear Polly."

Her lips parted. She put her hand to her throat, as though she felt a constriction there. She stood perfectly still while he kissed her gently on the cheek. Suddenly she dropped her head to his hand, which she held against her kissed cheek ; he saw the twin crescents of her short, thick lashes against her face which the starlight silvered, and, for the first time, thought her beautiful.

"Dear, dear Johnny. You're such a gentleman—I oughtn't to have let you." Before he grasped her intention, she laid her warm lips to the back of his hand. He made an inarticulate sound as he tried to draw his hand away, but, though anticipating the action, she held it tightly, and, drawing it to her bosom, covered it with both of hers. "I didn't mean what I said. You know—about wishing we hadn't."

"You ought to have meant it," he muttered.

A smile of penetrating sweetness lifted the corners of her lips.

"Shall we forgive each other everything, before we say good-bye?"

III

It was two in the morning. Harcourt Flood sat in his big, carved chair beside a dead fire, listening to the ticking of the clock. There were a dozen things he wanted to say, he wanted to do—and they were all unsayable, undoable. For the better part of a week he had been dumb, while things he had come—foolishly—to look upon as permanent quietly disintegrated about him. His initial error—he went on repeating it—was in taking the boy to live with him. Having, over a span of two decades, built up a habit of solitude, who but a fool would have allowed it to be broken—for a whim; for some soft, weak moment when sentiment triumphed over common sense.

No less idiotic, of course, was his present persuasion that the boy's departure was final. Now, there *was* folly, if you like! Where else should he go? Certainly not to any other member of his family, and he would not, for obvious reasons, stop on the Coast. Provided some other damned woman did not catch him on the rebound, what in the name of heaven should prevent his return to a place he looked on as his home?

From one point of view, of course, this Ashanti war was the best medicine he could have found for his present trouble. From another—a fellow in that frame of mind was just the sort to take idiotic risks. . . . Harcourt pulled his thoughts up short; no good dwelling on that aspect of the situation. Oh, let him go; let him get the poison out of his system—it was no use pretending he would be of any use to himself or to the business until he had got over that little slut who seemed to carry bad luck wherever she went! Rape: that's what women like that wanted—to pay them out for the men they rape of their hearts and souls. Like to see one of 'em try it on with me! She'd get all she bargained for, and something beside. Damn fool—Roan; serve him right. Never could pick his women.

Johnny. . . . Wonder what he was up to, that night he went out from here. Seven in the morning when he got in—where did he spend the night? Wouldn't say, of course; close as a clam. None of my business. Ought to have gone with him, I suppose—but you can't butt in. Different, if we'd been the same age. If I'd been Joe Prior. I wonder where he is.

Ought to go to bed. What's the good? Go down to see him off, I suppose—on that blasted tub of Runstables.' A nice sort of trip he'll have—might just as well have waited till next month, for the *Anaki*. No good talking to them—have to do it their own way.

The door opened quietly.

"Who's that?"

Johnny, in his dressing-gown, answered, "Me." As he came into the range of the lamplight, Harcourt grunted.

"Huh! You. A nice job you'll make, of getting up in the morning. What time did you tell them to call you?"

"Five o'clock. I've been to your room; I thought you'd be asleep." He shivered, glancing towards the grate. "Fire's out, is it?"

"What d'you want?" asked Harcourt.

The clock ticked loudly in the pause.

"There's something I've been making up my mind to tell you. I don't want to—but I don't want your feelings to be hurt by getting it from somebody else."

"Since when have you started to consider my feelings?" snarled Harcourt.

"Since always, I hope. I've got a lot to thank you for——"

"You have." He refused to be mollified. "You can thank me for letting you set out on this wild-goose chase—most people wouldn't!"

"Most people wouldn't be asked," was the grim reply.

"See here." Harcourt hoisted himself to an angle in the chair that allowed him to cover his nephew. "I haven't had much to say, so far, about this trip of yours, but that doesn't mean I've not thought—plenty. I'm quite satisfied you should find a way of making yourself useful to your country—it's your duty. But that ain't the whole of it. Siddown. Do you want a drink?"

Johnny shook his head.

"No, thanks." He found a chair.

"I don't know what use they're going to find for you, out there." It was the continuation of a soliloquy, aloud. "I've been trying to get hold of some of the official records on the outbreak of '74. There aren't any."

"*What?*"

"There aren't any," repeated Harcourt. "So now, maybe, you'll begin to realise what we're up against. There's not one recorded word about Wolseley's campaign except a couple of blue-books on the treaties and palavers; not a line about the action, about disposition of troops, about transport, about defence or attack. Wolseley'd got the Royal Welch, the Black Watch, a battalion of the Rifle Brigade and a detachment of blue-jackets; we—I've had it in confidence—have got nothing but nigger mercenaries, native levies and a handful of whites; and we're going in blind——"

"What about '95? Doesn't that give us a pointer?"

"When they let us walk straight through to Kumassi, not realising we were after Prempeh? Pah! That wasn't fighting," said Harcourt. "Now, see here, Johnny; I'm not a soldier, and I don't reckon to know anything about military set-up. But unless I'm very much mistaken, you're going into the biggest muddle anybody's ever seen. There'll be shortage of everything—including man-power—and communications bedlam. Wet season—you know what that means : bridges down, wires out of order, tracks submerged ; troops held up for want of provisions and ammunition —emergency staff driven crazy." He paused.

Johnny sat silent, his hands in the pockets of his gown, his legs in pyjama trousers stuck out in front of him : on the defensive—an unusual thing, with Hacky.

" To cut the cackle : up in the bush, you're worth one man—with luck. At Cape Coast, with your knowledge of native lingoes and organisation, you might be worth five. Now do you see what I'm driving at ? "

" I see. Actually, it'll depend on the C.-in-C., won't it ? I suppose we'll all come under the military at this point."

" God damme, do I have to say it ? You ain't to go soldiering ! I've got one——" Harcourt's jaw dropped, and a look of curious horror came over his face. He had been about to say, " I've got one son already in the fighting line ; " had it really come to this—that he accepted Johnny, also, as his son ? " Don't take me the wrong way, my boy." An uncertain gentleness in his tone shocked Johnny : made him look away. " I'm not trying to get between you and your sense of duty. It's the instinct of every decent person, when his country's at war, to pick up a gun. When economy's a condition of general survival, the fellow who wastes is as much of a traitor as the one who runs away."

" Well, that's not a matter for individual judgment, is it ? After all, if you're once in, you're just a parcel of war material——" His uncle's lifted hand checked him.

" Wait. We're both of us war material—in a longer and bitterer war than this dust-up with the niggers. And, for the present, we're a forlorn hope—that's what it comes to. I ain't saying the relief isn't on its way ; but it's got a long road to travel. You and I are the ones that have got to hold out, if the others lose heart and belief in the outcome of our struggle. You go into this Ashanti brawl, and what happens ? You make a present of your guts to some blasted nigger butcher—the guts that could have served your people long years after we've got the blacks swept back where they belong——"

Oh, Christ, that's not the way of it ; isn't there any chance of making you see that's not the way of it ? That " our " war, as you call it, isn't white against black, but human for human ? He felt an iron band pressing round his skull, as he realised the impossibility, for ever, of getting Harcourt to accept this aspect of their task. Yet what did it matter ? There was, after all, nothing illogical in two people with different objectives working to the same end, and Harcourt's objective was the sound one, from the point of view of popular sympathy.

" Now do you see why you've got no business to go battleaxing round the bush ? " Harcourt was growling. " I want you back here, as soon as this mess is cleaned up. Look ; I've been thinking things over." He had hitched his heavy body to the edge of the chair ; for all his white hair, the sullen, vinous bloatedness of his face, something shone out of him that Johnny had never seen before. " There's enough of us now—enough 'big' names—to form a company to work out a development scheme and put it to the Government—hey ? Let 'em come in if they want—as shareholders—but——" As the words poured out of him, Johnny sat and marvelled at the dynamic force which leapt from peak to peak of creation : that raised objections to its own arguments, only to annihilate them ; that discounted no trifle, yet admitted none as a barrier to its conclusions, which emerged at last, chiselled and neat as the work of the lapidary, from a welter of incongruous material. He sat silent, before the fruits of all those moody silences, those snarling criticisms, those brief, sneering rejections of the few ideas he had, now and again, put forward : silent, and moved, and endeavouring to account for Harcourt's sudden revelation of himself and the secrets of his mind.

" What about it—hey ? "

Johnny nodded, finding himself unable to speak.

" That'll get 'em, won't it ? " Harcourt was like a boy. " That'll show 'em we're out for blood, this time ! And that'll give you something to think about when you're through with rice consignments and the Vickers-Maxims that have got themselves mislaid between B.C.A. and the Base ! " he chuckled with satisfaction. " That's what I'll be getting on with, while you're away—in rough draft, of course. Mind you, I'll be wanting masses of detail—existing facilities, local material, labour costs, water supply, and so on ; this isn't the time for getting those. But you'll be the one responsible. I must see about office quarters ; we can't run this from Queen Square. You'll have to see to the staff——"

He glanced involuntarily to see whether Harcourt had been drinking, although knowing that the effect on him of alcohol was, invariably, taciturnity. But the decanter was three-parts full and his glass not emptied. It was disconcerting—this sudden gush of volubility from one who, on the few occasions when Johnny himself had indulged in what Harcourt was pleased to call " vapouring," had snubbed him into silence. " Don't fly before you can crawl—don't fly before you can crawl ! " He could remember no flight that could compare with these.

" So you'll have plenty to do when you get back—and now perhaps you'll give up your hare-brained notions of taking a relief column up to Kumassi while the C.-in-C.'s looking the other way ! " concluded Harcourt triumphantly.

It came to him, in a flash of light.

For a moment, as something knotted itself in his throat, Johnny had a terrified notion he was going to burst into tears. He felt his eyes swim, and the room and his uncle's figure opposite blurred themselves out in a brief haze. So that was it ! That was why old Hacky, for the last ten minutes, had been talking like a parrot—like a fool—like the grand old idiot that he was.

" What are you looking for ? "

" Thought I'd dropped something." Johnny rose and straightened himself to stand in front of Harcourt. His uncle's eyes, black, shining with misery in their pouches of discoloured flesh, looked up at him, and he saw love in them, and gave it back in his smile. " It's all right. I'm not going out with the faintest intention of getting myself killed."

The purple poured up from Harcourt's jowl to the roots of his white hair. His heavy lower lip sagged from the white line of his teeth.

" You—damn' fool ! " Johnny looked away quickly from the other's emotion. Presently he heard the decanter rattle on the lip of the glass, and knew the dangerous moment was past. " A quarter to five ! You'd better go and have your bath."

" That's just what I was thinking. And it's time you turned in. Well, sir——" He held out his hand ; Harcourt ignored it.

" What's that you came in to tell me ? "

" Good—God." He had forgotten it completely. His attention to Harcourt, the rush of emotion that had swept over him at the proof of his uncle's affection, had driven it from his mind. He stood for a moment, silent, aghast. Forgotten—that he was married. Could any such antic thing have happened to a man before ? His fingers, twitching in his pocket, encountered paper, and reminded him of something else he had forgotten. He brought it out, holding it towards Harcourt.

" This—you might give it to Miranda—sometime. Or keep it for me until I come back."

Harcourt took the envelope impassively ; lumbered across to his desk and felt in his pocket for the keys. As he stood there, bending over the drawer, the lamplight capping his head with silver, Johnny knew he could not tell him : could not, in this final moment, deal him a blow that would wound him to the core. Anger—that one would be prepared for : but not the moment of mute stupefaction that must follow the announcement : the startled look of pain, quickly covered by resentment, that he would be unable—perhaps for a second—to control. Somehow, one had not considered the possibility of hurting him ; his fury was to be taken for granted. I can't leave him, with that on his mind. . . .

Harcourt had locked the drawer and stood waiting. He said sharply :

" Are you owing money ? "

" No, sir—at least, nothing of importance. Gilbert's seeing to that for me. Well—I suppose we'd better say——"

" Go on and get your tub. I'll see you at breakfast."

May morning—with small clouds, still pink-feathered with dawn, tossed about the blue. Everything very distinct in the pure light—houses, people, the springing green opposite the Cathedral, the thin spire of St. Raphael's up river, the skeleton hulls in the shipbuilding yards. He could feel Harcourt's eye possessing it all, and the stir of the same possession in his own heart. He felt the old familiar thrill at the sight of the *Gloriosa* and the *Daldalus*, their wooden walls mnemonic of old splendour—or did he feel it ? Was it not a mechanical salute to emotions that were past ?

The *Cetus* lolled against the dockside, her black stack with the red and green Runstable bands, her dingy buff superstructure and the ochre throats of her cowls doing little to relieve her air of a disreputable deep-sea tramp. A momentary vision of the *Aldebaran* glimmered in Johnny's memory, and the contemptuous saying of the old-time sailor: "He's given up the sea and gone into steam." Harcourt was growling in his ear, "You'll have had enough of *her* by the time you reach the Coast!"

They shook hands dully. From the top of the gangway he looked down, and saw Harcourt looking up; saw him lift his hat and replace it on the square, white head, and saw him turn, and, dominating the few onlookers with his height, re-enter the car. The Panhard rolled solemnly out of the dockyard gates, and Johnny went down to his cabin.

BOOK FOUR

Gold Coast–Guerdon–Bristol –London

1900

CHAPTER ONE

I

Cape Coast Castle,
May 31st, 1900.

DEAR UNCLE HACKY,

You will have received my two cables—which I felt a bit guilty over charging to the paper! I am afraid they contained nothing which is not fully covered by Reuter's agents. The place is seething with rumours, with scares and counter-scares, but I would soon be in hot water, here, as well as with you, if I tried to pass off any of these as hard news. All I can say for the present is, this isn't a " rising," it's *war*, and it looks like being a long job.

Anyhow—Willcocks has arrived, and has done the very best thing possible in appointing one of the traders—Russell—as his Private Secretary; this has made a very good impression, and shows the Commandant not to be one of the hide-bound military. He is putting in a fine job of organisation; the cables are humming, and all Europeans have been called up for questioning. His first object is to establish an Advanced Base on the Prah River, where we can concentrate troops, ammunition and supplies, as we get them. (Talking of supplies, there's no free issue, yet, of Government rations, so everything has to be got from the stores, and you may depend these rascally locals are taking full advantage of the position.) The hell of this campaign, up to the present, is the absolute impossibility of keeping in touch with Base; the enemy has played mayhem with our wires, and we're mainly dependent on runners—you can guess what that means. All sorts of tales get around, of which the latest is panic in the goldfields, and there's a very grim story that Slater's column has been cut to pieces at Kwissa, and S. has lost his life; but this is not yet confirmed. Hall is much criticised for not having made a dash for Kumassi, but, leaving out the question of virtual suicide—Applin and Morris got in, failed to bring off the relief, and now the garrison, already near starvation point, is saddled with their upkeep, as well as with that of its original occupants. Willcocks is determined not to move until he has all the material of victory in his hands, and this, I'm ready to bet, will involve him with some of the hotheads and ignoramuses at home, who, of course, expect an immediate miracle from his appointment.

Our greatest trouble, however, is carriers. The civil authorities have refused to pass a compulsory labour ordinance, being afraid of starting a flare-up among the coastal blacks, so now, most of the available supply having been mopped up by Hall's column, we're dependent on volunteers. Of course there aren't anything like enough—the word Ashanti sends them straight to earth!—and we are at a total standstill, until we get the reinforcements promised from Lagos. Hall's lot, that he took up to Fomena for the palaver, ratted on him, and now he's cut off, with twenty thousand Ashanti between him and Kumassi, and those treacherous beasts the Adansi blocking his retreat to the Prah.

It's raining like blazes, and each day's delay means an appreciable increase in our problems. Reports keep coming in that the Prah is rising and that the roads get worse day by day. A nice look-out when we get started !

I say "we," because it's perfectly obvious I'm doing no good by stopping here, and I have decided to find some way of going up with the main column. Europeans are badly needed, for the maintenance of order in the transport lines, and at Prahsu I shall at least be in touch with our active forces, and will see, as well as hear, most of what goes on between the Base and the various fighting contingents. I don't forget the last talk we had, and you may be assured I will take all the precautions you would wish me to take. I know those wouldn't include anything that meant failure in duty.

This will all be stale news, by the time you receive it, but I will continue to cable, and will write whenever there is a chance of a letter getting through. I'll be glad of some home news, when you have time to drop me a line.

Your affectionate nephew,

J. Flood.

II

Seen from the decks of H.M.S. *Magpie*, the town was a child's drawing in white chalk on a gunpowder grey background ; storm-water, shooting from the sewers, carved gullies in the rain-pitted litter of the foreshore, and the sky was pulled down on the roofs like a dirty blanket. It had stopped drizzling, but everything dripped. Over British Headquarters the flag was twisted into a rope of washing, and the red fezzes of sentries were sodden to the colour of dried blood.

In the town itself, progress, except on one's feet, was impossible ; the crowds were like black flies, beaten down by the rain, the gutters lined with refugees from up-country ; water ran round and over them, where they squatted in their soaked clothes, mindlessly accepting discomfort for the sake of safety. The white coifs of two nuns flickered over them like butterflies ; the nuns had baskets and a little rice—it was the miracle of the loaves and fishes, without the miraculous increase. Others looked on resentfully ; they had no business there, those victims of unreasoning panic ; none was from the danger-zone north of the Prah. They had bolted—bringing their vermin, their diseases, possibly their leprosy, into the town. There had been some attempts to keep them out, but they had just pressed in, by force of numbers. They were crusted in the alleys like bugs.

Through the vast, disorderly supply dump that the town had become wandered distractedly the members of emergency staffs, their confusion increased by the excited officiousness of coloured assistants; trying to locate the goods for which they were individually responsible. In the swarming forecourt of Headquarters where Johnny waited—cursing the weight and clammy heat of the mackintosh he wore to save the trouble of carrying it—a babel of clipped English speech rattled in his brain like dried peas on a drum; he had given up trying to join one sentence to another, or to imagine how the madhouse of which, unwittingly, he had become an inmate might be reduced to military coherence.

"I say—I wonder if you could tell me where I could get a sword and a water bottle? I've been scoutin' round for the last twenty-four hours. . . ."

"Any word from Minter?"

"No—line's down; Acting Director's gone up to Esumeja. What's that—a carrier chit? Sorry, old boy, you're unlucky."

". . . and a lovely bout of bellyache in the cantonments! They've got rice for twelve hours, and somebody's been selling 'em epi!"

"Well, how the blazes is one to drill them, if there's no shells? Half my men haven't even seen the 75-mm.; we've spent the whole ruddy day, breakin' it down and settin' it up—every ruddy thing but firin' it. . . ."

"No, old boy—no carriers, until Cardew's Timmanis get in from Sierra Leone."

"Twenty-five bob, if you'll believe me, for three tablets of Vinolia—and six for a stick of shaving soap! High time we commandeered these stores, if you ask me."

"Hell, no, I'm not a billeting officer; tell him to look after himself. Who sent for him, anyhow?"

"Beef, biscuits, quinine; go on. Try Accra."

"My dear old chap, it's frightfully nice of you; but *have* you ever travelled with a two-mile column?"

"Been trying for ten days to get a passage for my wife. Damn' nonsense; they ought to be thankful to get civilians out of the way."

". . . and the message took two days from Prahsu. I ask you—seventy miles! Wires are like a ball of knitting, after the kitten's been at it."

". . . left for Fomena with five hundred and got there with thirty-five. It's what I keep on saying: what's the good of putting niggers in charge of niggers?"

"Khaki—who the blazes wants khaki? Blast the khaki; I want cartridge belts. Not a damn' bit of leather in the town and all our stuff swollen up with the infernal wet!"

"Yes, sir—strictly speaking, the allowance is eighteen carriers—eight hammock boys per officer. Bother is, these plaguy Fans have got the jitters and won't go up beyond the Prah. Mansu's supposed to be sending some, but . . ."

"I say—this Berkefeld I was issued: there's something wrong with the works. Can it be mended, or do I put in for another?"

"No carriers, no carriers, no carriers; hell, are you hard of hearing? —*No carriers*."

" . . . reckoned with sixty rounds apiece we could afford a dozen practice rounds ; and before you could say Jack Robinson, the beggars had fired off fifty-two ! Well, you know Hausas . . ."

" Hallo—what's this ? "

Tramp, tramp. Tramp, tramp. A steady squelch of bare feet and a sudden surge of the crowd carried Johnny into the opening of the sculptured gateway. Gallimaufry of tattered blue uniforms broke here and there into bran-new khaki, tight-buttoned across its owner's proud chest. Mud everywhere—spurting head-high between the toes of runners : spattering pill-boxes rakish above the flash of white teeth : caking itself in pads on bare shins. A faint thrill of excitement went through the spectators.

" Who are these ? "

" Melliss's Nigerians : soldiers of the Queen, m' lads ! They look something like it, at any rate. Better batch than Hall's——"

" They need to be. Anything more come through about Slater, by the way ? "

" Only the confirmation. Poor devil."

" Look here ; is there any chance of seeing the Adjutant ? " Having passed through the stages of optimism, self-consciousness and pessimism, to something approaching indifference, Johnny had no compunction in putting the question, for the tenth time, to the speaker whose broad shoulders were blocking his view of the passing column. As the other turned, he took in the insignia of rank on a sleeve level with his eyeballs ; that the owner of a pink and brown schoolboy face, with a dab of chicken-coloured fluff on the upper lip, should be a captain was no anomaly in the Frontier Forces.

" Not an earthly, my dear fellow." A gleam of recognition came into a pair of lively, nondescript-coloured eyes. " Mr. Flood, isn't it ?—Sorry ; 'fraid even the majesty of the Press won't work this time. Unless "—as an afterthought—" you happen, by any chance, to have half a dozen hammocks about you ? "

" Is it hammocks now ? " Johnny smiled dimly.

" We've managed to raise ten ; that leaves one surplus."

" I'm sorry, I can't manage hammocks. I say "—as the other, sketching a half-humorous salute, was turning away—" you couldn't give me a line to go on, could you ? I've got to see somebody—it's not paper palaver," he added.

A slight crease of responsibility appeared between the officer's fluffy brows.

" I'm afraid I can't help you. We've got an utter shambles on at present—half a dozen chiefs catching it hot and strong because the carriers they promised haven't turned up. If you take my advice, you'll pack it up, whatever it is—and drop in to-morrow, if you happen to be passing. We may have got over our headaches by then——"

" Or found a new one."

" By Jove, you've got something there ! " The frown faded into an easy chuckle. " I'll have to be off. You mayn't just have noticed it, but there's a sort of slave-driving atmosphere round here, since the arrival of the dear old Commandant that doesn't suit my simple nature at all. Believe me, I've been trying for the last twenty-four hours to get out and buy a toothbrush; it's like being a hunted butterfly. Oh Lord, what's it this time?" he broke off to groan, as a dishevelled figure whose sweat-soaked shirt was coming out of its trousers at the back thrust through the crowd towards them. Johnny recognised one of the shipping clerks—one of the few, he thought enviously, who had been lucky enough to get themselves accredited jobs with the military. Like all the rest whose work kept them in the small close cells where the clerical staff operated, he had the half-blinded look of a creature crawling from its burrow into the light.

"I've been trying out that varnishing notion of yours, sir—Captain Paget: but it looks like it's no good."

"Damn. Let's look." Paget snatched the paper the other was carrying from his hands. "Damn—blast—it's sticky!"

"Gum won't dry off in this muggy weather."

"And what the blazes good'll these things be after five minutes in the rain?" muttered Paget disgustedly. He dropped the map in the mud and twitched out his handkerchief. Johnny had time to recognise the object of his annoyance before it was obliterated by a passing foot.

"It's no good anyhow—probably. These maps, you know—they're only a sort of joke. Maybe that's why they do them on paper, and not on linen," he offered.

The bleared eyes of the messenger peered at him through their red rims: an octoroon, Johnny guessed, after a quick glance at fingernails.

"Excuse me, sir—they've been looking for you."

"Who's been looking?" His heart gave a tick; could it be that all the time-wasting, the sheer, aimless hanging about of the last ten days was over? But the other shook his head.

"Dunno—they were calling your name, 'bout half an hour ago."

"Right—I'm coming."

"My dear chap." Paget's hand fell solemnly on his shoulder. "Don't be *silly*! He's probably got it all wrong. Go on, Jones, go and wash yourself: the varnish has got into your brains. Take it from me," said Paget, as the bleary-eyed one shambled away, "he's made a mistake. Orders are, no civilians until we've cleaned up this little affair with the chiefs. I've got no sort of affection for the nigger gentry, but I confess my heart bleeds for Mr. Bongo-Wongo and his friends this morning. Do you happen to know a razor-faced police pundit of the name of Morris?"

"Morris of Charlestown?"

Paget nodded.

"Give me my choice between facing a half-section of Ashanti on the warpath and *that* one and I'll plump for the fuzzy-wuzzies without blinking an eyelash. A frightful fella! I shake like a jelly each time I catch his eye. I fancy we'll get those carriers."

"I bet you will!" The cloud of depression and ineffectuality lifted; Johnny grinned from ear to ear at Paget's disgruntled face.

"You do know him?"

"Yes; he's a grand fellow."

"You're a better man than I am, Gunga Din," said Paget respectfully. "Oh lord, oh my, look at this!"

A string of chiefs came trotting across the forecourt; no particular degree of sapience was needed to detect that they were pleased to regain their liberty. There was a notable lack of jauntiness in their bearing. Johnny caught Paget's eye and laughed outright. The latter bit his lip, then shrugged his shoulders.

"All right; it's up to you—if you care to chance your hand. Down the lobby—second door on the left. And for the lord's sake don't say I sent you!"

The first bit of luck that's come my way, he thought, as he opened a door into a whitewashed cell, every available inch of whose space was taken up with trestle tables, its walls lined with the iron specie boxes that accompany an army on the march. Outside a barred window passed and repassed the fixed bayonets of sentries below in the street. The place smelt of kerosene oil and natives. Morris looked up as he entered—but a Morris thinner and yellower of face than he remembered him. As their hands met, the Commissioner said:

"I wondered when you'd show up."

"I didn't even know you were here, sir!"

"Well, what are *you* doing?" Morris asked presently.

"Nothing—much. I'm supposed to be here for the paper——"

"Special correspondent?" Morris cocked an eyebrow.

"They've got to find some name for it."

"Well, you're not complaining of news shortage?"

"There's a damn' sight too much news, sir—of the wrong sort," he found himself blurting out. "Too many mares' nests and too few chances of investigating them. My editor won't thank me for sending back fairy tales."

"What do you expect?" Morris shrugged his shoulders. "There's a war on. I suppose you want to get up to the Prah."

"I want something to do," said Johnny shortly. "To put it plainly, sir—this job of mine's a farce. We're too far from the fighting; by the time news filters down here, it doesn't even bear any relation to what actually happened. I get my story written, get ready to cable it, and by that time half a dozen other versions have come along. There's no time to sort out fact from fancy——"

Morris made a slight movement of impatience.

"I don't want to waste your time, sir; but there's surely more ways I could be of use than hanging around Cape Coast, waiting for some real news to break?"

"I should have thought so. I suppose you've tried?"

"I've been running round in circles ever since I got here, trying to find somebody who'd give me a job. The ones that have got jobs in their pockets haven't got time to see me, and the others——" he stopped; there was no need to tell Morris about the others, who appeared to think that the first duty of the *Diorama* correspondent was to further their private interests by helping them to evade military restrictions on the use of the jealously reserved lines of communication between Cape Coast Castle and the outer world.

" I'll give you a piece of news—*not* for your paper. Willcocks is leaving on the fifth."

" What ? The day after to-morrow ?" This, indeed, was news, and, on the face of it, almost incredible. " But—but, sir, what about troops ?"

The Commissioner's eyes evaded his companion.

" Three hundred Nigerians, eight officers and non-coms. Leaving for Prahsu in thirty-six hours. You see," explained Morris carefully, " they're getting hungry, in Kumassi."

He wondered if he had heard aright. Three hundred natives and eight white men—against fifty thousand Ashanti ?

" Not counting the hundred and seventy Hausas," Morris was saying, " and the Moshi cavalry, that managed to get themselves shut up in the Fort last week, we've got about a thousand troops, spread out over a hundred and forty-five miles. Of course there'll be reinforcements, as time goes on. Meanwhile "—his mouth twitched under the crisp moustache—" time goes on ! "

" What about recruiting ? "

" Recruiting ? Levies, do you mean ? "

" No—whites. There must be thousands of them along the coastal belt——!"

" I think most of them are here." Morris's tone was serious, but his eyes twinkled. " Several hundred, at any rate—all clamouring for guns ! It takes up an appreciable amount of somebody's time, getting them sorted out and sent back where they came from. Some will probably be organised into some kind of a defence force—if it gets that far ; they've picked out a few for guides and linguists—those are, mainly, the missionaries. It's largely a problem of expediency, you know. Most of them know as much, or more, than the military about handling the native ; for obvious reasons, none can be given any sort of command."

" Of course they're untrained ; but everybody out here can handle firearms. Couldn't we form a kind of Volunteer brigade ? "

Morris shook his head.

" Even if they could spare officers for the command, you can't send townsmen tramping through the bush. We can't afford liabilities in this campaign."

(" You don't happen to have any hammocks about you ? " The ribald inquiry revived in Johnny's memory. " I've managed to raise ten——" Ten ; mentally he portioned them out. No, they could afford no liabilities, this side of the Prah.)

" What's the position about carriers, sir ? They're in pretty short supply, aren't they, since the Sierra Leone police went up to the goldfields ? "

" They'll be here ; I've just been having a little chat about them."

Morris chuckled. "The problem is, who to put in charge of them? The beggars skedaddle on the least pretext and of course their own headmen can't hold them together. As a matter of fact"—his fingers drummed the papers on which they were resting lightly—"I have suggested sending our own civilians up with the lines. It might be better for morale. . . . You'd better be seeing about your equipment."

"You're sending me?"

"You'll have to report—all I can do is recommend you. There'll be seven or eight hundred in the line; if you get three hundred up to the Prah, you'll not be doing so badly." He raised his hand as Johnny began to stammer his thanks. "Don't make any mistake, Johnny; it's a rotten job. But it'll take you up to the Base, and you'll get your news piping hot—instead of with the chill off it! But don't blame me"—he rose, and Johnny knew he was being dismissed—"if you're not allowed to put all of it into your cables."

Questions buzzed in his brain. "Get your equipment." What kind of equipment? The first thing to be done was to find out what would be wanted, the second to acquire it. The first was not easy—every person he asked having different views on the essentials of an up-country journey, and Johnny's instinct being, as always, to travel as light as possible; and the second, he was to discover, was all but impossible. He had realised, within a few hours of arrival, the folly of his persuasion that he would be able to supplement the hastily assembled odds and ends of his outfit from the stores on the Coast. The shops were cleared; round their doors a few unlucky latecomers, like himself, buzzed like bees about deserted hives; the storekeepers sat sullenly among their empty shelves, cursing the order that forbade their replenishment until the requirements of the military had been met.

He spent the rest of the day trudging from point to point, now bargaining for a pair of second-hand puttees, now trying to bulldoze a native tailor into altering a coat that someone had ordered, and had left behind in his sudden departure. The material was the cheapest kind, as supplied for the troops: there was not a yard of good cloth or a foot of leather left in Cape Coast. He plodded on, paying double and treble value for inferior or partly worn-out goods. A ramshackle pile of objects lay on the floor of his room at the end of the day; two essential items had evaded his utmost search. No hammock, no filter. He dedicated a regretful thought to Maskelyne and Cook—which led his mind to Kershaw, "somewhere up-country"—according to the usual, unreliable channels of information—looking after communications.

In the darkness, under the slow, persistent rain, the crowds, anæsthetised, crawled from one end of the town to the other; crawled back again. All through the night the crawling would go on, and the endless question, "News? Any news?" bubbling on lips and staring in eyes. Cape Coast Castle was a vast listening ear, with the brain behind it dead.

III

June 5th, 1900. As the darkness thinned into a clammy dawn, the ant-heap of the town stirred faintly, gave up, a few at a time, its dazed inhabitants. Along the middle of the street were deposited the loads, beside which squatted the carriers, in the depressed silence that overcomes their kind when faced with a task from which there is no escape ; all sizes, both sexes, they squatted in their dank cloths, waiting the signal for departure. A powdery drizzle descended from the clouds behind which, as day advanced, heat started to gather : sucking up moisture in steam, not only from the earth, but from the silent multitude which gathered along the route of departure. A little body of troops received the order to fall in, and shuffled to their place in the line which had formed in the heart of the town.

Trying to look, and to feel, martial, Johnny went along his carrier line : unable to escape from recollections of games of "soldiers" played by himself and Dorset and Gilbert, and of "uniforms" furnished from Vicky's dressing-up chest. As his eye went over the sub-human multitude for which he and a lank North Country man, named James, were responsible, his brain struggled towards actuality.

There was no cheerful randan of a military band to enliven the time of waiting ; no shouts, no waving of flags or handkerchiefs—because that is not the way of the native. A gaping attention, a few brief, furtive good-byes and but a faint attempt at a cheer from the Europeans greeted the little knot of officers who came out of Headquarters and went quietly to their places ; a dull, whispering hum swelled for a moment into a chatter of recognition, on the appearance of the one on whom the fates of all depended : the short, grey-faced man whose limping progress took him, with the help of a stick, to the head of the column. His hammock was waiting, but he vetoed it with a gesture ; whatever might come, beyond the boundary of the watching town, splints would not prevent Willcocks of Burma from leading his little army on the first stage of their woeful pilgrimage. The little heroism there was in the scene it was his duty to provide, and there was no white man who did not pay mental tribute to the cost of providing it.

The headmen were yelling ; carriers, heaving themselves reluctantly to their feet, were shouldering their burdens. A bark clicked the Hausa troops to attention, and a couple of British non-commissioned officers attempted to lend an illusion of smartness to the meagre spectacle by pacing along the ranks, hollow-backed, with swagger-sticks in the crook of their arms. As the bugles rang out, the sun, by one of the erratic tricks of Nature's stage-management, forced itself through the clouds and burned its way down the barrels of sloped rifles. The immense arms of the regimental drummer swung out in a preliminary flourish and three hundred sets of white teeth flashed into an involuntary smile. Forward—march. *Dum, dum, dum. . . .*

The great, grunting file of the carriers was before him and behind him, like a shabby crocodile. As they swung through the slums of the native quarter, Johnny felt himself part of a miracle : the miracle of Willcocks's main column for the relief of Kumassi.

Presently the town fell behind. The sun blazed down. Ahead, smothered in its own steam, the forest belt simmered in the heat of noon.

IV

North of the Prah River, and north of the lands belonging to their treacherous allies, the Adansi, Ashanti was leaving no stone unturned in its preparations for the reception of the enemy. After a short sharp lesson at Esiagu, several defaulting generals had been executed and the fighting forces strengthened in equipment and personnel. In the war camp of the Commander-in-Chief the main concentration, however, was on Intelligence. Fifty priests, summoned to a grand fetish palaver, were given plainly to understand that it was up to them to fix victory, or face consequences, to themselves and their families, unpleasant in the extreme.

With the whole-hearted co-operation of the local populace the priests got down to their business in the market-place : a live sheep was pegged down with skewers, as a preliminary, and a token batch of hand-picked young warriors daubed with the blood. During the ritual capering—from which the general public was excluded, but which took in a series of gun volleys, the tossing of small packets of gold dust and pulped yam into the air and the fashioning of a number of highly potent ju-ju—every member of the community, from its elders to barely toddling infants, found some way of contributing to the fetish atmosphere, which, as time wore on, thickened over the priests and their occult occupations. A bevy of spirited young maidens, fresh from the fattening huts, rushed about whooping, with knives stuck through green pawpaws, representing the heads of the enemy. Little boys got themselves smacked for chanting the words—or as much of them as they could remember—of the song composed on the outbreak of hostilities. It was against the law for any but the army to sing it, but all the children had been hanging about the camps ever since the fighting began, and had picked up the tune and part of the verse like little parrots :

> " The Governor came on a peace palaver.
> He demanded money and sent white men
> to bring him the Golden Stool,"

sang one lot, and were answered by another :

> " Instead of money
> the Governor shall have the white men's heads
> sent to him at Kumassi."

And both together, with a great deal of gleeful stamping :

"The Golden Stool shall be washed clean in
white men's blood !"

It took six hours for the priests to produce assurance of total victory for Ashanti, and cost the exchequer eighty-one pounds English, seventy loads of salt, twenty goats, twenty sheep, seventy bottles of rum and fifty female slaves. All responsible agreed it was money well spent ; it created an immediate access of confidence among the allied tribes and checked a subversive tendency among the jittery minority, when the lo-koli drummers got to work and sent the glad tidings chattering through the bush.

There was a great deal of singing and dancing that night, and long after the exhausted civilians had settled down, the camps kept it up, tossing the old war ditties from fire to fire : making old folk wag their heads and tell each other that good times had come again.

"Do you hear the buffalo moving in the forest ?"

"We hear him."

"We are like the buffalo in strength and in bravery."

"We also are like him !"

"We also are like him," came rustling from toothless gums, as old hands felt in the dark for spears long set aside. "We also are like him !" —adolescent youths nudged each other and joined in. "We also are like him," children drew their lips away from their mothers' dugs to lisp. The halt, the sick, the blind—even those monstrosities to which the bush gives birth in its remote fastnesses—joined that night in the asseveration of Ashanti's greatness, that streamed up on the smoke of its camp fires into a starless sky.

At the rate of three-quarters of a mile an hour, and in silence, a thin, wet serpent, more than a mile in length, was working its way through the bush. Every now and then the serpent broke, scattered itself, and eventually united again. Onward it travelled, with inexpressible languor, dragging its links of bronze, of copper and ebony, its sides of sodden drab-green, patched here and there with scales of metal, round trunks of mahogany, of odum and nyedua ; tangling itself in networks of vine ; brushing moistures from the silver stems of orchids.

From time to time it sank, belly-deep, in slime ; it submerged itself in swamp, it became a chain of dark nodules, bobbing erratically across a race of water. Mist swallowed it. It dissolved in the stenches raised by its passing. Gathering foulness, it reformed itself, and continued on its way.

Torn, it bled ; stung, it writhed ; maimed, it halted. And at last it reached the Base.

CHAPTER TWO

I

SELINA, in these days, was virtually immovable. A victim of the new. "S-shaped" corset, the bulk of her increasingly heavy body lifted and pushed forward, her posterior thrust back from the waist which, as someone unkindly observed, was a mere optical delusion, the invention of her modiste—she resembled, in her high arm-chair, nothing more than a plump, comatose pigeon. Yet, despite the creamy folds of chin pleated into the boned collar of her gown, she retained a kind of beauty. Even Harcourt had been heard to refer to his sister-in-law as "a fine woman." Harriet, more pungent in her descriptions, called her a "harem type," and, to Miranda, her mother was a gardenia, heavy with perfume, faintly tinged at the edges with decay, yet beautified by its very decadence. It never occurred to Miranda at any moment to establish any kind of human relationship with Selina.

"There's Miranda. Dear me, I wish she wouldn't take that bird about with her all the time. She's beginning to look like a witch," yawned Selina, as her daughter limped along the terrace, the merlin chained, as always, to her fist.

Vicky looked up sharply, as though about to speak; but she changed her mind and her lips tightened. She, in the last few weeks, had begun to look more than her age. And yet—any person who had had the honesty and the temerity to point out to her that a period of deep anxiety and distress had afforded Vicky the happiest time of her life would never have been forgiven. Amidst all the shock and humiliation which her youngest brother's conduct had inflicted upon the family, Vicky had proved the tower of strength to which the others—even Dromore—had clung; she tasted at last, in full measure, the reward of her devotion.

In Vicky, Dromore sought and found the understanding so painfully lacking in his wife; on Vicky, Harriet, reluctantly, had come to lean; to Vicky, Harcourt came, grumbling, for some modicum of the common sense conspicuously lacking in other adult members of the family. It was to Vicky that Ethel Flood had written a long, carefully-worded letter of sympathy, and Vicky who dealt, in a dignified fashion, with the uneasy commiseration of neighbours, while the gale of scandal beat about the walls of Guerdon, until it wore itself out, or was diverted by newer dramas. The importance of Miss Victoria Flood was no longer a tacit affair, it was overt, triumphant, and its effect was seen even in the angle of her Sunday bonnet, the increased stiffness of her sturdy spine. It was felt in an access of antagonism to her sister-in-law Selina, the cool amusement of whose lowered eyelids Vicky felt she had not earned! *She* had not wanted to usurp Selina's office; but as Selina chose, almost contemptuously, to pass it over to her—she, Vicky, was not the one to shirk her duty and her responsibilities.

" She really ought to be a little more *soignée*, at her age," Selina was complaining. " Why doesn't somebody tighten her suspenders? Do look at that left stocking——! "

" It's the ' bad ' leg," said Vicky shortly. " I expect she is feeling the strain—like the rest of us."

" It looks to me," said Selina, with one of her rare flashes of clumsy humour, " as though the elastic was feeling the strain. Where's Ethel? " she asked impatiently. " Don't tell me she's feeling the strain as well! "

" I expect she is resting; they are going down to Mamma's for tea. Selina——" She stopped to moisten her lips.

" Well; what? "

" How can you be so indifferent——? " burst out Vicky. " A little kindness—it is surely not too much to expect a little kindness——! "

Selina gave her a curious look.

" Do you want kindness? "

" I? Certainly not! " Vicky bridled.

" I didn't mean you in particular; I meant all of you," explained Selina.

" And why do you persist in saying ' you,' instead of ' we '—as though we were of no concern of yours whatever? Whether you choose to consider it so or not, you are now a Flood, and the mother of Floods. You've got no right to—to stand aside, like the Sadducees. And it hurts Drummy very much," she concluded with asperity.

" Drummy enjoys being hurt." A strange smile curved Selina's lips.

" What nonsense! How can you say such a thing? "

Again she gave her secret, subtly malicious smile.

" To change the subject—what did Venetia say? "

" Oh. . . . He told you he was seeing her? "

Selina's fine brows arched themselves.

" Whatever may be his vices, Drummy is usually correct; you'll admit that."

" Tscha! " snorted Vicky; she had no use for the expression " vices " in connection with her brother Dromore.

Selina looked at her with a faint glint of irony beneath her sleepy eyelids. When Gilbert gets married, I think I'll go and live with them. Then you will be mistress here, and it will really be much more comfortable for everybody. It would have been amusing to say this aloud, but she decided, on second thoughts, to reserve it for a future occasion.

" Well; is Venetia going to divorce him? "

" No; she isn't," said Vicky, tight-lipped.

" Of course she isn't," said Selina on a soft, satisfied note. She plucked negligently at a thread on the ruffled flounce of her gown. " Would you mind passing me the scissors? And she's not taking him back, either; if I know anything of Venetia."

" Knowing Venetia myself," retorted Vicky with spirit, " I had not expected her to show so much good feeling—without some very powerful inducement."

"Good feeling?" Selina appeared to taste the expression. "It implies so much and is capable of so many misinterpretations."

"Good feeling," spat Vicky, "means one thing only: preserving our dignity—which, in this case, depends on Roan's social reinstatement——"

"At Venetia's expense?"

"Not at all. Venetia knows perfectly well that she's in an invidious position herself. If she takes him back, all the scandal will die down—in time. It would never have arisen but for her own disloyalty."

"I wonder," murmured Selina.

"You know as well as we do that most of their quarrels were over her extravagance! She was *ruining* him," said Vicky with conviction.

"I used not to like Venetia," mused Selina. "I'm quite surprised to find how much I'm in agreement with her, these days. I really can't see why she should make a burnt offering of herself in order to save your faces."

"Burnt offering! Do you know Drummy and Hacky offered to pay all her debts—all the bills she has run up, since leaving Roan?" Vicky leaned forward with a dark flush on her face to tell her.

"Well—well—well!" Selina's eyes were wide open at last. "How very, very much that must have amused Venetia," she murmured, her own face was bright with enjoyment.

"I absolutely fail to understand you," said Vicky icily.

"Do you?"

"I don't know what's changed you," she stammered. "We used to be such friends; now—we might almost be—strangers."

"We might—mightn't we? Well, go on: Venetia, of course, refused the bribe"—she dismissed Vicky's bitterly reproachful look with a smile—"and Drummy was deprived of his olive branch. Well, he must have looked very odd in the rôle of the pigeon."

"I suppose you mean 'dove,'" snapped Vicky. "Dromore is going to Paris."

"What on earth for?"

"In the hopes of bringing Roan to his senses."

Selina put her head on one side.

"Really? And has anybody thought anything about Emily Temple?"

"The less one thinks of her, the better," said Vicky, thin-lipped.

"Oh, probably." Selina's tone dissociated her from argument. "I was only thinking that if I were a man," she said dreamily—"if I were Roan," she amended—"and somebody came preaching to me about what I should, or should not, do, in an affair involving my—well, whatever it happens to involve, in Roan's case——"

"Well?"—as Selina paused to consider the matter.

"I should probably," smiled Selina, "use my fists! Drummy would look very odd, wouldn't he—reading the lesson on Sunday with a black eye?" She paused as Vicky rose. "Are you going? You might see if you can find the boys," she said fretfully. "I suppose they're mewed up in Gilbert's room; I think, when Dorset's on a visit, he might pay a little attention to his mother."

"Dorset and Gilbert went over to the White Pool to look at the fish," said Vicky coldly, and left the room.

Selina laid her hand to the *point d'Alençon* cascading from the square yoke of her bodice, and decided she felt faint. She had felt faint a number of times lately and blamed the congested atmosphere of her surroundings for it. She made the immense effort of rising. Her heavy torso achieving its balance over her moulded hips, the train of her gown spread behind her, Selina, like a meditative fantail, strutted to the cabinet in the corner of her room.

II

"Polly."

She had called three times, not daring to raise her voice too high on account of the sick woman, before the door opened and Polly hurried down the path, trying to pat her disordered hair into neatness, to fasten the cuffs which were rolled above her elbow.

"I'm sorry; have you been calling a long time?" She stood by Marcella's head, hiding her face against the soft muzzle.

"How's your mother?"

"Just about the same. She has such bad nights."

"She wants a herb pillow," said Miranda instantly, "like Aunt Vicky made for Grandmamma. I'll ask her to make another, shall I? And plenty of fresh air;" she glanced up at the small closed window, almost hidden in a tangle of roses. "Why don't you open it? Sick people need lots of fresh air."

"Because——" She bit her lip. Because all the flies swarm in from the midden: that was the answer. A sudden vision of Guerdon bedrooms flashed into her mind; of linen she had helped to spread, of down pillows she had tossed, of lofty ceilings and breezes billowing curtains of muslin and lace into the rooms. This was what "being ill" meant to Selina Flood, in her scented dressing jacket, in the great bed, converted by its towering canopy and the dais upon which it was placed into a kind of a throne. This was the picture called up by Miranda, when she spoke of "being ill." How should Miranda visualise a lean-to roof, a couple of foot-square window spaces, almost on a level with an uneven floor, the makeshifts which lack of room, rather than poverty, foist upon the unprivileged?

She had never known shame, or had cause to know shame, of her home before. It was not shame she felt now, so much as a painful sense of disparity—far removed from envy, for envy was not in her. But she was Johnny's wife, and Miranda was his sister, and the feeling of inequality hurt her pride, as she imagined it might hurt his. She was silent, her head bent over the cob's, the sun spangling the back of her neck with golden freckles.

" When are you coming up to ' the house ' ? It's beastly, without Johnny."

" Have you heard from him ? " Deeper she ducked her head.

" No ; there hasn't been time yet."

" How long do letters take ? "

" It all depends ; nearly three weeks. If he's missed the mail, it might be a month. Come back with me for tea, Polly ! Oh—I suppose you can't, because of your mother. Well, can I have tea with you ? I've had about enough of the family, since Johnny went away."

She crimsoned. Tea, for visitors, had been a rich, elaborate meal in the parlour ; had been glittering china, a profusion of home-made cakes and scones, of honey and preserves ; in summer strawberries and cream. The teapot of Sheffield plate, belonging to Aaron Bowling's mother ; Ellen's silver tongs and spoons, initialled, part of her dowry when she was married. The snowy cloth, perforated with drawn thread and edged with crochet—Polly's own handiwork ; the lustre bowl, packed with zinnias, like a bonfire in the middle of the table. Tea, now, was a snatched mug on the bare corner of a kitchen table already laid for the men's evening meal. Once, I wouldn't have minded ; now—because of Johnny—it's different.

" Help me down," Miranda was saying.

" There's—there's not very much ; I've not done much baking since Mother was ill," she faltered.

" I only want some milk and some bread and honey. What are you having ? You look as if you could do with a good sit down."

She brought a tray to the parlour, where Miranda, with some difficulty, had been persuaded to wait. How queer the room seemed : almost dead, with the unopened windows, prisoning its scent of beeswax and lavender bags, and the piano closed. She muttered an apology as she pushed the casements open—" Nobody uses this room much now "—and poured Miranda's milk into a cup. She was conscious of her crumpled gown, of patches of damp under her arms, of an absence of the daintiness on which she had prided herself—for which there was no longer any time. She thought she caught Miranda's eyes, with an expression of surprise, of delicate distaste in them, and blurted :

" I'm all in my dirt, because I've been giving the upstairs a scrub. There's such a lot of things to be done——"

" It's absolutely intolerable, at home, since Johnny went away." Miranda waived the subject, her jaws champing on a crust of new-made bread.

" Is it ? " She found she had no taste for food.

" Of course it is ; who do you think I've got to talk to ? It was bad enough, not having Emily——"

" How—how's Miss Emily ? "

" I don't know. She never answered my letters. And then——"

" Now, now ; what's the matter ? " Polly's arm had gone round her shoulders instinctively. It stiffened there. Miranda. Miss Miranda. My *sister* . . .

" You won't repeat anything I say, will you? I mean, not to anyone at ' the house.' "

" I've not seen anybody for weeks."

" Doesn't Ames come to see you any more?" Miranda interrupted herself to say in surprise.

" No, I don't see any of them," she insisted, with a violence that deepened the surprise.

" But I thought he was courting you, Polly. Have you had a quarrel?" persisted Miranda.

" Oh, goodness, no. I just don't have anything more to do with any of the boys. There isn't time," she muttered.

" Oh well, *I* don't know." Scowling, Miranda drummed with her fingers on the table. "*You* never told me," she accused.

" I've not seen you, have I, dear? What were you beginning to tell me about Miss Emily?"—I ought to say "Emily," and I ought to say "Miranda;" I'm Johnny's *wife*. Sometimes I can't believe it; why has it just become impossible to believe, now I'm talking to Miranda, that I'm so fond of?—who's always been fond of me? A sudden impulse swept over her, to tell Miranda; she dragged herself back from it, with horror.

" You know," Miranda was saying, " what happens to our letters at ' the house.' We put them in the hall, then they're put in the letter-bag, and it's taken to Papa. He puts his own letters in and locks it, and one of the grooms takes it to the post office."

She knew; she nodded. The journey with the bag had provided her with opportunities for rendezvous in the past.

" Now and again—not very often—Papa looks through the letters in the bag. Well, there was one from me to Emily."

" So what happened?" she prompted as Miranda paused.

" I was sent for. I expected a ' row '; as a matter of fact he was quite nice—for him. But he said I wasn't to write to Emily again—ever."

" Whatever did you say?" Astonishment banished awkwardness.

" You know Papa—it's no use arguing with him," she said, shrugging her shoulders. " I did try to make him tell me what it meant, but he simply refused. I ' wasn't old enough to understand '! Such balderdash. It makes me furious, the way they treat me like a fool, because I'm lame and rather blind. As if it made any difference——!"

" We used to think he was so fond of Miss Emily. . . . Do you suppose he's vexed with her for refusing Mr. Dorset?"

" Good heavens, he'd have said something before, wouldn't he? Besides, he's as pleased as punch with Ethel—with Dorset's new wife."

" What is she—is Mrs. Dorset—like?" A pang of painful curiosity prompted the question.

" You saw her at their wedding, didn't you? Well, that's all there is. I mean, she's one of those people who are all ' outside '; like empty boxes. Ethel's a very grand box—like one of those caskets in the Big Drawing-room. She's got no heart, or soul, or feelings whatever—of course, that makes her exactly right for Dorset. They're stopping with us now," she added.

" Who—Mr. Dorset ? " Her heart gave a sickening leap.

" Ethel's going to have a baby. It's her last visit, before she settles down to incubate, or whatever they call it ! " sniffed Miranda.

In the tumult which shook her she missed the rest of the sentence. Dorset—who *knew*—here, now, at Guerdon. Would he come to see her ? Would he say something kind ?

Miranda was saying :

" —so I asked Aunt Vicky and she wouldn't tell me either. Naturally I'm not going to be cut off from my greatest friend without knowing what it means ! "

" What are you going to do ? " she forced herself to ask.

" I've written to Emily, telling her exactly what happened, and asking her to write back by return ; and I've brought the letter for you to post," said Miranda calmly. " Sometimes I give a letter to one of the servants, but it's always a bit risky. Who's this coming in at the gate ? " Miranda was looking across her shoulder.

" It's Cousin Jinny. She comes in sometimes, to sit with Mother and help me make the bed before she goes." Polly rose stiffly. " You'll excuse me for a minute, won't you—I must just go and speak to her ; she's very touchy about being taken for granted "—she smiled dimly.

" Polly, Polly——" Miranda caught a fold of her skirt as she passed. " I've had an idea. If she's here, you can walk back through the park with me, can't you ? "

" Oh no, dear—really, I couldn't ! " Her face burned. " I've got dozens of things to do—I've got to get the men's tea—they'll be in in another half-hour——"

" Half an hour ! " scoffed Miranda. " If we start now, you'll be back in less than that. Johnny always said you run like a rabbit ! "

" In this hot weather ? Phew ! " She blew a stray lock of hair away from her brow. The prospect of entering the park appalled her—yet she knew she would, in the end, be defeated. A kind of hopelessness soaked into her, while weakness and love made her surrender to the appeal, and a few minutes later they set out together towards the lodge.

" . . . There's Doss and Ethel. They've been visiting Grandmamma."

Straight into the trap. Her heart stood still. Dorset—who knew. She heard herself stammer :

" Now you're all right—they'll walk up with you—I'll turn back "—and felt Miranda' s bony fingers close over hers, on Marcella's bridle. She felt her knees give and her body flood with sweat.

Ethel Flood, her figure bulky despite its corsetting, was staring, saying something to Dorset, then turning towards a bed of lobelia, which she poked with the tip of her parasol. Like a pellet of lead in the heart, Polly received the message, *She knows too* ! The broad sweep of the avenue and the calm façade of the Dower House, smitten with evening sun, rose and waved ; she was obliged to support herself against Marcella's gleaming shoulder.

Dorset, broad, heavy in his light-coloured country tweeds, turned crimson ; he appeared to hesitate, then, biting the short, upturned moustache which made a savage line above his lips, he crossed the lawn sharply towards Miranda, whom he addressed, ignoring Polly, who remained as though frozen, her hand still on the bridle of the cob.

" What are you doing here ? "

" I've been having tea with Polly." Her eyes widened in astonishment at his tone.

" Come on—come straight on." Still ignoring Polly, he seized the bridle roughly, jerking it in the cob's mouth. Small, stolid, Marcella resisted, tossing her head.

" Don't do that, you idiot ! " cried Miranda ; the movement, slight as it was, had sent a jarring anguish through her spine. In her rage, she lifted the switch and cut at Dorset's angry, crimson face ; his anger leaping to meet hers, he snatched it from her, broke it in half and tossed it into the bushes.

" By God, you little vixen ! You deserve your ears boxing ! "

" You dare ! Just see if you dare ! " she screamed. " You with your filthy manners—can't you say ' Good afternoon ' to Polly ? And take your hand off my reins ; I don't want any help from you. Polly ! " she shrieked ; but Polly was twenty yards away. " Polly," she called ; and the fugitive figure broke into a stumbling run. " My God, I don't know where you learn your beastly manners——"

" That'll do." He had recovered his temper ; guessing he had hurt Miranda, he was a little ashamed. He gave her the deep, grey-eyed smile on which he had learned to rely for disarming his enemies. " I didn't mean to jog you, Winkle. Gad, what a little spitfire you are ! " His long-lashed eyes were burning close to hers ; she drew back from them and from his handsome, high-coloured face, with a grimace of disgust.

" Don't push your face at mine ! "

" And don't talk to me about bad manners," he purred. " Now, listen : you're not to have any more to do with that girl. Will you remember that ? "

" Pooh ! I don't take orders from you," she defied him.

" No ? Then perhaps you will take them from Aunt Vicky."

" You're cracked," said Miranda coolly. " It's a pity if Ethel's making you more of a snob than you used to be, Doss. And it's a pity she never saw you and Polly having fights on Grandmamma's croquet lawn, when we were all children ! If you want to cut your old friends, pray do ; you won't get me to follow your example." In one of her rare fits of stubbornness, Marcella chose to ignore the kick on her sturdy barrel and remained stock-still. " Get on, you damned horse ! " muttered Miranda furiously.

Dorset held the bridle with the peculiar pleasure he always found in asserting himself, calmly, without heat or malice, over the defenceless.

"You like Polly Bowling, don't you?"

She found herself suddenly cold and quiet, like Dorset.

"What about you?" she heard herself saying; the words surprised her, because it was as though someone had borrowed her tongue, her lips, to speak them. "What about sneaking off to meet people, secretly, in the park? What about kissing them——?" It was a shot in the dark; she was almost as much taken aback as he, to see it had found its mark.

"You—little—spy!" It came in a whisper, incredulously.

She felt her teeth chattering, as her lips split over them in an ugly grin. It had only been a guess; it was almost terrifying to find it had been accurate.

"All right," said Dorset viciously. "Now, listen to this. If you have any more to do with Polly Bowling, you'll be sorry: both of you. And she'll be the one who'll pay for it. I can do Polly a—great—deal—of—harm"—he dropped a negligent emphasis on each of the syllables. His lips curved into their surfeited smile; he clapped the cob on the shoulder. "Think it over," he recommended, as Marcella started off on her dogged trudge up the avenue.

Polly leaned against a tree, her hand clasped to her bosom. So that was how it was to be; he, who had kissed, had shown her. She felt sick with humiliation, and the horror of the future swept over her in a heavy wave. Mother. . . . If Mother dies, I can't stop here, possibly. Father'll kill me. I'll have to get away.

III

Roberts's six weeks of enforced inaction at Bloemfontein, which cost him eight thousand men by enteric and endemic diseases, had come to an end. At the beginning of May, on the war maps which, in the spring of 1900 had become a standard feature of almost every English home and office, the little flags had started their swift progress northward with Buller and Methuen, Hamilton and French. On June 6th, Harcourt Flood, in common with thousands of his fellow-countrymen, nailed his little Union Jack into Pretoria and drew a breath of satisfaction.

Along the Backs and in the town there were few signs of excitement; a flag or two appeared, a few pedestrians resurrected the cockades they had worn on Mafeking night, the trade in celluloid buttons revived and beer houses were lively; but, after that twenty-four hours of jig-making in which, barely three weeks ago, Bristol had let off its patriotic steam, Pretoria came as anti-climax. Harcourt snorted as he gave orders for the flag to be broken on the staff that slanted over the porch in Queen Square.

"Well, that's the start of the finish, eh, Hacky?" It was Samson Killick, fresh from a visit to Mr. Searle: his old-fashioned mutton-chop whiskers brushed up smartly, a button with "Bobs's" head on it stuck in his lapel. Samson's eldest son had been mentioned in dispatches: regarding which, Samson's false modesty allowed it to be inferred that the capture of

Cronje, Wolverans, Albrecht and the forty-odd field cornets and commandants who, at Paardeberg, surrendered to the British, although attributed in various quarters, was in reality due to the dash and gallantry of Lieutenant Bill Killick of the 12th Brigade. " Hey, Hacky ! How about a bottle of ' the boy ' ? " beamed Samson, and slapped his friend smartly on the shoulder.

Harcourt took a sour view of the exuberance, but went to his cupboard —passing, as he did so, another war map. His eyes squinted away from the solitary dab of red, white and blue—stark contrast to the bristle of tricolour on its neighbour. God damn the Ashanti—and damn Sam Killick, with his cockahoop airs, just because he, like about a hundred thousand other people, had got a son in the fighting line !

The cork came out with a pop, covering Harcourt's hand and wrist with foam before he could direct the wine into the glasses. Sam's spurt of schoolboyish laughter added to his ill-humour ; he responded sullenly to the toast of the day.

" ' Bobs '—eh ? "

Harcourt drained his glass and set it down brusquely.

" Have you seen Baker ? " He had had enough of Lord Roberts's achievements for the present.

" Baker—— ? " Samson gaped. " Nay," he said innocently. " I just been round seeing how they were getting on with the new wing of the Asylum." A flicker passed over the other's face. " It'll be all shipshape for the opening, next month. A grand job : a real grand job they're making of it—"

" They'll need to ! " A mirthless guffaw broke from Harcourt. " So you ain't seen our Lord High Chancellor of the Docks Committee ? You ain't heard, perhaps, that we're paying seventy thousand seven hundred and fifty for twelve and a half acres of land for a timber wharf on the Floating Harbour ? If that don't fill your new wing when the taxpayers hear of it—call me a Dutchman ! "

Samson whistled softly. No wonder old Hacky was surly ! He stole a look at his companion. Yes, there was no question about it : Hacky was looking his age—and more. He had changed a lot in the last month or two—no, it was earlier than that the change had set in. When he began chasing this West African hare of his. When he bought the old *Di* and set up as a newspaper proprietor. Hacky had bitten off more than he could chew and was showing the effects.

A tap at the door, a snarl from Harcourt—" Come ! " and old Derbin tottered into the room. On him Samson turned his usual geniality.

" Hallo, Derbin ; we're having a drink to Pretoria and Lord Roberts. You'd better join us."

" It's very kind of you, Mr. Killick," piped the old man. " You'll have to excuse me—this hour of the morning—my internals. Sir "—he turned to Harcourt—" Prior is back, sir."

" . . . What do you say ? "

Harcourt turned slowly. To himself he was saying : What's this about

—this ridiculous thing I'm feeling—this . . . He turned, and as his heavy eyes met those of his old servant, the thought shot into his mind : Derbin *knows*. Derbin knows. How should he know? Does old age bring with it some kind of clairvoyance, in compensation for the things it forces one to relinquish? Derbin was old—almost beyond the computation of age ; and now, for the first time, Harcourt found himself realising that this old man, who had actually served his grandfather, had grown imperceptibly into his life, along with his traditions. He was not a man who dealt in intimacies, and it came to him as a shock that, unknown to himself, and in some fashion beyond his control, an intimacy had established itself between him and the bent figure which stood in its attitude of customary respect between him and the corner of his desk.

" What do you say? " he had asked ; and Derbin had not answered, because he knew there was no need. He stood there waiting, with the June sunshine turning the black stuff of his suit to green, and a fold of the flag caught softly by the breeze under the sash of the open window behind him.

" You'd better fetch him up—and get another glass." His sullen mouth had twitched sheepishly into a smile.

" I took the liberty of telling him to follow me upstairs, sir—so he could take his time. The stairs are a little awkward, sir, with his disability," old Derbin was mumbling.

" Wounded, is he? All right, fetch him in, fetch him in." He crossed the room to the other window—the one overlooking the Backs—and stood for a moment with his back to the room, staring furiously through the mist that had gathered across his eyes. All the water prickled and danced with sunlight, there was a kind of wild, sweet, irrational gaiety in the air. It was on such a morning he had proposed to Isobel, thought Harcourt—and cursed his memory. He heard a curious tapping sound, heard Samson say : " Well, well, my boy—well, well ! " with a queer note in his voice, and swung round.

He opened his lips and found he could not speak. Words were smitten from him by the spectacle of the tall, lanky figure swinging between its crutches, with a trouser-leg neatly pinned up over a stump that ended a few inches below the short jacket. The grin and the upstanding flame of hair were all that remained of Harcourt Flood's recollections of the boy who might be his son.

" Siddown." They had gripped each other's hand, and he had recovered from the absurd emotion.

Joe grinned, hitched his crutches aside in a very expert fashion, and lowered himself into one of the vast chairs which had evoked Harriet Flood's irony. It is safe to say that it was the first time any member of the office staff had ever been offered a seat in the Chairman's presence. The heightened colour of Joe's thin face showed his embarrassment at the honour. He was almost too overwhelmed to accept the glass of champagne which was given to him on a nod from Harcourt.

" Well, Joe ; welcome home." The two men raised their glasses, and Joe, crimson to the gills, followed their example.

" Thank you, sir—thank you, sir." He coughed as the effervescence of the wine tickled his nostrils.

" It was one of them pom-poms—made a real mess of my leg," he admitted presently. " Well, might have been worse, mightn't it, sir ? I'm a bit dot-and-go-one just now, but I'll be all right when I get my new leg, shan't I ? "

" That'll be all right," growled Harcourt. He shot a sidelong glance at Killick. What about *your* son ? the glance said. " How did you manage to get back ? I thought they were only sending the officers home and keeping the men in hospital."

" That was another bit of real luck ! " Joe's face radiated his conviction that an especial dispensation of Providence had governed his experiences in the Transvaal. " You see, sir, I was orderly to Captain Strachey, and we both got popped at the same time ; but the Captain's—his wasn't much of a do, as it turned out, and he decided to stop out there, and it was him that fixed for me to have his passage back in the hospital ship, because I wasn't any good, as you might say, and it was better to get fellows like me out of the way to make room for the ones that wanted the hospital beds. Sir, what's the news about Johnny ? "

" Well—you know he's at Cape Coast Castle ? " said Harcourt.

" I heard something about it when I got back, but I've not heard from him at all. When did he go ? "

" Last month," said Harcourt shortly. " You've probably missed the letter ; you'll be hearing, one of these days. Well, Joe, you'd better let me know when you want to start work."

" That's a good young fella," Killick was saying, as Joe's crutches clicked on the polished boards of the landing on his way downstairs.

" Of course he's a good young fella. What the hell 'ud he be doin' in my office if he wasn't ? " snarled Harcourt ; but his surliness had lifted. If anyone had told him that the sun was shining more brightly, the air was lighter and his brain clearer because a red-haired junior clerk had got back from South Africa—he would have said they were mad.

IV

The whole town seemed patched with brightness as, swinging between the crutches, he pressed eagerly towards its narrow, familiar streets. Barely five months since he had left it—and what were five months in the life of Bristol ?—yet it seemed as though a small section of eternity had cloven the past from the present. Johnny would have understood. . . . That was the only shadow on his return : the absence of Johnny. It would have been good on this, the first morning, to have taken their favourite walk round the old city walls ; to have tipped their hats as usual to Brennus and Belenus, and, having completed the circuit, to wander on to the slums of Castle Green which, for Joe and Johnny, bore still the imprint of Godfrey of Coutance, of all the pageantry of the Normankings. Presently, when they had fixed his new leg, he would be able to do all that again. Now, although the hour was not yet eleven, the morning was hot, and the effort of supporting his long limbs on the crutches brought sweat out on Joe's brow.

He stood still to mop it away. The close air was layered with familiar odours, with the smells of fruit and fish, of new bread and coffee freshly ground ; and the pavements crowded with housewives. In the cluster about a fishmonger's marble slab, a straw boater, a print blouse gathered smartly into a broad belt of buckram and a clear soprano voice caught at Joe's memory.

"I'll take the sole—and I want it filleted, if you please." The speaker swung round, bumped lightly into him, said, "Sorry !" and followed it with a gasp. "*Joe !*"

He saw her eyes widen, go to his crutches and, incredulously, to his stump. The colour drained from her cheeks.

"Oh—*Joe.*"

"Why, Polly." He, too, found himself speechless, struggling with the sudden tightness in his throat.

Her eyes had filled ; with a strange feeling of apartness and wonder he watched them overflow, watched them pour their stream of crystal down her whitened cheeks, watched it dripping on the bosom of her blouse. He had never seen a woman cry in that way before ; he watched it, fascinated, unable to connect it with himself.

"Oh, Joe." Shyly she put out her hand and touched his that gripped the crutch.

"Why, Polly, fancy meeting you," he managed, foolishly, to say.

"Why didn't you tell me ?" she whispered.

He recovered himself with an effort.

"Tell you—what—about my silly old leg ? Ho, that's nothing. Well, Polly, how are you ?"

"Oh, dear—oh, poor, poor Joe !" She had snatched her handkerchief and was holding it pressed to her face to conceal its distressful quivering. He began to be embarrassed, to stiffen himself against her pity.

"Oh, just you wait ! I'll be dancing the Lancers as good as anybody before I've done !"

Polly made a noise between a laugh and a sob.

"It's like you, Joe, to be plucky."

"Well, what's there to be plucky about ? I've got one sound hopper, haven't I ?—and that's more than some of our chaps can say. It's a real treat to see you, Polly. I hadn't expected that much luck, my first morning at home."

She had hastily dried her eyes and the warm pink was returning to her face.

"Joe—I've got to hurry or I'll miss the bus ; but you'll come out and see us, won't you ?"

"Yes, I will—if it's all right, Polly."

She went crimson as she had formerly been white.

" Of course it's ' all right ' !—I mean—I'm very busy, you know, since Mother got ill."

" Perhaps I'd be in the way."

" Don't be silly." She turned quickly to take her parcel from the fishmonger. " We'll see you, then—on Sunday ? "

" I'd like to see you to the bus, if you don't mind me walking with you."

" Well, Joe——" She hesitated, her hand twitching nervously as she rearranged the contents of her basket. Guessing at what was in her mind, he said :

" Maybe I don't get along fast enough ; I wouldn't like to make you miss it."

She muttered : " Good-bye, Joe," and was gone, fluttering, into the crowds, before he had time to ask her what he had intended : whether she had heard any news of Johnny. He saw no more of the streets of Bristol as he swung his way back by Cathay to Ship Lane.

In the little stuffy kitchen he found his meal ready. The good-natured, easy-going Puckles had welcomed him with open arms, and it was the wife's suggestion that the truckle bed he had occupied so long should be brought down to the sitting-room, to spare him the difficulty of the steep and narrow stairs. She placed a steaming and fragrant dish on the table as Joe came in.

" Beefsteak pudding ? Phew ! A pity Johnny's not here, Ma ! Remember how he used to go for your Kate and Sidney ? " he chuckled.

She made no reply, heaping the plates with their big helpings of suet and gravy, and with new potatoes swimming in butter that made Joe smack his lips.

" Where's Dad ? Out on a job ? "

" Ay ; he'll not be in till tea-time. Now get on with that—and don't let me have any leavings to clear up when you've done ! "

" Leavings ? No fear," Joe promised her, as he picked up his knife and fork. Ten minutes later he gave her a triumphant grin across an empty plate. " That good enough for you, Ma ? How about some more potatoes ? You know," he went on, as she went to the pan on the hob, " it's going to seem rum without Johnny. Haven't you had any word from him yet ? "

" No, we haven't." Her good-humoured mouth had stiffened.

" Oh well, you know what it is. Mails take a long time from the Coast —and the war'll be making a difference. Think of old Johnny out there— among the niggers ! "

" Listen here, Joe." The tartness of her voice made him look up quickly ; she was standing at the end of the table, her knuckles resting on it, and a dull, purple flush had run up to the thin roots of her dark hair. " Once and for all, I don't want to hear no more about that young fella. Decent we are, an' decent, please God, we'll always be ; and this house isn't for the likes of him or his click."

While Joe sat aghast, his jaw dropping, she lowered herself into the rocking-chair at the side of the hearth ; her brow knitted, her arms folded, she swung slowly backwards and forwards.

" Since you come here I been a mother to you, and so I was to that young Flood. You never seen anything, either of you, that wasn't a good example to the pair of you. Maybe Puckle takes a glass too much now and again, on a Saturday night, but you never saw or heard anything from him that would do you harm, or any other young person, be it male or female."

" No, that's true enough—but what's all this about, Ma ? " Mystification lay on Joe's brow ; what the devil had Johnny—in the past a prime favourite with Ma Puckle—been up to ? "

" We always warned you, both of us, that there was plenty of trouble to be had without looking for it by heedless young chaps like you ; and I know as Puckle spoke to you, Joe, right sharp, over some of the company you was keeping on the sly——"

" All right, Ma ; but what's it got to do with Johnny ? He never went with girls—I'll take my oath on that ! "

" You'd better save your oaths," she snorted. " Fetched a woman in here one night—that's what your friend Johnny did——"

" Rot ! " cried Joe.

" And don't you ' Rot ' me. The pair of 'em—drunk as lords—a-laying on your bed——"

" You must have gone clean daft ! " he shouted. " Johnny never did such a thing in his life. It's a damned lie, Ma, and I don't know what's come over you to believe it. Good Lord above, if you don't know Johnny better than that, after all these years—it's preposterous," muttered Joe, as he thrust the plate with the untouched potatoes away from him.

" And you better take care how you call me a liar, young man ! " She had stopped swinging and sat stiffly gripping the arms of the chair. " Puckle'll have something to say to you—— ! "

" I didn't call you a liar. I said it was a lie, and I couldn't understand your believing it. And no more I can't," repeated Joe, his face redder than hers, his eyes bright with rage.

" I s'pose I can believe my own eyes, can't I ? Come in at one in the morning, after we missed the last train from Bath—which we'd been to see Puckle's aunt that's got the tea-shop—and every step of the way we'd walked, and like to drop, the pair of us ! And there's a light in your old room—me heart stood still. ' Burglars ' ! I says to Puckle. Huh—burglars ! There they was—the pair of 'em——" Mrs. Puckle paused to draw breath. " Your friend Johnny Flood—and the other was one of them two pill-garlicks you had to tea before you went away."

" *What ?* That Miss Livingstone—that young lady from Mercer's ? " gaped Joe.

She shrugged her shoulders.

" Don't ask me what her name is ! The madam—for two pins I'd've given her in charge ; but for getting the house a bad name, that's what I'd have done—don't *you* make any mistake ! " she added viciously. " Coming into decent folks' places as if they was knocking shops! I'd've put 'em both in the street——"

"But—wait a minute——" Joe's head was spinning. "I can't get this —Johnny wrote me he'd gone up to live with his uncle in Berkeley Square—how could he——?"

"Huh—he'd know better than take his fancy woman to Berkeley Square, wouldn't he?"

"But he'd never . . . How could he know you and Dad were out?" persisted Joe. "You know as well as I do, he'd never have brought a girl here—hang it, Ma, he wouldn't have done it anyhow. It's not Johnny's line of country—there's something rum somewhere—it doesn't make sense, any of it." He rubbed his hands wildly through his ruffled hair.

"Sense or nonsense, whys and wherefores—I don't want to hear anything more about it." The chair clacked back on its rockers as she got up. "Johnny Flood's not coming back here again, and we're having no more young women to tea. So that's the end of it. And now you can sit there and read the paper while I wash up."

For the next half-hour he held the newspaper before his face without understanding a line of its contents. The clash and splash from the scullery, the clatter of the children running back to Infant School added to the confusion in his brain. The whole thing was unbelievable—was like some kind of an evil nightmare: simply because it was Johnny. Fellows did behave in that way, of course—he, Joe, had no grounds for superiority—but not Johnny. And even that little Miss Livingstone—Polly's friend: Polly would not make friends with a girl of that kind. Did Polly know anything about it? Was that what had made her seem—for the first time he admitted it—awkward, and a little anxious to get away from him this morning? And was it the explanation of Johnny's long silence——? Why should it be? What had it got to do with him, Joe? Or with Polly, come to that?

A dark, uneasy sense of mystery settled upon him, to escape from which he again seized his crutches and went out to seek the clean breeze blowing along Radcliff Parade.

V

With a distracted glance at the clock, she flung her hat off and rushed at the oven to see whether the hotpot she had left there had gone dry; she rattled the poker under the stove and ran for the great pan of potatoes that must be boiled in time for the midday meal—and gasped with shock as she glimpsed from the window the dour, advancing figure of her father. She would be late again!

It seemed to Polly that her life had become a scramble, trying to think of something for her mother's comfort, trying to remember all the duties which now devolved on her. Always late and always forgetting, she had become a shuttlecock between her father's sour silences and her mother's anxious reminders. A taciturn man, Aaron Bowling, with small sympathy for youth and gaiety—he seldom complained, but, during his little time indoors, sat glumly silent, unresponsive to attempts on the part of his womenfolk to lighten the atmosphere his presence darkened. With her mother there to support her, Polly was immune from this gloomy influence ; alone, she found it insupportable, and, half-ashamed, would steal upstairs to the hot, darkened room where Ellen's leaden face turned towards her on the pillow.

"Your hair looks as if it could do with a good brush."

"I expect it does, Ma dear."

Pity for the querulousness of sickness restrained a sharp reply, and tears were not far from the brightness of Polly's eyes as they fell on the stark remains of her mother's vigour, sunk in the feather mattress which, for all their care, gave off its faint, unwholesome stench of staleness and disease. Oh, Ma, why should it have come to this?

Compunction for all those carefree years that had turned her into a "young lady" quickened Polly's efforts and controlled her irritable distaste for the task of nursing ; but there were moments when she came near to hatred for her father, and bit her lips to hold back her resentment of him. Why, instead of laying his hot, unbathed body nightly by his wife's side—it could not be good for either of them and must add to Ellen's discomfort—could he not sleep in the other room? Yet some shy perception of the inviolable privacy that controlled the relationships of her parents held her back from suggesting it. Trying sometimes to freshen the room by burning lavender twigs, or sprinkling Cologne water on Ellen's pillow, she thought, with an angry envy, of Selina Flood's great room up at "the house," and wondered why comfort and decency should be a prerogative of the rich and denied to the poor ; and then was obliged to concede that riches had little to do with it—save that want of them had withheld from Aaron Bowling the education which would have refined his perceptions.

"I met Joe Prior in town this morning," burst from her when, leaving her father to get on alone with his meal, she carried up the invalid's tray. "Oh, Ma, the poor fellow's lost a leg! Isn't it shocking? I couldn't help bursting out crying at the sight of him."

"I warrant Joe's no less a man for it," said Ellen feebly. She pushed her plate aside. "I've got no appetite this morning."

"Oh, Ma! And I went down specially to get you that piece of sole," mourned Polly.

"Why don't you marry him?"

"Marry—Joe?" she gasped. "No, Ma dear ; I told him I wouldn't, before he went to South Africa."

"It's foolish of you." Ellen sighed. "I'd like to have known you'd got him to look after you."

She rushed from the room ; stood panting for a moment on the landing, then ran downstairs, snatching up a duster as she passed through the kitchen, with a glance at her father as he bent over his plate of food.

"What's the matter with you? When are you going to have your dinner?"

"I've had as much as I want—I've got jobs to do."

Had there really been a time when a whole afternoon passed in ironing a print frock, in playing the piano, in reading a story, perhaps in slipping up to "the house" for tea in the servants' hall and a brief flirtation with one of the grooms or gardeners on the estate? She stood, sometimes, aghast before the drudgery which was the record of the twenty-four years of her mother's married life. There now seemed something wicked in her own heedless, happy progress: in the gay Bristol interlude, that ended. . . . No. From that her mind still shuddered away.

Had she once had time to enjoy the summer?—thinking herself "busy" when she took their dinners to the men in the fields; when she joined in the haymaking, taking as her due those sly looks of admiration for a figure displayed in all its ripeness by the light tossing of the dried grass; when feeding the calves was a merry diversion instead of an onerous duty?

All that sunshine, all that laughter had nothing to do with the Polly Bowling who dragged her weary limbs to bed by daylight; who had barely time to say her prayers before she fell asleep; who was shaken back to consciousness when dawn was hardly in the sky, to stumble downstairs, to light the kitchen fire and make the cup of tea her mother craved, before starting the housework which had to be done—according to its mistress—before the farm work began. Was there a time when she came drowsily conscious to her mother's voice, waking her with that cup of tea? She blushed to remember it.

So long as Polly could remember, they had had no indoor help but a sluttish village girl to scrub the floors and swill out the dairy. Beds to be made, slops emptied, rooms "turned out," or dusted, in rotation. "I hope you're keeping the parlour decent." Sick of the extra labour it entailed, one day she emptied the canterbury of its sheaves of music and packed them away in a cupboard; when would she ever play again? Her hands were stiff and rough with unaccustomed labour. "You'll have to be lime-washing the scullery one of these days." Oilcloth and brasses to polish. Meals to prepare. Washing up, washing up. Poultry and pigs to be fed. Eggs to collect and count. Butter to be made up in pats for market—mercifully she had found a woman to do the churning. Scalding the churns—a duty Ellen delegated to no one and about which she was ceaselessly exercised.

Family washing, family mending—while all around the earth put on its summer beauty; spread itself with the creamy snow of clover and the wine-red of trefoil; fields rippled with the singing green of wheat, the blue of oats, the silvery haze of barley; and the air filled itself with pollen and the small grey moths that fly out of dried grass.

At least, she reflected thankfully, as she whisked her duster round the shelves of that complicatedly hideous piece of furniture known as a "chiffonière," which was the pride of Ellen's heart, one had little time for thinking. (The plants had not been watered ; the musk lay, soft and ragged, over the edge of its pot, and the blossoms of the primulas had withered into their green cups.) And Joe was coming, on Sunday. Joe . . . a pang shot through her, gripped her momentarily with nausea ; oh, poor, poor Joe ! So big and active ; last year he had helped with the harvesting, heaving the sheaves of corn up on the wagon—stronger and even quicker when he had learned the knack of it than the farm hands. Something—she struggled for a simile—something *godlike* about his big, happy movements, the swing of his hips and shoulders, his hair bursting from its townsman's sleekness into ringlets of bright copper about his freckled brow. Standing beside him had been like standing by one of the good farm beasts, with its own sweetness of heat and health on it. Just for a moment or two she had fancied herself in love with Joe ; had imagined him kissing her, putting his big, freckled arm round her waist, courting her, the way other boys had done, but Joe was too shy to do. He could only love her with his eyes—poor Joe !—and, partly because his restraint provoked her, she could never stop teasing him.

Polly's eyes misted with self-reproach as she thought how very, very kind she would be to Joe on Sunday.

CHAPTER THREE

I

THE white man in charge of the serpent stumbled at its tail. For forty-eight hours no clear, clean draught of air had entered his lungs, and he had forgotten the shape and colour of the sky. His conception of a world beyond the impenetrable web of the forest had worn thin. Sound had reduced itself to a squelch of unshod feet, to the subhuman grunt and wheeze of the carrier line, to the whine of a sloth and the screech of a parrot. Sight was a blur of green. The stench of rotted vegetable matter was driven like a plug into the nostrils.

Movement was the mechanical thrust of one foot before another, hampered by suction and by the blind network of roots. Sometimes there was water. Sometimes the giant trunk of a tree had dropped itself across the barely distinguishable track. There was the weight of a mackintosh, coated in mud to the chest, and the drag of a torn boot, letting in mud to mingle with blood. Up and down, up and down the line. How many men missing from this gang, how many from that ? The endeavour to memorise the faces of company captains, of gang leaders, of individual carriers, many of whom had lost, or deliberately thrown away, the arm-bands meant to act as marks of identification. A brief spell of rest in a hammock—but rest that was not rest, with responsibility gnawing at the brain—then back again to the patrol.

“ Three hundred carriers ? ” Johnny took a purely formal glance at the chit in his hand. He had made, since his arrival, another journey, twenty miles back, to Fesu, to take over carriers. He knew what to expect.

"One thirty—odd."

"It says three hundred here." What the hell? One had to give an imitation of efficiency.

"Sure. That's when we left Mansu."

"You've dropped a hundred and seventy?"

The European handing over grew tired of the game.

"There's your rice. It's mouldy. We got no covers."

"Have you fed them?"

"Not yet."

"Right. We'll go straight off."

"On empty bellies?" The other lifted his eyebrows. "You'll have the rest of 'em dropping——"

"Let them drop," said Johnny grimly. He had had enough, by now, of carrier lines to know that full bellies mean trouble, and that the carrier, like the camel, is capable of existing on his own interior nourishment.

He went down the squatting lines and spoke shortly to each gang. Behind him went the two Hausas who had come down with him. The carriers sulked and ducked their heads. A native company captain boldly demanded rice.

"There will be rice at the end of the march. And"—he let the Colt swing gently in his right hand—"he who breaks line between here and the end will need no rice. I say it."

It was half-way through the palm tunnel between Fesu and Prahsu that he shot the first man. It had not seemed possible, to shoot a man in cold blood, but, when the time came, it was as though, without his own volition, the Colt spoke for him.

Like all carrier convoys, the line was split into companies, and the companies into gangs, each under its own leader. The length of the line and the narrowness of the track, allowing only of single file, made it virtually impossible to control more than a short section at a time. Before leaving Fesu, he had already marked down one gang in particular and its headman as a potential trouble centre and had placed himself immediately behind them. Twice this lot had broken, twice downed its loads and tried to scatter, and each time he had fired over their heads. The third time they had evidently decided that the shots were only tokens and that it was worth risking. Johnny dropped his man in the very act of leaping for the tangle; he fell back in midair like a shot squirrel. He knew the act was not "in order"; that one was not supposed to fire on carriers; and did it cold-bloodedly. He kicked the squealing victim to his feet and had him thrown into a hammock. It took nearly an hour to reassemble the wildly disordered and now badly frightened gang, but when they reached their journey's end only five, apart from the extremely noisy sufferer in the hammock, had risked the hazards of their guardian's aim.

Stumbling towards the ramshackle rest-house that had become Base

Headquarters, Johnny mechanically took note of changes. When he had first arrived the grass was shoulder-high ; it crawled up to the house, formed a barrier like loose-woven canvas to progress, gave up innumerable insects and was rank with malaria. When crushed by the loads, it gave off a fetid odour, like a sickly manure. Within forty-eight hours of leaving the coast, he had developed a hatred of the colour green ; never in any circumstances, he resolved, would he have anything green about him in future. At all points of the compass the horizon was obliterated by bush ; a yard or two from the beaten track you were midway between ankle and knee in a stinking water—the rising Prah : the Prah which stood for safety, for it marked the boundary of enemy country, and for discomfort, since its steamy moisture fed the monstrous vegetable growth and hatched the tsetse breeding in the swampy patches along its margins.

But the grass had fallen. Slowly—round the rest-house whose upper floor, split into three compartments, served as hospital, staff quarters and sleeping room for the Europeans, and whose ground floor was crammed with stores and ammunition—the grass had been beaten down by an emplacement of tents, of mud and bamboo huts and of stands, partly roofed over with plantain leaves, for the carriers' food. In place of the vast chaos he had left behind him there was some semblance of military order, of a big camp preparing for action. Nothing left out, reflected Johnny, as he passed the latrine screens, round which loped a brace of grinning Hausas —bar the troops. Where the Hausa lines had been, when he went back to Fesu, was a patch of yellowed grass and mud. There must be some more— somewhere ? Possibly they had been shifted on to drier ground.

He let himself settle into a rickety chair with the caution and quiet of one surprised at finding himself capable of sitting at all : his satisfaction only slightly shaken by the descent of a large clot of mud and sodden vegetable matter from overhead. Over his oaths and the laughter of the rest, a single voice expressed in irony the general opinion of officers' quarters, as represented by a gimcrack cubicle whose roofing was already liquefying in pools on the flooring beneath.

" Good old Public Works ! "

" What's yours, Flood ? "

" What have you got there ? "

" Swiss milk, water, rum "—with gusto. " A good old Doctor ! Ought to wash out the dregs of that dev'lish awful stream we came through yesterday. Demmed if I've not still got half a dozen tadpoles rushin' about inside me ! Got your mug ? "

" No fear. Mine's whisky."

" There ain't any sparklets," warned the other. " Well "—he swizzled vigorously—" here's to the jolly old enemy ; and let's hope he'll give us a livelier time, when we meet him, than we've had so far."

" You don't need to worry," a voice spoke dryly. " The Ashanti, when he gets going, 's quite a fighter. Any mail ? " he turned to Johnny to inquire.

The latter shook his head, swigged back the whisky the other passed him, and dragged himself up again. Friendly as they were, he knew, in their confined space, his room was preferable to his company. He would get a bath. . . .

A simmering dusk settled on the camp. Shortly after sundown the first crack came, and the bush danced and blazed in blue lightning. As the wind rose it filled itself with the crackling whine of parting roots. Here and there a great tree fell and the reverberation of its fall shook the huts and sent creatures of the forest leaping for shelter. In one of the camps across the Prah the lightning touched off a gunpowder dump ; rocks and tree stumps and human fragments were hurled above the dark vegetable canopy presently to be lashed into ribbons by the rain. A telegraph wire, ripped from its couplings, whipped round and neatly decapitated one of the broncocephalic dotards, of which each village had its quota, as he was snuffling his panicstricken way home.

Save, however, by the weak-minded, the storm was taken seriously, but created no panic. The bush conceded that Tando was having trouble with some of his family, but that the matter did not concern human beings. Ashanti, Adansi, Denkera and the rest of them sat snugly under their thatch —more snugly, in fact, than the inhabitants of the rest-house at Prahsu, now licked by the rising river, its surrounding jungle mashed into swamp by the sudden downpour, its frail structure shaken by the gale, pinned to the earth only by the weight of its occupancy.

Jammed in their quarters by an indescribable clutter of baggage, which barely left room for the erection of camp-beds, men listened to the storm and shrugged their shoulders on the destruction of their work of the last four days ; hospital tents ripped up and whirled like gigantic kites to rest on tree tops ; grass huts reduced to heaps of mud ; bags of rice, sodden on their bamboo stands, burst, scattered and already sprouting on the steaming earth. There was little conversation—partly because of the noise of the gale and partly because each man's heart was heavy.

The full account of the defeat at Dompoassi had come through : Carter's retreat to Kwissa, with fifty per cent casualties, had brought home, even to the congenitally lighthearted, like Paget, the deadly nature of the campaign. There were details : Edwards, loading and firing his gun, ramming the charges in with his walking-stick, until he fell wounded ; Roupell, shot through both wrists, continuing to carry ammunition with his forearms ; the gallantry of Sergeant Mackenzie of the Seaforth Highlanders, leading that last wild charge on the stockade, when his commanding officer had lost his eye—that made each man pray secretly that he might not, when his time came, fail to maintain the brave pace set by his comrades.

Somewhere, out in the downpour, was Melliss, with his little company of one hundred and fifty men, beating his way to the relief of Carter at Kwissa ; somewhere else, another hundred struggled hopefully towards Fumsu. Once, already, they had been turned back on an ambush scare, and again they were sent forth. In the end room, a sick man, responsible for them all, could barely lift a hand to take the cables as they came in.

Two or three of his companions were writing letters ; no one knew when, or if, they would get to the coast. Johnny, with a writing-pad on his knee, sat staring at a blank page.

Joe, in South Africa, wondering why he had had no answer to his last letter. Still with his fond, obstinate heart set on Polly—not knowing he had been betrayed by his best friend. How write to Joe ?

It was impossible to set on paper the confession of his treachery ; equally impossible to write and to make no confession ; to ignore the past. Yet how could he say bluntly : " I have married the girl you love ? " His imagination gave him, with too great vividness, Joe's pleasure at seeing his handwriting on the envelope ; his saving the letter, perhaps, " for a treat," until he had a quiet opportunity of opening it ; and then—the fatal sentence, leaping like an asp at his heart. Supposing it were to arrive when the Sixth Division was going into action ; or when he was sick, or—though heaven forbid—wounded ? He knew, at last, that it was utterly impossible to send such a letter ; that he must either keep silence or force himself to write the usual friendly epistle that Joe would be expecting, and hoping for : though his gorge rose at the hypocrisy of the act. He knew the peculiar poignancy of a letter from home to a man on active service : how a trivial expression, or the omission of a hoped-for phrase, strikes with an exaggerated sharpness on the susceptibilities of the reader. For Joe's sake, the easier path of silence must be rejected ; would he not already be fretting for news from his friend ?

Then—when they met ; when, face to face with Joe, he made his confession : that was not the end, for the explanation had yet to be given. And could never be given. So there could never again, even if Joe forgave him, be confidence between them. A spasm of bitter regret seized him, shook him, and passed : but not completely. In his headlong impulse to make reparation for an act of which, at the time, he had barely been conscious, had he sufficiently considered Polly ? Would they not, both of them, have been wiser to have waited until the violence of their reactions—his compunction and sick self-disgust, her panic of confusion—had subsided ; until they were calm enough to think quietly about the future, to decide, mutually, whether there was no other course open to them than the desperate one which, at the moment, had seemed the only solution of their problem ?

Poor Polly ; was she now agonising, as he was doing, about it—about that fateful moment which had bound two utterly incompatible people irrevocably together—unless they found a way out as foreign to a Flood as it was to a Bowling ?

Yet what else, in the circumstances, could they have done ? Had he been staying at home—had he, even, been sure of his return—he would, he knew, have persuaded her to wait : to make sure, first, that circumstances had bound marriage upon them. But there had been from the first no question—at least, in his mind—of leaving Polly to the hazardous future with no form of security for her and for the child she might bear. They had had to marry, for his credit as well as for her own. Surely even Dromore must see that the bad old legend of his grandfather's time must not be revived by a Flood of the younger generation? Surely the proof that his son had behaved like a man of honour must, in time, soften Dromore's attitude to the pair of them? For himself, Johnny, it did not matter; on Polly's account it was vital. Even more so, in the case of her child.

Most of his companions were asleep, although the rattle of the rain was still like artillery. He discovered he had cramp, smothered a grunt, and moved into another position. It was too late, now, to begin a letter to Joe. He ought also to write to Harriet, and to Miranda; notes would do—there was no point in harrowing them with descriptions of his present situation. And he must send some sort of vindication of his departure from Cape Coast Castle to Harcourt—and a line to Whittick! He began to scribble:

"I am sorry the suddenness of coming out here left me no time to see, or even to write to you. I'm afraid we must postpone the appointment with Dietrich. I hope this miserable business will be settled before long, and without too much bloodshed on both sides.

"Luckily, I managed to get supplies of your prescriptions from Savory and Moore's, and hope they, with the old standby, quinine, will see me through. Would order more to be sent out, but think it very doubtful they would reach me, as I have not the slightest idea what my movements will be, or what turn events will take. There is rather a pandemonium on, and communications are very bad."

He hesitated for a moment before adding, at the foot of the page:

"Queer as it seems, I have been practically free from the other trouble since about a week before I left home. It looks as if Dietrich might not be needed, after all."

II

The carriers from Sierra Leone arrived, bringing a smallpox epidemic which filled the hospital tents and overflowed into as many huts as were habitable after the night's downpour. All available labour was pressed into the reconstitution of the ruined camp—during which operation most of the coastal carriers seized the opportunity to bolt, and were considered good riddance; their panic shown by not waiting to get their money, they would have been useless on the other side of the Prah.

In the walking column of mud that appeared on his left, Johnny recognised Paget. Although, in spite of their interdependence, both military and civilians preserved a slight bar of formality in dealings with one another, this had all but disappeared between Paget and Johnny: the former having discovered a strong liking for the "game little devil" who "went on trudgin' all over the place with those unseemly bloody carriers." The liking was heightened to respect, almost amounting to awe, by Johnny's fluency in the vernacular, and, consequently, his ability for getting what he wanted with less trouble than the majority. Paget, he knew, was disgruntled ; hoping to have been sent out with Melliss, he had been kept at the Base, to take over the command of the next batch of troops, when (if ?) any such arrived.

"Heard the latest ?" he lingered by Johnny long enough to inquire. Johnny turned from the trench a bunch of Mendis were clearing round the hospital tents. They had all been sick, were small, weak and worked feebly—which was why they had not gone up with one of the departed columns. You had to keep on at them to get anything done : a nasty, disheartening, brutish kind of job.

"No ; what's doing ?" he asked hopefully, wondering if a grain of precious news had come through, and whether, in that case, he had any chance of getting at the telegraph.

Paget gave a muffled chuckle.

"Dear old Commandant's found a new game for us—going around, blandishing the chiefs into contributing supernumerary man-power for the reinforcement of the troops. Otherwise, raising levies. A dreary little job." He ended on a grimace.

"Sounds that way. Particularly if the chiefs don't feel like contributing." Their eyes met, exchanged a look of understanding. "What about training the levies ? Raw bush nigger's not likely to be good war material—up against fighters like the Ashanti."

"You're too right," sighed Paget. "I suppose they'll allow us a Hausa non-com. or two, to help us whack them into shape. By which time, please goodness, the siege will have been lifted and the wogs have calmed down. Though it *did* flash across my mind——" He stopped, biting his lip.

"That it's going to be a long do ?" Johnny turned to curse a Mendi who was malingering, and turned back. "Looks like it," he admitted briefly.

"This popping a couple of hundred at a time into the bush—well, it's something like dropping a pinch of mustard seed into a bin of corn, ain't it ? A pony to a shilling you find your seed again, what ? Ha, ha," observed Paget, and dug thoughtfully at the mud with the point of his walking-stick.

Johnny handed over, with a sharp word to the headman, and the pair of them made slowly back towards the house, from which a smell of midday chop diffused itself among the other scents of the clearing.

"Actually," said Paget, "there are few things I look forward to less than meeting a bad-tempered detachment of Ashanti ; it seems their style of warfare's too, too unsporting."

"I don't suppose you'll find the tribes, as a whole, sticking to the rules," Johnny admitted.

The other nodded gravely.

"If the worst comes to the worst, I don't mind setting fire to a village or two, and chivvying a few selected old men, women and children round the huts. I suppose we'll have to find some use for the levies. That, at least," said Paget, on a note of reason, " is the dear old Commandant's idea."

" Not take them as a war-head, I suppose ? "

" ' Use the troops directly on the enemy, then send in the levies to harry and burn villages, destroy crops and do all possible general damage.' " He quoted glibly from authority. " If you know of a more poisonous little job of work for an officer of Her Majesty's forces, tell me about it. Not," said Paget bitterly, " that I'm likely to get it. A skin like mine's much too precious to be risked under fire ! So far as I can make out, I'm to sit on the Prah, counting out bags of rice and chasing carriers each time they try to bolt. Some frightful ass told the Commandant I won the half-mile at my prep. I admit I've got a turn for speed, but I'm a bit doubtful of my form when it comes to bush paths."

Before the day was over, however, his gloom was dispelled. Once more he sought out Johnny—the latter, this time, snatching a brief sleep on top of one of the baggage piles.

" Hi, Flood : listen. We've got a real job to do."

" When do you start ? " He struggled back through the heavy drowsiness of physical exhaustion. There was a kind of beauty in the gaiety of Paget's face pushed close to his.

" Pull yourself together, man ; the Commandant wants you."

" *Me ?* " He had an idea that he just existed, somewhere on the periphery of the Commandant's consciousness, but, save for a brief, sharp interview, when he gathered that Morris's credentials had been accepted, and that he was an accredited member of the transport column, he had never met Willcocks face to face.

" Listen : Bendick's out in the Omo country, raising levies ; he's sick, and his second, McGinty, 's dead. We've got to get a relief to him. I want you, along with me—we start to-morrow, at dawn. We've got to make sure of those levies—they're on our right flank : they'll link up with the Akim bunch under Benson and Wilcox. . . ."

He dragged himself to his feet ; clambered over the baggage piles that made an obstacle race of the route to the Commandant's quarters, and found himself facing Willcocks.

" Mr. Flood. You know what a native levy consists of ? " Propped up on his camp-bed, his face furrowed and leaden with fever and the nag of his injured leg, the Commandant wasted no time in preliminaries. Without waiting for Johnny to answer : " It is a motley mob of undisciplined riff-raff, the throw-outs of the tribe, or village, the rabble any chief or headman is glad to get rid of. They are armed with trade guns, slugs and powder usually ; in addition, of course, to native weapons, which few of them know how to use with any degree of skill.

" Their pay is what they loot. The people who supply them usually expect a grant of land in return for their loyalty and services. Care must be taken about these pledges, for they have got, sometime, to be honoured." He stopped again, with a pulse ticking in his cheek and the sweat pearling down from his short grey hair, although the evening was cool.

"That, however, has got nothing to do with you. I am told you have some knowledge of the Ewe dialects."

"Yes, sir. A little."

"Only a little?" snapped Willcocks. "For pity's sake, man! This isn't a time for modesty. We all know 'a little'; just enough to make us uneasy when we have to depend on the linguists. I was given to understand you were fluent."

"There are a great many dialects," said Johnny slowly. "I can make myself understood in three; I understand a couple more. And I know Hausa. I think they would combine into a pretty serviceable mixture, sir; unless, of course, we happened on some remote corner of the bush, where language, as such, is practically at a discount."

"Omo," said Willcocks; and his brows twitched up in query. Johnny felt his muscles stiffen.

"Yes, sir. I know Omo. I mean, the place. And the people."

"Then—are you prepared to go out with Paget?" As Johnny hesitated, he added, "I know what you are thinking, Mr. Flood: that you came out as a correspondent, and that if you go out with a minor contingent you risk missing the advance of the main column on Kumassi. That, of course, is perfectly true. You have your duty to your paper to consider."

"Yes, sir. That was what I had in my mind."

There was a brief silence.

"Well, you had better think it over. I have no intention of persuading you against your will, or your conscience. The farthest I will go is to remind you that every white man with knowledge of the country and the people is of inestimable value to us in our present shortage. Omo, situated on the Ashanti border and linking up with the nominally loyal Akim, is in a key position. We want those levies. Paget is a fine young officer, whose experience is not yet equal to his courage. I'll give you an hour to make your decision."

Thoughts raced through his mind like shadows: Reuter; the inevitable War Office dispatches, boiled down for the Press; the glory that would accrue to the newspaper man who was actually in at the relief of Kumassi; the forty to one chance that Kumassi would relieve itself before ever the main column got up there. There had been at least one report, well accredited, though it was contradicted later, that the garrison had broken out; that Hall had joined the Governor and that both were on their way south.

He rejected mentally the idea of personal glory. It was not that kind of war. It was a war in which nothing counted but duty to one's fellow men. As a unit in the main column he would be one of a hand-picked bunch whose individual equipment was equal, if not superior, to his own. That main column might even, in an impasse, be dependent on the levies which McGinty's death and the illness of Bendick had disorganised.

Even while the Commandant was saying, "Send Paget in," his answer was ready.

" I've decided, sir. If I can be of use, by going to Omo, naturally I'll go."

Willcocks's thin lips twitched into a smile under the cropped moustache. " Thanks. I ought to have told you : it's tricky going from here. You've got to cut through a corner of enemy territory, and the Akim aren't dependable. But Omo's supposed to be pro-British. It's Morris's district ; he said he'd vouch for them—as far as one can vouch for any of the tribes, under present conditions."

It was Paget's turn, that night, to go round the sentry posts. Johnny went with him. They clambered softly over the sleeping bodies of the others and squelched into invisible mud. It took a long time to get round the camp, but the challenges came punctually ; the Hausa guard was on the alert. In one of the hospital tents somebody had nightmare, or delirium. They paused to look in. The orderlies were struggling with a naked figure ; the shadows went leaping and writhing over the palely luminous canvas of their background ; finally the man was tripped and flung back on his fellow invalids of left and right. There were no beds. Every inch of the ground-sheets—so thick in mud and filth they were indistinguishable from the sodden earth—was covered with bodies, there was no room to step. Innumerable eyes, in pustulated faces, looked at the two white men without intelligence. Close to the tent flap two objects like mummies, swathed in canvas, witnessed to the toll, since nightfall, of the disease.

With a smothered exclamation Paget stepped sharply back on Johnny and apologised.

" Dev'lish silly—it gives me the horrors—in spite of vaccination," he muttered, shamefaced. They stumbled on twenty paces before he spoke again. " Well—another four hours—and we'll be off. And I don't mind admitting I'm damned glad ! If it's a choice between smallpox and the Ashanti, give me the wuzzies, any day."

They both stood in silence, straining their eyes to see, through the darkness, the almost imperceptible line where bush met sky. There was a lot of cloud, but an occasional star helped to define space from tree-tops. Johnny heard Paget draw a long breath.

" It's damned difficult to imagine, isn't it ? "

" What's difficult ? "

" In there "—he probably nodded his head, but the movement was lost in the dark—" all seething with blacks : dozens of them, probably, at this moment, scouting along the other bank, listening to our voices—what ? "

" It isn't likely," Johnny was able out of his experience to answer. " The blacks are scared stiff of the dark ; that's what would have given us an advantage—if we'd had white troops, enough of them to spare for a protective guard to the carriers. We could bring off a lot of surprises, if we kept going after sundown."

" As it is, the wuzzies'll do the surprising—ha, ha ! " The mechanical little laugh, with which Paget ended so many of his sentences, dropped like two tiny plummets of lead into the dark. " Well, how about turning in—— ? "

" Might as well." He said it grudgingly, knowing he would not sleep ; it was better out of doors, away from the stifling heat, the groans and restless movements of their companions.

" I dare say you've got a letter or two you want to write."

" A letter ? " He spoke vaguely.

" I've written to my *fiancée*. Mere formality—in case of fire ! " After a pause. " You've not got anything you'd like to leave behind—same principle ? "

" . . . No," said Johnny.

" You're not married ? "

" Why ? "

" My dear fellow, don't, for heaven's sake, imagine I'm prying into your private affairs ! " came Paget's voice out of the dark. " On the other hand, it's silly to pretend that this trip of ours is entirely a picnic, though the enemy doesn't appear, yet, to have broken in the Akim-Omo direction. What I mean to say is, either you, or I, might happen to step on something that went off bang, and, in that case—you see what I'm driving at ? "

" Yes—I see. I might write a letter sometime," said Johnny carefully. " Thanks for reminding me."

Lying in the dark, he wondered to whom to write a letter which might be the last he would ever write, and what in the world one was supposed to put in such a letter. A collective one, addressed to the whole of the family, would be absurd and could not fail to be stilted, since each of the readers would expect his own particular idiom which did not apply to the rest. No letter to Harriet, for example, could be acceptable to Dromore, and the kind of thing he wrote to Selina or Miranda would hardly suit Harcourt. And Polly would have no share. . . .

All those he loved . . . yet no one to whom, to the exclusion of all others, a letter was due. No one with a supreme claim on him, such as Lady Gwendoline Morley—he had read the superscription while undressing—had on Paget. In law, no doubt Polly ; poor Polly, who, beyond the fringe of her all-enveloping benevolence, cared no more for him than he for her. Polly would cry, and say Poor Johnny, and then all her anguish would rise into a great wave on behalf of her child. He knew suddenly that he must, at all costs, find out if Polly was going to have a child, and, after reflection, decided that there was nothing for it but to risk a letter to her. He could scribble it in the morning and arrange to have it sent by the next runner down to the coast. Polly—his next of kin ; wasn't that what they called a man's wife ? Polly, his next of kin ! The absurdity of the expression twisted his lips in the dark. No, it was impossible to write to Polly : to involve her in all the uproar that would accrue if someone else—her father, for instance—opened the letter. He simply must be there—Providence allowing—to stand by Polly's side, for her protection, when the moment came to declare the truth.

For the first time, coherently, he allowed himself to contemplate the future : which meant, almost undoubtedly, a complete break with all the associations of Guerdon, if not of Queen Square. It was possible, although not probable, that Harcourt would keep him in the office ; in which case a little house in, or near, Bristol, would furnish all their needs. But if Harcourt chose, for his own imponderable reasons, to espouse the Guerdon cause, he, Johnny, would be looking for work, and it might be lodgings or rooms in a farm house for Polly and the baby ; or it might mean leaving that part of the country altogether and building a new life among strangers. Surely, however, Harcourt's devotion to the cause to which they were both dedicated would forbid so drastic a cleavage ?—and his contempt for Guerdon and all its standards incline him to look leniently upon one who had shown, in so marked a fashion, his repudiation of them ? Harcourt had no use for women, and it was hard to say whether Polly's bonny looks, her good manners and the gaiety of her disposition would go any way towards softening the old man and earning his forgiveness of their act of deception.

Polly would make a good wife, a sweet wife, and, please God, he would be good to her. But something—some wild, romantic impetus—had gone out of living. He refused deliberately to associate it with one whose name should never again, if he could help it, cross his lips.

When the Reveille sounded and heads were lifted reluctantly from the rolled-up bundles that served the majority for pillows, Paget, looking across the room, saw Johnny silhouetted against the pale light of the window. He was scribbling on a pad propped against the window ledge. Odd little man ; to whom after all had he decided to send a letter ?

CHAPTER FOUR

I

THE two women stood motionless, listening to the *fiacre* clopping lightly away from the tall iron gates, with their interwoven design of vine and trellis. Then there was the sound of the gates being locked and the lantern above them went out with a blink. The shuffling tread of the night porter carried him back to his lodge under the twin flights of steps meeting at the porch on the mezzanine. The courtyard filled itself with the liquid blue-green of summer night, and a street lamp, catching the cones of blossom on a lilac, turned them to a pale silvery grey.

The windows on the balcony were wide open. Sophie turned back into the room, after looping the yellow moiré curtains back with their silken cords. She lifted and set aside a cushion, in which, to her imagination, a faint trace of cigarette scent lingered.

"Would you care for a *tisane*, *chèrie*, before you go to bed ?"

"No, thank you, Sophie."

"Do not let me detain you. I always sit here and read a little until I begin to feel drowsy."

"Am I in your way ?"

" Naturally not." Her gown of embroidered tulle caught on the pile of the carpet and dragged back from her slim waist as she crossed the room.

" Sophie ! " The imperative note startled her attention from the book she had opened. " Have you nothing to say ? "

" To say . . . ? It is not a good time to begin saying things—at this hour of the night." But compunction drew her back to her companion's side ; she lifted her hand and touched delicately the young, hollowed cheek. " *Couches-toi, ma petite ;* we can say things to-morrow—if you wish."

" No—please ! You must say something—you must think something ! "

Sophie transferred her hand to her own cheek and leaned her head slightly against it. Finally she said :

" You looked charming and behaved most beautifully. What else ? I was proud of you ; of your good manners and your dignity."

" Is that all you can find to say ? " Emily reproached her.

Sophie sighed. She had hoped to postpone this conversation, but it was evidently not to be. She went slowly to the *chaise-longue* and lay down ; her head turned on the cushions, away from Emily, who, after a brief hesitation, made a little rush that brought her to Sophie's side and dropped her on her knees.

" Sophie. You are my best, my only friend. And you are tormenting me."

" What do you want ? " came at last, desperately, from the older woman.

" Want ? But you have just met the—the man I am going to marry," stammered Emily.

Sophie's head made an almost imperceptible negative movement before she turned to meet Emily's eyes. She opened her lips—and closed them.

" You will let me stop with you, until the divorce goes through ; won't you ? "

" And then—what ? "

" We will find a place of our own, of course. In Paris, I hope—where I can be near you and see you often. Or just outside. He told me he has friends at Versailles——"

" I am going to hurt you very much, *chèrie*, but I cannot help it." The reply had been long in coming ; Emily's breath fluttered, her fingers were curled into the palms of her hands.

" You cannot live in Paris," said Sophie de Séguin, " or in any place near Paris. It is quite out of the question. If you do not know that—he does."

" But—what do you mean ? " she gasped.

Sophie again turned her head away ; she could not, to those wounded eyes, say what had to be said.

" His Paris—which, if you marry, would be yours—is full of English people, who mix freely in society and who would soon make your position perfectly unbearable. You will not have the *entrée* to the Embassies, and a young Englishwoman who cannot make her *début* under the protection of her Ambassadress is at a disadvantage from which no other patronage can save her. *Chèrie* "—she caught the small, clenched hands and pressed them under her breast—" I must make you believe the truth of what I am saying! You would be no worse off in London than you will be here, as a young girl who, having been the cause of a divorce, has married her lover."

" But I have told you—— ! "

" That you are not lovers ? *Mon Dieu*, and who is going to believe that ? " cried Sophie. " London—what is it, after all, but a suburb of Paris ? It is a mere matter of hours, before a scandal in London becomes a scandal in Paris."

" Oh, surely not—— ! "

" I am speaking of your Paris, not of mine. There is not very much contact between the two, although they mix on formal occasions. And I assure you, dearest Emilie, ' French ' Paris is very quick to exclude a young woman who is not *bien vue* by her own countrymen."

After a moment Emily said piteously :

" Then where will we go ? "

Sophie was silent.

" I don't understand," she whispered. " You—and Papa——"

" Listen, *chèrie*. Your Papa, apart from being a man—to whom all things are forgiven !—was a very distinguished person at the Embassy. He had the style and outlook, and spoke the French of a Parisien. He was so much sought after that he could have afforded, if he had chosen, to be as irregular in his private life as he pleased. But he had too much good taste to offend a society to which he was proud to belong."

A ghost rose in the silence that followed her words.

" You were a very little girl when he died, *chèrie* : but surely you remember your father ? Can you imagine him, in any circumstances, acting other than chivalrously, to a woman young enough to be his daughter ? "

" But Roan—— It was his suggestion I should come to you ! " Catching the implication, she defended him indignantly. " He has done everything, everything in the world, to protect me ! Candleby—it was all my fault what happened at Candleby ; many a person, I am sure, would have washed his hands of the whole affair ! "

" I hardly think so poorly of him as that. As for his chivalry," said Sophie dryly, " it is in another category. Shall we, perhaps, not discuss chivalry in connection with your—friend ? "

" Ah—you don't like him," cried Emily, with sadness.

" That is to be childish," Sophie pointed out. " If we begin on that subject, it will be morning and we shall still have got no further ! "

" All the same, you don't." For the first time a faint note of antagonism put Sophie on her guard. " Naturally, I realise he is not in Papa's position, to command consideration from what you call ' *tout Paris* ' ; but he has many friends——"

" Who are likely, also, to be friends of yours ? "

" Perhaps you don't know "—with a pathetically youthful attempt at dignity—" how things have altered in England—in spite of the Queen.

Quite a number of what they call the 'Marlborough House set' have divorced and re-married, without its affecting their position in the least."

"Yes, I have heard that," agreed Sophie, "and there are plenty of *divorcées* in our society; but they are not your kind of people, or mine. As to young girls—you must know that our standards are equally as strict, if not more so, than yours. No girl of blemished reputation has the smallest chance, in this country, of making a reputable marriage; her husband's title cannot prevent her becoming a *déclassée*—a fact of which every man is aware. Frenchmen rarely marry for love; they marry for the sake of the heir and to enhance their own prestige."

"There is no question of my marrying a Frenchman." Her lips were pouted stubbornly.

"Happily—no. But the kind of English to whom you are accustomed—you call them 'the best people,' is it not?—are even stricter in Paris than they are in London. It is, perhaps, their way of protecting themselves against the charge of libertinage which is vulgarly brought against us! I have often been amused," said Sophie with a faint smile, "to see people who, at home, allow themselves a certain liberty, behaving here with the greatest circumspection; for fear, I suppose, of forfeiting their credit with their Embassy."

"What hypocrisy!" cried Emily indignantly. "And you——?" she continued. "How did they treat you, when you and Papa——" She caught back the words, blushing at the crudity of the wording.

"I, also, was in a position of privilege," admitted Sophie. "I had, to begin with, the protection of my husband's name——"

"But all your friends must have known? I remember the afternoons you drove with Papa in the Bois, and the parties you made for Longchamps; and Sunday mornings, after church, when you joined Papa and me and Nounou for an apéritif at Rond-Point, then you would drive us home to avenue Gabriel, and drop Nounou and me, and take Papa with you for *déjeuner*——"

Sophie made a slight gesture, as though these memories were too painful.

"Do you not know the difference between what people think and know and what they say? We were two well-mannered people who took pains, always, never to give occasion for gossip, and whose separate and public lives were important enough to each of us to make up for our necessary times of separation. All the same"—she sighed—"you must not think it was easy. It is never that, for the woman, even when it may be, for the man. It calls for much self-denial, self-control; and it is only a great passion that makes it worth while."

"Sophie"—the hard note had gone out of Emily's voice; she nestled more closely to her friend—"why did you not marry Papa, after Mamma died, and you were free?"

"When lovers marry," came the answer, slowly, "it is usually because romance is dead; or because they are obliged to do so, by circumstances; or because they are so young—God help them!—that they believe love is eternal. What could marriage have added to what your father and I shared, over all those happy years ? " There was gaiety, this time, in her smile. " It is like adding an ingredient to a dish that is perfect already and ruining it ! "

" Oh God," breathed Emily, " how happy you must have been. Please tell me : was Papa the first one you had loved ? "

" I told you I never loved my husband." Sophie's lips twitched again. " But one does not reach the age of twenty-eight—my age when I met Everard Temple—without various romances ! He was my first, and my last, lover," she concluded simply. " After Everard, there could be—no one. You believe me, *chérie* ? "

The pressure of Emily's hand answered this without words, but a spasm crossed her face as she whispered :

" Love is so *terrible*."

" Yes ; it is terrible. And so is God," said Sophie unexpectedly. She felt Emily recoil. " And we cannot live without either."

" No—no ; of course not." Emily got up abruptly ; she went out on the balcony, to press her palms on the cool, faintly dewy rail and look down into the deep blue-green pool of the courtyard ; the pale spires of lilac, floating like water-lilies on the darkness, recalled the lily-pool at Guerdon, and she started back as from a physical hurt. " How long does it take to get a divorce ? "

" I do not know—in the English courts. I believe a long time. Perhaps a year."

" My God ! " Panic was written all over her as she came back into the room. " But I must get married before then ! " gasped Emily.

" And supposing the wife will not divorce him ? " said Sophie coolly.

" Oh, but she will. I know Venetia—I mean, I have met her. She is charming," said Emily, clutching at her confidence.

" Has she a lover ? " asked Sophie practically.

" Oh—I don't know," Emily was obliged to confess.

Sophie shrugged her shoulders.

" A *chic* woman does not usually care to part with a husband, unless she has something effective to put in his place," she pointed out. " Tell me, *chérie* : why are you so anxious to marry a man you do not love ? "

Emily's delicate face crimsoned.

" Oh, but—I do ! "

" *Il y a du louche dans l'affaire*," muttered Sophie. She also rose, walked the length of the room, and turned on Emily. " There is only one reason for a young girl to marry a man with whom she is not truly in love ; to improve her position." Relenting, she came back to lay her hand on the other's shoulder. " *Chérie*, you have told me the truth, is it not ? You are not his mistress ? "

" No, Sophie ; truly I am not."

" Then, most dear child, what good can it bring you ? "

" What else can I do ? " she whispered.

" We can think of that later. But I beg you to believe me : so far as regaining your former position is concerned, it is of no use at all to marry Roan Flood."

"He will, at least, look after me." At last tears flowed; Sophie gathered her in her arms.

"My little Emilie, my pretty bird, you have others, beside him, to look after you." She drew the girl beside her on the sofa. "Ah, how like your mother you are! I knew her, you know, very slightly. How sweet she was! Sweet, cool, hiding her emotions under a tranquillity just like yours—but, oh, what wild impulses it concealed. She was indeed fortunate, in her marriage to your father, who understood and protected her in every mood."

"Is it strange, then, that I long for protection?"

"Shall I tell you exactly what it will be like if you marry Roan Flood?"

". . . The only circumstances," ended Sophie, when she had finished her dolorous picture of couples who had done what Roan and Emily proposed to do, "that could make all this tolerable—it could never be more —would be such a passionate love on both sides that nothing and no one in the world any longer had meaning for either. *No one in the world*," emphasised Sophie.

During the long silence that followed she thought of the man who had just left them: the sophisticated, charming man, patently in love with Emily Temple. No word had passed between the three of them that had any bearing whatever on the situation; they might have been three casual acquaintances, sharing the elder woman's hospitality. As an exercise in deportment it could not have been bettered—and Sophie appreciated deportment. He had kissed her hand at parting, and Emily's, with the right degree of deference for the woman who was his hostess and the woman he loved. Had she, perhaps, imagined the one look he gave her? It was so swift she could not be sure of it; but an impression remained with her, that in that fraction of a second, he had asked her pardon, her understanding and her mercy on them both. What insolence! She had felt her soul crystallise against him. She knew the type—fatal, always, to young girls; past-masters of the delicate flirtation, of the flattering look, that transforms the shy *débutante*, fresh from her governess, into the *dame du monde*, and sets her young suitors at a disadvantage. Don Juan of the schoolrooms! but, for once, hoist with his own petard. She had felt her smile of farewell, cruel with satisfaction.

Incredible, that Emily, with all her experience and her opportunities, should have fallen for those jaded attractions. Very good-looking; but *un peu rastaquouère*. Not much breeding behind those excellent manners. A peculiarly attractive voice—but nothing, surely, to capture the daughter of Everard Temple?

Somewhere—there was an explanation. Emily Temple: an acknowledged prize of the London season, flinging herself away on a man who (if he maintained his present pace) would be in a bath-chair by the time she was in her prime. That, to Sophie de Séguin, did not make sense. Sophie-like, she set herself to unravel the puzzle.

They were aware, simultaneously, of a change in the lighting. They looked with astonishment at Sophie's lamps, under their shades of frilled silk, paling in the dawn. What do I look like? wondered Sophie, looking at the girl opposite her. She has no beauty left, apart from her bones. Emily—the dark coil of her hair loosened, the accordion-pleats of her gown of pongee silk, coloured like an orchid, crumpled—shivered; her thin young arms were goose-fleshed, her face slightly yellow in the dawn twilight. Sophie moved stiffly to extinguish her lamps, and the ghostly luminance departed from the room. The dawn came in, clear and fresh and simple.

"The servants will be asleep; can you manage your bath?"

"Yes, thank you."

"Sleep well, *chérie*." Sophie touched the ruffled hair lightly; the two stood for a moment, breast to breast. "You shall not be disturbed until you ring," promised Sophie.

How incredible a story, thought Sophie, as she brushed out her long, dark hair—and how like her mother! There must be a streak of madness somewhere: that stubborn tenacity of loving—the crazy pursuit of a phantom! To love one man because he resembled another . . .

The future she set resolutely aside. Some way must be found of ministering to a mind diseased; but she must wait for the revelation. If love —the love of Everard's child—could effect anything, such love would not be lacking; but Sophie was too much woman of the world to underestimate the difficulty of her task. The Cullens—they could not entirely be discounted; although, being of age, Emily had no technical obligation to her adopted parents, there was gratitude to be considered.

Some of the phrases she had used to Emily came back to her, causing her a pang on account of their cruelty.

"A woman, if she is in love, can build her whole life round a man; no man, if he is worthy of the name, is satisfied with a woman, save in the first few months of passion."

"No matter how great his loyalty, he can never raise you to his position; on the contrary, that very loyalty will oblige him to descend to yours."

No anger, no denials; after the first few moments, no attempt to argue. *She does not love him!* So much was balm to Sophie's sore heart that ached the more for each barb she planted in the girl's.

And so dawn came—with Emily in her gown of that decadent green which was fashionable that year, like a plant battered by rain; her dark-ringed eyes half-stupefied, weak with languor, the blood drained out of her.

Sophie coiled her hair and allowed the loosened garments to fall round her ankles. As she stepped out of them she glanced at the little clock on her dressing-table.

. . . A door on the landing—pale blue and white, with the early sun slanting across it—clicked as she passed; then opened. Emily stood there in her white peignoir, incredulous.

"Sophie! Where are you going?"

She buttoned her glove as she answered, smiling:

" To mass. I hoped you would be asleep."

There were soft stirrings about the house, a clink, a tinkle, the cautious pad of a slippered foot.

" To mass—— ? "

" I nearly always go at seven o'clock. *Au revoir, chérie.*" An impulse made her turn at the head of the stairs. " Would you like to come with me ? You can—if you don't take too long to dress."

" I can slip something on—I've only taken off my gown ! " Her face had lost its deadness ; her eyes fixed with a humble eagerness on Sophie's face, she tugged at the satin ribbon of her belt.

" I will wait for you downstairs," said Sophie.

The fountain had been turned on in the courtyard, and along the street a watering-cart was laying the powdery dust the sweepers had left behind. There was an exquisite purity of unsullied morning in the air.

II

" They're doing their best to make a sort of prisoner out of me," scribbled Miranda,

" ——*but I'm not going to put up with it.* You know the old gazebo we used to play in, that's all broken down now ? There's the thicket behind it, and an oak tree that got struck in the storm the summer before last. *Do* try and meet me there. I've got nobody else now but *you.* I'll be there every evening somewhere about six o'clock. That's the time I go out with my hawk, and they're used to the idea. Don't *you* let me down.

" MIRANDA."

" P.S.—I've got a letter from Johnny to show you. He is all right, so far."

Polly carried the letter—brought down by one of the under-gardeners —in her pocket all day long. Each time she touched it a shiver went through her, and she whispered, *I can't, I can't!* Each time the thought of Miranda, waiting, depending on her, sent a fresh stab of pain into her heart. She had never been in the park since the meeting with Dorset—not even in that small strip bordering on the high road through which ran a right-of-way which Dromore, and the second Hercules before him, had vainly striven to set aside. The village was tenacious of its privileges—they were few enough ; so in spring and summer of every year, small children gathered primroses, wood hyacinth and asphodel inside the high, mossy wall that ran round the whole of the Guerdon demesne ; lovers lay there and it was more or less taken for granted that when one of the village girls got " into trouble " the park was responsible.

Although, thanks to her friendship with the gamekeepers, she was free of the farther reaches, and, with the boys and Miranda, had penetrated into the glades that sheltered the fallow deer, Polly knew well the " cut through the park," as it was known locally ; had strolled there demurely with many a rustic swain, and even with Joe when, in a gracious mood, she saw fit to accede to his hinted desire to avoid the company of the farm. But the mere thought of the park—of Guerdon ground—now made her shudder ; it was poisoned for her for ever, by the one who formerly had made it sweet. Miranda—she could not know what sacrifice of pride fulfilment of her demand entailed ; or what fevered throbbing it aroused in a wound still raw.

" Polly."

It was Joe. He had been out three or four times, encouraged by her welcome ; getting a lift in one of the carrier vans, or sometimes in a market wagon, out of Bristol, or chancing the omnibus and a possible pick-up along the road between Henbury and the farm. Always lively, always with some new trick to display his dexterity with the crutches ; making no claim on her for entertainment, contented to sit in kitchen or scullery while she rushed about her work, proud to make himself useful in any way she could devise for him. This time it was washing up ; propped on his crutches in front of the sink, wrapped in an old apron of Ellen's—because, as usual, he was wearing his best suit—he whistled and sang as he scoured pans and piled the clean crockery on the draining-board that sloped from the corner window.

As she turned at the sound of her name, he indicated with a flourish the result of his labours. Wretched as she was, she had to smile.

" Oh Joe, how grand ! It would have taken me hours—and I do so hate the pans. Now you must sit down and have a cup of tea——"

" How about a stroll ? "

" A stroll ? I can't leave Mother," she reminded him.

" You look as if you wanted some fresh air," he told her seriously.

" I get plenty of that—tearing about the yards ! " Her laugh had a little edge of bitterness.

He said, after a pause :

" Shall I tell you what I think, Polly ? I think something's upset you. I've not done anything I shouldn't, have I ? "

" Of course not, Joe." She felt his tenderness reaching out to her, enfolding her gently, and tears rushed to her eyes. Each time he came she was more keenly conscious of the support of his love ; it was terribly hard not to give love back when one received it in such measure. His long, manly patience and his fidelity were like warm hands laid upon her heart. He had not once spoken of marriage since his return, yet their relationship had become in some ways like that of a devoted married couple, his presence brought her peace, confidence and endurance ; she could feel herself trusting him, leaning on him, letting him share the road which, before his coming, had seemed as though it could not much longer be borne. The horrible encounter with Dorset, which was with her day and night like a living wound, even penetrating her sleep and repeating itself in dreams from which she woke herself with her moaning, had quickened her tenderness towards Joe ; hardly caring whether she betrayed herself, she clung to him for the balm his devotion brought to her pride, she allowed his arms to hold her above the bitter waters of her humiliation.

It seemed natural to tell him about Miranda's letter, which he read gravely before giving it back to her.

" You'll have to go, you know. What does she mean about ' making a prisoner ' ? " he wondered.

" I don't know. But—oh dear, it sounds as though she's in trouble. I don't know what to do——"

" Well, what's the matter with going to this place she talks about ? This oak tree ? Look, it says six o'clock. The milking'll be done "—he was proud of his acquaintance with the habits of the farm—" and they'll be having their tea. That cousin of yours will be here, won't she—— ? "

" No, no, I can't——" She broke sharply into his careful planning. " I can't go in the park—— ! "

She heard one of the crutches clatter on the brick floor and his arm went round her, hard, strong, drawing her close to the body which, although thin, was a man's body, strong and hard, with a man's will and passions. She drew in her breath with a little gasp as she felt the involuntary response of her own flesh to the embrace, and knew the colour had fluttered to her cheeks.

" Has anybody frightened you in the park ? " he was saying sternly, as though it were his right to know.

" Oh—no—— ! " she gasped, less aware of what she was saying than of the shocking sweetness of being held in that way by someone who cared for her.

" Because, if they have, I'll fix them. Wait till I get my leg : I'll fix them ! I promise you that," he muttered between his set teeth.

" Oh Joe—you're so sweet—I don't deserve it," she half-sobbed.

" You deserve all the ' sweetness,' as you call it, I've got. You know there isn't anything I wouldn't do for you—and Johnny," he told her—taken aback when her hands flew to her mouth, her eyes widened and her face whitened, as she thrust back away from him against the supporting arm.

" What do you mean—' and Johnny ' ? " She was hoarse with horror.

" Why, Polly, you know how Johnny and I are. There's nobody means much to me," he stammered, " except you and Johnny."

" Why did you have to bring him up ? " she cried.

" Well," said Joe in honest puzzlement, " I suppose it was Miss Miranda. You know he thinks the world of her. Yes "—he was looking at the letter, crumpled in her shaking hand—" I guess we've got to do something about that—on account of Johnny."

" I tell you, I can't ! " Carried away by panic, she stamped her foot ; she flung the ball of paper away from her towards the kitchen range.

" Pick up my crutch for me, will you ? " said Joe.

As she bent to do it she found herself wondering at this new, authoritative Joe, whose will she accepted with a meekness that astonished her. *Joe*—whom she had always teased, dominated, and a little despised for his humility. Was this really Joe whose command it was inevitable to obey?

" I'll come up the ' cut ' with you and then you can go off and meet Miss Miranda, and I'll wait and bring you back."

The heavy mouth, the level look were Dorset's—and yet not Dorset's. What was it about Joe that was so like a Flood, and yet—not like? No Flood, not even Johnny—poor Johnny!—had that implacable *kindness*, that left one helpless, save to obey their will.

" I didn't think you were coming," scowled Miranda.

She gasped, pushing the hairpins into her hair from which they had been dragged on her way through the thicket.

" Oh, Miss Miranda! You knew I wouldn't let you down!"

" I think they've gone raving mad at home," observed Miranda presently. " I'm to have a tea-party on Tuesday."

" But—but that's very nice, isn't it?"

" Don't be an idiot. You know I can't bear any of the people round here. *I* never made friends with any of them—*Polly*." She leaned forward with urgency to lay her hand on the elder girl's arm. " Shall this be our place—shall it? Let's meet here—and not tell anybody." Perhaps it was her own nervousness that made Polly sensitive to the strained, uncertain look—the un-Miranda-like hesitation in the parted lips, as though there were more to say and she could not bring herself to say it. Polly's arm went out instinctively.

" I'll do the best I can, dear. You know, it's not easy—the way things are at home."

" We've got to stick together!" Miranda was clinging to her. " It's always been we four, hasn't it?—you and I, and Emily, and Johnny. They've got rid of Emily; it will be you next, if we don't take care! We've got to—to outwit them between us. Until Johnny comes home." The green shade, the little hawk on the branch to which Miranda had transferred it, the creance dripping—small, blind witness to an undefined pact—sent a shiver through her as she answered:

" I must go, dear; really I must. Yes—I'll try to come again." Had Dorset and his wife gone yet? she wanted to ask, but the question dried on her lips. The branches lashed back as she forced her way through them and stumbled out to join Joe on the " cut through the park."

" Well? Was it all right?"

Again the longing welled in her to tell him everything, to surrender herself, once and for all, to his loving kindness that looked out at her from his honest eyes; and she fought it back. She muttered some nervous evasion that Joe, taking " girls' secrets " for granted, did not challenge; and they had walked some way in silence before he said:

" It's getting time we heard from Johnny."

" Oh—she'd heard."

" Miss Miranda? Well, that's fine!" He checked, his face brightening.

" Perhaps I'll be having a letter one of these days. I don't suppose he's had any of mine yet. Did she tell you what he said ? "

" He was at Cape Coast Castle—and it was wet," she mumbled. Joe chuckled, then grew suddenly grave.

" I wonder. . . . No, of course ; he's got to do what the paper tells him. . . ." He poked frowningly at a dark clump of ivy and periwinkle by the edge of the path.

" Well ? What about it ? " Her voice sharpened on the words.

" I'm wondering if he'll keep out of the mess. It wouldn't be like Johnny—if there was anything to be done."

" Do you mean the fighting ? But surely—he's a newspaper writer, isn't he ? They don't fight—surely ? " Her lips felt dry.

" They're not on the fighting force—but there were plenty of them in South Africa—did jolly plucky things—and got captured—and wounded," he brought out wretchedly. " You can't write about war without getting in the way of the guns," he muttered.

Although her heart had turned to ice she rallied him.

" But there's no fighting yet at Cape Coast, is there ? It's somewhere near the sea, where all the white people live, and that town where they've got the Governor shut up is right away inside, among the savages ! " So much she had managed to gather from the maps in the newspapers. " He *can't* be in danger ! " she insisted, almost angrily. " Miranda would have said——"

" I expect you're right." His eyes were heavy with doubt. " But—I'll be glad when he drops us a line."

" His uncle's heard, hasn't he ? "

He forced himself to smile.

" You won't get much out of Mr. Harcourt." Alone of the junior staff, Joe never made use of the Chairman's sobriquet ; Harcourt ceased to be " Old Iron-Guts " on a day unspoken but ever in the minds of both. " I guess I'm just fidgeting. I guess it's having been in the war oneself—seeing the way things go different from the way they're planned. Do you ever see the *Di*, Polly ? " he broke off to ask her.

" We don't get it out here." She shook her head. " I try to get it when I'm in town—sometimes I run into the library to have a peep, but somebody's nearly always taken it, and I don't like to ask ; it seems a funny paper for a girl to read."

" I'll bring it out next time I come," he promised. " There's a grand article this week—I bet Johnny's at the back of it and that some of those War Office nobs are going to be hopping mad when they read it over their breakfasts ! I can't remember how it all goes, but it's about the living conditions out there, and it ends up by asking whether the Government's going to give the army a square deal. By jinks ! " he added, as Polly was silent, " I wish you knew Johnny like I do, Poll ! He may be just a pint-sized little chap, but he's the greatest pal anyone ever had ; and if cutting off my right hand was ever any use to Johnny—well "—Joe covered an unwonted gush of sentiment with a laugh—" I reckon I'd manage lopsided.

"You know what I thought when I found they'd sawed off this old hopper of mine? I just prayed to God I'd show as much guts as Johnny would show, in my place——"

It was no longer to be borne.

"Joe!" She just managed not to scream it. "I'll have to run! You understand, don't you? Cousin Jinny's husband will be mad if she's not there to give him his supper——"

IV

She tossed in the hot darkness, pushing her uncombed hair away from her burning face, seeking a cool patch on the crumpled pillow.

The lonely silence of the house invaded the room, fluttered in her heart and her stomach, throbbed in her wrists and behind her knees. She pictured the couple next door—her parents: he, in his twitching sleep of over-exhaustion, flinging out a leg or an arm, the slow, animal-noise of the sleeping male tearing itself from his throat; she stiff and still, awake, taut with endurance. They, at least for a little longer, had each other! Did she ever, in the intervals of her pain, think of the days when there had been, for each of them, delight in sharing the same bed? Did his hand, in half-slumber, ever stray towards hers, unhappily sensing the time to come when it would no longer be there to hold? Or had they already gone so far, she into her house of pain and he into his house of mourning, that they had ceased to feel for each other anything but the kind of wondering impatience of those whose farewells said, are anxious for the end?

She felt her face crumpling, like a child's, to cry, as memories came back: of rocking on her mother's knee, nodding sleepily to the quiet toneless croon of her mother's voice: "Poor Shepherd Boy, 'tis time to leave the mountain;" "Two little kittens, they lost their mittens;" "There is a green hill far away" . . . The scoldings, the kissings, the sure certainty that behind scolding lay love that nothing—no pertness, no disobedience, none of the misdemeanours indulged in only for mischief's sake—could ever diminish. Times of childish sickness and tender care; little festivals, planned by love, and prepared for by hours of sewing, with pride in every stitch; pride repressed "for her own good," but burning deep in the eyes, for later achievements; words of warning spoken across a heedless head, and shed lightly as drifting May blossom; love, trust—trust . . .

She found herself crying stormily, noisily, and stuffed the sheet into her mouth, for fear it should be heard next door. Too late, now, to confess. All that anxious love and pride—all finished; nothing for it now but to go on deceiving. And they said people knew, after they were dead. Oh Mother—oh Ma—couldn't you come back, just for a moment, before it's too late, and let me tell you—let me explain? Just to put your arms round me once more . . .

Her hands, softly battering the coverings as though they battered at her mother's door, were still. It was too late. Ellen had already gone into her house of death, that lacked death's peace, and there was no place there for her daughter. Oh Ma, no place for Polly? No, no place; because you have not trusted me. . . .

Her mind leapt wildly, chaotically, towards the future: fluttered like a panic stricken bird among unknown terrors. Who would befriend her? Not her father: stricken at the foundations of his stony pride by her desertion of her own people. Not Johnny's family, with Dorset as its symbol; Miranda, perhaps—but what power had a little girl against adult decision?

"You'd better be making up your mind to marry Joe Prior," her father had said, as he picked up the candle to go upstairs. It was the only word he had spoken all the evening; she had accepted it, for a moment, with fluttering relief, as a sign he did not expect her to remain with him, when her mother was gone. Thank God, thank God! She could not have stayed with the cold, silent man, to be his farm-house drudge until Johnny came back.

Joe—with his constant loving it would be so terribly easy to return!

"Don't go, don't go," she had wanted to cry to him, like a child left in the dark, when he said good night to her from the vehicle which was taking him back to Bristol. "Don't go in *that*!" she wanted to scream, as, incredulously, she recognised the Dower House dogcart—old Mrs. Flood was always sending her servants with messages at strange hours into town. She stood as though frozen, forgetting, until it was almost too late, and they reached the bend in the lane, to return his cheery wave.

Don't go; don't go. I've got no one but you to love me. A wild desire to run after and stop him—a crazy feeling that he was in danger from her enemies—had to be fought back, before, her head swimming, she turned back to the house. Too late, too late to claim that fond, protective care. Joe—and Johnny; Johnny and Joe; the pair of them who had been so good to her; whom she had equally betrayed.

CHAPTER FIVE

I

AT the end of twelve hours they had walked themselves to a standstill, and the bush was packed in round them like layers of green cotton-wool. The foliage overhead let through a continuous leakage of rain. Umbrellas were an impossibility, and the wet heat of their mackintoshes made Paget feel, he said, as though he had a portable steam bath hung round his neck.

"For two pins I'd imitate them"—he nodded at the carriers, jogging along with the wet pimpling their backs. Every now and again the pimples joined and shot a miniature cascade down the hollows of their spines. "Has it, by any chance," he inquired carefully, "struck you that we're lost?"

"I'd not be surprised."

"We ought to have hit that village about two hours ago."

"We could be avoiding it." In the eyes of both, as they met, was the same thought: of their total dependence on the figure that led their tiny cavalcade.

They went on in silence, because talking wasted energy. Then there was a strip which was almost dry; where the tree-trunks were thin and straight, and there was no undergrowth, because the tops were so closely interwoven that hardly any light came through. The dry twilight would have been agreeable, but for the noise their feet made on the shale and bits of twig and bark whose crackling rang in their ears and set their teeth on edge.

One of the carriers crashed, with a noise like an explosion, into an old game-pit, and they got him out. Then an hour went by in crossing a small swamp. For part of the way Paget was up to his chest and the greeny-black syrup was licking Johnny's chin. When they came out, the leeches were hung round their necks like fat bundles of globular seaweed and glued over the backs of their hands. Everyone sat down and started disembarrassing himself of leeches. Johnny helped Paget to dig a tick out of his thigh; it had got its head well in and blown itself out like a plum; Paget gave a yelp as the stab ran down his leg. A carrier started intestinal cramp and rolled about screaming; two of his friends held him while Johnny dosed him. Suddenly, while he was touching the man, rubbing his swollen belly, trying to relieve his agony, he felt a gush of almost unbearable pity, directed not merely to the sufferer but to them all.

Coming up from the coast, he had steeled himself against pity; had schooled his mind deliberately not to think of individuals, not to regard his line as anything more than a link in the machinery of war. But here it was different; of their little company of twenty-two one began to distinguish faces, to attach, here and there, a name to a pair of eyes, milky blue-over-black, or to some trick of movement, or to an oddly shaped head. One forgot their slyness, their indolence and their crass stupidity and was conscious only of a touching helplessness, a hopeless dependence that reached timidly out from grey, from green, from blue-black or brown-black faces, from faces the colour of ash or the colour of dung. Almost everyone had some kind of sickness on him : a disease of the eyes or nose, ulcerated thighs, various stages of syphilis. One, eyed nervously and avoided by the others, had decided to die ; Johnny recognised the symptoms of the melancholia that no scientist has ever been able to diagnose, and marked its victim uneasily as a danger-spot, for this sickness is known to spread like the plague and may infect a whole community. He had heard of travellers coming upon a whole village of the dead, with no mark or sign of violence to account for their mysterious extinction.

He did what he could ; nipped the guinea-worm in the leg of one of the Kroos with a bit of split bamboo, gave it a twist—and they went on. It was beginning to be dark, and, apart from themselves, they had seen no human being since midday, when they came on a jittery little colony, on the move, like themselves, but in the opposite direction.

There was some argument with their guide : as a result of which they had quitted the main track, and seemed, so far as Johnny could judge, to be taking a deep, northward bend. He had misgivings, but, knowing it was folly to argue with a guide, kept them to himself. His head was splitting, his eyes felt as though they had been replaced by live cinders, and he could feel the temperature jigging up, although he had taken the precaution of an injection, immediately before setting out. It was no use ; he was in for a fever dose. He wondered how long he could keep going, or whether it would be better to give in now, and risk temporary immobilisation in a place where they were in no particular danger, rather than be caught somewhere where they were obliged to speed. He was relieved when Paget said :

" We'd better make this our halt." The carriers had already started to show uneasiness at the approach of the dark ; there were twenty-two of them, but only three, so far, had bolted, and, apart from the boy with snake-bite, the others were healthy.

It had not rained for an hour, and they had reached a patch of high ground. While Paget's orderly, Mahmoud, set up the two camp-beds, and contrived something with bushrope, tarpaulins and a dank roll of mosquito netting between some convenient boughs, the two Hausas—all they had been able to spare from the Base—got a fire going. It smouldered bitterly, reluctantly, and gave out almost no heat, but they crouched round it, letting their clothes steam, while Mahmoud made tea in an old kerosene tin. The water refused to boil and the leaves floated like bits of hay in reddish-brown liquid. Mahmoud heated a can of bully beef, and Johnny broke bits of biscuit into the gravy and tried to eat them, but soon gave it up. A griping pain ran into his bowels. He let Paget give him a double tot of rum, and vomited it. He felt Paget lifting him.

Several times during the night he got the impression they were travelling ;

he felt the jolt, jolt of the hammock and heard the boys grunt, but knew this must be imagination, because nothing would induce them to continue the journey after nightfall. Sometimes light cut at his eyes like a knife, and he rolled over and buried his head in his arms. Then there was movement like the rocking of a ship, and a variety of unidentifiable noises. Somebody lifted his head up and held a vessel of some sort to his lips. The liquid it contained—whatever it was—ran down on his chin and chest and he gave a groan of disgust.

When he opened his eyes, Paget was there, smoking a pipe and looking down on him.

" Hallo."

He tried to sit up, and was defeated by weakness. He felt himself grinning sheepishly.

" I must have had a fever go."

" That's about it."

" Thought I was in for it—last night. Blast it. I suppose it's time we were on the move."

" Take your time."

" We ought to be getting on, though—shouldn't we ? "

Paget's hand on his shoulder pressed him back.

" There's no hurry—now."

" What do you mean—' now ' ? " His mind, working slowly, arrived at the question.

" Another half-day can't make much difference. Take it easy, old boy. When we do start, we may have to keep going."

A pang of apprehension went through him. He stammered :

" How long—have we been here ? "

" This makes the third day."

" Oh, my God—Bendick——"

" Keep your hair on." Paget let himself drop easily on the edge of the camp-bed, pushed a cigarette in Johnny's mouth and gave him a light. Johnny was glad not to have to do something that would betray the unsteadiness of his hands. " You see—what with one thing or another—it was better to wait."

" Why the hell didn't you put me in the hammock—— ? "

" My dear fellow, I'd have done it in a jiffy. If that blasted guide hadn't ratted."

Johnny digested this in silence.

" The morning after we arrived," went on Paget, in his pleasant, rather high-pitched voice, " he just wasn't there. So as there was no point in our getting ourselves completely lost—prob'ly running our heads into an ambush—I sent back for another. I didn't want to go back myself, with the carriers—and prob'ly drop half of them on the way ; and one man travels faster than a line. If the dear old C.-in-C. has had my chit, the other man ought to be along—almost any moment."

" Supposing he doesn't turn up ? The runner mightn't get back to the Base—or anything."

" That," admitted Paget, " raises quite a problem. That village we were looking for—it's gone over to the Ashanti."

" How did you find that out ? "

" Mahmoud and I took a little trip, round and about, yesterday," was the airy reply, " and we came across one or two of the locals. I couldn't understand their lingo, of course, but they all looked as if they'd been seeing ghosts, and, according to Mahmoud, it seems the enemy's been getting quite busy round this quarter. So far as I could make out, they were trying to tell us the way to go, but I'm sorry to say, old boy, the whole thing was lost on me, and Mahmoud's never seen the bush before in his life : apart from only being able to understand one word in ten of the local *parlez-vous*."

Johnny swore fluently.

" Of course—I would choose a time like this to crock ! "

" Well—it seemed wiser to play for safety, in the circumstances. It will do no good to Bendick, if we all get lost in the bush."

" We ought to have got there twenty-four hours ago ; isn't that it ? "

" More or less," admitted Paget. " That, of course, is, if we'd kept to the main track. Unfortunately, that infernal little party we met, back near Fenge, disorganised the schedule. Now—there isn't the dimmest clue to where we are."

How many miles had they come already ? The twistings and turnings of the latter part of the journey defied all reckoning. Neither could the compass be of help, since it was impossible to tell whether they now stood north or south of the place for which they were aiming. They might even have overshot it. Omo lay north-east of Prahsu ; how far north-east had they travelled ? The waterways afforded no guide—mere trickles, and even dry riverbeds, having swollen into torrents.

" We'll give it the rest of the day," Paget was saying. " If nobody turns up, we'll start out at daybreak. After all, the damned track's got to lead somewhere—— ! "

Even if into enemy territory.

II

Night once again. The nights had begun to seem longer than the days. There was something eternal in those hours of darkness, with the bush pinned all round them, full of tricklings and gurglings : with the occasional cough of a leopard or the whine of a baboon. But the rains reduce animals, like human beings, to stillness ; there were none of those babblings, shrieks, noisy chases that take place under a clear moon.

They had done very little talking ; the mind of each was on Bendick at Omo, trying, single-handed, to hold on to his levies : the levies Willcocks depended on for the flank movement that was to help in the relief of Carter at Kwissa. If Bendick succumbed, like his junior officer, McGinty, or even if he went down with a bad attack of fever, there would be no one to hold the rabble that represented the gutterscrapings of Omo: nor was it out of the question that, like dogs turning on a wounded one of their tribe to tear him to pieces, the levies might turn on one whose helplessness put him at their mercy. Certainly they would break, and the work of weary months would be undone, Bendick and Willcocks deprived of the support on which they were counting.

It was diabolical, sitting there motionless. It was madness to set out—perhaps in a totally wrong direction—with the sure knowledge that, at the first threat of danger, the carriers would dump their loads and vanish: which meant going on without provisions, without any of the things necessary to preserve life to that unpredictable day when they reached Omo. Paget had been back, with one of the Hausas, to look for the main track, which they had abandoned—so far as it was possible to judge—some twelve or fourteen miles back; but in the tangle of bush paths that crossed and recrossed this part of the forest, there was little hope of finding the right one. And when darkness fell, and no one had arrived from Prahsu, each knew, without speaking to the other, the deadliness of the enterprise to which they were committed.

That night Johnny dreamed of Emily, as he had never done before.

"Flood. Flood. Wake up. The dawn's here."

Like a man who has just received a blow on the head, he found himself struggling towards consciousness of his surroundings. Paget was shaking his shoulder, and he muttered:

"All right, all right, let me alone; I'll be awake in a minute"—and sat for a moment on the edge of the bed, with his head in his hands, trying to collect himself, to subdue the ache in his breast which had come with the realisation that he had been dreaming.

"Are you all right? Will you be fit to travel?" Paget was asking anxiously.

He nodded, opening his eyes. The tree trunks were spectral with dawn, the humid chill of the bush made him shiver. While he stood, rubbing his face with his hands, feeling the bristle of three days' growth on his chin and the immense discomfort of his unbathed body, Mahmoud brought him a mug of tea that smelled and tasted largely of rum. He gulped it back, watching the boys moving about hastily in the grey morning mist, that hung thickly about the clearing, held down by the leaf-canopy overhead.

Paget called him over to one of the chop-boxes, which he and Mahmoud had got open, and pushed tins of canned meat and packets of biscuit at him.

"Put as much as you can get into your pockets; it's no use depending on these damned niggers. Five more of them got away in the night; when they find out we're travelling without a guide, they'll be off like the wind. We'll have to take some of the specie as well, but it's no use weighing ourselves down unduly. I'm going to send you on with the line, and stop behind with Mahmoud and bury the bulk of the stuff; it'll be the first thing they'll drop, if they get a scare. Go on about a mile, then wait for us to catch up ; it won't take long, but I don't want them to see where we plant it. *Sure* you're fit ? "

" Yes—so long as we can take it easy. I'll feel better after something to eat. See here : a mile's a fairly long way and these tracks seem to wander all over the place. How about our pegging it out ? I could use strips of an old shirt, or something. Then you'd be certain not to miss us."

" It's not a bad idea," Paget conceded, after thought, " though I'm not keen on blazing the trail for the benefit of anybody who may be around. However, I shan't be long, and it's better than losing one another. Have you got a flask, by the way ? "

" Powder, or liquor ? "

" Both, if it comes to that ; but I was thinking of whisky. We ought to split the bottle between us."

" You fill your flask. It's only a half-bottle, isn't it ?—one of the flat ones ? I can get it in my hip pocket."

" Massa." Mahmoud was at his master's elbow. " Dem headman, he fit for palaver."

" No fit." Paget promptly shook his head. " Tell headman I fit for kick his backside, unless his blasted line's ready by the time I've had chop."

" Dem headman," persevered Mahmoud, having shifted from his left foot to his right, and back to the left again, " plenty sick. All same boys. Got humbug in um belly. No lib for start."

" What did I tell you ? " muttered Paget, as he screwed the top on his flask. " Somebody's told them we're going on without a guide——"

" My pigeon," murmured Johnny. He stiffened his knees, which, since waking, felt like jelly ; the various packages he had disposed about his person weighed disproportionately on his weakened frame, but he supposed he would get used to them. " All right ; we'll move off now. Do you want the Hausas ? "

" No, take them with you—but, dammit, you've had no breakfast—— ! "

" I'll get something while we're waiting for you. I know these beggars ! " He smiled dimly. " The longer they hang about, the more trouble they'll think up ; the only thing's to keep 'em on the move."

" Right-ho. Mahmoud and I'll get along faster than the line—you'll not have to wait long for us. Well—good luck, Flood."

They shook hands casually. Ten minutes later, with a Hausa in front, himself in the middle, immediately behind the trouble-making headman, and a Hausa to bring up the rear, the line moved off. The air was heavy with rain, which had not yet started to fall ; but the track, which continued to be dry, was the best they had struck so far, although narrow, only allowing for single file, and effectually barricaded on either side with a wild luxuriance of tie-tie. From the beginning there were accidents : the kind of accidents that occur when a carrier line is unwilling. A load was dropped, its lashings came undone and its contents were scattered and took an unconscionable time to reassemble. A boy caught his big toe in a root, pitched headlong, and his pretence of being knocked out lasted a good ten minutes before the toe of Johnny's boot convinced him that unconsciousness was not a paying game. The headman twice tied himself in knots and rolled about in the track ; each time he had to be given time to relieve himself before the line moved on, because it was not safe to leave him behind. The very absence of disquieting sound or incident heightened, in some way, the atmosphere of panic, which Johnny felt each time he stepped out of the line to fasten a strip of rag to something at the side of the track. Each time he did this, he took pains gravely to explain to those within earshot that it was white man's ju-ju, meaning that no danger could overtake them from behind ; but he felt them unconvinced. The mere fall of a leaf would be enough to start a stampede, which there would be no means of checking : since there was no means of knowing how near they might be to the enemy, to whom the firing of guns would betray their position.

Suddenly he knew, *It's here.*

The line ahead of him had halted ; was bunching, trying to double on itself ; he heard the crash of loads being dropped. Instead of the backs of heads there were mouths and eyes wide with fright and struggling bodies, bearing back on him. He shouted across his shoulder to the Hausa in the rear, steadied himself astride the track with a Colt in each hand, jabbing the barrel of the left into the ribs of the headman in front of him and aiming direct at the first of the fugitives in the line : praying meanwhile that the Hausa at the head would not fire before getting the order and bracing himself to take a rush which, unless checked by the sight of the firearms, would bowl him over like a ninepin.

The narrowness of the track was, however, in his favour. Seeing the muzzle of the Colt, the first man, losing his head, swerved and flung himself at the tie-tie, which held him back as though it had been wire netting. Those behind him were doing the same : grovelling, wrenching, scratching, even biting at the walls of their green prison, at one end of which was terror and at the other death. Johnny saw a leg disappearing like a black snake : one man gone—two—three—he flung a glance across his shoulder, saw the Hausa struggling with four men, saw him hit two across the head with the butt of his rifle, saw them drop, and the others escape ; took the hint, knocked the headman out with a blow at the base of the scalp—the only vulnerable spot—and, scrambling across the loads, managed to reach the first Hausa in time to knock the rifle out of his hands, just as he was about to fire. He then found out what was wrong.

Across the clearing, into which the track broke briefly, had passed, evidently at no distant moment, an armed column. The earth was mashed into a muddy pulp, there was the usual débris of a marching army—broken weapons, abandoned cooking-pots, pieces of shields, oddments of hide and cat's-tail, dragged probably from a warrior's skirt. There was worse. Human fragments led him to the centre of the clearing, on which Ashanti had set its unmistakable seal in the pegged-out remains of one of its victims ; in its mutilations, in the genitals stuffed between the grinning jaws of the corpse. The breath choked in his throat as he realised it had been a white man, though its nakedness made it impossible to say of what rank or walk in life. His mouth had gone very dry and he forced himself to swallow once or twice. The Hausa at his elbow had gone the powdery grey of frightened native, but he was standing his ground, and Johnny remembered the notorious courage of these native troops. The other Hausa had come up at the trot ; while he stood with eyes widening in horror at the grisly spectacle, Johnny spoke sharply in the men's own tongue.

"The carriers have gone ? "

"There are five who sleep, of whom the headman is one," was the succinct reply.

The utmost to be hoped was that some of the fugitives had run into Paget, and that he had succeeded in turning them. Yet what use under heaven was a panic-stricken carrier line ? he asked himself, as he moved about the clearing, trying to guess, by the condition of the ground, how long it was since the Ashanti column had passed. Not long ; for although the ground was pulpy, the deeper ruts had not filled up with water. It was about an hour and a half since the last heavy shower had fallen. Some time within the last hour and a half. That might mean—he felt his scalp tingle—within the last half-hour ; that the final stragglers were still within earshot. He made himself bend and touch the corpse ; it was cold. That, of course, meant nothing. But it ought to be buried. Paget—that meant Mahmoud—had the shovels. Paget—who should surely have caught up with them by now.

Slowly the conviction dawned on him that they had come much farther north—nearer enemy territory—than they imagined. It had been madness, of course, to leave the main track which—according to the map—led by way of three rivers almost to the borders of Omo country ; then there was a big swamp, which forced them to take a loop northwards, and this should have been their only danger area. Now, for all they knew, they were in the very heart of enemy country : either among the dangerous Adansi, or the dubious Akim—who, so far, had not made up their minds on which side to play, but, under Ashanti pressure, were as likely to go over to the enemy side as to stand by their promises of loyalty to the British. There was only one course of safety : to make, by the compass, due south, for at least half a day's journey, then turn due east, and chance getting, from a friendly or neutral village, directions that would take them straight up to Omo. He had reached this conclusion when he discovered that the Hausas were whispering together and that he himself was virtually tiptoeing about the clearing ; the absurdity of it shook a smothered laugh out of him—but he knew it was no time or place for laughter. The Ashanti might be within a mile ; a shiver of impatience went through him, as he looked down the track by which they had arrived, in the vain hope of seeing Paget and Mahmoud hurrying towards him.

To kill time, he sent the Hausas back to collect what they could of the loads the carriers had dropped : directing them mainly with gestures. There was no need to caution them ; they worked practically in silence, sweat beading their faces, as they staggered back with the chop-boxes, the ammunition chests and the white man's baggage, of which there was mercifully little. The rain had started again, and came whispering down, filling the clearing with its thin grey curtain and blurring the arcades of the tree trunks before the tie-tie began: whispering of solitude, of the immensity of distance from fellow beings, of the imponderable hazards of the bush. . . .

The heart almost shot out of his mouth, when the sound came which, above all, he had dreaded, for which, subconsciously, he had been waiting: the crack of an Army revolver, that split the silence and sent a flock of birds shrieking and clattering havoc to the whole of the surrounding forest.

III

Although it was mobilising, the village wanted, if possible, to keep out of the fighting. Only one thing makes a village eager to fight: confidence generated by a powerful ruler, a well-seasoned army of warriors, a strong priesthood and a smart witch-doctor, with all the latest resources of his profession at his fingertips. Omo had none of these. Omo was only just recovering from its débacle of the previous year; it was badly shaken by a police inquiry; it had been trying, hard, to behave itself, and those who did not feel like behaving had cleared out. It was considered wiser, on the whole, not to inquire where they had vanished to, but rumour had it that some of them had gone up to Ejesu, to join forces with the Queen-Mother's party: the link-up between Ya Ashantua and the previous rulers of Omo forming part of the by no means savoury reputation which the latter enjoyed.

The new chief, elected by the people, and approved, *faute de mieux*, by the Commissioner, as the best of a poor bunch, was anxious, plausible, and, like most chiefs, had a keen eye to the main chance. He had been given clearly to understand that any failure in loyalty to the Great Queen would be punished by loss of office; moreover, that the triumph of Ashanti would mean the total extermination of a tribe so precariously situated as Omo, right on the Ashanti border. Once let the Ashanti gain control of the northern district, round and about Kumassi, and there would be nothing to prevent their ramping south-east, and even extending their territory down to the coast.

So it was with great relief that he learned the war was moving northward, and that Omo was likely to be overlooked in the great drive for Kumassi, where the supporters of the Great Queen were converging to take the brunt of the attack. Abuakwa was anxious for the war to be over, so that he could turn to the consolidation of his own position, which he was touchily conscious was not commensurate with that of previous rulers of Omo who, although not officially kings, had enjoyed royal prestige and privileges not usually conferred upon mere tribal leaders.

When approached about levies, Chief Abuakwa was in a jam. He had a young, promising bunch of warriors, that he wished to reserve for his private use later on; he did not want in any circumstances to have them offered up as gun-fodder to the Ashanti. But he badly wanted a strip of additional territory on his northern border, and it would be good to get it without fighting for it. He therefore took council with his captains, with the result that, at the cost of a few raids, a bribe here and there and a threat to some vacillating headman, the bush gave up some nine or ten score denizens, duly presented, as levies, to the representatives of the Great Queen. On a wet June morning, these paraded on the clearing outside the chief's stockade.

After a moment's stunned contemplation—" Are they human ? " Lieutenant McGinty inquired with awe of his superior officer. Captain Bendick, a little more hardened to the bush-dweller, gave it as his opinion that, all evidence to the contrary, they fell within that category.

Two days went by in sorting out the obvious detritus : the deformed, the too evidently diseased, the freaks—which included a boy with his feet and shinbones set back to front below the knee-joint, and a dwarf whose enormous head bobbed like a bladder of discoloured lard on his narrow shoulders ; a couple of lepers in an advanced stage of the disease and a boy whose entire head and face were covered with a revolting mass of pustulated matter—and in having a series of arguments with Abuakwa, who took the high-handed attitude that he had been asked to produce levies ; there were levies ; and what about it ? He refused point-blank to part with any of his trained fighting men, who would be needed for defence, if the war drifted Omo way. The white men were defeated ; they had no powers of impressment.

At the end of a week's training, a nucleus of about twenty could distinguish, after some thought, their right hands from their left, and were made leaders of the flitter-headed majority. Unless otherwise occupied, in scratching, digging out ticks, or simply staring around them, about a third of the entire company (by now reduced from two hundred to seventy) could be persuaded, by a shout, to shamble a few steps forward, and, by another shout, to shamble a few steps back. A " right turn " or " left turn " produced chaos, in which fifteen or twenty got knocked down, turned sulky and refused to play. While one squad was exercised, the others were supposed to sit and watch ; mostly they shambled away among the huts, pilfering what they could lay their hands on, scrounging food or merely rubbering at the strange, urban customs which, to many, were as much of a novelty as the life of the coast towns was to up-country inhabitants. This created constant ill-feeling among the villagers, furnished material for endless complaints and wasted as much time as went to the training of the squads. People kept vanishing, and others, out of curiosity, drifting in, to vanish in their turn.

By the end of the week, Captain Bendick, having lost a stone and a half and gained a temperature which, if charted, would have resembled a silhouette of the Andes, observed that he now knew what made a man stage a massacre. McGinty, usually appreciative of his superior officer's humour, smiled palely. Unaware of the microbe he had collected, it did not seem worth while to mention that he was feeling like death. The feeling fulfilled itself within forty-eight hours. Captain Bendick was by himself: one white man in charge of seventy—more or less—raw bush savages, under the critical and unsympathetic eye of a chief who, conscious of the demoralising effect these interlopers were having on his own people, made no bones about suggesting that Cappi Bendi should remove himself and his training centre to some spot where they would cease to be a charge on the resources of the community.

Reeling with quinine, Cappi Bendi continued manfully to wrestle with the problem of dexter and sinister, and to wonder if his message had ever reached the Base. Now and again, when fever had relieved him, for an hour or two, of his command, he had lightheaded bets with himself. The chances of support reaching him in time, starting at evens, mounted, as time went on, from three, to seven, to forty to one. Cappi Bendi was a very sick man; recognition of the fact was in the eyes of the orderly who took over the squad on the morning when the white man pitched face down on the parade ground and was carried back to his tent.

CHAPTER SIX

I

IT was a burning day. He was red and beaded with sweat and the dust had laid a grey powder up his dark trouser-leg and over his solitary boot. He had had to walk, from the omnibus stop; it *would be* a day like this, when nothing came by, to give him a lift along the road. He stopped to pull his cap off when he saw the drawn blinds, then, after a moment's hesitation, swung himself round by the yard gate and stood at the back door.

"Oh Joe——!"

"Don't bother about me," he said quickly. "I'll just sit down a minute—you don't have to pay any attention to me——"

He was in the rocking-chair, mopping the sweat out of his eyes, and she was beside him, on her knees, her head on his shoulder, her arms cast about him; he could feel the softness of her breast, pressed to his side; he held her tightly, stroking her hair.

"It's the first chance I've had for a good cry!" she told him apologetically, and found him taking the handkerchief from her hand and gently drying her eyes. "Dear Joe! I'm sorry——"

"You can always depend on me, Polly; you know that, don't you?"

"Of course I do, Joe." His tenderness started her tears again. She sprang up at the sound of a knock on the front door. "That's what it's been ever since breakfast!" and hurried down the narrow hall to answer it.

The breath caught in her throat as she recognised Miss Victoria Flood. Johnny's aunt. My aunt. She found herself unable to speak, as, with a little gesture of helplessness, she invited Vicky into the parlour.

Vicky, being Vicky, said all the right things ; better, she managed to infuse some genuine warmth into them. It was easier, much, to feel warmly towards this drenched and subdued Polly than to the bouncing young woman whose contours reminded her, always unpleasantly, of some of the more indelicate subjects of the seventeenth-century portraitists.

" God comfort you, my poor girl. Try to remember His goodness to your dear mother ; she has been spared a great deal of suffering."

" Yes—thank you very much for all the things you sent her." She tried painstakingly to remember what one ought to say. " The—the funeral's on Saturday."

" The Squire will certainly be there. By the way," said Vicky, turning at the door, " if you or your father are wanting any black, I am sure we can find something. I should think my size would fit you—with a little alteration."

" You're very kind ; we've got all we want." Her hand trembled and her face flamed as she closed the door. Accept patronage—old clothes ! —from Johnny's aunt ? Never !—if they went in rags !—which was not likely in the case of a farmer's daughter.

" Polly," said Joe, as he was leaving, " I thought you'd like to know —I've got my leg. I've not got used to it yet—that's why I didn't have it on to-day. But I'll be as spry as a grasshopper in a few weeks' time—— ! "

" Oh, Joe, that's grand ! You'll come and show us, won't you ? "

He nodded gravely.

" And I'm starting work next week. Mr. Harcourt's put up my wages. I'll be getting five bob more——"

" I *am* glad." Her hand lay on his shoulder. " It shows he appreciates you !—and so he ought," she added stoutly, as the colour rose in Joe's earnest face.

" I only mentioned it "—his thick lips were trembling—" so you'd know—I could look after you—if you ever wanted it," he brought out, with difficulty.

The day, full of the small horrors that gather about a house of death, drew to its close. The two old almshouse women, who laid everybody out ; the carpenter, and the vicar, and a constant procession of villagers, with their bunches of flowers and their insatiable greed for mortuary details. And through and in despite of this stream all the work of the farm had to go on, all of that centring round the house depending on Polly. She was giddy with fatigue and could barely support herself on her tired and swollen feet by nine o'clock, when a tap on the door announced the village dressmaker to fit the " black " for the day of the funeral.

They could not go into the parlour, for the sofa had been made up as a bed for Aaron Bowling. As they groped up the narrow stairs, the heat from the upper floor bore down on them, heavy with an intolerable sweetness of flowers. Although the door of the death-chamber was closed, the scent seeped under the door and through ill-fitting joists and cracks in the walls ; the house was sodden with it. Her hand shook as she set the oil lamp down on the chest of drawers, and started wearily to drag off her skirt and bodice.

"There's not much room to see, but so long as the hem's straight it doesn't matter," she murmured, steeling herself against the clammy touch of the woman's fingers, the sickly-sweet breath that puffed now and again on her exposed shoulder-blades.

All her life she had hated Miss Monk; hated the look of her, the smell of her and the pretentious fuss she made over fittings; hated her inquisitive ways and the small malicious gossip, of which she made always the tittering disclaimer: "Not that *I'd* ever believe a word of it!" It had seemed to Polly, even as a little girl, that the very material Miss Monk handled was poisonous with her malice.

"'They say' Mrs. Flood *takes too much*; shocking, isn't it, for a lady in her position? Not that I believe a word of it.

"'They say' that Miss Emily, that was supposed to marry Mr. Dorset, 's turned out a regular—well! Looked as if butter wouldn't melt in her mouth; who'd ever have thought it? Not that I——

"'They say' Mr. Roan and his wife—that was the one looked like an actress, wasn't it? Tt, tt, I'm sure in *my* young days ladies—*real* ladies—didn't dress like that. 'They say' she——"

"You're sticking a pin into me!"

Why, suddenly, should she feel impelled to defend these people, who would never do as much for her, against the tattle of the village? She tightened her lips, her hate renewing itself, as the venomous mumble went on.

The hot, stiff material, with its canvas interlinings and rough seams, pricked the soft flesh of her armpits, and the sour smell of crêpe added to her disgust. Miss Monk's mouth was full of pins; when she spoke it was in a hissing whisper—her usual form of deference to a house of mourning; she breathed loudly, because she always enjoyed death; it excited her. Something else was exciting her, on the present occasion.

"That will do, Miss Monk, won't it?" Polly tried to speak pleasantly. "Except the waist. What's happened? It looks rather lumpy—to me." Miss Monk was notorious for her resentment of criticism; it was wiser to qualify fault-finding, when the latter was unavoidable.

"Lumpy? Oh, I left plenty at the seams—if that's what you mean"—a titter came through the pins—"on account of *letting out*!"

"Letting out——? But my waist hasn't altered—if anything it's thinner——"

Her voice died away, as she felt the woman's intention coming at her, like small arrows, barbed with ice. Not that *I'd* ever believe there was any truth in it!

Deaf, dumb and blind, while another ten minutes went by, of sticking in pins, plucking them out, and unnecessary—surely?—manœuvres with the tape-measure—she was conscious only of the question hammering in her brain. How can she know, when I'm not even yet sure myself? And slowly, as the fearful prescience of village gossips dawned on her, she shrank.

A ring of hunting dogs, led by Miss Monk !—closing in on her, yapping' with triumphant, slavering jaws.

Lotty, the blacksmith's girl : even the doctor had said she was not pregnant, and the woman who spread the tale had had to make public apology to the victims of her malice. And then, after all, Lotty *had* had a baby. . . . You were helpless among these old wives, and old maids, whose minds held a single, prurient thought. . . .

" I'll see it's up here in good time. Your poor mother ! Ah well, *she's* had a happy release ! " was Miss Monk's parting shot, as she stumbled into the darkness in which Polly plunged her by the slamming of the door. I wish you'd break your neck, you meddling old vixen !

Weary as she was, and aching in every limb, sleep again deserted her. She lay in darkness, hearing her father's snores mounting through the ill-fitting boards from the parlour : telling herself that she, a married woman, had every right to produce a baby ; thinking of what he would do to her, when she was obliged to tell him the baby was a Flood. Thinking of other Flood babies who had been born in peace and pride across the park. When the swain sharps the scythe. . . . Supposing Johnny did not get back in time ?

The sly glances, the avoidance of meeting her eyes were, she told herself on the day of the funeral, sheer imagination. She had, before leaving the house, examined herself very closely in the little glass of her bedroom, and was satisfied that nothing showed ; how should it, so soon ? The ugly black costume, the heavy, crêpe-trimmed hat, which had been her mother's, were unbecoming and made her look pale. No wonder I look pale ! thought Polly, after all these weeks. Yet, sure as she was of her appearance, she knew with quivering certainty that Miss Monk would have spread her poison : that the company gathered about the grave was there, in part to pay tribute to the dead, but equally to pry at Ellen's daughter ; and that there would be more jealous satisfaction than pity in the hearts of those who, for years, had resented " that stuck-up girl of Bowling's."

She had bidden Joe go straight to the church, not try to join the long, dusty procession which followed the farm cart, and, trusting her to tell him what she really wanted him to do, he had obeyed her. She had a moment's poignant regret, as she stepped out into the hard, hot sunshine. If her father had offered her his arm, or even given her a look . . . ! But he was shut into his house of mourning, and had barely spoken to her since Ellen died. How could it be true, she wondered, as her mother had always maintained, that he loved and was proud of her ? She could remember no word of affection from him, since the days of her childhood ; no caress other than the stony Good-night kiss which had grown into a habit she disliked, but dared not break. No, she could not stay there, alone with her father ; duty was not enough, without love to ennoble it.

All the people, in their rusty, country black, standing about the grave ; the relatives, with mourning bands on their arms ; the boys with whom, as a girl, she had flirted, now grown men—married, most of them, with families ; the companions of her days in the village school, married, several proudly, righteously pregnant—Joe, as a stranger, had put himself modestly in the background ; why could he not have come forward, to stand by her side ? She reminded herself she had no claim on him, nor he on her, and a lump rose in her throat.

The gently waving tree branches, the bees humming in silver flight over the grass on the graves, the familiar stones with names she had known from childhood, the vicar's droning voice, the dignified figure of the Squire —her father-in-law ? Oh, impossible !—all induced in her a sense of dream, of unreality. She had no desire to cry, to expose herself or her feelings to these people—in future her enemies. Suddenly it shot into her mind that she was seeing them for the last time.

On her return she got quickly into her working overall, for there is no time for the niceties of mourning on a farm. Cousin Jinny and one or two of the neighbours had helped her briefly to preside over the cold foods laid out on the long kitchen table ; someone complimented her on the great meat pie, someone else on her scones and pastry. She made nothing of their praise ; as farm-house funerals went, she knew there was nothing in particular about Ellen's ; that the " collation " fell, if anything, below the expected standard. But, in making her preparations, she had not cared ; the primitive orgy of " eating a man into his grave " had always revolted her.

"No, nothing," she had answered, to Joe's offer of help. " The women will wash up for me. And Cousin Hancock has to get back to town early ; I've told him to be sure to give you a lift. You'd better see if he's got the mare harnessed yet——" Nothing mattered but to get him away quickly, quickly : if possible, without saying good-bye !

But he plunged her in confusion by asking if he should, as usual, come out to-morrow.

" Oh—not to-morrow—p'raps—Joe ! " she stammered. " I'll let you know—but I think—to-morrow—I'll try and get a bit of rest——" She gulped ; it was not easy to lie, to his guileless, faithful eyes.

" All right ; then it'll be to-morrow week. I'm starting work again on Monday."

To-morrow week : that gave her time to breathe—to think how she should write to him. She gave him a quick, tremulous smile, and sped away.

The same sense of dream that had possessed her at the graveside followed her through her evening duties. It was after ten o'clock when her father shut himself into the parlour, and she sat down at a corner of the kitchen chamber, with pen and ink, and the lamp at her elbow, to write him a letter.

She wrote it several times, tearing up the versions, despairing at last of finding anything to redeem its inevitable baldness.

" Dear Father,

" I have gone away for a while, because I cannot bear the

farm without Mother. I am sorry for the inconvenience this will cause you, but I expect Jinny Higgs will find time to look after you until you have found someone to take my place. Tabby is giving the place a good clean up. I have fed the animals and collected the eggs. I think you'd better have a look at Buttercup ; one of her udders seems to be sore. I've laid the table and put dinner on. I hope it won't be spoiled by the time you get in. The bed in my room is made up.

" There's no need to worry, as I am all right. Perhaps I'll send you an address later on. Give my love to Joe Prior and tell him not to worry. People are sure to gossip, but don't pay any attention, because it will not be true. You know I have never told you a lie. I will write as soon as I can. I don't like leaving you alone, but I don't feel you need me, except to do the work, and other people can do that just as well. So good-bye for the present, Father.

" Your daughter,

" POLLY."

She had tried to put " with love from," and to qualify the " daughter " with " affectionate " : but some impulse towards complete sincerity forbade the misuse of words. You could not write those things to a person you were, virtually, deserting. Yet she cried a little, sentimentally, as she signed her name ; it would have made it easier, in some way, just then to have loved the cold, hard man who, by some inexplicable chance, was the author of her being. As she put the writing materials back in their drawer, she thought : He'll get that to-morrow, when he comes in for dinner, after I'm gone.

II

The grey, Sunday stillness of Paddington Station lay about her. She had wakened hurriedly, to find the door of the compartment open and the companions who were there when she went to sleep, at some moment after the train left Reading, gone. Drifting with the rest of the travellers past the ticket collector, she was brought up sharply, and the last drowsiness driven from her eyelids, by the realisation that she had not the faintest idea of the next step to be taken.

She had meant to have it all planned out by the time the slow, Sunday train reached London ; it was the heat and her own weariness that had defeated her. There was no means of conveyance, on Sundays, to Bristol from the village ; had there been, she doubted she would have ventured to make use of it. Stealing out of the front door, peeping up and down the lane to make sure it was empty, before rushing through the opposite stile, to take advantage of the cover of the hedgerow, she had known she must walk : must escape at least two miles, before daring to take advantage of the easier going of the highroad. Grasses twisted themselves into the laces of her boots, pollen laid a golden blur round the hem of her skirt, the sun, mounting ever higher and higher in a cloudless sky, moistened her brow; she had to stop and unbutton Miss Monk's horrible jacket.

She did not dare to look at the beauty of surrounding earth as she sped on her way, the Japanese holdall, containing all she could bring away of her by no means meagre wardrobe, and her umbrella growing heavier and heavier in her hands. Noon had passed by the time she staggered into Temple Mead Station, her hands shaking so much that she could hardly take the money out of her purse, to pay for her ticket. And the first half-hour in the railway carriage had passed, mainly, in trying surreptitiously (for she was not alone) to remove the stains of her former journey from her shoes, from her gown. She wished she had remembered to get into a "Ladies Only"; it would not have been so embarrassing, in front of a carriageful of women, to dust off her skirts, to rub the patent leather caps of her boots down the backs of her stockings, to try with a moistened handkerchief, but no mirror, to clean away the shiny patches she could feel, on her brow and at the corners of her nose. She was too shy to cross the other passengers and make her way down the corridor to the lavatory; she had never been in such a place on a train before, and, although she had heard of it, felt doubtful it existed. Supposing some men were standing in the corridor when she went along?

Stiff, at first, with confusion and excitement, sleep eventually had its way with her; and now she stood on Paddington Station, biting her lip, frowning a little with perturbation, unconscious, for once, of curious or considering glances directed towards her comely figure, of masculine feet that trailed, slowed down, and, in one or two cases, took to hovering, awaiting the glance, which, in her innocence, she might have given, that could be interpreted as an invitation.

Although inexperienced in travel, Polly, however, was not without common sense; she knew, thanks to her apprenticeship in Bristol, that it was imprudent to catch the eyes of strangers. She straightened her shoulders, stiffened her flat young back and gripped her holdall, doing her best to look calm, composed and mistress of the situation. If only her brain would work faster—originate some movement—supply her with a clue which she could follow, if only to the entrance to the station——! It worked fast enough to enable her to reply promptly to the Salvation Army girl who came up to her, with: "Do you want some help, dear? Is anybody meeting you?" "Yes, thank you; I shan't have long to wait"—and a moment after regretted her own folly. She might at least have got an address—or even spent a night in a hostel, which would have given her a chance to look round.

But when she turned, to change her mind, the Salvation Army girl had disappeared; empty as the station was, few as were the people who seemed to travel on a Sunday, there were no signs of the familiar scuttle bonnet and scarlet ribbon. She drew a slight breath of alarm.

"Care to share a cab, dear?"

She started round, to meet a pair of lively brown eyes, and to recognise one of her former companions in the railway carriage: a girl of about her own age, of whom, seated in the farther corner, on the same side as herself, Polly had only caught an occasional glimpse, as the young lady—evidently a seasoned traveller—jumped up to raise or lower a window, as they were about to run into or out of a tunnel. Several times she was forestalled by gallantry; this was usually followed by an exchange of badinage whose worldly flavour roused Polly's admiration and lowered her head, to hide a smile. Apart from these interludes, her brown-eyed *vis-à-vis*, up to now, had been, to Polly, a pair of high-heeled button boots, elegantly crossed at the ankles, the glimpse, beneath the hem of a black nuns-veiling skirt, of a black and red striped taffeta petticoat frill, and an occasional whiff of pungent perfume. She extended her observation candidly to a small, heart-shaped face, which experience did not yet enable her to label as Cockney, surmounted by a pompadour, in its turn supporting a plateau of the fashionable burnt straw, from the centre of whose crown spouted a double fountain of cock's feathers, curving down on either side towards the wearer's high cheekbones. A white tulle bow under a piquant chin, four-button brown kid gloves and as many bracelets, mainly of the curb variety, with chased padlocks, hearts and coins, as could conveniently be crowded on to a pair of slim wrists, completed Polly's first impression of the stranger whom, forty years later, she was still to call her friend.

"Which way were you going? I've got to get right over Waterloo Bridge; it's a dickens of a cab fare"—her teeth flashed briefly—"but we might share it, if you happen to be going that way."

Polly smiled slowly: liking the speaker, liking her easy way of extending friendliness to a stranger.

"I don't know where I'm going," she said, and chuckled.

The other girl's mouth opened.

"You don't? Go on!" she invited, with patent incredulity.

"I don't. I was going to try and find some lodgings——"

"Look here: is this straight?" The girl's brows knitted. "You come all the way up from Bristol—yes, I saw you getting in—and you've got nowhere to go?" As Polly nodded, she demanded fiercely: "What have you come up for? You're not"—her sharp eyes quickly took in the whole of Polly's figure—"you're not in the profession, are you?"

Polly was not sure what "the profession" meant, but shook her head.

"I just thought I'd look for—some sort of a job." She felt it sounded silly, and her eyes fell.

"Come on," she heard the girl say abruptly. "All the cabs'll be gone—Sunday's a hell of a day—is that all the baggage you've got?"

III

In years to come there was to be the first floor in Pimlico; the St. John's Wood cottage; a "maisonette" in the region beginning to be genteelly known as West Kensington; Ranelagh—one of those little red-fronted villas with minute balconies, overlooking the polo: these interspersed with interludes in Brixton, off the Tottenham Court Road and in the subfusc regions behind Victoria Station. There was English's (the locals still called it Belmont's), the first of the twice-nightlies, down in Hackney ; the Star of Bermondsey, that you could see when you arrived at Spa Road Station, on the South Eastern ; and so on, in a mounting grade, until—at last !—the Alhambra. There was all the beauty of Leicester Square and the West End, before gas lighting was abolished ; and Gatti's, in Villiers Street, under the Arches ; and Romano's, where the girls went on in their wigs, after the performance, to supper with their stage door beaux.

But, for Polly, " her " London was always that short stretch of thoroughfare that extends beyond Waterloo Bridge ; took in the first two blocks on either side and focused the small, intensive, ardently exciting life which presented so breath-taking a contrast to any she had previously known. Right up to the outbreak of the Second World War, whenever she was not to be found, those who knew her well would say resignedly, " Polly's gone to Waterloo." She would be found, wistfully conducting a *recherche du temps perdu* among the ghosts of a vanished world—knowing as well as anyone that the world she had known and loved now deployed its activities in St. Martin's Lane, and up and down Charing Cross Road. Drawn back by memories to the old York Hotel with its circular bar at the back, where the contracts used to be signed, she would sip her port, hoping each time the door swung open that it would admit one of those remembered figures—either dust, by this time, or absorbed into the limbo of Elstree which Polly, like most of her contemporaries, hated and feared. These were her sentimentalities, of which no reasoning, no representation of cold facts, could break her.

Or she might stroll along the deserted Sunday pavement, oblivious of the notice she attracted in her elegant tailor-made, the spray of cattleya on her lapel, and the silver fox draped negligently over one arm : looking up at the windows over what once was Driver's Stores, or at the church of St. John the Evangelist with its litter-strewn steps : remembering Sundays when those steps were knee-deep in confetti and rice ; when she and Bella, leaning gleefully on their elbows, had watched from opposite the coster weddings ; pearly kings and queens driving up in their decorated donkey carts ; dancing on the pavement ; feathers and bright shawls.

Over dinner at Cavour's, a far-away look would come into her eye, her hand remain suspended, in the act of squeezing the muslin-bagged lemon over her caviare.

" What's the matter, Polly ? "

" Nothing, dear. . . . I was just thinking of me and Bella, getting our penn'orth and ha'p'orth on Saturday night." " A penn'orth and ha'p'orth of *what* ? " some amused listener might inquire. On him the reproachful toleration of her glance would rest for a moment.

" That's what it was *called*, dear ; a bowl of stewed eels in parsley sauce and a spoonful of mashed—three ha'pence. That *was* a meal." Sighing, she turned to the waiter, holding the bottle in its cradle for her approval. " No, George," she would say fretfully. " That's not the one his lordship recommended the other day. And for Christ's sake see the woodcock's tender to-night; the last one I ate here was like a fossil!"

Too timid, to begin with, to wander far afield, Polly discovered there was plenty to be seen from the windows over Driver's; plenty to occupy her eyes and her wits in her bird's-eye view of life in the Waterloo Bridge Road. There were always loiterers, she discovered, on the corner by the York Road-Stamford Street crossing; on Fridays, Saturdays and Mondays the loiterers became a crowd, men and women, too well dressed to belong to the working classes of the neighbourhood, yet not well enough to place them among what Polly naïvely described as "gentry." Seen at close quarters, something else distinguished them: for all the smartness, the men, and some of the women as well, were not quite clean: a greasy yellowish-reddish shadow ran along the hair-line, a smear of dark blue or brown round the eyelid, or a grain of greasy black spangled the eye-corner nearest the nose. The girls' faces were heavily powdered and their mouths usually a rich red; the powder lay in a white mask as far as the chin-line, leaving the under part of the jaw, and the throat, dusky by contrast.

But they seemed nice, quiet people, well-mannered and cheery, as they idled in the sunlight; she wondered what kept them there, sometimes for a whole morning, walking a few yards along, then a few yards back; disappearing, perhaps, for a short while, but always returning; going into the saloon bar—girls as well as men!—and coming out again, to take up their mysterious vigil on the pavement. Sometimes there seemed to be a little excitement; once a girl's shrill voice—"Aren't you lucky?" floated up through some pocket of momentary silence in the hum of the Waterloo Road.

"Oh yes, that's the 'Junction.'" Bella, questioned, seemed to find this a sufficient explanation. Or, "I'll just slip along to the 'Junction'; never know your luck, do you, dear? The printing goes in to-morrow." Ashamed to say that this was as intelligible as Greek to her, Polly nodded, and tried to look wise.

Strange world, strange people, strange vocabulary.

"Where'd you get your capella, dear?" A few days after her arrival, Bella put her head on one side and surveyed her new companion's headgear.

"My—what?"

Bella burst from laughter into song:

"'Polly cocked his mince,
Hasn't been seen since,
Polly took his best capella dooey,
He scapa-ed his littari,
Nanty parkered his munjari
And His Jills is nantivari'd in the yooey!'

You know 'Polly cocked his eye,' don't you—in *The Geisha*? 'Cocked his mince'—mince pie—eye: d'you get me, Steve? Capella—hat.

'Where did you get—that—hat?'" chanted Bella, as Polly, slightly stunned, tried to follow the explanation.

"Oh—I know I'll have to get a new one. There wasn't time, when I left home."

"I can lend you one of mine, for now, if you like?"

"That's all right," said Polly simply. "I can afford one. Perhaps you'll help me to choose it. I'm not sure what they're wearing—but I'd like it to be nice."

Bella explained that the two rooms in which, from the hour of their arrival, Polly felt at home, were rented by her and her mother—"Marie Belloni. She's out in the number twos, with *The Geiesha.* Marie Belloni—you know——"

"You don't mean—the actress?" with a gasp of incredulity, as memory rescued a name from the bill boards.

"Bella Belloni: that's me. Don't bother, ducks; you won't know it. I'm still in the wines and spirits! Never mind; I bet I won't be the first that's gone from the 'Junction' to the top of the bill," was the cryptic rejoinder. "Well, here we are, and here, so far as I'm concerned, you're welcome to stay, until the tour's over, and my Old Dutch gets back from the road."

By the following Sunday she was capable of translating this: she knew that Bella's reference to the wines and spirits bore no relation to the liquor trade: that it meant that her name appeared in the smallest print among the advertisements on the back page of what Polly had always called a programme, which, to Bella was a bill. She knew that Poverty Junction was the corner to which the lesser music-hall people went to pick up an odd date, to meet an agent or a manager.

Each day bringing its new experiences, puzzling, sometimes a little stupefying, often amusing—there was little time to fret over the past. To be sharing lodgings with a girl of her own age, to be free at every moment to follow her own inclinations, at first almost took Polly's breath away. Constantly humiliated by her own ignorance, ashamed to admit how little she understood of Bella's conversation, she managed to keep up a small dignity of her own by helping in the housework. She was paying so little for her board and lodging that she could not believe it was enough; five shillings, Bella earnestly declared, covered more than everything. Accustomed to the rich and plentiful fare of her home, she did not see how this would feed her for more than a day or two; Bella's way with a penn'orth of pot-herbs and half a pound of sevenpenny pieces from the New Cut had yet to be revealed to her, and, at the end of a week, although the food was different, she had to admit that she was well and appetisingly fed.

Bella, lavishly untidy, indifferent to disorder in her surroundings, content to spend the day (unless going to the "Junction") in a dressing-gown, was equally content to lean back and watch Polly tidying their living-room.

"I can see you come from a good home, Miss Bowling!" she grimaced.

"Well—what about yourself?"

" Pro digs ? Combined chats ? Some old cat of a landlady that got five bob a week for looking after me while Ma was working ? Poops ! " returned Miss Belloni. A glint of curiosity shone briefly in her bright eyes before she lowered her lashes. Like the majority of people in her profession, she had too much good taste and kindliness to pry into Polly's private affairs ; but she constantly wondered what had brought the big, simple country girl up to London, and, on a day Polly mentioned her father, thought she had found the explanation. The mother dead, and a step-mother on the horizon ; don't blame her ! thought Bella.

Sometimes they took the halfpenny bus across the Bridge to Somerset House, minced their way along the Strand and across Trafalgar Square, where they set their watches by Dent's clock on the corner of Whitehall ; then on up the Haymarket to Regent Street for an orgy of window-gazing.

" Oh, Bella ! " breathed Polly, before a window full of gloves, which had drawn her from the more dashing attractions of the jeweller's into which Bella was poring.

A pair of white kids ! It had occurred to her that here, where no one knew her, she might, without want of respect to Ellen's memory, add a touch or two to relieve the dead black of her mourning. A pleated muslin front ? She had played with the idea of copying Bella's tulle bows, but decided they would not suit her. Besides, unless they were absolutely fresh —as Bella's seldom were—they looked slovenly.

" They'll cost you threepence each time you have them cleaned," said Bella doubtfully, in reference to the gloves.

But she had to have them. With that touch of white, and the white sailor Bella had persuaded her to borrow—since she refused to wear a colour, and it seemed a pity, as black did not suit her, to spend money on another black hat—she felt neat, " London-y " and suitable. Even Miss Monk's hideous costume seemed to fit better—and she must certainly not, for the present, think of buying another. Thus, out of necessity, was born in Polly that taste for severity in clothing which suited her so well, and, to the end of her days, distinguished her from her more fancifully attired contemporaries.

A good many heads were turned, to follow their demure progress ; the old gambit was tried—" Excuse me, miss, haven't we met before ? " and received by Polly with an expression of elaborate unconsciousness, spoiled by her explosive giggle at Bella's prompt come-back : " No, I've never been on Broadmoor." Bella was marvellous ; she had an answer for everything.

And at last they would giggle their way on to one of the horse trams, and, at the sight of the Shot Tower, resume their lives, not of West End butterflies, but of serious young women, dependent on their work and their wits for such glimpses of the gayer life as they enjoyed. They always avoided Poverty Junction on their return from such expeditions, sauntering along on the left-hand side of the road for a look in the theatrical costumiers, at photographs dashingly signed—" Gratefully yours, Kate Carney " ; " Ever yours, Vesta Tilley " ; " Sincerely, Marie Lloyd."

"No waiting on the Junction for them!" Bella's lips were pressed together; Polly saw her give a sharp little nod to a window on the opposite side of the road. "All right; you'll be seeing Bella Belloni, one of these days."

"Who are you speaking to?" Polly looked round for the object of Bella's address.

"Didn't I ever show you? That's Didcott's, over there: Hugh J. Didcott, that handles the topliners."

"Handles——?" she faltered.

"Agent, ducks, agent. Fifty-two weeks' work a year, two halls a night and your own brougham: that's what Didcott stands for. He was the one that found Vesta Tilley her name—you know: 'The Vital Spark.'"

"I suppose he's—he's too busy, to handle—everybody," observed Polly, with naïve tact. Bella's laugh rang through the clatter of the traffic as she thrust her hand through Polly's arm and pinched it affectionately. "You're a perfect *cure*! But you're a darling," she added affectionately. "Come on; let's go home. I want to try some of my new numbers."

A song was a number; Polly had already added the word to her growing vocabulary. Bella flung her hat on the sofa and littered the floor with sheets of music. No vocalist, in the strict sense of the term—her turn was the popular one of "impersonations"; her piquant little face could assume, in a moment, the very lineaments of the subject of her imitation, her gestures, her deportment fell mysteriously into line, as her voice varied from a crow to a flute in accordance with the necessities of her theme. Polly vamping an accompaniment, Bella capering among the furniture—Joe Elvin unexpectedly joined the company:

"So they stuck me on top of a Forder cab,
Told me I looked 'all there,'
They told me to take it down Regent Street
And round St. James's Square.
I was going along in the Strand, you know,
Near St. Martin's church,
When I cannoned against an onnamibus
And it toppled me off my perch."

Or Kate Carney, with:

"He takes me up in the gallery almost every night,
Buys me whelks and oranges and swears I'm his delight.
He shouts Bravo to every Pro, and as we rambles 'ome,
He plays the chorus of every song on a fagpaper an' comb."

Or the idol of all idols—to Bella, as to all of her worshipping public, just "Mahrie." It was so long since she had sung that Polly's voice felt stiff and rough, but the tune and the rhythm were irresistible. When Bella swung into the chorus for the second time, Polly let herself go:

"And the fellows all chi-yike
When they see me on my bike,
But I'm as cool as any icicle.
When a spoony cove says this,
'Mahrie, I should like a kiss!'
I only say, well—kiss my bicycle."

III

But there were times when her blithe spirit failed her; when she ached with homesickness and with grief for her mother; when she thought of Johnny, and tried hard to realise that he was her husband.

How could anyone of whom one knew so little be a husband? All the contacts of their childhood melted or misted by time—there opened between them, as they grew up, a formal though friendly gulf created by their different backgrounds. Free as each was from snobbery, each tacitly admitted the gulf, which only a strong community of interest could have made it possible, or worth while, to bridge. Joe formed a bridge, of a kind; but they had done little more than call to one another along this slender line of communication. (Joe: she had sent him two postcards, one of St. Paul's and the other of Westminster Abbey; and then had gone into a panic, wondering whether they would enable him to trace her.)

It was as impossible for her to imagine Johnny's private life, the people with whom he was intimate, as it was, she supposed, impossible for him to imagine hers. Alternately longing for and dreading his return, Guerdon was the nightmare that haunted her sleeping and her waking hours. She was always on the run from the thought of it; from the memory of Dorset's *hating* face. To think that she had ever believed herself in love with him; the thought made her blush, inside; it was as though her head and her face and her stomach were all lined with a burning red plush, that grew hotter and hotter and prickled. Dorset, who had kissed her in the park—who had fooled her into loving him with a love which, although she had never in her life seriously hated anyone, she now felt could very easily turn to hate, on her part as well as on his. "Don't cheapen yourself, Polly," had been a frequent saying of Ellen's. She had never known what it was to feel cheap, before that look of Dorset's, which soiled her, marked her down, and flung her aside. Oh, Joe, Joe, Joe!—whom I despised because of Dorset. Poor Joe, who needs me, now, to look after him.

She had told Bella nothing—because there was too much to tell, and to talk was only to probe a wound. Open as she was by nature, and prone to take the world into her confidence, she could not have borne Bella's interest, her sympathy, her eager questioning. The only thing that made their living together possible was Bella's ignorance—which, to do her justice, she had never attempted to relieve. All Bella knew was that Polly wanted to find "a job"; like most professionals, however, she was much too centred in herself, in the hazards of her own career, to worry about

Polly's. She was, apparently, perfectly content to have Polly's company, and took it for granted that, if the latter chose idleness, she could afford it ; at any rate, for the present, until she " got over her trouble." It was easy to fall in with Bella's noisy gaiety, to use it as a cloak to cover misgivings she tried to suppress.

Mr. Johnny—Johnny, as, of course, he was now : she tried to picture him among the nig—Negroes. The newspapers she saw carried very little about the Ashanti war ; South Africa was blazoned on their front pages. But she had sent him her address and asked him to write to her. The agent at Cape Coast Castle, whose address he had left inside the envelope of money—which also contained her marriage lines and her wedding ring —would surely know where to find him. It would be a comfort to receive even a word or two, to say he was well and, perhaps, when she could expect him home.

All these reflections brought an undercurrent of gravity into Polly's liveliness. As the novelty of her new environment wore away, she became neither happy nor unhappy ; often absentminded, with sharp phases of anxiety about the future, which quickened her longing for Johnny's return. He seemed at least something to lean on, something of her own. Sometimes she wondered wistfully if they would ever grow to love each other ; yet, strange as it seemed in one whose imagination usually served her well, she was totally unable to picture them sharing a home, going to bed every night in the same room, building round themselves the small intimacies which were her conception of married life.

And she began to be worried by the dwindling of the money Johnny had left her. It was the shops, of course. She could not resist them—as she could not resist the flower girls, or anybody who petitioned her for alms. There had to be a bunch of roses or cornflowers to " brighten up " the sitting-room, a bottle of scent for Bella, and a fowl as an occasional treat for week-ends—although Bella shrieked that three and sixpence was a shocking price to pay for a hen. When she indulged herself in a length of spotted veiling, shame made her drop a sixpenny bit in the hand of the beggar who waited on the threshold of the shop. Gloves ; she seemed always to be buying gloves, and handkerchiefs, and losing both.

While Bella pursued mysterious interests of her own, and, " the Junction " failing temporarily to produce the expected dates, went off for a couple of nights with *The Geiesha* company—which had arrived as near town as Watford—she wandered into the West End and found herself, as usual, without a handkerchief : which gave her the guilty excuse to enter Robinson and Cleaver's, outside which she happened to be at the moment she discovered her loss. Sauntering, pretending to be a lady of wealth and leisure, her lips parted with envious rapture among the snowy gleam of linen and damask ; catching an assistant's eye, she inquired haughtily the price of monogrammed napkins ; sniffed, " Oh, I required something of *much* better quality," and swept on.

Waves of muslin, clouds of Shetland wool, swansdown, eiderdown, cobwebs of lace and lawn. . . . Polly caught her breath. Her baby !—

which was behaving so well, she could almost forget it was there. She ought to be collecting things for it!—a reflection which so sobered her that the trimming and lace counters, usually her downfall, offered no temptation as she hurried out, forgetting the reason of her entrance.

Her baby. Avoiding the flower girls, she crossed the Circus firmly and turned down Lower Regent Street. She would no longer risk the fatal attraction of the shops, but would cut through by the little side streets to Trafalgar Square and catch the tram along the Strand. When her bootlace became untied in one of the alleys between Jermyn Street and Haymarket, she looked modestly behind her, before setting her foot on a low window-sill of polished brass, into which she casually glanced when the repair was accomplished.

It lay on a sheet of cottonwool, among a heap of other trinkets: a clump of little silver bells attached to a chased silver cone set on a handle of branch coral. A baby's rattle.

Five minutes later she had it, wrapped in tissue paper, in her handbag. It had cost three pounds. She felt sick with her own extravagance; sick, and a little frightened. It was the first thing she had bought for her baby. Where could she hide it from Bella?

Sitting in the horse tram, a flashy person opposite ogled for her attention; she raised the newspaper she had bought from the vendor on the corner of Duncannon Street in defence against his advances. It was some little time before she noticed that she had folded it back at the employment columns. Wanted——

"——a Good Parlourmaid; age about 24; tall; no fringe; not less than 12 months good character from last situation——"

No use. . . .

"Housemaid; age 20 to 25; wages £18, no beer; no fringe; must be strong, active, willing, early riser. Only those with long character need apply——"

She crumpled the page impatiently. Typewriters—she couldn't type. Pastrycooks. Experienced fitters. Waitresses——

"Refined Assistant required for Millinery. . . ."

She sat there, staring at it. Yes, there was no question about it; she had got to find some work—quickly.

CHAPTER SEVEN

I

IT was almost a day since they had discovered the loss of the compass ; the one thing they had had to depend on. It must have gone while they were wriggling through a patch of low-growing, thorny scrub, when one of Johnny's flap-pockets was torn away. They did not notice until they had gone nearly a mile ; useless, of course, to go back and look for it. It just meant that their chances were reduced so much lower. At least it relieved them both of the obligation of cheerfulness, of pretending to take it for granted it could not now be long before they reached a village, or met some person who could be persuaded to act as a guide. It allowed them to look calmly at death, to get, as it were, on friendly terms with it. Oddly enough, they both felt much better, after establishing this relationship with the imponderable. Like discovering, in an embarrassing companion, whom both had affected to ignore, qualities that entitle him, at least, to consideration. Two's company, three's none ; yet, having accepted the third, each felt himself relaxing, as though some portion of his load had been transferred to the newcomer.

Death. The man with the scythe. When the swain sharps the scythe. Odd thoughts went flickering through Johnny's mind. Now and again it was as though he saw their shadowy third—a black man, of course. He had just reached the point of surprise that the face of death should turn out to be the kind, handsome face of Osei, when he became aware of Paget, standing still, looking at him.

"I think it's to the right." He answered the question in the other's eyes."

"Toss you for it."

They tossed. Johnny called heads, and the coin came down tails on the back of Paget's hand. Paget gave in unexpectedly.

"Go on—make it right. Damned if you've not got more direction-sense than I have."

They looked at one another. Paget said, after a silence :

"I had a nightmare like this—once." And they went on.

Perhaps because there were only three of them—Johnny, and Paget, and the black man Death—the forest seemed to have grown much taller, and the tracks nearly imperceptible. The only good thing about that was that it showed they were not on a frequented route. He thought : It's like being an ant, crawling about in the roots of jungle grass ; he wondered if the ant had the same sensation of helplessness. Paget went first, most of the time, being the heavier, and Johnny, following with his head thrust in to the small of Paget's back, added his weight to the thrust of the other against the obstruction of the vines.

Things had become very bad for them both. They were stung from head to foot, and the pain of their swollen limbs reduced progress to a crawl. Paget's right arm had swollen so badly that they had had to cut the sleeve away. It was now a big, misshapen bolster, ending in a clump of purplish bananas ; he had no use of his right hand. Johnny was a reeling bag of skin and bone—disgusted with the body which thus played traitor to him. He had, now and again, a dull shock of surprise at his own weakness. I must be damned out of condition. The wiry frame on which he depended felt soft. Every now and then, everything blacked out ; each time it cleared, he was surprised to find himself still walking, propped by Paget's sound arm.

That was how it had been since the crackle of muskets that followed the sound of Paget's revolver—fired in the attempt to stop the stampede of the carriers ; and the carriers had swept over him, and Mahmoud had been knocked down, and, falling, split his skull on one of the boxes dropped in the flight. One of the shots had found a Hausa ; the other, leaping blindly at the bush, had received—what ? There was a scream, and then there was silence. Then Johnny fired three times, at random, for there was nothing to see ; and this, apparently, had frightened the enemy, for there was no more sound, and only the figure of Paget appeared, blundering towards the clearing.

Paget had wanted, at first, to force the five " sleeping " carriers, now recovering from their coma, to come on with them, but had been persuaded to leave them to their own devices. The hardest thing was the enforced abandonment of the stores, and the dubious prospect of reaching friendly territory before their meagre reserves of food were exhausted.

The nervous strain of their advance had long given way to exhaustion. Each had given up thinking of the enemy, save in terms of swamp, of tree trunk, of insect life, of snakes and of rain. The true enemy, each knew, was his own waning strength ; but for Bendick, thought Johnny, he would have been content to sit down and die. Harcourt—Harriet—Miranda—and Polly and her child, drifting across his mind, were other arguments, of course, against dying.

It was dark. And then it was light. " Moon," said Paget briefly. Moon. He blinked at it, without belief. Moon ? " Food," said Paget : " You'll have to get it out of my pack." Food : that tasted of must, of heat ; that had, somehow, to be put into a hole in one's face which had got mislaid among the swellings caused by bites. Like posting a letter in the dark. Feeling one's way across an area of numbness like a sheet of metal and chancing on the hole—at last.

" Smoke," said Paget, and he felt something pushing against his hand which he recognised by its shape as a tin. He heard a croak come out of his mouth : " Is it safe ? "—and remembered that nothing was safe and nothing unsafe ; all that had ended with the end of time. He fumbled a cigarette out of the tin and felt for the box of matches. He counted the matches with his fingers : eleven. Eight broke before he got a light. The scent of the cigarettes mounted sweetly into the air ; life revived with it.

" . . . Well," said Paget. " I suppose somebody's doing something—somewhere."

" . . . Do you suppose," said Paget, " there's anybody else in this bloody great wood, besides us ? "

" . . . What do you bet," said Paget, " that the dear old Governor is enjoying a cosy B. & S. at Accra, by now, and the rest of them kicking themselves for missing the fun of busting our way to Kumassi ? "

The moonlight ebbed and flowed out of the banks of cloud. Both men's hands went involuntarily to the revolvers as there was a nearby scramble, followed by a long, mewing whine. Something shook down a patter of dry twigs and bark on their heads and went bounding with long, elastic leaps that swung down the boughs to mark its passing. Silence came back, and was disturbed again by a chatter of tree-frogs from some unseen patch of swamp.

" Do you see what I see ? " asked Paget cautiously.

The muscles of his neck seemed to be a long time in functioning.

" That light—dodging about those tree trunks ? Some sort of insect. Probably means we're close to water."

" Ah," said Paget, on a note of undisguised relief.

" . . . I was thinking," said Paget, " about some of the things I'd like to have done. I'd like to have seen something of the world. And of course I'd have liked——"

" Well—what ? "—as he paused.

" It sounds cracked ; I'd have liked to have had a son. Gwendoline and I should have been married, last April."

" Why weren't you ? "

" Her people wouldn't hear of it. My being sent out here—and one thing with another. Pretty hard lines on a girl—to lose her husband as soon as she gets married. I see the point, of course. Still—it's hard lines. On both parties." Johnny saw the tip of the cigarette glow as Paget pulled on it. " We'd got it all fixed up, before I went to Sandhurst. Not officially, of course. Had to get her mother's consent. You never sent that letter by the way ; or did you ? "

" No," said Johnny, after a pause.

Paget asked diffidently : " Was it to a girl ? "

" No." There was another pause before he added : " It was to my son."

" You—lucky——! Well, well ; when were you married ? "

" Last month." Could it be true ? It seemed like a century ago.

" Oh. Ah." The situation seemed to call for tact.

" He's not born yet."

" Oh—I see. Ha-ha. You'll have to——" After a break, he ended the sentence. " I was going to say, you'll jolly well have to make me one of the godfathers."

" Thanks ; that would be grand." He took no notice of the implication behind the conditional. Presently Paget said :

" I wonder what it is makes a fellow so keen on having a son ?—I mean, apart from the old genealogical tree, and the family estates, and all that sort of thing? I mean, I've known lots of chaps who haven't a brass farthing to leave, or even any particular sort of record to worry about—go absolutely crazy over the idea of a son. Biological—what? Jolly old human instinct seeing to the survival of the race; I suppose that's it, when you come to boil it down."

"Plus," said Johnny, and wondered if he would some day be telling his son about this conversation in an African forest.

"Plus—what?"

"'John Brown's body lies a-mouldering in his grave, and his soul goes marching on.' Isn't that what you're after, really—the idea of going on living, in your son?"

He could feel Paget's stiff, soldierly brain wrestling with the suggestion. Presently he went on:

"Most people start something—or, as you've just said—set up some record—that they hope their sons will carry on, after they're gone. Perhaps"—he stammered a little—"it's only a memory, or—or a belief. Something, anyhow, that made life worth living for them—something that stands for truth——"

Paget was looking at him in a puzzled way.

"What a queer chap you are, Flood. I dare say there's something in what you say. If I'd had a boy, I'd have liked to have made him a soldier."

Johnny said abruptly:

"Feel like pushing on?"

He heard Paget's "Ha-ha," soft, vacuous, in the dark.

"Bloody silly—what? You and I—without a notion where we are, or where we're making for—just crawling on, like a couple of silly beetles——"

"I felt more like an ant, a while ago. Beetle'll do, though. Yes: definitely beetle—since chop!" "His soul goes marching on"—in the form of a beetle; he forced his creaking body to its feet.

He had not realised how his ear had tuned itself to the noises of the bush: to the insect sounds, the animal sounds, the water sounds and that indescribable non-sound, non-silence that forms the basis of them all: which he identified vaguely as the sound of growth, of vegetation spawning, rooting, throwing out its shoots, uncoiling its tendrils. He had actually seen a flower bud open with a crack, a vine, grown too strong for its host, lash out and lassoo the nearest support. And what he now heard belonged to none of these. His hand, reaching back, found and bit into the muscle of Paget's thigh, felt it stiffen in response. Would the message of his fingers reach Paget's brain and prevent him from speaking? With infinite caution, his hand still gripping the big thigh-muscle, he took a step back; felt Paget's body accept the signal; went on pressing back, and back, until twisted stems and branches allowed them to drop, as through a hole in a basket, into whatever lay behind. More rents, stings, stabs into outraged flesh. Crouched, not daring to move, even to ease their positions, they saw the open glade where they had been standing fill itself with a sudden glare of moonlight, as, ripping itself clear of cloud, the moon rode for a moment, high and angry, over the bush.

For both, it was the first sight of the native in war-paint. The line came close ; so close that they could not only see the ochre tiger-stripes transforming each face into a mask, the diamond-shaped palaver-marks and the horned headdresses of the leaders ; but could catch the smell of raw hides and rancid grease and hear the clok-clok of bones which, on one man, made a necklace, on another a girdle. A piercing stench of fresh blood and a cloud of flies accompanied a couple who, between them, carried what looked like a side of raw meat ; one ducked his head to lick it, the flies zoomed furiously, and the other made a noise like a laugh. All moved with a loose, padded spring, half walk, half trot, and the majority carried guns : the Dane, or—loot, no doubt, from a previous raid—the Lee-Metford.

Remembering schoolboy yarns, of watchers being betrayed by the glitter of their eyeballs, he had managed to get his hand up to shade his eyes ; Paget, he saw, had copied him. Paget was in an excruciating position, half crouched, half sitting, the greater part of his heavy weight carried on his left arm : how long could he carry it ? The misshapen right hand, like a five-pronged tuber, was stuck up before his face. Surely no human being could hold that attitude for more than seconds. Johnny, who had begun by counting the line, found himself counting the seconds—the split fragments of time that remained before Paget's strength gave way, and his noisy collapse delivered them into the hands of the enemy.

More, and more, and more of them ; a whole bloody army. Between the pair of them a loop of tie-tie hung down, as thick as a man's wrist. Something was holding the line up ; two or three, immediately in front of their hiding-place, halted. Fifty-eight, fifty-nine—less than a minute—Christ—Paget's arm was quivering. . . . The tie-tie drew itself back, with its curled-up tip swinging rhythmically from side to side, just in front of Paget's hand. Johnny felt his eyelids, swollen with bites, pushing at the flesh behind them ; his jaw dropped and stiffened.

The head of the snake and his hand shot out simultaneously. Catching it cleanly under the jawbone, he actually heard the venom spatter, as the weight of the creature dropped itself on him, bearing him against Paget ; and had a glimpse of Paget's eyes, like gooseberries mounted on balls of ivory, as the thought went through his mind : That's finished it. He felt the supporting bulk of Paget give—then there was a kind of bloodshot eternity, in which the one vital thing was to keep his grip on the neck of the snake, and the one sentient thing the agony in the bones of his arm, which it was crushing to pulp—followed by the incredible realisation that they were still undiscovered : that the discipline and strength of the body against which he was flung, assisted by Paget's fortitude in pain, had brought them a few more seconds of respite.

Another thing in their favour was the slight commotion into which, for some reason, the line had been flung ; something had gone wrong ; there were gallopings backward and forward, mutterings—it was evidently important not to make noise. But there was sufficient of a muffled hubbub to enable the two men in hiding to take a risk ; and it was Paget who, using his left hand, dragged the knife from the sheath on Johnny's hip and, with a blow more lucky than dexterous, severed the snake's head from its writhing body.

For a sweating moment they listened to the beheaded body lashing the dry brush at their feet in its final reflexes. Heads turned, hands pointed, a horrific face, painted with pale horizontal bars like a gridiron, even thrust itself among the leaves, all but within touch of Johnny's outstretched hand ; but the noise made by a fighting snake was too familiar to evoke more than a passing curiosity. Some message came down the line, and, while Johnny and his companion still sweated, it was gone like a puff of smoke.

Paget's muscles gave way at last, and he dropped with a crash that checked the beat of Johnny's heart ; supposing they heard, and turned back ? But the strain had been too much ; like Paget, he lay for a while, prone on the earth, the clothes of both filling with ants, with microscopic torments, to which neither was in a condition to pay heed. Presently he felt Paget pushing his flask into his hand ; there were only a few drops left in it, his own was all gone. He made a pantomime of refusal ; speech would not come. The crushed arm was like a boil. Paget thrust the mouth of the flask against his teeth. . . .

The moon had gone in again, and it was very difficult to see.

" Why in blazes can't it rain ? " he had recovered sufficiently to mutter.

" Hell," said Paget, " haven't we got enough, without rain ? "

" It was the moonlight brought that lot out. A bit of a downpour and they'd scuttle like hens."

" What—the Ashanti ? "

" Who says they were Ashanti ? This isn't Ashanti country ; if they are, they've got no business to be. More likely one of the revolted tribes —taking a chance of a bit of private raiding while their bosses are busy elsewhere."

" Dammit, I thought they were Ashanti. I was feeling a lot better for having met the Ashanti. I'd rather given up believing there was such a thing : you know—like the dodo, and the great sea-serpent, and the gryphon : what ? " Paget's irrepressible frivolity had reasserted itself.

He said reflectively : " A new track means easy going."

" What—on the *facilis decensus* principle ? " Paget's fluffy eyebrows, oddly mixed with the lank streaks of his hair, puckered.

" Might be." Johnny forced a smile. " On the other hand——"

" I get you. Given the choice between Avernus and this damned unsociable greenery, I think, by now, I'd plump for the hot spot. They're bound, of course, to be going somewhere. Either back to their own village —which wouldn't be so good from our point of view : what——? "

" I don't fancy so. That little party, unless I'm mistaken, is looking for trouble. The sort of trouble that might be useful for us."

" Don't be cryptic, my dear chap," complained Paget. " Let's be moving ; and, while we move, put it into words of one syllable. It's beginning to strike me "—he dropped his hand for a moment on Johnny's shoulder—" you're in charge of this expedition, not I."

" Rot," muttered Johnny.

" Rot be damned. Why aren't you a soldier, Flood ? You've been worth a packet to us, out here."

Each let out a strangled yelp as the bush crackled with musketry. It seemed for a moment as though the shots came from all round them, and Johnny's instinct was to fling himself on his face ; Paget, however, remained stock-still, across the path. Crack, bang, and an occasional flash ; prolonged volleys, ragged bursts, as from individual marksmen, more volleys —witnessed to the joyful inebriation of the native with a gun in his hand, and advertised the enemy's richness in ammunition. As the boom of an immense explosion shook the earth and lit the bush into a momentary likeness to painted scenery, he heard Paget yell, " Look out ! "

They had barely time to fling themselves at a tree, up which Johnny's lightness assisted him in swarming, while Paget's great weight and his poisoned arm dragged him down ; with Johnny's help he managed at last to straddle a branch, and sat there, with the sweat rolling off his face in drops the size of peas, and dripping on the fantastic spectacle below.

Antelope, leopard, hyena, panther, gorilla—all swept by terror into monstrous companionship ; above them the branches swung down and cracked beneath the flight of panic-stricken apes. A shrieking canopy of bush fowl, channelled by the undergrowth, fled with them, swooping over the indistinguishable river of pallor and darkness, of stripe and spot that flowed along the bush path on which, a few moments before, the two men had been standing. The air was rank with terror, stank like a hundred zoos with the exudations of fear.

" Look out, look out ! " Paget was shouting again, as the forest seemed to bend under some tremendous onslaught. A noise of trampling and rending, the crash of a tree trunk which, in falling, dragged with it its draperies of parasites : dragged them across the two men clinging to their branch, caught them as in a net—half-smothered Paget's scream. Choking, his eyes streaming from the lash of leaves, Johnny was aware of the approach of a mountain. A grey mass, crusted with lichens, was rolling down on them ; an opening fissure asphyxiated them with fetid air ; a wild, volcanic glint, on a level with his face, was recognised belatedly by Johnny as an eye, as the elephant rolled on—and they found themselves swinging in the hammock of vines which alone had prevented them from being mashed out under its feet.

Then came a howl which ploughed into human entrails, draining them of all but fear : a howl that jagged itself with shrieks of a frightful despair, as the sky, and the treetops, and the fitful moonlight filled themselves slowly with the colour of blood.

II

A message had gone out from Kumassi—and disappeared in transit, like most messages—that unless the garrison was relieved by the 15th, it was lost.

On the 16th, a lot of entertainment was afford to the surrounding bush by the firing of star-shells and rockets, intended as a signal to the troops supposed (erroneously) to be concentrated at Ordahsu. Ashanti squatted on its haunches for a free firework display; only a sophisticated minority was qualified to point out that, as fireworks, it was a poor show: that the rockets did not bang and that the star-shells, after crawling a few feeble yards up the firmament, merely let out a discouraged fizz and dropped back to earth. The residues were picked up in various camps with yells of delight—wrongly interpreted by anxious listeners as terror. It is to be feared there was a great deal of wishful thinking in Kumassi, where the white occupants of the Fort were still gallantly giving each other dinner parties on diminishing stores, and games of whist helped to divert attention from indelicate rumbles rising from empty stomachs.

Ostensibly in strict secrecy, preparations were going forward for evacuation along the Patasi-Terrabum-N'Kwanta road. Thanks to the native traders—who were doing very well with matches at two shillings a box, a 2-pound tin of beef at £2 16*s*., a 7-pound tin of flour at £3, and a single biscuit, ten shillings—details of these were known to every bush scallywag between Kumassi and the Prah.

The few odd kings who had discovered that loyalty would procure them sanctuary in the Fort had begun to get flustered; old Opoku Mensa's death from perfectly natural causes, right back in May, was now recalled as an ill omen, and the reduction of rations for kings, Hausas and servants to a third of a pound of meat and half a biscuit a day was regarded as boding ill for the future. A few levies that the kings had been persuaded to send out on food raids had their skins warmed by neighbours who took a poor view of people who wanted the best of both worlds.

There was also the business of the box-god, which, at the beginning of the month, had suddenly withdrawn its favours from its subjects. Ejesu, which treated its spirits properly, not keeping them in boxes, to be liberated only by the turning of a handle, but doing them proud with rum, calico and an occasional goat or hen, wagged its head sagely over the failure of the gramophone. No more Rule Britannia inside the Fort—or anywhere on the Gold Coast, if spirits meant anything. A people that did not know how to treat its fetish was not fit to govern the well-behaved children of the bush.

Every bit of this news filtered down to Omo: which also knew all about the panic among the European miners in the Corporation goldfields; how many had bolted, and that the manager was a brave man, but that he badly needed supporters. And that Denkera, Bekwai, Swedru, Dengiasi, Mampon, Juabin and N'Koranza, having received rich presents, had contributed levies, and that farms in Ashanti, Adansi, Kokofu and other districts had been obliged to feed them. And exactly what spot Beddoes, and Burroughs, and Melliss, and various other scattered detachments had arrived at in the bush (such information, in fact, as had not got through to the Base), and all about Wilson's Nupes carrying his body from Dompoassi to Kwissa, and back again, thirty-three miles to Fumsu, before they found a burial place for it.

And, up at Kumassi, bananas at three shillings apiece, and three shillings for a couple of plantain leaves, tied round an infinitesimal portion of manioc dough.

All these things were known, and the time, to a split second, that the evacuating party, including the white women, left Kumassi in a thick white fog ; and the hot reception they got at Patasi, and Marshall's death, and Leggett's, and hosts of highly irrelevant matter which would, however, have held plenty of significance at Prahsu, or in the Bekwai garrison. It was very amusing at Omo, fully advised on all these matters, to hear of Burroughs rushing his troops to Bekwai, Wilkinson executing a flank movement by Obuassi, and the shambles at Kokofu, where a couple of companies became confused and fired into each other—all for the sake of getting the Governor, by now jogging comfortably down to meet his old friend Quashi N'Ketya of N'Kwanta, out of Kumassi !

There were also rich rumours of sums varying from fifty to a hundred pounds English being offered for messengers, although none of such being paid : the post of messenger being a notoriously unlucky one, owing to the amount of spirits, blood, ju-ju and other hazards, in addition to the Ashanti, scattered about the bush in war time. It was only the most avaricious who would undertake it, and they, in most instances, changed their minds, or had them changed for them, in some unpleasant fashion.

Chief Abuakwa pondered these matters seriously. Like several of the less war-minded chiefs whose villages were situated more or less out of the immediate war zone, he inclined to the opinion that the war was nearly over. The Governor having got away, there would surely not be much more fuss about Kumassi. The thorn in his flesh, as she had been to his predecessors, was old Ya Ashantua, at Ejesu.

Ya Ashantua had, early in proceedings, been chased out of her war camp at Abercoom. She had put up a hard-luck story, and, having given an undertaking to behave herself, had been allowed to retreat on her fetish town.

The war, so far as that part of the country was concerned, had degenerated, largely, into a series of neighbourly squabbles : the local Ashanti being themselves divided, some professing loyalty to their rulers, others holding that it would pay better to back the British. Ya Ashantua, albeit ca'ing canny, was like a pea on a red-hot griddle. Up and down, round and about she went, wearing out her carrier, the stink of the pipe clamped between her few remaining teeth like an oriflamme ; gibbering here, laying down the law there, rudely giving her opinion of war captains who groaned each time the familiar figure jogged into sight, its skinny legs dangling over the carrier's arms, its skinny arms throttling his neck, its face of an evil old monkey poked over his shoulder, so that it was as though a two-headed monster were approaching. Children squealed and fled before the coming of the Ashanti queen.

The imprisonment of the young king at Kokofu was too much for her ; she had long had her eye on Kokofu. She sent a message saying that she was depending on her old friend and ally Omo—a number of whose warriors had already flocked to her standard—for support in the consolidation of her power.

Abuakwa was in a cleft stick. As a newcomer, installed, not so much by the public will as by Morrissi, he knew his situation was precarious. And Ya Ashantua had brought forward a powerful argument in favour of her proposal. She professed to know the present hiding-place of the Omo Basin, which, in the débacle of the previous year, had mysteriously vanished. Given the Basin (of which Ya Ashantua actually knew no more than she did, since it was in the secret keeping of Morrissi, who felt it had been the cause of quite enough trouble already, and would be appreciated as a fern-holder by his old aunt at Much Wenlock) his authority over the people would be assured.

Abuakwa was very much put out about the war, in general. War, in his opinion, was for the increase of personal wealth and territory. He saw no point, either in bolstering up a bumptious neighbour, or in incurring that neighbour's ill-will on behalf of an external Power which had done nothing in particular for himself or for his district. He was extremely anxious to get all these tiresome levies, who were eating the village out of hearth and home, away from his immediate vicinity, and he was perturbed about the death of Cappi N'Ginti. It was extremely likely Cappi Bendi would die also ; he was down with the white man's sickness and there were strange reports about his conduct. How if he, Abuakwa, were held responsible for these things ?

Abuakwa sighed, and prepared to play the old historic game which, as any chief would tell you, is the only way to keep upsides with all parties : the game of running with the hare and hunting with the hounds. Cappi Bendi dead, and the levies melted back into the bush (where many had retired already), someone might start awkward inquiries. Someone might even come along and start the whole bothersome business all over again —there was nothing more pigheaded than a white man, when he wanted something. The obvious thing to do was to lie as low as possible ; give Cappi Bendi a good burial, and see that the news of his death did not leak out until there was no risk of disagreeable repercussion.

In pursuit of this policy, therefore, he sent for a squad of his most active young tree-climbers and despatched them into the bush, with instructions to cut down all the wires along which the British sent their messages. He also, as a sop to his warriors, gave them *carte blanche* to execute a small practice raid on an unimportant neighbouring village, whose chief and headmen had been removed owing to a divergence of opinion with Authority, which had elected, in that district, to stake its fortunes on British victory. The village was in a state of disorder and virtually undefended ; the raid would put the warriors in a good temper and have sound publicity value.

The warriors returned with the news that all was neatly accomplished, including the capture of a white man, who had taken it on himself to mend wires the boys had been cutting. They hoped, as a mark of approval, they would be allowed the white man's head.

Abuakwa hummed and hawed ; the situation was a delicate one. Authority took a poor view of the head custom . . . on the other hand, Authority was very busy indeed, elsewhere, and it was important to keep the warriors in a good humour. Well, just for this once, they could. Having anticipated the decision by several hours, the culprits returned suitable thanks. The head was on view the same evening, outside the fetish house. By next morning, a tale was round, that the head had been recognised, and there was a certain amount of fluster, which Abuakwa dealt with summarily. The alcohol was finished, and the stoppage of trade meant there would be no more gin and rum, except at extortionate prices, until the war was over ; but there was plenty of palm wine. Abuakwa ordered double rations of palm wine to be served out to the whole village. While Omo hiccuped its way into blissful oblivion, he sent word to Ya Ashantua that he was prepared for palaver.

To the noise of drums, the artless yowling of happy Omo and the smell of cooking meat, Captain Bendick prepared to render his soul up to God.

III

. . . Above all, there was the smell of burning, mercifully over-riding the rest. The fluttering in his knees and wrists, the overpowering nausea which had seized him, when they came on the aftermath of the raid, subsided gradually ; what helped most was, of course, Paget's air of irritable matter of fact. It was, he remembered, a soldier's business to take a scene like this for granted.

"Damn their silly eyes—now there's nobody left to direct us ! " he was mumbling, having completed a tour of the still smouldering village, whose fires, blended with the moonlight, gave them as much or more light than they needed. The earth round the huts was sodden—not with rain ; for the most part there was a deadly stillness, but now and again, in the shadows, there was a feeble movement, a crawl, a flap, the slither of something trying to drag itself deeper into sanctuary. Omo had done its work very thoroughly ; the residue—so much as was visible—reminded Johnny of some kind of ghastly picture puzzle : the kind of thing the boys used to cut out with their fretsaws and set their friends to piece together. Every now and then a long shudder ran through him ; he could not bring himself to follow Paget over charred, unrecognisable fragments, and over others, only too recognisable, either to sight or touch—that had once been human. The remains of the huts were piles of ash, soft, dusty, holding the heat like braziers : the two men could feel it through their boots. Here and there they kicked up a red heart of fire, and tried to trample it into the sodden ground.

" They ran a cordon round the village and then fired it. Come on, Flood ; this will be pretty damned unhealthy——" He broke off, as Johnny's hand closed on his arm.

" Listen."

The moon was now very low, but steady ; the clouds had dragged themselves away to the west, where they hung in turrets of blackness against the green of the sky ; it could not be much longer to dawn.

Outside the ruined stockade, across the clearing between it and the bush, two figures wavered, followed by a straggling carrier line.

" Now, who in blazes——? "

The thinner and more feeble of the two figures seemed to reel, and to support itself briefly by its sturdier, petticoated companion ; but their hands remained linked together, and they were presently heard to be singing. Something between a croak and a groan, that went before them, resolved itself, as they drew nearer, into a tune, into words, which Johnny recognised, with incredulity.

" Thou Whose Almighty Word
Chaos and darkness heard——"

" My God—it can't be—it can't——"

" Spirit of truth and love——"

" Oh, my God—my God : Cousin Charlotte——! "

" Wait a minute ; find some place for Hananiah to sit down."

Paget caught him in the act of falling.

" Hold on, sir ! " He lowered the fainting man to the ground.

" We've been walking nearly twenty-four hours. He'll be better when he's eaten." While they exchanged glances of horror, wondering what the bare mouthful which remained of their rations would do for two starving people, a gaunt travesty of the Charlotte Gummeridge he remembered stared with red-rimmed eyes across their shoulders, and her face was blasted with a smile. " ' For His mercy doth endure ! ' There's fire."

Fire, and food. At first Johnny and Paget held back : each ashamed and afraid of depriving the others.

" If you imagine my housekeeping isn't equal to a couple of visitors——! " grunted Charlotte, as she ladled stew into tin plates, delegated by mutual assent, to the " Visitors "—" Thanks ; Hananiah and I will share the pot ; we prefer it that way."

" Who is the famous old grenadier ? " Paget took an opportunity of whispering to Johnny.

" I told you : my Cousin Charlotte—Mrs. Gummeridge."

" You ain't pulling my leg, are you ? "

Johnny shook his head. They ate in silence, curiosity numbed by hunger and exhaustion. Charlotte was, characteristically, the first to recover. She scrambled to her feet, with a glance at the sky, just thinning towards dawn. The towering trees around them were reluctantly shedding their blackness, dragging themselves loose from the web of night ; the birds had started, there was a breathlessness of withheld rain in the air.

" While you others are digesting, I'll take a look round."

" Oh—er—Mrs. Gummeridge ! " This brought Paget hurriedly to his feet to face her. " I wouldn't—you know—if I were you ! An African village after a raid isn't exactly a place for ladies."

Her big, sullen mouth twitched into a smile as she looked up at him. " I'm a missionary, not a lady ; don't you know the difference, young man ? "

" I don't admit it," was the gallant rejoinder, which turned the smile to a scowl. Charlotte Gummeridge had no use for pretty speeches, or for young men who produced them in circumstances like the present.

" We're a good half-day off our track, and my husband's got to have a sleep before we start to push on," she growled at him.

" Push on—where ? Excuse me, ma'am, but "—embarrassed, he touched his uniform ; not, however, hoping it would carry much authority with Cousin Charlotte.

" To Prahsu, of course."

" . . . but that's days away ! " gasped Johnny.

" Days ? We'll be there, God willing, by this time the day after to-morrow." The expression on their faces softened her own, as she looked from one to the other. " I suppose you've been going in circles ? It's difficult, when there's no sun."

" But where have you come from ? "

" Diloli—up near the Ashanti-Omo border. The villagers ran away into the bush," she said casually, " but our own boys—the mission pupils —were very loyal." She glanced at them proudly. " There's been a lot of massacre round that district—not war, in the proper sense of the term, because our troops haven't got there : but the chiefs and head-men get drawn off to the war camps—and that means disorganisation—and internal squabbles for power——" She interrupted herself with a gesture of impatience ; plainly she was anxious to be gone.

" And you say you're going to Prahsu——? "

" I suppose we can make ourselves useful there, can't we ? " she snapped. " Then we saw the fire. We'd have been here sooner, if Hananiah would have made use of his hammock. Of course he wanted to spare the boys ; none of them are trained for carrying—it's been a hard trek for them to-day."

" And for you. Won't you take a rest, Mrs. Gummeridge—before you go on ? "

She gave him a look of stony displeasure.

" You don't suppose, young man, that we've come this long way out of our way to gape at a burned-out village ? " Turning her back on him, she beckoned to two of the mission boys, who clambered to their feet; Johnny saw the first-aid boxes strapped to their belts.

"I suppose I'd better go with her," muttered Paget. "Do you think she knows what she's in for——?"

"She knows; and I'm going myself," said Johnny grimly. "You'd better stick here, with Gummeridge. When he's had a sleep, you may get some information out of him. Diloli's not so far from Omo; he may know how things are going up that way."

The rain began again while they picked their way through the shambles of the village: even more ghastly in grey dawn than under the light of the moon. Moonlight dramatised, while daylight dragged away the last vestiges of drama, leaving only offensive statement. Already the hothouse moisture of the bush had brought up a fetor that hung like steam among the ruins. Refusing to accept his lead—he had hoped a little to spare her—she trudged ahead; sometimes summoning the boys, sometimes stooping to lift out of the way, with her bare hands, the unspeakable, which might conceal something with life in it. Shamed, sickened, praying his own body might not betray him, praying for some share of her fortitude, he stumbled after her. Suddenly she rose, triumphant, with the live body of an infant in her hands.

"That's the first!" She had not uttered before; but the look in her eyes, as she placed the little whining thing in his arms, was, to Johnny, like the look of God.

The sum of their finding, at last, was four babies, one of which died as they lifted it from the ash in which it was buried; a young woman, who seemed at first to be an idiot, and who had to be held, to prevent her running away; and a man so old that his wits had gone also, who had been protected by the heap of mutilated carcases which had been piled on top of him. There was no milk to give the babies, the raiders having killed or driven away the village herds. Charlotte sent one of the boys back to warm up a spoonful of the patent food she carried, apparently, for such emergencies as these, and sat down to minister, with Johnny helping her as well as he could. The rain, now, came down in lances, and soaked them to the skin.

No conversation, and only the briefest of comments, passed between them, while they did what was necessary. The native woman, having been fed and jolted back to her senses, such as they were, by a few astringent remarks from Cousin Charlotte—whose tone conveyed the purport in which her language failed—was given the babies to hold; now only two, for a third had yielded up its frail life on a gasping breath—and was hustled towards the shelter of the trees by the mission boys.

Johnny and Charlotte looked at each other: her face the colour of lead, where it was not black, skirt and petticoat in ribbons to the knee, a hank of reddish-grey hair hung over one shoulder in abandonment at odd variance with the primness of the bonnet perched above it; the thin black death's-head of his face covered in a five days' stubble that hid from her all of the dapper young man she remembered as her kinsman. The flesh and garments of each were blackened by the charred wood among which they had been moving.

" You're getting frightfully wet," he heard himself stammer idiotically.

She looked down at herself vaguely.

" It was the canoe. . . . Of course we oughtn't to have taken it; the river was too high. Hananiah swam well; very well indeed." It was as though she were dreaming.

He swallowed something in his throat.

" Cousin Charlotte: can you forgive me?"

She stared at him blankly—and seemed to come awake. In place of answer, she dropped her big hand heavily on his shoulder.

" What are you doing up here, Cousin John?"

" We're trying to get up to Omo." He accepted her change of subject without comment. Between two Floods, isolated by fate in a foreign country, there could be no enmity. " Bendick's in trouble, up there, with his levies; we're supposed to be"—he grimaced—" the relief."

" What—are you in the Army?" She seemed, for the first time, to take in the khaki.

" No; I should say, not officially. They sent me up with Paget, to do the talking. We've mucked it, so far." He gave her a brief outline of their wanderings since leaving Prahsu.

" It's easy enough from here," she told him. " You just keep on until you find the river, then follow up the main stream until you get there. It's a little more than a day's journey; that's all. We'd come back with you; but I've got to get Hananiah down to the coast, if I can. If God wills," she corrected herself. Her face was that of an old woman. " It was always Hananiah who did our planning," she added with unconscious pathos, " in the past."

" He's a very sick man, isn't he?" He pitied her.

She gave him a curious look.

" He's been sick a long time. That's why we left Charlestown. We ought to have put in for furlough, but we heard about the Diloli mission. We're very short of workers in this part of the field. He insisted——" She sighed and rubbed her hand over her brow in the way he remembered.

" What's right? What's wrong? Perhaps you were right, about Thomas. Hananiah never recovered from that. He kept on saying he had to atone. He's going to atone, by the look of things—with his life. You'll say, that's right——"

" Cousin Charlotte—I beg you——"

" All his work, all his sacrifices, all his devotion, don't count, for Hananiah, because of that one slip," she said accusingly. " I'm telling you, because you're against the missionaries. You think we care less for the human creature than for his relationship to Christ. . . .

" We've both got the same idea in our heads," she went on, a little confusedly. " You and me, I mean. We're both guilty people. We're both trying to work it out, in our own ways. I've read some of your *Diorama* stuff; I don't agree with all of it. I don't think you're fair to the Government; I don't like to think of those articles of yours being read by coloured people, up and down the Coast. But that's only my opinion. It doesn't count—any more than yours counts, about what *we* are trying to do. We offer them Jesus; you offer them railways and landing piers. Which, in the end, will mean most, to Africa?"

"Neither will mean a thing," he answered her, "unless Africa accepts it of her own free will. Don't you see, Cousin Charlotte? You've got to build up your human being, as a human being, before he's fit to decide whether or not he wants Jesus. All you people are doing, under present conditions, is force a new superstition on them. The whole teaching of Christianity is against the West African's theory of life, as it stands at present: a theory based on the survival of the fittest, on an eye for an eye and a tooth for a tooth, which obtains over nine-tenths of the country to-day. You've got to show them the *practical* value of civilisation, before you can ask them to accept our doctrine of mercy, of loving-kindness and love."

"You mean, you've got to make them feel it *pays*," was her bitter rejoinder.

Generations of Floods spoke in the reply.

"Why must a thing that 'pays' be discredited? You've missed our object; *my* object, I ought to say—because the people I work with don't see it quite from my point of view. I want West Africa to pay for the black people, as well as the white. I want things to be better on the Coast because until *we* can live here at our best, *they* can't benefit by our being here. Until we've shown them what it means—living according to our morality and our laws, what's the use of taking them a religion that's in direct opposition to the beliefs that govern them and their own society?"

Her eyes were narrowed, her mouth set, her hands clenched, as though to put up a physical resistance to his arguments.

"You'll never break down my sense of values, Cousin John!"

"I would never try," he said quietly. "One value, at least, we've got in common: that both white and black carry within them the seed which makes them equal in the sight of God. Most intelligent people accept that—in theory. In practice, it falls down, as a rule. Cousin Charlotte"—he hesitated—"you said just now I was against the missionaries. Will you forgive me if I say something? If you'd take your religious message to the white population, that's got some sort of traditional preparation for it, and confine your work among the natives to healing and helping, you'd be doing more for Christianity than you're doing in your churches to-day."

She opened her mouth, and closed it again. She said abruptly:

"We must get some rest, both of us," and turned on her heel. As they started back towards the others, she muttered, "You have a good heart, Cousin. It's a pity you haven't got more faith."

On a patch of ground higher and not so sodden as the rest they all slept. It was mid-morning when Charlotte roused them, but grey as dusk with rain and the overhanging darkness of the trees. The stench from the nearby village had grown appalling.

" We'd better be pushing on. The boys have got chop ready."

Over the meal, final instructions were exchanged. The Gummeridges were to take a full explanation to the Base of what had happened to Paget's expedition, the report of which Paget had hurriedly scribbled out on a leaf torn from his notebook. It was Hananiah who inquired whether they had any letters, which he could probably send down to the coast from Prahsu.

Paget said that, if they could wait, he would be very glad to scribble another line to his fiancée.

" What about you, brother ? " His hand in the breast pocket of his tattered coat, Hananiah turned gravely to Johnny.

He hesitated. On the envelope he had carried in his pocket since leaving Prahsu, there was no address ; he had not known how to direct it. An impulse came to him to destroy it. Then he changed his mind, pulled out a pencil and scribbled the one word, " Polly."

" If you'd send that—some time, with a covering note, to Joe—Joseph Prior, care of our firm in Bristol—I'd be grateful, sir." A feeling of curious finality swept over him, as he watched Hananiah push it into his pocket.

They ate, and then, led by Hananiah, the four of them, followed by the mission boys, prayed. The noise of the beating rain muffled Hananiah's weak voice ; water soaked into their knees and down the backs of their necks ; all had temperatures, all were numb and—save Hananiah—dumb with discomfort ; the babies wailed. Then they shook hands—not only with each other but with the boys.

It took them about an hour to reach the river, the hazards of the journey augmented by the trails of telegraph wire which, every now and then, was looped across their path. Along the bank of the river the going was fearful, much of the time up to the armpits in swamp. They were obliged frequently to rest ; Paget's arm, which Charlotte had lanced, and then bandaged for him, was in a sling and gave him hell ; he walked for hours on end to a smouldering accompaniment of oaths. They had given up all attempt to maintain conversation.

" Now which blasted way is it ? " The continuity of the swamps, the strain of getting through them, had forced them, at last, on to higher ground, away from the guiding thread of the river ; and again they were lost.

Johnny lifted an unsteady hand and pointed ahead.

" That way—where the chap's looking at us."

" What chap ? There's nobody," said Paget sharply.

" Yes, there is "—he broke into a stumbling run—" he knows—if we follow him—we'll be—all—right——"

It was afternoon on the following day when they reached Omo. He had hardly dared to recognise the lay-out of the land, as the swamps gradually receded and they found themselves on relatively dry ground. They stumbled from bush into clearing, two antic figures, covered in black slime from head to foot, vilely smelling. He heard Paget croak :

" I don't see signs of any levies "—and dragged himself to the stockade, before pitching headlong.

When he came to his senses, he was lying on a pallet of branches and skins in one of the huts. He wondered if it was the one he had occupied the last time. Only a faint, reddish glow redeemed the place from total darkness; he smelt the familiar scent of bush-light.

"Are you there, Paget?"

"Yes." After a pause, "Bendick's dead. And buried."

"What about the levies?"

"Cleared out."

"What did Bendick die of?"

"Fever, by the sound of things. He left a note." A short honk of mirthless laughter came out of the dark. "It was rather interesting. Poor old Bendy! A great man, but no hand at French."

"French!" It took a moment or two for the implication to penetrate Johnny's mind. He turned painfully towards Paget's voice to inquire: "What's French got to do with it?"

"I'll show it you in the morning. I think this is how it goes: 'Held the levies as long as possible. Reward Abuakwa for assistance and compensate for damage, rationing, etc.' Then poor old Bendy took his splash into French: 'Pas un mot de verité dans tout ça, ce chef est mauvais bête, ne lui donnez pas un sou, il fabrique quelquechose avec la vieille fille à E . . .'—I suppose that stands for Ejesu——"

"But what's he want to put it in French for?"

"Because, my dear old boy, this chief, who wears a Norfolk jacket over his petticoat, and is about the nastiest specimen I've met so far, speaks English—or the gibberish that passes for it on the Coast. He probably reads it as well. I suppose he was afraid to suppress the note. So here we are: and we've got to start over again with the levies—from zero."

CHAPTER EIGHT

I

Dear Uncle Hacky,

It is more than six weeks since I had any news from home, and I have, of course, no means of knowing whether you have received any of my letters. The last I sent down by runner was almost certainly lost, as we have had no word of any kind of his arrival at the Base. I shall therefore repeat what I put at the beginning of each of my letters, and you can leave the page out, if you have already seen it.

I know that you will be displeased with me for the action I have taken, and can only give you my word that, so far as the campaign is concerned, we know little less here than we did at the Base. With the troops scattered as they are, over an area so vast that it baffles description, and in present weather conditions, co-ordination is practically non-existent. If our news gets poor representation in the Press, I can assure you that ignorance, not indifference, is to blame. It was very soon borne in on me that I was of considerably less value as a newspaper man than as one more European with some slight experience of the country. I therefore (as I put in my earlier letters) took on the conduct of carrier lines, and later, on the Colonel's suggestion, accompanied Paget's relief expedition as a linguist. I would like to make it clear that this was much against my personal inclination, which was to stop at the Base and go out with the main relief column, as soon as it was ready ; but with the shocking shortage of officers and troops it becomes a matter of conscience to fill up any hole in organisation which occurs, and for which one is considered suitable.

We have now been up here nearly six weeks, on the most hopeless task that any man was ever set. On our arrival, we were told that Bendick and McGinty were dead, and the levies they had been sent to raise had scattered. So Paget and I had to start from scratch, and a nice job it has been !

The chief is a slippery party, who blows hot and cold—I imagine according to the news he gets from surrounding districts. (It would be amusing, if it were not galling, to find that these up-country tribes are much better informed on the campaign than we are ourselves.) One day he promises us a hundred men, the next day he has changed his mind, and tells us to apply to the king. There is, of course, no king of Omo, of which I was fortunately aware, the Stool having been abolished many years ago ; but there is evidently some person of whom this chief, Abuakwa, is very much in awe, and we have a pretty good suspicion who it is : the old Queen Mother at Ejesu. Abuakwa is agreeable, in rather a cheeky fashion, but makes it quite plain he does not want to be responsible, either for the raising or the maintenance of levies.

To cut a long story short, we have trekked for miles, interviewing kings, chiefs and headmen ; having to put up with every kind of sharp practice and impudence, and sorely handicapped for want of military support, and the pomp and circumstance the native expects of the British. When Paget tries (through me) to recruit the men direct, they say, " Ask our chief." When we see the chiefs, they say, " Ask the king." The kings say, " Ask the chiefs "—and so it goes on : like a grim kind of version of Hunt the Slipper.

The outcome of all this is some fifty gibbering nondescripts, that Paget is trying to drill into a bodyguard, having inherited from poor Bendick nothing but a solitary orderly, who, having had Army training, performs prodigies of valour, and is the only person in whom it is possible to place any confidence. When you find a good native, he *is* good ; but I have had plenty of cause to alter my opinion of " the noble savage," and of his superiority to the people along the Coast. The Omo tribe seems shockingly to have deteriorated, since the death of their former chief ; apart from the chief's bodyguard—an upstart, insolent lot—they are the most unpleasant samples of humanity it is possible to imagine : the majority of very low mental standard, barely removed from idiocy, and riddled with every sort of disease. Their habits are piggish and they are utterly untrustworthy, in every respect.

Paget's squad resists instruction in the most remarkable way ; they are lazy beyond belief and arrant cowards. The only way of inducing a martial frame of mind is to organise Hooray parties, and let them yell their heads off. I must admit that the caterwauling they set up, when encouraged by Paget, is of a most horrific nature, and would paralyse me, if I happened to be on the opposite side ! But if it comes to a real show, heaven help us. They are totally undisciplined and quite impossible to hold.

One of our minor trials is the intolerable cockiness of the natives, which we have learned to connect with a British reverse. It is mortifying beyond words to know they have access to information which is denied to us. Some busybody has chopped the telegraph wires to ribbons all over a ten-mile radius from our present situation ; I suppose the repair squads have their hands full, keeping the lines open between the Base, Bekwai and the various concentrations of Regular troops. From Paget's orderly I got an extraordinary story of a white man who appears—apparently from heaven—and " makes the wires speak." I can't get it out of my head this may be Kershaw ; it would be like him to go freelancing round the country, thumbing his nose at Administration and doing a particularly nasty job just for the sake of doing it. I wish he would turn up here. It is hellish, being dependent on runners, who ask the most extortionate prices—half of which they demand in advance, and are supposed to claim the remainder when they return, which they seldom do. Our specie, which we managed to recover from the place where we were obliged to bury it, on our way up, is rapidly melting away, and goodness knows what will happen when our funds are exhausted. The native traders are behaving very badly, and charge exorbitant sums for the mere necessities of life ; the maintenance of the levies alone presents a problem which grows more acute every day, as our only real hold on them is through their stomachs, and if rice gives out they will certainly bolt back to their various villages, leaving us high and dry.

Paget is bored and angry ; I most earnestly hope and pray we may not be called upon to take part in any action, which can only mean a holocaust. It is nearly a fortnight since we had any communication from the fighting areas. My opinion is that the war is probably over by now, and that we have been forgotten.

Harcourt laid down the thin sheets of paper with an oath. Slumped in his chair, his hands, with the square, finely tended nails, spread on the desk before him, he stared into vacuity. Sick with apprehension, he was also furious : furious with himself, as well as with Johnny ; furious, because he ought to have foreseen the outcome of allowing Johnny to go out to the Coast under present circumstances ; furious, because it was all his fault. . . . No ! Why should he blame himself?—he, who was also a victim : his plans shattered, his work thrown back, the whole impetus of his projects brought to a standstill, on account of a worthless slut of a Society girl, trailing ruin, as she trailed her muslin skirts, over all with whom she came in contact. Snake-woman !

Because of her, Johnny was rotting away in African jungle. Roan, resigned from his clubs, was, according to his last letter, existing in the South of France, on the fringe of that dubious society composed of those who, from one cause or another, are not quite acceptable by their peers at home. Fool, thrice-damned fool, at his age, to let himself be ruined by a woman. Woe to all Floods who came under the influence of women. Isobel, and her falsity. Venetia, whose extravagance and frivolity had, from the first, encouraged the worst in Roan. Selina—did Drummy know about her ? Even Harriet, by her contemptuous disloyalties, had, it seemed to Harcourt, in this bitter mood, contributed to the downfall of Floods. Hatred of all women rose in him like gall.

It was in this unpromising frame of mind that he received Derbin, when the latter shambled into his room.

" . . . and send Prior to me," he concluded his sharp dismissal of the trivia the old clerk laid before him.

" Yes, Mr. Harcourt."

" Well ? What are you waiting for ? Send him," said Harcourt, as the old man did not move.

" Mr. Harcourt . . ." The old hand went out towards the corner of the desk, and respectfully withdrew. " Excuse me, sir . . ."

" What is it ? " Outwardly impassive, he was roused, wary, on the defensive against some note in the other's voice.

" Prior is a good clerk. War has queer effects—sometimes—on young men. Shock . . ."

" Confound you, can't you speak out ? "

" I would not have mentioned it, sir, but that you are bound to notice it for yourself. I hope I do not presume, Mr. Harcourt : Prior is a *very* good clerk. But he is under the influence of drink."

After a silence :

" Is this the first time it has happened ? "

" No, sir, I am sorry to say."

" Why haven't you reported it ? "

No answer.

" You'd have done it, fast enough, if it had been one of the others, wouldn't you ? " sneered Harcourt.

The red-rimmed eyes met his ; still the old man did not reply.

" You—old—spy," whispered Harcourt.

Presently he rose and went to the opposite end of the room ; then, turning and lowering his head like a charging bull :

" There is no place in this business for a toper—whoever he may be. Send him to me."

. . . He heard the clumsy clack of the artificial leg ; the uneven step crossed the polished boards a little way, and halted. Harcourt turned with his hands in the pockets of his trousers ; his feet apart, his shoulders thrust up towards his ears increased the formidability of his stature. The youth before him lifted his eyes indifferently, and indifferently allowed them to fall again. Harcourt glowered disgustedly at the blotched face, the puffy eyelids, the dingy linen and uncombed hair ; they did not require the confirmation of the stale smell of beer Joe had brought into the room with him.

" What do you mean, by coming to business like that ? "

Sullenly silent, Joe stared at the floor-boards.

" You stink," muttered Harcourt. " You're drunk—aren't you ? "

" I was—last night "—defiantly.

" And how many more nights ? "

" I don't know. Five, perhaps—or six."

" You have the effrontery to admit it ? "

" You asked me." In the thrusting lower lip, the resentful eyes, Harcourt recognised himself, and sickened. The words, " You're dismissed," trembled on his lips ; he found himself unable for the moment to speak them.

" So that's how you squander your Army pay."

" I sent my pay to "—Joe looked up ; caught Harcourt's eye, read danger in it, and stammered—" away."

In the silence that followed, the kindly, blowsy ghost of Kitty Prior rose between Harcourt and Kitty's son. So the Yankee marriage had not turned out as she expected—that she took money from her son ! In the sourness of his mood, Harcourt drew an evil satisfaction from the conclusion.

" What do you think of yourself—hey ? What do you think of yourself ? "—for the sake of something to say, he mumbled lamely.

There being no possible answer to such a question, Joe returned to his contemplation of the polished oak at his feet.

"Throwing away your prospects: making a pig of yourself!" Harcourt let himself drop into the chair. What to say to the fellow—what to say? He stared resentfully at the scattered pages of the letter he had meant to tell Joe about—Joe, who often asked him for news of Johnny. "What the devil do you want to be such a fool for?"

Suddenly they rushed back to him—his reflections before Joe came into the room; his face grew purple as he smote the desk with his clenched fist.

"I know all about it—God damme, it's written all over you! Some damned woman business——! Get out of my sight—get out of my sight!" roared Harcourt, as Joe lifted his head, his dropping jaw and his face, which had gone the colour of ash, to meet the onslaught of the speaker's rage. In the transport of his fury, every vein in his body throbbing as though it might burst, Harcourt was hardly aware of the figure which, after an instant's stupefaction, dragged itself to the door.

It was some moments before he had sufficiently recovered himself to open the rest of his correspondence, and it was with a snort of impatience that he recognised the small, smug handwriting of his son-in-law from Liverpool.

> ". . . Owing to pressure of work, we have engaged two female typewriters. Although it is the first time females have been employed, the experiment is, so far, successful. The women, who are of sober character and responsible years, work behind a partition erected for that purpose at the far end of the main office."

He dragged a sheet of paper towards him and scrawled:

> "Typewriters to be dismissed, with week's pay. No females to be employed in future in any department."

and signed it, viciously: his declaration of eternal war against the poisonous sex. A petty form for such declaration to take; ashamed, yet stubborn, he threw it into the basket for outgoing mail, and opened the next envelope.

> "DEAR SIR,
>
> "In reference to your esteemed inquiry of the 12th ult. we enclose a list of Office Premises in the City District which we consider might meet the requirements of your Organisation, and shall be glad to arrange for access at any time named as convenient by you or your representative. Trusting that we may be of service to you,
>
> "We remain, Yr. obedt. servants,
>
> "MAYER, STRAUGHAN & HUGHES,
>
> "Land and Property Agents."

He let it fall from his hand. His organisation. What organisation was there, with its vital unit thousands of miles away?

Damn' nonsense, his mulish common sense returned, to this reflection. God help West Africa, if its future were dependent on a youth in his transient twenties! The organisation was *there*—in a mounting bank balance, in filing cabinets, in stacks of correspondence, in the accounts of a newspaper whose returns he studied each week—not wholly with satisfaction. Sales were rising—but not fast enough. There was a weak link, somewhere. Could it be in himself? His egoism took umbrage at the thought. But as he set his name to the reply the knowledge was with him, like a worm coiled in his innermost, that his pride disdained to acknowledge—that without that young faith, that young integrity, *without Johnny*, the thing, for him, was dead. He would go on—yes, by God!—in the face of all hell. West Africa and the West African trade must be made secure—for the sake of Great Britain; for the sake of Bristol. But it would be a machine, and not a man, that went fighting on—until Johnny came home again.

"I've got a bad bit of news for you, Hacky," said Samson Killick, over their lunch at the club. "I'm afraid we've lost Patcham's business. It's the way I said: Cruikshank's taken it to Runstable's."

Harcourt grunted. He had nothing to gain by pointing out that it was the fourth of their big customers they had lost in six months to the rival firm.

II

She had offered herself with confidence to the proprietor of the little millinery shop in an alley off St. Martin's Lane; her experience at Mercer's, although not among the hats, would surely stand her in good stead.

It took Polly little more than twenty-four hours to discover that her business was less to sell hats than to act as a decoy for masculine strollers who appeared to take a strange interest in a window ostensibly devoted to the display of millinery. She did not understand the strange business transacted, under cover of ribbons, veilings and plumes, at the far end of the dark little shop: although it seemed to her odd that gentlemen should come in, and give orders for hats for their lady friends, without bringing the lady friends to try them on. Instead, they wanted to see them on her; but it was not at Polly's head they looked, when she lifted her arms and obligingly posed, in one model after another.

Candidly enjoying her own reflection, Polly was willing to put on hats all day: much more interested in the set of an osprey or a bunch of violets against her crisp pompadour than in the spectators. She had never, outside of fashion plates, seen such hats before, and envied the occasional actress whose admirer brought her in, to purchase a "Madame Pearl" creation. "Madame Pearl," a red-haired Jewess, took small part in the selling; her rôle lay in the mysterious cabin behind the model stands, from which she would occasionally sally forth, to make a rush at Polly, or at one of the other sales girls, tilt a hat on one side, or pull it forward, and go back muttering to her den at the back of the shop.

"By Jove, a corker!"

"It's a love, isn't it?" Her hand to the sweep of ruby velvet under the upturned brim of the "love," Polly turned on the speaker her innocently stupid smile.

"Like me to buy it you, little girlie?" A sly hand caressed her ribs.

She felt as if someone had punched the breath out of her body; she turned crimson.

It was not the first offer she had had, of a "present" from the customers; others she had laughed aside, conscious of titters from the other girls, and of a sharp frown from Madame Pearl. The head saleswoman, who alone showed her a faintly contemptuous friendliness, had drawn her aside. "You'll be getting yourself into trouble if you don't look out." "What for?" The other sniffed disdainfully; Polly thought she might be pretty, if she left off the bright pink patches on her cheeks and the blue shadows on her eyelids. Still, they probably helped to show off the hats. "I don't suppose you're selling hats for a hobby, are you?" scornfully inquired the girl, as she swept away.

Polly was puzzled. A hobby? She was selling hats for a living. Not much of a living; Madame Pearl paid poor wages, and Polly often wondered how the girls managed to afford the new trinkets, the silk stockings, embroidered garters and smart new glacé shoes they were always displaying. Miss Connie, the head girl, had even turned up, one morning, with a little enamel watch, pinned to her bosom with a true lover's knot of what every one declared to be *real* turquoises! Were they all getting commissions—for which she, in her stupidity, had forgotten to stipulate? She resolved to find out.

But no one had ever touched her like that before. Glaring with rage, Polly dragged off the hat, flung it down, regardless of its fragility, and stalked into the back of the shop. She heard laughter behind her, and the shrill torrent of Madame Pearl's apologies to the customer. Burning with indignation, she did not care.

But during the scolding that followed, she had time to think of her lack of experience: of the difficulty, for a girl as ignorant as herself, in finding employment, and she gave in, although with misgivings, when she was ordered to take a box of models "on approval," to an address in Chandos Street.

". . . and I don't expect you to bring any of them back!" Madame Pearl threatened her, as Polly pushed her arms sulkily into her coat.

"Four—and the cheapest five guineas? I can't make people buy, if they don't want to spend all that money," she muttered.

"It's about time you knew your business, miss! If you've not learnt it, we'll find somebody who does, at the end of the week."

She climbed four dirty flights of stairs to ring a bell, and felt her heart miss a beat when the door was opened by a man in shirt sleeves, in whom she recognised her tormentor of the morning.

" Come along inside, little girl." A pair of indecent eyes revived her former disgust.

" I—I'm supposed to see Miss Vandeleur."

" That's right—Vivvie's waiting for you."

There was no means of avoiding the compulsion of a hand that went to the back of her waist. She was propelled into a dingy sitting-room, crowded with furniture : with standard lamps in pinked taffeta shades, with soiled cushions, with smoke-stained draperies, with the debris of untidy living. A stale stench of spirits, of Egyptian cigarettes, of patchouli contracted Polly's fastidious nostrils. She refused an invitation to sit down, clutching her boxes, watchful, on the defensive.

" Vivvie's in the bathroom ; she'll be here in a minute." His smile, meant to reassure her, increased her panic. " How about having the ta-tas ready to show her ? "

She fumbled with tapes and tissue paper. It chanced that the first to hand was the creation of the morning ; she gasped as she brought it out, and tried to hide it, but her companion was too quick.

" So you brought your favourite ? Cunning little girl ! Put it on. It's not Vivvie's style, but I'd like her to see it on you."

She obeyed, her eyes avoiding his, and avoiding the big, fly-spotted glass over the mantelpiece. She heard him draw in his breath.

" A tip-topper—by gad ! But take your coat off—it spoils it."

" Why—why bother, if M-Miss Vandeleur isn't likely to want it ? " she stammered—knowing he was right : that Miss Monk's clumsy, crêpe-trimmed collar must ruin the look of any kind of headdress. While she hesitated, she felt his hands softly drawing the collar away from the back of her neck, tried to jerk them off, and was caught from behind by the shoulders.

" Now what's the matter ? You mustn't be nervous, my dear ; that's not the way to sell hats ! " He was chuckling. She felt the coat being pressed down, over her upper arms, slipping into the crook of her elbows. " Wait a minute : something's caught——"

She leapt from him with a cry as the muslin collar band of her blouse and the buttons that fastened it between her shoulder-blades were ripped open.

" Stand still—you little simpleton ! Don't you know a hat like that wants a woman's neck and bosom to show it off—— ? "

She did not know how she managed to snatch herself away, or how she found herself outside the door in which his clumsy and belated lunge had failed to be in time to turn the key. She was on the stairs, sobbing, trying to cover herself decently—she had left the hats : would Madame Pearl get them back, or the money ? Would she set the police on her ?—plunging blindly from landing to landing, hearing the oaths of her pursuer—he was elderly and heavy, and hadn't his coat on : surely he would not dare to chase her into the street ?—then her heel caught on a step, and she was falling, rolling, bumping. . . .

" Now then ; what's going on here ? "

It was Polly's luck that the passer-by who had paused on the threshold was a policeman. Faint sounds of a withdrawal above suggested that the occupant of the fourth floor was not anxious to invite the attentions of the law. In her relief, Polly's face crumpled, and she let out a howl like a baby.

"What's all this about?"

"I—I stepped on my skirt. I think I've broken every bone in my body!" She realised, as the law ponderously produced its notebook, what a fool she had been to say that. "No, no, I was only joking. It's just my ankle—I'll be all right in a minute."

Bella was out, luckily, when she limped round to the side door in Boyce Street and dragged herself up the steep stairs to their apartment. She did not want to have to tell Bella about her adventure, feeling that to do so would be to invite the other's scorn (though concealed by kindness) for her naïveté. She had made such a big boast of being "able to look after herself," when Bella had expressed some misgivings of the neighbourhood in which she had found her employment! Her skirt was covered with dust—she felt ashamed to think she had walked through the streets, looking such a sight; the heel of her shoe was nearly dragged off, and one of her stockings was torn from shin to knee; she must hide these evidences before Bella's return.

She got into the bath—the water was tepid; it was only hot at week-ends—and sat there, examining her bruises and abrasions; wondering if the baby was all right. . . .

Presently she made herself a cup of tea, and settled, somewhat painfully, on the couch, to read until Bella came in. The Belloni household was not strong in literature; most of Bella's reading, and that of her mother, consisted of *The Stage* and *The Era*, an occasional sixpenny novelette, and the girls' twopennies Bella picked up from the paperman's stall at the closed entrance to Waterloo Station, under the bridge. Polly read *A Girl's Decision*, *Magda Lorrimer's Secret* and several instalments of a serial which Bella's fancy for making spills had robbed of its conclusion; yawned over *Six Suggestions for Decorating Your Dinner Table*—without, however, wondering how many of the readers of *Meta's Weekly* gave dinner parties; drew the dubious assurance from *What the Stars are Saying*, that Taurians would have a pleasant surprise, about the middle of the week, and financial benefit towards the end—a glance at the date of the paper, three months old, disposing of immediate hopes, and memory failing to supply any special advantages accruing in the week to which it referred. A rough map of the heavens, however, captured her attention, and, forgetting the monthly variation of the constellations, she sought eagerly for Taurus: Taurus, with its big red star, of which she had forgotten the name, which, in some mysterious fashion, linked her with Johnny, wherever, at this moment, he might be.

Because the paper was an old one, dated in April, she found Taurus easily, away towards the right-hand periphery of the circle: and that must be the great star, Aldebaran—she murmured its name aloud as she bent over the page, and liked the sound of it. Aldebaran ; a pretty word, a pretty name. Suppose she were to call her baby, conceived under that same star, Aldebaran ? No ; she relinquished it. It was not fair to give children—especially if they were boys—odd names ; it made the others laugh at them. And, anyway, the name could not be decided until Johnny came home. Still no word. . . .

Bella, who had had, except for a couple of odd dates, a fortnight " resting," came home in high feather.

" Got the week at English's, dear ! " she announced, as she spun herself through the door. " Saw old English himself—tried to get the top of the bill : what a hope ! He's putting me on second turn, so I can ' work another hall ' ! Oh yes, Bella Belloni can take her pick of the halls all over the West End ! Still—you never know your luck ; p'raps it'll be the brougham next week and a bottle of champagne after the rag's down," she gasped, tossing herself into a chair.

It seemed a good moment to take the bull by the horns.

" That's a good thing—as it's my turn to be out of a job."

" They've given you the sack, ducks ? " The sympathy in Bella's tone could not quite disguise her astonishment that Polly had ever managed to meet the exigent standards of a West-End firm.

" I walked out ; I didn't care for the customers."

Bella gave her a shrewd look. It was not her way to ask questions, or to pass comments, without invitation ; that was one of the good things about living with Bella. An impulse of gratitude made Polly spring up—not without a gasp—at the bruises she had forgotten—to give her a hug.

" I'm so glad about your good luck, Bella. I wish I'd got your talents and—and your experience." Before she could control them, the tears flooded into her eyes ; she rushed into the bedroom and slammed the door.

After supper, the girls went down to the Hero of Waterloo, where Bella proposed to celebrate her good fortune by standing treat. The night was warm and blue, and gilded by the street lights ; across the river Whistler was leaning on the wall of the Embankment with Walter Greaves at his elbow, thinking about one of his Nocturnes—not that Polly or Bella knew about that, or would have cared if they had known. They paused on the corner of Buckley Street, to watch the big coloured man who swallowed lighted matches, chewed up wine-glasses, ate coal and performed other digestive feats that brought him the coppers of fascinated bystanders ; and wandered on to the Hero of Waterloo, whose landlady, a friend of Bella's, made them welcome in her parlour behind the saloon bar, to which only the privileged were invited.

" Hallo, Jock "—" Hallo, Jim "—" Hallo, Harry." Bella's greetings displayed familiarity with the company. " My friend Miss Bowling," formally introduced, needed, apparently, no other sponsoring. The heat of the room, the " rounds " lavishly ordered by Bella's acquaintances, who would not hear of the girls paying their share, the patter of the piano, cheerfully commandeered by an individual in a check suit, exhilarated Polly, as her cheeks flushed with repeated glasses of port. Bella, her skirts gathered up in her hand, mincing along the narrow alley left by the chairs, was singing—*He takes me up in the Gallery.* An enraptured audience drew —*Sarah, Sarah, make up your mind, now do* from her as an encore, and applauded the wistful little tune to the echoes.

"Now, Miss Bowling—Miss Bowling; won't Miss Bowling oblige?"

"Oh, I couldn't——!"

"Go on, Polly: give them *Kiss my Bicycle,*" urged Bella, generously giving away her most successful number.

She had risen, but she shook her head; that was Bella's. Moreover, she wasn't sure of it; less sure than ever, with all these strangers looking on, and the floor roking slightly under her feet.

"I—I don't suppose you know *Walking in the Zoo,*" she stammered, to the accompanist.

"Don't you make any mistake, miss," came a roar from behind her. "Give him the key—Harry'll vamp to anything!"

"*The Stilton, sir, the cheese, the O.K. thing to do*——" would they know an old-fashioned thing like that?

"*On Sunday afternoon is to toddle in the Zoo.*"

An encouraging shout, and two elderly men and a good-natured looking woman sitting with them, swung into the verse:

> "'Week days may do for cads, but not for me and you,
> So dressed right down the road, we'll show you who is who!'

"Chorus, gentlemen!

> "'Walking in the Zoo,
> Yes, walking in the Zoo,
> The O.K. thing on Sunday is the walking in the Zoo!'"

Applause, laughter, Bella's delighted, unenvious face.

"Why, Polly, you've never done that before! You sly thing——!"

. . . Then, with the unaccountable swing of mood that takes place in such company, the atmosphere turned sentimental. A tall, lugubrious individual rose to his feet, to deliver, with immense lachrymosity, *When the Church Bells Chime.* A seafaring visitor was persuaded, without difficulty, to contribute *Rocked in the Cradle of the Deep.*

"I can sing again, if you like," volunteered Polly, bemazed, bemused by her own success, as much as by the port, which had, by now, gone well to her unaccustomed head. She bent to murmur to the accompanist. There was some shuffling among sheaves of music, produced from the interior of the piano stool; a ragged score was produced, and propped up on the stand. The first chords were played, and a hush fell upon the audience.

"Falling leaf and fading tree . . ."

"Christ!" One of the customers in the saloon bar turned to his companion. "Listen to that voice. . . . Here, a minute, Ma!" He beckoned to the landlady, who had reappeared behind the counter, after attending to her guests.

In answer to his gesture, she drew aside a curtain masking the little window from the parlour into the bar, and the two men looked through —at a tall, full-bosomed girl who, with her hands linked before her, the tears streaming down her face, and down those of her listeners, sang Tosti's *Good-bye* in a voice to break the heart.

It was evident that Polly and her audience were drunk ; equally evident that she had " got " them with that rare combination of vocal technique and genuine emotion that an audience, however unsophisticated, is quick to feel and to which it is prompt in producing its response. Of the two men in the bar, of whom both had had " sufficient," one had quickly recovered his sobriety. It was a long time since they had had a voice like that on " Poverty Junction."

" Oh no, I couldn't—possibly——! " Polly found herself giggling, and was checked by Bella's clutch on her arm.

" It's no good talking to her now," Bella was saying tersely. " Can't you see she's tipsy ? Ta-ta, Bill ; we'll see you in the morning."

III

" Mamma, I wish you would come up and speak to Miranda. Nobody can do anything with her."

" What do you mean ? " The raising of Harriet's fine eyebrows implied that, in her day, they did not speak of " not being able to do anything " with a girl just out of the schoolroom. " Surely, her mother——? "

" Selina is not at all well "—Vicky nervously evaded the question ; her mother gave her a curious look. How much did Victoria know, or not know, of Selina's unwellness ? Surely Vicky, although a spinster, had sufficient intelligence to recognise certain unmistakable symptoms ? " I'm afraid Miranda is seldom at her best with her. And this last escapade of hers——! "

" Of Selina's, or Miranda's ? " inquired Harriet coolly.

" Of Miranda's." Vicky caught her breath, remembering that she had been taught never to say " of course " to her mother. " Miranda has been very difficult for some time. We noticed it first, over Emily Temple."

" Yes ? " said Harriet, as her daughter paused.

" One of those exaggerated, schoolgirl friendships," said Vicky, who had heard of, but never experienced, such things. " Most unfortunate, of course—although no one could have foreseen the turn events would take——"

" Naturally not," was the nonchalant reply.

" Drummy put a stop to the correspondence, and Miranda appeared to think she had a grievance——"

" I must say I fail to see why Dromore found it necessary to interfere ; why not have allowed it to die out of its own accord ? I should not imagine Emily Temple had any desire to keep up communication with our family."

" No doubt Drummy felt he was acting for the best," said Vicky, with the prompt loyalty she brought to any aspersion on her favourite brother. A faint smile flickered on Harriet's lips ; it was always worth while dropping that bait, for the amusement of seeing Vicky rise. " And the next thing we found out was that she was meeting that Bowling girl secretly ! "

" That, at least, need cause no disturbance, need it ? I understand the Bowling girl has left home."

" Left home ! " Vicky's eyes rounded. " Run away from home—a somewhat different thing. With her poor mother hardly in her grave——"

" Well, I suppose that may have had something to do with it." Harriet moved impatiently ; she was always restive under village gossip.

" There is quite a different account in the village—and I always said Polly Bowling would come to a bad end ! " said Vicky viciously. " Their lease is up, by the way, and Drummy has decided not to renew it. I'm afraid he's thinking of selling some land——"

" We were talking about Miranda," her mother reminded her.

" Oh yes—Mamma, would you ever have expected Miranda to be so deceitful ? And that, I'm afraid, is not the worst. She has actually been carrying on a correspondence with a—a black man ! "

" *What ?* " This, at last, was startling.

" Boko—Bofo—that person Johnny brought here. She's been receiving letters, and posting them on the sly——"

" And how is it this has not been found out before ? " asked Harriet, when Vicky had completed her account of Miranda's delinquency.

" I'm afraid everyone has been too upset, to pay much attention to what Miranda was doing," admitted Vicky. " The shock of—of Roan, and Selina's delicate state of health, and—oh yes : our anxiety about Johnny, since Harcourt brought us the news of his really very thoughtless departure into the fighting zone—— ! " Harriet's face stiffened. " I've really felt it my duty," said Vicky, on a slightly defensive note, " to devote as much time as I could to Drummy ; to spare him as much as I could of effort and anxiety ; to try and rouse him from the sad state of melancholy into which he has fallen. Perhaps I've a little neglected Miranda—but little did I think—— ! "

" And what made you think ? " She spoke harshly, for she knew herself guilty ; Johnny's last words to her, " Keep an eye on Winkle for me, will you, Grandmamma ? " rose in her memory to reproach her. And she had always cared for the child ; only her selfish absorption in her own misery, the endless, gnawing apprehension for the grandson she loved, which robbed her nights of sleep and her body of its strength during the daylight hours, had drowned all else. The only one of them all she cared to be with was Harcourt, sensing, under his harsh common sense, a torment similar, although surely not equal, to her own.

" There were some loose boards under the carpet, in Miranda's bedroom ; we had to send for the carpenter. When they were lifted up, the letters were there—all tied up in bundles ! Miranda was out, so the housemaid, very properly, brought them to me." To the question in Harriet's eyes, she replied, " Oh, I must admit there was nothing objectionable in them ! Bofo—Boko—oh dear, I never remember his silly name—evidently knew better than to write anything improper. There were, as a matter of fact, only three letters from him ; the rest were from Johnny and Emily Temple. I was rather shocked, Mamma, to see, from one of his letters, that Johnny was aware of this correspondence, between his sister and—a Negro ! "

" You had better order the brougham," said Harriet, after a pause.

The house had a curious air of doom, she thought, as half an hour later, she and Vicky mounted the steps into the silent hall. Even Vicky appeared to feel it. She looked round her uneasily.

" How quiet it seems, doesn't it—since Dorset was married, and now Gilbert's gone to town : I suppose he'll be the next to get married—although I'm afraid that will upset Selina."

As they crossed towards the stairs, the door of the library opened, and the master of Guerdon came out into the hall. Dromore indeed had altered, and presented a sorry spectacle, even to the habitually unsympathetic eyes of his mother. " As usual, he is dramatising himself ! " thought Harriet, but felt a touch of pity for him, as she held up her cheek for his kiss. His broad frame was shrunken, his shoulders were consciously bowed, as though, like Atlas, they assumed the support of the world. It was a jaded version of the Prince Consort that Dromore presented ; as though aware of it, he turned his eyes towards the consolation of Vicky's understanding face, even while kissing his mother.

Harriet braced herself. Really, it was ridiculous, the way they insisted on turning Guerdon into a house of mourning, simply because Roan had made a fool, and admittedly, a villain of himself, by running away with Emily Temple ! Ridiculous, and, in the final analysis, degrading.

" I've come to see Miranda," she said briskly.

Dromore's large, grey face could hardly turn greyer ; but he raised one hand, and dropped it, as though Miranda's name deprived him of the little strength he had in reserve for the answering of comments. He took a few wavering steps back towards the library, turning in the doorway, hollowly to address his sister.

" When you have taken Mamma upstairs, Victoria, I should be obliged if you would join me in the library."

" Of course, Drummy," answered Vicky, with that tenderness in her voice that no one evoked except her eldest brother. Harriet was obliged to bend her head ; they had had nearly three months of it—and how they were enjoying it !

" Is she in her bedroom ? " she inquired, thinking of the torn-up flooring, as they reached the gallery.

" Oh yes, the men had finished by lunch-time "—Vicky spoke vaguely, her thoughts, as her mother realised, with Dromore.

The long gallery, flooded with light from its western windows, spread before them its vista of the magnificence created by Matt, and added to by his son, the second Hercules. Harriet's lips twisted slightly, as she gazed down the tunnel of brocade and gilt, crowded, like Westminster Abbey, with inferior statuary ; she remembered bursting out laughing when she was brought to it, as a young bride, and the poor view Hercules, whose mind—it was, after all, his wedding night—was on other matters, took of her amusement ; so poor a view that she had never dared, as she had at the moment intended, to try and persuade him to part with some of those preposterously modest, Canovan atrocities, to which she much preferred Matt's savager taste, as displayed on the upper panels.

Curiosity prompted her to lay her hand on one of the carven doors leading to the "state apartments."

"It seems a long time since I looked in here."

Vicky opened it for her.

"I'm afraid it's all in curling pins. Drummy has not the heart, these days, to do much entertaining."

"Nor is likely to do much in the future." Harriet withheld the words out of compassion for Vicky, who probably knew as much as she did of Guerdon's prospects, under the new regime of economy which, so Harcourt had informed her, he was enforcing. She stepped forward into the vast drawing-room, which, with its curtains drawn, its carpets rolled, its furniture covered with dust-sheets and its immense lustres in muslin bags, looked more like a showroom in a deserted museum than a room dedicated to social gaiety. She took a few more steps across the parquet and, on an impulse, dropped a curtsey ; turning to see her daughter staring at her in astonishment.

"Mamma——?" faltered Vicky, on a note, almost, of alarm.

"I just felt it was—suitable." No need to explain to Vicky that her salute was to the ghosts of the old ladies Centlivre, hovering in the shadows—biding their time. Harriet gave a little nod as she walked out through the door. Perhaps you'll not have so long to wait, after all. . . .

"Miranda."

The figure lying face downwards on the bed took no notice. On the bedpost, the little hawk quivered beneath its hood.

"Miranda, here is your Grandmamma."

"You had better go down to the library," said Harriet, after a brief contemplation of the motionless figure.

She waited until the door was closed, then crossed the room, and sat lightly on the edge of the bed. Still Miranda did not move ; and Harriet did not touch her, for she had an immense respect for genuine grief ; for its pride, its decency, its utter rejection of trivial consolations. She could guess from Vicky's bald recital, a little of it : imagine how a nature, driven in on itself by physical defects, deprived through physical weakness of normal development, fastened with a passion out of all rational proportion upon the objects of its few loves. Emily was one, Johnny another ; possibly Polly Bowling, who had been her childish playmate, was another ; if so, no one would ever know it from Miranda. And Osei Bofo—what loneliness of heart had ever driven the child to so unlikely a confidant?

A deep compunction, filling Harriet's heart, made her lay her hand, without speaking, on Miranda's ankle. The thinness and sharpness of the bone made her look down quickly. Suddenly she made her decision. This girl, this little sister whom Johnny loved, to whom so many of his anxious thoughts were dedicated ; this feeble plant, all but crushed out among a rank growth against which Harriet knew what it was to struggle . . . by heaven ! It was time to put a stop to it.

" Miranda." Because her heart was melted within her, Harriet's voice was curt. " All this is very foolish, and we have now got to behave ourselves."

" What do you mean by ' all this ' ? " A voice came, after a long silence, out of the pillow.

" I can't possibly talk to the back of your head," said Harriet practically. " Would you like me to help you to turn over ? "

" I can help myself," muttered Miranda, after another pause. Harriet averted her eyes from the too-evident struggle. When she looked up again, Miranda was lying on her back ; there seemed to be nothing of her face but a pair of empty eyes.

" What have *you* come to take away from me ? " the eyes asked. Harriet's looked at them steadily.

" You are no longer a little girl. You are old enough to be told anything you like to ask."

" I don't want to ask anything—thank you," added Miranda, as an afterthought.

Harriet tried again.

" I feel it is time I had a change. I have been thinking of going to London."

" London—in August ? "

A glint of approval came into Harriet's eyes ; it pleased her, that her granddaughter should be aware of the incongruity of the suggestion.

" It was more unlike Guerdon than any place I could think of," she confessed ; a smile twitched the corner of her mouth. " Unless one considered going abroad ; and I've begun to feel a little too old for that."

Miranda stared at her grandmother for a moment ; then stretched her arm above her head and lifted her hawk down. The glove, as usual, was on her left hand. As she stroked the bird's flags to calm its fluttering, looking across its small blind head at Harriet, the implication was complete : *You too !* Well, I suppose you won't take this ? .

" Can you suggest any other place ? " inquired Harriet.

Miranda shrugged her shoulders, as to say the choice did not concern her.

" Then I think it shall be London ; after all, it is nearly September, and I shall need some time to get ready ; I have got out of the way of travelling, in the last few years. I want you to come with me," said Harriet, casually.

" . . . Me ? "

" I said you were no longer a little girl ; and you are quite old enough to be an agreeable companion. It wouldn't amuse me at all, to go away alone, with a maid."

" But . . . but I can't leave my hawk. I'm all he's got," she stammered.

" I don't quite know how one deals with a hawk in London," said Harriet, after reflection. " But I don't doubt something can be arranged. I wouldn't allow it to most people, child, but I find I'm—lonely. That's between you and me." She got up briskly from the bed.

Miranda's cry followed her to the door.

" Oh, Grandmamma, don't go—please ! See—I'm putting him down : I want to kiss you ! "

Presently the two stood hand in hand : each in her own fashion had recovered her self-possession, her thin armour of self-defence : and each was aware of the weak spot in the other's, as well as in her own.

" So we'll go to London," said Harriet, gruffly for her, " and that, I think, will be a great deal more sensible than stopping here, worrying ourselves sick over Johnny."

" Oh—you too——" she gasped.

" What do you suppose ? " snapped Harriet.

Miranda's hand tightened in hers.

" It does make a difference—to know there are two of us——! " She gave a quick, nervous smile. " Johnny'd like to know, wouldn't he ? "

" Johnny shall know," said Harriet, after a pause.

CHAPTER NINE

I

" KEEP to the straight numbers ; you don't know enough, yet, to put ' character ' over. It's a bit too like a swarry at the parish hall," Bella had advised her, with the candour of good will.

" But I can't make them laugh, with the straight stuff ! "

" Never mind about making 'em laugh. What you'll sell yourself on for the present, ducks, is your voice and the way you look. Go slow on the laughs. There's laughs *and* laughs," said Bella dryly. " You'll look well if they give you the One, Two, Three ! "

So when, in a stuffy little room full of tobacco smoke, Polly gave her first audition, in front of three men who eyed her, as she afterwards said, as though she were a doubtful piece of meat, and with sweat running into the palms of her tightly clenched hands, she remembered Bella's advice. She did not attempt to be " funny," but concentrated on producing her voice to its best advantage and speaking her words distinctly—a point whose importance Bella had impressed on her. " Concert artists may be able to get away with the blarble-arble-arble stuff," she had warned. " But no halls audience will stand for it."

And the outcome was her first date—for a little hall she had never heard of (although she knew, by now, most of the reputable names) in Camberwell. The offer was couched in no flattering terms by a stout person who barely looked at her, shrugged his shoulders, said it was a gamble, but you never knew what " they'd " fancy next ; anyhow, he supposed *his* hall could stand it for a night, the money was ten bob, and—as an afterthought—she'd do her turn in one.

(" Told me I could do my turn in one—sauce ! ' Christ,' I said to him, ' is that all ? ' " Snatches of conversation between Bella and her friends came back. . . .)

She drew herself up, the discovery that she was at least an inch taller than the person who, in so unmistakable a fashion, down-rated her abilities, lending her assurance.

" Christ," said Polly, in her rich, good-humoured voice, " is that all ? "

A guffaw broke simultaneously from the three men. One, with a cigar between the first two fingers of a not immaculate hand, tapped her on the shoulder with the other fingers and winked.

" You'll do, dear. You won't get a band rehearsal—see ?—because it's only a fill-in. Think you can manage ? "

Polly gasped ; she had forgotten the band.

" Oh, yes, I'll manage," she gulped.

" You'd better," was the grim rejoinder. " All right ; you've got plenty of noise to give 'em ; give it—all of it—see ? Our audiences don't want all those finiky ' pianos ' and ' dimins ' you seem to be so fond of. And—here, Miss What's-Yer-Name-On-The-Bills : make yourself look nice—eh ? The customers want something to look at, as well as something to hear."

This nearly finished her. Her new acquaintance, gained under Bella's ciceroneship, with the halls had shown her that there was nothing in her wardrobe which by any stretch of the imagination could, from a music-hall manager's point of view, be described as " nice." Nor, generous as Bella would certainly be, in offering her own garments, would anything of Bella's meet across her chest or round her waist. She set her teeth, however, nodded her head, and fled back to the Waterloo Road with the new problem.

" I'll tell you what "—the ever-resourceful Bella was prompt with a suggestion—" I bet my Old Dutch has got something that will do. Let's open that old basket of hers ; we've got to rig you up somehow."

Presently Bella was panting :

" Go on, push down your chemise and get all those tapes and shoulder-straps out of sight."

" But—Bella—I can't show all that ! "

" Don't be soppy ; a singer's got to wear evening dress."

" Perhaps it will come up a little bit higher, when we alter the hooks," she murmured—aghast, yet fascinated, by her reflection in Bella's glass .

Never before had the pink-pearl gleam of her flesh been revealed as in Marie Belloni's gown ; it was a Carl Druschki rose bursting out of a holder of bright blue satin ! The boning of the sleeveless bodice gave her more bust and waist than she had ever known she possessed ; the skirt, springing over her hips and flowing like the inverted blossom of an immense morning glory about her feet, was heavy with its incrustations of silver passementerie and diamanté, its ruffled taffeta lining ; a cascade of silver "dewdrop" tulle descended from the proud shelf of her young bosom, accentuating its fullness, and was caught on the left side by a five-inch sunburst of theatrical paste. Bella had thrown three ropes of "pearls" round her neck, and was now rummaging in the basket.

"You ought to have a hat."

"A hat, with evening dress?"

"Here we are!" Triumphantly she fished a battered skeleton of chiffon and wire out of the depths. "Looks a bit rocky, but we'll soon do it up with flowers. Things look all right across the floats—even when they're practically rags," Bella assured her. There were plenty of "rags" about the blue satin gown, but the effect was dazzling ; overwhelmed by her own magnificence, Polly could hardly tear her eyes from the glass. "Now get that off," chided Bella. "You know we've got none too much time, and there's all the hooks to be altered and mend that tear in the lining ; you don't want to get your foot in it as you're going off, and take a header into the big drum!"

All through the afternoon they worked feverishly with their needles. Polly's eyes kept going to the clock ; she had now begun to feel very much as though she were marching towards the guillotine ; she kept nervously clearing her throat.

"Don't do that!" snapped Bella. "You'll be as hoarse as an old crow. Here—suck a piece of toffee."

At seven Bella started to make her up—a fresh shock for Polly, in the discovery that she had got to go through the streets with paint on her face. But Bella had to get down to Bermondsey ; she lingered as long as she dared, then had to rush, leaving Polly half-stunned, feeling as though she were waiting for her death sentence. At a quarter to ten, sweating from every pore, Bella's masterpiece in Leichner and ricepowder already in ruins, for she dared not retouch it, she stood in the wings, waiting for her entrance. She was quite numb, by now—and thankful for it : not knowing that numbness is the most dangerous mood in which an artist can face an audience. All she wanted was to get it over. . . .

They had given her a ticklish spot on the programme—between the last of the comics and the acrobats ; half of the audience had collected its hats, and were half-risen in their seats, when the chairman announced, "In the regretted but unavoidable absence of our old friend Billy Mackintosh, Miss Polly Bowling has consented to oblige. Miss—Polly—Bowling!"

The new name caught the fancy of a few, and checked departure : it sounded like a female comic. But there was a mere patter of perfunctory applause, and she was well into the first verse of her song before those who had not wandered too far from their seats dropped into them again, deciding they might as well have their money's worth.

It was odd, on Friday morning, to find herself on Poverty Junction with Bella—who, with her present and another week fixed, had no need to be there, but had staunchly rallied to the support of her friend. Even though nothing came of it, there was a thrill in being a " pro," in treading that famous pavement in her own right. She had so often been there with Bella that she had picked up several acquaintances ; they came up, with the generosity of their kind, to congratulate her, to wish her good luck ; they had heard, it appeared, that she had " knocked 'em in Camberwell." Aware that she had not " knocked 'em," Polly remembered Bella's cautions against undue humility. " Don't you make any mistake, dear : the world rates you as you rate yourself—especially in the profession. Tell 'em you've been booked for a return date in October ; I don't mind betting you'll get one. His Jills'll keep his eye on you, now you've broken the ice."

Despite the crack she had made in it, Polly found the ice held remarkably well—for nearly a fortnight. She began to get frightened, for her money was nearly done, and she detested the prospect of being dependent on Bella's generosity. Then she began to pick up an odd date here and there. Still set on comedy numbers, she worked hard, with Bella's help, over her old stand-by, *Walking in the Zoo*, and one or two others, and added *Soldiers of the Queen*, which practically every artiste had in her repertory, in deference to patriotic feeling. All this time she never had her name on a bill—even among the wines and spirits—because she was usually rushed in to fill the gap left by the defection of some other artist.

But the most she earned in a week was a pound, of which Bella refused to take a penny, saying she would need all she could get, for expenses, and could pay back, if she liked, as soon as she got a genuine engagement—until the beginning of September : when, out of heaven, so it seemed, came an offer of a week at the Kilburn Empire. The prospect of receiving, on Saturday morning, eight golden sovereigns was enough for Polly ; it was Bella who pointed out the true significance of this engagement : that Polly had got herself, for the first time, on to one of the big booking circuits, and that she might now look forward with something like confidence, to other dates, both in London and in the provinces. " You might even find yourself working Bristol Hippodrome. You've got further in these few weeks than I got in my first four years," declared Bella, with pride so far removed from jealousy that Polly, who had paled at her previous suggestion, flung her arms round her neck.

" I wouldn't have—without you to help me."

" Poops. Now, I tell you what you've got to do ; you must have some postcards, to leave with the agents and send people that ask for your autograph."

" Christ—who's going to do that ? " gaped Polly.

" Plenty of people—before you've done. And shut up Christing around," virtuously said Bella, whose own vocabulary was invariably coloured by the light-hearted blasphemy of her professional surroundings. " You've just picked it up like a poll-parrot, and it doesn't suit your type."

When the photographs came, Polly was torn between gratification and doubt.

"They've thinned down the fat part of my neck and given me more nose!"

"It's all right, they're good publicity," decided Bella, and smote the breath from Polly by advancing the money for six dozen. "It's cheaper to buy in quantity; these will last quite a time—until you can afford some better."

"I should think they'll last the rest of my life," giggled Polly. She had been smitten by a sudden inspiration. It was dangerous—but she found it irresistible. After Bella had gone out, she seized one of the postcards, wrote across its right-hand corner, in the fashionable slanting style set by Marie Lloyd, Vesta Tilley and their rivals, "With love from Polly," added the words "Kilburn Empire," and the date when she would be working there, on the reverse side, slipped it into an envelope and addressed it to Mr. Joseph Prior, 6 Ship Lane, Bristol.

II

When the runner came in, they had been drilling the levies for eleven hours. "Drilling" was a name for it. It was Johnny who, when Paget had gone into blinding, swearing hysteria at the end of three weeks' attempt to drive into the mahogany heads of the guileless children of the bush the elements of their duty as a protective army, suggested that the only thing to do was make a kindergarten game of it.

"Drill" was trotting round the so-called parade ground, shuffling to a standstill at "Halt" and starting erratically forward at "March." It was scuffling doubtfully a few paces forward and a few paces back, on "Right turn" and repeating the process on "Left turn," varied by a mild version of the Rugby scrum and a lot of giggling. "Fall in single file" was a game of twos and threes, "At the double" an invitation to the majority to squat comfortably on their heels and watch, with obliging grins, the agreeable spectacle of two white men, with fists clenched and elbows bent, sprinting hopefully round the clearing, on the off-chance that somebody would take it into his head to imitate them. Nobody was so silly. Even a bushman knows that nobody in his right mind runs round and round, after nothing in particular, in a temperature like a steam bath.

"Fire," on the other hand, was a riotous success; it involved firing off from the hip (for no right-minded native gets in the way of the recoil from his gun) a museum collection of shooting pieces obligingly supplied (for about three times cash value) by a local trader: accompanied by wild yells, a lot of anticking about and screams from members of the party who—as invariably happened—got scorched by the powder. Yes, "Fire" was a winner. Johnny suggested keeping it for a treat at the end of other manœuvres. "Good drill—Fire. Bad drill—no Fire," he solemnly tried informing the levies; who thereupon went into sulks and started picking lice out of each other's hair.

It was Johnny's idea to split the levies into two companies, led by Paget and himself respectively, to storm and to hold an improvised stockade. This successfully disposed of any theories he might formerly have held about the toughness of the savage. Somebody always stubbed his toe, and retired, whimpering ; a private feud developed between two friends, one of whom had, carelessly, walloped the other in the eye with the butt of his hunting spear, and the action was held up, while the rest gathered round to watch the two settle the matter, usually with fisticuffs and a peculiarly nasty upward jab with the knee, that gave Johnny a jolt in the pit of the stomach each time he saw it used. By this time, both he and Paget had begun to grasp the distinction between raw bush native, who is a hunter, but not a natural fighter, and the in-bred, highly-trained members of the fighting forces.

Then there was the ambush game : played in a patch of bush close to the village. The levies knew a great deal more about ambush than either Johnny or Paget, and let it be seen that they considered the latter's ideas childish. They were going to conduct ambush on their own lines, not on the white men's, if occasion arose. There was no objection to that, as Johnny pointed out to Paget ; the more use one could make of the natural ability of the native, the better. Unfortunately, ability was at par. The only design which became apparent, as training proceeded, was the levies' intention, at any price, of saving their own skins ; on this point they were crystal-clear.

All this to-do of co-ordinated movement, of left and right, of leaping to attention at a command, was just white men's eccentricity. The levies were tolerant, but uninterested. They continued to drill—sometimes under the lofty regard of Abuakwa's warriors : with whom they exchanged grins, bursts of laughter, and occasionally rude remarks, when the white men's efforts proved more than usually ineffectual.

Paget had tried to get the co-operation of Abuakwa and some of his captains in the matter of disciplining the irregular troops. Abuakwa called a meeting of the captains, made Paget, through Johnny, explain just what he wanted of them, nodded his head gravely, and promised, on behalf of his warriors, whatever aid was wanted.

When, however, it came to redeeming the promises, there was always a hitch. The captains were in conference, or the head captain (too magnificent a person to concern himself with levies) had sent them on a reconnoitring expedition, or it was a special fetish day and all the army had to stand by for ritual dances. It was plain, at last, that Abuakwa had not the smallest intention of associating himself with the levies—apart from collecting the money for their rationing and demanding from time to time additional sums in compensation for damage said to have been done by them. These demands, which grew more frequent as it dawned on the inhabitants of Omo that anything lost, stolen or destroyed might be put down to the levies, and replaced free of charge, wasted much time and were usually productive of acrimony on both sides. Paget eventually hit on the expedient of suggesting that a record be kept, and presented, on the departure of the irregulars, when he would examine it and make settlement in agreement with his findings. This arrangement Abuakwa was induced, on payment of a considerable *douceur*, to accept ; he was, himself, rather tired of haggling over a cooking-pot, somebody's favourite calabash, the screen of fish some too-trusting individual had left behind his hut to dry. He agreed that a lump sum would be more acceptable—and leave him more profit, after settling these trivial claims. The atmosphere, although strained, was not actively antagonistic, and, apart from coming and lolling uninvited in Johnny's or Paget's huts, fingering their belongings and either asking for point-blank or annexing anything that took his fancy, Abuakwa had ceased, latterly, to make himself a nuisance.

This, then, was the position on the morning that they were taking advantage of the first spell without rain for weeks, to give the levies what Paget called a good grilling, when a figure in a loincloth and nothing else but its hunting knife dipped through the tie-tie immediately behind where Johnny was standing, and made signs for attention.

" Halt ! " bawled Paget ; adding, " Stand at ease," merely as a matter of form, as the levies never did anything else. His eyes, and Johnny's, were bolting out of their heads, for, since they brought the levies back to Omo, and settled down to the training, no communication whatever from the outer world had reached them, although they had several times dispatched messages—without knowing, however, whether they ever reached their destination.

Both were close to the end of their tether, immensely reduced by want of European food. Although some of the chop boxes they had had to abandon were recovered (this was one of the few concessions Abuakwa had made—for a consideration—to their convenience) and Paget had gone back, in a hammock, with the carriers, to look for and exhume the buried specie, their supplies had been exhausted for several weeks, and their stomachs were ravaged with manioc flour, with half-raw meat—cooked in the casual Omo fashion of wrapping it in plantain leaves and leaving it to look after itself under a heap of ashes—and with river fish. The meat was invariably fly-blown, and not unseldom maggoty. Eggs, for some reason, were always bad ; it was Paget who produced the interesting theory that the Omo egg, even warm from the layer's body, was charged with sulphuretted hydrogen generated by the age of the bird that produced it.

Unripe plantains afflicted them both with attacks of dysentery, and rice filled their bellies and intestines with wind. But for such game as they managed to shoot—both were so weak by now that their marksmanship had deteriorated—they must have starved ; edible flesh, for some reason, was rare round Omo—or was combed out for the use of the chief, his household and those of the heads of the village. Monkey they could neither of them bring themselves to eat ; it was too like cannibalism. And local fish was so rank in flavour—brought on, moreover, such torments of thirst—that they could eat it only in very small quantity. For drinking they were reduced to palm wine—although among Bendick's leavings (much of which had been looted before their arrival) they had discovered the remains of a case of claret. The heat had fermented it and all save one of the bottles had burst. They had saved the residue—half vinegar, half yeast—for what it represented, and solemnly drank the Queen's health in about a thimbleful apiece each night at sundown.

Johnny had held to the hope for some time that they might be able to get a message to Charlestown ; then realised that, apart from the fact that Morris was not there, having been called up on the Staff of the Base Commandant, and that his substitute, though doubtless a man of good will, would know little of the district or the people, Charlestown, since the beginning of the rains, was isolated by its swamps ; that, although relatively close as the crow flew, it was in all probability no more accessible than Prahsu itself—besides the unlikelihood of its carrying any organisation for the collection or dispatch of military supplies. He wondered, often, what his friends were doing : guessing that most of them would have left, to offer their services at British Headquarters.

Paget's big, finely-conditioned body was down to a rail—although its innate healthiness had, in time, triumphed over the poisoned arm, which Bendick's orderly had cleaned and fomented with some of the mysterious herbal eluctuaries of the bush. He was more disturbed about Johnny, whom sometimes, while pretending to sleep, he watched—hitching himself about the hut like a little, very old, very sick monkey, very cunning in disguising its feebleness. They had both had spells of fever—Paget's the heavier of the two—but Johnny's were more disquieting, and unlike anything Paget had ever seen. In his bouts of delirium Johnny would get up, dance and gibber, go out in the bush (if he were not prevented) and come back, talking with a gravity so complete that it was difficult to realise he did not know what he was saying, about " blood." Once he declared, with perfect seriousness, that he had seen " spirits," one of whom had told him Abuakwa was not to be trusted. As the fact was self-evident, Paget shrugged it aside. And he was always mentioning a " face."

But all their tribulations were forgotten, as they flung themselves at the runner, who, unrolling his loincloth, produced a packet which Paget snatched from his hand.

" Oh my God ! " There was something like a sob in his voice. " Letters—— ! "

He tossed a handful to Johnny, who found himself peering incredulously —his sight had grown very bad ; continuous bites along the lids had permanently inflamed them, and set up an infection in both eyeballs that kept him rubbing them—at the handwriting of Harriet, of Harcourt, of Miranda, of his father, of Dorset. He stood clutching them, not quite able to make himself believe in them ; feeling that they made, each of them, some kind of demand on him ; not quite sure of himself, or of them ; feeling his brain strain, as it strains from a nightmare towards intimation of reality ; wondering, presently, if he would be able to see to read them, or whether he would have to ask Paget. . . .

" Come on, old man." Paget's arm lay across his shoulders ; he heard him laugh, a little unsteadily. In Paget's hand, also, was a packet of letters —but in the other hand, the hand he held under Johnny's nose, was something that looked to Johnny like a tiny fuzz of dirty cottonwool. He had not seen the runner produce, from some cavity of his anatomy, that which meant more to them, even, than letters from home. "Weren't we saying, last night, we could do with a magnum of the dear old widow? Here's our magnum; let's get inside and draw the cork."

Legs, thought Johnny, as, having dismissed the levies, they went back to the hut, were odd things. There was something fascinating about the way in which they operated, as it were, quite independently of any control on the part of their owner: jerking forward, one, two, one, two, with an occasional hitch, of course: a slight tendency, now and again, for one to get in the way of its partner; but working, on the whole, surprisingly well in double harness. Amazing things . . . legs. . . .

Paget had spread the crumpled ball of tissue paper—evidently, at some time, the protective sheet of a book illustration—flat on the table, and, sprawling between chair and table, prepared to decipher the close lines of indelible pencilling with which it was covered.

"Good God! Just listen to this:

"'This is the third attempt to get through to you, and no one seems to know whether you are still at Omo. The last man came back with news you had left——'

What did I tell you? He must have come while we were away, collecting the levies, and of course Abuakwa didn't say we were returning. If I don't find some way of settling the hash of that blistering chief, when we get out of here, my name's not Alden Galahad Paget."

"It's not, is it?" One of the difficulties, he had lately discovered, was keeping one's mind on essentials. It went dodging, like a butterfly, over any attraction.

"Frightful, of course. My Mamma came, unfortunately, under the Tennysonian influence, at rather a crucial moment for my future. Shut up," grinned Paget, "and listen:

"'We have been hoping to hear your wires were up again, as a man called Kershaw has been reported as working round your district. Unfortunately he is one of those unsatisfactory although well-meaning people who prefer to operate independently of military authority, and we therefore have no official record of his movements. As, however, it is many weeks since he was heard of, it is to be feared the worst must be assumed.'

Silly ass!" put in Paget, in parenthesis. "Why the dickens can't these fellows realise the trouble they cause——?"

"That's the sort of chap Kershaw was. If a job wanted doing"—Johnny heard himself saying—"he used to do it. He used to say, if it needed putting through the departments, it showed it wasn't necessary, after all."

"Did you know him?"

"He was my chum—last time I was out here."

"Too bad. Well now——

"'We take it Omo is still loyal, and that your work with the levies is proceeding according to plan.'

That," observed Paget, "is what I should call an unjustifiable assumption. Touchin', ain't it—the childlike confidence some people have, that you've only got to wave your malacca, and a protective army rises, full-armèd from the sod?"

"Ladies present," murmured Johnny, his eyes on Harriet's envelope. "You mustn't use rude words."

Paget gave him a look. Was Johnny going to hold out? He returned to his reading.

"'Please commit these orders to memory. On the morning of the 17th prox., a column leaves here under Gibson with the object of seizing a village called Kwetti, about ten miles from Ejesu, S.W. Here we hope to be reinforced by Harriman's column, as the position is important and heavy resistance is expected. It is by no means certain that Harriman can get there in time.'

Now, that's better; a touch of uncertainty humanises the situation.

"'The eventual objective, of course, is Ejesu, which, despite the nominal surrender of the Queen, is suspected of being a centre of disaffection, as well as an important fetish town, the capture of which would have great effect on the enemy. It is imperative to secure the best possible support for Gibson's Mendis, whose morale is in some degree dependent upon a conclusive victory at Kwetti.'

Now for it!

"'You will therefore leave Omo, with whatever troops you have in training, and converge on Gibson at N'Buri, which is about three miles south of Kwetti and not more than a day's march from Omo, through country which is said to be heavily ambushed, falling in at the rear of the column and proceeding with it to Kwetti: where you will, in accordance with Gibson's orders, follow the customary procedure with the levies.'

A delicate touch—customary procedure; I like it.

"'As much depends on the execution of this manœuvre, it is

expected no effort will be spared to make it successful. God bless you —and grant this does not fall into enemy hands! Send back word if you receive it.

"'The letters came in yesterday. Hope they contain news that will put you both in good heart for the prospect ahead.'"

They sat in silence, neither moving. Presently Paget put out his hand, picked up the paper again and screwed up his eyes to read the final words, carried into the eighth-of-an-inch margin the writer had left.

"'Would stress importance of fully trained scouts and strong point to your own column.'"

Suddenly his veneer of lightness cracked.

"Christ Jesus! 'Fully trained scouts'!"

"They're all bushmen; that part of the show may work," Johnny murmured.

"'A strong point to your column.' Why not tell us not to forget our pocket handkerchiefs? 'In the disposition of an army on the march, the best place for the medical officer and stretcher party is immediately behind the millimetre gun escort,'" Paget quoted bitterly from a famous authority. "What in blazes do they imagine we're taking Gibson, in support of his blasted Mendis?"

When the storm wore itself out, Paget rose, a little sheepishly and picked up his mail.

"Well, old man, I'll leave you to your letters. See you later—when we'll work out *how* we'd dispose a relief column, *if* we'd got a relief column, *when* we're called on to produce a relief column! This trip to Kwetti's going to be the prettiest hare-an'-hounds I've taken part in since I left 'the shop'—if you ask me."

As, so far, his legs, which seemed to have assumed entire control of his person, did not require him to get up, Johnny opened his letters.

No use. The lines just ran into one another, blurred in violet, or blue, or black, across the page. He would have to have patience, until Paget had got through the bundle of his own correspondence, which he had carried off to his hut. It was like sitting behind a sheet of clouded glass, on the other side of which were gathered all those one loved; whose embraces one longed to receive, whose voices one longed to hear. The thickness of the glass cut off the voices, as its opaqueness hid all but a faint movement of impatience, as though they were as eager to get to him as he to reach them and the reassurance of their loving hands. Suddenly a single word—"Dearest"—in Harriet's writing, leapt at him from the page. Dearest . . .

Abruptly, he assumed, for once, authority over his legs, and forced them to carry him out of the hut.

He had got in the habit of wambling into the village, where the appearance of the little bearded white man no longer caused any sensation. In his few spare moments (when the legs did not decree otherwise) he got pleasure of a kind in wandering among the huts, in watching the kittenlike gambols of the children—in marking the changes which had come over the village in the short time since the days of Akosua and her son Kufi. Omo had degenerated ; the want of a powerful authority was in the air. Allowing for the damage done by a particularly severe rainy season, the place looked bedraggled ; the superb, three-tiered slope of the Hall of Justice had sometime caught fire, and had not been repaired. Such energies as Omo could spare from lounging, eating, squabbling and so forth it had put into the strengthening of its stockade, and in building two strong defensive outposts along the main approaches to the village.

Omo was prepared for war, although it had no intention of starting it. Omo was, moreover, hard up ; rubber production being at a standstill and no trade coming up or down the river. They struck Johnny as a shiftless, lackadaisical lot—apart from the army, which, glossy on the best of the food, the best of accommodation and the best of the young women, went peacocking around, looking down their noses at everybody—including the white men. If it came to that, the white men could look down their noses —and did. Paget frankly hated the populace ; Johnny behaved, a good deal of the time, as if it were not there. But his duties as liaison officer between Paget and the chief, and Paget and the heads of the village, brought him contacts denied to the former, on account of his ignorance of the language.

There was the young man N'Timidi : a sedate, secretive youth, usually among the spectators when the levies were drilling. He, unlike the majority, was impressed by white authority. Johnny had guessed his secret : that behind the receding brow, the fathomless, ophidian eyes there smouldered a steady ambition towards leadership. He had tried to make use of this ambition in enlisting N'Timidi's help in the drilling. N'Timidi made no bones about his refusal ; he said with a directness that was refreshing, after the slippery ways of the war captains, that, the chief having shown himself indisposed to concern himself with the levies, it would be bad policy for him, N'Timidi, to associate himself with their training. Johnny, unlike Paget, saw his point, and respected it ; he found N'Timidi, in other respects, polite, obliging and superior to the common run of the village. He got in the habit of conversing with him, in a mixture of dialect, mission English and pantomime, eked out with the few Hausa words N'Timidi had picked up during Bendick's time. In this way he came by various useful scraps of local information, and it was through N'Timidi that they got the occasional flashes on the progress of the general campaign which were all they had to depend on ; although Johnny noticed that the Omo man was careful in confining his bulletins to the distanter phases of the war. He had nothing whatever to impart that could be of the least use in helping them to find out how things lay in the immediately neighbouring districts.

" They say, N'Timidi "—he had come on his acquaintance cleaning off the remainder of a skillet of manioc dumplings which his wife—a young woman of surpassing ugliness and no intelligence whatever—had just given him for his supper—" they say," said Johnny, settling down in the rather familiar fashion that always gave Paget a shock (" My dear fellow, you can't be cosy with the natives ! " " Why not ? " " Discipline, my dear man, discipline ! Doesn't look well, you know—squattin' on your haunches, as if you were a bally nigger." " What do you expect me to do ? Cart an arm-chair around with me ? "—one of their few, and trifling, disagreements), and picking up the instrument which, for want of a better name, he called the drum-fiddle—" They say that there is, in these parts, a very remarkable man." Whereupon he dipped his hand into the calabash of water at N'Timidi's elbow, pushed it into the old barrel which is the belly of this exotic instrument, seized the stick which is its clapper, and to his satisfaction produced at one go the boom and the screech for which the drum-fiddle is distinguished.

This furnished his excuse for visiting N'Timidi, a notable drum-fiddler, who, flattered by the interest Johnny evinced in his musicianship, was pleased to teach Johnny the art of the instrument, together with the variety of wails and howls with which the virtuoso of the drum-fiddle enriches his performance. Paget's face, on a day he came on them at it, as Johnny had just mastered his yowling, formed one of the latter's brighter recollections of their association. Still, as he later pointed out to Paget, that was the time he got out of N'Timidi the vital information about the trader who had powder to sell, and the exact price it was policy to offer for it.

" I know of none such." N'Timidi smiled careless appreciation of the progress of his pupil and leaned back to listen. " For what is this man remarkable ? "

" It is said," said Johnny—after the usual hither-and-thithering he employed to work up his companion's curiosity—" that he can take the strings that carry the white men's messages into distant parts, and which, from one cause or another, have got broken ; and that he can put them together and make them speak."

" Such a man," admitted N'Timidi, " there has been, and I have heard tell of him. But it was not in this moon."

For nearly an hour Johnny persevered, working nearer and nearer the subject of his inquiry, playing skilfully on N'Timidi's weak spot, his vanity, which could seldom resist the insinuation that he was a man of greater knowledge, sense and discretion than the majority of his co-villagers, and had access to information withheld from them.

It was dark, and the fires and bushlights gleaming fitfully among the huts, when he returned to Paget.

" Where the dickens have you been ? And do you mean to say you haven't opened your mail yet ? "

His legs were more than usually erratic when he approached the table at which Paget was sitting. He heard himself laughing a little, and put his hands hurriedly up to his face, to smother the laughter : for it was no laughing matter he had brought to Paget—and brought them hurriedly down again, for he had never quite got accustomed to the feeling of the hairy mat which, now two or three inches long, covered his face. On their arrival they had found, among other things, Bendick's razors, which Paget used daily ; but he had felt it was wiser, in Omo, not to cut his beard, which was a safeguard against his chance recognition by any survivors of Morris's purge, when he disbanded the supporters of Omo's former leaders.

" The dispatch said—it said "—he stammered—" something about Omo still—being loyal ; didn't it ? "

Paget was staring at him.

" Kershaw—Kershaw——"

" Pull yourself together, Flood." Paget had risen, was frowning down on him, as Johnny, still babbling Kershaw, groped in his pockets. Kershaw ?

Memory flashed back : Kershaw—the man Johnny had spoken of as his chum—the man who—was it possible ?

His hands were on Johnny's shoulders, shaking them.

" You don't mean Kershaw has turned up ? That we've got the wires again ? "

Johnny shook his head ; his hands were shaking as he dropped the grisly refutation of Omo's loyalty on the table between them. Paget's jaw fell, his face drew itself into an expression of horrified disgust, as he looked at the big, clumsy denture, obviously from the upper jaw of a European.

" Tha-that's Kershaw ! " babbled Johnny. " I saw them in a glass by his bed, every night."

" It's possible—he could have dropped them," muttered Paget, after a few moment's contemplation of the hideous object.

" N'Timidi bought them—from the boy who stole them from his head —when it was set up inside the fetish house."

In the look they exchanged, the danger they were in stared naked from each man's eyes.

CHAPTER TEN

I

"CHEERS!" observed Captain Gilbert Flood to his brother, Mr. Dorset Flood, who said "Cheers!" back. They lifted their glasses to one another with the rich satisfaction of two gay young bachelors, temporarily engaged in the enjoyable process of "painting the town red."

For Dorset had regained, briefly, his bachelor status. The *ennui*, for a person of his tastes, of having a wife about to enrich the family tree by the production of a new generation (and making rather more fuss about it than a Flood wife was expected to make) had resulted in his adoption of Gilbert's suggestion of a few days in town on his way to the moors—where he anticipated the double distinction of being hailed as the best shot in his host's party and the importance accruing to a young husband who has just received news of the birth of an heir. The "few days" had stretched out to a fortnight. "*All* your letters have been forwarded to Drumlochrig," wrote Ethel petulantly, "and I only learned by chance from Grizel Macdonald that you have not arrived yet! What *are* you two doing?"

"What *are* we doing?" Dorset winked solemnly at his brother, on receiving the foregoing. Gilbert cast his eye over it and chuckled.

"I don't know, I'm sure, old boy; but, by gad, you've dropped years since we came up from the country!"

Dorset verified this by a look in the glass, by pulling down his waistcoat and by his smile of secret satisfaction. His first bachelor trip since he married (he took considerable credit to himself for this)—there was no question he had kept his form. Gilbert, too—though less nippy on his pins than he was before he got his wounds, poor old boy—was the best of company, and there was no pick-me-up in the world like the morning bottle of champagne for putting a couple of overnight roisterers on good terms with themselves and the world they favoured by existing in it.

"By gad, you know, it's good—to be away from Guerdon." Gilbert, a little more battered than his brother, refilled his glass. "I must say the place is like a morgue; the pater really has made heavy weather of Uncle Roan's business."

"Nothing to what he'll make of Johnny's business, when *that* one's exploded!" Darkness descended abruptly on Dorset's brow. "The more I think of that, the more I see red——!"

"Don't think about it, old boy," advised Gilbert. "Sorry I brought it up. Sufficient unto the day—what? There's many a slip—and all that sort of thing——"

"You know, he always was the damnedst fellow. The devil of it is, I was always so fond of him. But he certainly made it as difficult as possible—do you know, he once actually told me he hated Guerdon?"

" Guerdon ain't what it was." Gilbert fell into the gloomy key of his companion. " What with Uncle Hacky croaking from the battlements every time he comes near the place, and the pater in a permanent blues—it's about time you took over."

" That's another damned thing." Dorset took a cigarette out of his case and clipped the case viciously back in his pocket. " Ethel doesn't care for Guerdon."

" None of 'em do," said Gilbert comfortably. " Grandmamma loathed it, and so did Uncle Hacky's wife, and Aunt Venetia. Makes no difference ; it's the family seat."

" And an infernally costly one," his brother muttered. Gilbert's jaw dropped.

" You don't mean—— ? "

" I don't mean I'm not as fond of it as you are ; but it's no good blinking the fact that the place is eating money, and that it will continue to do so, at the present rate of things. Think of the to-do we've just had with the drainage ; think of that antediluvian heating system—that practically lifts you off your feet each time you cross one of the gratings, and leaves your teeth chattering unless you're sitting right on top of a fire ! Think of all those damned foot-baths—because the structure won't carry a modern plant. Even when we built on the new rooms over the stables, they only put in one bathroom for the five. And the estate itself—tenants always grizzling about their cottages, something always wrong somewhere, and money, money, money going down the drain. And who's getting any fun out of it ? I'm devoted to Guerdon, but at this rate, old boy, it's going to be very little better than an expensive ruin, by the time I inherit."

" I thought—Ethel——" Gilbert paused delicately.

" Ethel, unfortunately, has a father—and a mind for business. Pretty dam' funny that ! " His teeth flashed briefly in his hard, handsome face. " We don't usually marry female financiers, do we ? I see her point, in a way ; her old boy bought us this smashing place in Hampshire, and I admit she's made a marvel of it ; her taste's extraordinary and nothing satisfies her but ' the latest.' Did I tell you we had some newspaper fellow in the other day, to know if he could take photographs of the interiors, for some damned magazine ? A fine thing, if an English gentleman's no longer to enjoy the privacy of his home ! I got rid of the bounder pretty sharply."

" Well—there's always Flood and Company." Gilbert easily voiced the general creed.

" Is there ? " Dorset gave him a sharp look. " With Hacky pouring all our profits into his wild-cat West African scheme ?—which might come off, I grant you : the old boy's shrewd—but what's the use of this long-term planning, when demands are immediate ? "

" You—you wouldn't get rid of Guerdon, would you ? " A note of uneasiness had come into the other's voice.

" Great heavens, no. But I might keep it for the hunting, and close or let it for the rest of the year. Sell off some of the land ; by putting that into the house, we might get it habitable in time. I must talk to Ethel about that. By the way—I persuaded Papa to sell the Bowling farm, and all that acreage. In view of future events, I thought it rather a neat stroke of business. The fellow who's buying means to live there and farm the land himself. So the Bowlings are out," concluded Dorset, with satisfaction.

"Pretty good," said Gilbert, with an admiring glance at his brother. "Bowling's a surly brute, anyhow; the hunt has trouble with him every year." He glanced at the clock and pushed himself to his feet. "Look here, we're going to be late! We promised to take the girls down to Henley and they'll have to be back in decent time for their shows."

The meeting at Paddington Station, of the young men in boating flannels and blazers, the girls in "river" creations, followed the prescription of most afternoons since the two had been in town; the journey down to Henley, the punt on the river, the tea-basket, Dorset's prowess with the punt-pole completed the picture. Summer was nearly over; the slim, fallen leaves of the willows lay in swirls on the backwaters. The rising mists drove them back to town earlier than had been their custom on previous jaunts.

Leaning against her admirer, Miss Kitty murmured:

"You'll be in front to-night, won't you?"

"Of course," purred Dorset, who had no intention of being anywhere of the kind. Four times was enough for any George Edwards show, and there was no point in staring across the footlights at a young lady one had been privileged to view at much closer and more interesting quarters.

"Romano's?" cooed Miss Kitty.

"Is that what you'd like?" smiled Dorset, narrowing his eyes at her in a way that made her catch her breath.

While they changed their clothes:

"You're at the Gaiety to-night, I suppose?" inquired Gilbert.

"No?" Dorset's disclaimer had a rising inflection meant to indicate that he was at the disposal of any more attractive suggestion.

"Oh—I thought I heard you telling Kitty you were. Dulcie's brougham's broken down, or something, and I promised I'd drive her to her theatres. We could pick up Kitty later on and have a bite of supper at Romano's?" He produced it as brightly as though it were not what they had been doing every other night for a fortnight.

"As a matter of fact, I believe she's got something else on."

"Has she? By Jove, old boy, she's taken a toss for you!"

The fact being self-evident, Dorset shrugged his shoulders.

"Perhaps Dulcie will bring one of her friends along."

Opera hats and tails; white gloves, gardenias in the buttonhole: "Coo, look at the mashers!" from hovering urchins, as, having deposited Miss Dulcie at her stage door, they strolled to the front of the house and into the dress circle bar—emerging just in time to hear Miss Dulcie's numbers.

"Don't be late, whatever you do; my second house is Kilburn—I only just make it in time," she had exhorted them, in bidding *au revoir*.

" Where the deuce is Kilburn . . . ? "

Because the programme-seller happened to be pretty, Dorset gave her half a crown, waved the programme aside with a smile that stained her cheeks with crimson, and the pair of them made their lordly way into the bar. His order of champagne was a tacit apology to his unconscious brother. It had been very amusing in the cab—Dulcie leaning against Gilbert, her glittering eyes avoiding Dorset, gracefully slouched with his back to the horse ; her hand tightly clasped in Dorset's under cover of her evening cape (paid for by Gilbert). It was the kind of joke Dorset enjoyed ; it meant nothing beyond the fun of bringing that absent glitter into Dulcie's eyes, of making her restless. . . .

The procedure was the same as before ; after Dulcie's turn, they sauntered round to the stage door to wait for her. A slight drizzle had started, and they went inside, to light cigars and prop up the box of a doorkeeper who looked suspiciously at the two " West-End johnnies," conspicuously out of the usual run of patrons of the Kilburn Empire. Hangers-on of Dulcie Debenham's. Well, she was one of the new sort—not like good old Lottie—good old Kate. Catch *them* trailing chaps round in their broughams, instead of saving themselves up for the customers !

" Who's that ? "

A full, round voice ran through the door marked " Stage " across the passage. Dorset started, shot a quick look at Gilbert, strode across and swung the door open.

Through the dark screens of the wings, in the narrow slot of brilliance that was the stage, stood the figure of a young woman. While he stared at it incredulously, a stage hand, his attention caught by the draught and the penetration of voices from the passage, shouted :

" Keep that door shut ! "

" By God, did you see ? "

" See what ? "

" *Polly Bowling.*"

" You're binged, old boy," said Gilbert easily.

" Binged be damned. Polly—Bowling : by God ! Well ! " said Dorset with a satisfaction so deep that he was virtually glossy with it. " If I can't cook that slut's goose after this, and get poor old Johnny out of his mess—call me a Dutchman ! "

" Poor ole Johnny." Gilbert, actually, was much more " binged " than his companion. " Wonder where he is to-night ? " he mumbled, with the sudden sentimentality of the unsober.

" I wish he'd stop his nonsense with the blasted niggers, and come home ; I can't help worrying about the silly fellow. Pull yourself together, old boy : here's Dulcie."

" They gave you a good hand to-night, dear." One of her companions on the bill greeted Polly as she came off.

" I didn't think I was so good. Something seemed wrong, somehow —and who the hell let that draught in ? " said Polly, recovering herself. " I thought it would cut my shoulder-blades off ! "

"A couple of topper-and-tails johnnies—behaving as if they'd bought the act. Maybe they had?"—with a nudge.

"No bloody fear!" said Polly, who had by now absorbed the vocabulary no less easily than she had absorbed the customs of her environment.

"I was only teasing you, ducks. Well, night-night. Working next week? That's good; don't let 'em put you on again after Dulcie Debenham!"

It was pouring, and the distance to Waterloo Bridge Road seemed endless; the weight of the Japanese hold-all, into which she had learned skilfully to pack her hat, dress, and the make-up box Bella had given her, increased, as she trudged to the tram. Some day, perhaps, she would be at the top of the bill, with a brougham of her own—when the outlook was particularly dark, Polly always tried to cheer herself with such visions; but they were more than usually lacking in conviction to-night. She could, this week, have afforded to take a cab, but had decided not to do so; she was owing too much to Bella, and had sworn to herself to make Bella take at least four of the eight pounds she would collect the following night. Friday—and, so far, only one odd date booked for next week; that meant Poverty Junction in the morning—and it looked like being wet. She had intended to come up to the West End and buy a few more things to add to the little pile which was slowly growing at the bottom of her drawer in Bella's chest. Thank God Bella wasn't inquisitive, and not addicted, like a great many girls, to "borrowing." She would never open anyone's private drawer. But she might have found . . .

Bella was home, and had supper ready by the time she got in. She crawled in, dropping the hold-all, and began, with fingers stiffened by carrying that and her umbrella, to unbutton her mackintosh coat.

"It's a sodding night."

"Never mind," said Bella cheerfully, as she lifted the stewpan from the trivet to a wad of newspaper she had placed on the corner of the table. Polly looked, but held her peace. When she got supper, the table was carefully laid, the food "dished up," the stove cleaned of any splashes that might have accumulated on it in the course of her cooking. Bella scoffed at such niceties. "The food tastes just the same, doesn't it?" she would justify her own more casual methods. "You'll be all right when you've had your supper. Open the stout—there's a duck. Well, what were they like to-night?" came her usual inquiry, after an interval in which she satisfied her hearty appetite and Polly scattered the bits of meat and vegetable indifferently about her plate.

"I don't know. There was something queer about it. I felt as if"—she paused—"as if somebody was looking at me."

Bella's face stiffened.

"Let's see: what's the Empire hold?" she inquired, with mock gravity. "Two thousand five hundred, is it? Well, allowing for the bar-crawlers—you silly juggins!" She burst out laughing, in which, for a moment, Polly joined.

"I know—I'm dippy. It was just a nasty feeling I got, that's all."

" Well, never mind nasty feelings ; I've got a bit of good news for you. Billy wants to see you in the morning ; it's Hoxton, next week. You'll be on the bill with Wee Minnie Mills. You've seen her, haven't you ? There's a bitch ! " said Bella, with conviction. " She's got a great girl in her twenties, that one of the Allegro twins—you know, the wire-walkers—goes with ; and Minnie won't let them get married because she says how the hell's she going to do child impersonations when all the world knows she's a grandmother ? "

Polly sat silent, while the spate of Bella's chatter flowed, at last, to a finish, in a yawn.

" Well, I'm ready for my downy." As she lowered her arms, stretched above her head, she looked curiously at the averted head, the listless attitude of her companion ; her voice softened. " Is anything the matter, duck ? Don't you feel well ? "

Polly turned her head slowly.

" I'm going to have a baby."

There was a pause, before Bella said quietly :

" I know."

Her heart leapt and the colour raced up her cheeks, as she gasped :

" Does it show ? "

" I've known a long time. Yes, dearie, it's beginning to show," said Bella compassionately.

" I shan't be able to go on working ! "

" Oh, you'll be able to work for a long time yet. We'll have to find you another dress—that's all : not so shiny, with a bit more drapery down the front." Bella came behind her and put her arms round her shoulders, giving them a squeeze. " Don't you worry ; me and the Old Dutch will see you through."

" I wish—my husband would come home."

" Your—— ? " Bella's jaw dropped.

" My husband." Polly turned quickly. " You didn't think I wasn't married, did you ? "

" Hell—it wasn't my business to think," gasped Bella. " Well—to think of your being *married* ! " She gave a little laugh, of relief as well as apology. " Does he know about—this ? "

" I wrote him a few weeks ago ; he mayn't have got it, yet. He's out in Ashanti." Like most people, she pronounced it " Ash'n-tee " ; she had a vague recollection that Johnny had called it something else, and expected to correct her pronunciation on his return.

" Jesus ! " said Bella. " Well "—she caught at the philosophy which had supported her and her mother throughout their vicissitudes—" never mind, dear ; you'll see—it will all come right in the end. And now we've got that off our chests—come on to bed, or Billy'll think you've not got enough life in you for Hoxton ! " Although her curiosity was fully roused, her tact would not let her question Polly further. Something was obviously wrong, somewhere—a quarrel, perhaps ; Polly would never lie to her about being married. Trouble with his people—or hers. A farmer's daughter—Polly had let *that* drop. And a tommy—Bella took it for granted ; of course—and her family thinking she had married beneath her. The kind of thing that was put right by the birth of a grandchild—particularly if it happened to be a boy. Oh yes, Polly would be all right.

" Come on, duck—let's give each other's hair a good brush, before we settle down. Nothing like the good old whalebone for soothing sorrows away ! "

But when they got into the bedroom, she saw that Polly was too tired to share the hair-brushing, and began quietly to help her to take off her clothes. As she twitched the ribbon of the bodice, a crumpled paper fell from the warmth of Polly's bosom ; Bella bent, picked it up and handed it back to her.

" Oh—thank you. It doesn't mean anything ; I was only carrying it —for luck."

A question she was immediately ashamed of herself for asking burst irrepressibly from Bella's lips.

" Is it from your husband, dear ? "

" No. It's from the man I ought to have married," said Polly, so wearily, so indifferently, that Bella's heart was wrung. Oh lord, this was a mess. " There's nothing wrong about it," Polly answered her troubled look. " I just sent him one of my photographs, and the hall where I was working. This was waiting for me when I went to band rehearsal last Monday. Poor old Joe—I only carry it for luck," she repeated, as she laid it under the pillow where, unknown to Bella, each night it had rested. After a silence :

" Are you in love with him, ducks ? " asked Bella, rather diffidently.

" With *Joe* ? "

" Well, you don't generally sleep on a letter, unless you're pretty ' gone ' on the person who wrote it," Bella pointed out, with reason.

" No, it's not that in the least," Polly hastened to assure her. " It's just—Joe's like part of home. I suppose I get a bit homesick, sometimes."

" But you're not in love with him ? " Bella persisted. Polly was sitting on the edge of the bed, tying the bow on the end of her long plait of hair. Her fingers were suddenly still.

" What is it—being ' in love ' ? " Her brows puckered above her tired eyes. " I mean, what's the difference between loving somebody and being ' in love ' ? "

" Oh, go on ; you know." Bella's tone showed that she scorned the quibbling.

" I don't believe I do."

" Do you mean to say you've never been really—soppy about a fellow ? "

A dark tide of crimson rose to the roots of her hair.

" I was—once."

" But it wasn't Joe ? "

" No, Bella ; it wasn't Joe," whispered Polly, as she swung her feet under the bedclothes and blew out the candle.

II

6 Ship Lane, Bristol.

Dear Polly,

My word it was fine to hear from you. And the photo is a corker though not quite the Polly I remember. I feel like showing it to everybody, then I say No, I'll keep it to myself. Perhaps there'll be another one for exhibition some day ? ? ? N.B.—I don't ask much do I ! ! !

So you're on the stage at last. I know you always said it's what you'd like and I'm very, very glad for your sake. I wish I could come to London and see you but there's only Saturday afternoons and I've had some extra jobs lately. I'll explain that later on. But it means I don't like to ask off for the present so you'll understand and not expect me. One of these days I'll be turning up with a bunch of flowers like a regular stage-door johnny. (I can see myself.)

Well, Polly dear, I don't expect you know what a relief it's been hearing from you. Silly-like, I'd worked myself up into a state. I ought to have known I could trust you. I don't know how to put it, but I think I understand what it must have been like for you at home without your mother and you just feeling you couldn't stand it any longer. I wish I could have helped you. I went up that Sunday week after you had gone but didn't see anybody except Dick your cowman who told me your father was upset which of course he would be and no doubt you'll be writing to him soon.

I must explain about the Saturday work or you will think I might go on and find some way of coming up to London which you know there is nothing I would so much like to do.

To tell you the truth I got in a bit of trouble a few weeks ago misbehaving myself and thought I was going to get the sack but Mr. Harcourt is a trump. He told me what he thought of me which wasn't any less than I think of myself. I wondered a long time if he would think it cheek but I wanted to show him I appreciated not being sacked as I fully *expected and deserved* to be. So I went and said I didn't want any pay but if I could work Saturday afternoons to make up for the firm's time I'd wasted I'd be only too glad—as I knew Johnny did a lot of odd jobs for him he's got nobody to help him with now. Well you know the Chairman or rather you don't. He hummed and hawed and growled for a bit and seemed to think I'd got something up my sleeve, i.e. doing a good thing for myself and I think I made a mistake in mentioning Johnny's name because nobody's all right for the Chairman but Johnny.

But I managed to convince him in the end that I wasn't trying to grind an axe of my own so here I am on Saturdays, mostly doing errands, addressing envelopes and making copies of letters. Not much of a job but so long as it shows I'm willing I don't care. I think the Chairman misses Johnny a lot which we all do. It's not the same with him away. *I might say the same about somebody else.*

Now I have a piece of news that I hope won't come as a shock to you.

A week ago last Sunday I went out to your father's place, to see whether there might be any news, and found everything cleared up all ready for a *sale*. Dick told me the farm had been sold over your father's head and he had gone to live for the time with your cousin Jinny. The buyer was taking over all the farm stuff and all the household furniture and personal things were being sold. It looks a dirty trick to me, and the village is buzzing with it and the Squire (Johnny's father) is very unpopular. Dick's opinion is he had had it in his mind a long time ; wasn't there some trouble last winter about the hunt coming across your land ? But I suppose he didn't like to act while your mother was still alive. Anyhow this is what dropped like a bolt from the blue about a month after you went away.

Well, Polly, I didn't know what to do. If I'd known where to get in touch with you, I'd have sent a telegram. I knew you'd be upset at all your mothers things going and I didn't know what to do because I couldn't get to the sale and if I had there wasn't much £ s. d. to put up against the other buyers. I thought about your piano of course but that was out of the question. So I asked Dick to bid for me for some little thing and mentioned one or two I knew you cared about. In the end I've got your mother's tea caddy the tortoiseshell one with bits of ivory stuck in it and if you send me your address I'll post it on. You may know all about the sale, etc. Anyway I hope I did the right thing.

My second piece of news is a few lines from Johnny. They must have been written months ago because Mr. Harcourt told me the other day he's now all up among the savages. I hope he's all right. He asked after you specially. What about sending him one of your postcards ? You know he was always nearly as fond of you as I was. I think that photo would look grand stuck up in the tent and give the niggers something to think about ! They would probably make a fetish of it. How do you fancy yourself as an Ashanti queen ?

Now, Polly, dear, I think this is all. I'm hoping for a letter soon (you see I'm a regular Oliver Twist !) but understand how busy you must be. Love and a big X from

Ever your sincere friend,

JOE.

P.S.—My new leg is a corker ! "You should see me dance the polka" (not quite—yet).

She smothered a groan in the sheets, for fear Bella was not asleep. Oh Joe ! Oh Johnny !—my two sweet, sweet friends. Oh, Johnny, darling, do come home quickly, and let's get this tidied up, for all our sakes. Relieve me of my burden of deceit. Protect your baby and me from your people until we're strong enough to look after ourselves. I'll never harm you by clinging on to you, Johnny, if it's better for you I should go away. Just let me earn enough to keep myself and the baby, and we'll go right, right away, and you can go back to the people to whom you belong. It's not fair you should have to fight our battles—you'd always be beaten, by Dorset, and your father.

Presently she folded her trembling hands.

Our Father . . . protect Johnny. Don't let any harm come to him among the Ash'ntees. Bless him, and me, and our baby, for Jesus Christ's sake. Amen.

III

Saturday afternoon. The big office was empty, the desks cleared of their working-day load of pens, pencils and papers. Joe laid down his pen and leaned back, to refresh himself with a look at the photograph which, on those lonely Saturday afternoons, was always under the lid of his desk. He might as well have had it out, propped up in front of him ; no one ever came in. But it might—nay, would !—have kept him from concentrating as he ought to do, on his self-imposed task.

Polly. He tried to picture her, with white fluffy stuff round her neck, as in the postcard, acting in the theatre. (To Joe, any appearance on the professional stage was "acting.") They had not caught it badly—that bonny smile of hers, and the "Come hither" tilt of her head, that made the light shine all the way down the parting in her hair ; that was a new way of doing her hair—well, there was no doubt about it suiting her. What was she wearing ? What happened down below the fluffy stuff ? he wondered naïvely, that looked as if—almost as if—she had nothing else on ! Some photographer's trick, of course—that wouldn't be Polly ! —and it certainly was pretty.

It was not for Joe to know that Polly, at Bella's instigation, had arranged to be "done" in Marie Belloni's gown, showing off her handsome shoulders and the apple-like curves of her breasts ; but that last-moment modesty, assisted by the memory of some picture she had seen, accounted for the cloud of tulle. It was as well for Joe ; the other would have upset him, roused misgivings, reminded him of the winks and nudges which accompanied the mention of any woman who "acted on the stage." No, Polly was not one of those ; you had only to look at the photo to see she was as modest and simple a girl as ever.

He allowed himself, usually, five minutes at three o'clock, to dwell upon her picture ; but barely two had passed when a rattle and the opening door made him fling the postcard into his desk and slam the lid.

My word, how old the Chairman looked, and how sick. The gleaming poll of snow-white hair had lost its arrogant lift ; with the droop of his shoulders, instead of the towering figure he always presented, Harcourt seemed no more than an average tall man. The pepper-and-salt tweeds hung slackly on a body that seemed to have shrunk ; the unhealthy, leaden-purple jowls sagged on his invariable black stock. When Joe jumped to his feet, Harcourt stared at him as though he were seeing a ghost.

"I'd forgotten you were here. Get on—get on with what you're doing." He stood there, vexed, irresolute, looking around him as though seeking something that ought to have been there ; looking—it flashed into Joe's mind—for Johnny.

The great mahogany desks on which (despite Harriet's animadversions !) no sacrilegious clerk had dared scratch his initials, stood empty : the far one by the window Johnny's—before he had gone up to work in the Board Room, so as to be near his uncle, if the latter wanted him. I wonder how he knows ? thought Joe, as Harcourt went and sat down there ; never in his memory had the Chairman noticed where anyone sat, except old Derbin, in his cubbyhole like a glass loose-box, beyond the fireplace.

Harcourt sat there as though he were alone, his heavy, dissatisfied face dropping forward, his back rounded, his elbows on the desk and his hands—the handsomest thing about him—folded : sat there, staring. Not at Joe, not at anything in the room. Just staring.

Joe did not like to move ; he thought of the noise his pen made, screeling along the foolscap. Something was going on he was afraid to disturb. So he sat with his pen in his hand and his head down, and, apart from the ticking of Matt's big clock, there was not a sound in the room. When, out of the corner of his eye, he ventured to steal a glance, Harcourt's hands were sliding slowly up and down the lid of the desk, as though he were stroking it.

Presently he got up, and lumbered to the door.

" Go home, boy. You've been here long enough."

" Please, sir, I haven't quite finished."

" I said, go home."

" Yes, sir." His face burning, Joe prepared to obey.

" You've got a home, haven't you ? "

" Oh yes, sir ! "

" That Ship Street place—— ? "

" Yes, sir, I'm still there."

" Do they look after you ? "

" I'm very comfortable indeed, thank you, sir." He hoped his tone did not betray his astonishment at the unheard-of solicitude. After a moment's hesitation. " You're sure I can't do any more ? I generally stop on until four o'clock. If—if you want anything taking to Berkeley Square, I'm going to the library."

" Why are you going to the library ? "

" I generally pop in to have a look at the papers, sir. I like to see what they're saying about—the war." Both understood it was not to the Boer War he was referring.

" You see *The Diorama*, don't you ? " glared Harcourt.

" Yes, sir. I just like to keep an eye on the others as well."

" . . . You'll see some files on my desk. You can bring them up to the house. I'm going back myself." Why not ? What was there to detain the Chairman of Floods, in Queen Square, on a September afternoon ?

Half-way across the Parade he stopped, leaning irascibly on his stick, for Joe to catch up with him.

" What do you want to lag behind for ? "

" I—I didn't know I was to walk with you, sir," stammered Joe ; it would never have entered his head to do so, although, so expert had he become in the management of the artificial leg, that he could easily have kept pace with Harcourt's measured tread.

Harcourt gave a curious look at the well-brushed red head, the face which had lost its freshness of colour along with the youthful chubbiness which Joe had tried to counteract by growing a moustache. The moustache, with its long, waxed points—Harcourt's abomination—was clipped back, now, to a mere bristle; the objectionable flourishes about Joe's appearance had vanished. Not good-looking, or even gentlemanly, but an honest, plain fellow with the dignity of his own simplicity. Joe wondered why the Chairman grunted. Harcourt had had enough of so-called "gentlemen."

It was the first time he had ever entered the house in Berkeley Square, but Harcourt seemed to take it for granted he would follow him into what Joe supposed was the study. The big, dignified room—so filled with Flood relics that it was almost a Flood museum—was a little overwhelming.

"Thank 'ee," said Harcourt.

Joe could not, as he turned, resist giving one look round the room—which was the room of Johnny, as well as of Harcourt: at the dim portraits of Johnny's ancestors, at the Chippendale, and the ship models, and a score of objects whose purpose or history he could not recognise; but which seemed, for a moment, to be calling out to him, in some language whose sound was familiar, although he could not distinguish the words.

"How'd you like to go to Liverpool?" Harcourt's voice spoke suddenly behind him.

Joe caught his breath. Liverpool? He knew, from the point of view of the office, that it was promotion; that the big building in Water Street housed what was spoken of, in whispers, as the "live" end of Flood and Company; that the Chairman's son-in-law was described as a go-ahead manager, who was "all out" to pull Floods ahead of their big competitors. Sneer as he might at new-fangled methods, Harcourt admitted their virtue, by sending up his most promising people, from time to time, for a "rubbing-up" in Water Street. And one or two, latterly—it was shameful to admit it—had not returned, but, when their time was up, had left Floods for employment in other Liverpool firms. Disloyal; scandalous. Joe had fully shared the indignation of some of the older clerks at this treachery, which must have struck deep at the Chairman's pride in the Company. It was long since anyone had been sent to Liverpool; he knew it was proof, not only of his own advance in the firm's estimation, but of Harcourt's confidence. But it had come on him out of a clear sky, and for the moment he did not know how to answer it.

"I—to tell you the truth, I had never thought of it, sir." He knew it was a bad answer; that the Chairman did not like havering. He looked for inspiration out of the window; to the trees that waved gently on Brandon Hill. "Bristol——" he murmured, and stopped. He was not looking at Harcourt, to see the momentary softening on the older man's face.

"That'll do; you can go. We'll have a talk—one day."

As the rap of the artificial leg crossed the tiling of the hall, the old question rose in Harcourt's mind to torment him. As usual, he thrust it aside. What was the use? No one would ever know. Except Kitty Prior. And who in his senses would accept her word? He was briefly angry with himself for bringing Joe into this house—then anger submerged itself again in misery. Johnny—Johnny—Johnny. When are you coming home?

Fool; to come back here, where loneliness pressed in on him, as it had done ever since Johnny went away. That was why he had spent the afternoon at Queen Square—much good he had done by it. The work he had intended to get on with lay untouched, while he walked up and down, or stood, looking down the river with eyes which, for the first time in his life, did not see it. And then—contemptibly—to get Joe Prior to come back with him, simply because he had not the guts to walk into the empty house alone! What the devil had come over him? Harcourt sneered at himself, looking at his watch.

There was time to drive out and have a cup of tea with his mother—no, damnation! She was in London. What a woman of her age wanted, gadding to London—and in the month of September—heaven only knew. Craze for spending, manifesting itself in a new direction. And Miranda with her; tt-tt! What the pair of them were up to was no concern of his, but the bills were. Drummy—Drummy had looked pretty green, when he heard that his income from the firm would be halved in the near future; must have come as a shock, for he had hardly shown any spirit in disputing it. Still moping about Roan. Well . . .

Johnny. It seemed as if, to-day, he could not get the boy out of his mind. Ought to be ashamed of himself, rum-busting round the Coast, with a hundred things of more vital importance waiting to be got on with. Niggers! Couldn't he see it was the Army's business to wipe that up—as no doubt they would: though in the War Office's own sweet time, and, of course, as economically as possible. Nothing so cheap, in the estimation of Governments, as flesh and blood. With luck, that was one of the things that would be altered, when his scheme got into its swing; its swing that was being interrupted by that infernal young Johnny—who'd sooner pump lead into niggers than keep his mind on a job by which, if things turned out properly, lead-pumping might be avoided in future.

He found himself staring at the corner where, when they were together, Johnny usually sat; at the chair which had come to be Johnny's, at the revolving bookcase usually stacked with Johnny's books of reference, papers, pipes, tobacco jars and inconsiderable litter. It was coldly tidy. Cursing the officiousness of servants, Harcourt took out his keys and opened his desk; taking out the leather-covered volume in which, from time to time, he summarised the progress of his scheme. Here, in a nutshell, easily produced for the benefit of any person showing interest, was the essence of an enormous correspondence, of a financial project tortuous in its details, but clear as crystal to a mind like Harcourt's: a balancing of fact against fantasy, a nicely calculated estimate of human, as well as material, values.

It would have surprised some of those who thought they were "cutting ice with Hacky" and "in on a good thing," if they could have seen the contents of his secret ledger. "J. L. promises £5000. Lord P.—Banker's order £200 p.a. for ten years. Good. B.—Anxious to acquire shares. *Not on your life.* R.F.C. (Hull) 4 pages, suggesting modification of Clause XVI. Seems sound. One of J.'s discoveries ; must ask him." Damn.

He forced himself down to the work neglected, that afternoon, at the office : which included a summary to be presented to a Cabinet Minister, providing the essential background to a question to be asked, with luck, in the House. Let one at least safeguard oneself, if possible, against a plea of ignorance rising from incomplete information !

Promises of support from So-on and So-on and So-on ; big names. Look well on a directors' sheet ; the directors' sheet of . . . what to call it ? West African Consolidated : some such name. Why couldn't Johnny be here to take his share in such discussions ?

Ought to have gone into the business of those offices. Suddenly he flung the ledger down. It did not seem as though he could settle to any planning. How long, now, was it, since there was a letter from Johnny ? It seemed odd, that Joe Prior had not heard from him ; the two were thick as thieves—another rum thing, if ever there was one ! The boy who ought to have been his son, and the one who—possibly—was. God had a sense of humour. Well—He needed it. But it certainly looked as if young Johnny was being slack about catching the mails. Too bad of the fellow ; he must know they were thinking about him.

Harcourt's worst moment was, however, to come : when, dinner having been announced, he went into the dining-room, gazed for a moment, incredulously, at the table, and furiously rang the bell.

"What in hell's name does this mean ? "

The servant, following the direction of an outraged gesture, let his jaw drop ; coloured, stammered, and made haste to repair his unforgivable mistake.

"I'm very sorry, sir—I couldn't have been thinking."

Not thinking ? What was the matter—that Johnny was so much in their minds that, four months after his departure, his cover was set, in its usual place, opposite that of the master of the house ? Harcourt poured whisky into his glass and gulped it. His appetite was gone. Presently he flung down his napkin, left the food on his plate, went back and locked himself into the study.

He took out of a drawer in his desk the small packet of Johnny's letters sent from Cape Coast ; two from Prahsu and the one he had managed to get through from Omo, which, by some unaccountable whim of communications or mails, had arrived ahead of one of the letters from Prahsu ; and settled to read them. He had already read them so often that they had lost authenticity ; it was like a stale book, that still interests, but leaves the reader profoundly unsatisfied because the interest is academic and lacks the emotion of a fresh and living theme. As he read, it was borne in on him that all the events described by Johnny were already so far in the past that they had ceased to hold significance for the present. In time of war, the incident of yesterday is by to-day, little more than legend.

Come home, home, home! his heart was crying, as he pushed the crumpled sheets back in their envelopes. Come home, you silly fellow, and sit there in your chair, and find out—as you know in your heart and conscience already—that there's more in life than a light-minded, treacherous girl. Wait until you're my age, my boy, and you'll thank God you got your lesson early, and found out in your youth the truth about women! Two men together, Johnny: that's the best life—especially when one's old and the other's young; the old one with his experience and the young one with his confidence in the future. Come on home, lad, and we'll show them what two men together can do, when they've got no damned female millstone round their necks——!

The packet jammed, as he was trying to push it back in the drawer, and, thrusting his hand in impatiently, to clear it, he found and drew out the closed envelope Johnny had asked him to give to Miranda.

His heart gave a tick, as he read the superscription: "For Winkle." To be given to her, if . . . . What balderdash! What on earth had come over the fellow? Of course he'd come back. . . . You're going to come back. . . . You'd damn' well better come back! He sat with his hand clenched upon Miranda's letter: rather ludicrously defying the gods; but with an angry feeling at the back of his mind that the gods were laughing at him.

A thing like this—his forefinger mechanically tapped the letter—was just inviting trouble. That might be called superstition, but the Chinese were wise people, and they held by it. To name evil was to invite its malign attention. To prepare for evil—that, surely, was no less indiscreet.

"For Winkle." Under the gummed flap lay words—fresh words—penned by Johnny: another bit of the boy, for which, Harcourt now owned to himself, he was greedy. He was tempted for a moment to tear up the envelope and its contents—written in an outrageous assumption; great God, it's not *going* to happen! He heard himself shout the words, and pulled himself together.

A letter for Miranda. Johnny was fond of the girl, of course—poor little beggar. What would you expect from a Westermain? That impoverished stock was bound to break down somewhere; good thing it had not been over one of the boys. She managed the three boys, then mishap after mishap, and, finally—Miranda. Pish. A woman who gave up at four children was not much to boast about. Granted, there had been only four of Harcourt's generation, but that was Harriet's stubbornness. His grandfather had had two—legitimately; he, of course, was gadding about all the time, and, no doubt, distributed his favours; but the line had started from that rich Barbadian litter of eleven which had been produced punctually and without complaint by a woman who had her husband's plantation to look after, instead of lolling on an invalid couch, like her modern counterpart!

Miranda—a girl, and therefore out of Flood reckoning. Harcourt knew nothing of his niece, beyond the fact that he had once or twice, latterly, noticed a look in her eye that reminded him of Johnny. A sullen young miss; minds warped, it was said, in accordance with bodies. All the same, she had enough right feeling to tell him about her letters from Johnny; she had read him bits not, the chit!—having the grace to hand him the letters, to read for himself. Still, that was her upbringing; Vicky should keep a tighter hand on her.

What on earth did the boy find to say to Miranda? He had become aware of an intolerable fanning-up of curiosity, that was partly curiosity and partly jealousy—that Johnny's thought should turn, in such a connection, not to his uncle, but to his little sister. There could be no secrets in it, he argued with himself; a manly youth does not have secrets with a little girl in the schoolroom. And suddenly, half in fury, half in disgust at himself, fully aware of the ignoble way in which he was behaving, Harcourt tore open the letter.

Ten minutes later he was sitting, livid, clutching the arms of his chair, his chest heaving, gasping:

"I've got to take care—or I'll be having a stroke"—as though care could save him from the results of his own inexcusable action.

IV

My Darling Winkle,

I feel rather silly, over writing this, and I hope you will never get it, but going out to the Gold Coast I have to make sure of certain things, of which the first is that you should know how much I love you, think of you and hope and pray for your happiness. It seems a funny thing to write, but I can't go without telling you that I have never known anyone quite so brave and that I am proud above all words of my sister.

It would be foolish to deny that I might possibly not come back. As you know, queer things happen in times of war, and, although I am only going out as a correspondent, appointed by the paper to Cape Coast Castle, which is at present our Headquarters, the Base may be shifted at any time, and I suppose I shall go with it.

What I have now to tell you will come to you as a great surprise, but I hope not as an unpleasant one. Polly and I were married, just a week ago. Dorset and Gilbert know, for I have left all the money part of it in Dorset's hands, and asked them both to look after Polly, if anything happens to me. There are reasons why we cannot make our marriage public, before I go away, and I am a little afraid that, if I don't come back, they may not tell you, as it is useless to suppose that both Polly's family and ours will not be very much put out. I know I can trust you, dear Winkle, to be kind to Polly and do whatever you can (I know it won't be much) to comfort and help her. I am deeply distressed by the thought of leaving her to face all this alone.

The other thing is—I have a kind of idea they will try to keep it from

Grandmamma ; or, on the other hand, they might drop it on her in some way that would upset her dreadfully. I would therefore like the news to come from you—unless something happens, and they forestall this letter ; in which case, please go at once to the Dower House and say and do what you can to make things better. Above all, assure Grandmamma of my lack of intent to deceive her, and of how sad I feel, in going away without taking her completely into my confidence. I confess I cannot imagine what will be her attitude to Polly ; if you can do anything to make it a favourable one, you know what a difference it will make to my wife (that's the first time I've written it ; how queer it looks !) and how everlastingly grateful I should be. Mrs. Bowling will probably be dead by the time you receive this, and I fear Polly will have no one of her own to turn to, except her father, who is not likely to be of much comfort, from the little I know of his character.

I write all this, dearest Winkle, with the most complete trust in your understanding, and in your loyalty to

Your most devoted brother,

John Flood.

When he could think at all, when the rage, and the despair, and the resentment in him had died down, Harcourt thought : Polly. Polly who ? He had to scramble through the letter again to find the answer, and it was a moment or two before memory supplied the full reply. Polly Bowling, daughter of the tenant who farmed the twelve acre. It was so long since he had left Guerdon, he concerned himself so little with the tenantry, that he had to think back far, to recall the Bowlings or their scheme in the Guerdon universe. Some dim recollection came to him, at last, that they had been unpopular with the manor ; that Bowling's " independence " was resented by Dromore, who liked his tenantry subservient ; but that they had connections with " the house " through the kitchens—knitted up, by the usual country intermarriages, with some of the Guerdon servants. He remembered a blooming wench of fourteen or fifteen, nodding her head at him in rather a saucy fashion, as she tripped along the bridlepath and he rode up to the house, some ten years ago, and Vicky, when she heard of it, saying, " Oh, Polly Bowling," in a way that promised Polly Bowling should be put in her place, for her want of proper deference to her betters. And something about a nurserymaid for Miranda. . . .

This—for Johnny. Let me not be mad—not mad, sweet heaven !

Time passed, while Harcourt fought a battle with his own violence and sense of betrayal : now hating, now loving, the one who had betrayed him. He sought, of course, his usual panacea, the brandy-bottle, but, for once, it failed him. The rich, consoling nectar turned to gall in his mouth. It was after midnight when he remembered the thing which had never failed : the river.

A clear moon floated over the familiar scene : so silent now, so clamorous by day. A few drunken sailors, trolling their way from King Street, back to the ships slumbering against the Redcliff wharf ; a frowsy prostitute or two, casting a hopeful glance towards the tall figure throwing its shadow before it on the cobbles, and deciding it was policy to make themselves scarce ; a cat, with a big river rat in her mouth, slinking on her belly back to her young in some cellar of the Backs.

It was low tide ; down on the dried mud, in every attitude of abandonment, lay, here and there, the derelicts of the shipping slump ; some sleeping, some trying to make love—sly, ineffectual fumblings, carried on in fear of the dockyards police, on duty above. From such squalor he turned his head in disgust ; it was not that he had come down to the river to find. He walked on ; by Broad Quay, Narrow Quay, the Grove, to the Welsh Back—round the three sides of the small, square peninsular on which, seventy years ago, Matt, the second Hercules, and Quentin had landed ; could it be only seventy years ? More than time separated that night of smoke and flame from the present ; a new world had groaned painfully into being—a new world, and a better one ? It was hard to say. He thought of Derbin—his solitary link with that past ; Derbin, who must be over ninety years old ! Only another three years, and he would have been born into the slave trade. Perhaps he was. Of those years with Matt, Derbin would never speak.

He stood on the Bridge, to look at a solitary star trembling near the spire of the Redcliff ; thinking of the beautiful church, and those of his family it enshrined. And remembered, suddenly : " J. R. Bowling. Faithful servant, good friend." Could it be, once again, that a Flood would profit by the fidelity of a Bowling ?

It all came back to him now, with the link between the names : two rather patronising young men, reining their horses at the gate of a farm, to jeer at the expostulations of an angry farmer, irate at the hunt which, the previous morning, had swept across his land. And Roan's contemptuous dismissal of the protest, with :

" It's a pity you've not got a bit more of the spirit of your ancestor, Bowling ! You don't seem to have any kind of loyalty to the manor, or sense of respect to the name of Flood."

" Loyalty works both ways. And may be that seafaring fellow had got something to respect," was the uncompromising retort, which Roan, in his high-handed fashion, had laughed off, with a not ill-natured, " Damned impudence ! " as they rode away. Roan held the same attitude to independence as himself : a not unrespectful toleration. It was Drummy—and, of course, Vicky, who always took Drummy's side—who could not stomach it.

Farmers and seafaring men ; not a bad background. Better, by God, than degenerated gentry, or the vitiated products of some fourteenth century baronial line, with nothing but their quarterings to recommend them ; their morals as worm-eaten as their staminas—looking down their Norman, or Plantagenet, or merely Elizabethan noses at the men who were fools enough to think them worth the purchase.

It . . . just . . . might . . . work.

He was afraid to admit a consolation, but, as he prowled down little streets whose name, Bristolian as he was, he had forgotten, Harcourt was thinking. It might work. It was, in any case, one more buttress between Johnny and the false, fictitious life of Guerdon—not that he needed it. It would bring at least one Flood back to his own earth, back to his true bearings. A farmer's daughter! She would hardly have the impudence to foist views, social prejudices, aristocratic pretensions on a husband she had tricked into marrying her—there could be, of course, no doubt about that. Johnny had made a slip, and had chosen a foolish way of putting it right—which might turn out not so foolish, after all. There was nothing whatever to indicate involved sentiments—thank God for that!—in the letter to Miranda. He had found himself a bedfellow who, apart from the conjugal relation, he could ignore. Could anything be more to his—and Harcourt's—purpose? No more stravaging about after women, and a wife who would take conception as a matter of course—not of sacrifice and heroism! And healthy children, to carry on his name.

Gradually his heart lightened. Drummy, of course, would be fit to be tied! It is to be feared Harcourt found little but amusement in the prospect of the reactions of his elder brother.

A twist, and the beginning of Redcliff Parade brought Harcourt once more in sight of the river. He drew a deep breath; only one familiar with Avon could have sensed that tremulous moment when the tide is on the turn; that all but imperceptible freshening of air, that quiver of the silver snake in her dark bed. Presently the rhythm would set in; the slow lift, the swelling, the swing of the masts, now still, against the stars, and the rigging, preparing itself to enmesh the dawn. O, Avon river. . . .

No shame, with only that witness, in letting the tears gush to the eyes, roll over, roll down the heavy folds of the face. A child, crying into its mother's bosom, Harcourt gripped the handle of his walking-stick, muttering, Come home. Only come home, home, home. Come, and we'll build a new Bristol; we'll tie the Gold Coast and Bristol together, so that the gold will flow up these sweet waters and lift our ships on shoals of gold! There'll be singing here and singing out there—yes, white men and black singing together. There'll be ships and there'll be landing piers and there'll be roads running right up into the heart of West Africa, and their merchandise coming down and ours going up; and the swamps will be drained away and in time there'll be railways, and white men and black working joyfully together, for the good of each other and the good of England, on whose good West Africa's good depends.

Neither a fool nor a poet, Harcourt's reflections, as he stood weeping beside the Avon, were not couched in these terms; but this was their emotional content.

Only come home, my boy, and we'll do the best we can, for Bristol and for the Gold Coast. Only remember I'm getting an old man, and I need the stimulus of youth—your youth—to keep me up to all it's in my mind to do.

CHAPTER ELEVEN

I

JOHNNY had taken what they called the dog-watch, on the levy lines, which were penned in a ramshackle stockade, lavishly hung round with old bits of metal, old tin cans, bells and various tintinnabulæ, to give warning of escape. Not that the levies seemed keen, now they had settled down to acceptance of their lot, on escaping ; but there was no point in taking risks. Relieved by Bendick's orderly, he stumbled towards the hut ; it was just after eight o'clock.

Paget was awake, and had made tea : mercifully, and by dint of the greatest economy, Bendick's tea chest, so far, had held out ; it was their solitary luxury. They used it with miserly care, going so far as to count the leaves : fifty for the strong morning brew (" and fifty as they come ; it's cheating to pick out the big ones ") and thirty for the can they shared before turning in. Paget said :

" There's something going on. Take a look down the street," he invited, as Johnny questioned this with lifted eyebrows.

" I don't see a thing."

" That's just it."

There was indeed something odd about the village, usually, at this hour of the morning, a scene of animation : an absence of the customary matutinal squawking and scutter, a strange tranquillity about the huts. An old, blind man, the village centenarian, had been pushed into his chair on the porch, a few young women drifted about with a sleep-walking air which would certainly have earned them a brisk spanking from the partners of their mats and bowls, if the latter had been waiting for their breakfast. Omo had a peaceful, even a smug, air.

" Drink up your tea and let's go and find Abuakwa."

" How the deuce they did it," confessed Paget, some half-hour later, " baffles me."

It was all but incredible that an entire regiment, including the chief's bodyguard and the chief himself, had, during the hours of darkness, moved out of the village as noiselessly as a cloud of smoke. No one knew where, or why they had gone. N'Timidi, questioned, shrugged his shoulders ; even he put up no claim, for once, to being in the confidence of the war captains. But there was a flicker in his eye which resolved Johnny to return and question him later, and an uneasiness which his air of indifference failed to hide. He turned at the first opportunity, and disappeared into his hut ; it was evident he did not want to be seen talking to Johnny under the attentive eyes of the civilian population.

The day went by in preparations for the march on Kwetti, which was to take place the following morning at dawn. The distance being short, it was fortunately unnecessary to carry a heavy equipment—levies being expected to forage for themselves for supplement to their rice ration, and there being no heavy armaments, such as the 75-millimetre, which requires thirty-two carriers for gun and carriage, and as many for ammunition; or the 7-pounders with their twelve and the Maxims with their eight carrier allotment. There was, of course, no Medical Department, with its freightage of hammocks and stores to consider. The levies were travelling light, each carrying, in addition to his firing piece, a machete, nominally for cutting the way into the bush, but just as likely to be used as a weapon in moments of exaltation.

Carriers had to be found for rations and for reserve ammunition; and it was agreed that Paget and Johnny should manage with two carriers apiece, for rations and bedding—kit having dwindled to so negligible a quantity that it could easily be rolled into the rugs and mackintosh sheets inherited from Bendick and McGinty. By exercising the most strenuous self-control, they had saved enough of the European rations for a three-day march, knowing it was impossible for them to travel on native food. The levies were to receive the customary half-ration—three-quarters of a pound of rice a day for each man of the flying column, and to supplement this with the yams, plantains and so forth found along the route.

Immediately on receiving his orders, Paget had started, through Johnny, to negotiate with Abuakwa for carriers, but at the end of four days had arrived at no satisfactory settlement. The problem now was to find some person of responsibility with whom to drive the deal to a conclusion. And this seemed all but impossible. Individuals, approached, nodded their heads eagerly at the prospect of pay, and Johnny was forced to correct Paget's optimistic impression that these were to be depended on. Allowing for ammunition, emergency rations (for the surest way to lose a levy is to fail to feed him) and the few possessions of the white men, they had worked it out that they might manage with ten, or, at the most, twelve carriers; less they dared not reckon, for fear of being a charge on Gibson's column. These, with two hammock boys—which meant that only one person could ride at a time—were the absolute minimum, and a ludicrously small number for a column on the march, whose carrier line usually numbers half as many again as the officers and men in the fighting line. The levies now numbered sixty-four, counting some thirteen or fourteen raw recruits, who, having just joined, largely for the fun of the thing, were likely to be more trouble than they were worth, but had to be counted in as, in the circumstances, no able-bodied man was dispensable.

By sundown the pair of them were blind with fatigue, and it was still questionable if they had any carriers, or whether those who, at considerable expense, and with much blandishment, had been persuaded to enlist, would have thought better of their bargain in the morning. As well as, and in despite of this preoccupation, the drilling had gone on all day. The levies, yelled at through megaphones and galvanised by bugles, had bounced, scuffled, knocked one another down, yelled, fired, and done everything but behave in the way a disciplined fighting unit behaves under command of its officers. Paget gave up at last ; at this rate he would not have a leg to carry him, in the morning. There were no pioneers, and the scouts were quite likely to go rambling off on ploys of their own, when they lost sight of the column ; but the Lord had willed it, and he had done his best. As an army, it was a farce ; except that a farce is usually something to laugh at, and there was little laughter in Paget's young heart.

" We'll have to start without carriers, if the worst comes to the worst," he told Johnny grimly. " That's to say, we'll pick out the ten biggest nitwits of our own lot, and make them carry."

" That'll start a fuss ! "

" It'll start more fuss if I show them my Colt ! We're going to get these bastards to Kwetti, or blow their brains out, individually ! At any rate, they can all carry their own rice."

" They'll have finished it between here and N'Buri, if they do, and have nothing left for the jaunt on to Kwetti ! " Johnny warned him.

" Oh, let them go on with empty bellies then—the god-damned, double-faced, lead-swinging sons of she-apes ! " spluttered Paget—knowing, as Johnny knew, that it could not be done ; that it was his duty to present his supporting force in as good fettle as it was possible to preserve them.

Johnny blinked at the sons of she-apes, lolling after their exertions in the sun which, for the first time for weeks, had elected to shoot an erratic gleam or two across the clearing. Nothing could be more innocent than their present occupations, of hunting fleas, of chewing pepper pods, of squashing beetles, while their rice was being prepared.

Yet each was capable, under pressure, or even under influence of one of the incalculable moods that govern the primitive being, of cutting out his eyeballs, of driving a knife through his cheek so that the blade pinioned his tongue, of lopping off his arms or his legs, of committing the ultimate violation on his manhood—of performing, in fact, a score of acts which, not immediately terminating life, made of it martyrdom—in a spirit, almost, of play. If these potentialities were in the levies, notoriously the weakest, the most cowardly, the least aggressive—except when assured of no counter-attack—of the fighting forces, what must Ashanti in all its glory be like ; the prowess of its trained warriors, to whom every variety of mutilation, every obscene outrage upon the victim delivered into its hands, was brought to a fine art?

Peering towards Paget, he wondered if these things were in his mind ; if he also knew fear, or whether his discipline of a Regular soldier and an officer had banished in him the weaknesses that go with the instinct of self-preservation.

As though something of his thoughts had communicated itself to the other, Paget said :

" I'd like you to know—I'd sooner have you with me than any other fellow I can think of. You're a grand soldier, Johnny. You mayn't think that's a compliment, but I don't know how to pay you a higher."

Johnny had fallen into an uneasy doze between dusk and daylight, when he was roused by Paget shaking his shoulder.

" Listen, Flood : we're in God's own mess. Hassan "—the orderly—" has just come to me with his eyes bolting out of his head ; he's overheard some chatter in the village. Abuakwa and his fighting gang have gone up to Ejesu, to join up with the Omo bunch that tied up with Ya Ashantua, after the trouble last year. Oh hell, I feel as sick as a dog ! What did we let them get away for ? "

" What could we have done to prevent them ? " His tongue felt stiff in his mouth, his brain struggled to grapple with the new problem. Presently he dragged himself off the bed, forcing a feeble smile. " I'll go and have a drum-fiddle session, if you like, and see if N'Timidi's got anything to add to your information."

" Ten to one he'll tell you a pack of lies," muttered Paget. " I've been wondering whether we ought to set off to-night. The sooner we join up with Gibson the better, if that cursed black's decided to play with the Ashanti."

" There are two things against that," pronounced Johnny, after consideration. " One, that you'll almost certainly lose the levies, if you try to make them march in the dark. You can't blame them," he added seriously, " when you remember the spirits. . . . There's blood, too, down that track to N'Buri ; I saw it myself, only a few nights ago."

" Go on," said Paget—who had given up trying to make Johnny out, about blood and spirits—impassively.

" The other thing is, we're as safe here as we'll be anywhere. You can tell by its quiet the village isn't expecting trouble ; and Abuakwa certainly isn't going to bring his friends down here, to bust up his own home town."

" You're probably right," admitted Paget, after an interval occupied in biting a nail. All ten, by now, were down to the quick ; he said he did it in his sleep. One fell into nasty habits—however hard one tried to cling on to something approaching a normal standard of decency. He did not add what was in his mind : that the delivery of those sixty odd scallywags in the proper quarter was a matter wrapped up in his personal honour, and that the prospect of letting Gibson down, if they should happen to have a fright on the way, had driven the sleep he badly required from his eyelids. There was at least a fifty-fifty chance that the levies would fight, when they found themselves part of a fully armed column : especially as the column itself would take the brunt of the fighting, leaving, with luck, little for the levies to do but work up additional horror for the scattered enemy by their yells and random shots, and be destructive—for which last they could be depended upon.

" All right ; let's turn in," he said shortly.

They went out for a last look at the lines before settling for the night. The levies, who knew they were marching in the morning, were sleeping like good children before a party.

II

How near an animal one can become! thought Johnny, as he lay scratching in the dark. They had kept themselves relatively clean, although the huts in which they slept were—as they had not been in Kufi's time—verminous.

Abominations of every sort crawled out of the walls of woven matting; dropped from the roofing; oozed up from the floor. The bedding they had shared out was full of lice; it was impossible to get it clean.

Their clothes were deplorable; Johnny's beard made him feel filthy, he envied Paget his smooth jaw—although, by now, the razors were in bad condition, and it seemed impossible to keep the blades from rusting, in spite of scrupulous drying after use and copious applications of oil.

One's body made ludicrous noises, let out the most nauseating smells. Paget, a few weeks ago, had gone down with an excruciating attack of blackwater fever, from which his recovery had nothing to do with the treatment he received. Bendick's medical stores were reduced to the most primitive; they had at least to give thanks that Omo, evidently agreeing on caution, had forborne large-scale looting until it was positive that Bendick would have no successor. They had found a guard on Bendick's belongings, and Abuakwa, smirking with virtue, claiming remuneration for his attention to Cappi Bendi's interests.

He lay there—now and again sweeping a spider away from his face—thinking of the men he and Paget were leading in the morning, into difficulty, danger, possibly annihilation, "for righteousness' sake." Of all paradoxes, this—that he, whose primary motive was peace, should be involved in an embroilment of the native against the native, with the object of his reduction, in another form, to the acceptance of British autocracy—seemed to him the most ironic. With this objective Matthew Flood had run liquor to the Coast, had entered into slim contracts with kings, had drunk blood brotherhood with one of them. . . .

How far back would the present struggle set his own purpose—his secret dream moving under cover of the project to which Harcourt and he had solemnly dedicated themselves: the dream whose goal was humanitarianism, not gain?

More antagonism to the black race; more confusion in the lay mind between the savage and the community, represented, to Johnny, by Osei—themselves to be rated as savage, because they were black. In dealing with a white enemy, the public had no difficulty in distinguishing between the pacific element and the belligerent rabble. And again—why rabble? Would the "rabble" of England defend it against invasion? Was it England's "rabble" that collected along her sea coast, to hold off Napoleon?

That the Gold Coast had been sold to the British by his ancestors was no affair of the present-day Ashanti. The African Companies and their monopolies, the Assiento of 1713, the schedule of 1752, Mungo Park and Sir Charles McCarthy's skull were no more remote from the successors of

Prempeh II than the present right of the British Government to contravene their ancient privileges, disturb their law system and exploit them and their ancient heritage to British advantage.

How much better off, so far, was Omo, for British intervention—even under the beneficient administration of Morris? What was the difference between miners, quarrying gold—their gold, at that—from the earth, and the labourers on Jonathan Flood's plantations in Barbados?

Ostensibly—freedom: an ironic word to the native, raised in the boundless freedom of the bush! Freedom: a fetish word, a little handful of dust—paid for in humble submission to a foreign administration, a foreign law, a foreign religion; in distasteful toil, only made tolerable because the pay was just sufficient to procure for them foreign dissipation, foreign liquor, foreign gewgaws. Yes, admittedly that's the way it is at present; but can't you see how much better off they will be when they settle down to the acceptance of our rule?

Better off—in what way? Come now; let's get away from slipshod generalisations. Better morally, materially, as human beings? Finer physical types, happier, more contented? Yes, yes, of course that's the idea: but how is it working out? Three hundred and seventy years after the first voyage to Guinea and Benin—three hundred and seventy since old Mr. William Hawkins, father of a more famous son, set out from Plymouth and "touched at the river of Sestos on the coast of Guinea, where he trafficked with the Negroes and took of them elephants' teeth and other commodities which that place yieldeth"—has West Africa any cause to bless the British name? Have the British left any permanent mark on this great continent apart from their offal-line along the coast?

And I—and I . . . His weary brain toiled on. I, who imagined I knew the answers to all these questions; who intended to spend the rest of my life in trying to get them put into practice—I, to-morrow, am committed to the very thing I most condemn: the imposing, by means of violence, upon an ultimately defenceless people, standards I believe in for myself, but not for them; laws I understand, but which to them represent injustice; retribution for crimes of which the principal one is their desire to maintain their independence—not with a moral, or a humanitarian, or even a religious object: but for gain, gain, gain!

To-morrow morning I offer up, in duty to my country, all my beliefs, all I have tried and that I hoped to do—so forgive me, God—and protect me . . .

At this point Johnny's temperature slid up above the hundred mark and relieved him of the trouble of thinking. Between ninety-nine and a hundred and three it jigged for the remainder of the night, and a great many people came into and out of the hut: Harriet and Miranda, and Joe, whose presence, for some reason, made him feel uncomfortable—he could not remember why; and Harcourt, and Doss and Gilbert—both very cheerful, paying almost no attention to him but talking away very hard across him, cracking jokes that made him want to chuckle; and, for a little while, embarrassing him painfully, Emily—only fortunately she did not recognise him ; as, indeed, how should she, through the scrub on his face ? There had been something, once, about Emily . . . suddenly it went through him like a knife. Emily—oh, my God ! My only love. He was screaming, fetching up great sobs like hard lumps out of his chest. . . .

Then there was no one there but Harcourt ; sitting by the bed, his big hand clasped round Johnny's. " I'm afraid I'm in a filthy mess, Uncle Hacky." " Never mind : get your bath—and be sharp about it. We've got a devil of a lot of things to see to this morning.——"

This morning. It lay in a silver web about the hut, and Paget was bending over him. Paget drew back, his face grave and disturbed ; his brow knitted with dissatisfaction at Johnny's appearance.

" You've been having another go, haven't you ? "

" I suppose so." His voice was oddly like an etiolated version of the squeal of the drum-fiddle. " I'll be all right—when I've had my tea."

" You'd better take the first lap in the hammock," said Paget.

Johnny's lips tightened ; to be accompanying Paget, not as a useful unit of the expedition, but as a liability, put the crowning touch to his humiliation. He knew, however, that it would not lighten matters to dispute Paget's decision. He muttered :

" Put me on the end of the line, then ; at any rate I can keep an eye on the tail."

" You'll go where the hammocks usually go—in the middle," snapped Paget. Johnny understood his companion's valiant determination to observe the military formalities, as far as was possible, with his rag-tag mob. Half a dozen weedy Omo youths and three women were standing by the baggage pile ; the youths sheepishly scratching their shins with their toes, grinning hopefully, and arguing as to who should carry the smallest load. When two melted away, Johnny felt no surprise ; carrying was just a little too much like work, for Omo.

The levies were on their toes. Not having the smallest capacity for thinking ahead, living wholly in the moment, the inebriation of being given their guns and promised lots of " Fire " left them without a qualm. They really did not look too bad, Johnny, peering at them, was thinking ; all were sticking out their chests and their bellies, laughing, chattering, throwing gags to one another, indulging in little prances of wellbeing and satisfaction in their own importance. There had been a great to-do of oiling and hairdressing ; the line stank to high heaven. Curious decorative appendages had made their appearance : a few mangy skins, some necklaces of teeth, a bristle of sharpened bones stuck into woolly scalps ; in conjunction with which the effect of British bandoliers and haversacks was rococo in the extreme.

So much for the equipment. Paget had spent a sleepless night, trying to convince himself that it was true, and not some kind of grisly nightmare, that at six in the morning he was starting out, with five dozen men, whom he was expected to deliver intact at a place described as one day's march from Omo through probably hostile country ; that he had no trained pioneers, and not more than a couple who had any idea of handling a felling axe or a saw ; that he could most certainly not trust his flankers ; that, in the event of their coming to water, they had not a single Berthon boat, to assist them in running a tie-tie rope from bank to bank, as support for the more timorous ; at the same time, that they must, as far as possible, keep to low levels, where water would collect, as by choosing higher and dryer ground, they would make themselves a target for the high-throwing guns of the enemy, who usually chose for his emplacements a ravine or hollow which gave him the advantage he lost in firing flat or downhill. A score of other precepts for bush-fighting, gleaned from his superiors, jagged and buzzed in this young man's mind, all of which, invaluable with Regular troops, he knew to be futile with his line of scallawags.

He wondered whether Abuakwa had swallowed the Timali yarn, and was ready to bet he had not. The track to Timali (so Johnny had gathered from N'Timidi) started off for about an hour in the same direction as Kwetti, then forked deeply south, while the Kwetti trail lay due north, more or less towards Ejesu. When the question of the carriers arose, they had paid a formal, explanatory call on Abuakwa, to state that the carriers were required for Timali. Ostensibly accepting this, Abuakwa nodded gravely. Paget wondered whether a savage ever winked ; he would have sworn to a tremor in Abuakwa's left eyelid.

Meanwhile, Gibson and Harriman, and perhaps even the Governor in Kumassi, were counting on him.

"You'd better hop in," he told Johnny, and lifted the bugle to his lips.

The line bounced forward, grinning, chattering, making enough noise for an excited boys' school let out for a football match. There would be no need to tell them to pipe down, thought Paget grimly, when the bush closed round them ; when, behind the bush-mats, hung either side the one-man path, the thinning of the scrub may harbour the sniper ; when, in each man's uneasy consciousness dawns, and grows, the feeling that he is being lain for at two yards ; when panic takes shape in the form of an observation ladder, or notches cut in the bark of a cotton tree. Gambolling good will would soon subside into sullen slogging, and the ten o'clock breakfast halt would supply the pointer to what might be expected for the remainder of the march to N'Buri.

Only let me get the perishers there ! he prayed inwardly. After that, they can run into holes, fall down and break their silly necks, dissolve into thin air—only so long as I can show Gibson I've brought them. . . .

Tree branches rocked and ropes of vine whipped across his face, while Johnny lay in the hammock. It was as well he was there, for his legs had packed up at last. Not that anyone would claim it was luxurious, to travel in a hammock. Carriers and hammock-boys were given the customary ten minutes' halt each hour ; at the end of which they started forward at a trot which did little for the comfort of the person they carried. After breakfast, thought Johnny, I'll walk. Meanwhile, he lay in the hammock, a little heap of skin and bone, so light that it was not surprising that the boys occasionally forgot they were carrying ; letting the wet branches soak him, shivering in the rain, light-headedly pretending he was on his way back to the coast—to the ship—to the sea—to the waters of Avon, sweeping up to Bristol town.

III

Abuakwa carried a large whip of elephant hide ; with this he was intending to keep his warriors well up to the mark, and himself conveniently in the background.

The bodyguard was silent, and a little moody. They were not sure, even now, about Abuakwa : whether they would not have done better, after all, to have gone off with their renegade comrades, who, flouting the new chief's authority, had joined a powerful and authoritative leader, who could assure them victory. Would the Ashanti now turn nasty, and dispose in practical fashion of Omo's tardy support?

Abuakwa was quite shrewd enough to guess what they were thinking. On the other hand, he was proud of his fighting force and sure of the impression it would make on Ya Ashantua and her war captains, when they set eyes on it. He stood a little way off the track, allowing the line to pound past him, just for the sake of the thrill that company gave him : few of them under six feet in height, picked for their superiority to the ruck of the forces : masked with ochre, some with horned helmets that suggested fabulous animals of the bush ; all furnished with belts, with necklets or with bangles of the bones of Omo's former enemies ; freshly anointed with blood that ran glistening among the cicatrices, or clotted into points the skirts of leopard skin ; well-armed with Danes, as well as with the knives and spears essential in close fighting.

Abuakwa himself was an imposing figure : hung from shoulder to knee in tails of wild cat, his chest and arms loaded with the insignia of chieftainship—bracelets and chains of teeth, of carved ivory, of metal plaques and of small fetish objects, guaranteeing his safety—not that Abuakwa meant, as has been stated, to leave that to charms. The spirits help those who help themselves ; no tribe, from a fighting point of view, is worth anything deprived of his chief. Omo should not lose its chief. Abuakwa grinned graciously at his favourite of the young war captains, who cast a glance of envy, not wholly devoid of calculation, at the chief's headdress of rhinoceros horn shooting forth above the tiger-striped, yellow and black oblong of the brow.

He was especially gracious to the intelligence department, jogging along, somewhat hampered by its occult paraphernalia, on the end of the line. He had spent a lot of public money on the fetish crowd ; there was no question of their support, their credit being at stake, not merely with Omo itself, but with the entire province, and all the scattered Omo people between the capital and the borders. His decision to sweep Omo over to the side of Ashanti was the outcome of long and expensive consultations with this gentry—whose duty it was, now, to convince his supporters of the wisdom of his action. Unfortunately, Omo, as a whole, was not amenable to abstract conviction ; what it needed was a good, sound, practical demonstration. . . .

During the halt for food, Abuakwa summoned the captains for a short palaver. Although Ejesu had shown suitable appreciation of Omo's decision to support the cause of Ashanti, all possible pomp and circumstance must be preserved, in order to demonstrate to that brow-beating old hag, Ya Ashantua, that Omo was not there to be kicked around and given the dirty work to do, while her own warriors were pushed into all the positions of importance and treated as the cocks of the walk.

In this the captains, albeit cautiously, concurred.

The old tartar, Abuakwa continued, must be shown the difference between the renegade Omo she had so far been harbouring, the *déclassé* residue of a fallen régime, and the true Omo, militant and powerful, Basin or no Basin, and insistent on its proper share of all advantages accruing through victory to the Ashanti cause.

Wa, said the captains ; that was all right.

In order, pursued Abuakwa, to mark the difference between Omo proper and its big-mouthed deserters, some definite gesture was needed ; something which, for once and for all, would convince Ejesu of the value of Omo's support.

The captains looked thoughtful ; the young one who had an envious eye on Abuakwa's rhinoceros horn observed—in rather a roundabout way, for he did not care, as yet, to prejudice his standing—that, as war leaders, they were concerned rather with action than with policy.

True, admitted Abuakwa ; but it was as well to understand the policy which underlies action ; and that nothing was more likely to increase their prestige with the Queen of Ashanti than their arrival with proofs of a successful attack on an enemy column.

This caused an outbreak of chatter, from which, as it died down, emerged the points, first, that eager as Omo was to fight, and confident of its prowess, the company, in comparison with that which many tribes could put in the field, was small ; that there would be no opportunity, in the small time before they were due at Ejesu, to build stockades, to create observation posts, to link up with other war camps in order to ensure the supplies of war material on which a successful action depended. Moreover, that although, given time for these preparations, victory was to be taken for granted, an unprepared attack could only result in ignominious retreat before the superior armaments carried by the enemy.

Again Abuakwa agreed, hardly less delighted, by now, with his own superior intelligence than contemptuous of the dim-wittedness of his captains. Were they not conscious of the effect to be made—and hardly to be achieved by the smartest of military formations—by the trotting into Ejesu of a company reeking with fresh blood, redolent of triumph over a vanquished enemy?

This they could have had before leaving home, but for the dictates of prudence, and the indiscretion of having too many witnesses to an unorthodox procedure. Out in the bush—a mere half day's march at a tangent from the direction in which they were travelling—lay the easy solution.

"And have we not in our blood—we also—the blood of Ashanti?" With a fine wild outflinging of the arms, Abuakwa concluded his peroration: and, with a smile of satisfaction, watched the fire he had lighted course from man to man.

IV

"We lost time at that perishing stream." It was Paget, glowering at the gathering dusk.

They had lost more than time. Owing to the incomparable clumsiness of the carriers, baggage had been dropped and lay irrecoverable in a man's depth of river mud. Their single hammock, swept from the boys' hands by the race of the water, had gone swirling downstream, despite Paget's wild attempt to rescue it. They decided, after confabulation, that it was not worth while to set to and improvise another; Paget calculated that they could not, now, be more than an hour's march from N'Buri, and Johnny professed himself equal to walking. Tired as they were, each was stimulated by the prospect, after their long isolation, of joining up with their comrades of the regular forces; their hearts lightened, as they pressed on down the long tunnel, at the end of which was welcome—safety—support.

It seemed too good to be true that they had, so far, met with no obstruction. A few scares, a shot or two from some freelance sniper, at first flustered the levies, then had the excellent result of steadying them. The instinct of self-preservation held them together, and, in between obstacles, got a better pace out of them than either of the white men had hoped for. Obstacles—mainly fallen trees, and, as has been seen, the stream—accounted for a few serious delays; it had taken the seventy travellers—including the carriers, one of whom proved a better pioneer than carrier, and developed an altogether unsuspected ability with the axe—more than two hours to chop and scramble their way through the branches of a huge nyedua, matted and hung about with its parasites: like forcing their way through a gigantic ball of string. Weak as he was, Johnny almost despaired of making it; he actually hung for a few moments, impaled by the sharp end of a sliced-off bough, and had the indignity of being pulled off by one of the women carriers—each of whom had, so far, shown herself worth half a dozen of the boys.

But they had been travelling twelve hours; it was, by the waning daylight, after six o'clock, and the levies were getting restive for their evening rice. No earthly power would move them after nightfall; they would just squat and dither, see spirits and work themselves gradually into a state of demoralisation, if allowed, now, to break the line. Gibson and his Mendis ought, by now, to have arrived at N'Buri.

According to Hassan, they themselves should have been there by "three-quarters sun-time," which they understood as about the middle of the afternoon. It was imperative, not only to keep up the march but, if possible, to increase pace for the last lap of the journey which would bring them out of the bush to a place of human habitation.

For the last hour Johnny had found it impossible to keep his place in the column. He kept dropping back and back, cursing himself, cursing the uneasiness he was causing Paget. At the latter's orders, he had tried the experiment of being carried pick-a-back, but, owing to the clumsy indifference of his carrier, the nonchalance with which the latter drove his unhappy passenger against and through any entanglement they encountered, he soon abandoned this method of transport. Feebly, with blood running down his face, neck and arms, he swore at the carrier and demanded to be set down, refusing with oaths Paget's offer to carry him. "How can you, you bloody fool——?"

How could Paget carry—working continually up and down the line, to make sure it remained intact: covering twice its distance, and looking already like a dead man with fatigue?

"Keep it up, old man." He was fretfully conscious of an arm thrown round him, heaving him over a barricade his sight was too far gone to identify. He heard his own voice creak.

"Oh, for Christ's sake get on with your own job"—and was unaware of ingratitude—and of loving Paget—and of hating him—and of a green blur in his brain—as though the tie-tie tendrils had forced themselves inside his skull and were palping and gripping and knitting themselves about his brain; and of Paget's voice in his ear—like a whisper—like a shout—like thunder—and a whisper again . . .

"——doing—my job. Come on—keep it up—KEEP IT UP—*keep it up*——"

Keep it up. Lurch, stumble, swing half-way round, step, step, keep it up.

"Why?

Why—I've finished! I've done my part——!

Suddenly, it seemed, his brain had cleared and cooled itself; from a shrivelled nut it expanded, to make room for a single, distinct thought. He went on a little farther, carrying the thought carefully, like something precious: like a drop of dew, slowly collecting other drops.

I've done it—so it's all right. Done, done, done. Take it easy, Johnny, because you've done, done, done.

So when Paget came back again, it was a matter of common sense to say:

"Go on. I'm going to take my time."

Paget's face—green-ivory in the tree-light. Hard like a bone. Like a carving. Like the Yoruba head. Distant and far away. Knowing what had to be done. Darkness slipping between the tree trunks, coming up in whispering hosts behind the leaf curtains. Get the column to Gibson.

"We'll see you—later on."

Paget's face—green-ivory—about a hundred years old. Their hands met automatically—and there was nothing in the brief contact between the palms.

" See you—presently."

The line, trotting off, was sucked into the dark-green serpent-jaw of the track, was gulped. A patch of shrub gemmed itself surprisingly with faint points of light. The lights shifted. Went out. Get the column to Gibson. Paget's job. Racing against the darkness.

He sat down for a short rest : hugging his knees, tucking his beard into his chest, looking up under his eyebrows. There was a patch of glimmer on a nearby tree trunk. A slow smile broke on his lips, of salutation to his old companion, the Face. All right. You win.

Darkness coming now very quickly : filling in the spaces between tree trunks like slim bodies, coiling down like snakes crawling on its belly, pouring itself over the leaves and dripping from the great silver cornucopæ of the vines. Darkness beating the earth with a drum of implacable feet, darkness—tiger-striped——?

He lifted his head, his eyes widening ; his hand found the Colt—but for some reason could not hold it steady. It was important to be quick. And the best way of steadying it seemed to be to push it against the side of his head.

EPILOGUE

London

1901

"I SUPPOSE you don't feel like coming—back."

She had prepared herself for the question, and gave her answer quietly.

"No, Joe. I shan't come back. I've made other plans, and I'd sooner —sooner—not——" She caught her lip in her teeth.

She would not say that she would "sooner not" be within the reach of those who, during the six months of her widowhood, had shown her, unmistakably, that she had nothing to hope for, in sympathy or in understanding, from her husband's family. She would not come back, to be "Mrs. Flood" in Bristol: a centre of gossip, a source, perhaps, of embarrassment to her own relations and of trouble for Miranda. No. Not even if Joe asked her to marry him. Which he had not.

She felt a little hurt by the omission. But he was probably feeling, as she felt: too stunned, too confused for love. She wished he would say what was in his mind; what lay behind his distant, steady look—like that of a stranger—which reached her across a gulf which had opened between them on the day she admitted. . . . She wondered if she had grown to look as old as Joe looked, since that day.

Yes, thought Polly: I look old, and ugly.

In which she did herself an injustice. Actually, she had never come so near beauty, was never so nearly to approach it again, as during those months whose painful and humiliating experiences had robbed her cheeks of their colour and stripped away the flesh, so that all the bones stood out in their wholesome simplicity. She was blind to the grave dignity which had grown about her with her grief, and with her anxiety about the future. Nor did it ever occur to her that her refusal to justify herself had conferred upon her the unconscious nobility which all selfless actions confer on those who perform them.

"Did you read it?" she asked suddenly.

"Read what?"

"The letter he sent you—for me?"

"Of course I didn't," said Joe coldly.

"I'd like you to—please."

She held it out to him, and went to sit down on the farther side of the room. She sat there, rather like a child that has been put in a corner, her hands clasped tightly in her lap, her head bent, as in acceptance of punishment.

He stood, with the thin sheets of paper crumpled in his hand, thinking. Thinking—strange as it might seem—of Harcourt.

Polly and Johnny, the two he had most dearly loved—who had betrayed him. And Harcourt, who, knowing nothing of its significance to him, Joe, had been the first to tell him of the betrayal. Harcourt, who, for his own obscure motives, had stood by him. Harcourt . . . my father? Oh God, if only I knew!

It was Johnny who mattered, to Harcourt; and for Johnny nothing—nothing in the world—could make up. One could only try . . . for the sake of one's love. For the sake of one's love.

"My Dear Son,

"It is hard luck we do not know each other, but I like to think of you reading this some day, and wondering what sort of a fellow wrote it, and how we would have got on together.

"When they give you my letter, I suppose you will be about fourteen: the age I was when I ran away to sea. I don't know if you feel like running away, but if you do I hope you won't, because you must think about your mother. Don't forget that is up to you, as I'm not around to do the looking-after for you. That is the first thing I want you to keep in mind, and I think I'd better put you on your honour about it. In a way it's not fair, and it makes things more difficult for you, but I'm afraid you've just got to take it. I remember pretty clearly that fourteen and round-about isn't the happiest or the easiest time in one's life, and I would like to be there, to give you a hand. As I can't, I leave it to you, and trust you to do your best.

"This isn't an easy letter to write, because I haven't the least notion what kind of a fellow you are, or how you feel about anything, and I don't want to write anything that sounds pompous, or would be likely to give you the impression that I am dictating to you.

"As you are a Flood, I'll take a chance and assume that you're like the rest of us: stubborn, headstrong and self-confident. Those are all good qualities, used in the right way, and I like to think of you inheriting them. I wish to God I had more to leave you.

"Your upbringing will be very different from my own, and for that you have to blame your father; mind you don't ever make your mother responsible for it. There may be times when you envy those born to a state of life I would have tried to give you—not because, in the light of later experience, I think it is particularly desirable, but because one naturally wants to make things as good as possible for the people one cares for. So, if I'd been about, I would probably have indulged you, and I might have 'spoiled' you a bit—but not much. Because the best times I have had were among people who lived hard, and who got all their satisfaction out of beating circumstance.

"I am writing to you now, less as my son, than as a Flood of Bristol. You will get a glimmer of what that means if you go into the Redcliff and look at our tablets. I wish I could write it all down for you—all that lies behind those names: all the examples and all the warnings. But it would take too long, and I would probably get some of it mixed up.

" Old Hercules (I'd like you to have been called Hercules but you can't, because I'm a younger son, and the name only goes to the sons of eldest sons) was your five times great-grandfather ; that's your Bristol root. His son Jonathan went to Barbados and became a planter, and the family did not come back to Bristol until your great-grandfather Matthew's time. (He was the second cousin of Matthew the Abolitionist.) You have got relatives in Cuba, called Rodríguez, and I expect there are still connections in Barbados, and probably in the United States. I've never had time to work these out, and I only mention it in case you should visit there one day, and perhaps come across some of them.

" At all events, I want you to remember we are Bristol Floods, and that Bristol made us, and we owe it all we can bring to it.

" Well, son, I don't know what you are, or what you want to be ; but, as you are a Flood, I'll assume you are interested in trade. Some people look down on trade, forgetting what they owe to it. Trade is the lifeblood of our country, and you may be proud of yourself as a Flood, as a Bristolian and as an Englishman, if you contribute to it ; for you are helping to support everything an Englishman thinks ' worth while '—the monarchy, the British Constitution and the power of the British Empire, wherever that extends.

" Trade means money, which, at some time in their lives, most Floods have enjoyed ; and money means power. If ever you have power, if ever you have wealth—don't forget those who have contributed to it. See, if you can, that they are better off for serving your interests. I don't mean better off in the material sense, only—but better *as human beings*. We Floods owe a big debt to humanity. You'll understand that when you know more about our family history. If you ever get out to the West Coast of Africa, try and remember what I say. Don't be too quick to accept ready-made valuations. Don't—as a minor point—ever speak of a black man, or think of him, as ' a nigger.'

" I think this is about all, except as regards me. I wish I were leaving you a fine record, of which you might be proud, but there hasn't been time. It may be presumption on my part—even to think I could have effected anything. I suppose the only way to look at it is—it's better to have a hard try, even if you don't succeed, than just let things slide. There's always the chance you might set a ball rolling. I can't remember if indifference is among the Seven Deadly Sins. If it isn't, it ought to be.

" Tell the truth. Be loyal to your friends and just to your enemies. Try to make sure that nothing you do is prompted by self-interest, but governed by your own sense of right and wrong. If you can honestly say you've lived up to those principles, never mind what the world thinks of you ; you're a success.

" God bless you. Look after your mother. That others beside yourself may live to be glad you were born is the earnest wish of your father,

" JOHN FLOOD."

As he folded the pages together, he said blindly :

" It's just like Johnny."

Presently he said :

" If you ever want me, Polly—you know where to find me."

" Yes, Joe—bless you. Dear Joe. You'll come and see the baby, won't you, before you go ? "

The occupant of the cradle, hungry, set up a lusty howl.

" Sh, baby—sh, Debby—sh, Mama's precious ! "

She lifted her face, luminous with tears, to his.

" Debby—Aldebaran. The name's all right, isn't it, for a little girl ? "

THE END